Expiration Date

TIM POWERS

EXPIRATION DATE

Copyright © 1996 by Tim Powers

A Baen Book

Baen Publishing Enterprises
P.O. Box 1403
Riverdale, NY 10471
www.baen.com

ISBN: 978-1-4814-8408-4

Cover art by Adam Burn

First Baen printing, June 2018
First Baen mass market printing, June 2019

Distributed by Simon & Schuster
1230 Avenue of the Americas
New York, NY 10020

Printed in the United States of America

10 9 8 7 6 5 4 3 2 1

For Brendan and Regina Powers,
wonderful friends and family

❦

And with thanks to Chris Arena, Skot Armstrong, Gloria Batsford, Brian Bilby, Jim Blaylock, Phil Dick, Aaron Dietrich, Mike Donohue, Anthony Foster, Kendall Garmon, Tom Gilchrist, Jaq Greenspon, Ken Lopez, Joe Machuga, Ed McKie, Denny Meyer, Chris Miller, Dean Moody, Dave Moran, David Perry, Serena Powers, Sam Riemer, Megan Robb, Randal Robb, Roger Rocha, Lew Shiner, Fred Speicher, Kate Sanborne, Roy Squires, Kirsten Tierney, Ed and Pat Thomas, and Dan Volante—

—And with gratitude to Art, Bill, Bob, Dave, Dennis, Doug, Frank, Greg, Jane, Jody, Joe, Joel, Mac, Mario, Michael, Nick, Peggy, Rich, Tom, William, and the rest of the 1924 gang— and especially Charlie.

Expiration Date

BOOK ONE
Open Up That Golden Gate

TRENTON, NJ—Thomas A. Edison, the inventor of the light bulb, whose honors have included having a New Jersey town and college named after him, received a college degree Sunday, 61 years after his death.

Thomas Edison State College conferred on its namesake a bachelor of science degree for lifetime achievement.

—*The Associated Press,*
Monday, October 26, 1992

CHAPTER 1

"But I don't want to go among mad people,"
Alice remarked.
"Oh, you can't help that," said the Cat.
"We're all mad here. I'm mad. You're mad."
"How do you know I'm mad?" said Alice.
"You must be," said the Cat, "or you
wouldn't have come here."

—Lewis Carroll,
Alice's Adventures in Wonderland

WHEN HE WAS LITTLE, say four or five, the living room had been as dim as a church all the time, with curtains pulled across the broad windows, and everywhere there had been the kind of big dark wooden furniture that's got stylized leaves and grapes and claws carved into it. Now the curtains had been taken down, and through the windows Kootie could see the lawn—more gold than green in the early-evening light, and streaked with the lengthening shadows of the sycamores—and the living room was painted white now and had hardly any furniture in it besides white wood chairs and a glass-topped coffee table.

The mantel over the fireplace was white now too, but the old black bust of Dante still stood on it, the only relic of his parents' previous taste in furnishings. Dante Allah Hairy, he used to think its name was.

Kootie leaned out of his chair and switched on the pole lamp. Off to his left, his blue nylon knapsack was slumped against the front door, and ahead of him and above him Dante's eyes were gleaming like black olives. Kootie hiked himself out of the chair and crossed to the fireplace.

He knew that he wasn't allowed to touch the Dante. He had always known that, and the rule had never been a difficult one to obey. He was eleven now, and no longer imagined that the black-painted head and shoulders were just the visible top of a whole little body concealed inside the brick fireplace front—and he realized these days that the rustlings that woke him at night were nothing more than the breeze in the boughs outside his bedroom window, and not the Dante whispering to itself all alone in the dark living room—but it was still a nasty-looking thing, with its scowling hollow-cheeked face and the way its black finish was shiny on the high spots, as if generations of people had spent a lot of time rubbing it.

Kootie reached up and touched its nose.

Nothing happened. The nose was cool and slick. Kootie put one hand under the thing's chin and the other hand behind its head and then carefully lifted it down and set it on the white stone slab of the hearth.

He sat down cross-legged beside it and thought of Sidney Greenstreet in *The Maltese Falcon,* sweating furiously, hacking with a penknife at the black-painted statue of the falcon; Kootie had no idea what might be inside the Dante, but he thought the best way to get at it would be to simply shatter the thing. He had glimpsed the unpainted white base of the bust just now, and had seen that it was only plaster.

But breaking it would be the irrevocable step.

He had packed shirts, socks, underwear, sweatsuit, a jacket, and a baseball cap in his knapsack, and he had nearly three hundred dollars in twenties in his pocket, along with his Swiss army knife, but he wouldn't be *committed* to running away until he broke the bust of Dante.

Broke it and took away whatever might be inside it. He hoped he'd find gold—Krugerrands, say, or those little flat blocks like dominoes.

It occurred to him, now, that even if the bust was nothing but solid plaster all through, as useless as Greenstreet's black bird had turned out to be, he would still have to break it. The Dante was the . . . what, flag, emblem, totem pole of what his parents had all along been trying to make Kootie into.

With a trembling finger, he pushed the bust over backward. It clunked on the stone, staring at the ceiling now, but it didn't break.

He exhaled, both relieved and disappointed.

Dirty mummy-stuff, he thought. Meditation, and the big tunnel with all the souls drifting toward the famous white light. His parents had lots of pictures of that.

Pyramids and the Book of Thoth and reincarnation and
messages from these "old soul" guys called Mahatmas.

The Mahatmas were dead, but they would supposedly
still come around to tell you how to be a perfect dead guy
like they were. But they were coy—Kootie had never seen
one at all, even after hours of sitting and trying to make
his mind a blank, and even his parents only claimed to
have *glimpsed* the old boys, who always apparently snuck
out through the kitchen door if you tried to get a good
look at them. Mostly you could tell that they'd been
around only by the things they'd rearrange—books on the
shelves, cups in the kitchen. If you had left a handful of
change on the dresser, you'd find they'd sorted the coins
and stacked them. Sometimes with the dates in order.

At about the age when his friends were figuring out
that Santa Claus was a fake, Kootie had stopped believing
in the Mahatmas and all the rest of it; later he'd had a
shock when he learned in school that there really had
been a guy named Mahatma Gandhi, but a friend of his
who saw the movie *Gandhi* told him that Gandhi was just
a regular person, a politician in India who was skinny and
bald and wore diapers all the time.

Kootie wasn't allowed to *see* movies . . . or watch TV,
or even eat meat, though he often sneaked off to
McDonald's for a Big Mac, and then had to chew gum
afterward to get rid of the smell.

Kootie wanted to be an astronomer when he grew up,
but his parents weren't going to let him go to college. He
wasn't sure if he'd even be allowed to go to all four years
of high school. His parents told him he was a *chela*, just
as they were, and that his duty in life was to . . . well, it

was hard to say, really; to get squared away with these dead guys. Be their "new Krishnamurti"—carry their message to the world. Be prepared for when you died and found yourself in that big tunnel.

And in the meantime, no TV or movies or meat, and when he grew up he wasn't supposed to get married or ever have sex at all—not because of AIDS, but because the Mahatmas were down on it. Well, he thought, they *would* be, wouldn't they, being dead and probably wearing diapers and busy all the time rearranging people's coffee cups. Shoot.

But the worst thing his parents had ever done to him they did on the day he was born—they *named* him after one of these Mahatmas, a dead guy who had to go and have the name Koot Hoomie. Growing up named Koot Hoomie Parganas, with the inevitable nickname Kootie, had been . . . well, he had seen a lot of fat kids or stuttering kids get teased mercilessly in school, but he always wished he could trade places with them if in exchange he could have a name like *Steve* or *Jim* or *Bill*.

He lifted the Dante in both hands to a height of about four inches, and let it fall. *Clunk!* But it still didn't break.

He believed his parents worshipped the thing. Sometimes after he had gone off to bed and was supposedly asleep, he had sneaked back and peeked into the living room and seen them bowing in front of it and mumbling, and at certain times of the year—Christmas, for example, and Halloween, which was only about a week away—his mother would knit little hats and collars for Dante. She always had to make them new, too, couldn't use last year's, though she saved all of them.

And his parents always insisted to Kootie—nervously, he thought—that the previous owner of the house had coincidentally been named Don Tay (or sometimes *Om* Tay) and that's why the drunks or crazy people who called on the phone sometimes at night seemed to be asking to talk to the statue.

Terminator 2. "Peewee's Playhouse." Mario Brothers and Tetris on the Nintendo. Big Macs and the occasional furtive Marlboro. College, eventually, and maybe even just finishing high school. Astronomy. *Friends.* All that, on the one hand.

Rajma, khatte chhole, masoor dal, moong dal, chana dal, which were all just different kinds of cooked beans. On the other hand. Along with Mahatmas, and start some kind of new theosophical order (instead of go to college), and don't have a girlfriend.

As if he ever could.

You think it's bad that Melvin touched you and gave you his cooties? We've *got a Kootie in our* class.

His jaw was clenched so tight that his teeth ached, and tears were being squeezed out of his closed eyes, but he lifted the Dante over his head with both hands— paused—and then smashed it down onto the hearth.

With a muffled *crack* it broke into a hundred powdery white pieces, some tumbling away onto the tan carpet.

He opened his eyes, and for several seconds while his heart pounded and he didn't breathe, he just stared down at the scattered floury rubble. At last he let himself exhale, and he slowly stretched out his hand.

At first glance the mess seemed to consist entirely of angular lumps of plaster; but when he tremblingly brushed through the litter, he found a brick-shaped piece, about the size of two decks of cards glued together front-to-back. He picked it up—it was heavy, and its surface gave a little when he squeezed it, cracking the clinging plaster and exhaling a puff of fine white dust.

He glanced over his shoulder at the front door, and tried to imagine what his parents would do if they were to walk in right now, and see this. They might very well, he thought, go completely insane.

Hastily he started tugging at the stiffly flexible stuff that encased the object; when he got a corner unfolded and was able to see the inner surface of the covering he realized that it was some sort of patterned silk handkerchief, stiffened by the plaster.

Once he'd got the corner loose, it was easy—in two seconds he had peeled the white-crusted cloth away, and was holding up a little glass brick. The surfaces of it were rippled but gleamingly smooth, and its translucent depths were as cloudy as smoky quartz.

He held it up to the light from the window—

And the air seemed to vibrate, as if a huge gong had been struck in the sky and was ringing, and shaking the earth, with some subsonic note too profoundly low to be sensed by living ears.

All day the hot Santa Ana winds had been combing the dry grasses down the slopes of the San Bernardino Mountains, moving west like an airy tide across the miles-separated semi-desert towns of Fontana and Upland, over the San Jose Hills and into the Los Angeles basin, where they swept the smog blanket out to sea and let the inhabitants see the peaks of Mount Wilson and Mount Baldy, hallucinatorily clear against a startlingly blue sky.

Palm trees bowed and nodded over old residential streets and threw down dry fronds to bounce dustily off parked cars; and red-brick roof tiles, loosened by the summer's rains and sun, skittered free of ancient cement moorings, cartwheeled over rain gutters, and shattered on driveways that were, as often as not, two weathered lines of concrete with a strip of grass growing between. The steady background bump-and-hiss of the wind was punctuated by the hoarse shouts of crows trying to fly upwind.

Downtown, in the streets around the East L.A. Interchange where the northbound 5 breaks apart into the Golden State and Santa Monica and Hollywood Freeways, the hot wind had all day long been shaking the big slow RTD buses on their shocks as they groaned along the sun-softened asphalt, and the usual reeks of diesel smoke and ozone and the faint strawberry-sweetness of garbage were today replaced with the incongruous spice of faraway sage and baked Mojave stone.

For just a moment now as the sun was setting, redly silhouetting trees and oil tanks on the western hills around Santa Monica, a higher-than-usual number of cars swerved in their freeway lanes, or jumped downtown curbs to collide with light poles or newspaper stands, or rolled forward at stoplights to clank against the bumpers of the cars ahead; and many of the homeless people in East L.A. and Florence and Inglewood cowered behind their shopping carts and shouted about Jesus or the FBI or the Devil or unfathomable personal deities; and for a few moments up on Mulholland Drive all the westbound cars drifted right and then left and then right again, as if the drivers were all rocking to the same song on the radio.

In an alley behind a ramshackle apartment building down in Long Beach, a fat, shirtless old man shivered suddenly and dropped the handle of the battered dolly he had been angling toward an open garage, and the refrigerator he'd been carting slammed to the pavement, pinning his foot; his gasping shouts and curses brought a heavyset young woman running, and after she'd helped him hike the refrigerator off of his foot, he demanded breathlessly that she run upstairs and draw a bath for him, a *cold* one.

And on Broadway the neon signs were coming on and darkening the sky—the names of the shops were often Japanese or Korean, though the rest of the lettering was generally in Spanish—and many of the people in the hurrying crowds below glanced uneasily at the starless heavens. On the sidewalk under the marquee of the old Million Dollar Theater a man in a ragged nylon jacket and baggy camouflage pants had clenched his teeth against a scream and was now leaning against one of the old ornate lampposts.

His left arm, which had been cold all day despite the hot air that was dewing his forehead with sweat, was warm now, and of its own volition was pointing west. With his grubby right hand, he pushed back the bill of his baseball cap, and he squinted in that direction, at the close wall of the theater, as if he might be able to see through it and for miles beyond the bricks of it, out past Hollywood, toward Beverly Hills, looking for—

—An abruptly arrived thing, a new and godalmighty smoke, a switched-on beacon somewhere out toward where the sun had just set.

"Get a life," he whispered to himself. "God, *get* a life!"

He pushed himself away from the pole. Walking through the crowd was awkward with his arm stuck straight out, though the people he passed didn't give him a glance, and when he got on an RTD bus at Third Street he had to shuffle down the crowded aisle sideways.

And for most of the night all the crickets were silent in the dark yards and in the hallways of empty office buildings and in the curbside grasses, as if the same quiet footstep had startled all of them.

CHAPTER 2

❁

*". . . when she next peeped out, the Fish-Footman
was gone, and the other was sitting on the ground
near the door, staring stupidly up into the sky."*
—Lewis Carroll,
Alice's Adventures in Wonderland

KOOTIE TRUDGED back up the quiet dimness of
Loma Vista Drive toward home. He was walking more
slowly than he had been a few minutes ago on Sunset
Boulevard, and now that he had got his breath back he
realized that he was limping, and that his side hurt worse
than ever. Probably that punch in the stomach had
cracked a rib.

Tomorrow must be trash day—all the wheeled green
plastic trash cans were out along the curbs. His neighbors'
houses, which he had always scornfully thought looked
like 1950's-style Japanese restaurants, were hidden behind
the trees, but he knew that behind the ARMED RESPONSE
signs on the lawns they were probably all dark at this hour.
He was sure that dawn couldn't be far off.

He leaned against one of the trash cans and tried to ignore the hard pounding of his heart, and the tight chill in his belly that was making his hands sweat and shake. He could claim that burglars had got in, and kidnapped him because he had seen them, because he was a *witness* who could identify them in a *lineup;* they had panicked, say, and grabbed him and fled after doing nothing more than break the Dante. Kootie had managed to escape . . . after a fight, which would be how come his left eye was swelling shut and his rib was perhaps broken.

He tried to believe the burglar story, which he would probably have to tell to some policeman—he tried to imagine the fictitious burglars, what they had said, what their car had looked like, and after a few moments he was horrified to realize that the tone of the whole thing just rang with kid-ingenuity, like the "concerto" he had composed on the piano a year ago, which had sounded every bit as good and dramatic as Tchaikovsky to him at the time, but later was somehow just meandering and emphatic.

A kid just couldn't see the difference. It was like being color-blind or something, or preferring Frazetta to all those blobby old paintings of haystacks and French people in rowboats.

A grown-up would probably have been able to tell that Lumpy and Daryl weren't nice guys. *Well, shit, Koot my man, you can stay in my garage—it's right down here, nothing fancy but it's got a bed and a refrigerator—and you can work for me detailing cars.*

It had sounded all right.

And then *Pow!* behind a dumpster, and hard hands turning out his pockets while his knapsack was dragged off his back and all his carefully folded clothes were flung out onto the littered pavement, and a moment later Kootie was alone in the alley, snuffling and choking as quietly as he could and shoving his clothes back into the broken knapsack.

The glass brick had slid under the dumpster, and he had had to practically get down on his face and crawl to retrieve it.

At least he could still return that. And his parents *had* to take him back. He didn't care what punishment they would give him, just so that he could soon be in his own room again, in his own bed. Last night he had dreamed of going to college, of getting a "B.S.," which in the dream had meant something besides *bullshit*. The dream had given him the (stupid!) determination to finally put his (stupid!) running-away scheme into actual (stupid!) action.

He hoped he never dreamed again.

He pushed away from the trash can and resumed limping up the street, from one silent pool of agitated street light to the next. Go to bed and put it off until morning, he thought miserably. They might think I've spent the night at Courtney's house, and . . . No. There was the busted Dante to raise the alarm. Still, sneak into bed and deal with everything tomorrow morning.

The curb by his own driveway was bare—no trash cans. That wasn't reassuring. His mom and dad must be too upset to think of taking down the cans. But maybe they were off in the car right now, looking for him, and he'd be able to—

No. As he started limping up the white cement driveway he saw their Mercedes against the lights of the kitchen. And the leaves of the peach tree to the right of the house were yellowly lit, so his bedroom light was on too.

Shit, he thought with despairing defiance. Shit shit *shit,* and I don't care who knows it. At least there's no police cars. At the moment.

He tiptoed across the grass around to the garage on the north side of the house. The laundry-room door was open, spilling light across the lawn, and he crouched up to it and peered inside.

The gleaming white metal cubes of the washer and dryer, with the colorful Wisk and Clorox 2 boxes on the shelf over them, were so achingly familiar a sight that he had to blink back tears. He stepped in and walked quietly, heel-and-toe, into the kitchen.

He could see into the living room—and there were two elegantly dressed people standing by the fireplace, a man and a woman, and only after a moment did he recognize them as his mom and dad.

His dad was wearing . . . a black *tuxedo,* with a ruffled white shirt, and his mother had on a puffy white dress with clouds of lace at the wrists and the low neckline. The two of them were just standing there, staring at different corners of the room.

In the first moment of frozen bewilderment, Kootie forgot about wanting to cry. Could they have put on these crazily formal clothes just to greet him when he returned? His father's hair was *styled,* obviously blow-dryed up, and . . . and the hair was all black now, not gray at all.

Kootie took a deep breath and stepped out onto the deep tan carpet. "Mom?" he said quietly.

His mother looked much slimmer in the dress, and he noticed with disbelief that she was actually wearing eye makeup. Her calm gaze shifted to the ceiling.

"Mom," Kootie repeated, a little louder. He was oddly reluctant to speak in a normal tone.

His father turned toward the kitchen—and then kept turning, finally fixing his gaze on a chair by the hallway arch.

"I'm sorry," Kootie whimpered, horrified by this grotesque punishment. *"Talk* to me, it fell and broke so I ran away, I've got the glass thing that was inside it—"

His mother raised her white-sleeved arms, and Kootie stumbled forward, sobbing now—but she was turning around, and her arms were out to the sides now as if she was doing a dance in slow motion. Kootie jerked to a stop on the carpet, abruptly very frightened.

"Stop it!" he screamed shrilly. *"Don't!"*

"Fuck is that?" came a hoarse shout from down the hall.

Kootie heard something heavy fall over, and then clumping footsteps in the hall—then a homeless-looking man in a ragged nylon wind breaker was standing there scowling crazily at him. The big man's whiskery face was round under a grimy baseball cap, and his eyes seemed tiny. He blinked in evident surprise at the slow-moving figures of Kootie's parents, but quickly focused again on the boy.

"Kid, come here," the man said, taking a quick step into the living room. He was reaching for Kootie with his right hand—because his left hand, his whole left arm, was gone, with just an empty sleeve folded and pinned-up there.

Kootie bolted to the left into the green-lit atrium, skidding and almost falling on the sudden smooth marble floor, and though he clearly saw the two figures who were sitting in chairs against the lattice wall, he didn't stop running; he had seen the figures vividly but he hit the backyard door with all his weight—it slammed open and he was running across the dark grass so fast that he seemed to be falling straight down from a height.

His hands and feet found the crossboards in the back fence and he was over it and tearing through ivy in darkness, getting up before he even knew he had fallen— he scrambled over a redwood fence and then was just running away full tilt down some quiet street.

His eyes must have been guiding his feet on automatic pilot, for he didn't fall; but in his head, all he could see was the two figures sitting in the chairs in the atrium, *duct-taped* into the chairs at neck and wrist and ankle— his overweight mother and his gray-haired father, mouths gaping and toothless, eyes just empty blood-streaked sockets, hands clawed and clutching the chair arms in obvious death.

CHAPTER 3

". . . Just look along the road, and tell me if you can see either of them."

"I see nobody on the road," said Alice.

"I only wish I had such eyes," the King remarked in a fretful tone. "To be able to see Nobody! And at that distance too! Why, it's as much as I can do to see real people, by this light!"

—Lewis Carroll,
Through the Looking-Glass

PETE SULLIVAN opened his eyes after the flash, but seconds went by as he watched a patch of sky through the screened window of the van, and he didn't hear any thunder. He sat up in the narrow bed and wondered whether silent flashes behind one's eyes were a symptom of impending stroke; he had been unaccountably jumpy tonight, and he had played a terrible game of pool in the bar here after work, flinching and clumsy with the cue stick.

The thought of incipient stroke wasn't alarming him, and he realized that he didn't really believe it. He swung his bare feet to the carpeted floorboards and stood up—years ago he had replaced the van's stock roof with a camper top that raised the ceiling two and a half feet, so he was able to stand without bumping the top of his head—and he leaned on the little sink counter and stared out through the open window at the Arizona night.

Tonto Basin was down inside a ring of towering cumulus clouds tonight, and as he watched, one of the clouds was lit for an instant from within; and a moment later a vivid fork of lightning flashed to the east, over the southern peaks of the Mogollon Rim.

Sullivan waited, but no thunder followed.

The breeze through the screen smelled like the autumn evenings of his boyhood in California, a cool smell of rain-wet rocks, and suddenly the stale old-clothes and propane-refrigerator air inside the van was confining by contrast—he pulled on a pair of jeans and some socks, stepped into his steel-toed black shoes, and slid the door open.

When he was outside and standing on the gravel of O'Hara's back parking lot, he could hear the noise from the bar's open back door—Garth Brooks on the jukebox and the click of pool shots and the shaking racket of drink and talk.

He had taken a couple of steps out across the lot, looking up vainly for stars in the cloudy night sky, when a Honda station wagon spoke to him.

"Warning," it said. The bar's bright back-door light gleamed on the car's hood. *"You are too close to the*

vehicle—step back." Sullivan stepped back. *"Thank you,"* said the car.

The thing's voice had been just barely civil.

Sullivan plodded back to the van for cigarettes and a lighter. When he was back out on the gravel, the Honda was quiet until he clicked his lighter; then the car again warned him that he was too close to the vehicle.

He inhaled on the cigarette and blew out a plume of smoke that trailed away on the breeze. "Too close for what?" he asked.

"Step back," said the car.

"What vehicle?" Sullivan asked. "You? Or is there somebody else around? Maybe we both ought to step back."

"Warning," the thing was saying, speaking over him. *"You are too close to the vehicle. Step back."*

"What'll you do if I don't?"

"It'll go off like a fire siren, Pete," came a voice from behind Sullivan. "What are you teasing a car for?"

It was Morrie the bartender, and out here in the fresh air Sullivan thought he could smell the beer stains on the man's apron. "He started it, Morrie."

"It started it. It's a *car.* You've got a call."

Sullivan imagined picking up the bar phone and hearing the flat mechanical voice telling him that he was standing too close to a vehicle. "The power station?"

"Didn't say. Maybe it's some local mom pissed about her daughter being messed with."

Morrie had turned and was crunching back toward the lit doorway, and Sullivan tucked in his T-shirt and followed him. It wouldn't be some citizen of this little desert town—Sullivan was one of the apparently few tramp electricians who didn't get drunk every night and use his eight-hundred-a-week paycheck to sway the local girls.

Besides, he'd only been in town this season for a week. Last Friday he'd been bending conduit pipe and pulling wires at the Palo Verde Nuclear Generating Station a hundred miles west of here—and during this last week at the Roosevelt Station, outside of town, there had been too much overtime for him to do anything more than work, come back here to gulp a couple of Cokes and shoot a couple of games of pool, and sleep.

The noise of conversation increased when he walked in through the back door after Morrie, and Sullivan squinted in the sudden glare of overhead lights and neon beer signs. He walked to the bar, and Morrie was already behind it and tilting a plastic cup under the Coke tap. The telephone was on the bar with the receiver lying beside it.

Sullivan picked it up. "Hello."

"Pete? God, you're a creature of habit—every year working the same places at the same seasons." She sounded angry.

It was his twin sister, and his hand tightened on the receiver. "Sukie, what—"

"Shut up and listen. I'm at a hotel in Delaware, and the front desk just called me. They say somebody hit my car in the lot, and they want me to go down and give 'em insurance information. I—"

"Sukie, I don't—"

"Shut *up!* I woke up on bar-time, Pete! I was bolt upright a second before the phone rang, and then I felt the plastic of the receiver before my hand hit it! I could feel my pupils tighten up a second before I turned on the lamp! Nobody hit my car, I'll bet my life on it! She's *found* me, and she'll find you—she'll have people at the desk here waiting for me, and she's got people out there where you are, you *know* she does. And you know what she wants us *for*, too, unless you've managed to forget *everything*. *I'm* looking Commander Hold-'Em in the *eye* right now, if you care; this is for *you*. Go straight out of there, right now, and drive and—this call is through the goddamn front desk, I know they're listening—go to the place where we hid—a thing, some things, okay? In a garage? It's what you're gonna need if she's—wanting us again. For *any* purpose."

"I can't—"

"Do you know the thing I'm talking about?"

"I think so, the . . . where you can't hardly walk for all the palm fronds on the pavement, right? And you've got to crawl under low branches? Is the . . . thing still there?"

"*I've* never moved it."

"But I can't just walk away here, Sukie. I'd have to . . . God, go to Radiation Control and get a Whole Body Count, that takes twenty minutes right there, and for my paycheck—"

"*Walk away, Pete!* It's just a job."

"It's the Arizona Public Service," Sullivan told her evenly, "that's Edison-owned, just like all the utilities are—the east coast is all Con Ed, and the West Coast is California Edison, and even Niagara up there is on the Edison grid. It's all Edison, coast to coast. I'd never work for any of the utilities again."

"A.O.P., dude."

"Sukie, maybe somebody *did* hit your car," he began, then realized that he was talking to a dead phone. He hung it up and pushed it toward Morrie.

"Sukie?" the bartender said.

"My sister. Somebody ran into her car and she wants to make a federal case out of it." Sullivan was remembering how awkwardly he'd played pool earlier in the evening, and he was annoyed to notice that his hands were trembling. He pushed away the Coke. "Give me a shot of Wild Turkey and a Coors chaser, would you?"

Morrie raised his eyebrows, but hiked up the bottle of bourbon without remarking on the fact that this would be the first real drink Sullivan had ever ordered in the place.

Sullivan sat down at one of the stools and slugged back the bourbon and then chased it with a long sip of cold beer. It made him feel closer to his sister, and he resented that almost enough to push the drinks away.

But not quite. He waved the emptied shot glass at Morrie and had another sip of the beer.

I'm looking Commander Hold-'Em in the eye right now, if you care.

Commander Hold-'Em was Sukie's name for the Grim Reaper—Sullivan believed she'd derived it from the name of some poker game that she always lost at—and it was also what she had always called whatever gun she carried. For several years, in the old days in L.A., it had been a .45 Derringer with two hollow-point bullets in it. Commander Hold-'Em would certainly still be something as effective today. Sullivan wondered if she would kill herself before even going down to the front desk and making *sure* that the call had been a trap. Maybe she would. Maybe she had just been waiting, all these years, for a good enough excuse to blow her goddamned head off. And, of course, not neglect to call him first.

And you know what she wants us for, too, unless you've managed to forget everything.

For a moment Sullivan found himself remembering an enigmatic image from his recurrent adolescent nightmare: three cans of Hires Root Beer, sitting in beach sand, unopened forever . . . a man's voice saying, *You're not Speedy Alka-Seltzer—*

And he shuddered and thrust the thought away. He lifted his glass and took such a huge slug of beer that his throat ached sharply, and he had to sit rigid until the swallow had finally gone down. At last he could breathe again.

Now he could feel the sudden cold of the beer in his stomach. At least it had driven away the momentary memory. God, he thought, I'm turning into Sukie.

A.O.P., dude.

She'd been good at driving the L.A. freeways drunk—she always said that if you started to weave in your lane, you could cover it by accelerating as you corrected, and nobody would know you'd been out of control; it had become a motto of theirs—*Accelerate Outta Problems.*

Morrie finally refilled the shot glass; Sullivan nodded and took a cautious sip. I was *never* any good at shooting pool, he thought. Or else, I've always been fairly good at it, but I was just jumpy when I was playing earlier tonight. I can't accelerate out of this town, out of this job. Probably she made the whole thing up—giggling in a house somewhere right now, not in Delaware and not even owning a gun anymore—just to wreck my life one more time.

No way it'll happen.

He took a moderate swallow of the beer. I *could* just *resign* from this job, he thought. If I turn in my resignation to the general foreman, it won't be held against me. Tramp electricians are always getting "a case of red-ass" and moving on. I'd just have to sign out and get a Whole Body Count, wearing paper pyjamas and lying in the aluminum coffin while the counter box inches over me, measuring the rems of radiation I've picked up this year; then drive to California and retrieve the . . . the *mask*, and move on, to Nevada or somewhere. There's always utilities work for someone who's still in good with Edison.

But if Sukie's just jerking me around, why should I bother?

And if she's *not,* he thought, then there'll be people waiting for me to show up at the station, as she said. In fact, if bad guys were listening in on our call, at the front desk of her hypothetical hotel, then they'd have heard Morrie answer the phone here the way he always does, *O'Hara's in Roosevelt, Morrie speaking.*

It's a half-hour's drive from the Roosevelt Nuclear Generating Station to O'Hara's . . . if you're not in a tearing hurry.

Sullivan bolted the rest of the bourbon and the beer and walked out of the bar. Morrie would add the cost of the drinks to the rent on the parking space in the back lot.

As he trudged across the obliquely lit gravel, the sight

of the familiar, homely old van slowed his pace. He could just climb in, pull the doors shut behind him and lock them and get back into the fold-out bed, and tomorrow morning at eight be driving through the gate at the Roosevelt Station, waving his badge at the guard who knew him anyway, and then happily spend all morning tightening conduit bolts that would have to be ripped out and done again after the foreman noticed that the inspection date on all the torque wrenches had expired a week ago. Assured, meaningless, union work, at thirty dollars an hour. Where would he find another trade like it?

He jumped in surprise, and an instant later the Honda said, *"Warning—you are too close to the vehicle."* The breeze was suddenly cold on his forehead, and his heart was pounding. *"Step back,"* the thing went on. He stepped back. *"Thank you."*

Bar-time. It had not just been clumsiness at the pool table. He was definitely on bar-time again.

I woke up on bar-time, Pete!

That's what the Sullivan twins had called the phenomenon when they'd first noticed it, early in their years of working for Loretta deLarava in L.A.—Sukie had got the term from California bars that keep their clocks set about ten minutes fast, so as to be able to get all the drinks off the tables by the legal shut-down time of 2 A.M., and so drinkers experience 2 A.M. a little while before it actually occurs. The twins had spent a lot of nights in bars, though Pete drank only Cokes and the occasional beer, and he could still vividly see Sukie, wearing dark glasses at some dark corner table, sucking a cigarette and asking someone. *One-thirty? Is that real-time or bar-time?*

Sullivan stood beside the van now, his hand on the driver's-side door handle.

Finally, he unlocked the door and climbed in. The engine started at the first twist of the key, and Sullivan let it warm up for only a few seconds before clanking the van into gear and steering it out toward the road that would take him south to Claypool and the 60 Highway that stretched away west.

The sky flashed again, twice; and though he had rolled the window down as he drove past the glaringly lit front entrance of O'Hara's and then picked up speed on the paved road, he still heard no following thunder.

He touched the brake pedal an instant before the brake lights of the car ahead came on; and then he saw the next jagged spear of lightning clearly because he had already glanced toward where it would be.

Bar-time for sure. He sighed and kept driving.

Everyone experiences bar-time occasionally, usually in the half-conscious hypnagogic stage of drifting into or out of sleep—when the noise that jolts one awake, whether it's an alarm or a bell or a shout, is anticipated, is *led up to* by the plot of the interrupted dream; or when some background noise like the hum of a refrigerator compressor or an air conditioner becomes intrusive only in the instant before it shuts off.

The Sullivan twins had spent countless hours on bar-time during the eighties—it had seemed that they were always reaching for a telephone just before it would start to ring, and appearing in indoor snapshots with their eyes closed because they had anticipated the flash. Eventually they had figured out that it was just one more weird consequence of working for Loretta deLarava, but the pay had been good enough to make it, too, just a minor annoyance.

Pay. Sullivan glanced at his fuel gauge and wondered if he would ever be able to get his last paycheck from the power station. Probably not, if Sukie had been right about deLarava being after them. Could he get a job as a lighting technician again?

Probably not, if deLarava was still in any aspect of the film business.

Great.

Worry about it all later, he told himself, after you've got to Hollywood and fetched the mask—if it's still in that weird garage, if somebody hasn't planed off that hill and put up condominiums there.

Without taking his eyes from the highway rushing past in his headlights, he fumbled in the broad tray on the console beside him, found a tape cassette, and slid it into the dashboard slot; and as the adventurous first notes of Men At Work's "A Land Down Under" came shaking out of the speakers behind him, he tried to feel braced and confident. The intrepid traveler, he thought, the self-reliant nomad; movin' on, able to handle anything from a blown head gasket to a drunk with a knife in a roadside bar; and always squinting off at the horizon like the Marlboro man.

But he shivered and gripped the wheel with both hands. All the way out to Hollywood? The oil in the van hadn't been changed for four thousand miles, and the brakes needed bleeding.

Sukie had frequently, and apparently helplessly, made up nonsense lyrics for songs, and when the tape ended he found himself humming the old "Beverly Hillbillies" tune, and unreeling random lyrics in his mind:

> Sister said, "Pete, run away from there."
> She said, "California is the place you ought to be,"
> So he cranked the poor old van, and he drove to Galilee.

On the night of his sixteenth birthday, he had borrowed his foster-father's car and gone tearing around a dark shopping-center parking lot, and then the security guards had chased him for miles in their fake cop car, and at the end of the chase the furious guards had threatened to charge him with all kinds of crimes; nothing had come of it, and the only one of the wild charges he could remember now was *Intercity flight to avoid apprehension.*

And now here he was, twenty-four years later, his black hair streaked with gray at the temples, forlornly wondering how even an interstate flight could possibly let him avoid apprehension.

In the rearview mirror, he saw the back window flash white, and this time thunder came rolling and booming across the desert, past him and on ahead into the darkness, followed a moment later by thrashing rain.

He switched on the windshield wipers. Her real name had been Elizabeth, but she'd somehow got her nickname from Bobby Darin's "Mack the Knife"—the song had briefly referred to a woman named Sukie Tawdry. His vision blurred with tears and he found that he was weeping, harshly and resentfully, for the twin sister who had been lost to him long before tonight.

The unfamiliar liberation of drink made him want to stomp on the accelerator—*A.O.P., dude*—and hammer the flat front of the van relentlessly through the desert air; but he remembered that this first rain would free up oil on the surface of the highway, slicking everything, and he let the speedometer needle drift back down to forty.

There was, after all, no hurry. DeLarava would want to do her work on Halloween, and that was still five days off.

CHAPTER 4

❦

It was all very well to say "Drink me," but the
wise little Alice was not going to do that in a hurry.
"No, I'll look first," she said, "and see whether
it's marked 'poison' or not" . . .

—Lewis Carroll,
Alice's Adventures in Wonderland

LUMPY AND DARYL had not found Kootie's bag of
quarters in the knapsack's side pocket, and at dawn in an
all-night drugstore farther up Fairfax he had bought a
cheap pair of sunglasses to conceal his swelling discolored
eye. That left a little more than six dollars.

Kootie was sitting on a bus bench now, just because he
had been too tired to walk one more block. Maybe it
didn't matter—maybe all the bus benches in the whole
city looked like this one; or, worse, appeared normal to
normal people but would all look like this to *him*.

The bench was black, with a big white skull and crossbones painted on it, along with the words:

DON'T SMOKE DEATH CIGARETTES.

And he had seen packs of these Death cigarettes at the drugstore. The packs were black, with the same skull and crossbones for a logo. Could that actually be a brand name? What could possibly be in the packs? Little white lengths of finger bones, he thought, stained with dried blood at one end to show you where the filter is.

He was shivering in his heavy flannel shirt. The sunlight was warm enough when it was shining on him, but in the shade like this the air was still nighttime air—chilly, and thin enough to get in between the teeth of a zipper. Maybe when the sun got up over the tops of the storefront buildings this strange night would finally be all the way gone, and the bus bench would be stenciled with some normal colorful ad.

Maybe he could go home, and his mom and dad would be there.

(*In their wedding clothes, those two had to have been his real mom and dad, not the bodies duct taped into the chairs in the atrium, the bodies with their eyes—*)

He was shaking now, and he leaned back, gripping his elbows tightly, and forced the shuddering breaths into his lungs and back out. Perhaps he was having a heart attack. That would probably be the best thing that could happen. He wished his feet could reach the ground so that he could brace them on the pavement.

Back up on Sunset, hours ago when the sky had still been middle-of-the-night dark, he had tried several times to call the police. Maybe in the daytime he'd be able to find a telephone that worked right. Maybe maybe maybe.

The shivering had stopped, and he cautiously took a

deep breath as if probing to see if a fit of hiccups had finally gone away. When he exhaled, he relaxed, and he discovered that his toes could reach the pavement.

He brushed back his black curly hair and stood up; and when he had walked several yards to be able to stand in a patch of sunlight, he discovered that he was hungry. He could afford breakfast, but probably not much after that.

"You waiting for the 217 bus, kid?"

Kootie glanced up at the old man who had spoken to him. "No," he said quickly. "No, I'm . . . walking to school today." He shoved his hands in his pockets and hurried on south down the Fairfax sidewalk, forcing himself not to glance fearfully back over his shoulder.

That guy *looked* normal, Kootie told himself. He might have been just a man on his way to work, curious about this kid out by himself.

But Kootie remembered some of the people he'd met during this long, alarming night. An old woman pushing a shopping cart across a bright-lit supermarket parking lot had shouted to him, calling him Al, and when he had hurried away from her she had started crying; her echoing sobs had been much louder than her shouting, and he'd still been able to hear her when he was a block away. Later, ducking away from an old man that had seemed to be following him, he had interrupted a young bum, his pants down around his ankles, defecating behind some trash cans . . . and Kootie shook his head now to drive away the memory of seeing *rocks and bottlecaps* coming out of the embarrassed guy's butt and clattering on the asphalt. And one woman had pulled up to the curb in a gleaming XKE Jaguar and rolled down the passenger-side window and called out to him, "You're too young to smoke! I'll give you a hundred dollars for your cigar!" That time, *he'd* started crying because even though he couldn't understand what she'd meant, he had wanted to run to the nice car and beg the pretty lady for help, but her eyes and lips and teeth had been so glitteringly bright that he could only hurry away, down an alley too clogged with trash cans and stacks of wooden pallets for her car to follow.

Behind him now he heard the familiar puff of air brakes and the roar of a bus engine, and a moment later the big black-and-white RTD bus had gone grinding and sighing past on his left. Kootie distantly hoped that the old man had got aboard, and was going to some job that he liked, and that to him this city was still the malls-and-movie-billboards place Kootie remembered living in.

He watched the bus move ponderously through the lanes of morning traffic—what was down in that direction? The Farmer's Market, Kootie recalled, and that Jewish delicatessen where a big friendly man behind the fish counter had once given him samples of smoked whitefish and salmon—and Kootie saw a police car turn north from Beverly.

There was a pair of pay telephones in front of a minimart ahead of him, and he slanted his pace to the right, toward them, walking just fast enough so that he could be standing there holding a receiver to his ear when the police car would be driving past at his back. When he got to the phone he even went so far as to drop one of his precious quarters into the slot. I need time to think, he told himself.

He was imagining waving down the police car, or the next one that came by. He would let himself just hang on to the door handle and cry, and tell the officers everything, and they would all go back to Kootie's house on Loma Vista Drive. He would wait in the car with one of the cops while the man's partner checked out the house. Or else they'd radio for another car to go to the house, and they'd take Kootie "downtown."

And then what? Several times during his long night's trek he had paused to close his eyes and try to believe that his parents weren't dead, that he had just hallucinated all that terrible stuff about them being dressed up for a wedding in the living room and at the same time sitting murdered in the atrium, and about the one-armed hobo rushing up the hall and trying to grab him; and he had tried to believe too that the glass brick in his shirt pocket had nothing to do with the people he was encountering; and he hadn't once been able to believe either thing.

Could he believe them now, now that the sun had cleared the rooftops of the shop buildings across the street and all these distracted, ordinary strangers were busily going to work?

He could do an easy test. With a trembling finger he punched the 9 button once and the 1 button twice. I can still change my mind, he told himself nervously. I can still just run away from this phone—jeez, walk, even.

There was a click in the earpiece, and then a man's blurry voice: ". . . and I told him to just go fuck himself. What do you think of that? I don' gotta . . ." The voice faded, and Kootie was listening to the background murmur—laughter, mumbling, glasses clinking, someone singing. He could just barely hear a child's voice reciting, over and over again, "In most gardens they make the beds too soft—so that the flowers are always asleep."

Kootie's chest was empty and cold. "Hello," he said, in a voice that might have been too loud because he had to talk over the sudden ringing in his ears, "hello, I was trying to get the emergency police number—" It could still be all right, he thought tensely, *all* the L.A.-area phones could be crossed up in this way—but even just in his head, just unspoken, the thought had a shrilly frightened tone. "Who have I reached, please?"

For a moment there was just the distant clatter and slurred speech, and then a woman's voice, choking and thick, wailed, "Al? Al, thank God, where are you gonna meet me tonight? That supermarket parking lot again? Al, my legs've swelled up like *sausages*, and I need—"

Kootie hung up the phone without dropping it, and he was able a moment later to walk easily away down the Fairfax sidewalk; but he was surprised that the air wasn't coagulating into the invisible molasses that, in nightmares, kept him from being able to drag one foot ahead of the other.

It was all real. The sun was up, and he was wide awake, and that voice on the phone had been the voice of the old crazy woman he'd run away from in the parking lot, hours ago. His parents really were dead, obviously killed because he had broken the Dante and taken away the glass brick.

Kootie had killed them.

And even though the police wouldn't ever believe that, they would make Kootie do things—like what? Identify the bodies? No, they wouldn't force a *kid* to do that, would they? But he'd still have to make probably a million *statements*, which would either be true and sound crazy, or be lies and sound like a kid's lies; and eventually he'd be put into a foster home somewhere. And how would the telephones behave *there?* What sort of person would be in charge of the place, or soon come visiting? And if by then they'd decided he was crazy, they might have him in restraints, strapped down on his bed.

He recoiled away from a memory of duct tape.

If he just got rid of the glass brick, would all this stuff stop happening? But who would eventually *find* it, and why had his parents kept it hidden?

He remembered a Robert Louis Stevenson story about a devil in a bottle—it could get you anything you wanted, but if you died owning it you'd go to hell—and if you wanted to get rid of it you had to sell it for less than you'd paid for it, or it would come back to you even if you threw it into the ocean.

Was this thing worth money, could he *sell* it? Was *it* a "cigar"? If so, he could have gotten a hundred dollars for it from the Jaguar woman last night. It seemed to him that a hundred dollars was a good deal less than what he had paid for it.

There was a low, white-painted cinder-block wall around the little parking lot of a strip shopping center ahead of him, and he crossed to it and hiked himself up to sit on the coping. He glanced around at the wide, busy intersection and the sidewalks to make sure no one was paying any particular attention to him, and then he unbuttoned the pocket of his heavy flannel shirt and lifted out the glass brick. It seemed to *click*, very faintly deep inside, when he turned it in his hand.

This was the first time he'd looked at it in sunlight. It was rectangular, but bumpy and wavy on its surfaces, and even when he held it up to the sun he couldn't see anything in its cloudy depths. He ran a finger around its narrow side—and felt a seam. He peered at the side surfaces and saw that a tiny straight crack went all the way around, dividing the brick into two equal halves.

The two guys that had robbed him so long ago last night had taken his Swiss army knife, so he worked a fingernail into the groove and twisted, and only managed to tear off a strip of his nail. By holding the glass thing between his palms, though, with his fingers gripped tightly over the edges, he was able to pry hard enough to feel the two glass sections move against each other, and to be sure that the thing *could* be opened.

He pressed it firmly together again and took off his backpack to tuck the brick safely down among his tumbled clothes. He pulled the flap down over it all and then, since the plastic buckles had been broken last night, carefully tied the straps tight before putting the backpack on again. Maybe people wouldn't be able to sense the glass thing so easily now.

Like a gun, he thought dully, or a grenade or blasting caps or something. It's like they had a *gun* in the house and never told their kid even what a gun is. It's their *own* fault I somehow accidentally got them killed by playing with it.

If I open it—what? A devil might come out. A *devil* might *actually* come out. It wouldn't matter whether or not I believe in devils, or that my friends and the teachers in school don't. People in 1900 didn't think that radium could hurt you, just carrying a chip of it in your pocket like a lucky rock, and then one day their legs fell off and they died of cancer. Not believing something is no help if you turn out to be wrong.

He heard the short *byoop* of a motorcycle cop's siren and looked up nervously—but the cop was stopping way out in the intersection, and, as Kootie watched, he climbed off the blue-flashing bike and put down the kickstand and began directing traffic with broad slow gestures. The traffic signals had gone completely out sometime during the last few minutes, weren't even flashing red; and then even when the policeman waved for the southbound lanes to move forward, the cars and trucks and buses stayed backed up for another several minutes because nearly every driver had stalled and had to start up again.

As Kootie crossed Beverly, the sound of grinding starter motors was echoing among the lanes behind him like power saws.

CHAPTER 5

"Then you keep moving around, I suppose?"
said Alice.

*"Exactly so," said the Hatter, "as the things
get used up."*

*"But what happens when you come to the
beginning again?" Alice ventured to ask.*

*"Suppose we change the subject," the March
Hare interrupted . . .*

—Lewis Carroll,
Alice's Adventures in Wonderland

ONE OF THEM had finally been for real.

It had been two hours since the Greyhound bus had
pulled out of the dawn-streaked yard of the Albuquerque
station, subsequently finding the I-40 highway and
cranking its way up through the dry rock Zuni Mountains,
downshifting to follow the twisting highway among the
ancient lava beds, and booming down the western slope
to roar right through Gallup without stopping; but when

43

the bus finally swung off the I-40 at the little town of Houck, just over the border into Arizona, Angelica Anthem Elizalde simply kept her seat while most of the other passengers shuffled past her down the aisle to catch some fresh morning air and maybe a quick cup of coffee during the fifteen-minute stop.

She looked out her window. Though it was now eight-thirty, the bus was still casting a yards-long shadow, and the shadow pointed west. She shivered, but tucked her ladies' magazine into the pocket of the seat in front of her.

She had hoped to distract herself with its colorful pages, but had run aground on an almost hysterically cheerful article about how to cook squash, with a sidebar that addressed "Twelve Important Squash Questions"; and then she had been forced out of the pages again by a multiple-choice "Creativity Test," which gave high marks to the hypothetical housewife who, confronted with two mismatched socks after all the laundry had been put away, elected to (C) make hand puppets of them rather than (A) throw them away or (B) use them for dusting.

None of the listed answers had been anything like "burn them," "eat them," "bury them in the backyard," or "save them in case one night you answer the door to a stranger with bare, mismatched feet."

Elizalde managed a tight smile. She flexed her hands and wondered what work she would find to do in Los Angeles. Typist, again? Waitress, again? *Panhandler, bag lady, prostitute, a patient in one of the county mental hospitals in which she'd done her residency—*

—a felon locked up in the Sybil Brand Institute for Women—

She quickly fetched up the magazine out of the seat pocket and stared hard at a photograph of some happy family having fun around a swing set (—probably all of them models, really, who had never seen each other before lining up there for the picture—) and she thought again about turning back. Get off the bus at Flagstaff, she told herself, and catch the 474 bus, take it all the way back to Oklahoma City, be there by eight-thirty tonight. Go back to the big truck stop under the Petro water tower, tell the manager at the Iron Skillet that you were *too* sick to call *in* sick when you failed to show up for the waitress shift last night.

Get back on that old heartland merry-go-round.

For nearly two years she had been traveling, far from Los Angeles, working in restaurants and bars and small offices, along the Erie Canal from the Appalachians to Buffalo, and up and down the Ohio River from Pittsburgh to Cairo, and, most recently, along the Canadian River in Oklahoma. She'd celebrated her thirty-fourth birthday with half a dozen of the Iron Skillet waitresses in the bar at O'Connell's in Norman, twenty minutes south of Oklahoma City.

At least L.A. would be fairly warm, even now, in October, four days before Halloween. The Mexican street vendors in the Boyle Heights area might already be selling *El Día de los Muertos* candy, the white stylized skulls and skeletons—

(—*Shut up!*—)

Again she forced herself to stare at the family in the magazine photo, and she tried to believe that it really was a family, that they were genuinely enjoying some—

(—*long-lost*—)

(—*Shut up!*—)

weekend in the backyard, oblivious of this photographer—

. . . It didn't work. The adults and kids in the photograph just looked like models, strangers to each other.

Elizalde remembered driving the L.A. freeways at night, snatching an occasional glance to the side at some yellow-lit kitchen window in a passing apartment building, and always for one moment desperately envying the lives of whatever people lived there. She had always imagined hammered-copper roosters on the kitchen wall, a TV in the next room with "Cheers" getting innocent laughs, children sitting cross-legged on the carpet—

(—*Shut up.*)

That had never really worked, either. Maybe those apartments had all been vacant, with the lights left on. She folded the magazine and put it back.

A few moments later she jumped, and looked toward the front of the bus just before the first returning passenger stepped aboard, rocking the bus on the shocks. Elizalde sighed. No, she couldn't go back to Oklahoma.

For about twelve hours now she had been doing this, reacting to noises and jolts just before they happened. She'd been in bed when it started, and she'd awakened in her darkened apartment just before the clock radio had blared on. At first she had thought some mental clock had been keeping track of the time while she'd slept—she'd found herself remembering her grandmother's saying, *Es como los brujos, duerme con los ojos abiertos:* He is like the witches, and sleeps with his eyes open—but the effect had continued as she'd proceeded to get ready for work, so that she'd flinched before water had come out of the shower head, and nearly dropped her hair dryer because it had seemed to quiver animatedly in her hand just as she was about to push the On button.

Then she had begun blinking her eyes even before the tears welled up in them. She'd sat down on her bathroom floor and just sobbed with fright, for in the same way that she'd seemed to be anticipating physical events, she had now been afraid that an idea was about to surface in her mind, an idea that she had been strenuously avoiding for two years. Before she'd been able to distract herself, the idea had hit her: *maybe she had not, after all, had a psychotic schizophrenic episode in her Los Angeles clinic in 1990.*

And, bleakly, she had known that she would have to go back there and find out. Find out if: *one of them had finally been for real.*

Everybody was getting back on the bus now, and the driver had the engine idling. Elizalde let her head sink back against the high, padded seat, and she thought she might at last be able to get some sleep, during the twelve hours it would take the bus to plow on through Flagstaff and Kingman and Barstow to, finally, Los Angeles.

After all, it seemed that nothing could sneak up on her. *Soy como las brujas, duermo con mis ojos abiertos.*

Pete Sullivan clanked the gearshift into neutral and gunned the engine to keep it from stalling. He was stopped in what was supposed to be the fast lane of the

101, a mile or so short of the tunnel where the northbound Santa Ana Freeway would merge in. God only knew when he would get to Hollywood.

Though it was a non-holiday Friday morning, even on the westbound 60 the traffic had been jammed up—fully stopped much of the time, and occasionally speeding up and opening out in front of him for just enough moments to let him imagine that the congestion was behind him, before the red brake lights would all start glaring again ahead of him.

In the driver's seat of his van he was above most of the other drivers, and during the course of an hour, while his foot had moved back and forth from the brake to the gas pedal, he had watched the towers of Los Angeles rise ahead of him in the brassy light. The towers had been scrimmed to dim silhouettes by the smog, as if they were faded shapes in a photograph that's been left out too long in the sun—or, he had thought, as if the city had had its picture taken so many times that the cumulative loss of images had begun to visibly diminish it.

Like deLarava's ghosts, he had thought. Maybe the whole city has died, but is too distracted to have realized it yet.

The towers were clearer now, and it was disorienting to see big buildings that he didn't recognize—one of the new ones was a tall tan-stone cylinder, like a stylized sculpture of a rocket ship, and he wondered uneasily if he would still be able to find his way around the city's streets.

His window was open to the diesel-reeking air, and he looked down over his elbow at the center divider, which in the old days had generally just been a featureless blur rushing past. Flowering weeds, and even a couple of midget palm trees, were pushing up out of cracks in the concrete, and curled around them and the many Budweiser cans was an apparently constant web of brown tape from broken stereo cassettes; there were even a lot of *peaches* for some reason, bruised but unbitten, as if some citizen of this no man's land had left them there like Hansel and Gretel's bread crumbs.

Sullivan wondered what cassettes these were that drivers had so prodigally pitched out their windows, and he grinned nervously at the temptation to open the door and salvage some of the tape. It would be a cinch to clean it and wind it onto a fresh cassette-half. Would it all be the same kind of music, perhaps even all copies of the same tape? It occurred to him that the center divider looked like a miles-long shrine to primitive-but-urban gods; and he shivered and turned his attention back to the pickup truck in front of him, in the bed of which two Mexican girls were listlessly brushing their long black hair.

About an hour ago he had stopped peering ahead to see what wreck or freeway construction would be causing the traffic jam—apparently the freeways just snarled up without any definable cause these days, like the turbulence that would sometimes inexplicably shake a sump pipe at a power station even when all the air had been bled out of it.

In Los Angeles space is time, he thought—you don't say, *I'm thirty miles from downtown;* you say, *I'm half an hour from it.* If unpredictable turbulence has become a real, constant factor in traffic, then all the maps and clocks are broken (like the Mad Hatter's butter-clogged watch!)

and you can only make a hazy guess about how far it might
be from one point to another.

I'm a hundred years from Venice Beach, he thought,
and a thousand miles from Christmas Eve of 1986. Better
draw up a chart.

He pushed the thought away and concentrated on the
traffic.

The Brew 102 brewery proved to be gone. 102 had
been the only beer Sullivan had ever encountered that
had sediment in it, but he found that he missed the old
black-and-yellow sign, and he was further disoriented to
see half a dozen helicopters parked on the wide roof of a
building on the other side of the freeway. With the
glittering rocket still ahead of him, the whole place was
looking like a poster for some 1930's science-fiction
movie.

When he eventually gunned the van up the off-ramp
at Hollywood Boulevard, though, there were beat-up old
couches under the palm trees in the freeway border area,
and a dispirited-looking group of ragged black men, their
hair in ropy dreadlocks, were slouching there in the shade.
He half-expected to see chickens running around their
skinny ankles, and a fire in a split oil drum behind them.

The clocks and maps are smashed and ripped to bits,
he thought. Even though it was the *best* butter.

He drove west on Hollywood Boulevard, cautiously
pleased to see that though the names of many businesses
had changed—there was no Howard Johnson's restaurant
at Hollywood and Vine anymore—most of the actual
buildings he remembered had survived.

It seemed to him that it had always been like this, in the area from Franklin south to Melrose and beyond. Every building looked as if it had originally been used for something else. Even here on Hollywood Boulevard, the odd top corners of the storefronts were frequently broken or bent, showing old brick underneath, and between buildings he could see brick alcoves, way up and far back, dating from God knew when. Tiny ironwork balconies still stuck out on second and third floors, with probably nothing behind them anymore but empty offices.

Now that he was nearly there—only one turn remaining, a right onto Laurel Canyon once he'd got out past this tourist area of the boulevard—he was in no hurry to get to the ruins he and his sister had explored on that spring day in '86. At Wilcox he impulsively decided to turn north—and when he'd made the turn he saw that the Shelton Apartments had been torn down, replaced by some sprawling new pink apartment building.

He pulled the van over to the curb and switched off the engine for the first time since stopping for eggs and bacon in Blythe, four hours ago. Then for several minutes, while he lit a cigarette and stared across the street at the new four-story building, he tried to remember the old Shelton.

Like the Lido and the Mayfair, both of which were still standing a block farther up the street, the Shelton had had one of those big signs on the roof, separate ornate letters in line, supported by a lattice of steel beams, and had had a lot of the decorative cornices and balconies that architects never seemed to bother with anymore. The only eccentricities of this new place, the Hollywood Studio

Club Apartments, were inset windows and an apparent blanket policy of having all corners be rounded. A banner across the top announced $777 MOVES YOU IN! Probably not a bad price around here, he thought absently, these days. It had been while filming a documentary in the lobby of the old Shelton in the winter of '84 that he and his sister had finally got a strong clue about what Loretta deLarava really did.

DeLarava had hired the twins right out of college ten years earlier, and they'd been working for her ever since as "gaffers"—lighting technicians. DeLarava produced short-subject films—in-house instruction pieces for businesses, non-timely human-interest bits for news programs, the occasional commercial—and for twelve years the twins had spent their days driving to what seemed like every corner of Los Angeles, to lay cables and set up Genie lifts and hang lights over some beach or office floor or sidewalk.

DeLarava had been a disconcerting boss. One of the first jobs the twins worked on with her had been a short film about the vandalizing of Houdini's grave in Brooklyn in 1975—and deLarava had been the first to cover the event because it hadn't even occurred before she arrived. It had been deLarava *herself* who shattered the stone bust of Houdini in the Machpelah Cemetery and took a mummified thumb out of a hollow inside it, and who had dug two plaster hands out of the soil in front of the grave. The twins had of course not even been tempted to turn their new boss in to the authorities—but, apparently on a drunken whim, Sukie had stolen the thumb and the hands from deLarava's luggage on the drive back to the airport.

DeLarava had cried when she'd discovered the loss, and ransacked the car, and had even had to make new airline reservations because she insisted on driving back to the cemetery to look for the items, but Sukie had not ever admitted to the theft.

From the beginning, Sukie had taken a perverse pleasure in tormenting their boss, and certainly deLarava was an easy target. The fat old woman always wore a rubber band around her scalp, with her hair brushed down over it to keep it from showing, and after Sukie had discovered the habit she made a point of finding opportunities to bump the woman's head, dislodging the rubber band so that it sprang to the top of her head, making a wreck of her hair. And deLarava's clothes always had Velcro closures instead of buttons or zippers, and Sukie frequently managed to get the old woman's shoes or jackets attached to upholstered chairs or textured wallpaper, so that deLarava had to pull herself loose with an embarrassing tearing sound. And once, after a minute or so of silence during a drive, Sukie had glanced brightly at the old woman and said, "Yeah? Go on—? You were saying something about a picnic?"—as if their boss had just begun a sentence and then forgotten it—but deLarava had reacted with such fright to the disorienting gambit that Sukie had never tried that particular trick again.

At the Shelton they'd been filming in the lobby and in an upstairs hallway, and of course Pete and Sukie had arrived three hours before the rest of the crew to locate a 220-volt power source in the old building and set up the hydraulic lifts and hang the key lights. Sullivan remembered now that for an outdoor shot of the hotel they'd rented battery-powered lights made by a company called Frizzolini, and that Sukie had kept saying that deLarava had better be careful of getting her hair all frizzed. Possibly Sukie had been drunk already.

DeLarava herself had arrived early for that shoot. She would have been in her mid-fifties then, and for once she had been looking her age. She had always smoked some kind of clove-flavored Indonesian cigarettes that made a room smell as though someone were baking a glazed ham nearby, and on this morning, her chubby hands had been shaking as she'd lit each one off the butt of the last, sparks dropping unnoticed onto the carpet, and her pendulous cheeks had quivered when she inhaled. She had brought with her a whole hatbox full of props to distribute around the shooting area; Sullivan remembered pocket watches, a couple of diamond rings, even a feather boa, in addition to the usual antique, still-sealed bottles of liquor.

The project had been a short morbid piece on the suicides that had taken place in the old building; perhaps the film had been done on spec, for Sullivan couldn't now recall any particular client for the job, and he couldn't remember it having gone through the post-production or screening steps. Incongruously, they had been filming it on Christmas Eve. The old woman had never let a Christmas Eve or a Halloween go by without filming something, somewhere.

Sullivan wondered uneasily what she might have scheduled for this upcoming Saturday.

DeLarava had been interested in only two of the suicides that had taken place at the Shelton. The first was a woman called Jenny Dolly. Around the turn of the century, Jenny Dolly and her twin sister, Rosie, were a celebrated dance team, renowned for their beauty; but Jenny's face had been horribly scarred in a car crash in 1933, and she had hanged herself in her apartment here in 1941. The other suicide had been the actress Clara Blandick, who, one day in 1962, had got her hair fixed up and had carefully done her makeup and put on a formal gown and then pulled a plastic bag over her head and smothered herself. She was chiefly remembered for having played Auntie Em in the 1939 version of *The Wizard of Oz*.

Auntie Em, Auntie Em, thought Sullivan now as he puffed on his cigarette, echoing in his head the mocking voice of the Wicked Witch of the West in the movie.

And, he thought as he squinted through the smoke, a twin sister who killed herself. How're you doing, Sukie?

The shoot had been what gaffers called a bad-hang day. The lights had been plagued with "ghosting," the lamps glowing dimly even when the big old dimmer boxes indicated no power being transmitted, which called for a lot of laborious checks of the light board and all the cable connections; and then when the cameras were finally running, the shoot had repeatedly been interrupted by power surges and blackouts.

Apparently, a lot of people had died at the Shelton, he thought now.

Live and learn.

DeLarava had kept looking at her watch, though the clock on the lobby wall was accurate. Twice Pete had peered at her watch as she glanced at it, and both times it had been wrong—*differently* wrong: once it would read, say, 6:30, and a few minutes later it would be indicating something like 12:35. At one point, he had called Sukie over to one of the malfunctioning lights and in a low voice had told her about their boss's erratic watch.

Sukie had followed deLarava around the carpeted lobby for a few minutes after that, ostensibly to ask about the placing of the props and the fill lights, and then she had come back to where Pete was still crouched over the flickering lamp; and she had told him in a whisper that no matter which way deLarava was facing, the hour hand of her watch always wobbled around to point up Wilcox— north. It was a compass.

Shortly after that the music had started up. DeLarava had liked to have taped music playing before the cameras started running, even *during* takes for which the soundtrack would be entirely dubbed in later—she said it helped establish the mood—and the music was always something contemporary with the period the film was dealing with. Today it was Glenn Miller's "Tuxedo Junction," and she had decided to start it up early.

As the audiotape reels started rotating and the first notes came razoring out of the speaker grilles, deLarava had turned away from the twins and fumbled something out of her purse. She was clearly trying to conceal it, but both twins saw that she was holding a drinking straw— one of the striped ones marketed for children, with a flexible neck and some kind of flavor capsule inside it to make plain milk taste like chocolate or strawberry.

Sullivan pitched his cigarette out the window and

started up the van's engine. Stopped ahead of him was a battered old blue-painted school bus with the back doors open, and inside it, on wooden shelves and on the floor, were crates of bananas and tortillas and garlic and long, dried red chili peppers. A mobile third-world grocery store, he thought, a hundred feet from the Hollywood Boulevard sidewalk.

It reminded him of lunch, and he wondered if Musso and Frank's was still in business, a block or two west. He steered the van around the stopped bus and drove up Wilcox to make a U-turn back to the boulevard. Over the tops of the old apartment buildings in front of him he could see the Capitol Records building, designed long ago to look like a stack of vinyl records with a needle touching the top disk.

Vinyl records, he thought. The clocks and maps are definitely broken.

CHAPTER 6

"I dare say you never even spoke to Time!"

*"Perhaps not," Alice cautiously replied, "but I
know I have to beat time when I learn music."*

*"Ahh, that accounts for it," said the Hatter.
"He won't stand beating. Now, if you only kept
on good terms with him, he'd do almost anything
you liked with the clock."*

—Lewis Carroll,
Alice's Adventures in Wonderland

MUSSO AND FRANK'S GRILL, Hollywood's oldest
restaurant, was still in business on the north side of the
boulevard at Cherokee, and Sullivan parked around the
corner and walked in through the double wood-and-glass
doors and crossed to one of the booths under the eternal
autumn-scene mural and the high ceiling. The Tuesday
special was corned beef and cabbage, but he sentimentally
ordered a sardine sandwich and a Coors.

This had been his and Sukie's secret hideout; their

friends and coworkers had hung out in trendier places like the City Cafe and the Cafe Figaro on Melrose, or the Ivy down on Robertson.

In fact, he and Sukie had driven here in 1984 for dinner right after the Christmas Eve shoot at the Shelton, and during the drive Sukie had been loudly singing gibberish Christmas carols—*O car-bo-lic faith-less, poi-son-ously pregnant . . . O rum key, O ru-um key to O-bliv-i-on . . . Commander Hold-'Em, bone-dry king of a-angels . . .* and of course the old schoolyard song they'd got in trouble for singing in some foster home when they'd been seven, *We three kings of Orient are, trying to smoke a rubber cigar; it was loaded, it exploded . . .*

As soon as they'd got to the restaurant and been seated, Sukie had ordered a double Jack Daniel's, and Pete, though he had wanted a beer, had wound up with a Coke, because when the waiter had walked up to their booth Pete had been leaning forward and saying, "Coke?"

After the waiter had left, Sukie had grinned and said, "Coke what?"

Pete had waved vaguely. "What she was doing. Loretta, our dignified boss, snorting a straw along the old hotel wallpaper! Old cocaine mixed up in the dust, do you think?"

In reply Sukie had resumed singing some badly remembered lines from "We Wish You a Merry Christmas"—*"We won't go until we got some, we won't go until we got some, we won't go until we got some, so trot 'em out now."*

"What the hell, Suke," Pete had said, bewildered by her manic cheer.

"I figure that's what the Sodomites and—what would

you call 'em, Gomorrites?—were singing outside of Lot's house, you know? In the Bible, when all of Lot's neighbors wanted to bugger the angels that were visiting him. Loretta wouldn't go today until she got some, and she did get some—she sucked 'em up through that straw." The drinks had arrived then, and Sukie had drained hers in one long swallow and mutely signaled for another.

"Got some what?" Pete had said after a half-hearted sip of his Coke. "Angels? Angel dust? What?"

"Ghosts," Sukie had said impatiently. "What did you think? She snorted up a whole pile of ghosts today—did you see how much younger she looked when she finally got into her car and split? She looked thirty years old tonight, a *youthful* thirty, and she looked a goddamn *hundred* this morning. We somehow made it possible for her to draw a whole lot of ghosts out of the walls of that place and then snort 'em up her nose."

Pete hadn't wanted to start discussing ghosts with his sister. "She's, ah, something like a necrophilliac voyeur," he said. "There's probably a single word for it. She likes to go shoot films at cemeteries and places where people have died, and kind of rub her fingers in the dirt, we've noticed that in her before. Hell, I suppose there's somebody somewhere who watches the tape of Jack Ruby shooting Oswald over and over again. Getting off on . . . what, the thought that somebody really did die here. Creepy, but probably harmless, right? But I'm afraid she's going flat-out *crazy* now. Where does that leave our jobs? I mean, there she was, crouched over and snuffling along with a *straw,* as if some dead lady's perfume might still be in the wallpaper!"

"Pete," said Sukie, "I don't mean perfume, and I don't mean *metaphorical* ghosts. I mean there were real essences of dead people in that place, and she *consumed* them in some literal way, like a whale eating plankton."

Pete stared at her. "Are you saying," he asked carefully after a moment, "that you think she actually *believes* that?"

"God, you're an idiot sometimes. I'm saying that's what happened. She's *right* to believe it, she *did* eat a bunch of ghosts. Didn't she change, visibly, between eight this morning and nine tonight?"

Pete tried to smile derisively, but gave it up and let his face relax into a frown. "She did get something out of it," he admitted. "But come on, *ghosts?*"

The word hadn't sounded ludicrous in this dark wooden booth at Musso and Frank's.

"And," he found himself going on, "she is often . . . prettier and cheerier after a shoot. Still damn fat." He laughed uncertainly. "Do you suppose that's what she's been doing, all along? She never used a *straw* before. That we ever noticed, anyway."

"I'm sure she'd have liked it better if we hadn't seen her do that—but she obviously needed it too bad to be subtle this time. I bet she usually sucks 'em in through those damned cigarettes of hers—maybe ghosts are drawn to that clove smell, like kids to hot cookies. It *was* a flavored straw, you noticed."

Sukie's fresh drink arrived. Pete drained it himself, and Sukie glanced at her watch and then at the clock on the wall, and she asked for two more.

For a full minute neither of them spoke.

Pete was feeling the bourbon hit his fragile alertness

like static muddying up an AM radio signal. "And, of course, it would have something to do with bar-time," he said finally. "Ghosts are . . . if there *are* ghosts, they're certainly a very derailed crowd, in terms of time."

"Of course. And the electrical problems. We always have electrical problems, and she still not only doesn't fire us, but pays us way too much."

"We don't *always* have electrical problems," Pete said irritably. Then he made himself think about what Sukie had said. "Now you're saying it has to be *us?* Specifically, Pete and Sukie?"

"She acts like it, doesn't she? Has she ever once hired anyone else? Those props, those watches and things, those were lures; but for some reason she needs *us* to make her able to hook 'em. Did you keep on looking at her watch?"

"Not after the first business," he said glumly. Of course, Sukie would have, once he'd told her about it.

"When we finally got started filming, the hour hand was pointing straight to the section of wall she took her straw to, every time, and it wasn't north anymore."

Pete grinned weakly. "Compass needles point to ghosts?"

"Evidence of the old glazzies, droogie," she said, quoting the movie *A Clockwork Orange.*

Glazzies, he recalled, meant eyes. "Let's get some menus," she went on. "I may as well eat while I drink, and she'll want her precious twins all peppy and full of vitamins tomorrow."

Her precious twins, Pete thought now as he finished his sardine sandwich and drank off the last of the Coors alone in the booth on this sunny but cold morning eight years later.

The twins had continued working for deLarava for precisely another two years after that Christmas Eve; and Pete had eventually come to believe that Sukie was right about what deLarava had been doing at their shooting locations.

Neither of them, though, had seriously considered quitting. *What the hell,* Sukie had remarked more than once when she'd been drunk. *It's just exorcism, right? I mean, she inhales the ghosts and then they're gone— obviously, since she never goes back and does a shoot at the same place twice. We're exorcists, like that priest in that movie. And we didn't take no vows of poverty.*

No indeed, thought Sullivan now. DeLarava paid us damn well. And if she hadn't tried to get us *car-bo-lic faithless, poi-so-nously pregnant* to do that muscle beach feature in Venice, on *bone-dry king of angels* Christmas Eve in 1986, *won't go until we got one, so dredge him out now* we'd probably be working for her still, to this day.

He frowned intently at the check, tossed thirteen dollars onto the Formica table and walked quickly out of the restaurant into the chilly October breeze.

It had been *early* in 1986 when they had hidden the mask in the ruins up on Laurel Canyon Boulevard. Just a dried thumb and two plaster hands, but Sukie always referred to the set as "the mask."

Sullivan steered the van back onto Hollywood Boulevard, heading west again; there was still only the one more turn ahead. On the south side of the street stood a new McDonald's restaurant that looked like an incongruously space-age Grecian temple, but at least the Chinese Theater was still there in all its battered black and red byzantine splendor at Highland.

The boulevard narrowed after that, as it flowed west between big old apartment buildings and broad lawns, and around Fairfax the pavement of the eastbound lane was entirely ripped up for repairs, but the sun hung still a little short of noon in the empty blue sky when Sullivan reached Laurel Canyon Boulevard and turned right, up the hill.

The curling road had only one lane each way, and no shoulder at all between the pavement and the greenery hanging over bowed chain-link fencing, and he had to drive a good quarter of a mile past the place before he found a wider spot where the van could plausibly be parked without getting clipped by a passing car. And then the walk back down the hill was a series of lateral hops from the asphalt into the tall curbside grass every time a car came looming at him from around a corner ahead. Already he was sweating.

Even after six years, he recognized the section of chain-link fence he was looking for, and when he stopped and hooked his fingers through it and peered up the wooded slope beyond, he saw that the ruins had not been cleared away. Nearly hidden under shaggy palm trees and oaks, the broad stone stairway swept up to the terrace at the top of the hill, and even from out here on the street he could see many of the broken pillars and sagging brick walls.

He was breathing deeply, and wondering almost resentfully why no one *had* planed this off and put up condos or something. The real estate must be worth a fortune. At last he unhooked his fingers and stepped back.

Several NO TRESPASSING signs were hung on the fence, but it was widely split at one point, and among the tall weeds beyond he could see empty twelve-pack beer cartons and a couple of blankets and even a sort of little tent made from an upended shopping cart. Sullivan glanced up and down the road, and at a moment when no cars were in sight he ducked through the gap and sprinted to the shade of the nearest palm tree. He picked his way through a dense hedge of blue-flowered vinca, and after a few seconds noticed that he wasn't walking on dirt anymore—the soles of his black leather shoes were brushing dust and drifts of leaves off paving stones that had been laid in the 1920s.

The stairs were broad between the low corniced walls, but were thickly littered with bricks and chunks of masonry and the brown palm fronds that had been falling untended for five decades; and sycamore branches hung so low in places that he practically had to crawl from step to step. When he had scrambled up to the second landing he paused to catch his breath. The air was still and silent and fragrant with eucalyptus, as if Laurel Canyon Boulevard and all of Hollywood were very far away. He couldn't even hear any birds or insects.

A row of once-white marble pillars supporting nothing anymore ran along the top of a wall across the stairs from him, and below the wall a dead stone fountain poked up from a bank of dried leaves; the ruined architecture all looked Greek, or at least Mediterranean, and it occurred to him that time didn't seem to pass here—or, rather, seemed already to have passed and left this place behind. Probably that's why they don't tear it all down, he thought. It's too late.

He was now three-quarters of the way up the dusty, overgrown slope. To his right was a little stone bridge over a dry streambed, and though both of the wide cement railings still arched over the gully, the middle six feet of the bridge's floor had long ago fallen away. A weathered two-by-six beam spanned the gap, and he remembered that in 1986, at least, the beam had been sturdy enough to bear his weight.

He discovered that it still was, though it was springy and he had to stretch his arms out to the sides to keep his balance. On the far side he paused to wipe the dusty sweat off his face; he thought about lighting a cigarette, but looked around at all the dry brush and glumly decided he'd better not.

Then he froze—someone was moving around below him, clumsily, through the litter on one of the clogged side terraces. Sullivan couldn't hope to see the person through the shaggy greenery below, but in the weighty silence he could hear someone mumbling and scuffling around.

One of the bums that live here, he thought. It doesn't sound like a cop or a caretaker; still, the bum might draw the attention of such people, and I don't want to get kicked out of here myself before I retrieve the mask. They might fix the fence, or even post guards, before I could get back. This place is a historical landmark, after all, though nobody seems to pay any attention to it.

He tiptoed through the fieldstone arch ahead of him

and picked his way up a side stairway, which, being narrower, was relatively clear of debris. His fast breathing sounded loud in the still air.

There was another arch at the top, and he paused under it, for he was at the broad main terrace of the hill now, and he'd be visible crossing the cement pavement that stretched between the jungle below and the odd house in front of him.

The pavement was clear up here, and he let himself light a cigarette. Sukie, he recalled, had brought a flask, on that . . . March? . . . day in '86. That's right, March—it had been Good Friday afternoon, which had seemed like a good day for burials.

At first the two of them had thought that *this* house— this narrow, two-story building, brick below and stuccoed above, with castle-like crenellations along the roof as if the owner were ready to hire archers to repel attack from below—must be Houdini's mansion, and they'd been surprised that the famed magician would live in such a little place. Later they'd learned that this was just the servants' quarters. Houdini's mansion had stood a hundred yards off to the south, and had burned down in the thirties. But this was nevertheless a part of the old Houdini estate. It had been a fine place to hide the mask. "Hide a thumb in a place where there's already a lot of its thumbprints," Sukie had said.

Sullivan now stared uneasily at the house. The doors and windows were all covered with weathered sheets of plywood, but on the tiny upstairs balcony sat a flowerpot with a *green* plant growing in it. Had there been rain in

L.A. recently? The palm fronds he'd climbed over below had been dry as mummies. Was some homeless person *living* in this place?

He decided to hide here for a little while and see if the noises on the slope had been heard and might draw someone out onto the balcony.

Sullivan recalled that he and Sukie had nearly killed themselves struggling up the slope six years ago, for they'd been "on bar-time big time," as Sukie had said—they'd been feeling the roughness of a step underfoot before the shoe actually touched it, and the bark of a tree limb a second before the hand grasped it. But Sukie had been full of hectic cheer, chatting graciously with imaginary guests and singing misunderstood snatches from Handel's *Messiah.* Sullivan had been constantly whispering at her to shut up.

No one seemed to be home in the little castle. Sullivan relaxed and sucked on his cigarette, and he looked up at the brushy slope beyond the house. The upper slope had advanced visibly since his previous visit—broken dirt was piled up right to the stones of the arch at the south end of the house now, and a section of ornate marble railing stuck up crookedly above and behind the arch like a bleached rib cage exposed by a cemetery landslide.

He jumped suddenly, and as his cigarette hit the pavement he heard a voice from the stairway he'd just climbed: "By the hair of my chinny-chin-chin—"

Sullivan crouched behind the house side of the arch as the voice went on, "I'll huff and I'll puff and I'll eat you, billy-goat-gruff."

It's that bum, he thought nervously. He's following me,

and of course my gun is locked up back in the van.

Then he grinned at his momentary panic. Just a bum, he told himself. Forget him and go get the mask from the garage, which luckily is still standing. Sullivan stretched out his leg and stepped on the smoldering cigarette, but he was trembling, for the *billy-goat-gruff* remark had reminded him of the troll that had lived under a bridge in that old children's story. Maybe, he thought as he made himself maintain his grin, I shouldn't have walked across that board over the broken bridge back there.

He straightened up and stepped out into the sunlight and began walking across the old cement, careful not to kick any stray rocks.

The open-arched garage was a strange structure, too, entirely fronted with tiny inset stones and with two broad castle-like merlons on the roof; the inside walls were all stonework as well, and the back wall was concave, as though to provide good acoustics.

After only a few steps he whipped his head back around to the left and saw a skinny old woman come shuffling around the corner of the house. Her white dress looked as if it had been elegant before someone had spent years sleeping and apparently doing engine work in it, but all she was wearing on her stained feet was a broken pair of plastic zoris. The soles flapped on the cement as she hunched toward him.

"I suppose you don't want to lose your name?" she was calling anxiously.

Then Sullivan heard the bum scuffling quickly to the top of the stairs behind him. "Blow your house down!" he was cawing.

Sullivan broke into a run for the garage; he stomped
and skidded inside and in an instant, was crouched in the
shadows against the back wall, digging in the loose dry dirt
with his hands. It seemed to him that the dirt was colder
than it had any right to be.

"Where the *fuck*," he was keening to himself, just as he
felt the plywood board he and Sukie had laid over
Houdini's mask. He paused, even though he could hear
the bum wheezing his way across the driveway toward the
garage. It's not Houdini buried here, Sullivan reminded
himself; it's not even his ghost. He took a deep breath and
lifted the board away in a shower of powdery dirt.

And he saw that the life-size plaster hands and the little
cloth Bull Durham sack were still in the hole. If the bum
was just a bum, Sullivan could probably chase him away
by waving the plaster hands like clubs.

Even in his panic, he grimaced with distaste as he
tucked the sack into his shirt pocket, and then he made
himself snatch up the plaster hands, and he turned toward
the light of the entrance.

The bum from the hill slope was standing there, visible
at last, and Sullivan saw that he did have hair on his chin;
lots of it, white and matted. The man had his hands in the
pockets of an enormous ragged overcoat, and he was
rocking his head and peering in Sullivan's direction.

Sullivan's heart was pounding, for the man was clearly
puzzled to see him. "What do you want?" Sullivan
ventured. "How did you get in here?"

"I saw a guy—come in here," mumbled the old man,
"couldn'a had a hall pass, aren't they—I forget. Where'd
he go, anyway? I think he's the guy that stole my . . . my

Buick." He was scuffling backward in confusion now. "I'm still pissed about that Buick."

"He came in here," said Sullivan, trying to keep the shakiness out of his voice. "I ate him. And I'm still hungry." He could smell the old man now, the well-remembered tang of raw cheap wine oozing out through dead pores.

"Jesus God!" the old man exclaimed shrilly, his brown-mottled eyes wide. "*Ate*—him! I help out around here, ask anybody, I fold the newspapers—" He was flapping his shaky hands. "—rearrange the rocks and—branches, you know? Make it all neater." He bared teeth that seemed to be made of the same bad stuff as his eyes. "You can't eat me, not right on top of *him.*"

Sullivan jerked his head toward the slope and the ruined stairs. "Go, then."

Nodding as rapidly as a pair of wind-up chattering teeth, the old man turned and began limping rapidly back toward the stairs . . . Sullivan stepped out into the light, his heart pounding against the little bag in his pocket. The old woman had stopped a few yards away and was gaping at him uncertainly.

"I . . . was keeping your plant watered," she said. "In most gardens they make the beds too soft—so that the flowers are always asleep."

Sullivan recognized the line as something from the *Alice in Wonderland* books. So many of them he had read and somehow remembered them. Sukie had always said that the Alice books were the Old and New Testaments for ghosts—which Pete had never understood; after all, Lewis Carroll hadn't been dead yet when he'd written them.

"Fine," Sullivan told the old woman, making a vaguely papal gesture with one of the hands. "Carry on."

The old man had by now scrambled some distance down the side stairway, and in a birdy old voice was calling, "I got away-ay! I got away-ay!" in the *nyah nyah nyah-nyah-nah!* cadence of spiteful children.

Sullivan glanced back in distaste, then turned and looked past the old woman at the driveway that curled away down the hill to Laurel Canyon Boulevard. Best to leave *that* way, he thought. I haven't heard any sirens, and it's less important, now, that I not be seen. At least now I've *got* the goddamn things.

"Excuse me," he said, and stepped around the woman.

After a few moments, as he was trudging down the driveway, she called after him, "Are you animal, vegetable, or mineral?"

That was what the Lion had asked Alice in *Through the Looking-Glass*. "It's a fabulous monster!" he called back, quoting what the Unicorn had answered about Alice.

Don't I wish, he thought.

CHAPTER 7

❂

"I can't help it," said Alice very meekly. "I'm growing."
"You've no right to grow here," said the Dormouse.
                                        —Lewis Carroll,
                              Alice's Adventures in Wonderland

THE VAN SHOOK every time a car drove past it, but after carefully laying the plaster hands and the little bag with the dried thumb in it on the front seat, Sullivan climbed in the back and tossed the sheets and blanket and cushions off the unmade bed. The bed could be disassembled and partially telescoped to become a U-shaped booth with a little table in the middle, but when it was extended out like this, the boards under the booth-seat cushions could be lifted off, exposing a few cubic feet of unevident space. He hooked his finger through the hole in the forward board and levered it up out of its frame.

Inside the booth-seat box lay a couple of square, limp, plastic rectangles connected by two foot-and-a-half-long ribbons, and a gray canvas fanny-pack containing his .45 semi-automatic Colt and a couple of spare magazines.

He lifted out the fanny pack and hefted it. He hadn't shot the .45 since an afternoon of target practice in the desert outside Tucson with some of the other tramp electricians a couple of years ago, but he did remember cleaning it afterward, and buying a fresh box of hardball rounds and reloading all three magazines.

The strung-together plastic rectangles were meant to be worn around the neck while traveling, with one rectangle lying on the chest and the other back between the shoulder blades—right now he had about six and a half thousand dollars in hundreds in the one, and his union papers in the other. Sullivan always thought of the pair as his "scapular" because the linked flat wallets looked like one of those front-and-back medallions Catholics wear to keep from going to hell. He was always vaguely embarrassed to wear it.

He glanced toward the front of the van, where the three pieces of Houdini's "mask" lay on the passenger seat.

What would he put away in the seat box, and what would he keep out?

If he was going to drive straight back to Arizona and try to save his job at the Roosevelt Nuclear Generating Station, he would peel off a couple of hundred dollars to comfortably cover gas and food, and leave the rest of the cash hidden in the seat box here, along with the loaded gun, which was a felony to take across state borders; and the mask would be most effective where it was, out in the open. But if he was going to stay in Los Angeles for a while he'd have to allow for the possibility of being separated from, or even abandoning, the van—he'd want to have the cash and the gun *on* him, and the mask would have to be hidden from the sort of people who might get into the van and ransack it.

Another car drove past on Laurel Canyon Boulevard, and the van rocked on its shocks.

Stay in Los Angeles? he asked himself, startled even to have had the thought. Why would I do that? *She* works here, Loretta deLarava, and she probably still lives aboard the *Queen Mary* in Long Beach and commutes right up through the middle of the whole city every day.

I'd be crazy to do anything but leave the mask on the front seat and drive . . . anywhere. If I'm screwed with the Edison network I can still get electrician work in Santa Fe or Kansas City or Memphis or any damn place. I could be a plain old handyman in any city in the whole country, doing low-profile electric, as well as cement work and drywall and carpentry and plumbing. An independent small-time contractor, getting paid under the table most of the time and fabricating expenses to show to the IRS on the jobs where I'd have to accept checks.

And if I scoot out of here right now, I *might* not even be screwed with Edison.

Sukie's nonsense Christmas carols were still droning in the back of his head, and he found himself thinking about the last time he'd seen her, at the shoot at Venice Beach on Christmas Eve in '86. He had somehow not ever been to Venice before—he was certain—and of course he had not been there since.

But on that overcast winter morning he had *recognized* the place. Driving around in one of deLarava's vans, he had several times found himself knowing what he would see when he rounded the next corner: a gray old clapboard house with flowers growing in a window box, the traffic circle, the row of chipped Corinthian pillars lining Windward Avenue.

On this Christmas Eve of '86, big red plastic lanterns and garlands of fake pine boughs had been strung around the tops of the pillars and along the traffic-signal cables overhead, and the sidewalks had been crowded with last-minute Christmas shoppers and children, and dogs on leashes, and there had seemed to be a car in every curbside parking slot—but the pavements in his flickering memory had been empty and stark white under a harsh summer sun, and in his memory the shadows in the gaping windows and behind the bone-white colonnades were impenetrably black, all as silent and still as a streetscape in some particularly ominous De Chirico painting.

Under an overcast sky the real, winter ocean had been gray, with streaks of foam on the faces of the waves, but luckily deLarava had not wanted to actually go out onto the sand. Sukie was already drunk and wearing sunglasses, and Pete had been shaking as he set up the lights along the sidewalk.

They'd been supposed to be doing a short subject on the bodybuilders who apparently spent all their days lifting weights in the little fenced-in yard by the pavilion at the bottom of Windward Avenue, but deLarava's props had been old—a rented 1957 Buick, a *Gigi* movie poster to hang in a shop window—and she had had something else, too, that she'd carried in a shoebox.

(Sullivan was shaking now, holding the scapular and the gun. Idaho, he thought desperately, up in the Pelouse area where they grow lentils instead of potatoes. It'll be snowing soon now, and people always need electrical work done when it gets real cold. Or, what the hell, all the way out to the east coast, way out to Sag Harbor at the far end of Long Island—there was a lot of repair work of all sorts to be done during the off season, and you could hardly get farther away from Los Angeles.)

But helplessly he found himself remembering the moment on that chilly morning when deLarava had put down the shoebox on a truck fender, and Sukie had found an opportunity to peek inside it—and then had screamed and flung it away from her onto the sidewalk.

Pete had already spun around in sudden fright, and he'd expected to see something like a dead rat, or even a mummified baby, roll out of the box; but what had come spilling out of the box, tumbling across the looping electrical cables on the beachfront sidewalk, had been a well-remembered brown leather wallet and ring of keys and, somehow worst of all, three cans of Hires Root Beer. One of the cans rolled up against Pete's shoes, spraying a tiny jet of brown foam.

He and Sukie had simply fled then, mindlessly, running away up Windward Avenue. He had eventually stopped, winded, at a gas station somewhere up on Washington Boulevard, and had taken a cab to their apartment, and then driven his car to his bank, where he had cashed out his savings account. To this day he didn't know or care where Sukie had run to. Pete had been in Oregon by the next afternoon. Sukie had eventually tracked him down through union records, and they had talked on the phone a few times, but they'd never knowingly been in the same state at the same time again.

And now deLarava apparently wanted them back again. Sukie had obviously believed that the old woman intended to try the Venice "exorcism" again, with Pete and Sukie again present—voluntarily or not.

Sullivan tried to think of some other explanation. Maybe deLarava *didn't* want the twins back, hadn't thought about them in years, and Sukie's car had simply been hit by some random drunk, and the sudden onset of bar-time was caused by something that had nothing to do with deLarava; or deLarava might indeed want the twins back, but just to do the sort of work they'd done for her before, nothing to do with Venice; or she did want to do the Venice one again, but wouldn't be able to, now, because Sukie had killed herself. The old lady would be unable to do it unless she got a new pair of twins.

He bared his teeth and exhaled sharply. She might try to do it again, with some other pair of twins. Probably on Halloween, four days from now. Halloween was even better than Christmas, probably, for her purpose.

Well, he thought, in any case, I'm out of it. It has nothing to do with (—*a Hires Root Beer can rolling against his foot, wasting itself spraying a thin needle of foam out onto the sandy sidewalk*—) me.

For five full minutes, while cars roared past outside the van, he just crouched over the open underseat box.

Finally, with trembling fingers, he unbuttoned his shirt and draped the ribbons of the scapular over his head and onto his shoulders. After he had rebuttoned the shirt he flipped the black web belt of the fanny pack around his waist and snapped the buckle shut. Then he straightened up to go fetch the plaster hands so that he could put them away and reassemble the bed. The thumb in the Bull Durham sack he could carry in his shirt pocket.

CHAPTER 8

❖

"How are you getting on?" said the Cat, as soon
as there was mouth enough for it to speak with.
—Lewis Carroll,
Alice's Adventures in Wonderland

KOOTIE AWOKE INSTANTLY when he heard someone scramble over the wooden fence downstairs, but he didn't move, only opened his eyes. The scuffed planks of the balcony floor were warm under his unbruised cheek; by the shadow of the big old banana tree he judged the time to be about four in the afternoon.

He had found this enclosed courtyard at about noon; somewhere south of Olympic he'd picked his way down an alley between a pair of gray two-story stucco-fronted buildings that had no doubt housed businesses once but were featureless now, with their windows painted over; a wooden fence in the back of one of the buildings was missing a board, leaving a gap big enough for Kootie to scrape through.

Towering green schefflera and banana and avocado

trees shaded the yard he had found himself in, and he'd decided that the building might once have been apartments—this hidden side was green-painted clapboard with decoratively framed doors and windows, and wooden steps leading up to a long, roofed balcony. Someone had stored a dozen big Coca-Cola vending machines back here, but Kootie didn't think anyone would be coming back for them soon. He doubted that anyone had looked in on this little yard since about 1970. It was a relief to be able to take the adult-size sunglasses off his nose and tuck them into his pocket.

He had climbed the rickety old stairs to the balcony, and then had just lain down and gone to sleep, without even taking off his knapsack. And he had slept deeply—but when he awoke he remembered everything that had happened to him during the last twenty hours.

He could hear the faint scuff of the person downstairs walking across the little yard now, but there was another sound that he couldn't identify: a recurrent raspy hiss, as though the person were pausing here and there to slowly rub two sheets of coarse paper together.

For several seconds Kootie just lay on the boards of the balcony and listened. Probably, he told himself, this person down in the yard won't climb the steps to this balcony. A grown-up would worry that the stairs might break under his weight. Probably he'll go away soon.

Kootie lifted his head and looked down over the balcony edge—and swallowed his instinctive shout of horror, and made himself keep breathing slowly.

In the yard, hunched and bent-kneed, the ragged man

in camouflage pants was moving slowly across the stepping-stones, his single arm swinging like the clumped legs of a hovering wasp. The baseball cap kept Kootie from seeing the man's face, but he knew it was the round, pale, whiskered face with the little eyes that didn't seem to have sockets behind them to sit in.

Kootie's ears were ringing shrilly.

This was the man who had tried to grab him in the living room of Kootie's house last night—*Hey, kid, come here.* This was almost certainly the man who had murdered Kootie's parents. And now he was here.

The rasping sound the man was making, Kootie realized now, was *sniffing*—long, whistling inhalations. He was carefully seining the air with his nose as he made his slow way across the yard; and every few seconds he would jerk heavily, as if an invisible cord tied around his chest were being tugged.

Kootie ducked back out of sight, his heart knocking fast. He's been following me, Kootie thought. Or following the glass brick. What does the thing do, leave a trail in the air, like tire tracks in mud?

He is going to come up the stairs.

Then Kootie twitched, startled, and an instant later the bum began talking. "You came in here through the fence," said the bum in a high, clear voice, "and you didn't leave by that means. And I don't think you have a key to any of these doors, and I don't think you can fly." He laughed softly. "Therefore, you're still here."

Kootie looked toward the far end of the balcony; it ended at a railing just past the farthest door, with no other set of stairs.

I can jump, he thought tensely. I can climb over the railing and hang from as low a place as I can hold on to, and then drop. Scramble out of the yard through the fence before this guy can even get back down the stairs, and then just run until . . . until I get to the ocean, or the Sierras, or until I drop dead.

"Let me tell you a parable," said the man below, still audibly shuffling across the leafy yard. "Once upon a time, a man killed another man, and then he was . . . *sorry,* and wanted to be *forgiven.* So, he went to the dead man's grave, and dug him up, and when he opened the casket, he saw that the man inside it was himself, smiling at the joke.

"Hah!"

The balcony shook as a muscular hand grabbed the vertical rail-post in front of Kootie's eyes, and two shod feet loudly scuffled for traction on the planks, inches from Kootie's own feet; and the round face had poked up above the balcony floor and the bum's little black eyes were staring straight into Kootie's.

Kootie had rolled back against the wall, but now couldn't move, or breathe, or think.

The inches-away mouth opened among the patchy whiskers, opened very wide, and out of it grated a million-voice roar like a stadium when a player hits a home run.

Then Kootie had kicked himself up and was running for the far end of the balcony, but behind him he heard the fast-booming scuffle of the man scrambling up onto the planks, and before Kootie reached the rail, his head was rocked as the bum snatched at his curly hair.

Kootie sprang, slapped the balcony rail with the sole of his left Reebok, and was airborne.

Banana leaves were whipping his face, and he tried to grab a branch but only managed to skin his palm and go into a spinning fall. His knapsack and the base of his spine hit the hard dirt in almost the same instant that his feet did, and his head was full of the coppery taste of pennies as he scrambled on all fours, unable to work his lungs, toward the fence.

By the time he reached the alley, he could at least wring awful whooping and gagging sounds out of his chest, and could even get up onto his feet, and he hopped and hunched and sobbed his way to the street sidewalk.

A pickup truck with its bed full of lawnmowers and fat burlap sacks was groaning past in the slow lane, and Kootie forced his numbed and shaking legs to run—and after a few pounding seconds he managed to collide with the truck's tailgate, his knees on the bumper and his arms wrapped around the two upright metal tubes of a power-mower handle. At least his feet were off the ground.

But the truck's old brakes were squealing now, and Kootie was being pushed against the tailgate as the battered vehicle ground to a halt. He used the momentum to help him climb into the truck bed, and then, kneeling on a burlap sack that reeked of gasoline and the stale-beer smell of old cut grass, he waved urgently at the rearview mirror. "Go," Kootie croaked, "start up, *go!*"

Through the dusty rear window, he could see that the Mexican driver had put his elbow up on the back of the seat and was looking back at him. He was waving too, and mouthing something, no doubt ordering Kootie to get out of the truck.

Kootie looked back, toward the alley, and saw the one-armed bum stride out from between the two gray buildings into the brassy late-afternoon sunlight, smiling broadly straight at him.

Kootie sprang over the burlap sacks and banged his fist on the truck's back window, and he managed to scream: "Go! *Vaya! Ahora! Es el diablo!*"

The driver might not have heard him, but Kootie could see that the man was looking past Kootie now, at the advancing bum; then the driver had turned back to the wheel and the truck lurched forward, swerving into the left lane and picking up some speed.

Kootie peered behind them through the swaying fence of lawnmower handles and weed whips. The bum had slowed to a strolling pace on the receding sidewalk, and waved at Kootie just before the intervening cars and trucks hid him from view.

Kootie sat back against a spare tire, hoping the driver would not stop for at least several blocks. When he stretched out his legs his right ankle gave him a momentary twinge of pain; he tugged up the cuff and saw that it was already visibly thicker than the left ankle.

The ankle felt hot, too, but his stomach was suddenly icy with alarm. Am I gonna be *limping* for a while? he thought. How fast can I *limp?*

Five minutes later, the driver of the pickup truck turned into a Chevron station. He opened the driver's-side door and got out, and as he unscrewed the truck's gas cap he nodded to Kootie and then jerked his head sideways, obviously indicating that this was as far as he meant to take his young passenger.

Kootie nodded humbly and climbed over the tailgate. His right ankle took his weight well enough, but had flared with pain when he'd rotated it in climbing down.

"Uh, thanks for the ride," Kootie said. He fished the sunglasses out of his pocket and pushed them onto his nose.

"*Si,*" said the man, unhooking the gas-pump nozzle and clanking up the lever. "*Buena suerte.*" He began pumping gas into the tank.

Kootie knew that those Spanish words meant *good luck*. The sunlight was slanting straight down the east-west lanes of the street, and the shadows of the cars were lengthening.

Kootie was more upset about what he had to do now than he was by his injured ankle. "Uh," the boy said quickly, "*lo siento, pero . . . tiene usted algunas cambio? Yo tengo hambre, y no tengo una casa.*" Kootie wished he had paid more attention in Spanish class; what he had tried to say was, *I'm sorry, but do you have any change? I'm hungry and I don't have a house.*

His face was cold, and he had no idea whether he was blushing or had gone pale.

The man stared at him expressionlessly, leaning against the gas nozzle's accordioned black rubber sleeve and squeezing the big aluminum trigger. Kootie could faintly hear gasoline sloshing in the filler pipe, though the air smelled of fried rice and sesame oil from a Chinese restaurant across the street. Eventually the gas pump clicked off, and the man hung up the nozzle and stumped away to the cashier to pay. Kootie just stood miserably by the back bumper of the truck.

When the man came back he handed Kootie a five-dollar bill. *"Buena suerte,"* he said again, turning away and getting back into his truck.

"Thanks," said Kootie. *"Gracias."* He looked back to the west, and as the truck clattered into gear behind him and rocked back out onto the street, Kootie stood on the oil-stained concrete and wondered where the one-armed bum was right now. Somewhere to the west, for sure.

Kootie started walking eastward down the sidewalk. His ankle didn't hurt if he kept his right heel off the ground and walked tiptoe.

Sleep, he thought dazedly—where? There's no way I can go to sleep, stop moving. He'll catch up. Maybe I could sleep on a train—hop a freight.

Right.

Can I hide?

Most of the buildings in L.A. were low—three stories or shorter—and he looked around at the rooftops. Every one of them seemed to have a smaller house on top, in behind the old insulators and chimneys.

He's only got one arm, Kootie thought; maybe I can climb somewhere that he can't get to.

Right. With my sprained ankle?

Kootie was walking fairly briskly, and it seemed to him that he was just barely keeping ahead of panic.

He had passed many empty lots. He could describe the typical one now—fenced in with chain-link, with a few shaggy palm trees and a derelict car, and lines of weeds tracing lightning-bolt patterns across the old asphalt. Maybe he could get into a lot, and be ready to wake up and run when he heard the one-armed bum climbing the fence.

At the intersection ahead of him a man in an old denim jacket was standing on the sidewalk with a dog beside him. The dog was some kind of black German-shepherd mix, and the man was holding a white cardboard sign. When Kootie limped up beside them the dog began wagging its tail, and Kootie stooped to catch his breath and pat the dog on the head.

"*Bueno perro,*" Kootie told the man. He could now see that the hand-lettered sign read, in big black letters:

WILL WORK FOR FOOD—HOMELESS VIETNAM VET

"*Sí,*" the man said. "Uh . . . *cómo se dice* . . . *perro* is dog, right?"

"Right," Kootie said. "Nice dog. You speak English."

"Yeah. You got no accent."

"I'm Indian, not Mexican. India Indian. Anyway, I was born here."

The man he was talking to could have been of any race at all, almost of any age at all. His short-cropped white hair was as curly as Kootie's, and his skin was dark enough so that he might be Mexican or Indian or black or even just very tanned. His lean face was deeply lined around the mouth and the vaguely Asian eyes, but Kootie couldn't tell if that was a result of age or just exposure to lots of weather.

"Where do you two live?" Kootie found himself asking.

"Nowhere, Jacko," the man said absently, watching the traffic over Kootie's head. "Why, where do you live?"

Kootie patted the dog's head again and blinked back tears of exhaustion, glad of the sunglasses. "Same place."

The man looked down again and focused on Kootie. "Really? *Here?*"

Kootie blinked up at him and tried to understand the question. "If it was *here,* how could it be nowhere?"

"Hah. You'd be surprised. Act cool, now, okay?"

The light had turned red, and a big battered blue Suburban truck had stopped at the crosswalk lines. The driver leaned across the seat and cranked down the passenger-side window. "Nice dog," he said through a ragged mustache. "How you all doing?"

"Not so good," said the white-haired man standing beside Kootie. "My son and I and the dog been standing out here all day waitin' for someone who needs some kind of work done, and we'd like to be able to stay in a motel, tomorrow being Sunday and us wantin' to get a shower before church, you know? We're just six bucks short right now."

Kootie rolled his eyes anxiously behind the sunglasses. Tomorrow was Wednesday, not Sunday.

"Shit," said the driver. Then, just as the light turned green, he tossed a balled-up bill out the window. "Make it count!" he yelled as he gunned away across the intersection.

The white-haired man had caught the bill and uncrumpled it—it was a five. He grinned down at Kootie, exposing uneven yellow teeth. "Good job. So whatta you, a runaway?"

Kootie glanced nervously back up the street to the west. "My parents are dead."

"Some kind of foster home? Go back to wherever it is, Jacko."

"There isn't any place at all."

"There isn't, huh?" The man was watching traffic, but he glanced down at Kootie. "Well there *was* a place, I believe, a day or two ago. That's a Stussy shirt, and those Reeboks are new. Where were you plannin' to sleep? Any old where? You get fucked up bad around here, Jacko, trust me. Whole streets of chickenhawks looking for your sort. Nastiness, know what I mean?" He squinted around, then sighed. "You wanna move in with Fred and me for a couple of days?"

Kootie understood that Fred was the dog, and that helped; still he said quickly, "I don't have any money at all."

"Bullshit you don't, you got two bucks just in the last couple of seconds. Fred takes twenty percent, okay? Let's work this corner for another ten minutes, and then we can move up to Silver Lake."

Kootie tried to figure where Silver Lake was from here. "That's a long walk, isn't it?"

"Fuck walk, and in fact, fuck talk. We got a red light coming up again here. I got a car, and Fred and I keep moving. Trust me, you be doin' yourself a favor to ride along with us."

Kootie looked desperately at the dog's wide grin and brown eyes, and he thought about *keep moving,* and then he blurted, "Okay." He stuck out his hand. "I'm Kootie."

The man clasped Kootie's hand in his own dry, callused palm. "*Kootie?* No kidding. I'm Rightful Glory Mayo. Known as Raffle." Then, more loudly, he said, "Can we wash your car windows, ma'am? My boy and I haven't had anything to eat all day."

Raffle didn't even have a squirt bottle or a newspaper to wash windows with, but the woman in the Nissan gave them a dollar anyway.

"That's another forty cents you got, Kootie," said Raffle as the light turned green. "You know, we might do better if you ditched the shades—makes you look like a pint-size doper."

Kootie took off the sunglasses and looked mutely up at Raffle. He had no idea what color his eye socket was, but it was swollen enough to perceptibly narrow his vision.

"Well now, little man," Raffle said, "you've had a busy day or two, haven't you? Yeah, keep the shades—people will think I gave you that, otherwise."

Kootie nodded and put the glasses back on—but not before he had nervously looked westward again.

CHAPTER 9

"I only took the regular course."

"What was that?" inquired Alice.

"Reeling and Writhing, of course, to begin with," the Mock Turtle replied, "and then the different branches of Arithmetic—Ambition, Distraction, Uglification, and Derision."

—Lewis Carroll,
Alice's Adventures in Wonderland

RAFFLE was obviously pleased with the money they made during the next ten minutes, and he dug a laundry marking pen out of the pocket of his topmost shirt and, under the words HOMELESS VIETNAM VET, he added:

WITH MOTHERLESS SON

"We gonna make booyah bucks on this," said Raffle with satisfaction. "We probably be sleepin' in motels every night."

Kootie thought of sleeping on wheels. "I don't mind a

car," he said, struggling to keep the impatience out of his voice. He still hadn't seen the one-armed man, but he could imagine him watching from behind some wall.

"Good attitude," Raffle said. "Hey, we should be shifting locations—you want a beer?"

Kootie blinked. "I'm only eleven."

"Well, I'll drink it if you don't want it. Come on."

They walked across the street to a little liquor store, Fred following closely on their heels, and Raffle bought a bottle of Corona in a narrow paper bag.

"Let's head for the car," he said as they walked back out onto the sidewalk.

The car was a twenty-year-old mustard-colored Ford Maverick parked behind a nearby laundromat, and the back seat was piled with clothes and Maxell floppy-disk boxes and at least a dozen gray plastic videocassette rewinders. Fred hopped up onto the clutter when Raffle unlocked the door, and Raffle and Kootie sat in the front seats.

Raffle levered the cap off the beer bottle against the underside of the dashboard. In an affectedly deep voice, he said, "What's your name, boy?"

Catching on that Raffle was pretending to be someone else, Kootie said, "Mayo. Uh, Jacko Mayo."

"Very good." Raffle took a long sip of the beer. "We used to live in La Mirada, that's forty-five minutes south of here on the 5, okay? Four-bedroom house, only place you ever lived. I used to be a car mechanic, but your mom was a legal secretary and she made the real money, but she didn't have health insurance and when she got cancer we lost everything, and then she died. Nobody's likely to ask you for anything more than that, but if it ever comes up, just start crying. Can you cry if you have to?"

Kootie thought about it. "Easy."

"Great. Now are we black or white or Mexican or Indian or what?"

"To work for both of us? I'd just say—" He shrugged "—we're Angelenos. We just . . . grew up out of the sidewalks."

"Good. Don't remember no old days at all." Raffle tilted up the bottle and drained the last of the beer. "Now, there's some . . . things you're gonna have to just get used to seeing, okay? Like if you suddenly moved to . . . Borneo or Australia or somewhere, they might do stuff that you were always taught was bad, but it's okay there, right? I mean, as long as they don't say *you've* got to do 'em. *You* just consider it higher education."

"Right," said Kootie cautiously.

"Okay. There's a little nail in the ashtray, lemme have it, hm?"

Kootie found the nail and handed it to the man.

Raffle put the point of the nail into a little dimple in the base of the glass beer bottle, and then he picked up an old shoe from between the seats and whacked the head of the nail with it; the point was now inside the bottle, though the bottle hadn't broken, and Raffle twisted it back out, then blew through the hole.

"All us good Dagwood-type dads smoke pipes," he said. Then he reached under the seat and dragged up a box of Chore Boy scrubbing pads and prized a little cushion of steel wool out of the box. He tore off a bristly shred of the stuff and tucked it like a little bird's nest into the neck of the bottle, and then replaced the rest of the pad and pushed the box back under the seat.

"If you see a one-time," Raffle said, "don't change your expression or look around, but slap me on the leg."

Kootie remembered reading in the newspaper that *one-time* was a street term for policeman. "Is this," he faltered, "some kind of—no offense—dope thing?"

"Just say yo," Raffle agreed. Out of a hole in the double thickness of his shirt cuff he dug a tiny fragment of what seemed to be white stone, like a piece off one of the ones Kootie's father had spread around the plants in the atrium pots, and Raffle carefully laid it in the nest of steel wool at the top of the empty beer bottle.

Raffle slouched down in the seat and held the bottle up to the textured plastic head liner, which Kootie now noticed was dotted with scorch marks, and the man put his mouth to the little hole he'd punched in the bottle's base; then he flicked a long orange-plastic Cricket lighter and held the flame to the piece of rock as he sucked.

Kootie looked away as the bottle began to fill with pale smoke. His heart was pounding, but he didn't see any "one-times," and in just a couple of seconds Raffle had opened the door and rolled the bottle away across the parking lot.

Raffle exhaled, and Kootie smelled burned steel wool and a faint chemical tang. "Never hang on to a pipe," Raffle told him hoarsely as he began grinding the starter motor. "There's always another at the next liquor store."

"*Dagwood* probably saved 'em," said Kootie bravely.

Raffle laughed as the engine finally caught and he clanked the transmission into reverse. "Yeah," he said, still hoarse. "He probably had all kinds of oak pipe racks, full of cans and bottles. Blondie would dust 'em, and sometimes break one of the bottles and make him real mad—*I had that Corona broke in perfect, you bitch!*"

Kootie laughed nervously. Raffle made a left turn onto Fourth Street and angled into the far right lane to get on the southbound 110 Freeway.

"I thought we were going to Silver Lake," said Kootie. "Isn't that north?"

"Detour for medical supplies."

They got off three miles south at the Vernon Avenue exit, and Raffle parked in the empty lot of a burned-out gas station.

"The plan's this," he said as he rolled up the driver's-side window. "Me and Fred will be gone for twenty minutes or so. You keep the doors locked, and if anybody tries to mess with you, just lean on the horn until they go away, right? A one-time, roll the window down and smile and say you're waitin' for your dad. When we get back, it's dinnertime."

Kootie nodded, and Raffle grinned and got out of the car. He folded the seat forward so that Fred could scramble out onto the pavement, and then the door was shut and locked and the two of them had gone loping away down the sidewalk and around a corner.

Kootie realized that Raffle was going to go spend some of the afternoon's income on more drugs, but he never even considered getting out of the car and walking away. He remembered watching the riots on TV six months ago, and he imagined that the people around here would break his face off with bricks if they so much as saw him on the sidewalk.

He wondered what kind of food Raffle generally ate. Kootie was ready to eat just about anything at all.

He hiked up on the car seat and looked around. Dimly in the bay of the ruined gas station he could see the brown shell of a burned-up car, still raised up off the floor on the hydraulic lift; Kootie wondered if the owner had ever come by to see if any progress was being made on whatever repairs he'd brought the car in for. The tall palm trees along the sidewalks were black silhouettes against the darkening sky, and lights had begun to come on in shop windows up and down the street. Raffle's car smelled like unbathed dog, and Kootie wished he were allowed to roll down the windows. Big speakers were playing music somewhere not too far away, but all Kootie could hear was the pounding bass and a lot of angry, rhythmic shouting.

He sat back down. The one-armed bum would no doubt show up here, tracing the smell or warped refraction or abraded air or whatever effect it was that the glass-brick thing left as a track, but Kootie and his new friend—friends, plural, counting the dog—would be long gone.

He flipped the straps of the knapsack off his shoulders and dragged it around onto his lap and unknotted the straps. Then he dug around among the clothes until he found the glass brick.

He lifted it out and turned it against the windshield, trying to see the fading daylight through the murky glass depths. The brick still clicked faintly when he turned it, as though there was something hard and transparent inside. He rocked it in time to the incomprehensible music from outside. *Tick, tick, tick.*

He was pretty sure he should just pitch it—toss it into

the wrecked gas station and let the wrecked bum find it.
Or the lady he'd seen in the Jaguar last night—*"a hundred
dollars for your cigar"*—she could come and get it, and
have her tires rotated and burned up, as long as she was
here.

He gripped the glass thing in his palms the way he had
on the Fairfax sidewalk this morning; again he could feel
the halves of it shift when he pulled at it, and he looked
nervously at the street, but none of the cars driving by
stalled.

Prying hard and rocking the halves away from each
other, he soon had them almost completely separated.
One more tug, and the thing would be opened.

He thought again of the Robert Louis Stevenson story,
the one about the demon in the bottle. Here by the
burned-out gas station, though, in Raffle's car full of
Raffle's litter, on this alien street, it no longer seemed
likely that some kind of old-world monster would erupt
out of the little glass box.

He lifted off the top half.

And nothing happened. Inside it, laid into a fitted
cavity in the glass was . . . a test tube? A glass vial, with a
tapered black-rubber stopper. He put the halves of the
glass brick down on his lap and lifted out the vial.

He could see that it was empty. He found that he was
disappointed, and he wondered what the vial might once
have contained. Somebody's blood, mummy dust, gold
nuggets with a curse on them?

He twisted out the stopper and sniffed the vial.

CHAPTER 10

✿

Alice caught the baby with some difficulty, as it was a queer-shaped little creature, and held out its arms and legs in all directions. "Just like a star fish," thought Alice. The poor little thing was snorting like a steam-engine when she caught it, and kept doubling itself up and straightening itself out again, so that altogether, for the first minute or two, it was as much as she could do to hold it.

—Lewis Carroll,
Alice's Adventures in Wonderland

AS IF HE HAD plugged in the wires for the second of a pair of stereo speakers—as if he'd attached the wires when the second stereo channel was not only working but had its volume cranked up high—Kootie's head was abruptly *doubly* hit by the ongoing music from outside now; and he found himself somehow jolted, shocked, by the mere fact of being able to hear.

Dropping the vial, he grabbed the steering wheel and gripped it hard, gritting his teeth, cold with sudden sweat, for he was falling with terrible speed through some kind of gulf—his eyes were wide open and he was aware that he was seeing the dashboard and the motionless windshield wipers and the shadowed sidewalk beyond the glass, but in his head things clanged and flashed as they hurtled incomprehensibly past, voices shouted, and his heart thudded with love and terror and triumph and mirth and rage and shame all mixed together so finely that they seemed to constitute life itself, the way rainbow colors on a fast-spinning disk all blur into white.

It wasn't stopping. It was getting faster.

Blood burst out of his nose and he pitched sideways across the passenger seat onto his right shoulder, twitching and whimpering, his eyes wide open but rolled so far back into his head that he couldn't see anything outside the boundaries of his own skull.

Pete Sullivan jackknifed up out of the little bed and scrambled for the front seat—but when he yanked the curtain back from the windshield he saw that the van was *not* careening down some hill. He almost shouted with relief; still, he tumbled himself into the driver's seat and tromped hard on the emergency brake.

Ahead of him, beyond a motionless curb, half a dozen boys in baggy shorts and T-shirts were strolling aimlessly across a broad lawn. Their shadows were long, and the grass glowed a golden green in the last rays of sunlight.

Sullivan's heart was pounding, and he made himself wait nearly a full minute before lighting a cigarette, because he knew his hands were shaking too badly to hang on to one.

At last he was able to get one lit and suck in a lungful of smoke. He'd had a bad dream—hardly surprising!—something about . . . trains? Electricity? Sudden noise after a long silence . . .

Machinery. His work at the nuclear power plant, at the other utilities? The whole Edison network—Con Ed, Southern California Edison . . .

He took another long drag on the cigarette and then stubbed it out. The van was in shadow now, definitely not moving, and the sky was darkening toward evening. He breathed slowly and evenly until his heartbeat had slowed down to normal. Should he go find something to eat, or try to get some more sleep?

He had driven the van back down Laurel Canyon Boulevard and parked it here in the La Cienega Park lot, south of Wilshire. He had pulled the curtains over the little windows in the back and dragged the rings of the long shade across the curtain rod over the windshield and behind the rearview mirror, and had then locked up and crawled into the bed. He had apparently slept for several hours.

The boys in the park were at the top of a low green hill now, their laughing faces lit in chiaroscuro by the departing sun. Griffith's hour, Sullivan thought.

He fumbled in his pocket now for his keys. No way sleep, after that jolt. Dinner, then—but a drink somewhere first.

On the Greyhound bus, Angelica Anthem Elizalde had been dreaming of the ranch in Norco where she had spent her childhood.

Her family had raised chickens, and it had been Angelica's job to scatter chicken scratch in the yard for the birds. Wild chickens that a neighbor had abandoned used to roost in the trees at night, and bustle around with the domesticated birds during the day. All the chickens, and a dozen cats and a couple of goats as well, had liked to congregate around the trail of dry dog food Angelica's mother would spread by the driveway every morning. The half-dozen dogs had never seemed to mind.

It had always been her grandfather whose job it was to kill the chickens—he would grab a chicken by the neck and then give it a hard overhand whirl as if he had meant to see how far he could throw it but forgot to let go, and the bird's neck would be broken. Angelica's mother had tried it one time when the old man had been in jail, and the creature hadn't died. The chicken had done everything *but* die. It was screaming, and flapping and clawing, and feathers flew everywhere as her mother tried lashing it around again—and again. All the kids were crying. Finally, they had got an axe from the shed, a very dull old axe, and her mother had managed to kill the chicken by smashing its skull. The meat had been tough.

For the occasional turkey they would cut a hole in a gunny sack—her mother always called them guinea sacks—and hang the bird in it upside down from a tree limb, and then cut the bird's throat, standing well back. The sack was to keep its wings restrained—a turkey could hurt you if it hit you with a wing.

One Easter her father had trucked home a live pig, and they had killed it and butchered it and cooked it in a pit the men dug in the yard—the giant vat of carnitas had lasted for days, even with all the neighbors helping to eat it. For weeks before that, her mother had saved eggshells whole by pricking the ends with a hatpin and blowing the egg out; she had painted the eggshells and filled them with confetti, and the kids ran around all morning breaking them over each other's heads, until their hair and their church clothes looked like abstract pointillist paintings.

One of them had finally been for real—late in the afternoon her brother had broken a real, ripe, fertilized egg over Angelica's head, and when she had felt warm wetness on her scalp, and had reached up to wipe it off, she had found herself holding a spasming little naked red monster, its eyes closed and its embryonic beak opening and shutting.

Her dream had violently shifted gears then—suddenly there was clanging and lights, and train whistles howling in fog, and someone was nearly insane with terror.

With a jolt she was awake, sitting up stiffly in the padded bus seat, biting her lip and tasting the iron of her own blood.

It's . . . 1992, she told herself harshly. You're on a bus to Los Angeles and the bus is not out of control. Look out the window—the bus is staying in its lane and not going more than sixty.

You're *not* dead.

She looked up, beyond the rushing darkening lanes, to the flat desert that was shifting by so much more slowly. Probably the bus was somewhere around Victorville by now, still an easy sixty miles out of L.A.

On her panicked late-afternoon drive out of Los Angeles two years ago she had seen a Highway Patrol car behind her, just south of Victorville, and she had meticulously pulled off and let him go on by, and had had a hamburger at a Burger King alongside the freeway. Then she had driven the next dozen miles northeast on a side road paralleling the freeway, to let the cop get far ahead. Even on the side road she had stopped for a while, at a weird roadside lot among the Joshua trees where a white-bearded old man had assembled a collection of old casino signs, and big plywood caricatures of a cowboy and a hula dancer, and assortments of empty bottles hung on the bare limbs of scrawny sycamores, out here in the middle of the desert. Out of sympathy for another outcast, she had bought from him a book of poems he'd written and had published locally.

Now, biting her nails aboard a rushing Greyhound bus, she wondered if the old man was still there, wondered if Southern California still had room for such people.

Or for herself. She and the old man at the ramshackle roadside museum had both at least been alive.

The man known as Sherman Oaks screamed when the heat scalded his left arm, and he fell to his knees in the lush ice plant of the shadowy freeway island at the junction of the 10 and the 110.

After a few choking moments he was able to stand up and breathe; but his heart was pounding, and his left arm, still hot but at least not burning now, was pointed stiffly south. His right palm and the knees of his baggy pants were greenly wet from having crushed the ice plant.

Beyond the thickly leaved branches of the bordering oleander bushes, the flickering tracks of car headlights continued to sweep around this enclosed parklike area as they followed the arc of the on-ramp onto the southbound 110.

He ate it, he thought numbly. *The kid ate it, or it ate him.*

But I'll eat who's left.

He had come here to check his ghost traps. The trap right in front of him had caught one, but the ghost seemed to have fled when he had screamed. Sherman Oaks decided to leave the trap here—the ghost would come back to it in a few hours, or else another ghost would come. Sometimes he was able to bottle five or six from just one trap.

He had knocked the trap over when he had fallen, and now he righted it: a hand-lettered cardboard sign that read: SIT ON A POTATO PAN, OTIS. Other traps he had set up in this secret arbor included several more homemade signs—THE NOON SEX ALERT RELAXES NO ONE HT, and GO HANG A SALAMI, I'M A LASAGNA HOG—and scatterings of jigsaw-puzzle pieces on patches of clear dirt. Better-known palindromes, such as *Madam, I'm Adam,* didn't catch the attention of the wispy ghosts, and heavier items such as broken dishes seemed to be beyond the power of their frail ectoplasmic muscles to rearrange; but the Potato Pan and the Sex Alert and the Lasagna palindromes kept them confounded for hours, or even days, in wonderment at the way the sentences read the same backward as forward; and the ghosts would linger even longer trying to assemble the jigsaw puzzles.

Real, living homeless people seldom came here, knowing that this isolated patch of greenery was haunted, so he sometimes dropped a big handful of change among the jigsaw pieces—that trick would hold ghosts probably till the end of the world, for they not only felt compelled to put the puzzle together but also to count and stack the money; and apparently their short-term memories were no good, because they always lost count and had to start over. Sometimes, when he arrived with his little glass bottles, the ghosts would faintly ask him for help in counting the coins.

And then he would scoop the ghosts in and stopper the bottles tight. (It was awkward, using just his right hand; but sometimes he had actually seemed able to *nudge them along* a little with his missing left!) He had always known that he had to use glass containers—the ghosts had to be able to see out, even if it was only as far as the inside lining of a pocket, or they rotted away and turned to poison in the container.

He had his makeshift traps all over the city. In RTD yards under the Santa Monica Freeway, ghosts would climb aboard the doorless old hulks of city buses and then just sit in the seats, evidently waiting for a driver to come and take them somewhere; and they often hung around deserted pay telephones, as if waiting for a call; and sometimes in the empty cracked concrete lots he would just paint a big bull's-eye, and the things would gather there, presumably to see what sort of missile might eventually hit the target. Even spiderwebs often caught the very new ones.

Sometimes he got so many bottles filled that even his

stash boxes wouldn't hold any more, and he could sell the surplus. The dope dealers that catered to the wealthy Benedict Canyon crowd would pay him two or three hundred dollars per bottle—cash and no questions and not even an excitation test with a magnetic compass, because they had known him long enough to be sure he wouldn't just sell them an empty bottle. The dealers siphoned each ghost into a quantity of nitrous oxide and then sealed the mix into a little pressurized glass cartridge, and eventually some rich customer would fill a balloon with it and then inhale the whole thing.

The cylinders were known as *smokes* or *cigars,* slang terms of the old-timers who attracted ghosts with aromatic pipe tobacco or cherry-flavored cigars, and then inhaled the disintegrating things right along with the tobacco smoke. *Take a snort of Mr. Nicotinus, walk with the Maduro Man.* It had been considered a gourmet high, in the days before health and social concerns had made tobacco use déclassé. Nitrous oxide was the preferred mixer now, even though the hit tended to be less "digestible," lumpy with unbroken memories.

Sherman Oaks favored ghosts raw and uncut—not pureed in the bowl of a pipe or the cherry of a cigar, or minced up in a chilled soup of nitrous oxide; he liked them fresh and whole, like live oysters.

He opened his mouth now and exhaled slowly, emptying his lungs, hearing the faint roar of all the ghosts he had eaten over the years or decades.

The Bony Express, all the fractalized trinities of Mr. Nicotinus.

To his left the towers of downtown, among which he

could still pick out the old City Hall, the Security Bank building, and the Arco Towers, were featureless and depthless silhouettes against a darkening sky stained bronze by the returned smog, but the cooling evening breeze down here in the freeway island somehow still carried, along with the scents of jasmine and crushed iceplant, a whiff of yesterday's desert sage smell.

His lungs were empty.

Now Sherman Oaks inhaled deeply—but the kid was too far away. That old gardening truck had apparently kept right on going; he should have got the license number. But his left arm, still uncomfortably warm, was at least pointing toward the nearest loop of the track the kid was leaving. West of here.

The actual flesh-and-blood left arm was gone—lost long ago, he assumed from the smooth, uninflamed scar tissue that covered the stump at the shoulder. The loss of the limb had no doubt been a dramatic incident, but it had happened back in the old life that he knew only through vague and unhelpful fragments of dreams. He couldn't now even remember what name he might once have had; he had chosen "Sherman Oaks" just because that was the district of Los Angeles he'd been in when awareness had returned to him.

But he still *felt* a left arm. Sometimes the phantom hand at the end of it would feel so tightly clenched into a fist that the imaginary muscles would cramp painfully, and sometimes the "arm" felt cold and wet. When someone died nearby, though, he felt a little tingle of warmth, as if a cigarette ash had been tapped off onto the phantom skin; and if the ghost was trapped somehow, snagged on or in something, the phantom arm would warm up and point to it.

And even though he knew that there was not really any arm attached to the shoulder, Sherman Oaks found it awkward to walk through doorways or down bus aisles when the phantom limb was thrust out in that way. At other times the missing hand would for whole days at a time seem to be clutching his chest, and he would have to sleep on his back, which he hated to do because he always started snoring and woke himself up.

He squinted around at the darkening grove. He knew he should check the other traps, but he wanted to find the kid before someone else did; obviously Koot Hoomie Parganas had not yet reached puberty—that was why the boy couldn't absorb the super-smoke that he was overlapped with, even if he had actually inhaled it now. The unabsorbed ghost would continue to be conspicuous.

Sherman Oaks lifted his head at a sudden rustling sound. With muffled cursing and a snapping of oleander branches, someone was clumsily breaking into his preserve. Sherman Oaks tiptoed toward the intruder, but relaxed when he heard the mumbled words: "Goddamn spirochetes can't hear yourself think in a can of tuna fish. Yo bay-*bee!* Gotcha where they want 'em if it's New York minutes in a three-o'clock food show." And Oaks could smell him, the sharp reek of unmetabolized cheap wine.

Oaks stepped out into a clearing, intentionally stamping his feet. The stranger goggled at him in vast confusion.

"Get out of here," Oaks told him. "Or I'll eat you too."

"Yes, boss," quavered the stranger, toppling over backward and then swimming awkwardly back toward the oleander border, doing a thrashing backstroke across the ice plant. "Just lookin' to get my ashes hauled."

You got your ashes hauled years ago, thought Oaks as he watched the ludicrous figure disappear back onto the freeway shoulder.

But Oaks was uneasy. Even this sort of creature, the creepy old ghosts who had accumulated physical substance—from bugs and sick animals, and spilled blood and spit and jizz, and even from each other, sometimes—might go lurching after the boy, in their idiot intrusive way. They always seemed to find clothes to wear, and they could panhandle for money to buy liquor, but Sherman Oaks could recognize them instantly by their disjointed babbling and the way the liquor, unaffected by their lifeless token guts, bubbled out of their pores still redolent with unmetabolized ethanol.

They couldn't eat organic stuff, because it would just rot inside them; so they mindlessly ate . . . rocks, and bottle caps, and marbles, and bits of crumbled asphalt they found in the gutters of old streets. Sherman Oaks had to smile, remembering the time a truck full of live chickens had overturned on the Pasadena Freeway, freeing a couple of dozen chickens who took up messy residence on one of the freeway islands. Passing motorists had started bringing bags of corn along with them on the way to work, and throwing the bags out onto the island as they drove past. Several of the big old solid ghosts had mistaken the corn kernels for gravel, and had eaten them, and then a couple of weeks later had been totally bewildered by the green corn shoots sprouting from every orifice of their squatter's-rights bodies, even out from behind their eyeballs.

To hell with the ghost traps, thought Sherman Oaks. I can go hungry for one night. I've got to track down that kid, and that big unabsorbed ghost, before somebody else does.

The sky was purple now, darkening to black, and the *Queen Mary* was a vast chandelier of lights only a quarter of a mile away across Long Beach Harbor, throwing glittering gold tracks across the choppy water to where Solomon Shadroe stood on the deck of his forty-six-foot Alaskan trawler.

His boat was moored at a slip in the crowded Downtown Long Beach Marina, by the mouth of the Los Angeles River, and though most of the owners of the neighboring boats only rocked the decks on weekends, Shadroe had been a "live-aboard" at the marina for seventeen years. He owned a twenty-unit apartment building near the beach a mile and a half east of here, and even though his girlfriend lived there he hadn't spent the night on land since 1975.

He swiveled his big gray head back toward the shore. He had no sense of smell anymore, but he knew that something heavy must have happened not too far away— half an hour ago he had felt the punch of a big psychic shift somewhere in the city, even harder than the one that had knocked him down in the alley yesterday evening, when he'd been moving the refrigerator. And all of the stuffed pigs in his stateroom and galley and pilothouse had started burping and kept it up for a full ten minutes, as if their little battery-driven hearts would break.

A few years ago, it had rained hard on Halloween night, and he had climbed into his skewed old car and rushed to a Montgomery Ward's and bought a dozen little stuffed-pig dolls that were supposed to oink if you "GENTLY PET MY HEAD," as the legend had read on the boxes; actually, the sound they made was a prolonged burp. As soon as he had got back to the boat he had pulled them all out of their boxes and stood them on the deck, and they had soaked in the Halloween rain all night. To this day they still had the old-bacon mustiness of Halloween rain.

Now they were his watchdogs. Watchpigs.

Shadroe limped back to the stern transom and stared past the lights of the Long Beach Convention Center, trying to see the towers of Los Angeles.

He had been ashore today, dollying a second used Frigidaire to a vacant apartment on the ground floor of his building—the refrigerator he'd tried to install yesterday had fallen onto his foot, possibly breaking something in his ankle and certainly breaking the refrigerator's coils, and right there was a hundred dollars blown and the trouble of hiring somebody to take the damned inert machine away—and through an open window in another apartment he had caught a blare of familiar music. It was the theme song of the old fifties situation comedy "Ghost of a Chance," and when he had stopped to ask the tenant about it he had learned that Channel 13 was running that show again, every afternoon at three—by popular demand.

The sea breeze was suddenly chillier on his immobile

face, and he realized that he was crying. He couldn't taste the tears, but he knew that if he could, they would taste like cinnamon.

One night, and it looked like being soon, he would go ashore and stretch out and take a nap on the beach. Just so there was no one around. He really didn't want anyone else to get hurt.

And miles away to the northwest, out on the dark face of the Pacific, fish were jumping out of the water—mackerel and bonita leaping high in the cold air and slapping back down onto the waves, and sprays of smelt and anchovies bursting up like scattershot; fishermen working the offshore reefs noticed the unusual phenomenon, but being on the surface of the ocean they couldn't see that the pattern was moving, rolling east across the choppy face of the sea, as if something were making its underwater way toward Venice Beach, and the fish were unwilling to share the water with it.

"Jesus, Jacko did you get beat up again?"

Someone was shaking the boy awake, and for a few moments he thought it was his parents, wanting to know what had happened to the friend he'd been playing with that afternoon. "He was swimming in the creek," he muttered blurrily, sitting up and rubbing his eyes. "And he went under the water and just never came up again. I waited and waited, but it was getting dark, so I came home." He knew that his parents were upset—horrified!—that he had calmly eaten dinner and gone to bed without even bothering to mention the drowning.

He wanted to explain, but . . .

"Little man, you might be more trouble than you're worth."

A dog was licking the boy's face—and abruptly, as if across a vast gulf, the boy remembered that the dog's name was Fred; and then he remembered that his own name was Koot Hootie Parganas, not . . . Al?

His own memories flooded back, reclaiming his mind. He remembered that this was 1992, and that he was eleven years old, and until last night had lived in Beverly Hills—briefly he saw again the one-armed bum in his parents' living room, and his parents' blood-streaked bodies taped into chairs—and he knew that he was sitting in the car that belonged to his new friend, Raffle; and finally he remembered that he had opened his parents' secret glass vial, and had sniffed whatever had been in it right up into his nose.

His forehead was icy with sudden sweat, and he grabbed the handle of the passenger-side window crank, thinking he was about to throw up; then Fred clambered into the back seat, and leaned between the two front seats to lick Kootie's cheek again. Oddly, that made the boy feel better. He just breathed deeply, and alternately clenched and opened his hands. Whatever had happened to him was slowing down, tapering off.

"I'm okay," he said carefully. "Nightmare. Hi, Fred."

"*Hello, Kootie,*" said Raffle in a falsetto voice, and after a moment Kootie realized that the man was speaking for the dog. "Fred don't know to call you Jacko," explained Raffle in his own voice.

The boy managed a fragile smile.

Memories from a past life? he wondered. Visions? Maybe there was LSD in that vial!

But these were just forlorn, wishful notions. He knew with intimate immediacy what had happened.

He had inhaled some kind of ghost, the ghost of an old man who had lived a long time ago, and Kootie had briefly lost his own consciousness in the sudden onslaught of all the piled-up memories as the old man's whole life had flashed before Kootie's eyes. *Kootie* had not ever watched a playmate drown—that had been one of the earliest of the old man's memories.

A shout of Gee-haw! and the snap of a whip as the driver kept the six-horse team moving, tugging a barge along the Milan canal, and the warm summer breeze up from the busy canal basin reeked of tanning hides and fresh-brewing beer . . .

Kootie forced the vision down. Milan was the name of a place in Italy, but this had been in . . . Ohio? *and a caravan of covered wagons, which he knew were about to head west, to find gold in California . . .*

Kootie coughed harshly, spraying blood onto the dashboard.

"Oh, dammit, Jacko. You sick? I don't need a sick kid . . ."

"No," said Kootie, suddenly afraid that the man might order him out of the car right here. "I'm fine." He leaned forward and swiped at the blood drops with his sleeve. "Like I said, it was just a nightmare." He closed his eyes carefully, but the intrusive memories seemed to have trickled to a stop. Only the last few, the chronologically earliest ones, had hit him slowly enough to be comprehensible. "Are we gonna do some more business tonight?"

After a few moments Raffle gave him a doubtful smile. "Well, okay, yeah, I believe we will. After dark, and until ten o'clock, at least, a homeless dad-and-son tableau has gotta be worth booyah, out west of the 405 where the guilty rich folks live. You want to eat?"

Kootie realized that in fact he was very hungry. "Oh, yes, please," he said.

"Great." Raffle got out of the car, walked around to the front, and lifted the hood. "I trust you like Mexican cuisine," he called.

"Love it!" Kootie called back, hoping nothing was wrong with the car. His parents had often taken him to Mexican restaurants, though of course they had made sure he ordered only vegetarian things like chiles rellenos, not cooked in lard. He was picturing bowls of corn chips and chunky red salsa on a table, and he wanted to get there very soon.

Now Raffle was coming back and getting inside, but he had not closed the hood, and he was carrying a foil-wrapped package which, Kootie realized when the man sat down and began gingerly unwrapping it, was hot and smelled like chili and cilantro.

"Burritos," Raffle said. "I buy these cold in the morning and drive around all day with 'em wedged in between the manifold and the carb. Plenty hot by dinnertime."

Newspapers from underfoot turned out to be informal place mats, and silverware was a couple of plastic forks from the console tray; unlike Raffle's "pipes," the forks had obviously not ever been considered disposable.

Kootie made himself stop imagining a hot plate with a couple of enchiladas swimming in red sauce and melted cheese. This burrito was hot, at least; and the spices nearly concealed the faint taste of motor oil and exhaust fumes.

He wondered if the ghostly intruder in his head was aware of the events happening out here in Kootie's world; and for just a moment he had the impression of . . . of someone profoundly horrified in a long-feared hell. Kootie found himself picturing walking quickly past a cemetery at night, and being afraid to sleep for more than an hour at a time, and, somehow, sitting crouched on the cowcatcher of an old locomotive racing through a cold night.

Kootie shuddered, and after that he just concentrated on the burrito, and on thwarting the dog's cheerful interest in the food, and on the shadows on the dark street outside the car windows.

CHAPTER II

⚙

"You may not have lived much under the sea—" ("I haven't," said Alice)—"and perhaps you were never even introduced to a lobster—" (Alice began to say, "I once tasted—" but checked herself hastily, and said, "No, never")—"so you can have no idea what a delightful thing a Lobster-Quadrille is!"

—Lewis Carroll,
Alice's Adventures in Wonderland

IN WILMINGTON, the glow of dawn was held back by the yellow flares of the Naval Fuel Reserve burn, huge flames gouting out of towering pipes at the top of a futuristic structure of white metal scaffolding and glaring sodium-vapor lights; below it and inland, on the residential streets around Avalon and B Street, shaggy palm trees screened the old Spanish-style houses from some of the all-night glare.

Pete Sullivan tilted a pan of boiling water over his

McDonald's cup and watched the instant-coffee crystals foam brown when the water hit them. When the cup was nearly full he put the pan back on the tiny propane stove and turned off the burner.

As he sipped the coffee, he switched off the overhead light and then pulled back the curtain and looked out through the van's side window at this Los Angeles morning.

The money-scapular was pasted to his sweaty chest, for he hadn't known this area well enough to sleep comfortably with a window open.

Last night he had driven aimlessly south from his early-evening nap stop at La Cienega Park, and only after he'd found himself getting off the 405 at Long Beach Boulevard did he consciously realize that he must have come down here to look at the *Queen Mary*.

To put that off, he had resolved to have something good for dinner first, and then had been shocked to find that the Joe Jost's bar and restaurant on Third Street was gone. He'd made do with a pitcher of beer and a cold ham sandwich at some pizza parlor, disconsolately thinking of the Polish sausage sandwiches and the pickled eggs and the pretzels-with-peppers that Joe Jost's used to have.

At last he had got back into the van and driven down Magnolia all the way to the empty south end of Queen's Highway and stopped in the left lane, by the chain-link fence; he had slapped his shirt pocket to be sure he still had the dried thumb in the Bull Durham sack, and then he'd got out and stood on the cooling asphalt and stared through the fence, across the nearly empty parking lot, at the *Queen Mary*.

Her three canted stacks, vividly red in the floodlights, had stood up behind and above the trees and the fake-Tudor spires of the "Londontowne" shopping area, and he had wondered if Loretta deLarava was at home in her castle tonight.

The breeze had been cold out in the dark by the far fence, but he had been glad of his distance and anonymity—even if deLarava had been standing out on the high port docking wing and looking out this way, she couldn't have sensed him, not with the thumb in his pocket and the plaster hands in the van right behind him. Houdini's mask was only in effect draped around him right now; he wasn't really wearing it, wasn't a decoy-Houdini as the wearer of the mask was intended to be; but even so the mask would blur his psychic silhouette, fragment it like an image in a shattered mirror.

You've hurt my family enough, he had thought at her. *Fully, fully enough. Let us rest in peace.*

The beer had made him sleepy, and, after eventually getting back in the van, he had driven only a little distance west, across the Cerritos Channel and up Henry Ford Avenue to Alameda, which was called B Street down here in lower Wilmington, before pulling over to a curb and turning the engine off and locking up.

The rattling roar of a low helicopter swept past overhead now, and for an instant he glimpsed the vertical white beam of a searchlight sweeping across the yards and rooftops and alleys. Somewhere nearby a rooster crowed hoarsely, and was echoed by another one farther away.

Sullivan wondered if Los Angeles had ever been really

synchronized with the time and space and *scale* of the real world. Even finding a men's room, he remembered now as he sipped this first cup of coffee, had often been an adventure. Once in a Chinese restaurant he had trudged down a straight and very long flight of stairs to get to one, and then discovered that a number of doors led out of the tiny, white-tiled subterranean room—he had made sure to remember which doorway he had come in through, so that he wouldn't leave by the wrong one and wind up in some unknown restaurant or bakery or laundry, blocks from where he had started; and one time in a crowded little low-ceilinged Mexican restaurant on Sixth he had pushed his way through the restroom's door to find himself in a cavernous dark warehouse or something, as big as an airplane hangar, empty except for a collection of old earth-moving tractors in the middle distance—looking behind him he had seen that the restaurant was just a plywood box, attached to the street-side wall, inside the inexplicably enormous room. His Spanish had not been good enough to frame a question about it, and Sukie had been irritably drunk, and when he'd gone back a month or so later the place had been closed.

He lit a cigarette now and wondered if Sukie really had, actually, killed herself.

Remotely he remembered how close the two of them had become—after their father

died

when they were seven years old—during the years they'd spent in several foster homes. They had never had a "psychic link" or anything like that, but the world was so coldly divided between *us two* and *all of them* that the twins could read each other's moods instantly, even over the phone, and either one of them could unthinkingly and correctly order for the other at any restaurant, and the random letters on passing license plates would always suggest identical words to each of them.

Now Sukie was probably dead, and still his first response to the thought was *good riddance.* He was surprised and uncomfortable with the vehemence of the thought.

The twins had begun to differ when they were going to Hollywood High School, and it had become clear that the money their father had left them would be used up before they would finish college in about 1974. Sukie had never been interested in boyfriends, and she resented Pete spending money and time on things like dances. And the girls Pete went out with always dumped him before long, so the whole effort of trying to pursue romances really had seemed like a costly waste.

Eventually he had got a clue to why the girls had always dumped him.

He and Sukie had supported themselves through their last years in City College with jobs at pizza parlors and miniature golf courses and pet stores, but even after they'd graduated and got hired by Loretta deLarava for substantial salaries, they had continued to be roommates. Sukie continued to have no interest in the sex that was opposite to her, and Pete had continued to have meager success in pursuing the sex that was opposite to him.

And then in the summer of '86, Pete got engaged.

Judy Nording was a film editor who had done

postproduction work for deLarava since the late seventies, and Pete had got into the habit of drifting past the editing rooms when she would be working. Somehow, he had known that he'd be wise to do this visiting when Sukie was off on some solo errand.

Judy had been two years younger than Pete, but she had made him feel naive and stodgy and *incurious*—she not only knew everything about editing and mixing, but also knew nearly as much as he did about lights and colored gels and generator trucks and on-site electrical problems. And she was tall and slim, and when he strolled into her office she had a casual way of shoving her chair back and throwing one long blue-jeaned leg over the editing bench, with her ankle between the rewind posts, and the tight denim that sheathed her calf glowing in the glare from the light well. Her long blond hair was generally tied back in a braid.

He had been fascinated when she'd shown him things like the xenon-gas projection bulbs that worked under eight atmospheres of pressure, and that burned so hot that they reconfigured ordinary air into ozone, which had to be piped up through the ceiling by exhaust fans; and she had taken him down to the wide Foley stage in front of the screen in the projection room, and shown him the dozen floor-sections that could be lifted away to expose yards-wide movable wooden trays, so that the actors who were dubbing English dialogue onto foreign movies could audibly plod through sand while they spoke their lines onto the new soundtrack, or walk clickingly over marble, or even, if the last partition was lifted away, slosh noisily through a pool of water.

She had lived with half a dozen other young people in an old three-story Victorian house off Melrose, near the studio; even in '86 the house and yard had been fenced in with chain-link and barbed wire. Eventually Judy had given Pete a key to the front gate.

Sukie had been furious when he first spent the night there—but as it became clear that her brother and Judy Nording were actually likely to get married, Sukie had apparently changed her mind about the woman, taking her out for "girl lunches" and shopping expeditions.

Pete had been naively pleased that the two women were getting along, and he was seeing Judy every night.

Then one evening at Miceli's, an Italian restaurant off Hollywood Boulevard, Judy had been inexplicably cold and abrupt with him; he had not been able to demand or plead or wheedle the reason from her, and after he had sulkily driven her home and gone back to his and Sukie's apartment, he had shut himself into his room with a bottle of Sukie's Wild Turkey bourbon and had laboriously and painstakingly written a maudlin sonnet to his suddenly hostile fiancée. At about two in the morning he had opened the door, thrown all the drafts of the sonnet into the kitchen wastebasket, and lurched off to bed.

The next morning, he had been awakened at about ten by intermittent laughter and a harsh voice droning on and on, outside his bedroom window, in the alley; but he had not opened his eyes and dragged himself out of bed until he had recognized the lines the voice was reciting. Then, his face cold with nausea and disoriented horror, he had reeled to the window and squinted out.

Apparently, Sukie had taken out the trash.

Some ragged old man had found the drafts of Pete's sonnet in the Dumpster and, in mock-theatrical tones and with exaggerated grimacing, was reading the verses to an audience of about half a dozen unkempt men and women, who were bracing themselves on their shopping carts to keep from falling down with laughter.

Pete hadn't been able to work up the peremptory tone to tell them to go away, and neither could he bear to go back to bed and listen to more of the recital, so he had defeatedly set about showering and shaving and making coffee. He had eventually got to deLarava's studio at about noon—to discover that Judy Nording had quit. When he rushed to her house he was told that she had packed up her bed and stereo and books in a U-Haul trailer and had simply driven away. By nightfall he had established that none of her friends, nor even her parents in Northridge, would admit to knowing where she might have gone.

Upon hearing of it, Sukie had denounced Nording as a teasing, fickle bitch and probable sociopath; and under her indignation she had been obviously pleased and relieved.

In November, Pete had located Judy Nording—she'd been working for a news station in Seattle, and he had flown up there and surprised her on her front doorstep one rainy evening when she was returning from the studio. She had burst out sobbing at the sight of him, and he had walked her to a bar across the street. Over a calming gin-and-tonic she had stiffly apologized for disappearing the way she had done, but insisted that she had had no choice after finding out about his previous marriages, and his children, and his bisexuality. Sukie had told her all of it, Nording had assured him—Sukie had taken her to one last lunch and had shown her the wedding announcements, pictures of the many kids, and had even brought along a man who'd been one of Pete's ill-treated gay lovers. Sukie, Nording explained, had felt that she ought to know.

Now, sitting on the narrow bed in his van six years later, Sullivan winced as he remembered that *he had not been able to convince Nording that Sukie's stories had been lies.* It hadn't really mattered anymore, for Nording was by that time involved with some guy at the station, and Pete himself had begun dating a young woman who worked in a Westwood restaurant—but though he had laughed, and spoken earnestly, and shouted, and thrown a handful of change onto the table and waved at the telephone, during the course of a long half-hour in that Seattle bar, he had *not* been able to convince Judy Nording that he really was single, childless, and heterosexual.

Pete had been glad Sukie hadn't gone on to attribute to him something like heroin dealing, or murder, for Nording would probably have believed those things too, and called the police on him.

He had flown back down to Los Angeles later that night. Nothing about the scene he'd then had with Sukie in their shared apartment had gone the way he had indignantly planned. Sukie had cried, and told him why she had chased Judy away, and, hanging on to his jacket sleeve as he struggled toward the front door, had kept on telling him.

✳   ✳   ✳

He gulped the last of the hot coffee, and decided against another cup. Sukie had always had a couple of cups of coffee first thing in the morning, and then followed them with two or three cold beers "to keep anything from catching up."

He could see now that Sukie had been an alcoholic by the time they'd got out of college in '75. By the early eighties, when the twins had been working for Loretta deLarava for a while, they had been known to some of their friends as "Teet and Toot"—Pete was "Teet," for teetotaller, and Sukie was "Toot" for off-on-a-toot.

He was sure that he must have tried on a number of occasions to talk her into at least cutting back on her drinking, but this morning he could remember only one time. During a break at a shoot somewhere in Redondo Beach, years before she would wreck his engagement to Judy Nording, he had timidly suggested that one more slug from her bourbon-filled thermos bottle might be enough for the day, or at least for the rest of the morning, and she had said, "What you don't know can't hurt you." She had given him a strange look then—a sort of doubtful smile, with her eyebrows hiked up in the center and down at the outer edges, as if affectionately forgiving him for having asked a naively rude question, one that could have elicited a devastating answer.

He stubbed his cigarette out in a little tin ashtray on the narrow sink, then stood up and pulled his pants on. Later today he'd have to get a shower in some college gym, but right now he wanted to find some early breakfast at a place with an accessible men's room . . . and then have a look around the city.

He put on his shoes and a shirt and ducked between the front seats to pull back the windshield curtain. The windows of the houses on this street were still dark, though the dawn was beginning to fade the orange glow of the flares crowning the Naval Fuel Reserve.

As he sat down in the driver's seat and switched on the engine, he was suddenly, deeply certain that Sukie had indeed killed herself three nights ago. His heartbeat didn't speed up, and all he did was light another cigarette as he fluttered the gas pedal to keep the cold engine running, but quietly and all at once he had realized that for decades she had been wanting to be dead—maybe ever since their father died, in 1959.

A.O.P., dude. Accelerate Outta Problems. She hadn't exactly accelerated out of that one. It had taken her thirty-two years.

And now Sukie was a ghost. Sullivan hoped she would rest quietly and asleep, and not be searched out and snorted up by some East Coast deLarava, nor stay up, awake and agitated, and eventually grow by slow accretion into one of the lurching, imbecilic creatures such as he had seen at the Houdini ruins yesterday.

He let off on the gas pedal. The engine seemed to be running smoothly. He turned on the lights, squinted at the green radiance of the gauges, then clanked the engine into gear and nosed the van away from the curb into the still street. May as well head up to Sunset and see if Tiny Naylor's is still there, he thought.

In the Greyhound bus station on Seventh, Angelica Anthem Elizalde stood by the glass doors off to the street

side of the ticket counter, down at the end where the word
BOLETOS was printed very big over the small word TICKETS
on the overhead sign.

For the last several hours she had tried to nap in one
or another of the cagelike chairs, or peered out the doors
at the empty nighttime street, or paced the shiny linoleum
floor while humbled families gathered around Gate 8, to
eventually all pile aboard some bus bound for God knew
where, and then after half an hour or so be replaced by
more shuffling, apologetic, fugitive families. Their luggage
was old thrift-store suitcases, and cardboard boxes hastily
sealed with glossy brown tape, and woven nylon sausage
bags so stained that they might plausibly have contained
actual sausages; Elizalde kept expecting to see goats on
rope leashes, too, and wicker cages full of live chickens.

After some time she had convinced herself that the
hands of the clock on the wall did move, but she had been
wearily sure that they moved with supernatural slowness.
Without believing it very much at all, she had played with
the thought that she had died on the bus, that the jolt that
had waked her up as they'd been passing through
Victorville had been a massive cerebral hemorrhage, and
everything she had experienced since that moment was
only after-death hallucination; in that case yesterday's
eerie sensation of momentarily anticipating events had
probably been pre-stroke phenomena. This fluorescently
bright bus station boarding area, with its cage-chairs and
its chrome-and-tile restrooms and its jarringly jaunty
posters of rocketing buses, would be the antechamber of
Hell. This night would never end, and eventually she
would defeatedly join one of the crowds of departing

families and go away with them to whatever lightless
tenements and government-project housing Hell
consisted of. (She could offer her apologies to Frank
Rocha in discorporate person.)

But now, standing by the glass doors that faced
Seventh, she could see that the sodium-yellow-stained
blackness of the sky had begun to glow a deep blue in the
east; white lights shone now in the liquor store across the
street—presumably the employees were preparing for the
dawn rush—and a couple of the hotel-room windows
above the store were luminous amber rectangles. Los
Angeles was wearily getting up, she thought, shambling
to the bathroom, lip-smacking the false teeth into place,
strapping on the prosthetic limbs . . .

A whisper of cool breeze breathed between the
aluminum doorframes into the stale atmosphere of the
bus station, and somehow even down here south of
Beverly and west of the L.A. River, it carried a scent of
newly opened morning glories.

The day, the staring Western day, is born, she thought.
*Awake, for morning in the bowl of night has fired the shot
that puts the stars to flight.*

She jumped, and then the public-address speakers
snapped on to announce another departure.

With a rueful sigh she abandoned the notion that she
was dead. Another few cups of vending-machine coffee,
and then it would be time to start walking.

Lobsters and crabs had begun crawling out of the
Venice Beach surf at dawn.

Under the brightening tangerine and spun-metal sky,

the streets were still in dimness, and for a silent few moments at six-thirty a ripple of deeper shadows stepped across the uneven city blocks as the streetlights sensed the approaching day and one by one winked out. No-parking signs had kept the curbs of Main and Pacific clear all night, but on the side streets, and in the tiny dirt lots between houses, cars sat parked at whatever crooked angles had let them fit, and motorcycles leaned on their kickstands right up against walls and fence posts and car fenders.

On the rust-streaked walls of the old buildings, the little iron diamonds of earthquake-reinforcement bolts studded the old stucco. The painted Corinthian columns of the porticoed shop fronts facing Windward Avenue were faded in the half-light, and the littered expanse of the street was empty except for an occasional shapeless figure trudging along or stolidly pushing a trash-filled shopping cart. Occasional early-morning joggers, always flanked by at least one bounding dog, scuffed down the middle of the street toward the open lots facing the narrow lane that was Ocean Front Walk.

The lots were ringed with empty metal-pipe frameworks and cages that would be occupied with vendors' booths later in the morning, and the only color in the scene now was the vividly shaded and highlighted graffiti that was gradually engulfing the once-red Dumpsters lined up against the building walls.

Out past the stark volleyball poles and the cement bike trails was the open beach, not taking clear footprints now but showing clearly the sharp broken-star prints of bird feet and the crumble-edged footprints of joggers who had been out when the dew had still clung to the sand.

The waves were low and the blue ocean stretched out to the brightening horizon, undimmed by any fog. A jet rising steeply into the sky from LAX to the south was a dark splinter, with a point of white light at the wingtip shining as bright as Venus in the dawn sky. Fishing boats moved past in the middle distance as silently and slowly as the minute hand of a watch, and a fat pelican bobbed on the waves a hundred yards offshore.

And crabs and lobsters were climbing over the sprawled and trailing piles of coppery kelp. Seagulls shouted and glided low over the spectacle, their cries ringing emptily in the chilly air, and sandpipers swiveled their pencil beaks and high-stepped away along the surf edge. A shaggy golden retriever and a Great Dane had stopped to bark at the armored animals who had come clambering and antennae-waving up the sand, and the owners of the dogs stopped to peer and back away. More lobsters and crabs were tumbling up in the low waves, and the ones who had come out first were already up above the flat brown dampness and were floundering in the dry sand. A John Deere tractor had been chugging up the beach from the direction of the pier and the lifeguard headquarters, dragging a leveler across the night-randomized dunes and gullies, but the driver had put the engine into neutral and let the tires drag to a halt when he noticed the leggy exodus.

Then a wave began to mount, out on the face of the water.

It was a green hump against the horizon, rather than a line, more like the bow-swell of an invisible tanker aiming to make landfall here than a wave rolling in to crash indiscriminately along the whole length of the Santa Monica Bay coastline. Only when the pelican was lifted on it, and squawked and spread his wings at his sudden elevation, did the people on the beach look up, and then they hastily moved back up the flat beach toward the gray monolith of the Recreation Center.

The tall green swell grew taller, seeming to gather up all the visible water as it swept silently toward the shore. As the wave crested, and finally began to break apart into spray at the curling top edge and roaringly exhale as it leaned forward against the resistance of the air, a long form was visible rolling inside the solid water—and when the wave boomingly crashed on the sand, surged far up the slope in hissing foam and then was sucked away back to the receding sea, a big steely *thing* had been left behind on the brown, bubbling sand.

It shifted and settled, and then didn't move.

It was a fish. That much was agreed upon by the half-dozen people who timidly approached after the thing had lain inert on the sand for a full minute and no further big waves gathered out at sea—but the fish was twenty or thirty feet long and as thick as a thigh-high stack of mattresses, and its body and head were covered with bony plates rather than scales. No one in the knot of spectators could even guess what species it might be. It appeared to be dead, but it looked so like some monster from the pages of an illustrated book on the Cretaceous period that no one approached the thing within twenty feet. Even the dogs stayed away from it, and made do with bounding away to bark busily at the fleeing lobsters and crabs.

For a while, water leaked out of the fish's blunt face

from between its open, armored jaws, but now there was no motion at all to the creature.

An old woman in a parka stared for a while, then backed away from the big and vaguely repulsive spectacle. "I'll go get someone," she said querulously. "A lifeguard, or someone."

"Yeah," called a young man. "Maybe he can do CPR on it."

Up the slope, on the dry sand closer to the sidewalks and the handball courts and the sea-facing row of shops and cafes and blocky old apartment buildings, the panicky crabs and lobsters were turning in disoriented circles and waving their claws in the air.

BOOK TWO
Get a Life

Father got a lot of amusement out of lighting firecrackers, throwing them at our bare feet and making us dance when they exploded. He had it all his way one Fourth. After that we ganged up and made him take off his own shoes and stockings and do his dancing on the lawn while we three lighted firecrackers at his feet.

—Charles Edison,
The New York Times,
September 26, 1926

CHAPTER 12

"And what does it live on?"

"Weak tea with cream in it."

A new difficulty came into Alice's head. "Supposing it couldn't find any?" she suggested.

"Then it would die, of course."

"But that must happen very often," Alice remarked thoughtfully.

"It always happens," said the Gnat.

—Lewis Carroll,
Through the Looking-Glass

THE SKY WAS STILL PALE with dawn when Solomon Shadroe turned his old gray Chevy Nova left from Ocean Boulevard onto Twenty-First Place and immediately turned left again into the parking lot of his apartment building. From long practice he was able to do the maneuver smoothly, in spite of the car's rear end swinging out wide. The locator pins holding the rear axle to the springs had broken off long ago, and so the rear axle was no longer parallel to the front one; when driving straight ahead down a straight lane, the car was always at an angle to the center line, like a planing blade moving along a level board.

The three-story building dated from the 1920s, and had once been a hospital. The rooms were mismatched in size, and over the years he had cut out new windows and doors, laid two new floors across the elevator shaft to make three closets, and hung new partitions or torn old ones out, so no styles matched and no hallway and few rooms had the same flooring from one end to the other; but rents were low, and the place was shaded with big old untrimmed palm and carob trees, and the peeling stucco front was largely covered with purple-flowering bougainvillea. Any tenants that stayed long, and he had some who had been here for a decade or more, were the sort that would generally do their own repairs; the old-timers called the place Solville, and seemed to take obscure pride in having weathered countless roof leaks, power failures, and stern inspections by the city.

Shadroe parked on his customary patch of oil-stained dirt, clambered out of the old car, and limped ponderously to his office, pausing to crouch and pick up the newspaper in front of the door.

Inside, he turned on the old black-and-white TV set. While it warmed up he listened to the birds in the trees outside his office window—the mockingbirds seemed to be shrilling *cheeseburger, cheeseburger, cheeseburger*, and the doves were softly saying *Curaçao, Curaçao, Curaçao*.

Curaçao was some orange-flavored liqueur, he

believed. He couldn't recall ever having drunk any, and it probably wouldn't complement a cheeseburger, but for a moment he envied all the people who had the option of choosing that breakfast, and who would be able to taste it.

He sighed, picked up a cellophane bag, and shook half a dozen Eat-'Em-&-Weep balls—red-hot cinnamon jawbreaker candies—into a coffeepot, filled it with water from the faucet he had piped in last year, and put it on a hot plate to brew; then he lowered his considerable bulk into his easy chair and unfolded the newspaper.

The front section he read cursorily—Ross Perot was back in the presidential race, claiming that he had only dropped out three months ago because Bush's people were supposedly planning to wreck his daughter's wedding; "Electrified Rail Lines Would Energize Edison's Profits"; a Bel-Air couple named Parganas had been found tortured and killed in their home, and police were searching for their son, whose name Shadroe didn't bother to puzzle out but seemed to be something like Patootie, poor kid; country singer Roger Miller had died at fifty-six—that was too bad. Shadroe had met him a few times in the sixties, and he'd seemed like a nice guy. He was about to toss it and pick up the Metro section when he noticed something in a little box on the front page:

FANS SEARCHING FOR "SPOOKY" FROM OLD SITCOM

Attention Baby-Boomers! It worked for Father Knows Best *and* Leave It to Beaver *and* Gilligan's Island, *didn't it?*

Plans are afoot for another reunion show!

Led by independent television producer Loretta deLarava, fans of the situation comedy, Ghost of a Chance, which ran from 1955 to 1960 on CBS, are searching for the only elusive—and, some would say, the only indispensable—actor from the old show. They've been unable to locate Nicky Bradshaw, who played Spooky, the teenage ghost whose madcap antics kept the dull-witted Johnson family hopping. In the thirty-two years since the show's cancellation, the "Spooky" character has taken a place in pop mythology comparable to "Eddie Haskell" (Ken Osmond, Leave it to Beaver), "Aunt Bee" (Frances Bavier, The Andy Griffith Show), and "Hop Sing" (Victor Sen Yung, Bonanza).

Bradshaw, godson to the late filmmaker Arthur Patrick Sullivan, had been a child actor before Ghost of a Chance propelled him into millions of American living rooms, but he left showbiz in the mid-1960s to become an attorney. He disappeared in 1975, apparently under the cloud of some minor legal infractions on which he was due to be arraigned.

The police have had no luck in locating Bradshaw, but deLarava is certain that Spooky's many fans can succeed where the law can't! DeLarava wants to assure Bradshaw that most of the charges (all having to do with receiving stolen goods—for shame, Spooky!) have been dropped, and that his salary for doing the Ghost of a Chance Reunion Show will easily offset all lingering penalties. And—she adds with a twinkle in her eye—who knows? This reunion show just might develop into a whole new series!

✖   ✖   ✖

There was also the telephone number of a Find Spooky hotline.

Solomon Shadroe put down the front section of the paper and, with a steady hand, poured some of his Eat-'Em-&-Weep tea into a coffee cup. The dissolved candies gave the stuff the bright red color of transmission fluid. After a long sip he chewed up a couple of fresh ones out of the bag. The jawbreakers, and the tea he brewed from them, were all he had eaten and drunk for seventeen years. He never turned on the light when he went to the bathroom here, nor in the head on his boat.

Heavy footsteps clumped overhead, letting him know that Johanna was up. He reached across the table for his long-handled broom and, squinting upward to find an undented section of the plaster, thumped the end of the broom against the ceiling. Faintly he heard her yell some acknowledgment.

He put the broom down and fished a little flat can of Goudie Scottish snuff out of a pile of receipts on the desk. He twisted the cap until the holes in the rim were lined up, then shook some of the brown powder onto the back of his hand and effortfully snorted it up his nose. He couldn't smell or taste the stuff anymore, of course, but it was still a comforting habit.

He glanced at the three stuffed pigs he had set up on the empty bookshelves in here. They weren't burping right now, at least.

Can she find me, he thought. I live on water . . . but she lives right over there on the *Queen Mary*. I make Johanna do all the shopping, and anyway deLarava wouldn't be likely to recognize me these days. And she'd have a hard time tracking me—when I do drive, my car always points off to the left of wherever I'm really going. Still, I'd better take some measures. It would be hard at my age and in my condition to find another slip for the boat, and it'd probably be impossible ever again to get out to the Hollywood Cemetery and visit the old man's grave—though even now I don't dare sweep the dust and leaves off the marker.

When the knock came at the door he clomped his uninjured foot twice on the floor, and Johanna let herself in.

Shadroe inhaled. "Draw me a bath, sweetie," he said levelly, "and put ice in it." Again, he drew air into his lungs. "Today I gotta start re-wiring the units, and then I think I'll re-pipe the downstairs ones so the water's going north instead of south." His voice had gone reedy, and he paused to take in more air. "If I can find the ladder, I think I'll rearrange all the TV antennas later in the week."

Johanna brushed back her long black hair. "What for you wanna do that, lover?" The seams of her orange leotards had burst at the hips, and she scratched at a bulge of tattooed skin. "After the painting men the other month—your tenants are gonna go crazy."

"Tell 'em . . . tell 'em November rent's on me. They've put up with worse." *Gasp.* "As to why—look at this." He bent down with a grunt and picked up the front section of the paper. "Here," he whispered, pointing out the article. "I need to change the hydraulic and electromagnetic . . ." *Gasp* ". . .*fingerprint* of this place again."

She read it slowly, moving her lips. "Oh, baby!" she finally said in dismay. She crossed to his chair and knelt and hugged him. He patted her hair three times and then let his hand drop. "Why can't she forget about you?"

"I'm the only one," he said patiently, "who knows who she is."

"Couldn't you . . . *blackmail* her? Say you've put the eddivence in a box in a bank, and if you die the noosepapers will get it?"

"I suppose," said Shadroe, staring at the dark TV screen. It was set on CBS, channel 2, with the brightness turned all the way down to blessedly featureless black. "But nobody thought it was . . . murder, even at the time." He yawned so widely that pink tears ran down his gray cheeks. "What I *should* do," he went on, "is go to her office when she's there"—he paused to inhale again—"and then take a nap in the waiting room."

"Oh, baby, no! All those innocent people!"

Too exhausted to speak anymore, Shadroe just waved his hand dismissingly.

CHAPTER 13

"If I wasn't real," Alice said—half-laughing through her tears, it all seemed so ridiculous— "I shouldn't be able to cry."

"I hope you don't suppose those are real tears?" Tweedledum interrupted in a tone of great contempt.

—Lewis Carroll,
Through the Looking-Glass

IF YOU FOLLOW the Long Beach Freeway south from the 405, the old woman thought, you're behind L.A.'s scenes. To your left is a scattered line of bowing tan grasshoppers that are oil-well pumping units, with the machined-straight Los Angeles River beyond, and to your right, train tracks parallel you across a narrow expanse of scrub-brush dirt. High-voltage cables are strung from the points of big steel asterisks atop the power poles, and the fenced-in yards beyond the tracks are crowded with unmoored boxcars. It's all just supply, with no dressing-up.

Even when the freeway breaks up and you're on Harbor Scenic Drive, the lanes are scary with roaring trucks pulling big semi-trailers, and the horizon to your right is clawed with the skeletal towers of the quayside cranes. The air smells of crude oil, though by now you can probably see the ocean.

Loretta deLarava sighed and wondered, not for the first time, what the stark logo on the cranes stood for— ITS was stenciled in giant black letters on each of them, easily readable across the water from where she stood high up on the Promenade Deck of the *Queen Mary*.

Its? she thought. *What's?* Will *it* be coming back for its branded children one of these days? She imagined some foghorn call throbbing in from the sea, and the cranes all ponderously lifting their cagelike arms in obedient worship.

She gripped the rail of the open deck and looked straight down. A hundred feet below her, the narrow channel between the *Queen Mary* and the concrete dock was bridged by mooring lines and electric cables and orange hoses wide enough for a kid to crawl through. Down there to her left the dock crowded right up against the black cliff of the hull, and the morning shift was unloading boxes from trucks. Faintly, over the shouts of the seagulls, she could hear the men's impatient voices, not far enough away below.

The mechanics of supply and waste disposal, she thought. Always there, if you look.

She turned away from the southward view and looked along the worn teak deck, and she took another bite of the half-pound of walnut fudge she'd just bought. In a few hours the deck would be crowded with tourists, all wearing shorts even in October, with their noisy kids, stumbling around dripping ice cream on the deck and gaping at the glassed-in displays of the first-class staterooms and wondering what the bidets were for. They wouldn't recognize elegance, she thought, if it walked up and bit them in the ass.

During World War II, the *Queen Mary* had been a troopship, and the first-class swimming pool had been drained and stacked with bunks, all the way up to the arched ceiling. Before that, in the thirties, the ceiling had been lined with mother-of-pearl, so that guests seemed to be swimming under a magically glittering sky; but the top shelf of soldiers had picked it all away, and now the ceiling was just white tile.

She tried to imagine the ship crowded with men in army uniforms, and trestle tables and folding chairs jamming the pillared first-class dining room under the tall mural of the Atlantic, on which two little crystal ships day by day were supposed to trace the paths of the *Queen Mary* and the *Queen Elizabeth*. The crystal ships had probably been stopped in those days, with around-the-clock shifts of soldiers inattentively eating Spam below.

The unconsidered life, she thought as she took another bite of the fudge, is not worth living. And, in spite of herself, she wondered if the soldiers would have considered her.

The tourists didn't. The tourists didn't know that she lived aboard, on B Deck, in one of the nicest staterooms; they just thought she was another of themselves, fatter than most. And sometimes older.

Such tourists as might be around on this upcoming Saturday would at least see her in a position of some importance when she would be directing the filming of her *Ship of Ghosts* feature aboard the ship.

Her scalp itched, and she scratched carefully over her ear.

It was time to be starting for the studio. She wrapped up the end of the fudge-brick in the waxed paper it had been served on, tucked it into her big canvas purse, and started walking toward the elevators. She had of course been careful to leave the door of her stateroom not-quite-closed, so that a push would open it, and today there was a big, diamond-studded 18-carat gold bangle on the bedside table, right where the light from the porthole would show it off. Attractive to a thief, and too heavy for a ghost. And the doors of the Lexus in the parking lot were unlocked, with the key in the ignition. Maybe today she would wind up having to rent a car to drive to work in— there was an Avis counter in the lobby area of the ship.

On Halloween of 1967, the *Queen Mary* had made her last departure from England; and for these past twenty-five years the world's grandest ocean liner had been moored at the Port of Los Angeles in Long Beach, a hotel and tourist attraction now. The Cunard line had sold her to the city for 3.2 million dollars, and had insisted that the boilers be removed so that the ship could never again sail under her own power.

Under another name, Loretta deLarava had sailed aboard her in 1958, and had once danced with Robert Mitchum in the exclusive Verandah Grill at the stern, where you never ordered from the menu; the head waiter, Colin Kitching, would find you at lunch and ask what you'd like for dinner, and you could order anything you could think of, and they'd have it ready by eight.

The Verandah Grill now served hamburgers and Cokes and beer, and anybody on earth could get in. The tables and benches now were contoured sheets of vinyl-covered particleboard, and the floor was hard black rubber, with a herringbone pattern of bumps on it so people wouldn't slip on the french fries.

Her Lexus had not been stolen; and, unfortunately, the car telephone beeped at her while she was still on the Long Beach Freeway, within sight of the usual litter of old pickup trucks parked in the dirt by the river to her right and the usual half-dozen men on the banks with their fishing poles. DeLarava sometimes fished off the stern of the *Queen Mary*, late at night, and ate raw the big opal-eye perch and sea bass she occasionally hauled all the way up the side of the ship, but it never seemed to help. And these weary old men fishing in the poisoned Los Angeles River just seemed to mock her efforts.

She was soon crying as she held the telephone receiver to her ear, though her face as she stared through the windshield at the cars ahead of her was effortfully expressionless. More wrinkles she didn't need. She could only speak haltingly as she steered with her left hand.

"Are you still there?" buzzed the voice from the phone.

"I'm here, Neal." Why did the best vegetarian restaurant in Los Angeles have to have that name?

"So, they're going to meet us for lunch at Nowhere at

one," he went on. "Table for Obstadt, okay? They like the *Queen Mary* ghost show; be ready to defend this reunion-show concept, though, the 'Ghost of a Chance' thing, I don't think they view it as feasible yet." There was a click on the line. "You've got another call, Loretta—that's all I had. See you at Nowhere, at one."

"Right." The line clicked on Obstadt's end. DeLarava sniffed hard and blinked, then pushed a button on the back of the phone. "Hello?"

Over the background static of a portable telephone, she heard a steady echoing splashing. Whoever was calling her was doing so while urinating!

"Hi," came a voice, "is this Loretta deLarava?"

"Who is *this?*"

"Ms. deLarava? This is Ayres out in Venice Beach, and I don't know if this one is worth your time, but—"

"Are you *pissing* as you speak to me, Mr. Ayres?"

The noise abruptly stuttered to a stop. "No," Ayres said breathlessly. "No, of course not. Of course not."

"Good. What did you want to speak to me about?"

"Um. Oh, yeah—this may not be the kind of thing you told me to watch for, but a big goddamn fish just washed up on the beach this morning. It's about twenty feet long, apparently dead, and nobody can figure out what the hell kind of fish it is. And a bunch of lobsters and crabs crawled up out of the ocean at about the same time—they're still running around, some of 'em have got into the shops and the tennis courts. People are freaked."

DeLarava's heart was pounding, and all thought of Ayres's discourtesy was forgotten. That would have to be *him,* causing that, she thought. Coming back out of the ocean these . . . thirty-three years later. Of course this new damned smoke would finally be the beacon that would lead him ashore. And if Pete Sullivan is in town, that would also have helped draw him out.

"Thanks, Bernie," she croaked. She hung up the phone and began signaling for a lane change. She hadn't needed to ask *where* at Venice Beach.

She would have to call the studio and have them send a news crew to Venice, and then scoot south on the 405 to pick up Joey Webb at his creepy Signal Hill apartment. Good thing he never went anywhere.

She wasn't ready for this. Here was the old man coming out of the sea already—and Halloween was only three days off. It would definitely have to be *this* year, *this* Halloween. Would Joey *do*, would he be mask enough, all by himself? He'd probably be okay today, when she'd just be trying to see where the old man went, but what might happen on Saturday? Damn Sukie Sullivan anyway. Paranoid lush.

DeLarava's scalp was itching again, under the rubber band that encircled it under her brushed-over hair, and when she scratched, the rubber band slipped upward and jumped to the top of her head, where it sat slackly holding her hair up in an effect that she knew from past experience looked like a miniature thatched hut. She couldn't pull the rubber band back down into place before she got off the freeway—it took two hands, and she would want to fix her hair too.

She had started wearing a rubber band around her scalp when she turned forty (in 1966!), as a measure to keep her facial skin pulled taut. It had perhaps never worked very well for that purpose, but she had noticed that the cerebral constriction of it seemed to keep her thoughts aligned, keep her personality from fragmenting into half a dozen frightened little girls. And when old triumphs began (irrationally!) to shake up silty clouds of guilt and shame in her thoughts, a rubber band or two around her skull helped to slow the involuntary tears.

But fresh tears were leaking out of her eyes now. At least I've got an excuse to miss the Nowhere lunch, she thought. *Alert businesswoman, consummate professional; had to go cover the story of the crabs terrorizing Venice.* And maybe my stateroom will be robbed today.

In '46, when she'd had her other name and had still been waiting tables in Fort Worth, her little rented house had been broken into. The burglars had emptied her jewelry box onto the bed, and had flung her best clothes onto the floor, and had even left a greasy handprint on her not-yet-paid-off radio—*but they had not taken anything at all.* Obviously, she had had nothing, perhaps *had been* nothing, worth their attention.

The unconsidered life is not worth living. She had got consideration a number of times since then; she'd been robbed of diamonds, Krugerrands, fine cars—and she had gone to bed with a number of men, especially during her brief period of fame, and had even briefly been . . .

She shied away from memories of her marriage, and of a starkly sunny summer afternoon at Venice Beach.

But none of it had ever been enough to *confirm* her.

She knew it was Houdini's fault.

The southbound 405 was crowded, and she had to slow down to a full stop in the right lane. She sat there expressionlessly leaking tears for a full minute before the cars ahead of her began to move, and only then, too late to fix it, did she remember her disordered hair. She glanced at the driver of a Volkswagen trundling along in the lane to her left, and wondered if he was puzzled by her unusual coif, but he was oblivious of her. That didn't help at all.

The day after the day after tomorrow would be her seventy-seventh birthday. She had been born on Halloween in Grace Hospital in Detroit at 1:26 in the afternoon, in, apparently, the very instant that the famous magician and escape artist Harry Houdini was expiring in the same hospital.

And she had been robbed of her birth-ghosts, the psychic-shells of herself that had been thrown off in the stress and fright of being born. Those shells should have been instantly reabsorbed, like the virtual photons that electrons are always throwing off and then recapturing . . . but they had been caught by someone else, and so she had been tumbled out into this busy world with only a fraction of her proper *self*. The loss had to be connected with Houdini's death.

DeLarava hit the brake pedal again as taillights flashed red in front of her, and she thought about what Sukie Sullivan had said to her brother Pete on the telephone on Friday night, just before shooting her own drunken head off: *Go to the place where we hid—a thing, some things, okay? In a garage? It's what you're gonna need . . .* And Pete had said, *Where you can't hardly walk for all the palm fronds on the pavement, right? And you've got to crawl under low branches? Is it still there?* And Sukie had replied, *I've never moved it.*

DeLarava was sure that they'd been talking about Houdini's mask—the severed thumb and the plaster hands. The loss of them at Kennedy Airport in '75 had not been a random, tragic luggage theft after all—the twins had snatched the package, and hidden it from her. That, and the theft of her birth-ghosts, had been the only robberies that had ever hurt her.

A garage, she thought as she signaled for a lane change to the left, with palm fronds on the pavement and low branches around it. That could be nearly anywhere—and if Pete has recovered the thumb and the hands, there's no use in me finding the garage now anyway. And if he's carrying them with him, then he's masked and I can't track him.

At least not by psychic means.

But the old man is apparently out of the sea now, or at least emerging. Maybe I can catch him and eat him even without Pete being present as a lure. And though my twin set is broken, I ought to be able to get by, just with the help of Joey Webb. A real bag-full-of-broken-mirror schizophrenic is nearly as good a mask as a pair of twins.

And maybe this . . . this *lobster quadrille* will even draw Nicky Bradshaw out of hiding, him being the old man's godson and all, and the old man having got him his start in show business. Maybe I could have Bradshaw gassed or knocked unconscious. Do people dream, when they're unconscious? If so, I could probably be on hand to get live footage of one godalmighty fireball in Venice. It'd certainly be a more valuable bit of film to peddle to the networks than this feature on the lobsters and the dead fish.

It might even be possible for me to catch Nicky's ghost. I wonder how that one would taste, it having been in effect carried in a locket around his neck for seventeen years.

Neal Obstadt's offices were on the roof of the Hopkins Building on the corner of Beverly Glen and Wilshire, ten stories above the Westwood sidewalks and overlooking the tan blocks of the UCLA buildings to the west and the green lawns of the Los Angeles Country Club to the east. The walls of his consulting room were sectional cement slabs paneled with Burmese teak, but there was no roof, just a collapsible vinyl awning that was rolled back this morning to let the chilly breeze flutter the papers on the desk. Obstadt was slouched sideways in his thronelike chair, squinting up at an airliner slanting west across the blue sky.

"Loretta's a clown," he said without looking away from the plane. "Trying to eat the ghost of Jonah or somebody out of those fishes she hooks up from that puddle around the *Queen Mary.*"

The black-bearded man across the desk from him opened his mouth, but Obstadt held up a hand.

"Got to think," Obstadt said. "I need . . . what I need is a fresh viewpoint."

He pulled open a drawer and lifted out of it a thing that looked like a small black fire extinguisher. From his pocket he fished a thumb-sized glass cartridge, and he looked at the label hand-dremeled onto the side: HENRIETTA HEWITT—9-5-92.

"Was last month a good vintage?" he asked absently as

he laid the cartridge into a slot in the nozzle at the top of the black cylinder and then twisted a screw at the base of the slot until he heard a muffled hiss inside the cylinder. A plastic tube like a straw stuck out from the top of the nozzle, and he leaned forward over the desk to get his lips around it.

He exhaled through his nose for several seconds, then pressed a button on the side of the nozzle and inhaled deeply.

All at once:

Yellowed curtains flapping in an old wood-framed window with peeling white paint, hip and wrist lanced with flaring hot pain against the dusty carpet and the weight of the whole noisy planet crushing her sunken chest; only newspapers for years now on the big leather recliner by the TV, no one will find me, who'll feed Mee-mow and Moozh; Edna and Sam both moved away, back East, having had weddings of their own, but a string of Christmases before that with smells of pine and roasting turkey, and bright-painted metal toys; and their births, wailing little creatures wet and red-faced after the hours of anxious, joyful, expanding pain—(nothing like this constricting agony that was smashing her out of existence now like a locomotive rolling a fragmenting car in front of it)—and breath-catching nakedness under sweaty sheets in a palm-shaded Pasadena bungalow, a wedding in 1922, drunk, and driving the boxy new Ford around and around the little graveled traffic circle at Wilshire and Western; long hair easier to brush when the air carried the sulfur smell of smudge pots burning in the orange groves in the winter, and a schoolhouse and pet ducks in the flat farmlands out home in the San Fernando Valley, dolls made of wood and cloth, and smells of cabbage and talcum powder and sour milk; pain and being squeezed and choking and bright light—ejected out into the cold!—and now there was nothing but a little girl falling and falling down a deep black hole, forever.

Obstadt exhaled slowly, aware again of the sun on his bare forearms, the breeze tickling between the coarse gray hairs. He uncrossed his legs and sat up straight, his man's body still feeling strange to him for a moment or two. And, he thought, I now weigh one three-thousandth of an ounce more than I did a minute ago.

He took a deep breath of the chilly morning air. The memories were fading—an old woman dying of a heart attack, after kids and a long life. He knew that the details would filter into his dreams . . . along with the details of all the others. Nice not to have a wino or a crackhead for once.

"Loretta's a clown," he repeated hoarsely, dragging his attention back across the vicarious decades. "She wins chips in this low-level game, but never cashes 'em in to move up to a bigger table; though she'd obviously like to, with her Velcro and her vegetarianism."

He rubbed his fists over his gray crewcut, knuckling his scalp. "Still," he went on, "some big chips do sometimes slide across her table, and she's all excited about one now." He stood up and stretched, flexing his broad shoulders. "I'm going to take it away from her." He thought of brightly painted toys under Christmas trees. "Children," he said thoughtfully. "Does Loretta have any, biological or adopted? Find out, and find them if she does. Keep monitoring her calls." He looked at Canov. "What have you got on Topper?"

"Spooky," Canov corrected him. "Nicholas Bradshaw. I think the courts still have warrants out on him. We're pretty sure he's dead."

"Loretta's pretty sure he's not."

Canov made a tossing gesture with one hand. "Or she's trying to fake somebody out by *pretending* she thinks so. He does seem to be reliably dead. We got a broad spectrum of media out to do resonance tests at the houses he lived in, and in his old law office in Seal Beach, and they found no ringing lifelines that worked out to be him. The one that seems to be *his* thuds dead at around 1975, when he disappeared."

"What kind of *mediums?*" Obstadt hated faggoty overprecise language.

Canov shrugged. "Hispanic *brujas,* a team of psychics from USC, autistic kids, ghost-sniffing dogs, even; a renegade Catholic priest, two Buddhist monks; we fed LSD to some poker players and had them do sixty or seventy hands of seven-stud with a Tarot deck in the law office one night. We had some blind fencers in, and videotaped 'em, watching for spontaneous disengages, but we didn't see any dowsing effects. And all the EM stuff, TV sets and current and compasses, behave normally."

"Okay, so he's dead," said Obstadt, "and his ghost hasn't been hanging out at the places you checked. Is it wandering around?"

"Not if he died anywhere locally—it looks like he just dispersed, or was eaten. He published an as-told-to book in 1962, *Spooked,* but no copy we've found in libraries or bookstores or junk stores has any flyspecks on it at all, and we located a dozen copies of his high-school yearbooks, all of them with clean pages where his picture is. His parents were both cremated—Neptune Society—but his godfather's buried at the Hollywood Cemetery next to Paramount Studios, and we keep scattering dirt on the old man's marker, but the only time it's cleaned off is when the maintenance people do it."

Obstadt nodded. " 'Kay." He stood up and crossed the carpeted floor to an east-facing window. "And right now, go to Venice, will you? Check out this business with the fish and the lobsters."

CHAPTER 14

"I should like to buy an egg, please," she
said timidly. "How do you sell them?"
— Lewis Carroll,
Through the Looking-Glass

ONE OF THEM *had finally been for real.* Maybe.

Angelica Anthem Elizalde stood in the center of the
tiny *botánica* shop and stared resentfully at the morbid
items for sale. On one wall were hung a hundred little
cellophane bags of dried herbs, along with crude cloth
"voo-doo dolls" that cost two dollars apiece; on the
opposite wall, on shelves, were ranked dozens of little
bottles with labels like ABRE CAMINO and LE DE VETE DE
AQUÍ—"Road Opener" oil and "Stay Away Law" oil—and
aerosol spray cans labeled ST. MICHAEL THE ARCHANGEL
and HIGH JOHN THE CONQUEROR (*"Spray all areas of your
surroundings. Make the sign of the Cross. Repeat spraying
as necessary"*). In the glass case by the cash register were
a lot of books with colored pictures of Jesus and Our Lady

of Guadalupe and the Devil on the covers—one, called
Conjuro del Tobaco, by Guillermo Ceniza-Bendiga, was
apparently a handbook on how to tell the future by
watching the ash on cigars.

She had sat in the bus station on Seventh Street until
dawn, and then stashed her canvas bag in a locker and
walked east, over the Fourth Street bridge into the old
Boyle Heights area of L.A., where she'd grown up after
the move from Norco. When the police had brought
bloodied Mexicans into Lincoln Heights Receiving
Hospital, just a few blocks up Soto here, they'd always just
called the area Hollenbeck Division, but Elizalde had
liked the words *Boyle Heights,* and she had always tried
to focus on the old Craftsman and Victorian houses on the
narrow streets, and not on the bars and liquor stores and
ropa usada used clothing stores.

And she had always been somehow personally
embarrassed by *botánica* shops like this one.

The two young women behind the counter were
conversing in fast, colloquial Spanish, ignoring Elizalde.
Elizalde frowned, not sure how she felt about being
mistaken for an Anglo; but she just blinked around
impatiently and gave no indication that she understood
what was being said. One of the women assured the other
that the tourist would soon get bored and leave; the other
resumed the topic of laundry, reminding her friend that
Saturday was Halloween and that she had better not leave
her clothing out if it rained that night: *"La ropa estará
mojado en te espiritu, y olada mal por meses"*—The
clothes will be soaked in ghost-tea, and stink for months.

This is the vein, all right, Elizalde thought dourly. All

the creepy stuff that I was brought up to believe was
orthodox Roman Catholicism.

She remembered her surprise when a fellow student at
UCLA had mentioned being a Roman Catholic. Elizalde
had asked him how an intelligent person could really
believe, for example, that rolling a raw egg over a child
would cure fever—and then she'd been humiliated when
he'd assured her that there was nothing like that in Catholic
doctrine, and asked her where she had got such an idea.

She had of course chosen to laugh it off as a joke, rather
than tell him the truth: that her mother had viewed taking
Communion at church, and curing afflictions by rolling
eggs over sick people—or by burning cornflowers, or
eating papers with incantations scrawled on them—as all
parts of the same faith.

A plastic lighter and an open pack of Marlboros lay on
the glass counter; and Elizalde, reminded by the cigar-ash
book of a trick her grandmother used to perform,
impulsively laid a dime on the counter and took one of the
cigarettes. The women stopped talking and stared at her,
but didn't object when she lit it.

She puffed rapidly, not inhaling, and when she had a
half-inch of ash she tapped it off onto the glass and with a
fingertip rapidly smeared it into the shape of a six-pointed
Star of David. Then she puffed hard at the cigarette for a
full half-minute, while the two women on the other side
of the counter watched cautiously. Elizalde wiped her
right hand hard down the flank of her jeans.

Finally, she tapped the long ash into her dry palm; she
squeezed it, rubbed it around with her fingers, and
pressed her hand down onto the center of the star.

If this was done correctly, with the heel of the hand imprinting a beardlike semicircle and the curled-under fingernails scraping clean spaces that looked like shadowed eye sockets and then jiggling across the ash forehead, the result was a face that was plausibly that of Jesus, identifiable by the beard and a sketchy crown of thorns. Elizalde's grandmother had reduced grown men to tears with the apparently miraculous image.

Elizalde lifted her hand away—it had worked well enough.

One of the women crossed herself, and the other opened her mouth as if to say something—but then the ash pattern on the glass started to move.

Elizalde had glanced down when the women's eyes had gone wide and they'd stepped back, and at first, she'd thought a draft was messing up her crude picture; but the ash image was *reforming* itself. The jagged streaks that had been the crown of thorns became straggly lines like unruly bangs, and the broad smear of beard crowded up and became the jowls of a fat face. The ash around the eye gaps arranged itself in a finely striated pattern, representing baggy wrinkles.

Fleetingly, it occurred to Elizalde that her palms were too damp now to do the trick again. The blood was singing in her ears, and she gripped the metal edge of the display case because her sense of balance was gone.

She recognized the face. It was Frank Rocha, one of the patients who had died during that last group-therapy session at Elizalde's clinic on Halloween night two years ago.

Then the blur of the picture's mouth coalesced into

clarity like solid curds forming in vinegared milk—and the mouth opened, and began moving. It was of course silent, and Elizalde couldn't read lips, but she convulsively slapped her hand across the ash image, nearly hard enough to break the glass.

Her expression when she looked up at the two women must have been wild, for they backed up against the pay telephone on the back wall.

Elizalde dropped the cigarette onto the linoleum floor and ground it out with the toe of her sneaker. "*Yo volveré,*" she said, "*quando usted no está tan ocupado.*" I'll be back when you're not so busy.

She turned and strode out of the *botánica* onto the Soto Street sidewalk. The morning air was cold in her open, panting mouth, but she could feel a trickle of sweat run down her left-side ribs.

That *really was* Frank Rocha's face, she thought. God!

Her own face was as cold as if she had been caught in some horrifying crime, and she wanted to hide from this street, from this city, from the very sky.

She still had the letter from Frank Rocha in her wallet, in the hip pocket of these very jeans. She wanted to throw it away, throw the whole wallet away, every bit of ID.

One of them was finally for real, she insisted to herself even as she was furiously shaking her head and nearly sprinting away from the incriminating counter in the *botánica*. That last . . . *séance,* two years ago, actually fucking *worked.* It *did!* Dr. Alden, drunken old asshole, was *right* to make me resign. I should have listened to him, listened to the damned nurses, even though they were all wrong in their *reasons* for criticizing me. I *killed* those three patients who died in that clinic conference room, and I'm *responsible* for the ones who were injured, and the ones who are probably still in one or another of the state mental hospitals.

Angelica Elizalde vividly remembered the two times she had been called in to Dr. Alden's office:

"Come in," he had told her when she had walked down the hall to his ostentatiously book-lined cubicle. "Do please close the door, Dr. Elizalde, and sit down."

Alden had been the chief of the attending staff at the county hospital on Santa Fe in Huntington Park; he was a political appointee with unkempt hair and cigarette-stained fingers, and drunk half the time. Elizalde had been thirty-two years old, a psychiatrist with the title "Director of Medical Education for Psychiatric Training." She had been at the county hospital for two years at that time, and in '90 was making $65,000 a year.

And she had felt that she earned it. After her internship, she had stayed on at the county hospital for genuinely altruistic reasons, not just because it was the path of least resistance—the third-world-like situation provided experience that a more gentrified area couldn't give her, and she had wanted to help the sort of people who ordinarily wouldn't have access to psychiatric care.

Alden had reached across his cluttered desk to hand her a folded letter. "The charge nurse charged in here this morning with this," he said, smiling awkwardly. "You'd better read it."

The letter from the charge nurse to Alden had been a denunciation of Elizalde and her techniques; it concluded with, "Nurses and staff have lost confidence in Dr.

Elizalde and would not feel comfortable carrying out her orders in the future."

Elizalde had known that every hospital is virtually run by the nurses, and that no chief of staff could afford to displease them; but she had looked up at Alden defiantly. "My patients get better. Ask the nurses themselves how my patients do, compared with those of the other doctors."

Alden's mouth was still kinked in a forced smile, but he was frowning now. "No. I don't need to ask them. You must know as well as I do that your methods have no place in a modern hospital. Voodoo dolls! Ouija boards! And how many of those candles have you got on your shelves in there, the tall ones with . . . *saints,* and, and *God,* and the *Virgin Mary* painted on them? It's not helpful to—a *white-bearded* God, *Caucasian, a man,* leaning out of the clouds and holding a scepter! And Rastafari paraphernalia, Santeria stuff! Your office smells like a church, and looks like some kind of ignorant Mexican fortune-teller's tent!"

Abruptly, Elizalde wondered if she should have brought along a witness. In an even voice she said, "These methods are no more—"

"Voodoo dolls, Dr. Elizalde! I can't believe you credit such—"

"I *don't* credit them, any more than I credit Rorschach blots as really being pictures of monsters!" She had made herself take a deep breath then. "Really. Listen. By having patients do readings with cards and planchettes, I get them to be unself-consciously objective—about themselves, their spouses, parents, children. The readings let me see, without the patients having to *tell* me, the problems that deeply concern them, traumas that they subconsciously know should be exposed. A lot of people *can't do* the abstraction needed to see things in blots, or—or see motivations in situational sketches that look like old storyboards from 'Leave It to Beaver.' But if they've grown *up* with *these* symbols, they—"

"The subject is closed," Alden said tremulously. "I order you to resume the standard psychiatric routines."

Elizalde knew what that meant—see each patient for ten minutes at a visit, during which time she would be expected to do nothing more than look at the patient's chart, ask the patient how he or she was doing, assess the medications and perhaps tweak the prescription a little; nothing more than maintenance, generally by means of Thorazine.

She had left his office without another word, but she had not obeyed him. While the other psychiatrists' offices had all looked alike—the metal desk, the announcements taped to the walls, the particleboard bookcase, the toys in the corner for patients' children—Elizalde's office had gone on looking like a *bruja's* den, with the religious *veladoro* candles on the shelves, pictures of Jesus and Mary and filthy old St. Lazar on the walls, and Ouija boards and crystal balls holding down the papers on the desk. She had even had, and frequently used to good effect, one of those giant black 8-balls in the little window at the base of which messages like *Good Luck* and *True Love* would float to the surface when the thing was turned upside down. A simple "What do you think that's referring to, for you?"—with any of these admittedly morbid toys—had often unlocked important fears and resentments.

Some of the other members of the psychiatric team had frequently talked about raising "spiritual awareness" in their patients, and had liked to use the blurry jargon of New Age mysticism, but even they found Elizalde's use of spiritualism vulgar and demeaningly utilitarian—especially since Elizalde insisted that there was not a particle of intrinsic *truth* behind *any* sort of spiritualism.

Too, she had not been inclined to come up with the trendy sorts of diagnoses. It had been popular among psychiatrists then to uncover hitherto-unsuspected childhood memories of sexual abuse, just as ten years earlier all the patients had been diagnosed as having "anger" that needed to "be worked through." Elizalde was sure that guilt and shame were the next emotions that patients would be encouraged to rid themselves of.

She herself thought that guilt and shame were often healthy and appropriate responses to one's past behavior. And, so, she had again been called in to Alden's office.

This time, he had simply asked her to submit her resignation. He assured her that if she did not resign, she'd be "put on the shit list" with the Peer Review Organization and the National Register of Physicians—suspended from taking any Medicare or Medicaid patients, and thus unhirable at any hospital in the country.

He'd given her the rest of the day off to think about it, and she had paced up and down the living room of her Los Feliz house, determined to call "60 Minutes" and the *Los Angeles Times;* she would expose the county psychiatric system, rout the self-righteous nurses, get Alden's job. But by the next morning she had realized that she would not be able to win this fight—and at last she had driven to the hospital and mutely handed in her resignation.

Then she had gone into private practice. She found a chiropractor who agreed to let her rent his storefront Alvarado Street office on Tuesdays, and she worked as a secretary for a downtown law firm the rest of the week

Her Tuesday psychiatric business had been slow at first—two or three patients, sometimes a fifty-minute group "séance"—but good results earned referrals for her from local businesses and even from the county, and within six months she had moved into an office of her own, between a credit dentist and a car insurance office on Beverly. Soon she'd had to hire a receptionist to help out with correspondence and billing the insurance companies.

Finally, on Halloween night in 1990, she had held the last of her séance sessions. And it had been for real.

Elizalde had been walking west on the Whittier Boulevard sidewalk for the last several blocks, having fled Soto Street, and now she stopped.

In 1990, Frank Rocha had been living in a little bungalow-style house just north of MacArthur Park. Elizalde had called on him twice, in the determined, I-make-house-calls spirit she'd had at the time, and she thought she could find the place again.

He had had a wife, and . . . two daughters?

Standing on the sidewalk in the morning sun, Elizalde was snapping her fingers with controlled, fearful excitement. She knew that her two years of aimless wandering around the country had been just postponement; or not postponement but preparation, getting her strength back, for. . .

For the perilous and almost certainly pointless ordeal of making amends.

Amado Street, it had been. She would be able to find it once she had got to MacArthur Park. She took a deep breath, and then began walking, looking for a bus stop.

CHAPTER 15

⬙

"When the sands are all dry he is gay as a lark,
And will talk in contemptuous tones of the Shark:
But, when the tide rises and sharks are around,
His voice has a timid and tremulous sound."

—Lewis Carroll,
Alice's Adventures in Wonderland

SINCE THIS WAS IN EFFECT BREAKFAST, Pete Sullivan had ordered a Coors Light with his menudo. The beer was finished by the time the waiter carried the bowl of tripe stew to his corner table, so he waved the empty glass at the man.

"Another Coors," noted the waiter, nodding. From the moment Sullivan had sat down, the man had proudly insisted on speaking English. "That was *unleaded,* right?"

"Right," said Sullivan. "Right," he repeated quietly as the waiter walked back to the counter. Unleaded, he thought. That's the only kind of gasoline they sell now, so people with old vehicles like mine have to dump little jugs of lead substitute into the tank every time they fill up. Probably the term *unleaded* for light beer will still be in use long after leaded gasoline is forgotten, and everyone will assume that it's a corruption of some old beer term. *Uhnledden,* he thought blurrily. *The original light beer, brewed since the Middle Ages in the ancient German village of Bad Fahrting.*

There were two or three plastic bottles of shampoo now alongside the bottles of lead substitute in the box under the sink in his van, and he imagined strolling into the men's gym at City College up on Vermont and pouring the wrong stuff onto his head in the shower. He could claim it was a delousing measure. It probably would *work* as a delousing measure. But what would he tell the gas station attendant when he poured shampoo into the gas tank?

The shampoo had been only ninety-nine cents a bottle—logically—at the Arab-run ninety-nine-cent store he'd stopped at on Western. The ubiquitous little L.A. strip malls seemed to be all ninety-nine-cent stores now, as they had seemed to be all Mexican-style barbecue chicken places in the eighties.

Tiny Naylor's was gone, and so he had driven on down Sunset past the various coffee shops that he still thought of as *the chicken-hawk place, the A.A. and N.A. place, the rock-'n'-roll place, the punk-rock-hell place.* God knew what sorts of crowds they attracted now. Ben Frank's was still by the La Cienega intersection, and he remembered that it had been such a hangout for the long-hair-and-granny-glasses types in the sixties that the casting call ad for the Monkees' TV show had said, "Ben Frank's types wanted."

He had turned south on Highland and then east again on Melrose—and discovered that Melrose Avenue, though still animated, had died. He remembered when Flip, the huge used-clothing store, had burned in '83 or '84, and had then had an epic fire sale out on the sidewalk—kimonos and tuxedos and fedoras, all selling cheap in the hot sun and the loud rock music. Now there was a Gap clothing store, just like you'd see in any mall. In the early eighties, savvy Japanese had been scouring Melrose for old leather jackets and jukeboxes, and nervous tourists would drive by to look at the punks with green mohawks; now the funny hairstyles looked as if they'd been done at the Beverly Center. Like a government-subsidized avant-garde, Sullivan had thought as he'd tooled his old van down the crowded avenue, affluent disenfranchisement is just galvanic twitching in a dead frog's leg.

Once safely past the neighborhood of deLarava's studio, he had turned south on Western and driven down to Wilshire and followed it farther east, past the marooned Art Deco relics of the Wiltern Building and the Bullocks Wilshire, to Hoover Street; east of Hoover, Wilshire slants through MacArthur Park (Sullivan's father had always stubbornly gone on calling it Westlake Park, as it had been called before World War II, but today Sullivan sped through to Alvarado without thinking about the old man), and Sullivan recalled that the boulevard would end a mile or so ahead, just past the Harbor Freeway.

Here in this triangle between the Harbor and Hollywood Freeways were the narrow streets and old houses of the area known as the Temple-Beaudry district. Over on the far side of the freeways, on the hill above downtown L.A., the grand Victorian houses of Bunker Hill had stood until thirty years ago. Anonymous office towers stood there now; and on this side Sullivan saw new cleared lots and construction, and he knew that Temple-Beaudry would soon go the same way.

He had got off Wilshire and driven around through the pepper-tree-shaded streets, and had eventually found this place—a tiny Mexican restaurant called Los Tres Jesuses. Presumably, it was owned by three guys who each had the common Hispanic first name Jesus—pronounced *Hey-soos*, and usually, perhaps out of reverence, replaced with the nickname Chui—pronounced Chewy. "The Three Chewies" had sounded to him like a good place to get breakfast.

Snap, Crackle, and Pop, he thought now as he took a sip of his second cold beer. Manny, Moe, and Flapjack. Larry, Moe, and Culero. Sukie had called people *culero* sometimes—it meant, roughly, coward.

He picked up his spoon and dipped it into the hot menudo. Even the steam from it, sharp with garlic and onion and cilantro, was strengthening; in a few minutes he had eaten it all, chewed up every white rectangle of tripe and mopped up the last of the red, beefy broth with tortillas.

He wiped his forehead with the paper napkin and waved the second emptied bottle of beer at the waiter. He put it down and shook a cigarette out of the pack, and as he struck a match he noticed that the tin ashtray on the table had a crude felt-pen drawing of a skull in the dish of it, with, carefully lettered around the rim, the words L.A. CIGAR—TOO TRAGICAL.

It was a palindrome—L.A. cigar both ways, with toot in the middle.

Startled an instant in advance, he dropped the burning match onto the drawn skull, and the ashtray glared for a moment with a silent puff of flame, as if someone had previously poured a film of high-proof brandy into it.

The flame was out instantly, and the faint whiff of . . . bacon? . . . was gone as soon as Sullivan caught a trace of it.

Suddenly he was nervous—but a moment later all that happened was that a car alarm started up in the lot behind the bar. *Beep . . . beep . . . beep . . .* He smiled wryly—*Que culero,* he thought—but his hand was almost twitching with impatience for the third beer.

Then the bartender began clanging a spoon against a glass between the beats of the car horn: *beep-clang-beep-clang-beep . . .*

For a moment it was the Anvil Chorus from *Il Trovatore . . .* and with that the memories of his father had caught him.

You couldn't count on motors, their father had told Sukie and Pete a hundred times, sitting over chili sizes at Ptomaine Tommy's down on Broadway, or in line for the Cyclone Racer roller coaster way out at the Pike in Long Beach, or just driving the new Studebaker up Mulholland Drive along the crest of the Santa Monica Mountains to Topanga Canyon and back. *The camera had to be cranked at a steady speed even when you were crouched on a platform bolted to the front of a car spinning out around a turn, or on a boat in the Bering Sea when it was so cold that the oil in the camera was near to freezing solid. Some guys tried to use the second hand of a watch to keep rolling that foot of film per second, but Karl Brown told me the trick of humming the Anvil Chorus in your head— if you got that tune really tramping, they could swing you on a sling in a high wind from the top of a twenty-story building and you'd still have that crank turning sixteen frames a second as steady as a metronome in somebody's parlor.*

Their father had been Arthur Patrick Sullivan—known as A.P. or Apie, apparently because he liked to do feats of strength and had hair growing thickly on the backs of his shoulders—and he had started in the movie business in 1915, working as a cameraman and film technician in Cecil B. DeMille's barn at Vine and Selma in Hollywood. His bosses in those early days had been DeMille, Jesse Lasky, and Samuel Goldfish, who was soon to change his name to Goldwyn—but the infant movie business was chaotic, and Apie Sullivan had eventually become a producer and director at 20th Century Fox. For a cresting decade or so, he had made feature films with stars like Tyrone Power and Don Ameche and Alice Faye, but it had been obvious to the twins that he had been happiest in the days before sound stages and artificial set lighting. *They'd say "We're losing the light" when the sun would start to set,* he had often told the twins, *but that was Griffith's magic hour, that hour when the sun was just over the trees, and the buildings and the actors would be lit from the side with that gold glow.*

The 1920s had been their father's magic hour.

By the time the twins were born, in 1952, the old man had been on his third marriage, had subsided into doing documentaries and freelance ·editing, and was supplementing his income by buying and selling real estate out in Riverside and Orange County; but he had never moved out of the old Spanish-style house in Brentwood, and he had sometimes hung out at the Hillcrest Country Club with Danny Kaye and George Jessel, and had been proud that he could still occasionally get jobs in show business for the children of various old friends.

The waiter brought the third Coors Light, and Pete took a long sip from the neck of the bottle. Drinking in the morning, he thought.

Beth, as Sukie had been known until college, had always claimed to remember their mother, who died a year after the twins' birth. Pete had never believed her.

When the twins were seven, their father had got engaged to be married again. Kelley Keith had been thirty-three years old to their father's sixty-one, but she was a genuine actress, having had a few supporting roles in films like *We're Not Married* and *Vampire Over London,* and the twins had been impressed with her contemporary career as they had never been with their father's old movies. And she had been slim and blond with a chipmunk overbite and laugh-crinkled eyes, and Pete had been desperate not to let Beth know that he had fallen in love— he was certain—with their stepmother-to-be.

The four of them had seemed, to the twins at least, to do everything together—wading in the tide pools at Morro Bay to find tiny octopuses and to nervously stick their bare toes into the clustered grasping fingers of sea anemones, hiking through the pine woods around their father's cabin in Lake Arrowhead, having grand lunches

at the giant-hat-shaped Brown Derby on Wilshire. . .
Their father always ordered raw oysters and steak tartare,
and kept promising the twins that they'd be getting new
brothers and sisters before too long.

The wedding was held in April of 1959 at St. Alban's
Church on Hilgard. Sukie—Elizabeth—had been sulking
for weeks and refused to be the flower girl, and in the end,
it had been Shirley Temple's little girl, Lori Black, who
carried the bouquet of lilacs. The reception was at
Chasen's, and Pete could still remember Andy Devine
raucously singing "At the Codfish Ball."

And then, one afternoon that summer, their father and
his new bride had driven out to Venice Beach for a picnic.
The twins had *not* been along for this outing. Their white-
haired father had reportedly gone swimming, doing his
always-self-consciously-athletic "Australian Crawl" way
out past the surf line, and he had apparently gotten a
stomach cramp. And he had drowned.

Pete tilted the bottle up for another slug of cold beer.
After their father's death, Kelley Keith had just
disappeared. She had simply packed up all her belongings
and moved, and no one had been able to say where to.

Story of my life, Pete Sullivan thought now with no
particular bitterness. Later he'd heard a rumor that she
had gone to Mexico with a lot of their father's money.
Then he'd heard that she had got in a car crash down
there and died.

And so the twins had been put into the first of what was
to be a succession of foster homes. And eventually there
had been Hollywood High, and City College and no
money, and then the jobs with deLarava.

DeLarava probably has the license number of my van, Sullivan thought now as he swirled the last inch of beer in the bottle. Could she somehow have the cops looking for it?

He remembered a joke his father had liked to tell:
What do you make your shoes out of?
Hide.
Hide? Why should I hide?
No, hide! Hide! The cow's outside!
Well, let her in, I'm not afraid.

I'm afraid, Sullivan thought. *Yo soy culero.*

He had seen a pay telephone on the back wall by the restroom doors, and now he slid a couple of quarters from the scatter of change on the table and stood up. See if you can't establish a solider home base, he thought as he walked steadily to the phone. Clausewitz's first piano concerto.

Be there, Steve, he thought as he punched in the remembered number. Don't have moved.

He heard only one ring before someone picked it up at the other end. "Hello?"

"Hi," Sullivan said cautiously, "is Steve Lauter there please?"

"This is Steve. Hey, this sounds like Pete Sullivan! Is that you, man?"

"Or an unreasonable facsimile." Steve had been working at some credit union in the eighties. Sullivan wondered if he was about to leave for work. "Listen, I'm in L.A. for a couple of days, I was thinking we should get together."

"I can have a case of Classic Coke on the premises

when you get here," said Steve heartily. "Where are you staying?"

"Well," said Sullivan, grateful that Steve had so readily provided a cue, "I'm sleeping in my van. It's got a bed in it, and a stove—"

"No, you stay here. I insist. How soon can you be here?"

Sullivan recalled that Steve had been married, and he wanted to shave and shower before showing up at his old friend's door. "Aren't you working today?"

"I get Wednesdays off. I was just going to mow the lawn today."

"Well, I've got a couple of errands to run," Sullivan said, "people to see. This afternoon? I'll give you a call first. Are you still off Washington and Crenshaw?"

"Naw, man, I moved west of the 405, in Sawtelle where the cops don't pull you over if you're in a decent car. Let me give you the address, I'm at—"

"I'll get it when I call you back," Sullivan interrupted. "And I'll watch the speed limits on the way, I don't think I'm in a decent car."

"Make it soon, Pete."

"You bet. I'll bring some . . . Michelob, right?"

"It's Amstel Light these days, but I've got plenty."

"I'll bring some anyway."

"Are *you* drinking now? Old Teet himself?"

"Only when it's sunny out."

Steve laughed, a little nervously. "That's every day, here, boy, you know that. I'll be by the phone when you call."

After he had hung up, Sullivan stood beside the phone

in the dark hallway. His mouth tasted of menudo and beer, and he wished he hadn't left his cigarettes out on the table, for there was another call to make. A siren wailed past outside, and he slid his other quarter into the slot. He remembered the studio number too.

After two rings, "Chapel Productions," said a woman's voice.

Good Lord, he thought, that's new. "Could I talk to Loretta deLarava, please. This is Donahue at Raleigh." He wondered if deLarava still used Raleigh for special post-production work, and if Donahue was still there.

He had no intention of speaking to deLarava, and was ready to hang up if she came on the line, but the woman said, "Ms. DeLarava is at lunch—no, that's right, she's doing a timely in Venice. Might be a while."

Sullivan's face was chilly with sweat again, and he glanced at the men's room door, measuring the distance to it—but the surge of nausea passed. "Okay," he said, breathing shallowly, "I'll try later."

He juggled the receiver back onto the hook and swayed back to his table. Sitting down, he lifted the bottle and drank the last of the beer.

Order another? he thought. No. Can't A.O.P. in these narrow old streets, and you sure don't need a drunk-driving arrest. What the hell is she doing in Venice *today*? Halloween's three days off. At worst, this is just a reconnaissance scouting trip for what she'll be doing then—and maybe something timely really *is* happening there.

He thought about driving out there to see, and discovered that he could not.

CHAPTER 16

❂

"I'm sure I didn't mean—" Alice was beginning,
but the Red Queen interrupted her impatiently.
"That's just what I complain of! You should have
meant! What do you suppose is the use of a child
without any meaning?"

—Lewis Carroll,
Through the Looking-Glass

SOMETIMES KOOTIE *would be kind to the poor things,*
putting wooden croutons in the soup so that there would be
something they could eat at the dinner table; but today,
when he was trying to inoculate his children, he didn't want
the things around, so he was smoking a cigar made of paper
and horsehair. It tasted horrible, but at least there were no
indistinct forms hunching around the gate.

His children weren't cooperating—Kootie had got them
out on the lawn barefoot, and he was throwing little
Chinese firecrackers to make the children dance away
from their exploded footprints, but they were crying; and

when he set up a pole with coins at the top, his son Tommy
couldn't climb it, and Kootie had to rub rosin on the boy's
knees and shout at him before he managed it.

It hadn't been easy for Kootie to learn these tricks—he
was deaf and had to bite the telephone receiver in order
to hear by bone conduction. Now in the dream he was
biting one of the firecrackers, lighting it as if it was one of
the awful cigars, and when it went off it jolted him awake.

His warm, furry pillow was awake too—Fred had
scrambled up at the noise, and Kootie sat up on the pile
of video cassette rewinders in the back seat of Raffle's car.
Outside, bright morning sun lit the tops of old office
buildings. Kootie straightened the sunglasses on his nose.

"*That* roused the sleepyheads," said Raffle from the
driver's seat. "Backfire, sorry." He revved the engine, and
the whole car shook. "You were both twitching in your
sleep," Raffle went on. Kootie watched the back of his
gray head bob in time with the laboring engine. "I always
wonder what city dogs dream about. Can't be chasing
rabbits, they've never seen a rabbit. Screwing, probably.
I always used to want to do it with my wife doggie-style,
but I could never get her to come out in the yard."

Raffle was laughing now as he hefted the bottle of
Corona beer he'd bought late last night, and he wedged
it under the dashboard and popped off the cap.

Kootie pulled one of the rewinders out from under
himself, and as he dug in his pocket for a dime he peered
out through the dusty back window and tried to
remember what part of L.A. they were in now. He saw
narrow shops with battered black iron accordion gates
across their doors, drifts of litter in the gutters, and against

the buildings, and ragged black men wrapped in blankets sitting against the grimy brick and stucco walls.

He nervously pulled a dime out of his pocket and remembered that Raffle had called this area "the Nickel"—Fifth Street, skid row, just a block away from the lights and multilingual crowds of Broadway.

Raffle was chugging the warm beer, and Kootie was nauseated by the smell of it first thing in the morning, on top of the smells of Fred and last night's burritos. He bent over the gray plastic box of the rewinder and began using the dime to twist out the screws in the base of it. By the time Raffle had used the empty bottle as a pipe—needling the stuffy air with the astringent tang of crack cocaine and hot steel wool—and opened the car door to spin it out into the street, Kootie had worked the back off the machine and was trying to jam the blunt dime edge into the screw heads of the electric motor inside.

Raffle glanced back at him before putting the car in gear. "What *you* been snortin', Koot me boy?" he asked cheerfully as he steered out away from the curb. "A little *crank* up the nose to wake you up?"

"Nothing," said Kootie quickly, thinking of the ghost he'd inhaled at twilight yesterday. The ghost had surely been responsible for his peculiar dreams. Kootie certainly didn't have any children.

"Huh. Regular speed freak you are." The engine was popping and coughing, but Raffle was goosing the car forward down the curbside lane, tapping his foot rapidly on the gas pedal. "A speed freak, you leave him alone with a screwdriver and come back and find your stereo all over the apartment in pieces. This crack now, it's nothin' for kids, you understand, but it's harmless compared to speed." The light was green at Broadway, but he had to wait for pedestrians to wobble past before turning north. "Thing about speed, a guy cooks it up in a secret factory out in Twenty-nine Palms or somewhere, in the desert, you know? And if he's paranoid, which he usually is, with good reason, the paranoia gets in the speed, and when you snort it you wind up feeling what he felt when he was cooking it. You get his personality. They should have those priests make it, up here at St. Vibiana Cathedral on Second Street—spike the stuff with some sanka-titty."

For a moment Kootie pictured a breast that was heavy with decaf coffee, then realized that Raffle must have meant *sanctity*. Outside the car, the Broadway sidewalk was already crowded with bums and businessmen of, apparently, every nationality the world had to offer; all of them seemed busy, with concerns that Kootie couldn't imagine. How long, the boy thought unhappily, can I live out here on the streets like this?

The narrow ground-floor shops were all shoe stores and Asian restaurants and—of all things—travel agencies, but above the restless heads of the crowd stood antique iron lampposts with frosted glass globes, and fire-escape balconies zigzagging up the dignified brick faces of the smog-darkened buildings.

He looked down at the machine in his lap—and suddenly he didn't know what it was. Without deciding to, he found himself asking, "What does this thing do?"

Raffle glanced into the back seat. "Nothing, anymore, I guess. It's a video rewinder, was. To rewind movies, so you don't have to wear out your VCR."

"Movies?" Kootie stared at the plastic box and tried to imagine reels of cellulose nitrate film small enough to fit inside it. Then, "VCR," he repeated thoughtfully. Video-something, apparently. Video-cathode-rectifier, video-camera-receiver?

"Where did you grow up, boy?" said Raffle. "It hooks up to your TV set, and you rent movies to watch on it."

Kootie's heart was pounding, and he took off his sunglasses and ducked his head to peer out ahead, through the windshield, at the remote glass towers that intersected the yellow sky to the north. "What," he asked shakily, "has been the greatest invention since—" He caught himself. "—oh, say, in the twentieth century?" he finished.

He could see Raffle scratch the gray stubble on his brown chin. "Oh, I reckon . . . the thermos."

Kootie blinked. "The *thermos?* You mean like thermos bottles?"

"Sure," said Raffle expansively. "Hot things, it keeps hot. And cold things, them it keeps cold."

"Well," said Kootie helplessly, "yes . . ."

Raffle lifted his hands from the steering wheel for a moment to spread them in mystification. "So how does it *know?*"

Raffle was laughing again, and when Fred whined and licked his right ear he rolled down the driver's-side window so the dog could poke his head out from the back seat. Kootie leaned forward and took deep breaths of the chilly diesel-and-fish-oil-scented breeze.

"Where are we headed?" he asked.

"Civic Center, I think, wander around Spring and Grand and all, catch some of the effluent citizens who're on a break from jury duty or waiting in line for the matinee of *Phantom of the Opera*. Good guilt either way. And first a stop at the Market up here, get some good fresh tamales to put under the hood for dinner. There's Chinese too, but it don't last so good on the manifold."

"Tamales sound fine," said Kootie. "Uh . . . can I buy some firecrackers?"

"Firecrackers?" exclaimed Raffle. "On top of my felonies you want to . . . *purchase illegal explosives?*" Kootie had started to stammer an apology, but Raffle went on, "Sure, the boy can have firecrackers. And for breakfast, how about a slice of pepperoni pizza? *Let's have another cup of coffeee,*" he sang raucously, *"let's have another pizza pie."*

Kootie smiled uncertainly and nodded as Fred's tail thumped repeatedly against his cheek. Between two of the thumps he managed to get his sunglasses back on.

The first part of the morning was heady, nervous fun. Raffle parked the car on Third Street, and with Fred tagging right along they walked in the open front of the Grand Central Market, past the shoeshine stands on the sidewalk to the wide dim interior, where big live fish slapped on butchers' blocks and gray-haired little old women wolfed noodles from paper bowls with chopsticks and haggled over vegetables the like of which Kootie had never seen before. Raffle handled his party's purchases, joking in broken Spanish with the Hispanic fellow at the tamale counter and pausing for mumbled exchanges with a couple of overly made-up women who seemed to be just wandering around and whom Kootie took for hostesses.

Back out on the sunny sidewalk, Kootie and Raffle nibbled slices of hot pizza wrapped in waxed paper as they walked back to the car, while Fred trotted alongside carrying the bag of tamales in his mouth. Raffle had tucked a little flat square package into Kootie's shirt pocket in the market, and when they got to the car and Raffle bent over the hood, Kootie dug the package out and saw the Chinese dragon printed on the wrapper and realized it was his firecrackers. He tucked it into the hip pocket of his jeans.

Firecrackers, he thought bewilderedly. What do I want firecrackers for?

Kootie wondered if his dream was still clinging to him; all morning he had been flinching at voices and car horns and the whacks of the butchers' cleavers in the market, and until Raffle hoisted up the car hood Kootie was blankly staring at the low, sharp-edged cars that blundered incongruously through the lanes on this floor of the echoing valley between the buildings; the cars looked as though they'd been built to fly.

But when the hood had creaked up, Kootie leaned in over the fender and peered at the black engine. He could recognize the radiator, and vaguely the block, but he wondered why there were so many fan belts.

"Gimme the daily bread, Fred," muttered Raffle to the dog, who relinquished the bag he'd been carrying.

Beside the left wheel well a roll of aluminum foil was tucked in behind some square translucent box that appeared to have green water in it, and Raffle unrolled a yard of foil and wrapped the tamales tightly, then tucked them in under the air filter.

Kootie was delighted with the notion. "Automotive cuisine," he said. "They should design the engine with a box there, for baking."

"And hang a string from the radiator cap," Raffle agreed, "so you could steam ess-cargo." He patted the crumpled silvery bulge. "Think that's gonna stay wedged in there?"

Kootie didn't answer. He had just looked up into an enormous color photograph of his own face, and for a dizzy moment he couldn't guess the distance or the size of the thing. He blinked and bobbed his head, and then the image fell into its proper scale.

Behind Raffle and way above his head, in a wide metal bracket on the second floor of the building they'd parked in front of, a billboard had been hung—its bright and unfaded colors made it stand out from the weathered beer and cigarette signs around it.

The right third of it was a huge color blowup of Kootie's own fifth-grade school photo. And the words on the billboard were in Spanish, but the meaning was clear:

RECOMPENSA DINERO POR ESTE NINO PERDIDO,
SE LLAMA CUT HUMI
LA ULTIMO QUE LO VI LUNES, 26 DE OCTUBRE,
EN BULEVA SUNSET
$20,000 LLAMA (213) JKL KOOT $20,000
NO PREGUNTAS

Kootie began whistling, and he shuffled to the driver's side door and pulled it open, letting the thumb-button on the handle snap out loudly.

"Want me to drive?" he asked with a broad smile.

CHAPTER 17

※

*Alice thought to herself "I never should try
to remember my name in the middle of an
accident! . . ."*

—Lewis Carroll,
Through the Looking-Glass

RAFFLE WAS FROWNING at him in puzzlement over
the top of the hood. "No, Jacko," he said, slamming it down.
"Nor do I want Fred to drive. Get in on your own side."

"I can scoot across." Kootie got in the car and then
hiked and dragged himself over the console into the
passenger seat, so that Raffle's attention would be drawn
down at him rather than *up* toward the billboard. Kootie's
face was chilly with sweat, and his T-shirt was wet under
the heavy flannel shirt. He was whistling again to hold the
older man's attention, whistling Raffle's *another pizza pie*
tune because he couldn't think of anything else; he knew
that with his bad ankle he wouldn't be able to outrun
Raffle, if it came to that.

But now Raffle had coaxed the dog into the back seat, and had got in himself and closed the door. "Are all little kids as crazy as you?"

Kootie was glad that his sunglasses were hiding the alarm that must still be shining in his eyes. "I'm not a little kid," he said, hoping his heartbeat would slow down once the car got moving. "I'm an eighty-four-year-old . . . midget."

"Mayor of the Munchkin City," recited Raffle in a high, solemn voice as he cranked the starter, "in the county of the land of Oz." The engine caught, and the car shook.

"Follow the yellow brick *road*," quacked Kootie.

Raffle clanked the car into gear, nosed it forward, and steered it north again on Broadway. Kootie ruffled Fred's fur and stole a glance back at the receding white rectangle that was the billboard, and he wondered who was offering the $20,000 *recompensa*. One last quote from *The Wizard of Oz* occurred to him. "I don't think we're in Kansas anymore, Toto," he told Fred softly and self-consciously.

In the next two blocks they crossed over an invisible thermocline border, from hot, colorful third-world agitation into an area of tall, clean gray buildings, and streets with young trees planted along the sidewalks at measured intervals, and new cars and men in dark suits.

They turned left on Beverly and then parked in a broad pay lot off Hope Street. "We'll make booyah more than the seven bucks it costs to park here," said Raffle confidently as they piled out of the car and he opened the trunk to get his WILL WORK FOR FOOD—HOMELESS VIETNAM VET WITH MOTHERLESS SON sign; "so it's no problem parking on credick." (Kootie guessed that Raffle had derived his pronunciation of *credit* from the way people generally said *credit cards*.) The whoosh of trucks on the Hollywood Freeway, muffled by the tall hedge of the shoulder at the north end of the lot, was like low random surf on the lee side of a jetty.

They had slept in the car last night, and Kootie had noticed that Raffle slept only a few hours between medication runs. He hoped that tonight they might crash for a while in a motel—the sight of the Ahmanson Theater and the Mark Taper Forum and the Dorothy Chandler Pavilion, standing as imposing as foreign capitol buildings on the wide, elevated, tree-shaded plaza across the intersection of Temple and Hope, reminded him of the Los Angeles he used to live in, and he yearned for the gracious luxury of a shower.

Kootie limped across the asphalt of the parking lot, holding the end of the belt that was Fred's leash. The dog lunged at a couple of prancing pigeons, and Kootie tried to hop after him but turned his bad ankle and went painfully to his knees on the pavement. For a moment the world went from color to black-and-white.

"You're just gettin' beat to bits, Jacko," said Raffle sympathetically as he helped the boy back up to his feet. "Here, I'll take Fred."

Kootie wasn't crying, though the pain in his ankle was like a razory-high violin note, and he was sure blood must be trickling down his shin under his pants. "Okay," he managed to gasp, blindly handing Raffle the end of the belt.

As soon as Kootie was able to breathe smoothly he spoke, to show that he was okay.

"What 'work' do we do," he asked, "for food?"

The people who had given them stray one-dollar bills and pocket-warmed handfuls of change yesterday and last night had clearly been just paying an urban toll, but here he could imagine getting a *twenty* or two, and being given some actual *task*.

They stopped at the Temple Street curb. "Well," said Raffle, squinting around at the wide, clean streets, "you gotta *anticipate*. It's no good saying, 'I gotta go buy my gardening tools back out of hock' if the guy turns out to *have* gardening tools. The basic trick is 'Gimme forty bucks right now and I'll be at the address in a couple of hours,' see? With you along it should be easy. 'My boy's sick, I just need thirty bucks to stash him in a motel bed, and then I'll be right over.' A cough or two from you, and the guy's some kind of monster if he don't cooperate."

The light changed, and they crossed Temple, Fred tugging eagerly at the leash in Raffle's knobby fist.

"So, we don't do any actual *work* at all," Kootie said, relieved in spite of himself.

"Work is whatever you do that gets you a nice time, Jacko," Raffle said, "and you gotta figure out how to get the most for the least. Food, shelter, drink, dope. Some guys take a lot of R and R in jail, they don't mind those orange jumpsuits, but that ain't for me—my outstanding warrants are under different names, every one. In jail, speaking of your video rewinder, they start the movies at eight, but bedtime is nine, so you always miss the end of the movie. Could you live like that? And if you even smoke a cigarette—and one cigarette, in trade, costs you anywhere from four to eight items from the commissary, like soap or candy bars—a guy hiding in the air conditioning vent or somewhere tells on you, and then on the loudspeaker, 'Mayo, report to the front watch, and put out that cigarette.' You get a write-up, and gotta spend four hours scrubbing the toilets or something. Get two or three write-ups and you get a major—you don't get your early release date. The *good* life is this out here."

Kootie shrugged bewilderedly. "I'm sold," he said.

They were stopped now at the Hope Street corner curb, waiting for the east-west light to change, and several men in suits and a woman in a coffee-colored dress had drifted up beside them, chattering about whoever was singing the Phantom role today.

The words *I'm sold* went on ringing in Kootie's head as he stared to his right, back north across Temple.

The sky and the houses on the Echo Park hills and the greenery of the Hollywood Freeway shoulder all faded into a blurry two-dimensional frame surrounding the white, white billboard with the black lettering and the livid color photograph.

Kootie was icy cold inside his heavy flannel shirt. His ears were ringing as if with the explosions of the dreamed firecrackers, and he wondered if he would be able to run, able to work his muscles at all. It had not occurred to him that there might be more than one of the billboards—this affront had the disorienting dreamlike intrusiveness of supernatural pursuit.

The billboard was in English here, three blocks north of the first one:

CASH REWARD FOR THIS MISSING BOY

NAMED KOOT HOOMIE
LAST SEEN MONDAY OCTOBER 26ᵀᴴ
ON SUNSET BOULEVARD
$20,000 CALL (213) JKL KOOT $20,000
NO QUESTIONS ASKED

Kootie swung his head around to blink up at Raffle.

Raffle was staring at the billboard, and now looked down at Kootie with no expression on his weathered brown face.

The little green figure was glowing now in the screened box below the traffic signal across Hope, and the people beside Kootie stepped out into the crosswalk. Kootie found himself following them, staring at the crude silhouette in the box and hearing Raffle's step and Fred's jangling chain coming right along behind him.

"You'd get eight thousand," said Raffle quietly. "After my cut and Fred's."

"Damn Ford," said Kootie helplessly.

"We can get a Cadillac," said Raffle. "Hell, we can get a Winnebago with two bathrooms."

"I can't . . . go to them," Kootie said, involuntarily. *Why not?* he asked himself—I surely can't live in a damn *car* forever. Then he heard himself saying, "They'll eat me and kill you."

Kootie stepped up the curb, helplessly letting the theater-goers hurry on ahead, and turned to face Raffle.

Raffle was frowning in puzzlement. "*Eat* you?" he said. "And kill me?"

"Not you," Kootie said, speaking voluntarily now. "He was talking to me—he meant kill *me.*"

"That's what he meant, huh?" Now Raffle was grinning and nodding. "I get it, Jacko—you really *are* crazy. Your nice clothes and nice manners—you're the escaped schizo kid of some rich people, and they want you back so you can take your Thorazine or lithium, right? I'll be *rescuing* you."

Kootie, entirely himself for the moment, stared at the man and wondered how fit Raffle was. "I can just run, here." His heart was thumping in his chest.

"You got a bad ankle. I'd catch you."

"I'll say I don't know you, you're trying to molest me."

"I'll point at the billboard."

Kootie looked past Raffle at the momentarily empty sidewalk and street. "Let's let these cops decide."

When Raffle turned around, Kootie hopped up the stairs and broke into a sprint across the broad flat acropolis-like plaza, toward the curved brown wall below the flared white turret of the Mark Taper Forum; a walkway crossed the shallow pool around the building, and he focused on that. The tall glass facade of the Dorothy Chandler Pavilion was too far away.

Behind him he heard a yelp as Raffle collided with Fred, and then he heard the big man's shoes scuffling up the steps; but Kootie was running full tilt, ignoring for now the pounding blaze of pain in his ankle, and when he crossed the moat and skidded around the circular brown wall of the Mark Taper Forum he couldn't hear his pursuers.

Then he could. Fred's claws were clattering on the smooth concrete and Raffle's shoes were slapping closer. Kootie was more hopping than running now, and his face was icy with sweat—in a moment they'd catch him, and there was no one around who would help, everybody would want a piece of the $20,000.

Caught. Jagged memories crashed in on him—whipping his horse as he drove home at night past a cemetery while unsold newspapers tumbled in the back of the cart as insubstantial fingers plucked at the pages; crashing through the dark woods at Port Huron, pursued by the ghost of a recently dead steamship captain; fleeing west to California under the "mask" of a total eclipse of the sun in 1878, leaving no trail, sitting uncomfortably on a cushion on the cowcatcher of the racing Union Pacific locomotive, day after day, as it crested the mounting slopes toward the snowy peaks of the Sierras . . .

And too he remembered *expiring* in the bedroom of the mansion in Llewellyn Park in October of 1931, breathing out his last breath—into a glass test tube.

Anyone could eat him now, inhale him, *inspire* the essence of him. In his tiny glass confinement he had been taken to Detroit, and then eventually back out to California, and this prepubescent boy had inhaled him; the boy wasn't mature enough to *digest* him, unmake him and violate him and put his disassembled pieces to use for alien goals . . . but the people pursuing him *could,* and *would.*

If they caught him.

At this moment the boy was just a shoved-aside passenger in his young body, and the old man turned on the dog that came bounding around the curve of white wall.

✳   ✳   ✳

No more than *two* other people at the *worst*, thought Raffle, at the *very* worst, and that'll still leave sixty-six hundred for me, since dumb Jacko is forfeiting his share, making me run after him like this; I can knock him down and then start yelling, *Rightful Glory Mayo! Rightful Glory Mayo!*—no, no jail names here, use the real name—what the hell *is* the real name?—and then tell 'em to call 911, this kid's having a prophylactic fit, swallowing his tongue. I can take off my shoe and stick it in the kid's mouth so he can't talk, say it's a first-aid measure.

Raffle sprinted across the walkway over the shallow pool and skidded around the curved wall of the Mark Taper only a few seconds after Kootie had, and practically on Fred's tail—just as a deep *thump* buffeted the morning air.

And he clopped to a frozen halt, slapping the wall to push himself back.

The wall was wet with spattered blood that was still *hot*, and through a fine, turbulent crimson spray he stared at the portly old man, dressed in a black coat and battered black hat, who was gaping at him wide-eyed. Thinking *gunshot*, Raffle glanced down for Kootie's body, but saw instead the exploded, bloody dog-skeleton of Fred.

Kootie was nowhere to be seen.

The old man half-turned away, and then suddenly whirled and *sprang* at Raffle, whipping up one long leg and punching him hard in the ear with the toe of a hairy black shoe; the impact rocked Raffle's head, and he scuffled dizzily back a couple of steps, catching himself on the pool railing.

The old man's mouth sprang open, and though more

blood spilled out between the uneven teeth, he was able to say, *"Let's see you capture me now, you sons of bitches."*

Raffle remembered the boy having said something like *kill you and eat me,* and for this one twanging, stretched-out second Raffle was able to believe that this old man had *eaten* Kootie, and was now ready to kill *him,* ready to blow him up the way he'd apparently blown up the dog.

And an instant later Raffle had leaped the railing and was running away, splashing through the shallow pool, back toward the steps and the car and the smoggy familiar anonymity of the scratch-and-scuffle life south of the 10 Freeway.

The figure of the old man walked unsteadily to the stairs on the west side of the elevated plaza. A few of the people in line for *Phantom* tickets nudged their companions and stared curiously at the shapeless black hat, and at the black coat, which was coming apart at the shoulders as the arms swung at the figure's sides.

The well-dressed people in line had seen the boy run that way, pursued by the bum, and they'd seen the bum come running back, across the pool and right on past to the stairs, in a fright; but this old man was walking calmly enough, and there hadn't been any screams or cries for help. And the old man was disappearing down the parking garage stairs now, at a slow, labored pace. Clearly whatever had happened was over now.

The old man had thrown Kootie right out of his own body, into a pitch-dark room that Kootie somehow knew was Room 5 in the laboratory at West Orange.

The boy was panting quickly and shallowly, with a whimper at the top of each expiration. He wasn't thinking anything at all, and he could feel a tugging in his eyes as his pupils dilated frantically in the blackness.

As he slowly moved across the wooden floor, sliding his bare feet gently, he passed through static memories that were strung through the stale air like spiderwebs.

There was another boy in this room—no, just the faded ghost of a boy, a five-year-old, who dimly saw this dark room as the bottom of a dark creek in Milan, Ohio. He had drowned a very long time ago, in 1852, while he and his friend Al had been swimming. In the terror of being under the water and unable to get back up to the surface, in the terror of actually sucking water into his lungs, he had jumped—right out of his body!—and clung to his friend on the bank above. And he had gone on clinging to his friend for years, while Al had done things and moved around and eventually grown up into an adult.

Kootie shuffled forward, out of the standing wave that was the boy's ghost, and he was aware of Al himself now, who as a boy had simply walked home after his friend had disappeared under the water and not come back up; Al had had dinner with his mother and father and eventually gone to bed, without remarking on the incident at the creek—and he had been bewildered when his parents had shaken him awake hours later, demanding to know where he had last seen his friend. Everyone in town, apparently, was out with torches, searching for the boy. Al had patiently explained what had happened at the creek . . . and had been further bewildered by the horror in the faces of his mother and father, by their shocked incredulity that he would just walk away from his drowning friend.

As far as Al had been concerned, he had carried his friend home.

And in this room, thirty-seven years later, the friend had finally left Al.

Al was forty-two by then, though he had never forgotten the drowning. In this dark, locked room he had been working with Dickson on a secret new project, the Kinetophonograph, and late on a spring night in 1889 the two of them had tried the thing out. It was supposed to be a masking measure—and, actually, as such, it had worked pretty well.

Dickson had set up a white screen on one wall, while Al had started up the big wood-and-brass machine on the other side of the room; as the machine whirred and buzzed, the screen glowed for a moment with blank white light, and then Al's image appeared—already portly, with the resolute chin set now on a thick neck, the graying hair slicked back from the high, pale forehead—and then the image began to speak.

And the ghost of the drowned boy, confronted with an apparently split host, sprang away from Al and ignited in confusion.

Abruptly Kootie was back in his own body and remembered who he was, but he couldn't *see*—there was some hot, *wet framework* all over him. Shuddering violently, he reached up and clawed it off; it tore soggily as he dragged it over his head, but when he had flung it onto the railing of the cement steps he could see that it had been a sort of full-torso mask: the now-collapsed head of an old man with a coarse black-fur coat attached to the neck, and limp white fleshy hands lying askew at the ends of the sleeves.

Kootie was shaking violently. The morning breeze in the stairwell was chilly on his face and in his wet hair, and he realized numbly that the slickness on his hands and face was blood, a whole lot of somebody's *blood*. Profoundly needing to *get away* from whatever had happened here, he stumbled farther down the steps into the dim artificial light, unzipping his heavy flannel shirt. His throat was open, but he hadn't started breathing again yet.

Standing on the concrete floor at the foot of the steps, he pulled off the heavy shirt, which was slick with more of the blood; the nylon lining was clean, though, and he wiped his face thoroughly and rubbed his hair with it. Then he pushed the sticky curls back off his forehead, wiped his hands on the last clean patch of quilted nylon, and flung the sodden bundle away behind him. His backpack had fallen to the concrete floor, but at this moment it was just one more blood-soaked encumbrance to be shed.

The shirt he had on underneath was a thin, short-sleeved polo shirt, but at least it had been shielded from the blood. He scuffed black furry slippers off his Reeboks, wincing at the sight of the red smears on the white sneakers. *Good enough!* his mind was screaming. *Get out of here!*

He ran back up the steps, hopping over the collapsed organic framework, and when he was back up on the pavement he hopped over a low retaining wall, down to the Hope Street sidewalk.

He was walking away fast, with a hop in every stride.

The brief vision of normal life that the Music Center had kindled in him was forgotten—his brain was still recoiling from having been violated by another personality, but his nervous system had turned his steps firmly south, toward hiding places. The shaking of his heartbeat had started his lungs working again, and he was breathing in fast gasps with a nearly inaudible whistling in his lungs.

The old man's memories were still intolerably ringing in his head, and at every other step he exhaled sharply and shook his head, for along with the immediate clinging smells of dog and blood he could feel in the back of his nose the acrid reek of burned hair.

The little boy's ghost had exploded in an instantaneous white flash halfway between Al and the movie screen, charring the screen and putting a calamitous halt to the world's first motion picture, which, ahead of its time, had been a talkie.

A combusty.

Later, Al had explained the bandages over his burns as just the result of a crucible happening to blow up while he'd been near it, but of course the press had played it up.

The New York Times *headline for April 21, 1889, had read,* EDISON BURNED BUT BUSY.

CHAPTER 18

❦

*However, when they had been running half
an hour or so, and were quite dry again, the
Dodo suddenly called out, "The race is over!"
and they all crowded round it, panting, and
asking, "But who has won?"*

—Lewis Carroll,
Alice's Adventures in Wonderland

EVEN ON THIS WEDNESDAY MORNING in
October the Santa Monica Bay beaches were crowded—
with surfers in black and turquoise wet suits paddling
out across the unbroken blue of the deep water or
skating in across the curling jade-green faces of the
waves, and blankets and umbrellas and glossy brown
bodies thickly dotting the pale sand, and cars and vans
and bicycles glinting in the sun on the black asphalt of
the parking lots.

On the mile and a half of narrow grassy park on the
bluffs above Palisades Beach Road, just north of the Santa

Monica Pier, the villages of tents and old refrigerator boxes had drawn a crowd of tourists to mingle gingerly with the resident homeless people, for there was some kind of spontaneous revival meeting going on throughout the whole stretch of Sleeping-bag Town. Six or eight old women abandoned their aluminum-can-filled shopping carts to hop bowlegged across the grass, growling *brrrm-brrrm* in imitation of motorcycle engines or howling like police sirens; then all paused at once and, even though they were yards and yards apart and separated by dozens of people, all shouted in unison, "Stop! You're on a one-way road to Hell!" Ragged old men, evidently caught up in some kind of primitive Eucharistic hysteria, babbled requests that someone take their flesh and eat it; then all at the same instant fell to their knees and began swallowing stones and fistfuls of mud. Several tourists got sick. On the indoor merry-go-round at the Santa Monica Pier, children were crying and protesting that they didn't like the scary faces in the air.

A mile to the south, at Ocean Park, surfing was disrupted when nearly a hundred people went clumsily thrashing out into the water, shouting to each other and urgently calling out, "Sister Aimee! Sister Aimee!" to some apparently imaginary swimmer in peril.

And south of that, at Venice Beach, several trucks and a skip-loader had been driven around the Pavilion and down onto the sand, where, with police clearing the way, they slowly pushed their way through the crowd that had gathered around the big dead fish.

The thing was clearly dead—it was beginning to smell bad, and the crowd tended to be denser downwind of the fat woman who was feverishly puffing on one clove-scented cigarette after another.

None of the exhibitionist bodybuilders in the little fenced-in workout area had bothered to set down their barbells and get up off the padded benches to go look at the fish. And the girls in Day-Glo sunglasses and neon spandex went on splitting the crowd on Ocean Front Walk as they swept through on inline skates, and the jugglers and musicians stayed by their money-strewn hats or guitar cases. Attention can be briefly diverted by some kind of freak wonder, thought Canov as he leaned against one of the concrete pillars on the concrete stage, but these people know it'll eventually swing back to them.

From up on the stage he could see the signs on the storefronts above the heads of the crowd—MICK'S SUBS, PITBULL GYM FITNESS WEAR, CANDY WORLD/MUSCLE BEACH CAFE/HOT DOGS/PIZZA—and blocks away to the north, up by Windward, he could see the ranks of tentlike booths selling towels and sunglasses and hats and T-shirts and temporary tattoos. The direct sunlight was hot up here on the stage, though when he'd sidled over here through patches of shade he'd noticed that the breeze, bravely spicy with the smells of Polish sausage and sunblock, was nevertheless chilly. The LAPD officers ambling in pairs along the sidewalks were wearing blue shorts and T-shirts, but they'd probably been wearing sweats a few hours ago.

Canov wished he'd had time to change before driving out here, but deLarava had told somebody on the phone that she intended to come straight here herself, and Obstadt had ordered Canov to get to Venice quickly. Now here he was, dressed for the office, and his charcoal suit and black beard probably made him look like some kind of terrorist.

A massive concrete structure on broad pillars overhung the stage on which Canov was standing, and when he'd walked up to the thing and climbed up the high steps, he'd thought it was probably supposed to abstractly represent a man bent over a barbell; and behind it, squatting between it and Ocean Front, was a big gray garage structure that was shaped like a barbell sitting on one of those machines in an automated bowling alley that returned your ball to you. To Canov it all looked like some kind of surreal fascist physical-fitness temple in an old Leni Riefenstal documentary.

He turned his attention back out to the beach. DeLarava's film crew had begun piling their lights and microphone booms back into their van. Apparently, they were about to leave—Canov stood up on tiptoes in his Gucci shoes to make sure.

Why the hell, Loretta deLarava thought as she plodded heavily away from the fish, down toward the booming surf, are so many people out on the beach? Did *he* draw them, as cover?

Her shoes had come unfastened, with sand clogging the patches of Velcro, and she couldn't refasten them without a comfortable chair to be sitting in. And the white sun, reflecting needles off the sea and an oven glow upward from the sand, was a physical weight—she was sweating under her white linen sheath dress.

She paused and twisted around without moving her

feet, blinking when the salty breeze threw a veil of her hair across her face. I should wear the rubber band *on top* of my hair, she thought. "Come here, Joey," she called irritably.

Her bent little old assistant, ludicrous here on the beach in his boots and khaki jacket, crab-stepped away from the crowd down to where she was standing on the firmer damp sand. *He* never sweated.

"You're on a one-way road to Hell," he said, in a shrilly mocking imitation of a woman's voice. "*She* knew enough," he went on in his own voice, "to keep radio electricians around to screw. Total-immersion baptism to renounce the devils, and then she made sure to resurface under the spiderweb of radar-foxing moves. Rotor-fax devils," he droned then, apparently caught in one of his conversational spirals, "Dover-taxed pixels, white cliffs of image too totally turned-on for any signal *to* show. Too too too, Teet and Toot, tea for two."

DeLarava sucked on the stub of her cigarette so hard that sparks flew away down the beach, but there was no taste of ghost in the smoke. "What about Teet and Toot? Go on."

Joey Webb blinked at her. "They were here once, you said."

Perhaps he was lucid now. "Can you sense them, either of them? Can you sense their *father?*"

"Me sense a person?" Joey said, his voice unfortunately taking on his skitzy singsong tone again, "Aimee Semple McPherson swam out to sea here, and everybody thought she drowned. Two divers *did* drown, trying to save her, and she had to carry those ghosts forever, after that."

DeLarava had wanted Joey Webb to sift news of old Apie Sullivan's ghost from the turbulent psychic breezes, but he appeared to be hung up on Aimee Semple McPherson, the evangelist who had disappeared in the surf off Ocean Park in 1926; it had been big news at the time, but later the newspapers had discovered that she had just ducked away to spend a couple of weeks in anonymous seclusion with an electrician from her gospel radio station.

DeLarava sighed. Even as a film shoot, today's expedition had pretty much been a failure. The generator truck from the Teamsters Union had got stuck in the sand a couple of hundred feet short of the fish, so that cables had had to be run where people were sure to trip over them, and then there had been trouble with the Mole-phase lights, the tic-tac-toe squares of nine 5600-Kelvin lamps that were supposed to provide daylight-colored illumination to fill the shadows on people's faces; the lights had alternately flared and faded, and finally deLarava had told the cameraman to just shoot the bystanders with their eye sockets and cheek hollows gaping like caverns. God knew what the fish would come out looking like on the film.

Hours ago, Animal Control had sent a truck out to haul away the fish, but a bystander claimed that the dead monster was a *coelacanth,* some sort of living fossil from the Carboniferous Age, uncommon anywhere and never found in the Pacific Ocean. The Department of Fish and Game had arrived after that, and some professors had driven down from UCLA and were still arguing with anyone who planned to even touch the damned thing.

The news story, such as it was, was in the can, and deLarava had sent one of her people back to the studio with it, but she didn't want to leave the beach without learning whether old Sullivan's ghost had emerged from the sea yet—and if so, *where he was*. She wouldn't dare try to eat him until Saturday, but she could safely catch him in a jar now.

For what must have been the hundredth time, she glanced at her watch, but the compass needle was still jittering unreliably, pointing more or less at the concrete block of handball courts, which was north of her. Before the camera had started rolling she had stumped her way through the crowd around the site, peering constantly at her watch, but each of the six times the needle had pointed away from north it had been indicating some nearby grinning or frowning old lunatic in junk-store clothes—accreted, hardened old ghosts, whose stunted fields wouldn't even be detectable if they'd step back a yard or two.

Apie Sullivan's ghost would be indistinguishable from a death-new one, and *strong*, preserved for all these past thirty-three years in the grounded stasis of the sea. But tracking a new ghost, she thought now as she watched the quivering needle, is like trying to spot a helicopter in a city—you "hear" 'em from all kinds of false directions; they aren't truly at any "where" yet, and they're subject to "echoes."

But I'm not even getting any echoes. And Joey Webb isn't sensing him, and he would—Joey thinks they're angels or spirits or something, but he does reliably sense ghosts. Joey would know it if he was here.

And he's not here.

DeLarava dug in her purse and pulled out her wallet. "Joey," she said, "are you listening to me? I want you to stay here, rent a room at a motel or something, can you do that?" She slid a sheaf of twenties and hundreds out of the wallet and held it out toward him.

"Which motel?" said old Joey alertly, taking the money. "What name will he be using?"

"He's not going to stay at a motel, you—" She threw her cigarette away toward the waves, and coughed harshly, tasting clove in the back of her throat. "*He'll* be just a little wispy shred, like the cellophane from a cigarette pack, but not reflecting. Track him with a compass—he'll be dazed, wandering. Buy a jar of orange marmalade, dump out the marmalade but leave some smears in it for him to smell, and if you find him, catch him in it." She stared at the crazy old man anxiously. "Can you do all this?"

"Oh, *do* it, sure," he said with a careless wave. He shoved the bills inside his shirt. "What do you want me to tell him?"

"Don't *talk* to him," deLarava wailed, nearly crying with exhaustion and frustration. "Don't unscrew the lid after you've caught him. Just wrap him in your coat or something and call me, okay?"

"*Okay, okay.* Sheesh."

"You won't let him get past you? He mustn't get inland of Pacific Avenue, I can't afford to lose him in the maze of the city."

Joey stood up straight and squinted at her. "He shall not pass."

This would have to do. "Call me when you're checked in," she said clearly, then turned and began striding heavily up the sand slope, shoving her way between the bystanders.

When she had elbowed her way to the clearing in the center of the crowd, she paused by the thigh-high hulk of the coppery fish and looked down into its big, dulled eye. A living fossil, one of the UCLA professors had called this monstrosity. Hardly a living one, she thought. Though some of us still are.

She was on the north side of the dead thing, and she looked at her watch—but the compass needle pointed away behind her, northward.

She sighed and began pushing her way back out of the crowd. This was a waste of time, she thought. But maybe my billboards will have elicited a call about the Parganas kid. And I parked the Lexus way up on Main here— maybe somebody will have broken into it.

Sweat had run down from Canov's styled hair into his beard, and he scratched at it before it could work down his neck to his white collar. He was glad to see that deLarava was finally leaving, for a dozen children in swimsuits had climbed up onto the open-air stage that he'd chosen as a lookout post, and they'd started some skipping and singing game.

A big dead fish, Canov thought as he carefully stepped down the cement block stairs to the pavement. What can I tell Obstadt, besides that she hung around and looked at it and filmed it? This one's bigger than the ones she hooks and hauls up to the *Queen Mary* deck on dark nights, but she didn't catch this one, and she surely didn't eat it. Maybe she's just interested in fish. And the crabs and lobsters have all been picked up, or managed to return to the sea. I can't even bring him one, not that Obstadt would have any use for it, being a strict vegetarian.

"Can I buy a smoke off you, man?"

Canov turned away from the beach. A tanned young man who had been standing over by the volleyball nets had walked across the gray pavement to the stage, and now stood with one hand extended and the other digging in the pocket of his cutoff jeans. Canov thought he looked too healthy to be wanting nicotine.

"I haven't found any," said Canov. If it *was* a cigarette the man wanted, this answer ought to disconcert him. But instead of protesting that he didn't want a cigarette picked up off the sidewalk, the young man shook his head ruefully. "They're out today, though, aren't they?" he said, his voice just loud enough for Canov to hear it over the rap music shouting out of the black portable stereos on the sidelines of the volleyball games. "You can almost smell how they died."

Canov, never a user of the stuff known as "smokes" and "cigars," just shrugged. "I can smell that that fish died," he said inanely.

The young man glanced disinterestedly down toward the crowd by the shore. "Dead fish, yeah. Well, see you." And he began jogging away barefoot toward the bike path, doubtless searching for some other out-of-place-looking person standing around.

Police had cleared another path through the crowd,

and now a pickup truck with a cherry-picker crane in its bed had been driven down onto the sand, and Canov could see men in overalls trying to roll the fish over onto a long board. A big flatbed tow truck was parked nearby, and he wondered idly who had won custody of the creature.

He sighed and began walking over. Obstadt would probably want to know.

The fish was to be driven to an oceanography lab at UCLA. When the creature had been covered with a tarpaulin and roped down on the long bed of the tow truck, the driver slowly backed the truck out the way it had come, around the north side of the pavilion; the *beep, beep, beep* of the reverse-gear horn was drowned out at one point by metallic squealing, as one of the back wheels pinched and then flattened a blue-and-white trash can that had RECYCLE°RECICLE°RECYCLE°RECICLE stenciled endlessly around it, but eventually all four wheels were on pavement again, and the driver muscled the stick shift into first gear and began inching the big laboring old truck toward the Ocean Front curb, as policemen waved dozens of nearly naked people out of the way.

At last the truck reached Windward; and when the traffic thinned, out past Main, it drove up Venice Boulevard to Lincoln, and then turned north, toward the Santa Monica Freeway.

On the freeways, there you feel free.

As the truck ascended the on-ramp, grinding with measured punctuation up through the gears, the purple-flowered oleanders along the shoulder waved their leafy branches in a sudden gust; and sunlight flashed in the rushing air where there was no chrome or glass reflecting it, as if the ghosts of dozens of angular old cars accompanied the laboring truck.

In the steamy dimness under the flapping tarpaulin the jaws of the dead coelacanth creaked open, and a shrill faint whistling piped out of the throat as reversed peristalsis drove gases out of the creature's stomach. The whistling ran up and down the musical scale in a rough approximation of the first nine notes of "Begin the Beguine," and then a tiny gray translucency wobbled out of the open mouth, past the teeth, like a baby jellyfish moving through clear water.

A puff of smoke that didn't disperse at its edges, the thing climbed down over the plates of the fish's lower jaw, clung for a moment to the shaking corrugated aluminum surface of the truck bed, then sprang up into the agitated dimness toward the close tent-roof of the tarpaulin. The wind sluicing along the sides of the dead fish caught the wisp and whirled it back and out under the flapping tarpaulin edge into the open air, where hot, rushing diesel updrafts lifted it above the roaring trucks and cars and vans to spin invisibly in the harsh sunlight.

Traffic behind the flatbed truck slowed then, for suddenly the truck appeared to be throwing off pieces of itself: a glimpsed rushing surface of metal here, a whirling black tire there, glitters of chrome appearing first on one side of the truck and then the other, as if some way-ultraviolet light were illuminating bits of otherwise invisible vehicles secretly sharing the freeway. Then windshields were darkened in a moment of shadow as a long-winged yellow biplane roared past overhead, low over the traffic, with the figure of a man dimly visible standing on the top wing.

After no more than two seconds the plane flickered and disappeared, but before winking out of visibility it had banked on the inland wind, as if headed northeast, toward Hollywood.

CHAPTER 19

✦

"But then," thought Alice, "shall I never get any older than I am now? That'll be a comfort, one way—never to be an old woman—but then—always to have lessons to learn! Oh, I shouldn't like that!"

—Lewis Carroll,
Alice's Adventures in Wonderland

BACK IN HIS OLIVE STREET OFFICE after court, well in time for a healthful lunch, J. Francis Strube tossed his briefcase onto the long oak credenza and slumped his oversized frame into the padded leather McKie chair behind his desk.

He had an appointment this afternoon, some guy whose wife was divorcing him. The man had sounded almost apologetic on the phone, clearly reluctant to hire an attorney because he hoped his wife would abandon the divorce action and come back to him. Strube would sympathize during this first consultation, let the guy ramble and emote and probably weep; during later sessions Strube could begin to raise his eyebrows over the man's willingness to let the wife take so much stuff. Strube would interject, *Oh, she'll need it because she'll be doing a lot of* entertaining, *eh?* delivered in a tone that would make Strube seem like a sympathetically angered friend. *Well, if you want to let her have everything . . .*

Eventually, Strube could get a man to refuse to part with a vacuum cleaner that he might never have actually used, or possibly ever even seen. It took more time, but Strube preferred nurturing rapacity in these timid clients to flattering the egos of the villains who just wanted to ditch the old wife and marry the twenty-year-old *sex . . . pot.* For the latter sort, Strube would have to say, in tones of polite surprise, things like *You're* fifty? *Good Lord, you don't look a day over forty.* And, *How did you put up with this for so long?*

Anyway, the timid ones needed attorneys. What they initially wanted, like first-time Driving Under the Influence offenders, was to appear in court in humble *pro per*, not realizing that judges had all been attorneys once, and planned to be again after they retired, and wanted to make of these fools examples of how badly unrepresented people fared.

In a courthouse hallway this morning another attorney had told Strube a riddle.

Question: what do a lawyer and a sperm cell have in common?

Strube pursed his lips and leaned forward to pick up the newspaper that Charlotte had left on the desk. The telephone rang, but Charlotte would get it. Strube made it a point never to answer the phone on spec.

He waited, but the intercom didn't buzz. That was good, she was fielding whatever it was. He let himself start to read. He saw that Ross Perot was claiming to have backed out of the presidential race only because of threats from the Bush-campaign people. He smiled. Strube never voted, but he liked to see things shaken up. "Time for a Change!" was a political slogan that always appealed to him. He was about to flip the front page when he noticed the box at the bottom.

FANS SEARCHING FOR "SPOOKY" FROM OLD SITCOM

Strube read the story quickly, peripherally aware that his heartbeat was speeding up. When he had finished it, he pushed a button on the intercom.

"Charlotte!" he squeaked. "Get in here and look at this." No, he thought immediately, she might try to get the credit herself. "Wait, get me—" he began again, but she had already opened his office door and was staring in at him curiously.

She was wearing another of the anonymous dark jacket-and-skirt combinations to which she had been confining herself ever since he'd made a blundering pass at her six months ago. "Look at what?" she asked.

"Perot says Bush was going to wreck his daughter's wedding," he said absently, folding the paper and pushing it aside. "Did you read about that? Say, get me the telephone number of . . ." What had been the name of the damned snuff? Ouchie? "Goudie! Goudie Scottish Snuff, uh, Company. G-O-U-D-I-E. It's in San Francisco."

"Snuff?"

Strube raised the back of his pudgy hand to his nose and sniffed loudly. "Snuff. Like lords and ladies used to do. Powdered tobacco."

"Do you want me to call them?"

"No, just get me the number."

Charlotte nodded, mystified, and walked back out to the reception desk, closing his office door behind her.

If Nicky Bradshaw's still alive, thought Strube excitedly, *he's gotta still be doing that snuff; and it's a clue I'll bet not a lot of people remember. And I'll bet nobody but me remembers the actual brand name. God knows I ordered it often enough.*

Strube stood up and walked quickly across the carpet to the window overlooking Olive, and he stared down at the gleaming multicolored car roofs rippling through the lanes like beetles. Strube had a new BMW himself, but from up here it could look no different from any of the cars below him now. He was a member of Sports Club LA on Sepulveda—he had even got occasional business from his ad in the club's networking newsletter—and he was proud of his healthful diet regimen, years having passed since he had last eaten real eggs or bacon or butter or sour cream; and his apartment on Sunset was expensive, but . . .

Aside from his suits and the sectional furniture and some signed sailing prints on the walls, the apartment was pretty bare—in truth, about half of his worldly goods were in the goddamn credenza here in the office, along with the ceiling fan that he'd never taken out of its box and the routed cherrywood decoupaged J. FRANCIS STRUBE name plaque that a client had handcrafted for him and that he'd been embarrassed to put out on his desk because people might think he represented hippie dopers.

But he *could* be . . . the attorney who located Spooky.

Answer: each of them has one chance in two million of becoming a human being.

Of becoming somebody.

It seemed to him now that, when he was twenty and twenty-one, he had mailed orders to the Goudie Snuff Company as often as he had mailed solicitation letters to the people whose names and addresses had appeared on the thrice-weekly foreclosure lists.

He had worked as a legal secretary for Nicholas Bradshaw in '74 and '75 in Seal Beach. Bradshaw had handled mostly bankruptcy cases, which often came around to involving divorce and child custody, and young Strube had proved to have a natural knack for the tactics of family breakup.

Strube had planned to go into show-business law— after law school he had let his mousy brown hair grow long and had worn crazy little granny glasses, and he had gone to work for Bradshaw mainly because Bradshaw had once been an actor—but somewhere along the line Bradshaw had developed an aversion to the TV and movie business; and without a contact, an in, access, Strube hadn't been able to get any of the industry's law firms to consider taking him on.

Then after Bradshaw had just . . . *up and disappeared* . . . in '75, Strube had been left without any job at all. He had hastily gone to work for a divorce and personal-injury attorney, and passed the bar in '81. At last in '88 had been able to open his own practice . . . but he was still just disassembling families.

The intercom buzzed, and Strube walked back to his desk and pushed the button. "Yeah, Charlotte." He wrote down the 415-area-code number she read to him. At least Goudie was still in business.

Back in '74 and '75, Bradshaw had kept a box of snuff cans in his desk, and when he had paperwork to do he would open the box and lay out half a dozen cans, like a buffet, and sniff a bit of this one, a couple of snorts of that one, and a chaser of another. He had gone through so much of the stuff that he found it easiest to have his legal secretary order directly from the company.

Strube punched the number into the telephone.

Bradshaw had paid young Strube a generous weekly salary, and never cared what hour Strube came into the office or went home, as long as the work got done, and he had been lavish with bonuses—and, too, he'd always been paranoid, afraid of being findable, always varying his schedule and never divulging, even to Strube, his home address or phone number; wherever he was now, he clearly didn't want to be found. But . . .

"Goudie Snuff Company," chirped a voice from the phone.

"Hi, my name is J. Francis Strube. I'm in Los Angeles and I'm marketing a line of—" What, he thought nervously "—traditional Scottish products, tartan sweaters and walking sticks and so on, and I'd like to buy a copy of your mailing list."

Angelica Anthem Elizalde slumped wearily in the RTD

bus seat with her forehead against the cool window, and she watched the shops and old houses of Sixth Street, fogged by her breath on the glass, swing past in the sunlight outside.

She wondered if people still used the word *chicana*, and she wondered when and where she had stopped being one. The women in the seats around her were happily chatting in Spanish, and twice they had referred to her as *"la Angla sonalienta al lado de la ventana"*—the sleepy Anglo lady by the window. Elizalde had wanted to smile and, in Spanish, say something back about the long Greyhound ride across the desert yesterday, then had realized that she no longer had the vocabulary.

Her face was long and angular and pale, like a saint in an El Greco painting, and in her Oklahoma Levi jeans and her old Graceland sweatshirt she probably did look Anglo. It occurred to her that she probably even spoke with a bit of an Oklahoma accent now.

At one point during the long night at the Greyhound station—waiting for the dawn, not able to afford a taxi and not wanting to walk anywhere on the menacing dark streets—she had washed her face in the ladies' room, and had stared in the mirror at the vertical grooves in her cheeks and the lines around her eyes. Her face looked older than her thirty-four years, though the rest of her was somehow still as trim and taut as she'd been in her twenties—or even in her teens.

Immature? she wondered now as she watched the old houses sweep past outside the bus window. Say—she smiled nervously—arrested adolescent.

It seemed to her now that there had been something

naively Quixotic about her psychiatric career and her stubbornly terminal argument with Dr. Alden. In her private practice, in her own clinic, she had been able to make her own rules—and then had just fled the state and changed her name when the whole arrangement had blown up.

(Almost literally blown up—the fire department had managed to save the building.)

She had never married, nor ever had children. In idly psychoanalyzing herself, she had once decided that her "morbid dread" of pregnancy derived from the time when, at the age of three, she had climbed into an old milk can in the living room in Norco and got stuck—and, to hear her mother describe the event in later years, lost her mind. It was a three-foot-tall, forty-quart metal can that her parents had kept in the corner and tossed spare change into, and when toddler Angelica got stuck inside it, she had apparently had a severe claustrophobic reaction. After her father had failed to pull her out, and had failed to break the can open with a hammer (all of this no doubt compounding little Angelica's terror), Angelica's grandmother had been summoned from the house across the street. The old woman, who had luckily done midwifing for half a century, ordered Angelica's father to turn the can upside down, and then had delivered the toddler out of the can as though she were guiding a newborn baby out of the womb, head first and then one shoulder at a time. The afterbirth had been a shower of pennies and nickels and dimes.

Her mother had always told her how, apparently out of regret for having caused so much trouble, baby

Angelica must have awakened late that night and gone into the dark living room and gathered up all the spilled coins, separated them out by denomination, and then ranked them in stacks on a table; and her mother had forever insisted, with obviously sincere astonishment and pride, that the baby had even arranged the coins in chronological order of mint date, with the oldest coins on top.

Angelica had never believed that she had got up and moved the coins at all, but even as a child she had known better than to say so to her mother, who would probably have called the grandmother over again to do some distressing kind of homespun exorcism. Perhaps as a child Angelica had known that there were some borders that it was best not to include in one's maps. If so, she had recently learned it again.

The women in the bus seats around her this morning had no such compunctions. One woman was cautioning the others against leaving the living-room drapes open at night this weekend, and Elizalde at first assumed that it was a precaution against being shot in a drive-by shooting; and it might have been, partly, but after a few moments she understood that it was mainly to keep from calling to oneself the attention of the witches that would surely be flying around in *calabazas y bolos fuegos*, gourds and fireballs. Another woman said that she would be smoking cornhusk cigarettes every night for the next week or so; and one old grandmother in the very back seat said she'd be going out to Santa Monica on Friday night to feed her *piedra iman* in the sand and seawater. When Angelica Elizalde had been growing up, a *piedra iman* was a magnet; perhaps the term now meant something else.

Mundane borders too were commonplace with these ladies—secure in the supposed secrecy of the Spanish language, they casually traded adventure stories of how they'd stolen across the California-Mexico border, and a couple of them even discussed holiday plans to travel back and forth across it again to visit relatives in Mazatlán and Guadalajara, and they traded bits of advice for dealing with the *coyotes* who guided parties north across the broken wasteland of gullies and arroyos into the border cities of the United States.

Altogether they made Elizalde feel . . . incompetent and unworldly, a frightened fugitive with an out-of-date tourist's map. It should, she thought wearily, be the other way around. These women were housemaids, paid stingily in cash under the table, and they lived in the neighborhoods around Rampart and Union and the east end of Wilshire, where the families who were crowded into the shabby apartments did "hot bed" sleeping, in shifts, and Sunday dawns no doubt found these women stirring steaming pots of menudo for their hung-over husbands, who would have towels beside them to mop the sweat off their faces as they ate the spicy stuff. Elizalde had gone to college, and medical school, and had thought she had moved *up,* out of this world; now she wished she could trade places with any one of these women.

On the south side of the street, a sign over the bay door of a onetime gas station read CARREDIOS, and—in the few seconds it took her to realize that it was just a badly spaced and misspelled attempt at car radios—she read it as *carre dios,* which would mean something like the god of the course, the god of the run; and she had fleetingly thought of getting off the bus and going in there and lighting a candle.

She would have to be getting off soon anyway. Alvarado was the next stop. She sat up and tugged at the cord over the window, hearing the faint *bong* from the front of the bus, then got stiffly to her feet. Only a few blocks south of here was the office she had rented on Tuesdays, when she had first gone into private practice. Frank Rocha had been one of her patients even back in those early days, and later he had attended the group "seances" when she had opened her clinic up on Beverly.

She grabbed one of the upright steel poles as the bus squealed to a stop. What on earth, she thought helplessly as she let go and shuffled toward the opened back doors, do I think I'm going to *do* here? If his widow and kids even still live in that house? Apologize? Offer to . . . *help?* What money I've got I do need.

The letter in her wallet seemed to be heavy, seemed to be almost pulling her pants down on that side.

Do yardwork? Tune up the car engine?

Madam, she thought, suppressing a hysterical giggle, *I accidentally ran over your cat, and I want to replace it.*

Fine, but how good are you at catching mice?

She stepped down to the curb. Apologize, I guess. I can at least give her that, I can let her know that her husband's death has shattered me, that I'm aware that I was responsible for it, that I haven't been blithely forgetful of it.

As the doors hissed shut and the bus pulled away from the curb in a cloud of diesel smoke, Elizalde looked across the lanes of Sixth Street at the receding green lawn of

MacArthur Park. She sighed and turned away, toward a ripped-up construction site where, according to signs on the plywood hoardings, city workers were digging tunnels for the proposed Metro Rail; and she started trudging that way, north up the Alvarado sidewalk.

She recognized Rocha's house by the willow tree in the front yard. It must have had deep roots, for its narrow leaves were still green, while the lawn had not only died but gone entirely away, leaving only bare dirt with a couple of bright orange plastic tricycles knocked over on it. The old wood-frame house was painted navy blue now, with a red trim that Elizalde thought looked jarring.

Under these twittery surface impressions her mind was spinning. How on earth could she dare approach Mrs. Rocha?

How could she not? Only two nights ago, when she had weirdly begun reacting to events a second before the events happened, she had finally decided to *confront* whatever it was that had happened in her clinic on Halloween two years ago; and part of confronting it, as far as she could see, had to be facing the victims of it. Trying to make amends.

But she herself was a victim of it! Walking wounded! How would this ordeal—subjecting herself to this unthinkable meeting—be making amends to *Angelica Anthem Elizalde?*

Just to . . . *apologize?* No one would be better off.

But she was shuffling up the concrete walk toward the front porch. And when she had stepped up to the front door, she rapped on the frame of the screen. Brassy mariachi music was blaring inside. Peering through the mesh of the screen door, she could see the blue-and-pink flicker of a television reflecting in framed pictures on a living-room wall. The music and the colors both ceased at the same instant.

The gray-haired woman who appeared behind the screen stared at Elizalde for a moment, and then said something fast in Spanish.

"*Perdón,*" said Elizalde, as light-headed as if she'd just bolted a stiff drink on her empty stomach, "*estoy buscando por Señora Rocha?*"

"*Ahora me llamo Señora Gonzalvez.*" Her last name was now Gonzalvez, but this was apparently Frank Rocha's widow. Elizalde didn't recognize her, but after all she had seen the woman only once before, three or four years ago. She didn't recall her hair being gray then.

"*Me llamo Elizalde. Angelica Anthem Elizalde. Necesito—*"

The woman's eyes were wide, and she echoed, "Elizalde!" slowly, almost reverently.

"*Sí. Por favor, necesito hablar con usted. Lo siento mucho. Me hace falto . . . explicar que yo estaba . . . tratando de hacer—*"

"*Un momento.*" The woman disappeared back into the dimness of the living room, and Elizalde could hear her moving things, a shuffling sound like books being rearranged on a table.

Un momento? Elizalde blinked at the again-vacant rectangle of the screen door. One of us isn't understanding the other, she thought helplessly. This woman can't be Frank Rocha's widow, or else I can't have made it clear who I am—otherwise, surely, she wouldn't have just walked away.

"*Escúsame?*" she called. This was ridiculous. Her heart was thudding in her rib cage like fists hitting a punching bag, and her mouth was dry and tasted of metal. Hel*l-o*, she thought crazily, wondering if she might start giggling. I'm responsible for the death of *somebody's* husband around here . . . !

She curled her fingers around the door handle, and after a moment pulled it open against the resistance of creaking hinges.

On the mantel against the far wall an *ofrenda* had been set up, an altar, a figured silk scarf laid across a little embroidered cushion with framed photographs set up on it and around it, and two stylized, fancifully painted wooden skulls at either end of the display, like bookends. Preparation for El Día de los Muertos, the day of the dead. On the wall over it was hung a heart-shaped frame, its interior occupied by a gold-colored crucifix and a small clock face. She noted that the time was nearly noon.

She stepped inside, letting the screen door slap closed behind her.

Abruptly startled, she blinked her eyes shut—and a flash of red through her closed eyelids, and then a little mechanical whirring sound, let her know that the woman had taken her picture with an instamatic camera. To add to the *ofrenda?* wondered Elizalde in bewilderment as she opened her eyes and blinked at the woman's silhouette. But I'm not dead . . . Then her knees and the palms of her hands hit the carpet as a tremendous, stunning *bang* shook the room, and she was up and spinning and punching the screen door aside as another gunshot bruised her eardrums; she had clenched her eyes shut an instant before the shot, and so the splinters from the struck oak doorframe just stung her eyelids.

She felt one of her sneaker soles slap the porch boards—and then the porch had hit her again, and she was falling, and the dirt of the yard slammed against her hip and elbow as another *bang* crashed behind her and a plume of white dust sprang up from the sidewalk.

Rolling to her feet, she sprinted slantways across the barren yard and pelted away back south down the Amado Street sidewalk. She had to run in a slapping, flat-footed gait, for her feet kept feeling the impacts with the pavement before they actually occurred.

A one-story travel agency building, apparently closed, loomed at the corner on her left, and she skidded around its wall tightly enough to have knocked over anyone who might have been walking up on the other side—but the sidewalk, the whole narrow street, was empty.

In an alley-fronting parking lot across the street an old lime-green couch was propped against the back wall of another retail-looking building, and she crossed the street toward it—forcing herself to shuffle along, to stroll, rather than flail and stamp and wheeze as she had been doing.

Her lungs felt seared, and the back of her head tingled in anticipation of savage pursuit, but nobody had yelled or audibly begun running across the asphalt by the time she stepped up the curb and crossed to the couch.

She thought she could hide behind it, crouch in the cool shadow of it, until dark, and then creep away. Her teeth were clenched, and her face was cold with shame. *Why did I go there?* she was screaming in her head. *Why did I rip open her old wounds; and mine, and*—She remembered the shots, and rolling on the dirt, and running so clumsily, and she opened her eyes wide with the effort of forcing those things out of her attention, concentrating instead on the blue sky behind the shaggy palm trees and the telephone wires and the whirling crows.

Dizzy, she looked down and put her hand on the couch. The couch arm was fibrous and oily under her hand—*gristly*—but she realized that she had felt the texture of it only when she had actually touched it. The weird anticipation of sensations had apparently stopped when she had been crossing the street.

"Did you leave that here?" piped a close young man's voice, speaking in English.

Elizalde looked up guiltily. The back door of the building had been standing open, and now a fat white man with a scruffy beard was leaning out of it. He was wearing cutoff jeans, and his belly was stretching a stained example of the sleeveless undershirts she had always thought of as wife-beater undershirts.

She realized that she had forgotten what he had asked her. "I'm sorry?"

He peered up and down the alley. "Did you hear gunshots just now?"

"A truck was backfiring on Amado," said Elizalde, keeping her voice casual.

The fat man nodded. "So, is it yours?"

"The truck?" Her face was suddenly hot, and she knew she was either blushing or pale, for she had almost said, *The gun?*

"The couch," he said impatiently. "Did you put it here?"

"Oh," Elizalde said, "no. I was just looking at it."

"Somebody dumped it here. We find all kinds of crap back here. People think they can unload any old junk." He eyed the couch with disfavor. "Probably some big old black lady gave birth on it. And her mother before that. We got better furniture inside, if you got any money."

Elizalde blinked at him, trickles of disgust beginning to puddle in the scraped, blown-out emptiness of her mind. *And where were* you *born*, she thought—*on a culture dish in a VD lab, I'd judge.* But all she said was, "Furniture?"

"Yeah, secondhand. And books, kitchenware, *ropa usada.* Had Jackie Onassis in here the other day."

Elizalde had caught her breath at last, and she could smell beer on him. She nodded and made herself smile as she stepped past him into the store. "Yeah, she was telling me about it."

Inside were racks of pitiful clothes, bright cheap blouses and sun hats and colorful pants, that seemed still to carry an optimistic whiff, long stale now, of their original purchases at sunny swap meets and canvas-tent beachside stands. And there were shelves of books—hardcover junior-college texts, paperback science fiction and romances—and rows of family-battered Formica and particle-board-and-wood-veneer tables, covered with ceramic ashtrays and wrecked food processors and, somehow, a lot of fondue pots. A white-glass vase had been knocked over on one table, spilling a sheaf of dried flowers. *My* quinceañera *bouquet*, she thought as she looked at them. Withered roses, and husks of lilies, and a stiffened spray of forgive-me-nots.

"Begin life anew," advised the drunk bearded man, who had followed her back inside.

Life a-old, she thought. This was an accumulation of the crumbled shells of lives, collapsed when the owners had become absent, piled here now like broken cast-off snakeskins, some pieces still big enough to show outlines of departed personalities.

Well, Elizalde thought, I'm kind of a broken personality myself. I should hide in here for a while, at least long enough to see if cop sirens go past on the street outside, or angry Rochas or Gonzalvezes come bursting in. If they do, I'll just drape myself over one of these fine tables and be as inconspicuous as a skeleton hiding in a scrimshaw shop.

But nobody did come in at all, and the traffic outside was uneventful. The sunny October Los Angeles day had apparently swallowed up the gunshots without a ripple and was rolling on. Elizalde bought a Rastafari knitted tam—red, gold, black, and green—big enough to tuck her long black hair up into, and a tan size-fourteen Harve Benard jumpsuit that had no doubt had an interesting history. Three dollars paid for the whole bundle at the counter by the street door, and the bearded man didn't even remark on it when Elizalde swept the cap forward over her head and then pulled the jumpsuit on right over her jeans and sweatshirt. After she had pushed open the door and walked a block back south toward Sixth Street, she realized that she had taken on the humbled, slope-shouldered gait she remembered in many of her patients;

and she was pleased at the instinctive mimicry, during the few moments it took her to realize that it was not mimicry at all, but natural.

CHAPTER 20

❋

*"Don't keep him waiting, child! Why, his
time is worth a thousand pounds a minute!"*
—Lewis Carroll,
Through the Looking-Glass

HUNCHING AND HOPPING along the walkway that
flanked the Ahmanson Theater, moving in and out of the
fleeting shade of the strips of decorative roof so narrow
and so far overhead that they could serve as shelter only
against a preternaturally straight-falling rain, Sherman
Oaks followed his missing, pointing arm. The nonexistent
arm was so hot that the rest of him felt chilly, as if he were
reaching out the door of an air-conditioned bar in Death
Valley, out into the harsh sunlight. And he was sniffing
vigorously, for the boy Koot Hoomie Parganas had moved
through this place not long ago, and he could strongly
smell the big ghost that the boy carried.

Run, he read in the impressions still shaking in the air,
a long run, fleeing under a masked sun on the front of a

train, running . . . on all fours? With long nails clicking on pavement! What the hell?

His missing arm practically dragged him around the moat that encircled the giant wedding cake of the Mark Taper Forum, and then the stair railing across the pavement ahead of him seemed to be the only focused thing in the landscape; everything else, even the incongruous ragged pile of raw meat by the Taper's entry doors, was a blur. He was close!

At the top of the stairs he came to a full stop, and then cautiously peered down—and his heart began pounding still harder, for a *dead old man* was sprawled down there on the blood-smeared concrete stairs.

I should get right out of here, he thought—hop over this deceased old party and continue on the kid's trail.

But as he shuffled down the steps he realized that the thing on the stairs was not actually a man; it was a limply collapsed dummy, stitched into a coarse black coat of badly woven fur. But the imbecilically distorted face, and the white hands, seemed to be made of flesh—and the spattered and smeared blood looked real. It *smelled* real.

Oaks paused to crouch over the crumpled shell. He emptied his lungs through his open mouth, hearing the faint outraged stadium roar of all the ghosts he had inhaled over the years; and then he inhaled deeply, flaring his nostrils and tilting his head back and swelling his chest.

He caught the flat muskiness of ectoplasm, the protean junk that squirted out of mediums to lend substance to ghosts . . . but he smelled real flesh, too, and real blood.

Dog flesh, he realized as he sucked up more of the charged air. Dog blood.

No wonder he had caught an impression moments ago of running on all fours! Someone had vaporized a *dog* to get substance for filling out a figure too big and solid for ectoplasm alone. And a prepubescent kid wouldn't be able to provide much ectoplasm anyway.

The big ghost had done this, had made this thing. Why? The ghost must have perceived itself to be in some emergency, for this would have been a very stressful move.

Oaks stared down at the flat head of the thing. This would have to be a portrait of the big ghost that the kid was carrying: white hair, a pouchy and wrinkled face . . .

Who the hell was it? Probably someone famous, certainly someone powerful, to judge by the huge psychic field that his ghost projected. The face, broad and big-chinned and dominant even deflated on the steps here, looked vaguely familiar to Oaks . . . but from a *long* time ago. Briefly and uneasily, Oaks wondered how old he himself might be, really; but he pushed the question away and thought about the ghost who had left this thing here.

Whoever it was, he had died at the Parganas house on Loma Vista two nights ago—or at least that's where and when his spanking-new ghost had appeared, blazing in the psychic sky like a nova—and the Parganas couple had chosen to die horribly rather than tell Oaks anything at all.

Oaks stared at the blood on the steps here, and he remembered following the powerful new ghost's beacon all the way across town to that house in Beverly Hills on Monday night. By the time Oaks had got there, the ghost was gone, headed south, but Oaks had stayed to find out who it had been, and who had taken it away, in the hope of avoiding this weary labor of following every step of the thing's trail. He remembered his useless torturing of the middle-aged man and woman in that garden-type patio off the living room. As soon as he had taped the two of them into the chairs and started questioning them, they had gone into some kind of defensive trance; and Oaks, fearful of being caught there, had got angry and had cut them more and more savagely, and after he had finally cut out their very eyes he had realized that they had died at some point.

After that, still angry, he had set about searching the house. And then the kid had come home—very late, not far short of dawn—and when Oaks had gone into the living room, the dead couple's ghosts had been standing in there! Blinking around stupidly, but as solid as you could ask for, and them only an hour dead at the most!

He should have known right then that the big ghost had come back, and that it was the big ghost's promiscuous field that had lit up the two silly new ghosts in their wedding clothes. But the trail had been looped right back onto itself at that point, and too grossly powerful for Oaks to comprehend that it had doubled when the kid entered the scene. And anyway, the kid had taken off like an arrow out of a bow; and the boy had run out of the house *through* that garden patio, which could only have speeded him up still more.

Oaks hopped over the bloody mess on the stairs and stepped down to the cement-floored landing—apparently this was a parking level—but after a couple of steps he froze.

His phantom left arm wasn't pointing anymore; it had flopped nervelessly, and he couldn't feel anything at all in it. He tried to work the hand—usually when the arm was down by his side he could rasp the fingers against the hairy skin of his thigh, whether or not he happened to be wearing long pants—but the nonexistent fingers sensed nothing now but, perhaps, a faint cool breeze sluicing between them. The trail was gone.

Had the ghost freed itself from the kid and evaporated? That would be bad—Oaks was getting thin, and for the last thirty or forty hours he had been passing up the chance to eat smaller ghosts, in his anxiety not to miss this big feast. Or had the kid somehow all at once attained *puberty* this morning, enabling him to eat and digest the ghost himself?

Oaks's face was chilly with alarm—but after a moment he relaxed a little. Whatever had happened here, whatever it was that had provoked the ghost into whipping up this ectoplasmic mannikin . . . *the whole event must have been a terrible shock to the kid, too.* In his terror the boy might very well have just *clathrated* the ghost, convulsively enclosed it within his own psyche but not assimilated it—encysted the thing, shoved it down, walled it up tightly inside himself.

That could happen, Oaks knew; and if it had, the locked-in ghost wouldn't be detectable from the outside.

Like that one time when Houdini . . .

The fleeting thought was gone, leaving only an association: Jonah and the whale. Sherman Oaks hurried back up the stairs, stepping carelessly right on the limp face this time, and when he was back up on the pavement he hopped over a retaining wall by the valet parking driveway and strode away south on the Hope Street sidewalk.

Houdini? Jonah and the whale? God knew what memory had started to surface there—something from the time before he had come into this present continuity-of-consciousness three years ago, in the district of Sherman Oaks, from which he had whimsically taken this present name. Again, he wondered, briefly and uneasily, how old he might really be, and when and how he might have lost his left arm.

To his right, across the street, the elevated pools around the Metropolitan Water District building reflected the watery blue sky. Oaks calculated that the time could hardly be even an hour past noon, but the pale sun had already begun to recede, having come as far up above the southern horizon as it cared to in this season. North was behind him, and the thought prompted him to sneak a glance down at the pommel of the survival knife he wore inside his pants.

When he had stolen the knife, its hollow hilt had been full of things like fishhooks and matches. He had replaced that stuff with reliable compact ghost lures—a nickel with a nail welded to the back so that it could be hammered into a wooden floor, where it would confound the patient efforts of ghosts to pick it up, and some pennies stamped with the Lincoln profile smoking a pipe, another surefire ghost-attention holder—but he had valued the screw-on pommel, which had a powerful magnetic compass bobbing around in its glass dome.

But right now, the compass was pointing firmly,

uselessly, north. And his gone left arm was still sensing nothing at all. The ghost was effectively hidden inside the boy's mind now—Oaks was sure that that was what had happened—and, at least for as long as the ghost *remained* concealed, Oaks would have to track Koot Hoomie Parganas without any psychic beacons or Hansel-and-Gretel trails at all. And *now,* when he found the boy, he would probably have to *kill* him to get the big ghost out and eat it—and of course eat the boy's ghost too, as a garnish. A parsley child.

It occurred to Sherman Oaks that he might be smart to get to a telephone—and damn quick.

He walked faster, and then began jogging, hoping that in spite of his stained windbreaker and camouflage pants, he looked like someone getting exercise and not like somebody in murderous pursuit.

Clouds as solid and white as sculptured marble were shifting across the blue vault of the sky, south from the San Fernando Valley and down the track of the Hollywood Freeway, graying the woods and lawns of Griffith Park and tarnishing the flat water of the Silverlake Reservoir. Chilly shade swept over the freeway lanes and across the area of wide dirt lots and isolated old Victorian houses west of the Pasadena Freeway, and the squat wild palms shook their shaggy heads in the wind. Pedestrians around Third and Sixth Streets began to move more quickly . . . though one toiling small figure on the Witmer Street sidewalk didn't increase its pace.

Kootie was limping worse than ever, but he made himself keep moving. Raffle had been meticulous about divvying up their panhandling income, and Kootie had a pocketful of change as well as forty-six dollars in bills—eventually he would get on a bus, and then get on another, and eventually, ideally, sleep on one, and then tomorrow think of some durable sanctuary (—*church, stow away on a ship, hide somewhere on a "big rig eighteen-wheeler," go to the police, hide in a—*). But right now, he needed the sensation of motion—of ground being covered—that only working his legs and abrading the soles of his shoes could give him.

Kootie had stopped being angry at Raffle, and was instead panicked and dismayed at having lost the only person in Los Angeles, in the *world!*, who'd cared to help him. Kootie was certain that if he hadn't been such a stupid *kid*, he could somehow have talked Raffle out of turning him in, and they could right now have been driving to get Raffle's dope somewhere, happy in the car, with Fred licking their faces. Kootie winced as he stepped down off a high curb, and he wondered what Fred was doing now; probably right this minute Fred was sharing Kootie's own personal heated-up tamale with Raffle in some safe parking lot.

Kootie's pelvis and right hip ached, as if he'd recently tried doing one of those Russian crouch-and-kick dances and then finished with a full butt-to-the-floor split—but he was trying not to think about it, for the mysterious muscle strain was a result of whatever had gone on during the time he had been blacked out at the Music Center, when the ghost of the old man had been in control of his body.

God only knew what the old man had done. Fallen

awkwardly? Karate-kicked somebody? Kootie would have expected more dignity from *Thomas Alva Edison*.

There it was, he had thought about it. The ghost had been *Edison*—as in the SCE logo painted on the doors of the Halloween-colored black-and-orange trucks. Southern California Edison—the guy that invented the lightbulb. Kootie's parents had always told him not to play with lightbulbs, that there was a poisonous "noble gas" in them; in school he had found out that they'd been thinking of neon lights, and that neon wasn't poisonous anyway. But there had been a poison in the glass brick hidden in the Dante statue, for sure.

Noble gas my ass, he thought defiantly as he blinked away tears. You old . . . *shithead!* What were you doing in that test tube inside the glass brick anyway?

Duh, he thought, replying for the absent Edison, *I dunno.*

You got my mom and dad killed! And now everybody wants to kill me too.

Duh. Sorry.

Moron.

Kootie remembered the face on the top of the bloody framework he had pulled off himself, but a shudder torqued through him, almost making him miss his footing on the cracked sidewalk. It was apparently far too soon to think about that episode, and he found that he had focused his eyes on the stucco walls, bright orange even in the shadow of the clouds, of a ninety-nine-cent store on the corner ahead of him. Two pay telephones were perched under metal hoods on a post by the parking-lot curb.

Al, he thought nervously, quoting the old woman who had moaned to him out of the payphone receiver on Fairfax this morning, *where am I gonna meet you tonight?*

Al. Alva. Thomas Alva Edison. And in the hallucination he'd had—

Again, he shied away from the memory of being dislocated out of his own body—but he was sure that it had been the Edison ghost that the old woman had been trying to talk to. She had known the name—the nickname!—of the ghost Kootie had been carrying around. To the people who live in the magical alleys of the world, Kootie thought, that ghost must have been sticking out like a sore thumb.

But the ghost was gone now! Kootie had left it torn and deflated on the steps at the—

Involuntarily, he exhaled, hard enough to have blown out a whole birthday cake full of candles, if one had been here. (Raffle had told him that in these neighborhoods, they generally hung paper-skinned figures from trees on kids' birthdays, and then beat the things with sticks until they split apart, at which point the kids would scramble for the little cellophane-wrapped hard candies that spilled onto the dirt from the broken paper abdomens.)

The ghost was gone now, that was the important thing. Maybe telephones would work, for Kootie, now.

He flexed the fingers of his right hand and slowly reached down and dug in his jeans pocket for a quarter. Who would he call?

The police, for sure.

Kootie's teeth were cold, and he realized that he was smiling. He would call the police, and the one-armed bum wouldn't follow him anymore, not after the bum stumbled across the—

After the bum came to the end of the ghost's trail.

And then Kootie would be put in . . . *some* kind of home, finally, with showers and bathrooms and beds and food. Eventually he'd be adopted, by some family. He'd be able to see any movies he wanted to see . . .

His teeth were still cold, but he was sobbing now, to his own horror and astonishment. I want my *own* family, he thought. I want my own house and my own mom and dad. Maybe they aren't dead—*(in those bloody chairs)*— of course they aren't dead, they were standing in the living room in formal clothes *(ignoring me in such a scary way)* and probably they're the ones that hired the billboards and posted the reward!

He needed to know, he needed to throw himself somewhere *now*, and he ran to the telephones even though the pain of running wrung whimpers through his clenched teeth.

When he had rolled the quarter into the slot, he punched in 9-1-1.

After two rings, a woman's voice said, calmly, "Nine-one-one operator, is this an emergency?"

"I'm Koot Hoomie Parganas," said Kootie quickly. "My parents were—were robbed and beaten up, real bad, night before last, and there's billboards with my picture on 'em, and a reward—" Kootie was suddenly dizzy, and he actually had to clutch the receiver tightly to keep from falling. He swung around on the pivot of his good heel until his shoulder hit the phone's aluminum cowl. When he had straightened up, he had a quick impression that

someone was behind him, wanting to use the phone, but
he looked around and saw no one near him. "—a reward,"
he went on, "that's being offered for me. My mom and
dad live on Loma Vista Street in Beverly Hills and there
was—"

A man's voice interrupted him. "Parganas?" the man
said alertly.

"*Yes.*"

"Just a sec. Hey," the man said away from the phone,
"it's the Parganas kid!" More loudly, he added, "It's Koot
Hoomie!"

The phone at the other end was put down with a clunk
on something hard. In the background, Kootie could hear
a lot of people talking, and a clatter like a cafeteria. He
heard glass break, and a voice mumble "Fuck."

There was a rattling on the line as someone picked up
the distant phone. "Koot Hoomie?"

It was his mother's voice! She *was* alive! He was
sobbing again, but he managed to say, clearly, "*Mom,
come and get me.*"

There was a moment of relative silence, broken only
by mumbling and clattering at the other end; then, "Kethoomba!" his mother exclaimed. (Was she drunk? Was
everybody *drinking* there in the dispatcher's office?)
Kootie remembered that Kethoomba was the Tibetan
pronunciation of the name of the mahatma his parents
had named him after. She had never called Kootie that.
"Gelugpa," she went on, "yellow-hatted monk! Come and
get me!"

"Gimme that phone," said someone in the background.
"Master!" came the quavering voice of Kootie's father.

"We'll be out front!" Quietly, as if speaking off to the side of the receiver, Kootie's father asked someone, "Where are we?"

"*Fock* you," came a thick-voiced reply.

"Dad," shouted Kootie. "It's me, Kootie! I need you to come get me! I'm at—" He poked his head out into the breeze and tried to see a street sign. He couldn't see one up or down the gray street. "They trace these calls, ask the dispatcher where I'm calling from. Have 'em send a cop car here quick."

"Don't go outside!" called his father to someone in the noisy room. "Cop cars!" Then, breathily, back into the mouthpiece: "*Kootie?*"

"*Yes,* Dad! Are you all drunk? Listen—"

"No, *you* listen, young man. You *broke the Dante*—don' interrupt—you broke the, the Dante, let the light shine out before anything was prepared—well, it's your *son,* if you mus' know—"

Then Kootie's mother was on the line again. "Kootie! Put the master back on!"

Kootie was crying harder now. Something was terribly wrong. "There's nobody here but me, Mom. What's the matter with you? I'm lost, and that guy—there's bad guys following me—"

"We need the master to pick 's up!" his mother interrupted, her voice slurred but loud. "Put 'im on!"

"He's not here!" wailed Kootie; his ear was wet with wind-driven tears or sweat, and chilly because he was now holding the phone several inches away from his head. "*I* called. *My* name is Koot Hoomie, remember? I'm *alone!*"

"You killed us!" his mother yelled. "You broke the

Dante, you couldn't wait, and then the . . . *forces of darkness!* . . . found us, and killed us! I'm *dead,* your father's *dead,* because you disobeyed us! And now the master hasn't called! You're *bad,* Kootie, you're *ba-a-ad.*"

"She's right, son," interjected Kootie's father. "Iss your fault we're dead and Kethoomba's off somewhere. Get over here *now.*"

Kootie couldn't imagine the room his parents were in—it sounded like some kind of bar—but he was suddenly certain of what they were wearing. The same formal wedding clothes. In the background there, a little girl was reciting a poem about how some flower beds were too soft . . . and then a hoarse woman's voice said, "Tell him to put Al on, will ya?"

Kootie hung up the phone. The wind was colder on this street now, and the sky's gray glow made opaque smoke of the windshields on the passing cars.

His quarter clattered into the coin-return slot. Apparently, there was no charge on 9-1-1 calls.

And ten blocks east of Kootie, leaning against bamboo-pattern wallpaper at the back of a steamy Thai takeout restaurant, Sherman Oaks pressed another pay-telephone receiver to his ear.

At the other end of the line, a man answered, recited the number Oaks had called, and said, "What category?"

"I don't know," said Oaks, "Missing Persons? It's about that kid, Koot Hoomie Parganas, the one on the billboards."

"Koot Hoomie sightings, eh?" Oaks could hear the rippling clicking of a computer keyboard. "You speak English," the operator noted.

The remark irritated Oaks. Probably he had always spoken English. "Most people don't?"

"Been getting a lot of Kootie calls from illegal immigrants: *'Tengo el niño, pero no estoy en el pais legalimente.'* Got the kid, but got no green card. Looking for a second party to pick up the reward. There must be fifty curly-haired stray kids locked in garages in L.A. right now. One of 'em might even be the right one, though he hasn't been turned in yet, or this category would be closed out. Okay, what? You've got him, you know where he is? We've got a bonded outfit checking all reasonable claims, and a representative can be anywhere in the greater Los Angeles area within ten minutes."

"What I've got," Oaks said, "is a counteroffer." He looked around at the other people in the tiny white-lit restaurant—they all seemed to be occupied with their takeout bags and cardboard cartons, and even the obtrusive smells of cilantro and chili peppers seemed to combine with the staccato voices and the sizzle of beef and shrimp on the griddle to provide a screen of privacy for the phone. "You know smoke? Cigar? The Maduro Man?"

"It's a different category, but I can call it up."

"Well, I can put up—" Oaks paused to pull his attention away from the bright agitation of the restaurant, and he ran a mental inventory of the three major caches he kept, hidden out there in corners of the dark city; he pictured the dusty boxes of empty-looking but tightly sealed jars and bottles and old crack vials—he even had a matched pair, an elderly matrimonial suicide pact, locked up in the two snap-lid receptacles of a clear plastic contact lens case. "I can put up *a thousand doses* of L.A. cigar in exchange for the kid. Even wholesale, that's a lot more than twenty grand."

He heard more keyboard clicking. "Yeah, it is." The man sighed. "Well, for that we'd need a guarantor, somebody we've got listed, who can put up forty grand. Counteroffers have to be double, house policy. If we get that, we'll go ahead and list it under the Parganas heading. But the guarantor would have to do all the other work, like maybe putting a trap on the reward number phone and being ready to intercept anybody who, you know, might already have the kid and be trying to get the original reward. I don't have to tell you that hours count in this one. Minutes, even."

"I know."

Oaks looked down at the compass in the pommel of his knife—right now it was pointing up in the direction of Dodger Stadium, which was plain old north, but a few minutes ago it had joggled wildly and then, for what must have been nearly a full minute, pointed emphatically west. After that it had wobbled back to north, and he hadn't seen it deviate from that normal reading since.

During it all, he had felt no heat in his absent arm—but the compass had clearly registered a brief reemergence of the big ghost; and the ghost had been in the excited state, too, for ghosts didn't cast the huge magnetic fields when they were in their normal quiescent ground state. It *was* clathrated in the boy's psyche, and not dissipated or eaten. Oaks was achingly anxious to get off the phone and resume his jogging pursuit—westward!—but this insurance was worth a minute's delay.

"So, who's your guarantor?" the man on the phone was asking him. "Or do you have forty grand yourself, to put up instead of your smoke?"

"No, not me. Uh . . ." The street dealers he ordinarily sold to wouldn't have this kind of money ready to hand. He would have to go higher up. "You got a Neal Obstadt listed?" Oaks asked. "Under gambling, probably, I think that's his main business."

"Yeah, I got Obstadt." *(Clickety-click.)* "What do I tell him? Even for him, forty ain't just lunch money."

Oaks had heard Obstadt described as a heavy user, a good customer who was generally able to score the best specimens in the dealers' stocks. "Tell him it's from the guy named Sherman Oaks, the producer who brought you such hits as—I hope you're taping this?"

"Always got a loop going."

"Such hits as Henrietta Hewitt, the old lady who died on September fifth and whose kids were named Edna and Sam." It was a fairly long shot, but old Henrietta had been the best ghost Oaks had bottled lately, and anyway Obstadt might very well recognize Oaks's name and reputation. He might not, but the possibility of changing the Parganas listing was definitely worth this delay.

"I'll play it for him. I imagine he'll want to tape your voice himself, as your receipt for the money, if he goes for it. Are you at a number?"

"No, I'll call back in an hour. But if he authorizes it, you can list it on the board right now, can't you?"

"Yup. As soon as he says okay, it's on, and the . . . *mere mercenary details* are between you and him."

"Go," said Oaks, and hung up the phone.

Immediately, he wondered if he was making a costly mistake. He could easily get to all of his stashes within a hopping hour or two, but turning it all over to Obstadt's people would leave Oaks with approximately nothing. He might even have to kill a few street people to make up the full thousand bottled doses. But, of course, he wouldn't have to cough up the smoke unless he received the Parganas boy, and the big ghost inside the boy was clearly worth a thousand ordinary bottled dead folk. The nightly fresh catches in his traps would keep Oaks going until he could build up reserve stocks again.

He could feel his missing arm again, but it was just clutching his chest, and it was as uselessly cold as if it were cradling a bag of ice. He actually looked down at his grubby shirt-front and was remotely surprised not to see the fabric bunched by the clawed fingers. His compass was still pointing north.

The burning-plastic smells of sizzling shrimp and cilantro helped propel him across the linoleum floor and out onto the Figueroa sidewalk.

Oaks despised the processes of biological ingestion and digestion and elimination, and he generally lived on crackers, and bean soup fingered up cold and solid right out of a can, and water from unguarded hoses and faucets. His real sustenance was his ghosts, snorted up raw and new and vibrant from a hand-lettered palindrome or a pile of scattered coins, or—occasional serendipitous luxuries!—furtively inhaled in hospital corridors or from a body freshly tumbled on the street.

He remembered stalking the halls of County Hospital during the war, when every one of the hundreds of windows had been painted black in case of a Japanese air raid, and the ghosts of newly dead patients were too fearful to dissipate normally, and instead huddled in the corners of the halls, always faintly asking him, as he swept them into his bottles, "Are the Japs out there?" . . . And the maternity ward at Hollywood Presbyterian Hospital, where he had often been able to inhale the fresh-cast virtual ghosts thrown off by newborn infants in the stress of birth . . .

But it was now getting on to forty-eight hours since he had last "got a life"—which had been *before* he'd gone to the Parganas house. He hadn't even bothered to consume the ghosts of Kootie's parents after he killed them, so confident had he been that the big ghost must still be nearby; he had not wanted to waste the chase-time by pausing to eat those two minor items.

Out on the sidewalk he realized that the day had turned cold, and that the gray light would be diminishing toward evening before too long. Already the zigzag neon sign of a shoe store across the street was glowing yellow against the ash-colored wall. An orange-and-black SCE truck roared past, and he flinched away—from the roaring of it.

Those two minor items. Oaks would have been grateful for one such minor item right now. One lungful of real soul food, to keep away the Bony Express.

For he could feel the unrest of the ghosts he had consumed in the past. When he was forced to fast, they all became agitated, and his exhalations were more and more audibly wheezy with their less and less distant roars, as if they were all riding toward him—the Bony Express!—ever closer, over the midnight black hills of the unmapped borderlands of his mind, toward the lonely middle-of-nowhere campfire that was his consciousness.

His phantom left hand had crawled down his chest and now gripped his abdomen, squeezing so hard that Oaks was wincing as he hurried west along the Sixth Street sidewalk. He thought of making a detour, catching a bus up to—which stash was he nearest to?—the rooftop air-conditioning shed over the hair salon on Bellevue; but the thought of how strongly the compass needle had pointed west only a few minutes ago, and the memory of the collapsed face on the parking garage stairs at the Music Center, made him keep on putting one foot ahead of the other on the westward-leading sidewalk.

Mouth-to-mouth unsuscitation, with Koot Hoomie Parganas's body still twitching under him in protest at being so newly dead, and the two souls, the boy's and the big ghost, blasting hotly down Oaks's windpipe to his starving lungs.

Soon, he thought.

CHAPTER 21

"The little fishes of the sea,
They sent an answer back to me."
—Lewis Carroll,
Through the Looking-Glass

THE SUN was under the skirts of the dark clouds now, showing briefly on the western edge of the world before disappearing below the silhouetted hills of Pacific Palisades. Pete Sullivan was sitting by the leaded-glass window of Kendall's Sport Time Bar, and the long, horizontal rays of sunlight glowed red in the depths of the Guinness stout in the glass on the polished table.

He was waiting for his order of appetizers—fried mozzarella with marinara sauce and Buffalo chicken wings with celery and blue cheese dressing—but he had got the stout in the meantime because a teacher at City College had once told him that Guinness contained all the nutrients required to sustain human life. It was thick and brown and rich, though, and he planned to switch to

Coors Light as soon as he had emptied this glass and thus fulfilled his health duties. And this bar somehow didn't have any smoking area at all, so his next cigarette would have to wait until he got back into the van. A healthful evening all around.

Television sets were hung at several places in the darkness under the ceiling beams, but each one seemed to be tuned to a different channel, and the ones with the sound turned up loud weren't the ones closest to Sullivan. On the nearest screen he watched presidential candidate Bill Clinton moving his lips, while what he heard was whining electrical machinery and mechanical thumping from a farther speaker. Sullivan looked away.

His hands were still sticky from having washed them with Gojo hand-cleaning jelly at the tiny sink in the van. This morning, after driving around to pick up supplies, he had found an unfenced dirt lot east of Alameda, among the windowless plastic-works and foundries by the train tracks and the cement-walled Los Angeles River, and he had done some work on the poor old van.

The sun had still been glaring out of a clear October sky, and he had taken off his shirt and scapular and popped a beer from a fresh twelve-pack before opening the van's back doors and dragging out his tools.

The tire pressures were low, so he hooked up a little electric air pump to the battery with his jumper cables, and crouched beside each tire in turn, puffing a cigarette and sipping the chilly beer, and watched to make sure the cable clamps didn't touch each other as the pump wobbled and vibrated on the adobe dirt. Then he crawled under the van and dumped the oil, conscientiously draining the old black stuff into the kind of sealable plastic container that could be taken to an oil-recycling center, though unless someone was watching, he intended to leave the container right there in the middle of the field. A new oil filter, new spark plugs, and six quarts of Valvoline 20-50-weight oil finished the job.

L.A. air in the tires, he thought, and fresh oil in the engine. Nothing with any memories of fleeing Arizona— of driving to Houdini's wrecked old place—of fearfully crossing borders. And he remembered the old notion that after some number of years every cell in a human body had been replaced, every atom, so that the body is just a wave form moving through time, incorporating just for a little while the stuff of each day; only the wave itself, and none of the transient physical bits, makes the whole trip. Even a scar would be no more significant than a wobble still visible in an ocean wave long after the wave had passed the obstruction that caused it, while the water molecules that had actually *sustained* the impact were left comfortably far behind.

A.O.P., Sullivan thought now as he sipped his cloying Guinness. Accelerate Outta Problems. He had always been uneasy watching people *dig in*—the newlyweds committing themselves to a mortgage and a roof and plumbing, the brave entrepreneur leasing a building and getting boxes and boxes of letterhead printed up. Sullivan had owned the van for five years now, but he had owned other vehicles before that, and he would own others after the van met whatever its eventual terminal problem would turn out to be; the very books on the shelf over the top bunk were a wave form—paperbacks that were bought new, became bent and ruptured and yellowed, and eventually served as ragged whiskbrooms that went out with the trash they swept up, to be replaced by new paperbacks.

Sullivan had once read some Greek philosopher quoted to the effect that no man can step into the same river twice, because it's never again the same river, and he's never again the same man.

Thank God for that, Sullivan thought now as he beckoned to the waitress. On the nearest television screen, in front of some shabby house draped in yellow police-line tape, a concerned-looking newsman was frowning into the camera and opening and closing his mouth, seeming, because another set was turned up loud on a different channel, to be barking like a dog while someone kept saying, "Speak!"

Sullivan looked back down at the table. It was better with just the sound. Today he had set up his portable radio and cassette deck on the van floor, and on the noon news he had heard that some giant prehistoric fish had washed up on the shore at Venice Beach, and that lobsters had crawled out of the ocean and terrified people on the shore.

So there *had* been a timely at Venice. That was immensely reassuring. DeLarava's motive in going there *had* been just for a news story, and nothing to do with . . . anything else.

You're not Speedy Alka-Seltzer, you won't dissolve.

He cut off the intrusive remembered sentence before he could distinguish the voice that had *(long ago)* spoken it. Better to dissolve, he thought.

"And could I switch to a Coors Light now," he said aloud, for the waitress had brought the two steaming plates to his table, and lukewarm stout wasn't at all the thing for washing down garlic and Tabasco and blue cheese. "In fact," he added, "could I have two of them."

One of them to drink in memory of the surely dissolved ghost of Sukie, he thought.

Now that his head was ringing slightly with alcohol, he was comfortably sure that the wave form that had been his sister was safely dispersed and flattened out, and not carrying on past the death of the body that had maintained it. DeLarava only went to Venice today because her job happened to take her there, he told himself, and all the ghosts are laid.

Let it all dissolve. Scarf this hasty late lunch or early dinner, call Steve and go over to his house for a few more beers, and then just get out of L.A. All the old dirty shit is cleaned out of the van's works, and you've surely cleared all the old guilts and uncertainties out of your soul just by coming back here and looking around at the outgrown hometown.

Veni, vidi, exii, he thought, quoting another motto of Sukie's. I came, I saw, I left.

The sound vibrating out of the nearest speaker was some kind of mulitudinous roar like a crowded stadium, but on the nearest screen he could now see a beach, breezy basketball courts, a crowd of people in swimming suits standing and craning their necks . . . a brightly sunlit scene, not live.

Jarringly, it was Venice Beach—but obviously this was just a recap of the prehistoric fish story. Perhaps this film clip was deLarava's work. Sullivan's two beers arrived then, and with one of the chilly glasses clamped in his palm he was able to keep on looking up at the TV screen.

And a deep slug of cold beer helped him hang on to his mood of serenity. I *can look* at films of Venice Beach now, he thought steadily. All the old ghosts are laid.

As soon as the televised scene was replaced by a view of some new car leaning fast around rural roads, he drained the beer and took the other one with him as he got up—the food could wait—and walked back through the crowded tables to the hallway where the telephones and the restrooms were.

He dropped a handful of change on the wood floor, retrieved most of it and thumbed a quarter into the pay-phone slot, then punched in the remembered number.

Above belt-level wainscoting, the wallpaper was furry red velvet—and it fleetingly occurred to him that in spite of the beamed ceiling and the etched glass partitions around the booths, this place was probably too new for deLarava to find it worthwhile snuffling a straw in these corners.

The phone at the other end was ringing, and then it was picked up. "That you, Pete?" came a gasping voice.

"Sure is. Steve? I'm—"

"Where are you calling from, man?" Away from the phone he snapped, "I'm fine, dammit!" to someone.

"Well, I'm in a bar—in Westwood, I think, on Wilshire. A 'sports bar,' with TV sets hung all over the place, every one on a different channel. Loud. I can't wait to get to your place. And I don't think I'll be spending the night after all. I gotta get back to Arizona—"

"Okay, listen, I just this second dumped a whole panful of Beans Jaime dip all over myself, and it's *damn hot*. I've got to get back in the shower. Stay there for another half-hour or so, okay?"

"No problem, I've got some snacks—"

"Cool. That's good then. Shit, this stuff is like napalm! How's—I meant to ask, how's Sukie?"

Sullivan was glad that he had thought to bring a beer with him. After chugging a series of gulps, he gasped, "Fine. No, she's—well, I think she's dead."

"Jesus. You *think?*" After a pause, Steve said, "I always liked her. Well! Do something sentimental for me? Have a Kahlua and milk for me, in her memory, will you do that? Promise?"

It had been Sukie's favored breakfast drink. Sullivan nodded dutifully, imagining dumping Kahlua and milk into his stomach on top of the Guinness. He realized that Steve couldn't hear a nod, and said, "Okay, Steve. So, what's your address? I don't need directions, I've got a Thomas Brothers guide."

Steve gave him an address on La Grange Avenue, and Sullivan hung up and returned to his table.

The fried mozzarella had cooled off, but the Buffalo wings were still hot, and he dipped them in the marinara sauce as often as in the blue cheese dressing. When the waitress came by again, he ordered two more beers . . . and a Kahlua and milk, though he resolved to let the drink stand as a gesture rather than drink it.

He got hungrier as he diminished the fresh beers and ate the snacks, and after gnawing at the chicken bones he began chewing up the rehardened mozzarella. Just as he was considering ordering something else, maybe the Nachos Grande, the waitress walked up and told him he had a call at the bar.

He blinked up at her. "I doubt it," he said. "Who did they ask for?"

"A guy drinking a Kahlua and milk. You haven't touched it, but I figure you're who they want."

That has to be Steve, somehow, Sullivan thought uneasily as he pushed back his chair and weaved his way between the tables to the bar, on which a white telephone sat with the receiver lying next to it. He was reminded of the call he'd got at O'Hara's, back in Roosevelt, the call from Sukie that had started this pointless—no, this *cathartic*—odyssey, and after he had nervously picked up the receiver and said "Hello?" he was relieved to find that the voice on the other end was not Sukie's again. Then he realized that he hadn't listened to what this woman had said.

"What?"

"I said, is this Pete Sullivan," she said angrily.

"Yes. Are you somebody at Steve's house? I—"

"This is Steve's wife, and I'm at a pay-phone. He *scalded* himself dumping that dip on his leg! And in his hair! *Intentionally!* To have an excuse to give me a shopping list and get out of the house so I could call you from somewhere where those men wouldn't hear! Here's his note for you, his 'shopping list': *Pete—Call me back and say you cannot make it over to my house, please, Pete. And don't say on the line where you're going, and get out of there. Whatever it is, they want you alive. I've got a wife and kids. Good luck, but don't call me again ever after this next call.* That's his note, okay? This is the third damn *sports* bar on Wilshire that I've called, and now I've got to go to some store and buy some more frijoles and Jack cheese and stuff, even though I know we're not going to be making more Beans Jaime, thank God, just so this shopping trip will look genuine to those men! They'll leave when you call and tell them you can't come over, so call. And then just leave us alone!"

"Okay," he said softly, though she had hung up. The waitress was standing nearby, watching him, so he smiled at her and said, "Can I make a local call?" When she shrugged and nodded, he went on, "And could I have another Coors Light."

Again, he punched in Steve's number and, again, Steve answered it quickly. "Steve," Sullivan said, "this is Pete. I'm calling from a different bar, I'm up on Hollywood Boulevard now. Listen, man. I just won't be able to make it by tonight. And, ah, I'm gonna be leaving town—I'll catch you next trip, okay? Next year some time, probably."

As he carried his fresh beer back toward his table he wondered, without being able to care very much, if Steve's regrets had sounded any more sincere to "those men" than they had to Pete.

He was looking down and carefully watching each of his shoes in turn catch his forward-moving weight, for his spine was as tense as if he were walking along the top of a high wall.

He sat down heavily in his chair at last, and, just in case, hid the glass of Kahlua and milk under his tented napkin.

Those would be deLarava's men, he thought dully.

And I can drink all night long, or run to the van and drive to Alaska, and it won't change the obvious fact that she *is* planning, again, to—

He inhaled, drained the beer, and then dizzily exhaled.

—She is again planning to consume my father's ghost. For some reason, she can't just let him rest in peace.

She went to Venice today because of the fish business, sure, but the fishes must have been acting up because my father's ghost is coming back out of the sea; right there in Venice, where he drowned thirty-three years ago. Right back where it *started* from, he sang in his head.

DeLarava would like to have me—alive—as a lure. Not as part of a mask, the way Sukie and I used to work, but, for *this* one, as a lure.

With a shudder of revulsion, Sullivan remembered how fat and youthful and happy deLarava always was after sucking in some ghost through one of her sparking clove cigarettes.

Presumably one ghost was as good as another . . . so why was she again going after his father's? On that Christmas Eve in 1986, Pete and Sukie had both been uneasy with the fact of being physically present in Venice Beach, especially with deLarava, for it had been in the Venice surf that their father had drowned in 1959, when the twins had been seven—but it wasn't until well after noon, in the instant when Sukie had spilled the contents of the shoebox deLarava had brought along, that he and Sukie had known what ghost was indeed that day's particular quarry. DeLarava had probably been hoping to consummate the inhalation without the twins even suspecting, but the exposed wallet and key ring had been, horribly and unmistakably, their father's.

The old man had drowned, and they hadn't been there. And then Loretta deLarava had tried to eat the old man's ghost, and—as Pete Sullivan had realized only after having driven far up the featureless Interstate 5 toward San Francisco, and as Sukie must have realized at some point during her own flight—*they had fled without taking away the wallet and the keys.*

Sullivan held the cold beer glass tightly to keep his hands from shaking, and his face was cold and sweaty. In that instant, he completely understood, and completely envied, Sukie's suicide.

She'd had to do it. How could you hide forever in a bottle?—unless you became transparent yourself. Dissolved (—like Speedy Alka-Seltzer—) so that you were a waveform propagated all the way out beyond any scraps of physical material, even compass needles, that might move in response to the fact of you and thus betray your presence.

(He couldn't think about the three cans of Hires Root Beer that had also fallen out of the shoebox, one of which had rolled right up to his foot and sprayed a tiny forlorn jet of ancient brown pop across his shoe, but) he knew in the tightening back of his throat that he and his sister had betrayed their father on *that* day, that *chilly winter of 1986* day, by running mindlessly away and leaving the tokens of their father's ghost in deLarava's hands.

But I'm still alive, he thought, and I'm back in L.A. I've got to save him from her. And I can't possibly face him.

"—the ghosts of dead family members," said a placid

male voice from one of the television speakers, "but police investigators speculate that the apparently supernatural effects were caused by some electrical or gas-powered apparatus that may have exploded and caught fire, causing the blaze that gutted the psychiatric clinic and killed three of Dr. Elizalde's patients. Several others still to this day remain hospitalized for psychological trauma sustained during that Halloween tragedy."

Sullivan looked up at the nearest screen, but saw only football players running across a green field. He pushed his chair back and turned around, and on one of the farther sets saw a blond man in a suit standing behind a news-show podium. As Sullivan watched, the studio set was replaced with a still photo of a slim, dark-haired woman standing with raised eyebrows and an open mouth in a doorway. Her eyes were shut.

That looks like a bar-time snapshot, Sullivan thought as a chill prickled the back of his neck. *Whoever this woman is, she seems to have anticipated the flash.*

"And today," the newsman's voice went on, "nearly two years after that scam-gone-wrong, Dr. Elizalde is reportedly back in Los Angeles. Police say that this morning she went to the Amado Street house of Margarita Gonzalvez, the widow of one of the patients who died in the so-called séance, and drew a handgun and fired four shots! Mrs. Gonzalvez was able to snap this photograph of Elizalde shortly before the discredited psychiatrist allegedly began shooting. Police are investigating reports that Elizalde may subsequently have bought a disguise and stolen a car."

The scene changed back to the newscaster in the

studio, who had now been joined by another blond man in a suit. " 'Physician, heal thyself,' " said the newcomer solemnly. "A tragic story of misplaced faith, Tom."

"Certainly is, Ed," agreed the grave newscaster. "Though medical authorities now believe that many of the folk remedies dispensed at these *curanderias* and *hierverias* can actually be beneficial. It's the charlatans who prey on credulity, and exaggerate the reasonable claims, who give the whole field a bad name."

The newsmen were apparently segueing into a topical Halloween-related story about the upcoming Day of the Dead celebrations in the local Hispanic communities, and shortly they switched to film clips of stylized papier-maché skulls waving on poles, and dancing people wearing black and white face makeup and wreaths of marigolds. Sullivan turned back to his table, frowning at the spooklike figure of the napkin-draped drink. The dead woman's drink, the suicide's drink. He wasn't going to touch it.

Apparently, this psychiatrist's catastrophic "so-called séance" had been big news two years ago. Sullivan never read newspapers, so he hadn't heard about it.

She held a séance at her psychiatric clinic, he thought; on Halloween, a dangerous night even for a séance that might not have been meant to get real supernatural effects. And something sure enough happened—the surviving patients apparently saw "dead family members," and then there were fires and explosions or something, and three of her patients died. (Of course, the police would assume that the disaster was caused by some kind of goofy "apparatus" blowing up.)

If she *is* on bar-time, as that photo implies, it's certainly no wonder—she's now got ghosts guilt-linked to her, like all of us ghost-sensitives.

Sullivan had gathered from the news story that Dr. Elizalde had fled Los Angeles after the fire and the deaths. Why had she come back now, at another Halloween? Not to shoot at that widow, it seemed to him—if there was shooting, it was probably aimed at Elizalde. Elizalde probably came back here in some idiot attempt to . . . *set things right.*

Apologize to all of them, living and dead.

But . . .

It sounds to me as though she really *can* raise ghosts, he thought. Whether she's happy with it or not, it sounds as though she's a genuine, if accidentally ordained, medium.

She could probably raise the ghost of my father, and I could—insulated from him, at a *medium* distance, speaking through a screen like a shameful penitent in a confessional—warn him.

His heart was beating faster. Elizalde, he thought. Remember the name.

She'll be hiding now, but I'll bet she won't leave L.A. until after Halloween, until after her Quixotic amends are impossible again. She'll be hiding, but I'll bet I can find her.

He smiled bleakly into his empty beer glass.

After all, she's one of us.

Outside, in the westbound left lane of Wilshire Boulevard, a 1960 Cadillac Fleetwood slowed to a stop at the Westwood intersection.

Behind the wheel, Neal Obstadt could see that all the other drivers had their headlights on, so he reached out carefully and switched on his own. He liked to be the last.

A cellular telephone was wedged under his jaw, and in his right hand he held a Druid Circle oatmeal cookie from Trader Joe's. "You don't need to be fretting about over costs, Loretta," he said absently into the phone. "Your location accountant's an anal-retentive, and the production reports always balance. You've got the insurance and permissions. Worry about something else, if you've got to worry."

Obstadt had had various business dealings with deLarava for years, and he knew that this anxiety was what she called "checking the gates"—a cameraman's term for a last-minute, finicky checking of the lens for dust or hair. Still, he could hear her sniffling—and she'd been crying on the phone this morning, too—and it occurred to him that this agitation was out of proportion for the modest ghosts-on-the-*Queen-Mary* shoot she had scheduled for Saturday.

"You having a bad hair day, Loretta?" he asked. "Your big manhunt suffer a setback?" The light turned green, and he accelerated west, toward the elevated arch of the 405.

"*What did you have to do with that?*" shrilled her voice out of the phone. "He isn't *really* leaving the state, *is* he?"

Obstadt blinked, and smiled as he took a bite of the cookie. "Who, Topper?" he said around the mouthful. "Spooky, I mean—your Nicky Bradshaw. He left the state? I had nothing to do with it, I swear. I never even liked the show."

"Oh, *Bradshaw,*" she said, her quick anger deflating. "My . . . *manhunts* are doing just fine, thank you. I've got one snatch working right now that's going to be costing me *twenty grand.*"

"Good for you, kid, the big time at last." Obstadt glanced at the taped-shut Marlboro carton on the seat beside him. Twenty grand for a washed-up old prehistoric *fish?* he thought. Or did you give up on the fish? *I'm* spending *forty* grand to finance a snatch, buy the access to somebody else's snatch—but forty grand for a thousand primo smokes is the bargain of a lifetime. Jeez, though, cash!—in a cigarette carton that I've got to hand to some guy from the phone exchange, just for rerouting their reward listing of that missing Sockit Hoomie boy! The exchange people are reliable, but who, really, is this Sherman Oaks person? His *ass*'ll be smoke, if he hoses me on this. "So who is it that slipped through your fingers tonight?" Obstadt said into the phone.

"If everybody minded their own business," sniffed deLarava, "the world would go round a deal faster than it does."

Obstadt suspected that her line was a quote from one of the Alice-in-Wonderland books. Loretta liked old smokes that had hung around hotel lobbies for decades: Obstadt preferred them fresh. It was the old ones that quoted Alice all the time. Among the solid old bum-smokes on the street, the Alice stuff seemed almost to be scripture.

He was driving between the broad dark lawns of the Veterans Administration grounds now, with the Federal Building to his left and the cemetery to his right.

"Is it that fish?" he asked, taking another bite of the cookie. "Did you get outbid by the fish market man at Canter's?" So much for your bid to be the Fisher Queen, he thought—in spite of all your vegetarianism, and your 'youth treatments', and your Velcro instead of buttons and topologically compromising buttonholes.

"What are you eating?" deLarava demanded. "Don't speak while you're chewing, you're getting crumbs in my ear."

"Through the *phone*? I doubt it, Loretta." Obstadt was laughing, and in fact spraying crumbs onto his lap. "It's probably dead fleas. Don't you wear a flea collar under your hair?"

"Jesus, it's sand! Grains of sand! Has he been whispering to me while I napped? But I'll eat him—"

The line clicked. She had hung up.

He replaced the phone in the console cradle, and his smile unkinked as he drove under the freeway overpass, the cemetery behind him now. You spend all day at the beach, Loretta, he thought, you shouldn't be surprised to find sand in your ear.

Loretta was crazy, beyond any doubt. But—

Something big had happened two nights ago, at around sundown; he had had to excuse himself from dinner at Rusty's Hacienda in Glendale and go stand on the sidewalk and just breathe deeply and stare at the pavement, for all the ghosts he'd snorted up over the years were clamoring so riotously in his mind that he couldn't hear anything else; the Santa Ana wind had strewn the lanes of Western Avenue with palm fronds, and Obstadt had squinted almost fearfully southwest, over the dark hills of Griffith Park, wondering who it was that had so abruptly arrived on the west coast psychscape.

The intensity had faded—but now the street-smokes were all jabbering and eating dirt, and some kind of dinosaur had washed up in Venice, and deLarava couldn't stop crying.

Loretta's a clown, he had said this morning. *She wins chips in this low-level game, but never cashes 'em in to move up to a bigger table; still, some big chips do sometimes slide across her table; and she's all excited about one now.*

He stomped the gas pedal furiously to the floor, and bared his teeth at the sudden roar of the engine as acceleration weighted him back against the seat.

The fish? he thought; some Jonah *inside* the fish? The guy that maybe left the state? Nicky Bradshaw?

Who?

CHAPTER 22

❖

The snoring got more distinct every minute, and sounded more like a tune: at last she could even make out words . . .
—Lewis Carroll,
Through the Looking-Glass

AND WAY OUT EAST at the other end of Wilshire, out where multicolored plastic pennants fluttered along nylon lines strung above used-car lots, where old brownstone apartment buildings still stood on the small grassy hills, their lower walls blazing even in the failing daylight with bright Mexican murals, where neglected laundry flapped on clotheslines in the grassless courtyards of faded apartment complexes built in the 1960s, Kootie stepped up a curb, limped across the sidewalk away from the red glow of a Miller Beer sign in a corner bar window, and rocked to a halt against the bar's gritty stucco wall.

He was still intermittently talking to himself, and during the walking of these last several blocks he had even begun moving his lips and whispering the dialogue.

"I can't walk anymore," he panted. "I think I've ruined my foot—they're probably gonna have to just cut it off and put a wooden one on."

"Duh," he said thickly then, speaking for the absent ghost of Thomas Alva Edison, which he was certain he had left behind in a mess on the stairs at the Music Center, "well, I got wooden teeth. No, that was George Washington—well, I got a wooden head."

"I *saw* your head," Kootie whispered, his voice shaky even now as he remembered that shocking period of dislocation. "It was made out of old strips of beef fat." He mouthed the last two words with, it fleetingly occurred to him, as much revulsion as his vegetarian parents would have done. He jumped hastily to the next thought: "I'm gonna go in this bar—no, not to get a *cocktail,* you stupid old *fart!*—I'm gonna get somebody to call the cops for me."

Kootie was still holding the quarter that the pay telephone had given back to him two hours ago. He had been gripping it between his first two fingers and tapping it against the palm of his hand as he had walked. The rhythm of the tapping had been unconsidered and irregular, but now, probably because he had a purpose for the coin again, the tapping was forcefully repetitive.

"I don' wanna go in the bar," he said in his dopy-old-Edison voice, and in fact, Kootie didn't want to step in there. The memory was still too fresh of the lunatic phone call with—with what, exactly? The ghosts of his parents? It had been that, or it had been a hallucination. And his parents had seemed to be in a bar.

But if somebody *else* made the telephone call . . .

(He found himself picturing carbon; *black grains in*

a tiny cell at first, with a soft iron diaphragm that would alternately compress and release the carbon grains, thus changing the conductivity; but the grains tended to pack, so that after a while the conductivity was stuck at one level . . .)

If somebody else made the call it might go through, and not just be routed again to that bar from hell.

That call an hour ago had *started* to get through—Kootie was sure now that the first voice he had heard had really been the 911 operator, for after he had walked away from the pay phone he had seen a police car drive past slowly in the right-hand eastbound lane of what had proved to be Sixth Street. Kootie had wanted to go flag him down, but had found himself hurrying away across the parking lot instead, and pushing open the glass door of the ninety-nine-cent store, where he had then gone to the back aisle and crouched behind a shelf of candles in tall glasses with decals of saints stuck on the outsides.

He must have been afraid, still, of facing the police and deciding which sort of crazy story to tell them.

And then the shop manager had yelled at him, demanded to know what the boy was doing there, and in his feverish embarrassment Kootie had bought a bagful of stuff he hadn't wanted, just to placate the man: a box of Miraculous Insecticide Chalk, a blister-pack roll of 35-millimeter film, and a Hershey bar with almonds. They were all things displayed right at the checkout counter. The bag was crumpled up now, jammed inside his lightweight shirt.

When he had finally left the store and resumed limping east, away from the fading light, he had pretended that the imaginary ghost of Edison took the blame for Kootie having hidden from the police car. *Duh, sorry,* he had had the ghost say, *but I can't let the cops catch me—I've got library books that have been overdue since 1931!*

Now Kootie forced himself to push away from the wall and walk toward the bar's front door. He was chilly in the smoky evening breeze with just the polo shirt on, and he hoped the bar's interior would be warm.

(A glass lamp-chimney, blackened with smoke. When the black stuff, which was carbon, was scraped off, it could be pressed into the shape of a little button, and that button could be attached to the metal disk. In another room you could bite the instrument it was connected to, and, through your teeth and the bones of your skull, hear the clearer, louder tones.)

Kootie pulled open the door with his left hand, for the fingers of his right were still rapidly thumping the quarter into the tight skin of his palm. *Tap. . . tap . . . tap. . . tap-tap-tap . . . tap . . . tap . . . tap . . .*

An outward-bursting pressure of warm air ruffled his curly hair—stale air, scented with beer and cigarette smoke and sweaty shirts, and shaking with recorded mariachi guitar and the click and rattle of pool balls breaking across bald green felt. Yellow light shone in the linoleum under his Reeboks' soles as he shuffled to the nearest of the two empty barstools. The bartender was squinting impassively down at him over a bushy mustache.

"Do you have a telephone?" Kootie asked, grateful that his voice was steady. "I'd like to have someone make a call for me."

The man just stared. The men on the barstools around

him were probably staring too, but Kootie was afraid to look any of them in the face. They'll recognize me from those billboards, he thought, and turn me in. But isn't that what I want?

"*Teléfono,*" he said, and in desperate pantomime he raised his left hand in front of his chin as if holding an empty Coke bottle to blow hoots on, while he held his right hand up beside his head, the fingers extended toward his ear. "Hel-*lo?*" he said, speaking into the space above his left hand. "Hel-*lo*-o?"

His left hand was still twitching with the coin, and belatedly he realized that the rhythm it had been beating against his palm was the Morse code for SOS; and at the same time, he noticed that he was miming using one of those old candlestick-and-hook telephones, like in a Laurel and Hardy movie.

SOS? he thought to himself—and then, instinctively and inward, he thought: *What is it, what's wrong?*

An instant later he had to grab the padded vinyl seat of the barstool to keep from falling over.

Kootie's mouth opened, and for several whole seconds a series of wordless but conversational-tone cat warbles yowled and yipped out of his throat; finally, after his forehead was hot and wet with the effort of resisting it and he had inadvertently blown his nose on his chin, he just stopped fighting the phenomenon and let his whole chest and face relax into passivity.

"*Duh,*" came his voice then, clear at last. "Du-u-h," it said again, prolonging the syllable, indignantly *quoting* it. Then he was looking up at the bartender. "Thanks, boys," said Kootie's voice, "but never mind. All a mistake, sorry to have wasted your time. Here, have a round of beers on me." After a pause, Kootie's voice went on, "Kid, put some money on the bar."

Catching on that he was being addressed—by his own throat!—Kootie hastily dug into the pocket of his jeans and, without taking out his roll of bills, peeled one off and pulled it out. It was a five; probably not enough for very many beers, but the next bill might be a twenty. He reached up and laid it on the surface of the bar, then ducked his head and wiped his chin on his shoulder.

"Lord, boy, a fiver?" said his mouth. "I bet they don't get many orangutans in here. Who are these fellas, anyway, son? Mexicans? Tell 'em in Mexican that this was a misunderstanding, and we're leaving."

"Uhhh," said Kootie, testing his own control of his voice. "*Lo siento, pero no yo soy aquí. Eso dinero es para cervezas. Salud. Y ahora, adiós.*"

"Oh," he heard himself add, "and get matches, will you?"

"Uh, *y para mi, fosforos, por favor? Mechas? Como para cigarros?*"

After another long several seconds, the bartender reached out and pushed a book of matches forward to the edge of the bar.

Kootie reached up and took it. "*Gracias.*"

Then he could almost feel a hand grab his collar and yank him away from the bar, toward the door.

(*But even with the pressed carbon disk, if you were relying on just the current set up in the wire, there was clarity but no reach; all you had was a little standing system. To fix that, the changing current in the wire had to be just the cue for changes that would be mirrored big-scale in an induction coil. Then the signal could be carried just about anywhere.)*

"Trolley-car lines," Kootie heard himself say as he pushed open the door and stepped out into the cold evening again. Standing on the curb, he waited for the headlights of the cars in the eastbound lanes to sweep past, and then he limped out across the asphalt to stand on the double yellow painted lines in the middle of the street. His head bent forward to look at the pavement under his feet. His mouth opened again, and "Find us a set of streetcar lines," he said.

"There aren't any," he answered—hoarsely, for he had forgotten to inhale after the involuntary remark. He took a deep breath and then went on, "There haven't been streetcars in L.A. for years."

"Damn. The tracks make a nice house of mirrors."

Trucks were roaring past only inches from Kootie's toes, and the glaring headlights against the dark backdrop of the neighborhood made him feel like a dog crouching on the center divider of a freeway; and briefly he wondered how Fred was.

His attention was roughly shoved away from the thought. "After this next juggernaut, go," said his own voice as he watched the oncoming westbound traffic. "Have they always been this *loud?*"

"Sure," Kootie answered as he skipped and hopped across the lanes after a big-wheel pickup had ripplingly growled past.

On the north sidewalk at last, Kootie limped east, his back to the blurred smear of red over the western hills

under the clouds. Of course, he knew now that he had not
lost Edison's ghost after all, and he suspected that he had
known it ever since he had involuntarily hidden from the
slow-moving police car two hours ago; but the old man's
ghost was not shoving Kootie out of his body now, and so
the boy wasn't experiencing the soul-vertigo that had so
shattered him at the Music Center.

Actually, he was glad that the old man was with him.

"Well now," said his voice gruffly, "did you get the
firecrackers?"

Kootie's face went cold. Had those firecrackers been
important? Surely, he had lost them along with everything
else that had been in the knapsack or in the pockets of his
heavy shirt—but then he slapped the hip pocket of his
jeans and felt the flat square package. "Yes, sir!"

"Good boy. Haul 'em out and we'll squelch pursuit."

Kootie hooked out the package and began peeling off
the thin waxed paper. The things were illegal, so he looked
around furtively, but the TV repair shop they were stopped
in front of was closed, and none of the gleaming car roofs
moving past in the street had police light bars. "Why would
an orangutan go into a bar?" he asked absently.

"Sounds like a riddle. You know why the skeleton didn't
go to the dance?" Kootie realized that his mouth was
smiling.

"No, sir."

"He had no body to go with. Hardy-har-har. How
much is a beer these days?" Kootie's hands had peeled off
the paper, and now his fingers were gently prizing the
firecracker fuses apart. Kootie didn't believe he was doing
it himself.

"I don't know. A dollar."

"Whoa! I'd make my own. The joke is, you see, an orangutan goes into a bar and orders a beer, and he gives the bartender a five-dollar bill. The bartender figures, shoot, what do orangutans know about money, so he gives the ape a nickel in change. So, the creature's sitting there drinking its beer, kind of moody, and the bartender's polishing glasses, and after a while the bartender says, just making conversation, you know, 'We don't get many orangutans in here.' And the orangutan says, 'At four-ninety-five a beer, I'm not surprised.' "

Kootie's laugh was short because he was out of breath, but he tried to make it sound sincere.

"Don't like jokes, hey," said the Edison ghost grumpily with Kootie's mouth and throat. "Maybe you think it's funny having to pay four-ninety-five for a *beer*. Or whatever you said it was. Maybe you think it's funny that somebody could be trying for an *hour* to tell you what you got to do, but your intellectual grippers ain't capable of grasping any Morse except plain old SOS! Both times I proposed marriage, I did it by tapping in Morse on the girl's hand, so as not to alert anyone around. Where *would* we be, if the ladies had thought I was just . . . testing their reflexes? I knew Morse when I was fifteen! Damn me! How *old* are you?"

Kootie managed to pronounce the word "Eleven." Then, momentarily holding on to control of his throat, he went on, defiantly, "How old are *you*?" What with being unfairly yelled at, on top of exhaustion and everything else, Kootie was, to his humiliation, starting to cry.

"No business of yours, sonny." Edison sniffed with

Kootie's nose. "But I was a year short of seventy when I bet Henry Ford I could kick a globe off a chandelier in a New York hotel, I'll tell you that for nothing. Quit that crying! A chandelier on the ceiling! Did it, too. Did you see me kick that guy back there? What the hell have we got here?" Kootie's hands shook the nest of firecrackers.

"F-fire—" Kootie began, and then Edison finished the word for him: "Firecrackers. That's right. Good boy. Sorry I was rude—I shouldn't put on airs, I didn't get my B.S. until I was well past eighty-four. Eighty-four. Four-ninety-five! Oh well, we'll make our own, once we've got some breathing time. Breathing time. Hah."

Two black people were striding along the sidewalk toward where Kootie stood, a man in black jeans and a black shirt and a woman wearing what seemed to be a lot of blankets, and Kootie hoped Edison would stop talking until the couple had passed.

But he didn't. "You like graveyards, son?" Kootie shook his head. "I got no fondness for 'em either, but you can learn things there." Air was sucked haltingly into Kootie's lungs. "From the restless ghosts—in case the bad day comes, in spite of all your precautions, and you're one yourself."

The black couple stared at him as they passed, clearly imagining that this was a crazy boy.

"Leave no tracks, that's the ticket. I did all my early research in a lab on a train. Take your shoes off. Daily train between Port Huron and Detroit; in '61 I got a job as newsboy on board of it, so I could have a laboratory that couldn't be located." He sniffed. "Not easily, anyway. One fellow did find me, even though I was motivating fast on steel rails, but I gave him the slip, sold him my masks instead of myself. Take off your shoes, damn it!"

Kootie had not really stopped crying, and now he sobbed, "Me? Why? It's cold—" Then he had suddenly bent forward at the waist, and had to put weight on his bad ankle to keep from falling. *"Don't!"* He sat down on the concrete and then began defeatedly tugging at the shoelaces. "Okay! Don't push!" His hand opened, dropping the firecrackers.

Edison inhaled harshly, his breath hitching with sobs, and Kootie's voice said, brokenly, "Sorry, son. It's *(sniff)* important we get this done quick." Kootie had pulled off both his shoes. The concrete was cold against his butt through his jeans. "Socks, too," wept Edison. "Quit *crying*, will you? This is . . . ludicrous."

Kootie let Edison work his numbing hands, stuffing the socks into the shoes and then tying the laces together and draping the shoes around his neck. He straightened carefully, still sitting, and leaned back against the window of the TV repair shop. He half-hoped the window would break, but even with Thomas Edison in his head he didn't weigh enough.

"Your furt's hoot," spoke Edison, interrupting Kootie's breathing. "Excuse me. Your *foot* is *hurt*. I'll let you get up by yourself. Grab the firecrackers."

Too tired to give a sarcastic reply, Kootie struggled to his feet, closing his fist on the firecrackers as he got up. Standing again, he shivered in his flimsy shirt.

"Now," said Edison, "we're going to run up this street

here to our left—we're going to do that *after* you start to—no, I'd better do it—after *I* start dropping lit firecrackers on your feet."

At that, Kootie began hiccupping, and after a moment he realized that he was actually laughing. "I can't go to the cops," he said. "I got a one-armed murderer following me around—and a dope fiend cooking me dinner on a car engine, and my parents—and anyway, now *Thomas Alva Edison* is gonna chase me up a street barefoot throwing *illegal explosives* at my feet. And I'm eleven years old. But I can't go to the cops, hunh."

"I liked that trick of cooking on the engine." Edison had made Kootie's hands cup around the matchbook and strike a flame. "I'm saving your life, son," he said, "and my . . . my . . . soul? Something of mine." He held one of the lit firecrackers until the sparking fuse had nearly disappeared into the tiny cardboard cylinder. Then, "Jump!" he said merrily as he let go of it.

Kootie got his foot away from the thing, but when it went off with a sharp little bang his toes were stung by the exploded shreds of paper.

He opened his mouth to protest, but Edison had lit two more. Kootie's head jerked as Edison cried, "Run!" and then Kootie was bounding up the narrower street's shadowed sidewalk, both feet stinging now.

"*Fucking—crazy man!*" the boy gasped as another firecracker went off right in front of the toes that had already been peppered.

The next one Edison didn't let go of; he held it between his fingers, and the rap of its detonation banged Kootie's fingers as painfully as if he'd hit them with a hammer. "What the damn hell—" Kootie yiped, still leaping and scampering.

"Watch your language, boy! You'll have the recording angels hopping to their typewriters! Keep a clean mouth!"

"*Sorreee!*"

In the back of his mind, Kootie was aware that Edison's children had hated this, too, having their footsteps disattached from the ground; for an instant he caught an image of a girl and two boys hopping on a lawn as exploding firecrackers stippled their shins with green fragments of grass, and fleetingly he glimpsed how strenuous it had been to get Tommy Junior to shinny up a pole and grab the coins laid on the top—how Edison had finally had to rub rosin on the inside of the boy's knees so that he could get traction. It had had to be done, though, the children needed to be insulated every so often, for their own good.

He was hopping awkwardly, and the whoops of his breath burned his throat and nose. At least no one was out on this street at the moment; to his left, beyond a chain-link fence that he grabbed at again and again to keep his balance, dusty old hulks of cars sat in a closed bodywork lot, and the little houses on the opposite side of the street were dark.

One of Kootie's bouncing shoes had caught him a good clunk under the chin, and his ankle was flaring with pain, when Edison finally let him duck around a Dumpster in an empty parking lot and sit down on a fallen telephone pole to catch his breath. The nearest streetlight had lost power when Kootie had pranced past beneath it, and now as he sat and panted he watched the light's glow on the nearest cinder-block wall fade through red toward black.

Kootie's mouth hissed and flapped as he and Edison both tried to use it at once. Kootie rolled his eyes and relaxed, then listened to Edison gasp out, quietly, "If I was your father—I'd wash out your mouth—with soap."

Kootie had heard the phrase before, but this time he got a clear impression of a father actually doing that to a son, and he shuddered at the picture. Kootie's own father had not ever punished him physically, always instead discussing each error with him in a "helpful dialogue," after which the transgression was respected as having contributed to a "learning experience" that would build his "self-esteem."

"Well, that's plain *bullshit*," Edison went on in a halting whisper, apparently having caught Kootie's thought. "When I was six years old I burned down my father's barn—I was trying to . . . ditch a playmate who'd been following me around for a year or so; of course, at that age, I didn't know about tricks like blowing up your footprints with firecrackers!" He wheezed, apparently laughing. "*Oh*, no! Burned to the ground, my father's barn did, and my *little friend* was still no more ditched than my shadow was. What was I saying? Oh—so I burned down the barn, and do you think *my* father *discussed* it with me, called it a—what was it?"

"A learning experience," said Kootie dully. "No, I suppose he didn't."

"I'll say. He invited all the neighbors and their children to come watch, and then he damn well whipped the daylights out of me, right there in the Milan town square!"

Kootie sniffed, and from across all the subsequent

years of the old man's accumulated experiences, a trace of that long-ago boy's remembered despair and fear and humiliation brushed Kootie's mind.

For a long moment neither of them spoke. Then Kootie whispered, "Can I put my shoes and socks back on now?"

"Yes, son." He sighed. "That *was* for your own good, you know. We'll do better evasion tricks when we get the time, but the gunpowder cakewalk will probably have foxed your—what was it? one-armed murderer?—for a while. Slow him down, at least." Kootie's hand wavered out, palm down and fingers spread, and then just wobbled back to the splintery surface of the wooden pole. "You're tired, aren't you? We'll find some place to sleep, after we've taken one or two more precautions. This looks like a big city, we'll be able to do something. Before all this started up, I had the impression I was in Los Angeles—is that where we are?"

"Yes, sir," said Kootie. "Not in the best part of it."

"Better for our purposes, maybe. Let's move east a couple of blocks here, and keep our eyes open."

"Which way's east?"

"Turn right at that light. Need directions, always ask a ghost."

CHAPTER 23

"I have tasted eggs, certainly," said Alice,
who was a very truthful child; "but little girls eat
eggs quite as much as serpents do, you know."
"I don't believe it," said the Pigeon; "but if
they do, why, then they're a kind of serpent:
that's all I can say."

—Lewis Carroll,
Alice's Adventures in Wonderland

IN THE OFFICE on the ground floor of his apartment building, Solomon Shadroe had finally stopped staring at the horizontal white line on the television screen and had plodded to his desk to resume doing the month's-end paperwork.

He didn't like the line being there on the screen at all, but at least it had stopped flaring and wiggling.

At last he pushed his chair back from his desk; he had finished writing the October checks and had then laboriously calculated the balance left in the account. As he stared at the worn blotter it occurred to him that pencil shavings looked like scraps of garlic and onion skins—his desk looked as though someone had been chopping together a *battuto*.

Garlic and onions—he remembered liking them, though he couldn't remember anymore what they had tasted like. Something like fresh sweat, he thought as he stood up, and a fast hot pulse.

His cup of Eat-'Em-&-Weep tea was lukewarm, but he drank off the last inch of it, tilting the cup to get the last sticky red drops. He put the cup down on the cover of the old ledger-style checkbook and took a can of Goudie snuff out of the desk drawer.

As he tapped out a pile of the brown powder onto his thumb-knuckle and raised it to his nose, he looked at the high built-in shelf on which sat three of his stuffed pigs. They had been burping away like bad boys during the half-minute when the line on the TV screen had been acting up, but—he looked again to make sure—the line was still motionless, and the pigs were quiet now. Johanna had the radio on, and the only noises in the office were the rolling urgencies of Bruce Springsteen's "Dancing in the Dark."

"Too loud?" asked Johanna from the couch where she lay reading a ladies' magazine.

Shadroe took a deep breath as he inhaled the snuff. "No. Just finished it up. Utility bills eating me alive. Gonna feed the beasties now." He got to his feet and plodded to the shelves.

"Oh good. Beasties!" she called to the screened window. "Din din din!"

Shadroe pried two white paper plates out of a torn cellophane wrapper and laid them on the coffee table. Onto one he shook a handful of Happy Cat food pellets from a box on a chair. Then he dug a handful of smooth pebbles out of his shirt pocket and spread them on the other plate.

He had taken Johanna to the Orange County fair this summer, and in one of the exhibit halls his attention had been caught by a display called the "Banquet of Rock Foods Collection." The display had been an eclectic meal laid out on a lace tablecloth: on one plate sat a hamburger, pickles, french fries, olives, and what might have been a slice of pâté; on another sat a stack of pancakes with some jagged fragments of butter on top, with a sunny-side-up egg and two slices of underdone bacon alongside. There had been other things, too: a narrow roast turkey with ruffled paper socks on the ends of the drumsticks, a thin slice of toast, a boiled egg in an egg cup. The thing was, they were all rocks. Somebody had scoured deserts all over the west to find pieces of rocks that looked like food items.

He had wondered at the time if any raggedy old derelict had ever sat down at the table and tucked a napkin into his outermost grimy shirt. There had been a relish jar, Shadroe recalled, filled with tiny cubes of green glass—a spry old ghost could probably wolf down a spoonful of that before being hauled away.

In the months since, he had been putting out _two_ plates at night—one with cat food for the possums, as always, and one with delectable-looking rocks for the poor hungry old wandering ghosts. The rocks were often gone when he came back from the boat in the morning. In a catalogue recently, he had seen a set of Mikasa Parklane crystal candies, for a sale price of eighteen bucks, and he meant to get some to dole out during the cold nights around Christmas.

He had once read that Chinese people bury raw eggs in mud, and then dig them up years later and eat them. When he thought about that he was just glad that he couldn't remember taste, but apparently *Loretta deLarava* was not so fastidious—*she* didn't mind eating things that had long ago lost their freshness.

In his head he made up a lyric for the pounding Springsteen song:

Did your face catch fire *once?*
Did they use a tire iron to put it out?

It had been in 1962, on the set of *Haunted House Party,* that he had first met *Loretta deLarava.*

He'd been trying to make the shift from being a teen TV star to getting young-adult movie roles, but couldn't seem to shake the Spooky persona he'd acquired during the five years of "Ghost of a Chance." (People would keep asking to see him do the Spooky Spin, the dancelike whirl that, on the show, had always preceded his disappearing into thin air.) This was the fourth movie he'd worked in since CBS had canceled the series, and like the first three, it had been a low-budget tongue-in-cheek horror picture, filmed at a pace almost as fast as TV work.

The novice production assistant had probably been about thirty years old, though it was hard to be sure—she was already overweight even then, and her jaw and nose were noticeably misshapen even after evident reconstructive surgery. *(Did they use a tire iron to put it out?)* Her name was deLarava—she claimed that it had originally been two words but had been inadvertently combined into one, like DeMille's, by a careless ad-copy writer. She had quickly outgrown the modest PA chores—somebody else had had to be found to make the coffee and drive to fetch paper clips and saber-saw blades, for, within days of starting, deLarava was filling out time cards and writing the daily production reports. Her credentials were hazy, but clearly, she had had experience on a movie set.

"Sun's down," said Shadroe after putting the plates outside and coming back in and closing the door. "Draw me a bath, will you—" he paused to inhale "—sweetie?"

Johanna put down the magazine and sat up. She glanced at the television screen, but the line was still steady and motionless. "Not ice?"

"Ice," he said firmly. "A lot of it." He looked at the TV too, and sighed. *Can't wait till my alma mater actually goes nova,* he thought. "Ice every night," he went on in his labored voice. "Until Halloween's past. Anybody from the building," he added, "should come knocking, tell 'em I walked to the store, unless there's actual blood or fire."

" 'Sol,' " said Johanna in a drawling imitation of a tenant they'd had for a while, " 'I heard a *noise?*—in the *parking* lot?—so I shoveled your mailbox full of *dirt.*' "

The tenant had thought he'd smelled gas from a neighboring apartment, and, unable to reach Shadroe, had in a panic broken out all the windows in his own apartment. In the years since that tenant had left, Shadroe and Johanna had endlessly amplified on the man's possible responses to emergencies.

"Heh heh," said Shadroe levelly.

The couch springs twanged as Johanna levered herself up, and then the floorboards creaked as she padded barefoot to the next room; after a few seconds he heard water booming into the big old claw-footed cast-iron bathtub he had installed in there a couple of years ago. He used to take makeshift showers at dawn out behind the garages, holding a lawn sprinkler over his head, but a tenant had seen him one time and complained to the police—even though Shadroe had always been wearing jockey shorts when he did it—and anyhow he had had to stop.

Now he was wondering if even cold baths would work for much longer. He didn't speak to people face-on anymore, even if he'd just chewed up an Eat-'Em-&-Weep ball, because of the way they would flinch at his breath; and he knew that his ankle, onto which he had squarely dropped that refrigerator two days ago, couldn't possibly ever heal. He had wrapped it up tight with an Ace bandage, but it still hurt, and he wondered if he would be around long enough to get so tired of it that he would just saw the whole foot off.

He was only fifty-two years old . . . or would have been, if he had still had any right to birthdays. At least he wasn't a ghost.

Loretta deLarava obviously wanted to finish him off now—as she had smashed him seventeen years ago—after having taken aim at him all the way back in '62 on the set of *Haunted House Party.*

She had known who he was—Nicky Bradshaw, star of "Ghost of a Chance," godson to Apie Sullivan—but he had not realized who *she* was until that summer night when unseasonable rain had actually put rushing water in the L.A. River bed all the way up by the Fourth Street bridge, and the shooting of some zombie scene had had to be postponed.

Everybody had been sitting around in the big, chilly brick warehouse in which the indoor sets had been built, and deLarava had kept looking at her watch. That was natural enough, since by that time she was practically the second assistant director on the picture, but after a while she had lit up a corncob pipe full of some vanilla-scented tobacco and gone wandering out into the rain. He had heard her whistling old tunes out there, specifically "Stormy Weather," and when she had come back in she had ditched the pipe and had seemed to be stoned. At the time he had assumed that she'd been hiding the smell of grass or hash under the vanilla . . .

Though in fact she had seemed *wired,* as if on cocaine or an amphetamine. As soon as she'd got back inside and shaken back her wet hair, she had started talking nonstop in her hoarse, fake British accent—rambling on about her genius-plus IQ, and telling fragments of anecdotes that clearly had no point except to illustrate how competent she was, equal to any challenges and a master of subtle revenge upon anyone who might foolishly dismiss her as unimportant.

The monologue had sat awkwardly with the crew and the youthful actors, all of whom had until then thought pretty highly of her. Bradshaw had been napping in a nest of rags in the costuming room, but the change in the tone of the conversation woke him, and he had wandered sleepily out into the big room.

"I was married once," deLarava was saying airily. "He was a very powerful figure in . . . an industry I'm not at liberty to name. He gave me everything I asked for, we had a big estate in Brentwood and a whole fleet of classic cars! But he couldn't give me the gift I demand of a man—that I be the most important person in his life. His two children . . . *occupied that spot.*" (One of the crew wearily asked her what she had done about that, and deLarava simpered.) "We went on a picnic," she said, "and I fixed potato salad just the way he liked it, with olives and red onions and celery seed, but I used a jar of mayonnaise that had been sitting out opened for a few days. And he had an appointment later that afternoon. Oh yes," she went on as though someone had asked, "the most important appointment of his life. His precious children pigged down a lot of the potato salad, too."

"Jesus," someone muttered. "Did they all *die?*"

The question brought deLarava back from the spicy pleasures of the memory. "Hm? Oh no, they didn't . . . *die.* But for a while they definitely had nothing to think about except when Nurse . . . Nurse Loretta might find the time to attend to their sickbeds! I can assure you!" Her British accent had been broadening out to sound more Texan, and was practically a drawl when she added, "*That* time they really *were* pooped-out puppies."

At that moment, Bradshaw realized who she was. Her appearance had changed drastically in the intervening three years, but when she forgot the hoarseness and the affected accent he knew the voice even an instant before the *pooped-out puppies* phrase—which he had heard her say a number of times—confirmed it. Then she looked up and saw him, and her eyes widened and then narrowed momentarily as she visibly became aware that she had been recognized.

It's Kelley Keith, he thought in that first moment of surprise; it's my godfather's widow . . . fat and disfigured now . . . .

Only then did he consider what she had just said. *The most important appointment of his life.* And he remembered that the autopsy of Arthur Patrick Sullivan had mentioned spoiled potato salad in his stomach as the cause of the cramp that had caused him to drown, out past the surf line on that summer day in Venice in 1959.

Bradshaw had backed away without changing his sleepy expression . . . but he'd known that she wasn't fooled. She was aware that he—alone!—had recognized her, and that he alone had understood her oblique and inadvertent admission of murder.

After *Haunted House Party* was in the can, he had finally stopped trying to chase his earlier success in show business. He had enrolled in the UCLA law school, and two years later passed the California bar and moved to Seal Beach to practice real-estate law.

Sometimes during the ensuing decade, he had wondered if the advent of Loretta deLarava had scared him away from the movies . . . and then he had always recalled the artistic merits of *Haunted House Party*, and had wryly dismissed the suspicion.

He had stayed away from Hollywood, though, and had

gradually stopped seeing his friends in the industry; and even so, he was careful to keep his home address and phone number a secret, and to vary the route he took to his office, and to come and go there on no set schedule. He kept a gun in his office and car and bedside table. Superstitiously, he never ate potato salad.

And, in fact, it wasn't potato salad that she finally got him with, in 1975. It was a spinach salad with hot bacon dressing, and lots of exotic mushrooms.

When Johanna returned to her magazine, Shadroe, who hadn't called himself Nicholas Bradshaw since his "death" in '75, took one more look at the static television screen and then stumped into the little room where the tub was, and by the glare of the bare overhead lightbulb he stared with distaste down at the dozens of ice cubes floating in the gray water—like broken glass in a tub of mercury.

The sooner he took his bath and got out, the sooner he could be in his car and driving west on Ocean Boulevard to the marina, where he would climb aboard his boat and spend the long hours of darkness sitting and staring at another TV set switched to CBS with the brightness control turned down just far enough to black out the picture, watching the white line that would certainly be on that screen too, and listening for the burping croaks of his pigs.

Like every other night.

CHAPTER 24

"That's the effect of living backwards," the Queen said kindly, "it always makes one a little giddy at first—"

"Living backwards!" Alice repeated in great astonishment. "I never heard of such a thing!"

"—but there's one great advantage in it, that one's memory works both ways."

—Lewis Carroll,
Through the Looking-Glass

AT THE NORTHWEST CORNER of MacArthur Park, crouched under a pyrocantha bush in the shadow of the statue of General MacArthur, Kootie watched as his fingers opened his bag of purchases from the ninety-nine-cent store on Sixth Street. The box of insecticide proved to be MIRACULOUS INSECTICIDE CHALK—MADE IN CHINA, and inside it were two sticks of white chalk with Chinese writing stamped into them. An instruction sheet on flimsy paper was all written in Chinese figures, and Kootie leaned out of the shadow of the statue's base as his hands held the paper up close to his eyes in the leaf-filtered radiance of a streetlight.

"*'Directions for use . . .'*" he heard his own voice say thoughtfully. Kootie started to interrupt, "You read Chinese—?" but Edison took over again and finished, "*'. . . On floor, use enclosed chalk to write 'Bugs, kill yourselves forthwith'.'*"

Then Edison was laughing an old man's laugh with Kootie's boy's voice, and he flipped the paper over. "Kidding," Edison said. On this side the directions were in English. "*'The chalk is more effective to use at night,'*" Edison read, and Kootie could see that he was reading it correctly this time. "Well, that's handy, eh? *'Draw several parallel lines each two to three centimeters apart across the track which the insect used to take . . .'* I like 'used to,' as if the job's already done. Well," he said, folding up the instructions, "this will do some good, though it's a child's version of a device I set up in the Western Union office in '64 in Cincinnati, and later in Boston—a series of plates hooked up to a battery. That was for night work, too—I told everybody it was for rats or roaches or whatever they'd believe, but it was to get some rest from the damn ghosts."

Kootie caught a brief glimpse of memory: a big dark room in what had once been a downtown Cincinnati restaurant, copper wire connections arcing and popping all night, the harsh smell of the leaky batteries, and morose, transparent ectoplasmic figures huddled in the corners far away from the stinging metal plates.

Kootie's hands waved. "Get us back out to the sidewalk, will you boy?"

Kootie tucked the bag back into his shirt and then obediently straightened up and walked across the grass and stepped up to the sidewalk. He started to brush dirt off his pants, but found that he was crouching to draw a circle all the way around himself on the concrete with the stick of chalk. His lips twitched, and then Edison used them to say, "I'd better let you do it; spit in the circle. If I try it, you'll do something else at the same moment and we'll wind up with spit all down our chin."

Our chin? thought Kootie—but he did spit on the sidewalk before straightening up.

"Very well, *your* chin," said Edison. "Now crouch again and let me draw some lines."

Kootie squatted down, and then watched as his hand drew a maze of lines around the circle: parallel lines, spirals, radii from the circle's edge—until this section of sidewalk looked, Kootie thought, like the site of some hopscotch Olympics. Cars hissed past in front of him in the street beyond the curb, but the only close sounds were the click-and-scratch of the chalk and his own eager breath.

The chalk was being worn down to a stump as cartoon eyes were added, and more wheels were drawn, and crosshatch squares were carefully colored in. The production was a couple of yards wide now.

Kootie shivered. It was cold out here, and he didn't like having his arm stretched out for so long. "Will you be done when that stick of chalk is used up?" he asked hopefully. There had been two sticks of the chalk in the yellow-and-orange box, and he hoped Edison wasn't going to need the other one as well.

He was about to repeat his question when Edison spoke instead: "What? What is it now?"

"How much of that stuff have you got to draw?"

"Stuff . . ." Kootie's head was swung this way and that, and he had the impression that Edison was even more bewildered than he was by the convoluted designs he'd drawn on the sidewalk.

"Did *I*—" Edison began. He took a deep breath. "Yes. *There.* That'll stop any ghosts or ghost hunters who might pick up my trail."

As Kootie presumed to straighten up, he could feel his recent memories being ransacked. "And," Edison went on, "it might slow down your. . . *one-armed murderer.* Now—how much does a dinner cost around here? *Oaffg*—Never mind, what I meant was, let's find some place to eat." Kootie's head tilted to look down, and again their gaze swept the lunatic drawing. "After that we can come back here and—see if we've caught something to put in your film canister."

Only now did Kootie realize that his purchases at the ninety-nine-cent store might not have been his own idea and he wondered why Edison apparently wanted to catch a ghost. But the notion of dinner was compelling.

"I've been smelling barbecue for a while," he ventured.

"Good lad, I'm not getting anything . . . *olfactory,* myself. Lead the way, by all means—it's never a good idea to turn your back on your nose."

The thrilling blend of onion and peppers and lemon on the breeze seemed to carry at least the promise of warmth, and Kootie was briskly rubbing his arms above the elbows as he followed the smells across the Park View intersection and around a corner, to a doorway under a red neon sign that read JUMBO'S BURGOO & MOP TROTTER. Even from out on the street Kootie could hear laughter and raised voices from within.

"It's food," Edison assured him. "Southern stuff."

(Again Kootie got a memory flash—Spanish moss hanging from old live oaks along the banks of the Caloosahatchee as he chugged upriver in an old sloop, the winter house in Fort Myers among the towering bamboo and tropical fruit trees, cornmeal-dipped fried catfish served alongside corn on the cob that had crinkly hairpins stuck in the ends for handles . . .)

"And without any sense of smell I won't be able to *taste* any of it," Edison went on in an aggrieved voice as Kootie pulled open the screen door and stepped into the place. "I'd much rather have stayed deaf instead."

Redwood picnic tables were lined up on the flagstone floor, with a counter along one side of the room—ORDER at the near end, PICKUP at the other—and in the kitchen beyond that, Kootie could just see the tops of big shiny steel ovens. Framed hand-painted menus swung in the hot air above the counter, and the other three walls, dark old brickwork, were crowded with black-and-white photos that all seemed to be autographed. The cooks and the countermen and all the men and women and children at the tables were black, but for the first time since losing Raffle and Fred, Kootie didn't feel like an excluded fugitive.

"What can we do for you, little mon?" rumbled a voice above Kootie's head. Looking up, he saw the broad, red-eyed face of a counterman staring down at him.

"I'm going to have—" began Kootie, from habit wondering what sort of pulses and grains and vegetables they might serve here; then he finished defiantly, *"meat!"*

"Meat you shall have," the man said agreeably, nodding. "Of what subcategory and method of preparation?"

"Barbecue pork ribs," said Edison while Kootie was still trying to read the menu through the dark lenses of his sunglasses, "and the turnip and mustard greens with bacon dumplings—" ("Please," interjected Kootie breathlessly, just to be polite.) "And a big mug of beer—" ("N-n-no," Kootie managed to interrupt, "I'm too young, I'll just have a large Coke!") "And," Edison went on— (*"Not,"* said Kootie, who could see what was coming)—"a cigar," finished Edison in defeat, "dammit."

The black man was frowning and nodding. "Yes, *sir,*" he said. "Nothing wrong with *you.*" He was tapping keys on the cash register, which hummed and spat out a receipt. "Seven dollars and a quarter, that comes to."

Kootie gave the man a ten-dollar bill, keeping his mouth and throat firmly closed against Edison's outraged grunting.

The man gave him his change. "It'll be at the far end of the counter there, in just a minute. Do you think you can keep the number *twenty-two* in mind? Can you remember it even now?"

"Twenty-two," said Kootie. "Sure. Why?"

"Because that's the number that one of us up here will call, when your supper is ready for you to pick up. I can't see why that shouldn't be satisfactory to everybody concerned, can you?"

"No, sir," said Kootie. He limped to a table that was occupied only at one end by a couple of old men playing dominoes, and he wondered if he might ever get used to everyone thinking that he was crazy; then he wondered what schemes Edison might come up with for finding a place to sleep tonight, and to make money tomorrow. Remembering the chalk drawing, he hoped the old man's ghost wasn't going senile.

When his number was called and he went up to get his tray, his gaze was caught by a polished wooden box on the counter. A metal rod, hinged at the bottom, ran up the front of it, and a piece of paper had been taped to the rod, with L.A. CIGAR—TOO TRAGICAL hand-lettered vertically on the paper. On the counter in front of the box was a cardboard bowl of peppermints.

Kootie's gaze was snagged on the lettering. He read it downward, and then upward, and it was the same letters either way. This seemed important, this proof that moving backward could be the same as forward, that the last letter of a sentence could be not only identical to the lead-off capital letter but the very same thing. . . .

He realized that he had been standing here, holding the tray with the steaming plates on it and staring at the vertical words, for at least several seconds. He made himself look away and breathe deeply. "What," he whispered, "is it?"

"That's a cigar lighter," rumbled his throat as he crossed to his table and sat back down. "Well," he answered, "you didn't get a cigar, so forget about it."

Kootie made both of them focus on the food.

The ribs were drenched in a hot sauce that reeked of

tomato and onion and cider vinegar, and he gnawed every shred of meat off the bones and was glad of the napkin dispenser on the table. The greens only got nibbled, because Edison couldn't taste them and Kootie found them strong and rank, but he did eat most of the dumplings.

A mouthful of Coke ran down his chin onto his shirt when Edison opened his mouth to whisper, "My God, it's *fly paper!*"

Then Kootie watched his hands untuck his shirt to get at the bag and pull out of it the box of film. The film cartridge itself was dumped out onto the table, and Kootie's fingers snatched up the empty black plastic canister. Kootie was about to point out that the film was in the yellow metal thing, but Edison hissed, "That fella's going to light a cigarette!" Sure enough, one of the old men at the table had taken out of his pocket a pack of Kools and was shaking one out.

Kootie's head snapped forward, and then he couldn't tell if it was intentional or not when he drooled some Coke into the empty plastic film container.

"Get to the cigar lighter before he does," Edison whispered. "Go, or I'll motivate for you, this is too lucky a chance to waste."

His legs already twitching impatiently, Kootie pushed back the bench, got to his feet and wobbled over to the wooden box on the counter. *How does it work?* he thought.

Edison whispered, *"Don't* work it—act like you just came over here to get a mint."

Kootie started to say *Okay,* but had got no further than the "Oke—" when the ceiling lights dimmed and the air was suddenly cold; and he was distantly grateful when he felt his knees lock, for sudden dizziness had made the field of his vision dwindle like a receding movie screen. He thought he sensed someone big standing behind him, but he couldn't turn around.

" 'Kay," he managed to whisper.

Kootie watched his own hands. His left hand picked up one of the mints, and he could feel its powdery dry surface, like a big aspirin, even though he wasn't controlling the fingers—(It's like the opposite of when your hand's asleep, he thought)—and his right hand brought up the plastic container to catch the mint deftly when his left hand dropped it. Then his right hand slowly scraped the edge of the container up the metal rod at the front of the cigar-lighter box, as if trying to scratch off the taped-on paper.

Then the ceiling lights brightened again and all three of the cash registers began clicking and buzzing. Edison had capped the little container as quickly as if he had caught a bee in it. "Grab a mint," he made Kootie whisper. "Grab a whole handful, like you're just a greedy boy."

Kootie dizzily obeyed, and walked back to his table when his left foot began to slide in that direction. As he sat down, heavily, he heard one of the countermen demanding to know why all the registers were going through their cash-out cycles.

"Let's go before they figure it out," Edison said softly.

"Leave a tip?" put in Kootie. "They didn't bring it to the table," Edison pointed out impatiently.

As he rode his scissoring legs out of the restaurant, Kootie managed to wave one shaky hand at the counterman.

❊   ❊   ❊

The night outside was colder now, and the headlights of the faceless cars seemed to glow more hotly as they swept past. Edison, forgetful of Kootie's hurt ankle, was making him hurry, and the result was a bobbing, prancing gait. He had stuffed the plastic container into his front jeans pocket, but his left hand still clutched the mints.

"Did*jjj*—" began Kootie, but Edison clamped his teeth shut, then said, "Don't speak of it. I lit up the whole area—we've got to get clear of it."

Kootie was hurrying west on Wilshire, away from the spot where Edison had drawn the chalk patterns on the park sidewalk by the statue, and he caught a thought that might or might not have been his own: *A stupid use for chalk—that was just stupid—a* ghost's *idea of a ghost trap.* Apparently, the "flypaper" on the cigar lighter had been better.

Edison made Kootie glance up at a streetlight as he shuffled past under it, and Kootie understood that the old man was glad to see that the light didn't go out to mark their passage.

Ionic. From nowhere the word had come into Kootie's mind, and, at first, he thought of marble pillars with curled scroll-like tops. (Doric, Ionic, and Corinthian. Doric columns had just a flat brick at the top, and Corinthian ones had lots of carved grapes and leaves.) Then the notion of pillars disappeared, and he pictured a clump of little balls, with much tinier balls orbiting rapidly around the clump; when the tiny balls were stripped away, the clump—the nucleus—had a powerful electric charge. If it was moving, it threw electromagnetic waves.

These were not Kootie's thoughts, and they didn't feel like Edison's either. "Ionaco," Kootie said out loud. And suddenly the gleam of moonlight shining on the fender of a parked car ahead of them was not just a reflection, but an angular white shape, a thing; and Kootie's perception of *scale* was gone—the white shape seemed to be much farther away than the car.

The shape was rotating, growing against the suddenly flat backdrop of the city night, and it was . . . an open Greek *E*, a white spider lying sideways, a white hand with fragmenting fingers . . .

It was moving upward and growing larger, or closer.

It was a side-lit white face, an older man's face—with a white ascot knotted under the chin; and as Kootie stared, gaping and disoriented, the lines of a formal old claw hammer coat coalesced out of the shadows under the face, and an unregarded background shadow that might have been a building was now a top hat. Cars on the street were just blurs of darkness, moving past as slowly as moon shadows.

Kootie thought the image was some kind of black-and-white still projection—the light on it didn't correspond to the direction of the moon or the nearest streetlight—until the white mouth opened and moved, and Kootie heard the words, "I only have one left." The voice was low, and reverberated as if speaking in a room instead of out here on the street, and the lips didn't move in synch with the sounds.

The figure still seemed to be some kind of black-and-white hologram.

Neither Kootie nor Edison had kept the boy's body

moving. Halted, Kootie was aware of sweat on his forehead chilly in the night breeze. "One what?" asked Edison wearily.

"Belt." The ghost, for Kootie was sure that's what this thing was, opened its coat, and Kootie saw that the figure wore, as a sort of bulky cummerbund, a belt made of bundled wire. A little flashlight bulb glowed over the buckle. "Fifty-eight dollars and fifty cents, even now."

"We don't need a belt," Edison said; but, "What does it do?" asked Kootie. It was heady for the boy to realize that, on this night, he would believe nearly any answer the ghost might give.

"Well," said the ghost in its oddly contained and unsynchronized voice, "it *could* have cured Bright's disease and intestinal cancer. But it banishes paralysis and restores lost hair color and stops attacks of homicide. It's called the I-ON-A-CO, like the boy said. It's a degaussing device—you can sleep safely, if you're wearing it."

"I don't have fifty-eight dollars," Kootie said. For the first time since hurrying out of Jumbo's whatever-it-had-been, he opened his hand. "I've got mints, though."

The ghost came into clearer focus, and a tinge of color touched its white face. "Out of respect for Thomas Alva Edison," it said, and its words matched its lip movements now, "I'll take the mints in lieu of the money."

"He'd rather have had the mints in any case," said Edison grumpily. "And you never thought that *I* might want 'em."

"Is it okay," said Kootie before Edison could go on, "if I hold a couple out for Mr. Edison?"

"Well . . . a *couple*," allowed the ghost.

Edison again took over Kootie's tongue. "You have the advantage of me, sir. Your name was—?"

"Call me Gaylord." Pink-tinged hands appeared in front of the coat, and the two-dimensional fingers managed to unfasten the buckle—but when the ghost tried to pull the belt from around itself, the heavy cables fell through its insubstantial flesh, and clattered on the pavement; one of the hands wobbled forward, though, palm-up, and Kootie poured the mints into the hand, which was able to hold them. Kootie was careful to hold back two of them.

Kootie's hand slapped to his own face, and his mouth caught the pair of mints and chewed them up furiously. Then, only because it was his own mouth talking, he was able to understand the mumbled words "Pick up your damned belt and let's go."

Kootie crouched and took hold of the belt. The heavy metal bands of it were as cold as the night air, not warmed as if someone had been wearing it. As he straightened and swung it around his waist he noticed that it must have weighed five or six pounds, and he wondered how the ghost had managed to carry it.

When he looked around, he saw that he was alone on the sidewalk, and that the dark street with its population of rushing cars had regained its depth and noise, and no longer seemed to be a moving picture projected onto a flat screen.

Edison had swallowed the chewed-up mints. "I said let's go."

Kootie started forward again, trying to figure out the

working of the buckle as he limped along. "This is pretty neat, actually," he said.

"Poor doomed old things," said his voice then, softly, and Kootie just listened. "God knows where *we* are, the *real* us. Heaven or Hell, I suppose, or simply gone—in any case, probably not even aware of these lonely scramblings and idiot ruminations back here." Kootie's hand had pulled the capped black plastic film canister out of his pocket, and now shook the thing beside his ear. "I wonder who this poor beggar was. I invented a telephone, once."

Edison seemed to have paused, and Kootie put in, "I thought that was Alexander Graham Bell."

"I wasn't talking about that telephone. *Bell!*—all he had was Reis's old magneto telephone, a stone-age circuit with 'make and break' contact interruption, good enough for tones but lousy for consonants. Showing off in front of the King of South America or somebody at the Centennial Exhibition in '76, with his voice not hardly carrying along the wire from one end of a building to the other. He recited Hamlet's soliloquy—'For in that sleep of death what dreams may come/ When we have shuffled off this mortal coil . . . ' Two years later, with my carbon transmitter and *induction* coil, I held a loud-and-clear conversation with the Western Union boys across a hundred and seven miles, New York to Philadelphia!" Kootie snorted, to his own startlement. " 'Physicists and sphinxes in majestical mists!' A test phrase, that was, for checking the transmission of *sibilant syllables.* Think all that was easy? And *Bell* could *hear!* He had a very soft job of it."

Again, he held the black container up to Kootie's ear and shook it; the mint rattled inside. Then he put it back in Kootie's pocket. "Nymph," he said softly, apparently to the night sky, "in thy orisons, be all my sins remembered."

Kootie's footsteps had turned left, south down a side street, and the high reinforced windows of the buildings were dark. Up ahead on the right was a chain-link fence with some yawning lot beyond it. Kootie was rubbing his arms again in the chill, and he hoped Edison was feeling it too, and realizing that they'd need to find a safe place to sleep before long.

It occurred to him that Edison had not explained the telephone *he* had invented.

CHAPTER 25

❁

*There was a short silence after this, and then
the Knight went on again.*

*"I'm a great hand at inventing things. Now,
I daresay you noticed, the last time you picked
me up, that I was looking rather thoughtful?"*

"You were a little grave," said Alice.

—Lewis Carroll,
Through the Looking-Glass

IN THE GLARE of the streetlight at the southeast
corner of Park View and Wilshire, glittering flies were
darting around in the chilly air like metal shavings at a
machine shop. Sherman Oaks waved them away from his
face, keeping his mouth closed and breathing whistlingly
through squinched nostrils, for the flies were harkening
to the multitude-roar of his exhalations, and on this night
of all nights he was not going to condescend to consume
such trash even accidentally.

He had called the exchange back a couple of hours ago,

and the router had told him that Neal Obstadt had agreed
to putting up forty grand for the fugitive Parganas boy
against Oaks's pledged thousand doses of smoke.

The lady who had put up the twenty-thousand-dollar-
reward billboards had been eliminated from the exchange
listings, and replaced by Obstadt.

As a receipt, the router had played for Oaks Obstadt's
authorization message: *Yeah, tell this Al Segundo or Glen
Dale or whoever he is that I'll fade him—but if he hoses
me on the smokes, his own ass is smoke.*

Sherman Oaks had irritably got off the phone and
resumed his anxious search of the streets around Union
and Wilshire—

And then about an hour ago a glance at his knife-
pommel compass had shown the needle pointing west so
hard that it didn't wobble at all, and moved only to correct
for his own motion.

He had immediately thrashed his imaginary left arm in
a furious circle, but the only blinks of heat it felt were
weak and distant and *fleeting*—human lives flickering out
uselessly, in deaths that simply tossed the ghosts up to
dissolve in the air. Naive psychics were impressed when
occasionally they sensed this routine event, but Oaks was
only interested in the coagulant ghosts that hung around
and got snagged on something.

He hadn't been able to sense the big one. It must still
have been contained in the boy. But at least it was still
distinct and unassimilated, and, at the moment, it was in
its excited state, for his compass needle was pointing at it.

He had hurried west—and at Park View Street his
compass had gone crazy.

Someone, almost certainly the big ghost working the boy's hands, had drawn a lunatic ghost lure in chalk on the sidewalk, and had spat in the center of it; and now all the broken-down ghost fragments that inhabited the house flies around the MacArthur Park lake had swarmed out and were circling the intricate chalk marks as if trying to follow some prescribed hopscotch pattern in their flight. The ones that landed on the chalk lines seemed to be dying.

The flies alone wouldn't have hampered Oaks too badly, for their charges were very weak even in excited swarms like this; but when he stood on the Park View curb and looked down at the compass at his belt, he saw that the needle was jigging and sweeping back and forth across nearly ninety degrees of the compass face. From at least Sixth Street in the north to Seventh in the south, the city blocks ahead were *waked up*. Every ghost in every building was agitated and clamoring. Office workers tomorrow would probably be seeing magnetically induced distortions on the screens of their computer monitors, and if they'd left their purses in their desks they'd find that their automatic teller cards were demagnetized and no longer worked. And even hours from now the offices would still be chilly with the cold spots where the ghosts had drawn up their energies.

The big ghost must have stepped *way* out, at some point in this neighborhood, and just *damn flashed* the ghost populace, mooned them. That would energize and urgently draw every spirit lingering nearby. God knew why the big ghost had done it, for it couldn't eat any ghosts itself.

What, thought Oaks uneasily. You just wanted somebody to chat with? Or did you do it simply to fox my radar this way?

Sherman Oaks felt tense, nearly brittle, and he kept calling to mind the collapsed, hijacked, flesh face he had seen on the steps to the parking level at the Music Center this afternoon. Who the hell *was* that, who *is* this big ghost?

The threads of association trailed away back into the blankness that was his life before the awakening of consciousness in the district of Sherman Oaks three years ago. But he shook his head sharply. Enough idle chatter, he told himself, quit dishing the applesauce. If the compass is temporarily foxed, that only means that you're back on a limited-to-visual footing. Get your footing moving—you know you're on the right track, and you know he's close.

"So, what was the telephone *you* invented?" Kootie asked tiredly. He had walked down the side street, away from the streaking headlights of Wilshire, and was now staring through a chain-link fence at an enclosed paved yard that was shadowed from the intermittent moonlight by surrounding buildings.

"Well, I had to stop work on it. I found I was able to call people who hadn't died yet. What do you suppose this is?"

"*Hadn't* died?" Suddenly Kootie was uncomfortable with this conversation. "It's an empty lot."

"With, for once, no barbed wire on the fence. And it's got a couple of old cars in there, that look like they've been there since Ford first rolled them off the production line. Damn Ford anyway."

Kootie remembered having said *Damn Ford* when Raffle had seen the reward-for-this-boy billboard at the Music Center; and he realized that it must have been Edison talking then, and that he had been referring to Henry Ford, rather than to Raffle's car.

Kootie found that he had curled his fingers through the chain link, and was looking up and down the empty sidewalk. "What did Ford do to you?" he asked.

He wasn't really surprised when he began helplessly climbing the fence, but he had certainly not expected the old man to be so agile. "Ow!" Kootie exclaimed breathlessly at one point, "watch the right ankle!—Oh, sorry." The street was silent except for the rush of cars back on Wilshire and the immediate thrashing clang of the shaken chain-link.

Astride the crossbar at the top, Kootie's body paused to catch its breath. "When I was dying," said Edison, "Ford made my son catch my last breath in a test tube for him." In deference to Kootie's ankle, he didn't just jump, but climbed down the other side.

At last unhooking his fingers from the chain-link, Kootie hurried across the cracked pavement of the enclosed lot to the nearest of the abandoned cars. Shaggy night-blooming jasmine bushes overhung the car, and crumpled plastic bags had been shrink-wrapped by Monday's wind right onto the heavy leafy clusters, like butterflies captured in midflight poses against the fronts of car radiators.

When Kootie was crouched behind the fender, Edison went on in a whisper, "Oh, he meant well—just like he did when he built an exact replica of my Menlo Park lab, for his 'Light's Golden Jubilee' in 1929, the fiftieth anniversary of my incandescent lamp. That must have confused a whole nation of ghosts and ghost trackers—Ford reconstructed the entire lab, even using actual planks from my old buildings, with the old dynamos and half-built stock-ticker machines on the benches inside, and all the old tools. And he even erected a duplicate of the boardinghouse across the street! And he trucked in genuine red New Jersey clay, for the soil around the buildings! And there *was* a villain hanging around me in those days, trying to hook out my soul—I fed the fellow a poisoned apple!—and it was against such people that Ford was trying to protect me. Oh, it's hard to fault the . . . the generous, sentimental old fool, even now, now that I'm hiding in an empty lot in Los Angeles in . . . what year is it?"

"1992," said Kootie.

"*Good . . . God.* I died sixty-one years ago." Kootie had stopped panting after the exertion of climbing the fence, but now he was breathing hard again. "And I rattled my last breath into a test tube, which my son Charles then stopped up and *obediently* gave to Henry Ford." Kootie found himself staring at his hands and shaking his head. "Where did *you* get it?"

Into the ensuing silence, Kootie said, flatly, "My parents had it. Hidden inside a bust of Dante. They've had it forever. Had it."

"Inside *Dante*, eh? Just like I'm inside *your* head now. I guess I'm your built-in Virgil, though I've got to admit I don't really know the neighborhood. I wonder when we get to El Paradisio? Huh. Sounds like a Mexican speakeasy."

"So, Ford was trying to protect you."

"In his blundering way. Yeah, from ghosts and ghost hunters both—I stood out like a spiritualist bonfire. And—" Kootie's shoulders shrugged. "It was to *honor* me, too. A replica of the great man's lab, the great man's actual last breath! He was pleased to see his friends get *accolades*. He'd have been tickled to death—as it were—to know that I finally got a B.S." Kootie could feel his pulse thumping faster in his chest. "And not an honorary one, either—it was earned! The faculty examined seventeen portfolios of my research! And this was at *Thomas A. Edison State College*— if you please!—in Trenton, New Jersey."

"I . . . *dreamed* about that," said Kootie softly, "Sunday night." It, the thought of college, was the spur that finally made me put my run-away plan into action, he thought. Which has turned out to have put a lot of other stuff into action, too. "I must have been picking it up from you, you all worked up in the bust in the living room."

The laugh that came out of his mouth then was embarrassed. "I guess I *was* excited about it myself. A little. Not that I put any stock in academic honors." He shrugged again. "The news was all over the party line."

"Yeah," said Kootie, "I met some old lady that wanted to talk to you. Probably had a graduation present for you." Kootie sighed, feeling bad about dead people. "What are you gonna do with the ghost in the film can?"

Kootie could feel that Edison's mood was down too, and had been for the last several minutes; probably Kootie's own melancholy was largely induced in his surrounding mind by the suggestion from Edison's frail, contained ghost.

"The ghost in the film can," said Edison. "If he hasn't

died in there yet, we could talk to *him* on my telephone.
If we had my telephone with us, I could work it. You
might be able to as well—you strike me as another boy
who's carrying around some solid guilty link with a dead
person or two, hm?"

"I . . . guess I am." Kootie was too desolated and
exhausted, here in the dark empty lot, to cry.

"There now, son, I don't mean to stir it up." Edison had
Kootie sit down, leaning back against the car body. The
wind was rustling softly in the fronds of a stocky wild palm
on the far side of the car, and the only sound on the breeze
was the rapid *pop-pop-pop* of semiautomatic gunfire,
comfortably far away.

"My telephone," Edison said. "I got the ghost-
telephone idea when a spiritualist paid Marconi to buy my
Lehigh Valley grasshopper telegraph patents for him. It
was originally a scheme to make two-way telegraphy
possible on a moving train, by an induction current
between plates on the train and telegraph wires overhead,
with regularly spaced dispatcher stations along the way,
hence 'grasshopper.' *But*. . . they got a lot of random
clicking, some bits of which turned out to be . . . oh, you
know, idiot clowning: *Shave and a haircut, two bits,* and
Hey Rube, and the beats of the *Lohengrin* wedding
march and popular songs. Even so, I didn't figure it out
until the spiritualist bought the patents." He yawned.
"Up, son, I've got to set up the apparatus for our night's
worth of six signals."

Kootie didn't want to do any more work. Why was it
always *his* muscles and joints that took the wear and tear?
"What's a six signal? I bet we don't need it."

"Tramp telegraphers have to tap out a signal every hour, all night long. Called a 'six signal.' It's to show that you're still awake, alert, ready to participate. I used to just hook up a clock to a rotary saw blade, so it sent the signals *for* me, right on time, while I napped. *Up*, lad, it won't take but a few moments."

Kootie struggled to his feet one more time, and then he took out the chalk and, crouching, drew a big oval all the way around the car, which, he now saw, was a wrecked old Dodge Dart, of God knew what color under the dust of years. This time he drew arrows radiating out from the circumference, and he spit several times outside the wobbly chalk line.

"That'll make it seem that we're up and about, in a number of places," said Edison, "and for the night I can clathrate myself inside your head again—voluntarily this time!—with all hatches battened down. Then we'll be as damn hard to find as a gray hat in a rock pile." It seemed to Kootie that this simile had been derived from experience. "And we should sleep, and we should sleep."

Edison used Kootie's fingers to probe the car-door lock with a bit of wire he found on the pavement, but after a while he swore and tossed it away and just had Kootie punch in the wind-wing window with a chunk of concrete. Kootie's arm was just barely long enough for his stretched-out fingers to reach the lock-post button.

Kootie stepped back and opened the door—wincing at the echoing screech of the ancient hinges—and then he leaned inside, breathing shallowly in musty air that somehow nevertheless had a flavor of new houses.

The seats and floor of the car proved to be stacked with dozens of ancient gallon paint cans that someone had once halfheartedly covered with a stiffened drop cloth, and Kootie had to lift some of the cans out and set them down on the pavement just to have room to sit with his legs stretched out. He didn't know if the old man could feel the aching, stinging fatigue in his shoulders and knees—and in his hip, which pain he now remembered that the old man was responsible for—but Edison didn't argue when Kootie suggested that this was enough, and that they could sleep sitting up.

Kootie pulled the door closed—slowly, so that it wouldn't squeal again. The broken wind-wing wasn't letting in much fresh air, so he wrestled with the door's crank handle and managed to open the window several inches, enough to probably keep the fumes of mummified paint from overcoming him during the night. That done, he bent the old drop cloth snugly around his shoulders and shifted around until he found a position in which he could relax without setting off any big twinges of pain.

The empty lot was unlit, and it was very dark inside the old car.

Sometimes his father had come into Kootie's room at bedtime and had haltingly and awkwardly tried to talk to the boy. Once, after Kootie had supposedly gone to sleep, he had heard his father, back out in the kitchen with his mother, dejectedly refer to the conversations as "quality time." Still, it had been comforting, in its way.

"So, you fixed up this phone," he ventured now, speaking quietly in the close shelter.

"Hm? Oh, yes, that I did. Do you remember the story of Rumpelstiltskin? Your parents must have told it to you."

No. Kootie's parents had told him all about Rama and Koot Hoomie and Zorro-Aster and Jiddu Krishnamurti (in whose holy-man footsteps he had been intended to follow), and about self-realization and meditation, and the doings of various Egyptian holy men. But at least he had heard about Rumpelstiltskin in school. Thank God for school. "Sure," he said now, sleepily.

"Well, you remember that the little man didn't want anybody to know what his name was. That's important if a person is like you and me—misfortunate enough to be tethered by a stout leash of responsibility to somebody who's in the ghost world; it's like we've got one foot outside of time, isn't it, so that we react to noises and jolts just a split instant before they actually happen."

"You've had that happen too," said Kootie faintly, slumping farther down in the warming seat.

"Ever since I watched a playmate drown in a creek when I was five, son. So have a lot of unhappy people. And that . . . *antenna* we carry around makes us stand out to ghosts. They're drawn to us, and without meaning any harm they can attach themselves to us and sympathetically induce the collapse of *our* time lines—kill us, like a parasite that kills its host.

"People like you and me, if we manage to live long, have generally had a *wanderjahr,* a time of wandering around untraceably, often luckily giving a fake name and fake birth date, while we get the time to figure out what the hell's going on. I was a plug telegrapher when I was sixteen; that's like an apprentice, and for years I rode trains all over this country, because there was always ready work for any class of telegrapher during the Civil War. Blavatsky was doing her wandertime around then too: Europe, Mexico, Tibet. What you learn, if you're lucky, is that you need a mask if you're going to deal up close with ghosts. You can't let them get a handle on *you*, not anything. Real name and real birth date, especially. Those are solid handles."

Edison blew a chuckle out of Kootie's mouth. "One time in the early seventies, I had to go to City Hall in Newark to pay real estate taxes—last day, big fine if I didn't—and the fellow behind the desk was one of the big solidified ghosts, who had managed the no doubt difficult task of scraping together enough alertness to hold a county job, and he asked me what my name was. Hah! I had to pretend I couldn't remember! And pay the fine! My own name! Everybody in line thought I was an imbecile."

Kootie yawned so widely that tears ran down his cheeks, and it interrupted Edison's monologue. "So who did you call that was still alive?" he asked. "That must be embarrassing—'Hi, George, what are you doing there? Did you just this morning die or something?' "

Breath whickered out of his nostrils as Edison laughed softly. "That's just about exactly how it went. In 1921, I had got the spirit phone working: it required summoning back the ghost of my dead playmate—by then I had managed to cauterize the bit of him that had been stuck to me, sort of the way I'm stuck to you right now—and energizing him in a strong electromagnetic field. He was still my antenna. And then his augmented charge was amplified dramatically with an induction coil, and then he was . . . the operator.

"I was trying to call a man named William Sawyer, who had died forty years earlier; Sawyer was an electrical inventor who claimed to have come up with the electric lamp before I did, and wanted me to buy him out. I told him to go to hell. I just left him in the dust, and then he came around to my place when I was giving an exhibition, right after Christmas in, it must have been, '79. Sawyer came drunk, yelling and shouting that it was all fake, and he broke a vacuum pump and stole *eight* of the electric lamps, which I didn't have a lot of in those days. In the years after that, I had some opportunities to help him— and I didn't do it. I hadn't forgotten the theft and the vandalism, you see, and whenever I was asked about him I made sure to drip—I mean, made sure to drop—some unflattering statements about him. He turned into a drunk, and wound up killing a man, and he died before he could go to prison. So, forty years later, I was trying to get him on the phone to . . ."

Kootie's hands lifted. ". . . Apologize?"

After a few seconds of silence, Edison said, softly, "Yep." He exhaled. "But you get a crowd on that line, it's a *party line*, and everybody wants to talk. When they heard who was calling, somebody picked up, and I found myself talking to a mathematician who I had fired the day before! I was flabbergasted, and I said something like, 'Lord, Tom, did you kill yourself today?' All he wanted to do was recite poems to me, so I hung up and went round to his house. It developed that he had had a nervous breakdown, but had not in fact died. So I hired him back.

But I had learned that people can sometimes throw ghosts in moments of high stress, and those ghosts can sometimes wander away just exactly the same as though the people had died. They *are* the same."

"So . . . you quit work on the phone because of that?"

Suddenly agitated, Edison said, "Those aren't the *people*, the people you harmed, those ghosts. It's like trying to make amends to somebody's car, after they've parked it and walked away. Blavatsky was right when she claimed that the spirits called up by mediums are just animate shells. You can talk to the ghost of your dead uncle Bob, but Uncle Bob himself doesn't know anything about it. Chesterton said that, I believe." He shook Kootie's head. "What you've got to do is somehow *rehire* the sons of bitches."

Rehire my mom and dad? thought Kootie. "But . . . they're dead. What do you do about that?"

For nearly a whole minute there was silence.

Then, quietly, "Don't look at me, son, I'm one of 'em myself. Go to sleep now."

A fleeting impression of a candle being blown out and a door being closed, and then Kootie was alone in his own head again. Before loneliness could creep up on him he closed his eyes, and he was instantly asleep.

Beyond the dust-crusted glass of the car's windows, out on the sidewalk past the end of the lot and the chain-link fence, a silhouette came shuffling along from the direction of Wilshire Boulevard. Only one arm swung as it ambled along, though the torso rocked as though another arm were swinging alongside too. The head was turning to look one way and another, with frequent pauses to glance down at the figure's waist, but the silhouette registered no change in its pace as it walked on down the sidewalk, past the lot, and disappeared to the south.

CHAPTER 26

". . . I wonder what'll become of my name when I go in? I shouldn't like to lose it at all— because they'd have to give me another, and it would be almost certain to be an ugly one. But then the fun would be, trying to find the creature that had got my old name! That's just like the advertisements, you know, when people lose dogs—'answers to the name of "Dash", had on a brass collar'—just fancy calling everything you met 'Alice,' till one of them answered! Only they wouldn't answer at all, if they were wise."

—Lewis Carroll,
Through the Looking-Glass

BY ELEVEN O'CLOCK in the morning, Hollywood Boulevard was a crowded tourist street again, and it was the signs overhead—movie marquees, names of ethnic fast-food restaurants, huge red Coca-Cola logos, and the giant infantry soldier over the army surplus store—that caught the eye. But when Sullivan had driven down the boulevard at dawn, it had been the pavements that he had watched; empty lanes still blocked by last night's police barricades, litter in the gutters, and solitary junkies and long-night male and female prostitutes shambling wearily toward unimaginable refuges in the gray shadows.

Sullivan turned down Cherokee, parked his van in the lot on the south side of Miceli's and switched off the engine, and for a few minutes he just sat in the van and smoked a cigarette and sipped at a freshly popped can of beer. Thank God for the propane refrigerator, he thought.

Just because he had parked here didn't mean he had to eat at Miceli's. He remembered a Love's barbecue place on Hollywood Boulevard just a block or two away. He could even restart the van and go eat at Canter's, or Lawry's. What he *should* do, in fact, was get a to-go sandwich somewhere; he had no business blowing his finite money in sit-down restaurants.

It had been here at Miceli's, on that rainy night in the fall of '86 that he had had his last dinner with Judy Nording; the dinner at which she had been so distant and cold, after which he had gone back to the apartment he'd shared with Sukie, and had got drunk and written his ill-fated sonnet.

You're here to exorcise the ghost, he told himself comfortably as the cold beer uncoiled in his stomach. Prove to yourself that there's no more power to sting in those old memories—

And then he winced and took a deep swallow of the beer, for he remembered his real ghosts: Sukie, who for years had been so close a companion that the two of them were almost one person, their love for each other so deeply implicit that it could be unspoken, ignored, and finally forgotten; and his father, whose wallet and key ring *(and three Hires Root Beer cans)* he and Sukie had intolerably left behind when they had mindlessly fled deLarava's shoot in Venice Beach on Christmas Eve of 1986.

He had spent this morning at City College. He had showered and washed his hair in the cologne-reeking men's gym, setting his clothes and "scapular" and fanny pack on a bench he could see from the broad tile floor where the showerheads were mounted against the tile wall, so that he wouldn't have to rent an authorized padlock for the brief use of a locker, and possibly have to show some ID; and then he had got dressed again and reluctantly walked over to the library.

He'd made his way upstairs to the reference section, a maze of tall shelves full of ranked orange plastic file folders stuffed with newspapers and magazines, and endless sets of leather-bound volumes with titles like *Current Digest of the Soviet Press* and *Regional Studies,* and with some help he managed to find the long metal cabinets of drawers where the microfilm was kept.

He'd pried out the boxed spool of the *Los Angeles Times* from July to December of 1990 and carried it to a projector in one of the reading booths. Once the film was properly threaded and rolling, he sat for several minutes watching July newspaper pages trundle past on the glowing screen—advertisements, comics, and all—until he inadvertently discovered that there was a fast-forward setting on the control knob. At last he found the first of

November. (President Bush had "had it" with Saddam Hussein; the governor's race between Wilson and Feinstein was still too close to call.)

The Elizalde story was at the bottom corner of the front page: THREE DEAD IN CLINIC BLAZE. According to the text, a firebomb had been detonated in Dr. Angelica Anthem Elizalde's psychiatric clinic on Beverly Boulevard at 8:40 p.m. on Halloween night. The resulting three-alarm fire brought fifty firefighters from Los Angeles, Vernon, and Huntington Park, who put the fire out in forty-five minutes. Dr. Elizalde, 32, had suffered second-degree burns while trying to extinguish one of the patients who had caught fire; altogether, three of her patients had died, though only that one had died of burns; and five more were hospitalized with unspecified traumas. Police and the fire department were investigating the incident.

Sullivan had fast forwarded the microfilm to the November 2 issue. The story was still on the front page—now Dr. Elizalde had been arrested and charged with manslaughter. Several of the survivors of her Wednesday-night group-therapy session had told police that Elizalde had been conducting a séance when the disaster had struck, and that hideous apparitions had materialized in the air; and they claimed that one of the patients, a man named Frank Rocha, had spontaneously burst into flames. Fire investigators noted that Rocha's body had been *incinerated*. Police theorized that Elizalde had installed machinery to simulate the appearance of ghosts, and that this machinery had exploded during the fraudulent psychic performance . . . though they admitted that no traces of any such machinery had been found.

· The November 3 issue had moved the story to the front page of the second section, where it eclipsed the "Cotton Club" murder trial, which had apparently been hot news in 1990. Elizalde had raised her fifty-thousand-dollar bail, and then had apparently disappeared.

The descriptions of the Halloween-night séance were fuller now, and more lurid—the surviving patients claimed that ropes of ectoplasm had burst from the bodies of many present, and that spirits of eviscerated babies, and of screaming women and babbling old men, had then formed in the air over their heads; and Frank Rocha had exploded into white-hot flames. It was now revealed that several of the patients who had had to be hospitalized were in fact confined in psychiatric wards with acute psychotic reactions.

In the issue of November 4, it was confirmed that Elizalde had disappeared; police sources commented that until her arraignment they would not issue a bench warrant. Included in the article were quotes from an interview that the *LA Weekly* had done with Elizalde two months previous to what was now being referred to as the Día del Muerte Séance. "I find it effective," she was quoted as having said, "to use the trappings of the so-called 'occult' in eliciting responses from credulous patients. It has no more intrinsic value than the psychiatrist's cliché couch or the stained-glass windows in a church—it's simply *conducive.*" Police were still speculating that she had decided to enhance the effect by somehow staging dangerous, faked supernatural phenomena.

Sullivan had tucked the microfilm spool back into its

box and returned it to the drawer, and then located the cited issue of *LA. Weekly*—an actual paper copy, not microfilm—and turned the pages to the interview.

There had been a photograph of Dr. Elizalde in her consulting room, and, looking at it in the library this morning, Sullivan had winced. She was strikingly good looking, with long black hair and big dark eyes, but she looked more like a gypsy fortune-teller than a psychiatrist: the photographer had caught her smilingly underlit over a glowing crystal ball the size of a melon, and behind her he could see saint candles and all kinds of primitive little statues on shelves, and a framed print of Our Lady of Guadalupe.

The interview itself had not been so bad. He had made notes of some of her statements:

On ghosts: *"Well, of course when a person dies, actually that person is gone; a TV set that was used only to view PBS is no different from one that never showed anything but Sunday morning televangelists, once the two sets have been disassembled—they're both equal in their total absence now. But all of us who are still around have hooks in the memories of these dead people, unresolved resentments and guilts, and these things don't stop being true, and being motivational, just because the person that caused them is dead, has stopped existing. By having my patients strongly pretend—oh hell, briefly believe—that they can communicate with the dead collaborators in their pasts, I let them forgive, or ask for forgiveness—'give the pain to God'—and achieve peace. My patients don't forget the old wrongs endured or committed, but the memories of them stop being actively, cripplingly poisonous. My methods facilitate this by letting the patients* literalize *the old ghosts.* [ans. to quest:] *No, I don't believe in ghosts at all. I'm a rational materialist atheist. By the charged term 'God', I mean objectivity.* [ans. to quest.:] *My patients are free to. I don't preach.*

On men in her life: "*No, I—(laughter) physician heal thyself!—I think I'm still reacting against the machismo image of my father and my brothers. My father drank—I was thirteen when I figured out that his drinking was worst around February and March, when he'd get his vacation pay and his tax refunds—and he'd beat up my mother; and even on the farm out in Norco, he always had to have steak and salad and a baked potato and a couple of glasses of wine at dinner, and silverware, while the rest of the family got rice and beans. And my brothers and their friends were . . . oh, you know, khaki pants, polished black shoes, Pendleton shirts buttoned only at the top button with white T-shirts underneath, hairnets with the gather-point in the middle of the forehead like a black spidery caste mark. Tough—all the firstborn boys are Something Junior, and the fathers always had them out on the front lawn in a boxing ring made with a garden hose, sparring like fighting-cocks. And the boys and girls were supposed to get married and have kids as soon as possible. I've reacted against the whole establishment I was raised in, there—I'm not Catholic, I don't drink, and I don't seem to be attracted much to men. Oh—and not to women at all!—let me add. (Laughter.)*"

On why the crystal ball (if she's so materialistic): "*The stasis of the clarity, the clarity of the stasis—people look deeply for ghosts in pools where the agitation has passed.*

Tide pools seem to be the best, actually, literally, in eliciting the meditation that brings the old spirits to the surface; the sea is the sink of ghosts . . . that is, in the superstitious mind, mind you. Seriously, patients seem to find their ghosts more accessible in the shallow depths of actual ocean water. It's been worth field trips. Eventually I'd like to move my clinic to some location on the beach— not to where there's surf, you see, but pools of ordered, quieted seawater."

In the City College library, Sullivan had leaned back in his plastic chair and imagined the statements of a psychiatrist in some bucolic culture about a thousand years from now, when guns had survived as nothing but inert, storied relics: *Because of the legends still adhering to the objects known as "Smith and Wessons," I find that valuable shocks can be administered by pressing the "muzzle" of one such object against a patient's temple, and then ritualistically pulling the "trigger." I have here a specimen that has been perfectly preserved through the millennia. . , now, watch the patient . . .*

BOOM.

Boom indeed, he thought now two hours later in the Miceli's parking lot, as he finished his beer and dropped the cigarette butt inside the can. One of her patients must have been a ghost-connected person who acted as a primer, the charge being Halloween night and the hollow-point slug being a whole shitload of actual, angry, idiot ghosts. And the main target seemed to have been one of her patients who had died but hadn't realized it yet, so that he threw posthumous shock-shells when his lifeline collapsed, igniting his overdue-for-the-grave body. And then two others died of heart attacks or something, and everybody else just plain went crazy.

That must have been some night, Sullivan thought now as he levered open the van's driver's-side door and stepped down to the pavement in the chilly morning air. Well, maybe she's learned better now; here she is back in town, and, unless I miss my guess, the reason she's come back is to make amends—to a more literal sort of ghost than any she was willing to acknowledge when she gave that interview.

If I can *find* Dr. Angelica Anthem Elizalde, he thought, maybe she could be talked into doing another séance. She knows how, and I've got Houdini's mask, which has got to be big enough for both of us to hide behind. We could both deal with our ghosts *from behind the mask*, like Catholics confessing through the anonymizing screen in a confessional.

As he trudged up the sidewalk beside the brick wall of Miceli's, he wondered if Elizalde felt differently about the Catholic Church now. Or about drinking.

Or even about men, he thought as he pushed open the door and stepped inside.

Sullivan was sitting alone at a table down the hall from the entry and just taking a solid sip of Coors when someone tapped him on the shoulder.

He choked and blew beer out through his nose—and he dropped the glass, for his right hand had slapped his shirt pocket for the bag with the severed thumb in it and his left hand had darted to the loop on the fanny pack that would open the thing with one yank, exposing the grip of the .45 inside.

"Jesus, dude," came a startled, anxious voice, and a man stepped widely around from behind him, smiling and showing his hands self-deprecatingly. "Sorry!"

Sullivan recognized him—it was an old college friend named Buddy Schenk. "I spilled my friend's drink, sorry," Schenk said, looking over Sullivan's shoulder. "Could he have another? Uh—and I'll have one too." Schenk looked down at Sullivan. "Okay if I sit?"

Sullivan was coughing hard, but could inhale only with strangled, whooping gasps. He waved at the chair across from him and nodded.

"Beer in the morning," said Schenk awkwardly as he sat down. "You're getting as bad as your sister. And you're jumpy! You went off like a rat-trap! About gave me a heart attack! What are you so jumpy for?" He had unfolded a paper napkin from the table and was mopping up the foamy beer and pushing aside the curls of broken glass.

Sullivan tried to inhale quietly, and was humiliated to find that he couldn't. His eyes were watering and his nose stung. "Hi—Buddy," he managed to choke.

My God, I am nervous, he thought. If I'd known I was so scared of deLarava, I would have sat with my back to a wall. He wished he could smell something besides beer, for suddenly he wanted to seine the garlicky air for the scent of clove cigarettes.

The waiter who had earlier taken Sullivan's order for a meatball sandwich walked up then, and swept the soaked napkin and the broken glass into a towel.

After the man had walked away, Sullivan said, "Buddy,

you asshole," mostly to test his voice; and he could speak now. "It's good to see you."

Sullivan discovered that he meant it. This was his third day back in Los Angeles, and until this moment, he had felt more locked out of the bloodstream of the place than the most postcard-oriented tourist. It was a new Los Angeles, not his city anymore—the freeways didn't work nowadays, Joe Jost's was gone, Melrose Avenue was ruined, Steve Lauter had moved across the 405 and had guns pointed at his head, and the people Sullivan was most concerned about were dead people.

"Well, it's good to see you too, man," Buddy said. The waiter brought two glasses and beer bottles to the table, another Coors for Sullivan and of course a Budweiser for Buddy. "How's Twat?"

Sullivan smiled uncertainly, not sure if he'd misheard his friend or if the question was some vulgar variation on *How's business?* He looked over his shoulder and took a sip of beer carefully. "Hm?"

"Sorry, *Toot*. We used to call you two Twit and Twat sometimes."

Sullivan's momentary cheer was deflating, and he had another gulp of beer. "I never . . . heard that," he said.

"Well, you wouldn't have. Hey, it was all a long time ago, right? College days. We were all kids." Buddy laughed reminiscently. "Everybody figured Sukie had an incestuous thing for you, was that true?"

"I'm sure I'd have noticed." Sullivan said it with a blink and a derisive snort, but he found himself gulping some more of the beer. The glass was nearly empty, and he poured into it the rest of the beer in the bottle.

The old shock was still a cold tingling in his ribs. (He had read that the weight of the Earth's atmosphere on a person was fourteen pounds on every square inch of skin, and he thought he could feel every bit of the weight right now.) Sukie had been like the poor lonely ghosts, hopelessly trying to find that *better half.*

Old Buddy sure has a winning line of remember-whens, he thought.

"She's dead," Sullivan said abruptly, wanting to put a final cold riposte to Buddy's thoughtless needling before it went any further. "Sukie—Elizabeth—killed herself. Monday night."

Buddy frowned. "Really? Jesus, I'm sorry, man. What the hell have you—that's why you're alone. Were you with her? I'm real sorry."

Sullivan sighed and looked around at the Pompeii-style murals on the high walls. Why had he come here? "No I wasn't with her, she was in another state. I'm just in town for . . . business and pleasure."

"Sex and danger," agreed Buddy cheerfully, apparently having got over his dismay at the news of Sukie's suicide. Sullivan remembered now that for the few months that Buddy had stayed with them in '82, he'd always remarked, upon going out in the evening, *Off for another night of sex and danger!*—and when he'd drag back in later he'd every time shrug and say, *No sex. Lotta danger.*

"No sex," Buddy said now, grinning, "lotta danger. Right?"

"That's it, Buddy."

"You're having lunch, right? Lemme join you, it's on me and we'll eat ourselves sick, okay? Whatever you ordered already is just the first course. We'll drink to poor . . . Sukie. I'm supposed to be meeting a guy at noon, but I'll call him and put it off till three or so."

Sullivan was already tired of Buddy Schenk. "I can't be staying long—"

"Bullshit, you're staying long enough to eat, no?" Buddy was already pushing back his chair. "Order me a small pepperoni and onion pizza, and another beer, when you get your refill, okay?" He was calling the last words over his shoulder, striding away to the hallway where the telephone was.

"Okay," said Sullivan, alone in the dining room again.

He was agitated by the conversation about Sukie. And the insult to himself! *Twit* and Twat! And he was sure that he and Sukie hadn't picked up the Teet and Toot nicknames until . . . the early eighties, at the earliest. So much for the *we were all kids* disclaimer. It's not just thoughtless—why is he jabbing at me this morning?

Sullivan tried to recall when he'd last seen Buddy. Had Sullivan said or done something rude? Sukie might have. Sukie could probably be counted on to have.

His beer was gone, and he looked around for the waiter. A pepperoni and onion pizza, he thought, and another Bud and maybe two more Coors. It's always been Bud for Buddy.

Even the waiter had known it.

Sullivan's hands were cold and clumsy, and when he accidentally banged his fingers on the edge of the table they seemed to *ring*, like a tuning fork.

How had the waiter known it?

Oh hell, Buddy had probably been in here for a while,

and this one hadn't been his first. Or maybe he was a
regular, these days. Sullivan breathed deeply and wished
he had gone somewhere else for lunch.

Why was Buddy hanging around drinking beer at
Miceli's when he had a noon appointment somewhere?
Miceli's wasn't the sort of place one ducked into for a
quick beer.

Maybe the appointment was for lunch right here *at*
Miceli's, and Buddy had arrived early to drink up some
nerve.

Through the high window overlooking Cherokee, a
beam of reflected morning sunlight lanced down onto the
tabletop and gleamed on a stray sliver of broken glass.

Sullivan had certainly jumped when Buddy had tapped
him on the shoulder; grabbed not only for the gun but for
Houdini's mummified thumb, too. What had he been
afraid of? Well—that deLarava had found him.

Maybe deLarava *had* found him. Who was Buddy
calling?

Jesus, he thought, taking a deep breath. Where's that
waiter? You need a couple of beers bad, boy. Pa-ra-noia
strikes deep. You meet one of your old friends in one of
your old hangouts . . .

Both of which deLarava would have been aware of, just
as she'd been aware of Steve Lauter. Maybe there was no
one I knew at Musso and Frank's, day before yesterday,
just because that was Sukie's and my personal place. We
never went there with anybody else, so deLarava wouldn't
have known to plant an "old friend" informer there.

If Buddy's here to betray me, he might very well want
to pick a fight, to justify it to himself.

Sullivan stood up, walked around the table and sat down in Buddy's chair, facing the entry.

Are you seriously saying, he asked himself as his fingers tingled and he took quick breaths, that you believe deLarava has planted an old friend at each of your old hangouts? Restaurants, bars, parks, theaters, bookstores? (Do I have that many old friends? Maybe the roster is filled out with strangers who've each got a picture of me in their pockets.)

Oh, this really is paranoia, boy—when you start imagining that everybody in the city has nothing in mind but finding *you;* imagining that you're the most important little man in Los Angeles.

But I *might* be, to Loretta deLarava. If she really wants to capture and eat my father's ghost. And she has money and power, and the paranoid insect-energy to put them to directed use.

O'Hara's in Roosevelt, Morrie speaking, he thought, remembering his flight out of Arizona on Monday night, after Sukie's call. He had calculated then that it would take less than half an hour for bad guys to get from the nuclear plant to O'Hara's. He thought: how quickly can they get here, today?

Warning—you are too close to the vehicle.

Sullivan was out of the chair and walking toward the front door and feeling in his pocket for the keys to the van.

"Pete! Hey, where you going, man?"

Sullivan pushed open the door and stepped out into the chilly morning sunlight. Behind him he heard Buddy yell, "Goddammit," and heard Buddy's feet pounding on the wooden floor.

Sullivan was running too.

He had the van key between his thumb and forefinger by the time he slammed into the driver's-side door, and he didn't let himself look behind him until he had piled inside and twisted the key in the ignition.

Buddy had run to a white Toyota parked two slots away; he had the door open and was scrambling in.

Sullivan jerked the gearshift into reverse and goosed the van out of the parking slot, swinging the rear end toward Buddy's Toyota; the Toyota backed out too, so Sullivan bared his teeth and just stomped the gas pedal to the floor.

With a jarring metallic *bam,* the van stopped, and Sullivan could hear glass tinkling to the pavement as the back of his head bounced off the padded headrest. Luckily the van hadn't stalled. He reached forward and clanked the gearshift all the way over into low and tromped on the gas again.

Metal squeaked and popped, and then he was free of the smashed Toyota. He glanced into the driver's-side mirror as he swung the wheel toward the exit, and he flinched as he saw Buddy step out and throw something; a moment later he heard a crack against his door and saw wet strings and tiny white fragments fly away ahead of him. Then he was rocking down the driveway out onto Cherokee amid screeching rubber and car horns, and wrenching the van around to the left to gun away down the street south, away from Hollywood Boulevard. He slapped the gearshift lever up into Drive.

He caught a green light and turned left again on Selma, and then drove with his left hand while he dug the Bull

Durham sack out of his shirt pocket. Feeling like a cowboy rolling a smoke one-handed, he shook the dried thumb into his palm and tossed the sack away, then drove holding the thumb out in front of his face, his knuckles against the windshield. It felt like a segment of a greasy tree branch, but he clung to it gratefully.

Out of the silvery liquid glare of the cold sunlight, a big gold Honda motorcycle was cruising toward him in the oncoming lane. He couldn't see the rider behind the gleaming windshield and fairing, but the passenger was a rail-thin old woman sitting up high against the sissy bar, her gray hair streaming behind, unconfined by any sort of helmet . . . and she was wearing a blue-and-white bandanna tied right over her eyes.

Her head was swiveling around, tilted back as though she was trying to smell or hear something. Sullivan inched the thumb across the inside of the windshield to keep it blocking the line from her blind-folded face to his own.

Sweat stung his eyes, and he forced himself not to tromp on the accelerator now; the Honda could outmaneuver him anywhere, even if he got out and ran. (The shadows of wheeling, shouting crows flickered over the lanes.) And it was probably only one of a number of vehicles trolling between Highland and Cahuenga right now.

God, he prayed desperately as a tree and a parking lot trundled past outside his steamy window, let me get clear of this and I swear I'll *learn*. I won't blunder into predictable patterns again, *trust me*.

The 101 Freeway was only a few big blocks ahead, and he ached for the breezy freedom of its wide gray lanes.

Keening behind his clenched teeth, he pulled over to the Selma Avenue curb and put the engine into Park. He sprang out of the driver's seat and scrambled into the back, tossing the mattress off the folded-out bed. Buddy would even now be telling them that Sullivan was in a brown Dodge van, but they'd recognize him even sooner if he didn't have the full mask working. They would already have been given his name, his birth date, *too much of what was himself.* When he and Sukie had worked together, they had been a good pair of mirror images, being twins, and so there had been no solid figure for a ghost or a tracker to focus on; but now he was alone, discrete, quantified, discontinuous. Identifiable.

He had to grip the thumb between his teeth to bend over and lift the plaster hands out of the compartment under the bed, and he was gagging as he hopped forward and slid back into the driver's seat. He laid one plaster hand on the dashboard and grotesquely stuck the other upright between his legs as he put the van back into gear and carefully pulled out away from the curb.

The Honda had looped back, and now was passing him on the left. The riders hadn't had time to have talked to Buddy, but the old woman swung her head around to blindly face Sullivan, and peripherally he could see the frown creasing her forehead.

She's sensing a psychic blur, he thought; a mix of Houdini's birth and life, and my own. She won't be catching any echoes of Houdini's death, because the old magician was masked for that event, and got away clean even though he died on perilous Halloween. She'll be wondering if I'm a schizophrenic, or on acid—what it is that makes the driver of this vehicle such a psychic sackful of broken mirror. (He even felt a little different—his jacket seemed looser and lighter, though he didn't dare look down at himself right now.)

He groped through his mind for any remembered prayer—*Our Father. . . ? Hail Mary . . . ?*—but came up with nothing but a stanza of verse from one of the Alice-in-Wonderland books, a bit Sukie had liked to recite:

The sea was wet as wet could be,
The sands were dry as dry.
You could not see a cloud because
No cloud was in the sky:
No birds were flying overhead—
There were no birds to fly.

The motorcycle drifted past outside his window and pulled in ahead of him; through the close glass of the windshield he could hear the bass drumbeat of the motorcycle's exhaust pipes, and through the fluttering gray hair he could see the old woman's jaw twisted back toward him; but he kept a steady, moderate pressure on the gas pedal, though his legs felt like electrified bags of water. Was the driver of one of these cars around him seeing some signal from the old woman? Was he about to be cut off? They wanted him alive, but only so that deLarava could use him as lure for his father's ghost.

In a hoarse voice, he quoted more of the Alice scripture, thinking of Sukie and mentally hearing her remembered recitation of it:

Still she haunts me, phantomwise,
Alice moving under skies
Never seen by waking eyes.

The brake lights flashed on the transom of the gold motorcycle—but its rider leaned the heavy bike around in a U-turn and then accelerated back toward Cherokee, the diminishing roar of its engine rising and falling as the rider clicked rapidly up through the gears. Sullivan's jacket was heavy and tight again.

He spat the old brown thumb out onto the dashboard and gagged hoarsely, squinting to be able to see ahead through tears of nausea.

He turned left on Wilcox, and then right onto the crowded lanes of eastbound Hollywood Boulevard. Don't puke on yourself, he thought as he squinted at the cars glinting in the sunlight ahead of him. It looks like you got away this time. Now stay away. Hide. Buddy will have described the van, and might even have got the license number.

The thought of Buddy reminded him of the missile his old friend had thrown at the van as Sullivan had committed hit-and-run. Stopped at a red light, Sullivan now rolled down the driver's-side window and craned his neck to look at the outside of the door.

A branching pattern of viscous wetness was splattered from the door handle to the front headlight. It was clear stuff mottled with yellow and dotted with angular bits of white, and half a dozen vertical trickles had already run down the fender from the initial horizontal streaking.

Buddy's missile had been a raw egg.

The schoolboy-prankishness of the gesture was disarming. He egged my van, Sullivan thought; after I smashed the front end of his car! How could he have been colluding with deLarava at one moment and doing something as goofy as this in the next? I must have been wrong—poor Buddy wasn't guilty of anything but beery tactlessness back there in the restaurant, and then he must really have been calling some business associate when he went to the phone. I should go back, and apologize, and agree to pay for getting his car fixed. This was *pure* paranoia. Even the people on the motorcycle had probably just been—

No. Sullivan remembered the old woman sitting high up against the sissy bar, blindfolded against visual distractions and sniffing the breeze, and he couldn't make himself believe that the pair on the Honda had been random passersby.

He kept driving straight ahead.

East of Vine, the street stopped seeming to be Hollywood Boulevard, and was just another Los Angeles street, with office buildings and CD stores and boarded-up theaters, and red-and-yellow-blooming wild lantana bushes crouched in the squares of curbside dirt; but when he glanced out of his open window he saw, a smoky mile to the north against the green Griffith Park hills, the old white Hollywood sign—and for just a moment, to his still-watering eyes, it had seemed to read HALLOWEEN.

Not for two days yet, he thought, and he spat again to get rid of the taste of Houdini's thumb. I've got about thirty-six hours.

Just past Van Ness he turned right onto the 101 southbound. The freeway was wide open and cars were moving along rapidly for once, and he gunned down the ramp with the gas pedal to the floor so as to be up to speed when he merged into the right lane.

A.O. fucking P., he thought as he took his first deep breath in at least five minutes. *On the freeways, there you feel free.*

He remembered now, now that he was at long last experiencing it again, the always-downstream rush of driving along open fast-moving freeway lanes. Up here above the surface streets, above them even if the freeway was sluicing through a valley, the real world off to the sides was reduced to a two-dimensional projection of sketchy hills and skyscraper silhouettes, and you dealt with the *names* of places, spelled out in reflector-studded white on the big green signs that swept past overhead, rather than with the grimy stop-and-go places themselves; even the spidery calligraphy of gang graffiti markers, looping across the signs in defiance of barbed wire and precarious perches and rushing traffic below, were formal *symbols* of senseless-killing neighborhoods, rather than the neighborhoods themselves.

Other drivers were just glimpsed heads in the gleaming solidity of rushing cars in this world of lanes and connectors; space and time were abridged, and a moment's inattention could have you blinking at unfamiliar street names in Orange County or Pomona.

Sullivan had to find a place to stay, a place with a garage. After this, he couldn't keep living in the van out on the streets. And he wanted to be close to deLarava, without putting himself in the way of her possibly stumbling across him.

Just short of the towers of downtown he turned south on the Harbor Freeway, toward Long Beach and the Los Angeles Harbor . . . and the *Queen Mary*.

CHAPTER 27

"If it had grown up," she said to herself, "it would have made a dreadfully ugly child, but it makes rather a handsome pig, I think."

—Lewis Carroll,
Alice's Adventures in Wonderland

FRANCIS STRUBE'S black leather electric office chair was acting up. It was made by the McKie Company, which was supposed to manufacture the best race-car seats, and he had punched the button on the "comfort console" to pump up the lower-back region, but it had inflated out grossly, to the size of a watermelon, and in order to sit back with his shoulders against the top of the chair he had to push out his chest and belly like a pouter pigeon.

Ludicrous. He leaned forward instead, dividing his attention between the flimsy sheets of fax paper in his hand and the man in the seat across the desk. The Goudie Snuff people—after extorting a thousand dollars out of him!—had printed out their mailing list in some kind of minimalist dot-matrix, and Strube was afraid he'd have to get Charlotte to puzzle it out for him.

"But," said the client uncertainly, "would that be best for them?"

Strube looked up at him. What dreary aspect of the man's divorce case had they been discussing? Damn the chair. He pushed the "deflate" button several times, but the leather-covered swelling behind his kidneys didn't diminish; if anything, it swelled more. But he put patient concern in his voice as he asked, "Best for whom?"

"*Whom* we're talking about, Mr. Strube! Heather and Krystle!"

These, Strube recalled, were the man's daughters. He remembered now that custody of the children had been the topic at hand.

"Well, of *course* it would be best for *them*," Strube said, indicating by his tone that he was way ahead of the man, and had not lost track of the conversation at all. "*Our primary* concern is the well-being of Heather and Krystle." Strube had made a bad impression early on, when, having only read the girls' names on the information form, he had pronounced the second one to rhyme with *gristle* rather than *bristol.*

"But," went on the father of the girls, waving his hands bewilderedly, "you want me to demand alternating custody of the girls, a week with me and then a week with Debi, and then a week with me again? How would that work? They'd have to pack their clothes and . . . and toothbrushes and schoolbooks and . . . I don't even know what all. Every weekend! Would Debi be supposed to feed their goldfish, every other week? They wouldn't even know what was in the refrigerator half the time. The girls, I mean."

Rather than the goldfish, thought Strube. I follow you. "It's your right—and it's to their benefit," he said soothingly. "For two weeks out of every month they'd be living with you, in a normal, nurturing environment, away from that woman's influences."

He let his gaze fall back to where the fax sheets lay in a patch of slanting sunlight on the desk. Most of the customers for Goudie Snuff were shops, but there were a couple that seemed to be residential addresses. He noticed one on Civic Center Drive in Santa Ana, and drew a checkmark beside it. Santa Ana was just an hour away, down in Orange County—that could easily be where Nicky Bradshaw was hiding out these days. Strube reminded himself that he would have to scout all the likely addresses, and actually *see* Bradshaw at one of them; he wouldn't get the credit for having *found Spooky* if he just sent in half a dozen likely addresses.

And here was one in Long Beach. Why did so many people need to have snuff mailed right to their houses?

" 'That woman' is my wife," protested the client.

"For a while," Strube answered absently. Here was another address, in Southgate. How did somebody in Southgate afford a luxury item like Scottish snuff? "You did come in here for a divorce, you'll recall."

"Only because she filed! *I* didn't want a divorce! The girls staying a week with me, and then a week with her— this is fantastic!"

Strube looked up. "Well, you won't be paying child support for half the time. Besides, the arrangement won't last for very long. Your girls will hate it, and it'll wear Debi down, and then you can press for total custody." To hell with your girls, he thought; it'll protract the proceedings, and I'm paid by the hour.

The thought was suddenly depressing and he remembered yesterday's riddle about the lawyer and the sperm cell. He realized that he was hunched over the desk like some kind of centipede.

He spread his Nautilus-broadened shoulders inside the Armani jacket, and leaned back, lifting his chin.

And from the back of the McKie chair burst a sharp, yipping fart sound. A wordless cry escaped his astonished client.

Still sitting up straight, though he could feel the sudden heat in his face, Strube said, "That will be all for today."

"But—about the division of property—"

"That will be all for today," Strube repeated. He would press for a Substitution of Attorney tomorrow.

One chance in two million of becoming a human being. He could work with the studios, handle prestige cases for famous clients. *Swimming pools—movie stars.* He could start by representing Bradshaw.

The client had stood up. "What time . . . ?"

"Miss Meredith will schedule an appointment." I knew him in '74 and '75, which was more than ten years after he quit showbiz, Strube thought. I'm likelier to recognize him than any of his old Hollywood crowd is.

He maintained his stiff pose until the man had left the office. Then he let himself slump. He could check the Santa Ana address today. Maybe even the Long Beach one too.

* * *

Loretta deLarava was crying again, and it was taking her forever to eat her ham and cheese sandwich. She was in a window-side booth in the Promenade Cafe; out through the glass, across the blue water of the Pacific Terrace Harbor, she could see the low skyline of Long Beach with the boat-filled Downtown Long Beach Marina spread like a bristly carpet of confetti around the foot of it.

She preferred to eat in the employees' cafeteria on C Deck, four decks down, back by the stern; but she couldn't make herself go there anymore.

When the *Queen Mary* had been an oceangoing ship, that C Deck auxiliary room had been the men's crew's bar, called the Pig and Whistle, and she liked the airy brightness of the present-day cafeteria with the young men and ladies in the tour-guide uniforms chatting and carrying trays to the white tables, and the absence of obnoxious tourists. But yesterday, and the day before too, when deLarava had gone there, she had found herself in a low dark hall, with dartboards on the walls and long wooden tables and benches crowded with men, some in aprons and some in black ties and formal jackets. The men at the nearest table had looked up from their pint glasses of dark beer and stared at her in wonderment. She hadn't been able to hear anything over the throbbing, droning vibration that seemed to come up through the floor, and she'd realized that it was the sound of the ship's propellers three decks directly below her.

It had been the old Pig and Whistle that she'd seen, as it had been in . . . the sixties? Hell, the thirties?

And late last night she had left her stateroom and followed uncarpeted stairs all the way down to D Deck, and stood by the closed-up crew's galley by the bow and looked aft down the long, dim service alley, known to the crew in the old days as the Burma Road, that was said to stretch all the way back to the old bedroom service pantry and the hulking machinery of the lift motors by the stern. From far away in that dimness she had heard a lonely clashing and rattling, and when she had nerved herself up to walk some distance along the red-painted metal floor, between widely separated walls that were green up to belt height and beige above, hurrying from one bare bulb hung among the pipes and valves overhead to the next, she had seen tiny figures moving rapidly in one of the far distant patches of yellow light; children in red uniforms with caps—she had peered at them around the edge of a massive steel sliding door, and eventually she had realized that they were the ghosts of bellboys on roller skates, still skating up and down the old Burma Road on long-ago-urgent errands.

She had hurried away, and climbed the stairs back to her stateroom on B Deck, and locked the door and shivered in her bed under the dogged-shut porthole for hours before getting to sleep.

The sandwich was actually very good, with tomato and basil in among the ham and cheese, and she made herself take another bite.

The man sitting across the table from her was holding a pencil poised over the wide white cardboard storyboards. "You okay, Loretta?"

"Sure, Gene," she mumbled around the food in her

mouth. She waved her free hand vaguely. "Stress. Listen, we've also got to get a lot of footage of the below-decks areas—the crew's quarters, the section up by the bow where the service men were bunked during the war—it'd be a good contrast, you know? To all the glamour of the top decks."

"Well," he said, sipping nervously at a Coors Light, "I guess you can edit to a balance in postproduction—but we cleared it with the Disney people for just the engine-room tour and the pool and the staterooms and the salons. There might not be accessible power sources down in the catacombs, and God knows what their routines are—they might tell us it's too late to set it all up. It'd only be giving them two days' warning, if you want to get everything in the can Saturday."

"Well, we can at least do stills down there. A still photographer, and me, and my assistant carrying a portable stereo—that shouldn't disrupt any employees."

"You don't need music to shoot stills, Loretta. And how are you going to use stills?"

DeLarava had looked past him and seen Ayres standing by the cash register. She waved, and said, "I've got to talk to this guy, Gene. Do what you can, okay?"

The man stood up, taking the storyboards with him. "Okay. If the PR guy's in his office, I'll talk to him now, on my way out. I'll call you and let you know what he says. Tomorrow I'll be at the studio all day, and I'll be back here Saturday, early, to make sure they rope off the areas from the tourists. I still don't see why we had to *film* on Halloween. A weekday would have been less crowded."

"Will you not be questioning my *decisions*, Gene? You gentlemen all work for *me.*"

Gene left as Ayres walked up, shrugging as they passed each other, and deLarava was crying again; she wanted to scratch her scalp, but didn't dare, because she had stretched *three* rubber bands over it this morning. She had felt she had to, after the dream that had somehow left her to wake up crouched over the toilet in the stateroom's bathroom, whispering to the water in the bowl.

Ayres sat down and promptly drank off the last inch of the Coors Light. "Your old boy Joey Webb is crazy," he said. "He's out at all hours on the beach with a metal detector and a jar of orange marmalade, singing that 'Ed Sullivan' song from *Bye Bye Birdie.*"

"*Ed* Sullivan? The moron. He's not supposed to be looking for *Ed* Sullivan."

"Could I have another of these, please?" said Ayres to a passing waitress. To deLarava he said, quietly, "I found out some things about the Parganas couple."

"Okay . . . ?"

"Well, they were crazy too. The old man, named Jiddu K. Parganas, was born in 1929. His parents announced that he was the *jagadguru*, which is apparently like a messiah, okay? The World Teacher. Theosophical stuff. There was a guy he was named for, named Jiddu Krishnamurti, who was supposed to be it, but he shined the job on in '28. He got tired of the spirit world, he said, seeing ghosts crowding up the beaches all the time. Great stuff, hm? But *our* Jiddu, the one born a year later, didn't work out too well. When he was twenty, he got arrested for having burglarized the old house of Henry Ford, who had died two years earlier. The Ford executors hushed it up, but apparently Jiddu got away with a glass test tube. The Ford people hoked up another one to replace it, and nowadays the fake is on display in the Ford Museum in Greenfield Village in Michigan."

DeLarava's heart was pounding, and tears were again leaking out of her eyes. "Fake of . . . what?"

"It's supposed to contain Edison's last breath."

"*Edison?*" My God, deLarava thought, no wonder the psychic gain is cranked up so high around here since Monday! No wonder Apie is coming out of the sea, and every ghost in town needs only a sneeze to set it frolicking. I *guessed* that the Monday-night torture-murder wasn't a coincidence, and that the kid had run away with *someone* heavy—but *Edison!*

"Yeah," said Ayres blandly, "the guy that invented the lightbulb. Anyway, Jiddu married a rich Indian woman who was also into this spiritual stuff, and they seem to have formed a sort of splinter cult of their own, just the two of them. They bought the house in Beverly Hills, where they were killed Monday night. The police are aware of the place—they've had to answer a lot of complaints from the Parganases and their neighbors. A lot of drunks and bums used to come around demanding to talk to somebody named *Dante* or *Don Tay.*"

"That would have been the mask," said deLarava softly. "They kept it in a hollowed-out copy of *The Divine Comedy* or something." She waved at Ayres. "Never mind. Go on."

"Some comedy. Their kid, this Koot Hoomie that you're looking for, was born in '81. His teachers say that he was okay, considering that his parents were trying to raise him to be some kind of Hindoo holy man. Have you got any calls?"

"Hundreds," she said. "People have grabbed every stray kid in L.A. except Koot Hoomie Parganas." She thought of the boy out there in the alleys and parking lots somewhere, eating out of Dumpsters and sleeping all alone under hedges . . . and last night's dream came back to her, forcefully.

She was crying again. "I've got to get some air," she said, blundering up out of her chair. "Tell Joey Webb to keep looking—and tell him to keep an eye on the *canals.*"

The sea was too full of imagined ghosts, waked up and opposing her, and the carpeted corridors and long splendid galleries seemed suddenly bristly with hostile ectoplasm accumulated like nicotine stains over the decades, so she fled to the Windsor Salon on R Deck.

She liked the Windsor Salon because it had *hanging chandeliers*, not the lights-on-columns that stood everywhere else in the ship, big Art Deco mushrooms with glowing mica-shade caps. The Windsor Salon had been built after the *Queen Mary* had been permanently moored in Long Beach, had in fact been built in the space of one of the now-useless funnels, and so it could afford the luxury of ceiling lights that would have swung and broken if the ship had been out at sea.

No parties of tourists were being shown through the room at the moment, so she collapsed into one of the convention-hotel chairs and buried her face in her hands.

She had dreamed of a group of little girls who were

camping out on a dark plain. At first, they had played games around the small fire they had kindled up—a make-believe tea party, charades, hopscotch on lines toed across the gray dust—but then the noises from the darkness beyond the ring of firelight had made them huddle together. Roars and shouts of subhuman fury had echoed from unseen hills, and the drumbeat of racing hooves and the hard flutter of flags had shaken in the cold wind.

Perhaps the girls had gathered together in this always-dark wasteland because they all had the same name—Kelley. They had formed a ring now, holding hands to contain their campfire and chattering with tearful, nervous, false cheer, until one of the girls noticed that her companions weren't real—they were all just mirrors set up closely together in the dirt, reflecting back to her own pale, dirt-smeared face.

And her sudden terror made the face change—the nose was turned up, and became fleshier, the skin around the eyes became pouched and coarse, and the chin receded away, leaving the mouth a long, grinning slit. Kelley had known what this was. She was turning into a pig.

Loretta had driven herself up out of the well of sleep then, and discovered that she was kneeling on the tile floor of the little bathroom, crouching over the toilet and calling down, down, down into the dark so that Kelley might find her way back up out of the deep hole she'd fallen into.

There were no parking lines painted on the weathered

checkerboard of cracked concrete and asphalt behind the apartment building, so Sullivan just parked the van in the shade of a big shaggy old carob tree. He dug around among the faded papers on the dashboard until he found Houdini's thumb, unpleasantly spitty and dusty now, and then he groped below the passenger seat and retrieved the Bull Durham sack and pushed the thumb back into it.

With the sack in his shirt pocket and his gun snugged in under his belt, he pushed open the door and stepped down onto the broken pavement. Green carob pods were scattered under the overhanging tree branches, and he could see the little V-shaped cuts in the pods where early-morning wild parrots had bitten out the seeds.

This would be the sixth apartment building he checked out. When he had come down off the freeway at Seventh Street in Long Beach, he had quickly confirmed his suspicion that motels never had garages, and then he'd driven around randomly through the run-down residential streets west of Pacific and south of Fourth, looking for rental signs.

He had stopped and looked at five places already, and, no doubt because of his stated preference for paying in cash, only a couple of the landlords had seemed concerned about his murky, out-of-state, unverifiable references. He thought he would probably take the last one he had looked at, a seven-hundred-dollar-a-month studio apartment in a shabby complex on Cerritos Avenue, but he had decided to look at a few more before laying out his money.

He was down on Twenty-First Place now, right next to

Bluff Park and only half a block from the harbor shore, and he had just decided that any of these beachfront rentals would be too expensive when he had driven past this rambling old officelike structure. He wouldn't even have thought it was an apartment building if it hadn't had an APT FOR RENT sign propped above the row of black metal mailboxes. It looked promisingly low-rent.

Sullivan walked across the pavement now toward the back side of the building, and soon he was scuffing on plain packed dirt. Along the building's back wall, between two windowless doors, someone had set up a row of bookcases, on which sat dozens of mismatched pots with dry plants curling out of them, and off to his left plastic chairs sat around a claw-footed iron bathtub that had been made into a table by having a piece of plywood laid over it. He stared at the doors and wondered if he should just knock at one of them.

He jumped; and then, "Who parked all cattywampus?" came a hoarse call from behind him.

Sullivan turned around and saw a fat, bald-headed old man in plastic sandals limping across the asphalt from around the street-side corner of the building. The man wore no shirt at all, and his suntanned belly overhung the wide-legged shorts that flapped around his skinny legs.

"Are you talking about my van?" asked Sullivan.

"Well, if that's your van," the old man said weakly; he inhaled and then went on, "then I guess I'm talking about it." Again he rasped air into his lungs. "Ya damn bird-brain."

"I'm here to speak to the manager of these apartments," Sullivan said stiffly.

"I'm the manager. My name's Mr. Shadroe."

Sullivan stared at him. "You are?" He was afraid this might be just some bum making fun of him. "Well, I want to rent an apartment."

"I don't *need* to . . . *rent* an apartment." Shadroe waved at the van. "If that leaks oil, you'll have to . . . park it on the street." The old man's face was shiny with sweat, but somehow he smelled spicy, like cinnamon.

"It doesn't leak oil," Sullivan said. "I'm looking for an apartment in this area; how much is the one you've got?"

"You on SDI or some—kinda methadone treatment? I won't take you if you are, and I—don't care if it's legal for me to say so. And I won't have children here."

"None of those things," Sullivan assured him. "And if I decide I want the place, I can pay you right now, first and last month's rent, in cash."

"That's illegal, too. The first and last. Gotta call the last month's rent a *deposit* nowadays. But I'll take it. Six hundred a month, utilities are included . . . 'cause the whole building's on one bill. That's twelve hundred, plus a *real* deposit of . . . three hundred dollars. Fifteen hundred, altogether. Let's go into my office and I can . . . give you a receipt and the key." Talking seemed to be an effort for the man, and Sullivan wondered if he was asthmatic or had emphysema.

Shadroe had already turned away toward one of the two doors, and Sullivan stepped after him. "I'd," he said laughing in spite of himself, "I'd like to see the place first."

Shadroe had fished a huge, bristling key chain from his shorts pocket and was unlocking the door. "It's got a new refrigerator—in it, I hooked it up myself yesterday. I do all my—own electrical and plumbing. What do you do?"

"Do? Oh, I'm a bartender." Sullivan had heard that bartenders tended to be reliable tenants.

Shadroe had pushed the door open, and now waved Sullivan toward the dark interior. "That's honest work, boy," he said. "You don't need to be ashamed."

"Thanks."

Sullivan followed him into a long, narrow room dimly lit by foliage-blocked windows. A battered couch sat against one of the long walls and a desk stood across from it under the windows; over the couch were rows of bookshelves like the ones outside, empty except for stacks of old *People* magazines and, on the top shelf, three water-stained pink stuffed toys. A television set was humming faintly on a table, though its screen was black.

Shadroe pulled out the desk chair and sat down heavily. "Here's a rental agreement," he said, tugging a sheet of paper out of a stack. "No pets either. What are those shoes? Army-man shoes?"

Sullivan was wearing the standard shoes worn by tramp electricians, black leather with steel-reinforced toes. "Just work shoes," he said, puzzled. "Good for standing in," he added, feeling like an idiot.

"They gotta go. I got wood floors, and you'll be boomin' around all night—nobody get any sleep—I get complaints about it. Get yourself some *Wallabees*," he said with a look of pained earnestness. "The soles are *foam rubber*."

The rental agreement was a Xerox copy, and the bottom half of it hadn't printed clearly. Shadroe began laboriously filling in the missing paragraphs in ink.

Sullivan just sat helplessly and watched the old man squint and frown as his spotty brown hand worked the pen heavily across the paper.

The old man's cinnamon smell was stronger in here, and staler. The room was silent except for the scratching of the pen and the faint hum of the television-set, and Sullivan's hairline was suddenly damp with sweat.

He found himself thinking of the containment areas of nuclear-generating plants, where the pressure was kept slightly below normal to keep radioactive dust from escaping; and of computer labs kept under higher-than-normal pressure to keep ordinary dust out. Some pressure was wrong in this dingy office.

I don't want to stay here, he thought. I'm not *going* to stay here.

"While you're doing that," he said unsteadily, "I might go outside and look around at the place."

"I'll be done here. In a second."

"No, really, I'll be right outside."

Sullivan walked carefully to the door and stepped out into the sunlight, and then he hurried across the patchwork pavement to his van, taking deep breaths of the clean sea air.

That apartment back up on Cerritos looks good, he told himself. (This place is only half a block from the beach, and I could probably see the *Queen Mary* across the water from the cul-de-sac right beyond the driveway, but) I certainly couldn't count on getting anything done here, not with this terrible Shadroe guy blundering around.

He unlocked the van door, carefully so as not to touch the drying egg-smear, and climbed in. Mr. Shadroe was probably still sitting back there in the office, carefully writing out the missing paragraphs of the rental agreement; not even breathing as his clumsy fingers worked the pen.

Sullivan pulled the door closed, but paused with the key halfway extended toward the ignition. The man hadn't been breathing.

Shadroe had *inhaled* a number of times, in order to talk, but he had not been breathing. Sullivan was suddenly, viscerally sure that that was what had so upset him in there—he had been standing next to a walking vapor lock, the pressure of a living soul in the vacuum of a dead body.

What are you telling me? he asked himself. That Mr. Shadroe is a *dead* guy? If so, I should *definitely* get out of here, fast, before some shock causes him to throw stress-shells, and his overdrawn lifeline collapses and he goes off like a goddamn firebomb, like the patient at Elizalde's Día del Muerte séance.

Still uncomfortable with the idea, he put the key into the ignition.

Shadroe could be alive, he thought—he could just have been breathing very low, very quietly. Oh yeah? he answered himself immediately. When he inhaled in order to *speak,* it sounded like somebody dragging a tree branch through a mail slot.

Maybe he's just one of the old solidified ghosts, a man-shaped pile of animated litter, who drifted down here to be near the ocean, as Elizalde in her interview, unaware of how literally she was speaking, noted that the poor old creatures like to do. (*"Tide pools seem to be the best, actually, in eliciting the meditation that brings the old spirits to the surface . . .*") But Shadroe didn't quite talk crazily enough, and a ghost wouldn't be able to deal with the paperwork of running an apartment building; collecting rents, paying taxes and license and utility bills.

Okay, so what if he *is* one of the rare people who can continue to occupy and operate their bodies after they've died? What's it to me?

Sullivan twisted the key, and the engine started right up, without even a touch of his foot on the gas pedal.

I wonder how long he's been dead, he thought. If his death was recent, like during the last day or so, he probably hasn't even noticed it himself yet; but if he's been hanging on for a while, he must have figured out measures to avoid the collapse: he must not ever sleep, for example, and I'll bet he spends a lot of time out on the ocean.

("*. . . patients seem to find their ghosts more accessible in the shallow depths of actual ocean water. It's been worth field trips.*")

He didn't want to think, right now, about what Elizalde had said in the interview.

What would that blind witch on the Honda see, he wondered instead, if she were to come around here? With a dead guy up and walking around all over this building and grounds, insulting people's vehicles and shoes, this whole place must look like a patch of dry rot, psychically.

This place *would* be good cover.

And the location is perfect for me. And six hundred a month, with utilities included—and a new refrigerator!—is pretty good.

Sullivan sighed, and switched off the engine and got out of the van. When he had walked back across the yard and stepped into the office, Shadroe was still at work on the rental agreement. Sullivan sat down on the couch to wait, stoically enduring the psychically stressed atmosphere.

(*"Eventually I'd like to move my clinic to some location on the beach—not to where there's surf, you see, but pools of ordered, quieted seawater."*)

"If you'll take cash right now," he said unsteadily, "I'd like to start moving my stuff in this afternoon."

"If you right now got the time," said Shadroe, without looking up. "I right now got the key."

Sullivan had the time. He was suddenly in no hurry to go find Angelica Anthem Elizalde, for he was pretty sure that he knew where she would be.

At the canals at Venice Beach.

CHAPTER 28

"*I can't go no lower,*" *said the Hatter.* "*I'm on the floor, as it is.*"

—Lewis Carroll,
Alice's Adventures in Wonderland

SITTING IN A BUS SEAT by a sunny window, warmed by the noon glare through the glass and by the oversized fleece-lined denim jacket he had bought at a thrift store on Slauson, Kootie was too sleepy and comfortable to worry. He was sure that the last two days and three nights had aged his face way beyond that picture on the billboards, and, especially with the sunglasses, he was sure he must look like a teenager. The denim jacket even smelled like stale beer.

Keeping his face maturely expressionless, he cocked an eyebrow out the window at the *pollo* stands and the 1950's futuristic car washes along Crenshaw Boulevard. He would be transferring at Manchester to catch another RTD bus to the Dockweiler State Beach at Playa del Rey.

The boy had awakened at dawn, his eyes already open and stinging in the ancient paint fumes in the abandoned car, and he had recognized the stiff drop cloth under his chin, and the split and faded dashboard in front of him; he had clearly remembered breaking the wind-wing window the night before, and opening the door and climbing in.

But he hadn't recognized the city dimly visible beyond the dusty windshield this morning.

Cables and wires were strung so densely against the sky overhead that for one sleepy moment he had thought he was under some kind of war-surplus submarine-catching net; then he had seen that the wires were higher than he had thought, and separate, strung haphazardly from telegraph poles and bulky insulators on the high roofs of all the old buildings. And even through the grime on the glass he could see that they *were* old buildings—imposing brick structures with arched windows at the top and jutting cornices.

He knew he'd have to prove himself here, in spite of being virtually broke and so terribly young—here in Boston, his first *big city*—

Boston?

He reached a hand out from under the drop cloth and opened the door. It squeaked out on its rusty hinges and let in a gust of fresh morning air that smelled distantly of what he knew must be coal smoke and horse manure—and then Kootie was glad he was sitting down, for he was suddenly so dizzy that he grabbed the edge of the seat.

"You're," croaked his own voice, "don't tell me—Kootie." After a moment he said, voluntarily, "Right."

Then his voice went on, thickly, "I was dreaming. This isn't Boston, is it? Nor New Jersey yet. It's . . . Los Angeles." His eyes closed and his hands came up and rubbed his eye sockets. "Sorry," said his voice as his right hand sprang away from the painful swelling around his right eye.

When he looked around again, it was typical backstreet Los Angeles that he saw and smelled around him: low stuccoed buildings and palm trees, and the smells of diesel exhaust and gardenias; above a three-story building a couple of blocks away, crows were diving over the condenser fans of a big rooftop air conditioner shed and then lofting up on the hot air drafts, over and over again. Only a few wires drooped overhead from the telephone poles.

The night air had been cold, and Kootie's nose was stuffed—after he sniffed, his jammed-up sinuses emitted an almost ultrasonic *wheee,* like the flash attachment on a camera recharging.

"All this running around is doing you no good at all, son," Edison had croaked then. "And I'm not getting any fresher out here. To hell with New Jersey. Let's get to the sea. I'll be able to just go into the seawater, safely, and be gone; and you'll be free of me, free to go be a normal boy."

Kootie had not said anything then, as he climbed stiffly out of the car, stretched as well as he could with the heavy I-ON-A-CO cable belt constricting his waist, and limped toward the lot fence; but he thought the old Edison ghost could probably tell that Kootie didn't want to lose him.

"Where will I go?" asked Kootie softly now as he

clambered painfully down the steps of the bus exit and hopped to the Manchester sidewalk. "I'll need money."

All at once, into the muted early-afternoon air, *"You're young!"* shouted Edison with Kootie's shrill voice. "You're still *alive!* You can send and receive as fast as any of them!" Kootie was hobbling away from the bus stop as quickly as he could, not looking at any of the faces around him, his own face burning with embarrassed horror and all feelings of maturity completely blown away.

He caught a breath and choked out, "Shut up!"—but Edison used the rest of the breath to yell, "Skedaddle to the Boston office of Western Union! I've got to get to New Jersey anyway, to pick up my diploma!" Kootie was sweating now in the chilly breeze, and he had clenched his teeth against his own squawking voice, but Edison kept yelling anyway: "The usual job! Napping during night work, with the ghost repellers popping and the gizmo sending your sixing signals on the hour!"

Kootie tried to shout *Be quiet!* but Edison was trying to say something more, and the resulting scream was something like *"Baklava!"* (which was a kind of pastry Kootie's parents had sometimes brought home for him).

Kootie was just crying and running blindly in despair now, blundering against pedestrians and light poles, and he wasn't aware of slapping footsteps behind him until a pair of hands clasped his shoulders and yanked him back to a stop.

"Kid," said a man's concerned voice, "what's the matter? Was somebody *bothering* you? Where do you live? My wife and I can drive you home."

Kootie turned into the man's arms and sobbed against

a wool sweater. "The beach," he hiccupped. "The police—
I don't know where I've got to go. I'm lost, mister."
Blessedly, Edison seemed to have withdrawn.

"Well, you're okay now, I promise. I hopped out of our
car at the light when I saw you running—my wife is
driving around the block. Let's go back and catch her at
the corner, away from all these people here."

Kootie was happy to do as the man said. Several of the
people behind him on the corner were laughing, and
somebody called out a filthy suggestion about what he
should do once he had skedaddled to New Jersey and
picked up his "*dip*shit *dip*loma." It horrified Kootie to
think that adults could be the same as kids; and now even
Edison was drunk or had gone crazy or something.

As he walked along quickly beside the man who had
stopped him, Kootie looked up at his rescuer. The man
had short blond hair and round, wire-rim glasses, and he
looked tanned and fit, as if he played tennis. He still had
one hand on Kootie's right shoulder, and Kootie reached
up and clasped the man's wrist.

"Here she is, kid," the man said kindly as a shiny new
teal-blue minivan came nosing up to the Manchester
curb. "Are you hungry? We can stop for a bite to eat if you
like."

The passenger door had swung open, and a dark-haired
young woman in shorts had one knee up and was leaning
across the seat and smiling uncertainly. "Well, hi there,
kiddo," she said as Kootie let go of the man's wrist and
hurried to the minivan.

"Hi, ma'am," Kootie said, pausing humbly on the curb.
"Your husband said you could give me a ride."

She laughed. "Hop in then."

Kootie hiked himself up, and then climbed around the console to crouch behind the passenger seat as the man got in and closed the door. The interior of the minivan smelled like a new pair of dress shoes straight out of the Buster Brown box.

"Let's head toward the 405, Eleanor," the man said, "just to get moving. And if you see a Denny's—did you want something to eat, uh, young man?" The minivan started forward, and Kootie sat down on the blue-carpeted floor.

"My name's Koot Hoomie," he said breathlessly, having decided to trust these people. "I'm called Kootie. Yes, please, about eating—but some kind of takeout would be better. I get screaming fits sometimes. You saw. It's not like I'm crazy, or anything." He tried to remember the name of the ailment that made some people yell terrible things, but couldn't. All he could think of was *Failure to Thrive,* which an infant cousin of his had reportedly died of. Kootie probably had that too. "It's that syndrome," he finished lamely.

"Tourette's, probably," the man said. "I'm Bill Fussel, and this is my wife, Eleanor. Have you had any sleep, Kootie? There are blankets back there."

"No thanks," said Kootie absently. "I slept in an old car last night." Get to the beach, he thought; let crazy Edison jump into the sea, and then these nice people can adopt me. "Can we go to the beach? Any beach. I want to . . . wade out in the water, I guess." He tried to think of a plausible reason for it, and decided that anything he came up with would sound like a kid lie. Then, "My parents died

Monday night," he found himself saying to the back of Mr. Fussel's head. "In our religion, it's a purifying ritual. We're Hindus."

He had no idea whether it had been Edison or himself that had said it, nor if any of it was true. I suppose we might have been Hindus, he thought. In school I always just put down *Protestant*.

"A beach?" said Mr. Fussel. "I guess we could go out to Hermosa or Redondo. Elly, why don't we stop somewhere and you can call your mom and let her know we'll be a little late."

For a moment no one spoke, and the quiet burr of the engine was the only sound inside the minivan.

"Okay," said Mrs. Fussel.

"Where does your mom live?" asked Kootie, again not sure it was himself who had spoken.

"Riverside," said Mrs. Fussel quickly.

"Where in Riverside? I used to live there."

"Lamppost and Riverside Drive," Mrs. Fussel said, and Kootie saw her dart a harried glance at her husband.

Now Kootie knew it was Edison speaking for him, for with no intention at all, he found himself saying, "There are no such streets in Riverside." Kootie didn't know if there were or not, and certainly Edison didn't either. *Why are you being rude?* he thought hard at the Edison ghost in his mind.

"I guess she knows where her mother lives," Mr. Fussel began in a stern voice, but Kootie was interrupting.

"Very well, name for me any five big streets in Riverside."

"We don't go there a lot—" said Mrs. Fussel weakly.

I'm concerned with; what if we have an accident driving? We're both upset—"

"An accident? I won't have an accident. They can—"

"They're bringing *cash,* El! We can't expect them to be driving all over L.A. with that kind of cash, in these kinds of neighborhoods!"

"You're worried about *them!* They killed his—"

The minivan shook as something collided gently but firmly with the rear end, and then there were simultaneous knocks against the driver's and passenger's windows. Even from the back seat, Kootie could see the blunt metal cylinders of silencers through the glass.

That wasn't ten minutes, thought Kootie.

A voice spoke quietly from outside. "Roll down the windows right now or we'll kill you both."

Both of the Fussels hastily pressed buttons on their armrests, and the windows buzzed down.

"The boy's in the back seat," Mr. Fussel said eagerly.

A hand came in through the open window and pushed Mr. Fussel's head aside, and then a stranger peered in. Behind mirror sunglasses and a drooping mustache, he was nothing more than a pale, narrow face.

"He's taped in," the face noted. "Good. You two get out."

"Sure," Mr. Fussel said. "Come on, El, get out. You guys are gonna take the van? Fine! We won't report it stolen until—what, tomorrow? Would that be okay? Is the money in something we can carry inconspicuously?"

The face had withdrawn, but Kootie heard the voice say, "You'll have no problems with it."

Mrs. Fussel was sobbing quietly. "Bill, you idiot," she

said, but she opened her door and got out at the same time her husband did.

A fat man in a green turtleneck sweater got in where she had been, and the man with the mirror sunglasses got in on the passenger side. The doors were pulled closed, and the minivan rocked as the obstruction was moved from behind it, and then the fat man had put the engine into reverse and was backing out. He glanced incuriously at Kootie.

"Check the tape on the kid," he said to his companion.

When the man in the sunglasses stepped into the back of the van, Kootie didn't make any noises, but tried to catch his eye. The man just tugged at the seat belt, though, and then found the roll of tape and bound Kootie's ankles together and taped them sideways to the seat leg, without looking at Kootie's face.

Somehow Kootie was still just tense, no more than if he were one of only a couple of kids left standing at a spelling bee. After the man had returned to the front seat and fastened his seat belt, Kootie wondered what had happened to the Fussels. He supposed that they were dead already, shot behind some Dumpster. It was easy for him to avoid picturing the two of them. He looked at the backs of his captors' heads and tried to figure out who the two men could be. They didn't look like associates of the raggedy one-armed man.

Kootie was surprised, and cautiously pleased, with his own coolness in this scary situation . . . until he realized that it was based on a confidence that Thomas Alva Edison would think of some way to get him out of it; then he remembered that Edison seemed to have gone crazy, and in a few minutes tears of pure fright were rolling warmly along the top edges of the duct tape on Kootie's cheeks as the minivan rocked through traffic.

They may not mean to kill me, he thought. Certainly not yet. Our destination might be miles from here, and—

He tried to think of any other comforting thoughts.

—And there'll probably be a lot of traffic lights, he told himself forlornly.

CHAPTER 29

✺

*"I don't like the look of it at all," said the King;
"however, it may kiss my hand, if it likes."*
—Lewis Carroll,
Alice's Adventures in Wonderland

SULLIVAN had driven up the 405 past LAX airport, past one of the government-sanctioned freeway-side murals (this one portraying a lot of gigantic self-righteous-looking joggers that made him think better of the fugitive graffiti taggers with their crude territory markers), and then he followed the empty new sunlit lanes of the 90 freeway out to where it came down and narrowed and became a surface street, Lincoln Boulevard, among new condominium buildings and old used-camper lots.

The plaster hands were on the passenger seat and the Bull Durham sack was in his shirt pocket, above the sun-and-body-heated bulk of his .45 in the canvas fanny pack. He had bought a triple-A map at a gas station and studied it hard, and he had only nerved himself up to come to Venice by vowing to stay entirely out of sight of the ocean.

The canals, thin blue lines on the map, were only half a fingernail inland from the black line that indicated the shore, and it was in the surf off this little stretch of beach that his father had drowned in '59—and it was from there that he and Sukie had fled in '86, leaving Loretta deLarava in possession of their father's wallet and keys and the three cans of . . .

Nothing looked familiar, for he had been here only that one time, in '86. He managed to miss North Venice Boulevard, and had to loop back through narrow streets where summer rental houses crowded right up to the curbs, and parked cars left hardly any room for traffic, and then when he came upon North Venice again he saw that it was a one-way street aimed straight out at the now-near ocean; and though he was ready to just put the van in reverse and honk his way backward a couple of blocks, he saw a stretch of empty curb right around the corner of North Venice and Pacific, and he was able to pull in and park without having to focus past the back bumper of the Volkswagen in the space ahead of him.

He didn't want to be Peter Sullivan here at all, even if nobody was looking for him—presumably his father's ghost was in the sea only a block away, and that was enough of a presence to shame him into assuming every shred of disguise possible.

So he tied an old bandanna around the plaster hands and took them with him when he got out and locked the van. The sea breeze had cleared the coastal sky of smog, but it was chilly, and he was glad of his old leather flight jacket.

Two quarters in the parking meter bought him an

hour's worth of time, and he turned his back on the soft boom of the surf and stalked across Pacific with the hands clamped against his ribs and his hands jammed in his pockets. The plaster hands were heavy, but at a 7-Eleven store an hour ago, he had bought six lightbulbs and stuffed them into his jacket pockets, and he didn't want to risk breaking any of them by shifting the awkward bundle under his arm. He stepped carefully up the high curb at the north side of Pacific.

Almost there anyway, he told himself as he peered ahead.

He was in a wide, raised parking lot between the North and South Venice Boulevards, and past the far curb of South, just this side of a windowless gray cement building, he could see a railing paralleling the street, and another that slanted away down, out of sight. There was a gap there between rows of buildings, and it clearly wasn't a street.

He crossed the parking lot and hobbled stiffly across South Venice, and when he had got to the railing and the top of the descending walkway, he stopped. He had found the westernmost of the canals, and he was relieved to see that it didn't look familiar at all.

Below him, fifty feet across and stretching straight away to an arched bridge in the middle distance, the water was still, reflecting the eucalyptus and bamboo and lime trees along the banks. The canal walls were yard-high brickworks of slate-gray half-moons below empty sidewalks, and the houses set back from the water looked tranquil in the faintly brassy October sunlight. He could see a broad side-channel in the east bank a block ahead, but this ramp from South Venice led down to the west bank, and apparently the only way to walk along that side-canal would be to go past it on this side, cross the bridge, and then come back.

By the time he had walked halfway down the ramp toward the canal-bank level, he had left behind the gasping sea breeze and all of the sounds of the beach-city traffic, and all he could hear was bees in the bushes and wind chimes and a distant grumbling of ducks.

He had never cared to read up on this particular seaside town, but from things people had said over the years he had gathered that it had been built in the first years of the century as a mock-up of the original Italian Venice; the canals had been more extensive then, and there had even been gliding gondolas poled by gondoliers with Italian accents. The notion hadn't caught on, though, and the place had fallen into decrepitude, and in the years after World War II it had been a seedy, shacky, beatnik colony, with rocking oil pumps between the houses on the banks of the stagnating canals.

He was walking along the sidewalk now, and he'd gone far enough so that he could look down the cross canal. Another footbridge arched over the blue-sky-reflecting water in that direction, framed by tall palm trees, and a solider-looking bridge farther down looked as though it could accommodate cars.

City-planning types had moved to have the canals filled in, but the residents had protested effectively, and the canals were saved. The neat brickwork of the banks was clearly a modern addition, and many of the houses had the stucco anonymity or the custom Tudor look of new buildings, though there were still dozens of the old, comfortably weather-beaten California bungalow-style houses set in among ancient untrimmed palm trees and overhanging shingle roofs.

Two women and a collie were walking toward him along the sidewalk he was on, and though neither of the women looked particularly like the pictures he'd seen of Elizalde, he dug with his free hand into the pocket of his jacket and pulled out one of the lightbulbs and the paper 7-Eleven bag.

Sullivan noticed a brown plastic owl on a fence post, and it reminded him that he had seen another one on a roof peak behind him. Ahead, now, he spied still another, swinging on a string from a tree branch. And he could hear several sets of jangling wind chimes—maybe Elizalde was right about ghosts being drawn to places like this, and the residents had set out these things as scarecrows. Scare-ghosts.

"Afternoon," he said as he passed the ladies and the dog.

When they were behind him he slid the lightbulb into the bag and crouched over the pavement. He glanced back at the two women, and then swung the bag in an arc onto the cement, popping the bulb.

Both of the women jumped in surprise—*right after* the noise.

"Excuse me," he said sheepishly, nodding and waving at them.

He straightened and kept walking, tucking the jingling bag back into his pocket.

The white-painted wooden footbridge was steep, and

he paused at the crest to shift the Houdini hands to his left side. He was sweating, and wishing now that he'd left the things in the van.

The water below him was clear, and he could see rocks in it but no fish. There had been fish—

He was halfway up the sidewalk of the branch canal, staring at a bleached steer skull on the wall of an old wooden house (another scare-ghost!), and he had no recollection of having descended from the bridge or walking this far up.

Aside from the two women he had seen, who had since disappeared, there seemed to be no one out walking along the canals this afternoon. He looked around. Even the houses all seemed to have been evacuated—he hadn't even seen a cat. (His heart was knocking inside his chest.) The water was too still, the houses by the canal were too low, crouching under the tall legs of the palm trunks, and the silence wasn't *nice* anymore—it was the silence of a dark yard when all the crickets suddenly stop chirping at once.

Elizalde wasn't here, and he didn't want to meet whatever might be.

Without noticing it, he had already passed the footbridge on this canal branch, but the wider bridge was still ahead of him, and as he started toward it he saw a car mount it from the islanded side, pause at the crest, and then nose down the far slope—slowly, for the arch was so steep that the driver couldn't be able to see the pavement ahead of him.

Just A.O.P., dude, Sullivan thought.

He was clutching the plaster hands with both of his

own hands as he walked now, and it was all he could do not to break into a run. He didn't look back to make sure nothing was crawling out of the canal behind him, because he was sure that if he did, he would have to *keep on* looking back as he fled this place, would have to *walk backward* toward the bridge that led away to the normal city channels that were asphalt and not water, and something would manifest itself ahead of him, and then just wait for him to back into it.

His eyebrows itched with sweat, and he was breathing fast and shallow.

This is just a funk, he thought, a fit of nerves. There are other canals here *(Are there?)* and Elizalde might be on the sidewalk of the next one over, or the one beyond that; she might be stark naked and waving her arms and riding a goddamn *unicycle*, but you won't see her because you're panicking here.

So be it. She couldn't have helped me anyway. I'll find *some other* way to warn my father's ghost (this trip out here was an idiotic long shot) after I drive out of this damned town and find a place to relax and chug a couple of fast, cold beers.

His right shoulder was brushing against vines and bricks as he strode toward the bridge, and he realized that he was crowding the fences of the houses, avoiding the bank—horrified, in fact, at the thought of falling into the shallow water.

The way all sounds echo like metallic groans underwater.

He must have just dropped the plaster hands. He was running, and his unimpeded hands were clenched into fists, pumping the air as his legs pounded under him. From the shoulder of his jacket he heard a snap, and then another, as if stitches were being broken.

At the foot of the bridge he stopped, and let his breathing slow down. This bridge was part of a street, Dell Street, and he could hear cars sighing past on South Venice Boulevard ahead. Even if something audibly swirled the water of the canal now, he felt that he could sprint and be in the middle of the boulevard before his first squirted tears of fright would have had time to hit the pavement.

With a careful, measured tread he walked up the slope of the bridge, and he paused at the crest. Ahead of him on the right side of the street was the grandest yet of the neo-Tudor buildings, a place with gables and stained-glass windows and an inset tower with antique chimney pots on its shingled funnel roof. He was wondering if it might be a restaurant, with a bar and a men's room, when in the bright stillness he heard something splashing furtively in the water under the bridge.

All he did was exhale all the air out of his lungs, and then rest his hands on the coping of the bridge and look down over the edge.

There was someone crouched down there, beside a small white fiberglass rowboat that had been drawn up onto the gravel slope beside the bridge abutment; the figure was wearing a tan jumpsuit and a many-colored knitted tam that concealed the hair, but Sullivan could see by the flexed curve of the hips and the long legs that it was a woman. Blinking and peering more closely, he saw that the woman wasn't looking at the boat, but at the barred storm drain that the boat was moored to. She was swirling her hand in the water and calling softly through the grating, as if to someone in the tunnel on the other side of the steel bars.

"Frank?" she said. "Frank, don't hide from me."

Sullivan's heart was pounding again, and belatedly he wondered if he had *really* wanted to find this Elizalde woman.

For that had to be who this was. Still, he silently reached up to his coat pocket (the pocket flap felt rough, like cloth instead of leather) and fished out a lightbulb. Holding it by the threaded metal base, he swung the glass bulb at the stone coping of the bridge.

"*Yah!*" shouted the woman below, scrambling up and splashing one foot into the water; and the bulb popped against the coping.

She turned a scared glance up at him, and a moment later she had ducked under the bridge, out of his sight.

"Wait!" yelled Sullivan, hurrying down the landward slope of the bridge. "Doctor—" No, he thought, don't yell her last name out here, that won't reassure her. "Angelica!"

She had splashed under the bridge and was back up in the sunlight on the bank on the west side, striding away from him, obviously ready to break into a run at any sound of pursuit. A couple of ducks on the bank hurried into the water, out of her way.

"We can help each other!" he called after her, not stepping down from the bridge onto the sidewalk. "Please, you're trying to get in touch with this Frank guy, and I need to get in touch with my father!" She was still hurrying away, her long legs taking her farther away with every stride. She wouldn't even look back. "Lady," Sullivan yelled in despair, *"I need your help!"*

That at least stopped her, though she still didn't turn around.

He opened his mouth to say something else, but she spoke first, in a low, hoarse voice that carried perfectly to his ears but would probably have been inaudible ten feet back: "Go away. My help is poison."

Here I am in Venice Beach, he thought. "Well, so's mine. Maybe we cancel out."

When she turned around, she was pushing the knitted cap back from her face, and then she rubbed her hand down her forehead and jaw as if she had a headache or was very tired. "You know who I am," she said. "Don't say *your* name here, and don't say mine again." She waved him to silence when he opened his mouth, then went on, "You can follow me to the big parking lot if you like. Don't get close to me."

She walked back, past the foot of the bridge, and started up Dell Street, walking next to the slack-rope fence of the white Tudor house Sullivan had thought was a restaurant. When she had passed it and was halfway to the stop sign at South Venice, he started forward from the bottom of the bridge.

After a few steps, he stopped in confusion and looked down at his own legs.

He was wearing . . . someone else's pants, somehow. Instead of the blue jeans he had pulled on in the gym at City College this morning, he was wearing formal gray wool trousers. With cuffs. He crouched to touch them, and two more snaps popped loose from the sleeve of his coat, and then the sleeve was disattached, hanging down over his hand. The sleeve was wool too—he slapped dizzily at his sides—the whole garment was, and it was a suit coat. He couldn't help looking back to see if his leather jacket might somehow be lying on the bridge behind him. It wasn't.

He pulled the sleeve off with his other hand. The upper edge was hemmed, with metal snaps sewed on. He gripped the cuff of the other sleeve and tugged, and that sleeve came off too, with a popping of snaps. (He noted that he was now wearing a long-sleeved white shirt, no longer the plaid flannel he remembered.) The coat was convertible, it could be worn with the sleeves long or short.

Why, he wondered, would anyone want a short-sleeved formal coat?

Well, it occurred to him, a magician might. To show that he didn't have anything up his sleeves. Houdini was a magician, wasn't he? Maybe I didn't lose the mask after all—maybe I'm wearing it.

He breathed deeply, and watched the ducks paddling out across the water. He was still nervous, but the sense of imposed isolation, of being the only moving thing on a microscope slide, had moved on past him.

He looked at his hands, and in the middle of this dream-logic afternoon he wasn't very surprised, or even very scared, to see (though the sight did speed up his heartbeat) that his hands were different. The fingers were thicker, the nails trimmed rather than bitten, and the thumbs were longer. There were a few small scars on the knuckles, but the scars he remembered were gone.

He lifted the hands and ran the fingers through his hair, and immediately his arms tingled with goose bumps, for his hair felt kinky and wiry, not straight and fine as it normally did. But it was falling back into limp strands as he disordered it, and he could now feel again the constriction of creased leather around his elbows.

When he lowered his arms, he found himself catching the sudden weight of the plaster hands; he gripped them firmly and slung them safely under his left arm. A lightbulb broke with a muffled pop in the pocket of his leather jacket, but he didn't need the lightbulbs anymore.

"Um!" he said loudly, to catch Elizalde's attention. "Hey, lady!"

She stopped and looked back, and his first thought was that she was a much shorter person than he had originally thought. Then he realized that this was a different woman—plumper than Elizalde, and with curly dark hair unconfined by any sort of hat, and wearing a long skirt.

But it had to be Elizalde. "Look at yourself," he said— quickly, for the skirt was already becoming transparent.

The woman looked down at her own legs, which were now again zipped into the tan jumpsuit. And though Sullivan had not blinked nor seen her figure shift at all against the background of pavement and distant buildings, she was taller, as if she had suddenly moved away.

He hurried up the narrow sunlit street toward her, and she let him get within ten feet of her before she stepped back.

"You saw that?" he asked.

Elizalde's olive complexion had gone very pale at some

point in the last minute. She looked at the lumpy bandana Sullivan was carrying. "You're not another damned *ghost*, are you?" she asked.

"No, I'm as alive as you are. Did you see—"

"Yes," she interrupted, "both of us. God, I hate this stuff. Let's not talk until we've got the street between us and the canals."

He followed her as she jaywalked across the one-way inland-bound lanes of South Venice. On the far side she stepped up the curb but then walked on the dirt between the curb and the sidewalk, toward Pacific Avenue. Sullivan followed her lead, stepping over weed clumps and Taco Bell bags and bottles in brown paper bags. *Avoiding marked channels*, he thought.

They walked into the parking lot through a gap in the low wall. A red sign on a pole by the exit read WRONG WAY—STOP—SEVERE TIRE DAMAGE; and someone had crookedly stenciled SMOKE under the STOP.

"There's a canal running under this parking lot," Sullivan ventured to say when they had walked out onto the broad cement face of it, ringed at a distance by light poles and low apartment buildings and shaggy eucalyptus trees in the chilly afternoon sun.

"I can run in any direction from here," said Elizalde shortly; "so can you. And anyway, we're between two oppositely one-way streets, one facing the sea and one away. It should make us hard to fix. And you've got a powerful mask, haven't you? Big enough for two, as we saw."

"Someone . . . *focused* on us back there, didn't they?" said Sullivan. "And the mask came on full strength. Maybe because there *were* two of us, our fields overlapping, there beside your. . . 'stasis of clarity, clarity of stasis'."

Elizalde was sweating. Her jumpsuit was bulky and lumpy, and he realized, belatedly, that she must be wearing another outfit under it. She stared at him. "That's something I said, in that interview in *L.A. Weekly*. Who are you? Quick."

"I'm Peter Sullivan, I'm an electrical engineer and I used to work in film, which might give you some clues. I've been out of town, too, traveling everywhere in the country except California." He was breathless again. "Hiding from all this, from somebody who died. Well, I told you it was my father, didn't I? But this Halloween is—is gonna be a heavy one. I'll tell you frankly, there are people after me; but I'm sure you're smart enough to know that there'll be people looking for you too. I think you and I should work together, pool our resources. I've got this mask. And I've found a safe place to live, a waterfront apartment building that's in a sort of psychic pea-soup fog."

She wasn't looking convinced. Her dark eyes were still narrowed with suspicion and hostility.

"And I know this city real well," he went on lamely.

Her voice was stiff when she answered him. "I, too, am familiar with *Nuestra Señora la Reina de los Angeles*," she said.

I get it, he thought wearily. You're Mexican, you've got a blood-in-the-soil, soil-in-the-blood kinship with the place, and you don't need a gringo sidekick. Our Lady Queen of the Angels, he thought, and it reminded him of the garbled lyrics of one of Sukie's Christmas carols:

Commander Hold-'Em, bone-dry king of angels . . . Death, Sukie had meant, the Grim Reaper. In this kind of crisis, here in L.A., suddenly and very deeply he missed his twin sister, who had gone away with Commander Hold-'Em.

"Lady," he said, almost hopelessly, "I need a partner. I think you do too."

She frowned past him at the cars crossing in both directions over on Pacific Avenue . . . and abruptly he knew that she was going to refuse, politely but firmly, and just go away. Probably she wouldn't come back here, probably she'd go looking for Frank somewhere else, where Sullivan would never find her.

"Don't decide right now," he said hastily. "No, don't even speak. I'll speak. I'll be at Bluff Park in Long Beach tonight at eight. That's wide open, you can drive by in a cab, in a disguise, and if you don't like the look of it you can go right on past, can't you? Or, if you like, you can run away in the meantime, be in San Diego by then, be hiding up a tree somewhere. I'll be at Bluff Park. At eight. Tonight. Goodbye."

He turned his back on her and walked quickly away, toward Pacific and his van and, somewhere not too many minutes distant, some dark bar with a men's room.

O rum key, O ru-um key to O-bliv-ion, he sang in his head.

CHAPTER 30

✦

"How cheerfully he seems to grin,
How neatly spreads his claws,
And welcomes little fishes in,
With gently smiling jaws!"
　　　　　—Lewis Carroll,
Alice's Adventures in Wonderland

BUT I SWALLOWED HIM, thought Kootie dully for the dozenth time.

He was lying awkwardly across the back seat of the van, on his left shoulder, which had gone numb. His whole spine ached every time the van leaned around a corner.

I swallowed him, like the whale swallowed Jonah. (Well, I inhaled him, actually.) But can I throw up the ghost? Cough him out? Or will they really have to cut me open to get it? It's in my head!

At the Music Center yesterday, Edison had said, *They'll kill you and eat me.* Was that really what was going to turn out to be true?

The driver had looped a pair of headphones over his bald scalp, and from time to time he spoke into a tiny microphone that stuck out under his chin. The other man had found KLSX on the radio, and his head was jogging to some old rock song from before Kootie's time.

Kootie was shocked again by their indifference. Were they *used* to driving little boys off to be killed?

All at once his right elbow was pressed painfully into his ribs against the sudden restraint of the seat belt—the minivan was slowing. Kootie discovered that he couldn't sit up again, with his feet tied together to the side post of the seat. He tried to push himself up, but his left arm was as numb and uselessly limp as if it belonged to someone else.

"Low gear, and slow," said the man in the passenger seat, "and keep the wheels dead straight."

"I've driven up a ramp before," said the driver.

A grating clank jarred the minivan. The pressure against Kootie's ribs and right elbow was abruptly gone, and he was rocked back against the seat—the minivan had moved slowly forward, and the front end was mounting some incline; a ramp, apparently. Kootie couldn't see the windshield, but the men's heads were in shadow now, and the interior of the minivan was darker.

"As soon as the front wheels are over the lip, give it a boost, to clear the oil pan—then brake hard as soon as the back wheels are in."

"I've *driven* up a *ramp* before."

The motor gunned briefly and the front end of the minivan dropped, and Kootie was again flung against the taut seat belt.

The driver switched off the engine, ratcheted up the

parking brake, and opened the door—it clunked against something, and the metal echoes told Kootie that the van had been driven up into the back of a truck, like the ambulance in *Die Hard*.

Both of the men climbed out of the Fussels' van, shuffled to the back of the truck, and then Kootie heard them hop down to some pavement. After that, with an abrupt dimming of the already-shadowy light into complete darkness, he heard some heavily clanging metal things tossed inside and the clattering rumble of the sliding back door being pulled down.

Kootie's eyes were wide, and his straining to see something in the pitch blackness only made imaginary rainbow pinwheels spin in his vision.

They could have left me a light, he thought. He was clinging to the sense of the words, for his breathing and his heartbeat were very fast, and (even more than starting to thrash and scream with not any particle of control at all) he was afraid he would wet his pants. *A flashlight left on, I could have paid for the batteries. The van's headlights, they could have jumped the van battery later from the truck battery. A fucking Zippo lighter!—left flaming and wedged in the console somewhere.*

Usually, Kootie was uncomfortable using bad words, but today in this total darkness, he clung to it. *One fucking Zippo lighter,* he thought again. Above the tape, the skin over his cheekbones was cold and stiff with tears.

He waited for Edison to yell at him . . . but he caught nothing from the old man. Perhaps he had deserted Kootie too. Maybe now these men would let him go, if Edison had gone . . . ? Kid stuff nonsense.

The truck's engine started up now—it was louder than the minivan's had been. Through the padded seat under him Kootie felt the jar as the truck was put into gear, and then the whole mobile room was moving forward, with the minivan rocking inside it.

And a moment later, Kootie jumped, for suddenly, silently, there was a dim light in one corner of the truck— outside the minivan, up by its right front bumper, a moving yellow glow. Then he could hear dragging footsteps—heavy, an adult—on the metal floor.

The minivan door was pulled open on that side, and a face leaned in, waveringly lit from below by a flashlight strung to swing around the person's neck. The glittering little eyes were like spitty sunflower seeds stuck onto the white skin under the eyebrows.

"Let me tell you a parable," said the voice Kootie remembered. "A man walking down the road saw another man in a field, holding a live pig upside-down over his head under the branches of an apple tree. 'What are you doing?' asked the first man. 'Feeding apples to my pig,' said the second man. 'Doesn't it take a long time, doing it that way?' asked the first man. And the man in the field said, 'What's time to a pig?' "

Kootie's eyes were wide and he was just moaning into the clotted tape between his jaws. The whole truck seemed to be dropping away into some dark abyss, hopelessly far below the lost sunlit streets of L.A.

Mindlessly, Kootie shouted against the duct tape gag— "*Al! Help me, Al!*"

Sherman Oaks had called the exchange again at 4 p.m.,

and at last the operator had had something to say besides, *Nothing yet, dude.* The man had given Oaks a telephone number and had suggested that he call it at his earliest possible convenience. Oaks used his last quarter to call the number.

"Where are you?" some man asked as soon as Oaks had identified himself. "We got a van and a truck circling each other down in Inglewood, and if they have to drive around much longer, the man says your tithe goes up to fifteen percent."

"I'm at Slauson and Central, by the trainyards," Oaks said.

"Truck'll be there in . . . six or seven minutes. It's an Edison truck, black and orange—"

"*What?*"

"SCE—what we could get quick. Is that a problem? The truck's not stolen; the driver's real Edison, but he's on the network barter, and he was right in the area where they picked up the van. After we talked to him, he just called in Code Seven or something."

Oaks groped to find a reason for his inordinate dismay, and found one. "I need a big boxy truck, with ramps, that you can drive a car into! I've got no use for some damn boom or crane thing—" He was working up genuine outrage now. This *was* wrong. "I'll pay no tithe at *all* for some damn—"

"Jeez, man, this is the kind you want. Edison's got all kinds of vehicles, not just those repair things."

". . . Oh," said Oaks, feeling like a cloud chamber in which the vacuum had just been violated, so that rain was condensing inside. "Okay. It's just that . . ."

"Sure. Now listen, there's a gun in the back of the truck, along with the stuff you asked for. The driver insisted that this scenario be set up so it could look like a hijacking if anything goes wrong, okay? Don't touch the gun, it's got smeary untraceable fingerprints on it right now."

"But there *is* a knife there, too? I need a knife—" I can't kill the boy with a noisy *gun*, Oaks thought.

"Your knife's there too. Try to relax, will you? Get in touch with your Inner Child." The line went dead, and Oaks hung up.

He took a deep breath and let it out slowly, trying not to hear the shrill voices in the exhalation.

Outer child you mean, he thought—it's the Inner Old Man I want to . . . *get in touch* with.

In an *Edison* truck! The shudder that accompanied the thought bewildered him.

He bent and with his one hand picked up the cardboard box at his feet, then stepped away from the pay telephone to let one of the impatient crack cocaine dealers get to it.

The box rattled in his hand. Tithe, he thought bitterly. It's like taxing waitresses' tips—the man taking the cut can be trusted to overestimate the actual take. In the box, Oaks had packed ten little glass vials, which was supposed to represent a tenth of the garden-fresh ghosts he would collect during the upcoming month. He had brought it along in advance this way to "show humble."

He had stuck each vial into a condom. Obstadt had probably never seen the raw product before, and he would doubtless imagine that this eccentric packaging was standard in the trade. Nine of the vials were in Ramses condoms, but one was in a Trojan.

Safe sexorcism. The Trojan hearse. Oaks had no intention of paying any more tithe. If Obstadt was still just a dilettante, well, he could take up an interest in fine wines or something; if by this time he was actually riding piggyback on the Maduro Man, though, he would be in the same jam that Oaks had been in in 1929.

(This morning Oaks had begun to remember events from before 1989, and he had concluded that he was a good deal older than he had thought.)

After hurriedly gathering up the thousand smokes and handing them over to one of Obstadt's men, and then packing up these ten, he had had only four unlabeled ones left to inhale himself: four miserable, vicious, short-lived gang boys, as luck would have it, the sort of bottled lives he ordinarily disdained as *pieces a shit.* They hadn't done much to hold back the tumultuous army of the Bony Express, clamoring and shouting in Oaks's head.

In the turbulence, old memories were being shaken free of the riverbed of his mind, and wobbling up to the surface *(like the unsavory old corpse that had bobbed up in the Yarra River in Melbourne in 1910, right after the manacled Harry Houdini had been dropped into the river for one of his celebrated escapes; and it had been a natural, if distasteful, mistake to pounce on the ragged old thing, imagining that it was Houdini freshly dead at last).*

He remembered living in Los Angeles in the 1920s, when neon lighting was so new and exotic that its ethereal colored glow was mainly used to decorate innovative churches—the "Mighty I AM" cathedral, and Aimee

Semple MacPherson's giant-flying-saucer-shaped Angelus Temple on Glendale Boulevard. Under some other name, Oaks had been a follower of all kinds of spiritualist leaders, even joining William Dudley Pelley's pro-Nazi "Legion of Silver Shirts"—though when, as required in the Silver Shirts, he had been asked to give the exact date and time of his birth, he had given false ones. Actually, he had not known what his real birth date might be; and so, lest he might give the correct date and time unconsciously, he had been careful to give the published birth figures of a randomly chosen movie star.

(It had been Ramon Novarro, and Oaks had occasionally wondered, though never with remorse, if Novarro's brutal death in the early hours of Halloween, 1969, might have been a long-delayed consequence of that lie.)

And in 1929, he had somehow inhaled a ghost that had been stored in an opaque container; and the stinking lifeless thing had choked his mind, blocked his psychic gullet, rendered him unable to inhale any more ghosts at all. (He thought of the collapsed face he had seen yesterday on the steps down to the parking level at the Music Center up on Temple.)

Oaks knew that he had got past that catastrophe somehow. (A suicide attempt? Something about his missing arm? The memories were like smoke on a breeze.) Some psychic Heimlich maneuver.

The Edison truck had pulled up then, and a man in bright new blue jeans and a Tabasco T-shirt had opened the passenger-side door and hopped down to the pavement.

"Oaks?" he said. When Oaks nodded, he went on, "Here she is. Driver'll pull into an alley and let the van aboard, and then you got half an hour of drive-around time. More than that, and your monthly rate increases. What's in the box?"

Oaks held out the cardboard box on the fingertips of his one hand, like a waiter. "Next month's payment, in advance."

The man took it. "Okay, thanks—I'll see he gets it."

A new Chrysler had pulled in behind the truck, and the man carried the box to it and got in.

Oaks had looked bleakly at the orange and black and yellow truck—Halloween colors!—then sighed and walked around to the back as the Chrysler drove away. When he'd pulled up the sliding back door, he'd been grudgingly pleased to see the things he'd asked for laid out on the aluminum floor: a flashlight, twine and duct tape, and a Buck hunting knife. In the front right corner, he could see the gun the driver had apparently insisted on: a shiny short-barreled revolver. Won't be needing that, Oaks had thought as he'd grabbed the doorframe, put one foot on the bumper, and boosted himself up.

CHAPTER 31

◎

*And once she had really frightened her old
nurse by shouting suddenly in her ear,
   "Nurse! Do let's pretend that I'm a hungry
hyaena, and you're a bone!"*

—Lewis Carroll,
Through the Looking-Glass

EVEN BY STRAINING all his muscles, all together or against one piece of restraining tape at a time, Kootie had failed to break or even stretch his bonds; though he could reach his fingers into the pockets of his jeans.

The flashlight swung wildly as the man climbed over the passenger seat and leaned down over Kootie. He reached out slowly with his one arm, closed his fingers in Kootie's curly hair, and then lifted the boy back up to a sitting position. Then he sat down on the console, facing Kootie, and stared into the boy's eyes.

Kootie helplessly stared back. The one-armed man's round, smooth face was lit from beneath by the flashlight, making a snouty protuberance of his nose, and his tiny eyes gleamed.

"No ectoplasm left, hey?" the man said. "No dog-mannikin today?" He smiled. "Your mouth is taped shut. You'll be having trouble expiring, just through your nose that way. Here." He leaned forward, and Kootie wasn't aware that the man had a knife until he felt the narrow cold back of it slide up over the skin of his jaw and across his cheek almost to his ear, with a sound like a zipper opening.

Kootie blew out through his mouth, and the flap of tape swung away from his mouth like a door. He thought of saying something—*Thank you? What do you want?*—but just breathed deeply through his open mouth.

"My compass needle points north," the man said. "Your smoke is clathrated. You need to unclamp, open up."

He lowered his chin, pushing the flashlight to the side, and he held his right hand out so that it was silhouetted against the disk of yellow light high up on the riveted truck wall. Squinting up sideways at the projection, the man wiggled his fingers and said, with playful eagerness, "What would you say to a . . . *rhinoceros?*" He bunched the fingers then, and said, "Clowns are always a favorite with little boys." The thumb now made a loop with the forefinger, while the other fingers stuck out. "Do you know what roosters say? They say *cock-a-doodle-doo!*"

Kootie realized belatedly that the man was doing some kind of shadow show for him. He blinked in frozen bewilderment.

"Helpful and fun, but not very exciting," the man concluded, lowering his arm and letting the flashlight swing free so that it underlit his face again. "What could be more *exciting* for a lonely little angel than a flight *up* the hill to where the rich people live? Aboard a charming conveyance indeed! I believe I can provide a snapshot of that."

He stared into Kootie's eyes again, and hummed and bobbed his round head until the spectacle of it began to blur from sheer monotony. In spite of his rigid breathlessness, Kootie thought he might go to sleep.

All at once, the motion of the truck became jerky and clanging and *upward*, and the seat under him was hard wood. He opened his eyes, and jumped against his restraints.

Cloudy daylight through glass windows lit the interior of a trolley car climbing a steep track up a hill. Kootie's seat was upright, though, and when he looked around he saw that the trolley car had been *built* for the slope—the floor, seats, and windows were stepped, a sawtooth pattern on the diagonal chassis. A city skyline out of an old black-and-white photograph hung in the sky outside.

There was a little boy wearing shorts and a corduroy cap sitting in the window seat next to Kootie, and he was staring past Kootie at someone across the aisle. Kootie followed the boy's gaze, and flinched to see the round-faced man sitting there, still wearing stained old bum clothes but with two arms and two hands now.

"Where is the gentleman you boys came with?" he asked.

The boy beside Kootie spoke. "In heaven; send thither to see; if your messenger find him not there, seek him i' the other place yourself. But, indeed, if you find him not within this month, you shall nose him as you go up the stairs into the lobby."

"Hamlet to Claudius," the man said, nodding. "Showing as a youngster, then, eh? Why not?" He smiled at the boy. "What's the matter, don't you like my pan?"

"Not much," the boy said.

The man chuckled. From under his windbreaker he pulled a pencil that was a foot long and as wide around as a sausage, and with his other hand he pulled out a giant pad of ruled white paper. "At the top of the hill, I'll fill out the adoption papers on both you lads," he said affectionately.

The boy next to Kootie shook his head firmly. "I have a snapshot myself," he said.

Then the whole length of the cable car fell to level, silently; the front end down and the back end up, though none of the three passengers were jarred at all. It was just that the seats and floor were all lined up horizontally now, like a normal car. The gray sunlight had abruptly faded to darkness outside the windows, and flames had sprung up in little lamps on the paneled walls.

The car was longer and broader now, chugging along across some invisible nighttime plain. The man with the little eyes was sitting several rows ahead now, and he was wearing a ruffled white shirt and a gray cutaway coat. In the aisle next to him stood a tall black man—his clothes were as elegantly cut, but seemed to be made of broad teak-colored leaves stitched together.

From behind Kootie came a boy's voice: "Newspapers, apples, sandwiches, molasses, peanuts!" Kootie turned around awkwardly in the seat belt that was still taped to his wrists, and saw the boy in the corduroy cap. A big wicker basket was slung over the boy's arm now, and he was slowly pacing up the length of the car, looking straight at the two men at the far end.

"Where are we?" Kootie whispered when the boy was beside him.

"An hour out of Detroit," the boy said without looking down, "two hours yet to Port Huron. Sit tight, Kootie. Newspapers, peanuts!" he went on more loudly. There were only the four people in the train car.

The man who now had two arms was staring at the boy. "I *remember* this!" he said softly. "*You* were *him!* Christ, what *year* was this?"

For a moment, the boy with the basket paused, and Kootie sensed surprise on his part too. Then, "Apples, sandwiches, newspapers!" he called, resuming his walk up the aisle. The train car smelled of new shoes fresh out of the box.

The man got to his feet, bracing himself on the back of the seat in front of him against the train's motion. "Well enough, I'll blow down your straw barricades. Uh . . . papers?" he said, smiling and holding out his two arms.

The boy lifted out a pile of newspapers and laid them in the man's hands. The man turned to the open window and tossed the stack out into the windy blackness outside.

When he straightened up, he said, "Pay this boy, Nicotinus."

The black man handed the boy some coins.

"Magazines," the man said then. He took the stack of magazines that the boy lifted out of the basket, and threw them too out the window. "Pay the boy, Nicotinus."

Kootie sat on his wooden seat, his wrists moored in the stocks of the anachronistic woven-nylon seat belt, and watched as all the wares in the boy's basket were dealt with in the same way, item by item, sandwich by bag of peanuts.

Through it all the black man was staring intently at the man who kept repeating, "Pay the boy, Nicotinus."

When the basket was empty, it too went out the window in exchange for a handful of clinking coins. The boy put his filled hand into his pocket, then took it out and put his fist to his mouth for just a moment, as if eating one of the coins.

For a moment the boy stood empty-handed, facing away from Kootie, while the train rattled through the night and the glassed-in lamp-flames flared. Then he took off his shoes and coat and hat, and, barefoot, lifted them up and laid them in the man's hands.

The man's round face smiled, though his tiny eyes didn't narrow at all. He turned and pitched the clothes out the window, and then he said, "Pay the boy, Nicotinus."

The boy held out his hand one more time—and the black man seized it and threw the boy to the wooden floor.

Kootie was slammed sideways across the back seat of the minivan with a man's weight on top of him crushing his ribs, and he was choking and gagging on a bulky plastic cylinder that had somehow got into his mouth; the flashlight was jammed between their bodies somewhere, and he could see nothing in the darkness. He knew the man's face was right above his own because of the harsh hot breaths battering at his right ear and eyelashes.

Something was repeatedly punching him in the side over the steel-cable belt, audibly tearing the denim jacket. He knew it must be the blade of the knife, being stopped by the metal coils of the I-ON-A-CO belt; but the stabs were wild, and he was sure that the next one wouldn't be another blunted impact but a cold plunge into his guts.

He shoved his tongue against the flat bottom of the plastic cylinder in his mouth, but before he could spit it out to scream and bite, his jaws involuntarily clamped tight around the thing.

At the same moment, *No, Kootie!* shouted a voice in his head; it was Edison—and the boy train-vendor in the hallucinations had been Edison, too. *I'll do this!*

At that moment, the knife blade grated off of the top edge of the belt cable and the point of it stabbed against the bone of one of his ribs. Kootie sagged in ringing shock. But an instant later, he had inhaled deeply through his whistling nostrils, and then his head was whipped around to face the man who was killing him, and his lower teeth popped the lid off the plastic cylinder.

And he blew a hard exhalation straight up into the man's wide-open mouth.

The man drove a knee solidly into Kootie's stomach, so that Kootie's long exhalation ended in a sharp, yelping wheeze—but the man had jackknifed off the seat, boomed hard against the sliding door as the flashlight whirled around his tumbling body like a crazy firefly, and then he had bounced onto his belly across the console, kicking his legs in the empty air so that Kootie heard popping tendons rather than impacts. A moment later, Kootie cringed to hear him vomiting so hard and loud that the terrified boy thought the man must be splitting open his face, pop-gunning his eyeballs, his sinus and nose bones cracking out to fall onto the carpeted floorboards.

Kootie's left hand was gently slapping his ribs, and when his fingers found the knife grip they held on and then carefully pulled the blade out of the hole it had punched in the denim. Kootie winced and whimpered to feel the point pull out of his flesh and the edge violin across the coils of the belt, but he just held still, knowing it was Edison that was working his hand.

Kootie lay half on his side across the seat, and he could feel hot blood roll wet down across his stomach from his cut left rib. He nearly jumped when he felt wet steel slide past his right wrist, and then that hand had twisted and was free, and had snatched the knife.

At last he spat out the emptied cylinder, and he was sobbing with urgent claustrophobic fright. "Get me out of here, mister!" he whimpered. "Oh, please, mister, get me *out of here!*"

He was anxious to be just a cooperative passenger in his own body now—gratefully he felt his right hand cut free his left wrist, and then he was sitting up and bending over to cut the tape around his ankles.

The one-armed man had heaved himself forward with each abdomen-abrading retch, and now his feet boomed against the van's ceiling as he toppled over the console to the floor. *"Edison!"* he said loudly, grating out the syllables like cinder blocks. *"Wast—thee—agayn?"*

Kootie didn't know whether it was himself or Edison that worked the door handle and pulled back the minivan's sliding side door. He stepped out, down to the floor of the truck, rocking as if he were aboard a boat, and he groped his way in darkness to the rippling, sectional metal wall that was the truck's door.

The cut in his side was just a point of tingling chill, but he could feel blood weighing down the folds of his shirt over his belt, and a hot trickle ran down the inside of his leg.

"Kootie!" he gasped. *"Breathe slower!* You're going to make us faint."

Kootie's mouth snapped shut, and he made himself count four heartbeats for every inhalation, and four for every exhalation.

Without his volition, his right hand went to his side and pressed against the cut.

Behind him, he heard feet thumping and scraping—inside the minivan, the one-armed man was up.

With his left hand Kootie slapped hurriedly at the ribbed inner surface of the truck's door until he found a blocky steel lever, and he braced himself on his good foot and heaved the lever upward.

Dazzling sunlight flooded the truck's interior as the door clattered upward, folding along its track overhead. Without his sunglasses, the day outside seemed terribly bright.

Pavement was rushing past down there beyond the toes of his Reeboks, and he was squinting out at the windshields of oncoming cars; a low office building and a red-roofed Pizza Hut were swinging past off to his left. The people in the cars might be gaping, pointing at him, but their windshields were just blank patches of reflected blue sky.

Kootie glanced behind him, into the dimness of the truck's interior, and he could see the one-armed man crawling down out of the minivan headfirst, onto the truck floor. *Breathe slower!* Kootie reminded himself.

"What do I do, Mr. Edison?" Kootie cried, his voice not echoing now but breezing away in the open air.

He sensed no answer; and when he tried to let the ghost take control of his body again, he had to grab the bottom edge of the half-raised door, for his knees had simply buckled and he would have fallen out of the truck.

He had to step back then, for the truck was slowing down.

Kootie freed his bloody hand from his side and waved it broadly at the cars following the truck, mouthing *Slow down, I'm getting out! Don't run over me!* and pointing down at the street. He glanced down past his shoes—the street was still moving by awfully fast, and his belly and an instant later his neck quailed like shaken ice water.

You'll tumble, he thought; even if he slows a lot more than this, you won't be able to land running fast enough, and you'll tumble like a Raggedy Andy doll. He imagined his skull socking the pavement, his elbows snapping backward, shinbones split and telescoped . . .

He couldn't do it. But if he waited another couple of seconds, the one-armed man would be on him again. Then, with an abrupt hallucinatory burst of glaring red and blue flashes on his retinas, a gleaming black-and-white police car had surged into the gap between the truck's bumper and the car behind. A half-second segment of siren shocked his ears, and Kootie swayed backward again as the truck slowed still more, and Kootie saw the front end of the police car dip as it braked to avoid hitting the truck.

And Kootie jumped.

His kneecaps banged the hood of the police car, and his palms and forehead smacked the windshield, cracking it with a muffled creak; in nearly the same instant, with a boom that shook the very air, the windshield crystallized into an opaque white honeycomb as a hole was punched through it next to Kootie's bloody right hand.

Kootie's right hip and shoulder hit the windshield then, and the glass gave beneath him like starched white canvas. And another boom rocked the world as a hole was punched through the wrecked web work of glass near his upraised left knee; the windshield dissolved into a spray of little green cubes, and he was sitting on the dashboard.

He whipped his head around to squint ahead at the truck. The one-armed man's face was right above the truck-bed floor, and in his one hand wobbled the silver muzzle of a gun. As Kootie stared, a hammer-stroke of glare eclipsed the gun, and he felt a jolt in the police car as the boom of the gunshot rolled over him.

The police car was screeching to a halt now, slewing sideways, but Kootie was able to hang on to the rounded inside edges of the dashboard, and though he was rocked back and forth he was not thrown off; even when the car behind rear-ended the police car with a squeal and bang and tinkle of broken glass, he just lifted his shoulders and dug in with his butt and let his chin roll down and up.

The police car was stopped at last. The orange-and-black Southern California Edison truck was wobbling to the curb against further braking and honking horns from behind, and Kootie scrambled to the fender and hopped down to the asphalt. The pavement under his feet was so steady, and he was so torqued, that he had to take several hopping steps to keep from falling over.

A couple of people had got out of stopped cars and were hurrying up. "Has someone got . . . change for a telephone call?" Kootie shouted, to his own surprise.

"Here you go, kid," said a woman absently, handing him a quarter. She was staring past him, at whatever was going on with the police and the one-armed man.

"Thank you," Kootie said. He was wobbling dizzily as he stepped up the curb, and a man in a business suit called something to him. "Man back there," Kootie yelled, "bleeding bad. Where's a telephone?"

The man pointed at a liquor store and said, "Dial nine-one-one!"

Sure, thought Kootie wildly as he wobbled onward through the cold sunlight. Nine-one-one. I'd get to talk to my mom and dad again, drunk as fig beetles by now; Edison could shoot the breeze with the fat lady from the supermarket parking lot. At least I'd get my quarter back.

He glanced back, but the doors of the police car hadn't opened, and, blinking against the silvery glare of the sunlight, Kootie couldn't see the one-armed man. He wished he hadn't lost the sunglasses.

"Where are we going?" he whispered, with timid hope, when he had limped around the corner of the liquor store and was facing a long alley with Dumpsters and old mattresses shored up against the graffiti-fouled walls.

"Anywhere relatively private," Edison said, and Kootie exhaled and began sweating with relief—the old man was not only back, but seemed to be sensible again, and would now take care of everything. "Keep pressing your hand hard against the cut, it'll slow the bleeding. I need to get a look at this wound, and then we'll go buy whatever sort of stuff we need to get you repaired. And some liquor. I really don't think we can get by, here, without some liquor."

"Shit, no," said Kootie, stumbling forward down the alley.

His face was cold and sweaty, but he smiled, for Edison apparently wasn't going to scold him for his language this time.

CHAPTER 32

*"... How puzzling all these changes are! I'm
never sure what I'm going to be, from one minute
to another! However, I've got back to my right
size; the next thing is, to get into that beautiful
garden—how is that to be done, I wonder?"*

—Lewis Carroll,
Alice's Adventures in Wonderland

"DIOS TE GUARDE *tan linda,"* said Angelica Elizalde
softly into the sea breeze.

She had taken off her sneakers in order to wade out in
the low, breakwater-tamed surf of Los Angeles Harbor.
The lights of the *Queen Mary* rippled across the dark
water, and Elizalde shivered now when she looked at the
vast old ship out there by San Pedro.

She had walked down to this narrow stretch of beach
from the bus stop at Cherry and Seventh, and she was still
putting off the decision of whether or not to meet the
Peter Sullivan person up in the parking lot on the bluff.

She glanced at her watch and saw that she still had half an hour in which to decide.

She paused and looked back up the shore. A hundred yards west of her, the Mexican women's fire still fluttered and threw sparks on the breeze. She might just plod back there and talk to them some more. The bruises on her knees and hip were aching in the cold, and it would be nice to sit by the fire, among people who could hear her secrets and not consider her insane.

Elizalde had walked up to the fire when the sun was still a flattened red coal in the molten western sky, and in her exhaustion, her Spanish had effortlessly come back to her so that she was able to return the greetings of the women and make small talk.

She had smiled at the toddler daughter of one and the woman had touched the girl's forehead and quickly said, *"Dios te guarde tan linda"*—God keep you pretty baby. Elizalde had remembered her grandmother doing the same whenever a stranger looked at one of the children. It was to deflect *mal ojo*, the evil eye. But Elizalde also remembered that it was a routine precaution, and she smiled at the mother too, and crossed herself. Only after the mother had smiled back, and Elizalde had accepted the gestured offer of a seat on the sand beside the fire, had she felt hypocritical.

Veladoros, devotional candles in tall glasses, ringed the fire; and Elizalde soon learned that these women were here waiting for midnight, when, it then being the Friday before *El Día de los Muertos*, they would bathe their *piedras imanes* in the seawater.

Elizalde realized that she had not misunderstood the

word yesterday—it did mean magnets. Her new friend Dolores untied her handkerchief and showed her own, a doughnut-sized magnet from a stereo speaker. The best ones, Elizalde had gathered, were the little ones from old telephones—stubby cylinders, no bigger than a dime in cross section, that looked like the smoking "snakes" that her brothers had always lit on Cinco de Mayo and the Fourth of July.

Witches used the magnets as part of the ritual that transformed them into animals, she learned, but *piedras imanes* were good things to have around the house to attract good luck and deflect spells. The magnets needed to be fed—by tossing them into dirt or sand so that they became bristly with iron filings—and it was a good idea to immerse them in the sea on this one Friday every year.

As she'd sat there and listened to the gossip and the jokes and the occasional scolding of one of the children for playing too close to the fire, Elizalde had lain back against a blanket over an ice chest, and from time to time had made such answers and remarks as she imagined her grandmother would have.

And she heard stories—about a man in Montebello who had to wear sunglasses all the time because one night he had left his eyes in a dish of water in his garage and taken a cat's eyes to see with while he made a midnight cocaine buy and returned at dawn to find that the dog had eaten the eyes in the dish, leaving the man stuck with the vertical-pupiled golden-irised cat's eyes for the rest of his life (Elizalde had commented that, in fairness, the cat should have been given the dog's eyes); about how raw eggs could be used to draw fevers, and how if the fevers had been very bad the egg would be hard-cooked afterward; about *los duendes*, dwarves who had once been angels too slow in trying to follow Lucifer to Hell, and so were locked out of Heaven and Hell both, and, with no longer any place in the universe, just wandered around the world enviously ruining human undertakings.

Elizalde had already heard stories about *La Llorona*—the Weeping Lady—the ghost of a woman who had thrown her children into a rushing flood to drown, and then repented it, and forever wandered along beaches and river-banks at night, mourning their deaths and looking for living children to steal in replacement. As a child, Elizalde had heard the story as having occurred in San Juan Capistrano, with the children drowned in the San Juan Creek; but, in the years since, she had also heard it as having occurred in just about every town that had a large Hispanic community, with the children reputedly thrown into every body of water from the Rio Grande to the San Francisco Bay. There was even an Aztec goddess, Tonantzin, who was supposed to have gone weeping through Nahuatl villages and stealing infants from their cradles, leaving stone sacrificial knives where the children had lain.

These women that Elizalde had met tonight told a different version. Aboard the *Queen Mary*, they whispered, lived a *bruja* who had somehow lost all her children in the moment of her own birth, and then drowned her husband in the sea; and now she wandered weeping everywhere, night and day, eating *los difuntos*, ghosts, in an unending attempt to fill the void left by those losses. She had eaten so many that she was now very fat and they called her *La Llorona Atacado*, the Stuffed Weeping Lady.

Elizalde wondered what character of folklore she herself might fit the role of. Surely there was the story of a girl baptized once conventionally with water and once with a fertilized egg, who endured a second birth (out of a milk can!) in a shower of coins, and who fled her home to wander along far rivers, in a foredoomed attempt to avoid the ghosts of the poor people who had come to her for help, and whom she had let die.

What would the girl in that story do next, having journeyed all the way back to her home village?

She looked again at her watch. Ten of eight.

She turned her plodding steps across the sand toward the steel stairs that led up the bluff to the parking lot. It was time to meet Peter Sullivan.

Sullivan had parked the van in a dark corner of the lot, and had walked away from it to smoke a cigarette in the spotlight of yellow glare at the foot of a light pole a couple of hundred feet away. Moths fluttered around the glass of the lamp a dozen feet above his head, flickering and winking in and out of the light like remote, silent meteors.

He had arrived at Bluff Park early, and had made a sandwich in the van with some groceries he'd bought after his flight from Venice; and though there were still three or four cans of beer in the little propane refrigerator, he had been drinking Coke for the last couple of hours. He always felt that Sukie was in a sense *somewhere nearby* when he was drunk, and anyway he wanted to be alert if the Elizalde psychiatrist actually showed up.

He was watching the cars sweeping past on Ocean Boulevard, and wondering if he shouldn't just get in the van and head back to Solville—which, he had learned, was the name given by the other tenants to the apartment building he had moved into today.

Now that he was sober again—hungover, possibly— teaming up with this Elizalde woman didn't seem like such a good idea. If she was unbalanced, which it sounded like she had every right to be, she might just lead deLarava to him. How could he take her to Solville, expose that perfect blind spot to her, when she might be crazy? He remembered his first sight of her in Venice— crouched in the mud below the canal sidewalk—wearing two sets of clothes—talking into a storm drain—!

He took a last deep drag on the cigarette, then patted his jeans pocket for the van keys.

And Elizalde touched his shoulder.

Sullivan knew that he had felt the touch an instant before it had happened, and he knew it was her; but he stood without turning around, still staring out at the cars passing on Ocean Boulevard, and he exhaled the cigarette smoke in a long, nearly whistling exhalation as a slow snowfall of dead moths spun down through the yellow light to patter almost inaudibly on the asphalt.

He dropped the cigarette among the lifeless little bodies, stepped on it, and then turned to face her, smiling wryly. "Hi," he said.

She sighed. "Hi. What do we do now?"

"Talk. But not out here where we might draw attention, like we did this afternoon. That's my van over in that corner."

"Those . . . hands are in it?"

"Yeah. If they become *my* hands again, we'll know somebody's looking at us again."

They began walking across the asphalt away from the light, their swinging fingertips separated by three feet of chilly night air. Enough light reached the boxy old vehicle for it to be clearly visible.

To his own annoyance, Sullivan found himself wishing that he had washed it. "Somebody egged my van," he said gruffly. "Makes it look like I threw up out the window."

"While you were going backward real fast," she agreed, stopping to stare at the dried smear. "When and how did that happen?"

"Today." He led her around the front of the van to the side doors. "A guy, an old friend of mine, tried to turn me over to a woman who wants to eat my father's ghost; I think she wants to capture me, use me as a live lure. The old friend threw an egg at me as I was driving out of there." He unlocked the forward of the two side doors and swung it open. The light was still on inside—the battery could sustain a light or two for a full day without getting too weak to turn the motor over. "Beer and Coke in the little fridge there, if you like."

Elizalde looked at him intently for a moment, then stepped lithely up into the van.

She leaned one hip on the counter around the sink, and Sullivan noticed to his embarrassment that the bed was still extended, and unmade. I must not really have meant to meet her, he thought defensively.

"Sorry," he said. "I wasn't anticipating company." And what is *that* supposed to mean? he asked himself. He threw her a helpless glance as he climbed up and pulled the door closed.

"You've got to wash off the egg," she said, and for a moment he thought she had meant *on your face*. Then he realized that she meant the egg on the outside of the driver's door.

"Is it important?"

"I think it's a marker," she said, "and more than a visible marker. Like a magical homing device. Raw eggs have all kinds of uses in magic. I should get out of this van right now, and walk away, mask or no mask. You should too, in a different direction."

Sullivan sat down on the bed. "I've got a place we can go where the psychic static will drown out the egg's signal. I'm pretty sure. Anyway, there's certainly a hose at this place, we can wash it off." She didn't seem crazy, and he was tired of spinning through his own circular thought paths over and over again. "I think we should stick together."

"That's what Peter Sullivan thinks, huh." She stepped around him and sat down in the passenger seat, watching him over her shoulder. "Okay, for a while. But let's at least be a moving target." She looked forward, out through the windshield, and stiffened.

Sullivan stood up and hurried to the driver's seat with the key.

Outside in the parking lot, several people were

standing on the asphalt a few yards away from the front bumper, shifting awkwardly and peering. Sullivan knew that he and Elizalde had been alone in the parking lot a few moments earlier.

"Ghosts," he said shortly, starting the engine. "Fresh ones, lit up by our overlapping auras." He switched on the headlights, and the figures covered their pale faces with their lean, translucent hands.

He tapped the horn ring to give them a toot, and the figures began shuffling obediently to the side. One, a little girl, was moving more slowly than the rest, and when he had clanked the engine into gear, he had to spin the steering wheel to angle around her.

"Damn little kid," he said, momentarily short of breath. The way clear at last, he accelerated toward the Ocean Boulevard driveway.

Elizalde pulled the seat belt across her shoulder and clicked the metal tongue of it into the slot by the console. "I saw her as an old woman," she said quietly.

He shrugged. "I guess each of 'em is all the ages they ever were. He or she was, I mean. Each one is—"

"I got you. Put on your seat belt."

"The place is right here," he said, pushing down the lever to signal for a left turn.

The first faucet Sullivan found, on the end of a foot-tall pipe standing in weeds at the corner of the Solville lot, just sucked air indefinitely when the tap was opened. He walked across the dark lot to another, ascertained that it worked, and then drove the van over and parked it. He carried a big sponge out to scrub the outside of the driver's door, and then had to go back inside for a can of Comet, but at last all the chips and strips of dried egg had been sluiced off the van, and he locked it up.

Elizalde carried a beer in from the van to Sullivan's apartment, and when she popped it open foam dripped on the red-painted wooden floor. The only light in the living room was from flame-shaped white bulbs in a yard-sale chandelier in the corner, and Sullivan berated himself for not having thought to buy a lamp somewhere today. At least there were electrical outlets—Sullivan noticed that Shadroe had put six of them in this room alone.

Sullivan had carried the plaster hands inside, and he laid them against the door as though they were holding it closed.

"This is your safe place?" Elizalde's voice echoed in the empty room. She twisted the rod on the Venetian blinds over the window until the slats were vertical, then walked to the far wall and ran her long fingers over a patched section where Shadroe had apparently once filled in a doorway. "What makes it safe?"

"The landlord's dead." Sullivan leaned against another wall and let himself slide down until he was sitting on the floor. "He walks around and talks, and he's in his original body and he's not . . . you know, *retarded*—he's not a ghost, it's still his actual *self* inside the head he carries around. I believe he's been dead for quite a while, and therefore he must know it, and be taking steps to keep from departing this . . ."

"Vale of tears."

"To use the technical term," Sullivan agreed. "The place must be a terrible patch of static, psychically. The reason I think he's aware of his situation is that he's made it a terrible patch physically, too, a confusing ground-grid. All the original doors and windows seem to have been rearranged, and you can see from outside that the wiring is something out of Rube Goldberg. I can't wait to start plugging things in."

"Running water can be a betrayer too."

"And he's messed that up. I noticed earlier today that the toilet's hooked up to the *hot* water. I could probably make coffee in the tank of it."

"And have steamed buns in the morning," she said.

Her smile was slight, but it softened the lean plane of her jaw and warmed her haunted dark eyes.

"Hot cross buns," added Sullivan lamely. "Speaking of which, do you want to order a pizza or something?"

"You don't seem to have a phone," she said, nodding toward an empty jack box at the base of one wall. "And I don't think we should leave this . . . compound again tonight. Do you have anything to eat in your van?"

"Makings of a sandwich or two," he said. "Canned soup. A bag of M&M's."

"I've missed California cuisine," she said.

"You were out of town, I gather," he said cautiously.

"Oklahoma most recently. I took a Greyhound bus back here, got in late Tuesday night. Drove through the Mojave Desert. Did you ever notice that there are a lot of *ranches* out in the middle of the desert?"

"I wonder what they raise."

"Rocks, probably." She leaned against the wall across from him. "'Look out, those big rocks can be mean.' And on cold nights they put gravel in incubators. And, 'Damn!

Last night a fox got in and carried off a bunch of our fattest rocks!' "

" 'Early frost'll kill all these nice quartzes.' "

She actually laughed, two contralto syllables. "Don't get excited now," she said, "but your dead man's got the heat turned all the way up in here, and not a thermostat in sight." She unzipped the front of her jumpsuit and pulled down the shoulders, revealing a wrinkled Graceland sweatshirt; and when she pulled the jumpsuit down over her hips and sat down to bunch it down to her ankles, he saw that she was wearing faded blue jeans.

She began untying the laces of her sneakers, and Sullivan made himself look away from her long legs in the tight denim.

"I hope you don't trust everybody," he said.

Out of the top of her right sneaker she pulled a little leather cylinder with a white plastic nozzle at the top. It had a key ring at the base of it, and with the ring around her first finger she opened her hand to show it to him. "CN mace," she said with a chillier smile. "In case the soup is bland. I don't trust anybody . . . very far."

Sullivan discarded the idea of taking offense. "Good." He straightened his legs out across the floor and hooked a finger through the loop at the corner of the fanny pack that was hanging on his left hip; then, not knowing whether he was being honest with her or showing off, he pulled on the loop—the zippers whirred open as the front of the canvas pack pulled away, exposing the grip of the .45 under the Velcro cross-straps.

Her face was blank, but she echoed, "Good."

She had taken her shoes and socks off and pulled the

jumpsuit free of her ankles and tossed it aside. She stretched her legs, wiggling her toes in the air.

"But," Sullivan went on. He unsnapped the belt and pulled it from around his waist, and then slid the fanny pack across the floor toward the door. "I've decided to trust *you*."

She stared at him expressionlessly for a long moment, but then she spun the leather-sleeved cylinder away. It bumped the heavy pack six feet away from where she sat, and she said softly, "All right. Are we partners, then? Do we shake on it?"

On his hands and knees, he crossed the floor to her. They shook hands, and he crawled back to his wall and sat down again.

"Partners," he said.

"What do you know about ghosts?"

To business, he thought. "People eat them," he began at random. "They can be drawn out of walls or beds or empty air, made detectable, by playing period music and setting out props like movie posters; when they're excited that way, magnetic compasses will point to 'em, and the air around tends to get cold because they've assumed the energy out of it. They like candy and liquor, though they can't digest either one, and if they get waked up and start wandering around loose they mainly eat things like broken glass and dry twigs and rocks. They—"

"Produce from the Mojave ranches."

"Amber fields of stone," he agreed. "They're frail little wisps of smoke when they're new, or if they've been secluded and undisturbed. Unaroused, unexcited. The way you eat them is to inhale them. But if they wander around they begin to accrete actual stuff, physical mass, dirt and leaves and dog shit and what have you—"

"What have *you*," she said, politely but with a shudder, "I *insist*."

"—and they grow into solid, human-looking things. They find old clothes, and they can talk well enough to panhandle change for liquor. They don't have new thoughts, and tend to go on and on about old grievances. A lot of the street lunatics you see—maybe most of 'em—are this kind of hardened ghost. They're no good to eat when they get like that. I worked for a woman who stayed young by finding and eating ghosts that had been preserved in the frail state, in old libraries and hotels and restaurants. She lives on water, aboard the *Queen Mary*—"

"I just heard about her! And she drowned her husband in the sea."

Sullivan crawled across the floor again and picked up Elizalde's beer. "I never heard of her having a husband. May I?"

Elizalde had one eyebrow cocked. "Help yourself, partner. I just wanted a sip to cut the dust."

Sullivan took a deep swallow of the chilly beer. Then he sat down next to her, setting the can down on the floor between them.

"What do you know about séances?" he asked breathlessly. "Summoning specific ghosts?"

She picked up the can and finished the beer before answering him. "I know a turkey can hurt you if he hits you with a wing—you've got to have 'em bagged up tight in a guinea sack. Excuse me. With ghosts, you'd be smart to have some restraints in place, before you call them. They do come when you call, sometimes. Séances are dangerous—sometimes one of them is for real." She yawned, with another shudder at the end of it, and then she glanced at the two white hands braced against the door. Sullivan was thinking of the ghosts they'd seen in the parking lot a few minutes ago, and he guessed that she was too. "I'm not hungry," she said in a low voice.

He knew what she was thinking: *Let's not open the door.* "Me either," he said.

"You've got your leather jacket for a pillow, and I can ball up my jumpsuit. Let's go to sleep, and discuss this stuff when the sun's up, hmm? We can even . . . leave the light on."

"Okay." He stood up and took off the jacket, but then crouched and folded it on the floor just a couple of feet from her, and stretched himself out parallel to the wall.

She had leaned toward the window to pick up the jumpsuit, and then she stared at him for several seconds. The gun and the mace spray were islands out in the middle of the floor.

At last, she sighed and stretched out beside him, frowning uncertainly as she set the empty beer can on the floor between them. "You . . . read the whole interview?" she said as she slowly lowered her head to the bunched-up jumpsuit. She was looking away from him, facing the wall. "The interview of me, in *L.A. Weekly?*"

Sullivan remembered reading, *I've reacted against the whole establishment I was raised in, there—I'm not Catholic, I don't drink, and I don't seem to be attracted much to men.*

And he remembered Judy Nording, and Sukie, and his sonnet that had wound up so publicly in the trash. I suppose I've reacted, too, he thought. "Yes," he said gently.

As he closed his eyes and drifted toward sleep, he thought: Still, Doctor, you did try a couple of sips of beer.

the idling engine, Mrs. Fussel turned around in the driver's seat.

"He's a nice man," she said. Kootie could almost believe she was talking to herself. "We want to have children ourselves."

Kootie stared at the floor, afraid Edison would give her a sardonic look.

"Neither of us knows how to deal with . . . a child with problems," she went on, "a runaway, a *violent* runaway. We don't believe in hitting children. This was like when you have to hit someone who's drowning, if you want to save them. Can you understand? If you tell the people from the hospital—or wherever it is that you live—if you tell them Bill hit you, we'll have to tell them *why* he hit you, won't we? Trying to bite, and yelling obscenities. That means nasty words," she explained earnestly.

Kootie forgot not to stare at her.

"Your parents were murdered," she said.

He nodded expressionlessly.

"Oh, good! That you knew it, I mean, that I wasn't breaking the news to you. And I guess someone hit you in the eye. You've had a bad time, but I want you to realize that today really *is* the first day of your, of the rest of your—wait, you were living at home, weren't you? The story in the paper said that. You weren't in a hospital. Who's put up this reward for you?"

Kootie widened his eyes at her.

"Relatives?"

Kootie shook his head, slowly.

"You don't think it was the people that murdered your *parents,* do you?"

Kootie nodded furiously. "Mm-hmmm," he grunted.

"Oh, I'm sure that's not true."

Kootie rolled his eyes and then stared hard at her.

After a moment her expression of concern wilted into dismay. "Oh, shit. Oh shit. Twenty thousand dollars? You were a *witness?*"

Close enough. Rocking his head back and humming loudly was as close as Kootie could come to conveying congratulations.

She was saying, "Sorry! Sorry! Sorry!" as she got out of the seat and stepped over the console, and then she was prying with her fingernails at the tape edges around his wrists.

The tape wasn't peeling up at all, and Kootie didn't waste hope imagining that she'd free him. He wasn't surprised when keys rattled against the outside of the passenger door and the lock clunked and then Mr. Fussel was leaning in.

"What are you *doing*, El? Get away from—"

"He's a witness, Bill! The people that killed his parents are—are the ones you just called! Did you tell them where we are? Let's get out of here right now!" She hurried back up front to the driver's seat and grabbed the gearshift lever.

Mr. Fussel gripped her hand. "Where'd you get all that, El? He can't even talk. These people sounded okay."

"Then let's drive somewhere and let Goaty talk to us, and you can call them back if we're *sure* it's all right."

"*Mm-hmm!*" put in Kootie as loudly as he could.

"El, they'll be here in ten minutes. We can talk to them right here, this is a public place, he'll be safe. It's his safety

BOOK THREE
Hide, Hide, the Cow's Outside!

❈

I don't claim that our personalities pass on to another existence or sphere. I don't claim anything because I don't know anything about the subject; for that matter, no human being knows. But I do claim that it is possible to construct an apparatus which will be so delicate that if there are personalities in another existence or sphere who wish to get in touch with us in this existence or sphere, this apparatus will at least give them better opportunity to express themselves than the tilting tables and raps and Ouija boards and mediums and the other crude methods now purported to be the only means of communication.

—Thomas Alva Edison,
Scientific American,
October 30, 1920

CHAPTER 33

But it's no use now," thought poor Alice, "to pretend to be two people! Why, there's hardly enough of me left to make one respectable person!"
—Lewis Carroll,
Alice's Adventures in Wonderland

KOOTIE WOKE UP when a black man nudged his foot with a bristly push broom. The boy straightened up stiffly in the orange plastic chair and blinked around at the silent chrome banks of clothes dryers, and he realized that he and the black man were the only people in the laundromat now. Whenever he had blinked out of his fitful naps during the long night, there had been at least a couple of women with sleepy children wearily clanking the change machine and loading bright-colored clothing into the washing machines in the fluorescent white glare, but they had all gone home. The parking lot out beyond the window wall was gray with morning light now, and apparently today's customers had not yet marshaled their laundry.

"My mom will be back soon," Kootie said automatically. "She had to go back home for the bedspreads." He had said this many times during the night, when someone would shake him awake to ask him if he was okay, and they had always nodded and gone back to folding their clothes into their plastic baskets.

But it didn't work this morning. "I should charge you rent," said the black man gently. "Sun's up, boy."

Kootie slid down out of the seat and pulled his new sunglasses out of his jacket pocket. "Sorry, mister."

"You wouldn't know anything about some chalk drawings somebody did on the outside of the building, would you?"

Kootie put on the sunglasses before he looked up at the man. "No."

The man stared at him for a moment, then crinkled his eyes in what might have been a smile. "Oh well. At least it wasn't gang-marks from our Kompton Tray-Fifty-Seven Budlong Baby Dipshits or whoever they are today. And at least it was just chalk."

Kootie's head was stuffed and throbbing. "Are the chalk markings still there?"

"I hosed 'em off just now." Again, he gave Kootie the wry near-smile. "Figured I'd let you know."

Kootie started to stretch, but he hitched and pulled his right arm back when the cut over his rib flared hotly in protest. "Okay, thanks."

He limped across the white linoleum, around the wheeled hanger-carts, to the glass doors, and as soon as he had pushed them open and stepped outside, he missed the stale detergent-scented air of the laundromat, for the dawn breeze was chilly, and harsh with the damp old-coins smell of sticky trashcan bottoms.

A half-pint bottle of 151-proof Bacardi rum had cost him sixteen dollars yesterday afternoon—six for the bottle, and a ten-dollar fee for the woman who had gone in and bought it for him. By her gangly coltish figure Kootie had judged her to be only a few years older than himself, but her tanned face, under the lipstick and eyeliner and flatteringly acne-like sores, had been as seamed and lined as a patch of sunbaked mud. Edison had made Kootie tear the ten-dollar bill jaggedly into two pieces before giving one half of it to the woman prior to the purchase; he had laughingly said that this made her his indentured servant, but neither Kootie nor the woman had understood him. He had wordlessly given her the other half of the bill after she had delivered the bottle.

Edison had already had Kootie buy a roll of adhesive tape and a box each of butterfly bandages and "Sterile Non-Stick Pads," and then in a patch of late-afternoon sunlight behind a hedge on a side street off Vermont, Edison had pulled up Kootie's shirt to look at their wound, which had still been perceptibly leaking blood even though Kootie had been keeping his fist or his elbow pressed against it almost without a break since he had got away from the Southern California Edison truck half an hour earlier.

It was a V-shaped cut too big for him to be able to cover with his thumb, and Kootie had begun whimpering as soon as Edison started swabbing at it with a rum-soaked pad, so Edison had made Kootie swallow a mouthful of the rum. The taste was surprising—like what Kootie would have expected from film developer or antifreeze—but it did make his head seem to swell up and buzz, and it distracted him from the pain as Edison thoroughly cleaned the cut and then dried the edges, pulled them together, and fastened them shut with the I-shaped butterfly bandages.

Then, with a pad taped over the closed and cleaned cut, Edison had had a sip of the rum himself. When Kootie had floundered back over the hedge and started down the sidewalk, he had seemed to be walking on the deck of a boat, and Edison steered him into a *taquería* to eat some enchiladas and salsa and drink several cups of Coke. After that, Kootie had been sober but sleepy. They had found the laundromat, had furtively marked up the wall outside it, and finally had gone in to nap in one of the seats. The nap had continued, with interruptions, all night.

He shivered now in the morning breeze and shoved his hands into his pockets. He knew he must be sober, but the pavement still didn't seem firmly moored.

He felt his mouth open involuntarily, and he wearily braced himself for forcing it shut against some crazy outburst, but Edison just used it to say, grumpily, "Where are we now?"

"Walking on Western," said Kootie, quietly even though there were no other pedestrians on the sidewalk. "Looking for a bus to take us to a beach."

"*Final discorporation* is on my agenda today, is that it? Why did we have to go outside so early? It's cold. It was warm back in that automat."

Each spoken syllable was an effort, and Kootie wished Edison wouldn't use so many of them. "They washed the chalk off the wall," he said hoarsely. Cars were rumbling past at his left, and his voice wasn't loud, but he knew Edison could hear him.

"Ah! Then you're a clever lad to have got away quickly." Kootie's mouth opened very wide then, so that the cold air got all the way in to his back teeth, and he was afraid Edison was going to bellow something that would be audible to any early-morning workers who might already be in these shadowed tax offices and closed movie-rental shops—but it was just a jaw-creaking yawn. "I shouldn't stay out here, in my excited state, like this. Compasses will be wagging. I'll go back to sleep. Holler for me if you—*mff!*"

Kootie had stumbled on a high curb and fallen to his knees.

"What's the matter?" said Edison too loudly. Kootie took the ending *r* sound and prolonged it into a groan that rose to a wail. "Don't *talk* so much," Kootie said despairingly. "I can't breathe when you do." He sniffed. "I bet we didn't get one full half-hour of sleep last night without somebody waking us up to ask us something, or yelling at their kids or dropping baby bottles." He tried to struggle back to his feet, and wound up resting his forehead on the sidewalk. "I can still taste those enchiladas," he whispered to the faint trowel lines in the surface of the pavement. "And the rum."

"This won't do," came Edison's voice out of Kootie's raw throat. Kootie's arms and legs flexed and then acted in coordination, and he got his feet under himself and straightened all the way back up. Slanting morning sunlight lanced needles of reflected white glare off car windshields into his watering eyes.

"You're just not used to the catnap system," said Edison

kindly. "I can go for weeks on a couple of interrupted hours a night. *You* go to sleep, now—I'll take the wheel for the next couple of miles."

"Can we do that?" asked Kootie. He left his mouth loose for Edison's reply, but had to close it when he felt himself starting to drool.

"Certainly. What you do is stand still for a moment here, and close your eyes—then in half a minute or so, I'll open your eyes but you'll already have started to go to sleep, get it? You'll go ahead and relax, and you won't fall. I'll hold us up, and walk and talk. Okay?" Kootie nodded. "Close your eyes, now, and relax."

Kootie did, and he let himself fall away toward sleep, only peripherally aware of still being up in the air, and of the daylight when his eyes were eventually opened again. It was like falling asleep in a tree house over a busy street.

And his confused memories and worries wandered outside the yard of his control and began bickering among themselves, and assumed color and voices and became disjointed dreams.

His gray-haired father was at the front door of their Beverly Hills house, arguing with someone from the school district again. Sometimes Kootie's parents would keep him home from school when science classes prompted him to ask difficult questions on topics like the actual properties of crystals and the literal meanings of words like *energy* and *dimension*.

"We're saving it for the boy," his father was saying angrily. "We're not selfish here. In my youth I had the clear opportunity to become a nearly perfect *jagadguru*, but I sacrificed that ambition, I unfitted myself by committing a theft, so that the boy could become the *jagadguru* perfectly, in psychic yin-and-yang twinhood with one who was the greatest of the unredeemed seers. The unredeemed one won't be able to accompany our boy to godhood, but he will be able to achieve redemption for himself by serving as the boy's guide through the astral regions. Right now, the guide must wait—masked in the boy's *persona* ikon, as he will eventually occupy a place in the boy's *persona*. In order for the union to be seamless, it must occur after the boy has achieved puberty."

Kootie had heard his father say much the same thing to his mother, on the nights Kootie had tiptoed back up the hall after his bedtime. It all had to do with the Dante statue, and the drunks and crazy people who wanted to talk to Don Tay.

His father waved ineffectually. "Clear off, or I'll have no choice but to summon the police."

But now Kootie could see the man standing grinning on the front doorstep, and it was the one-armed man with the tiny black unrecessed eyes.

Kootie flinched, and the dream shifted—he was lying in the back seat of a car, half-asleep, rocking gently with the shock absorbers, on the undulating highway and watching the door handle gleam in reflected oblique light when the occasional streetlamp swept past out in the darkness. He was relaxed, slumped in the tobacco-scented leather upholstery—this wasn't Raffle's Maverick, nor the old marooned Dodge Dart he had slept in on Wednesday night, nor the Fussels' minivan. He was too warm and comfortable to shift around and look at the interior, but he didn't have to. He knew it was a Model T Ford. The driver was definitely his father, though sometimes that was Jiddu Parganas and sometimes it was Thomas Edison.

Kootie smiled sleepily. He didn't know where they were driving to, and he didn't need to know.

But suddenly there was a screech of brakes, and Kootie was thrown forward into the back of the front seat—he hit it with his open palms and the toes of his sneakers.

The dream impact jolted him out of sleep, and so he was awake when his palms and the toes of his sneakers hit the cinder-block wall an instant later; using the momentum of the leap he had found himself making, he flung one leg over the top of the wall, and before he boosted himself up and dropped into the dirt lot on the other side, he glanced behind him.

The glance made him scramble the rest of the way over the wall and land running, and he was across the lot and over a chain-link fence before he had taken and exhaled two fast breaths, and then he was pelting away down a palm-shaded alley, looking for some narrow L-turn that would put still more angles and distance between himself and the Western Avenue sidewalk.

A pickup truck had been pulled in to the curb, and five men in sleeveless white undershirts had hopped out of the bed of it to corner him; but what had driven the fatigue out of his muscles was a glimpse of the bag-thing one of the men was carrying.

It was a coarse burlap sack, flopping open at the top to show the clumps of hair it was stuffed with, and a battered Raiders baseball cap had been attached to the rim and was bobbing up and down as the man carrying it stepped up the curb; but the sack was rippling as if a wind were buffeting it, and harsh laughter was shouting out of the loose flaps. As Kootie had scrambled over the wall, the bag had called to him, *"Tu sabes quien trae las llaves, Chavez!"* and barked out another terrible laugh.

Kootie was beginning to limp now on his weak ankle, and his cut rib was aching hotly. He crossed a street of old houses and hurried down another alley, ceaselessly glancing over his shoulder and ready to duck behind one of the old parked cars if he glimpsed the bumper of a pickup truck rounding the corner.

"What was that?" he asked finally in a grating whisper, and even just forming the question squeezed tears of fright out of his eyes.

Even Edison's voice was unsteady. "Local witch-boys," he panted. "They tracked us with a compass, I've got to assume. I'm going to go under, clathrate, so they can't track me. Holler if you need me—"

"But what was that?"

"Ahhh." Kootie's shoulders were raised and lowered. "They . . . got a ghost, captured one, and had it animate the trash in that bag, apparently. It's got no legs, so it can't run away . . . but . . . well, you heard it? I was afraid you did. It can talk. Cheerful thing, hmm?" The bravura tone of Edison's last remark was hollow.

"It woke me up."

"Yes, I felt you wake up in the instant before we hit the wall. It's like hearing the tiny snap of a live switch opening, just before the collapsing electric field makes a big spark arc across the gap, isn't it?"

"Just like that."

Kootie was still walking quickly, and he could tell that it was himself placing one foot in front of the other now. "Where do I go now?" he asked, ashamed of the pleading note in his voice.

"God, boy—just walk straight away from here, fast. As soon as I'm below consciousness you should start looking for someplace to hide for a while—behind a hedge, or go upstairs in some office building, or hide in a boring section of the library."

"Okay," said Kootie, clenching his teeth and looking ahead to the next street. "Don't hide too deep, okay?"

"I'll be not even as far away as your nose."

CHAPTER 34

❄

"'Bring it here! Let me sup!'
It is easy to set such a dish on the table.
'Take the dish-cover up!'
Ah, that is so hard that I fear I'm unable!"
—Lewis Carroll,
Through the Looking-Glass

SHERMAN OAKS sat shivering in the early-morning sunlight on a wall beside the parking lot of an A.M.-P.M. minimart. His companions, two ragged middle-aged men who were passing back and forth a bottle of Night Train in a paper bag, were ghosts, old enough and solid enough to throw shadows and to contain fortified wine without obviously leaking. They were pointing at a skinny lady in shorts and high heels at the street corner, and laughing (*"FM shoes, 'fuck me' shoes, hyuck-hyuck-hyuck"*), but Oaks just clutched his elbows and shivered and stared down at the litter of paper cups and beer cans below his dangling feet.

451

He was starving. The four *piece-a-shit* ghosts he had inhaled yesterday were all the sustenance he had had for more than three days, and the Bony Express was a shrill chorus in his head and a seeping of blood from the corners of his fingernails.

He hadn't slept last night. He hadn't even been able to stop moving—walking along sidewalks, riding buses, climbing the ivied grades of freeway shoulders. During the course of the long night he had found his way to a couple of his secluded ghost traps, but though the creatures had been there, hovering bewilderedly around the palindromes and the jigsaw-puzzle pieces, he hadn't been able to sniff them all the way up into his head; they had gone in through his nostrils smoothly enough, but just bumped around inside his lungs until he had to exhale, and then they were back out on the dirt again, stupidly demanding to know what had happened. He had even inhaled over one of the antismoke crowd's L.A. CIGAR—TOO TRAGICAL ashtrays in an all-night doughnut shop, and got nothing but ashes up his nose.

He was jammed up.

The "big ghost" that had been shining over the magical landscape of Los Angeles for the past four days had been the ghost of *Thomas Alva Edison.* It had been *Edison's* face on the collapsed ectoplasm figure at the Music Center, the day before yesterday. And now Edison had *(again!)* fed Oaks a rotted ghost—and it had jammed him up, and he was starving.

Oaks looked up at the sky, and he remembered mornings when he had snorted his fill the night before, and had had more unopened vials ready to hand. I'd like it always to be six o'clock on a summer morning, he thought, and I'm in a sleeping bag on some inaccessible balcony or behind a remote hedge, and my feet are warm but my arms and head are out in the cool breeze and I'm sweating with a sort of disattached, unspecific worry, and I've got hours yet to just lie there and listen to the traffic and the parrots flying past overhead.

The police would be after him. He had run away from that confusion in Inglewood yesterday afternoon, but his shots had probably hit both of the cops in that patrol car, and his fingerprints were all over the inside of the SCE truck, and the van in the back of it. And the police probably still had his fingerprints on file; he now remembered that he had held several custodial jobs in hospitals, during the fifties and sixties, catching fresh death-ghosts and lots of the tasty, elusive birth-ghosts.

He'd have to get rid of the revolver—a "ballistics team" would be able to tell that it was the weapon that had fired on the police car. Oaks should have no trouble finding some street person who would take it in trade for some other (certainly less desirable) sort of gun.

But the police, unfortunately, weren't his main problem.

He twitched, and turned to the ghost sitting nearest him on his left. The man was breaking off fragments of mortar from between the cinder blocks of the wall, and eating them.

"You'll choke," Oaks rasped.

"Hyuck-hyuck. Choke on *this*," said the ghost, without any gesture.

"*I'm* choking," said Oaks. "If you choke on one of those rocks, a Heimlich maneuver could unblock it, right? How can I unblock a spoiled *ghost* from my *mind*-pipe? Do *you* know?"

The ghost wrinkled his spotty forehead in a frown, and then began counting off points on the fingers of one hand. "Okay, you got stones in your ears and a magnet up your nose, right? And toads have got a stone in their heads. The Venerable Bead. And plenty of people have got shrapnel and metal plates in them, and steel hips. Check it out. Learnest Hand Hemingway used to save the shrapnel that came out of his legs and put it in little bowls so that his friends could take the bits as souvenirs; and eat them, of course, to get a bit of Hemingway." He smiled. "Everything is a Learnest experience. The golden rule to be in-got at the College of Fortuitous Knox. Fort You-It-Us Knocks." (The unattained pun made the intended spelling clear.) "It's important to feel good about yourself. This morning I met somebody I really like—me."

"That's good," said Oaks hopelessly. "Tell him hello from me, if you ever run into him again."

There was apparently no help to be had from the ghosts themselves. Oaks was choked, and the only way *he* knew how to unjam himself was likely to kill him. This time. Instead of just costing him another limb.

He could remember all kinds of things now. He remembered that Thomas Alva Edison had choked him this way once before—or at least once before—in 1929. Small surprise that the flattened face on the Music Center parking-level stairs had looked familiar! No wonder the *Edison* logo on the side of the truck had upset him! He should have paid attention to his forebodings. Thomas Alva Edison had never been any good for him.

❊ ❊ ❊

As the shock-loosened memories had come arrowing up to the surface of his mind, one right after another, during his endless odyssey last night, Oaks had learned that he had always been an ambitious fellow, setting his sights on the most powerful people around and then trying to catch them unguarded so that he could snatch out of their heads their potent ghosts.

He had pursued the famous escape artist Harry Houdini for at least sixteen years—fruitlessly. Houdini had evaded every trap, had been effectively masked, psychically inaccessible, at every face-to-face confrontation. Houdini had even given protection to his friends: there had been a writer of horror stories in Rhode Island to whom Houdini had given his own severed thumb in June of 1924; Houdini had had his plaster mask-hands made by then, and could assume them and make them flesh any time he liked, and so he didn't need the original-issue thumb anymore, and besides, Houdini had probably known that he himself was only a couple of years from death at that point. In Los Angeles, Houdini had even picked up some kind of electric belt for this writer friend, an electromagnetic device that could supposedly cure all kinds of ailments, including Blight's disease and cancer—which pair of illnesses the writer died of in 1937, in fact, for he had been skeptical of the belt and disgusted by the thumb, and had got rid of them.

Houdini himself had been untouchable, a genuine escape artist . . . even though Oaks had eventually managed to arrange his physical death on a Halloween. It had been useless, for even in the moment of his dying

Houdini had eluded him. Trying to catch Houdini had always been like trying to cross-examine an echo, wound an image in a mirror, sniff out a rose in an unlighted gallery of photographs of flowers.

Houdini's parents must have known right from his birth that their son had a conspicuous soul, for they had taken quick, drastic steps to hamper access to it. Confusingly, they had given him the name *Erik*, which was the same name they'd given to their first son, who had died of a fall while still a baby; and within weeks of Houdini's birth, they had moved from Budapest to London to goddamn *Appleton, Wisconsin!*—and given an inaccurate birth date for him.

Slippery name, vast distance from his birthplace, and a bogus birthday. Worthless coordinates.

And the boy had compounded the snarling of his lifeline by running away at the age of twelve to be an itinerant boot polisher for the U.S. Cavalry. When that proved to be an unreliable career, he had just drifted, riding freight trains around the Midwest—begging, doing manual labor on farms, and learning magic from circus sideshows. With no real name or address or nativity date, his soul had no ready *handles*, and such ghost fanciers as might have been intrigued by the weirdly powerful boy were no doubt left holding a metaphorical empty coat while the boy himself was safely asleep in a probably literal outward-bound boxcar.

Sherman Oaks had certainly been pursuing Houdini by 1900, when the magician was twenty-six years old (Oaks had no clue as to how old he himself might have been), but Oaks had not ever managed to get Houdini's soul squarely in his sights.

head jerked down and he was wailing *"Hoo-hoo-hoo,"*
behind the tape, on and on, even though he could feel
drool moving toward the corner of his distended mouth.

"For . . . God's sake, William," said Mrs. Fussel in a
shrill monotone. "Have you gone crazy? You can't—"

"Pull over," the man said, blundering back up toward
the front of the van. "I'll drive. *This is the kid.* El, it's Koot
Hoomie Parganas and he's obviously an escaped nut!
They'll put him back in restraints as soon as we turn him
over to them! I'll . . . bite my arm, and say he did it. Or
better, we'll buy a cheap knife, and I'll cut myself. He's
dangerous, we *had* to tape him up. And it's *twenty
thousand goddamn dollars."*

Kootie kept up his *hoo-hoo*ing, and did it louder when
Mrs. Fussel turned the wheel to the right to pull over; and
then he felt his drooling mouth try to grin around the tape
as the three of them were jolted by the right front tire
going up over the curb. Edison's *enjoying* this, Kootie
thought.

Mr. Fussel slapped him across the face—it didn't sting
much this time, through the tape. "Shut up or I'll run a
loop of tape over your nose," the man whispered.

Edison winked Kootie's good eye at Mr. Fussel. Kootie
hoped Edison knew what he was doing here.

The Fussels found a place to park in a lot somewhere—
the windshield faced a close cinder-block wall so that no
passersby would see the bound and gagged boy in the
back of the minivan—and then Mr. Fussel picked some
quarters out of a dish on the console and climbed out,
locking the passenger door behind him.

After several seconds of no sound but the quiet burr of

nose. He heard tape rip, and then Mr. Fussel was taping Kootie's elbows and forearms to the seat belt.

Against the tape that his teeth were grinding at, Kootie was grunting and huffing, and after two or three blind, impacted seconds he realized that his lips and tongue were trying to form words; they couldn't around the tape, but he could *feel* what his mouth was trying to say:

Stop it! Stop it! Listen to me, boy! You might *die even if you calm down and stay alert, watch for a chance to run, but you'll* certainly *die if you keep thrashing and screaming like a big baby! Come on, son, be a man!*

Kootie let the mania carry him for one more second, howling out of him to swamp Edison's words in a torrent of unreasoning noise; finally, the muffled scream wobbled away to silence, leaving his lungs empty and aching. He raised his shoulders in an exaggerated shrug, held it for a moment, and then let them slump back down—and the panic fell away from him, leaving him almost calm, though the pounding of his heart was visibly twitching his shirt collar.

Kootie was motionless now, but as tense as a flexed fencing foil. He told himself that Edison was right; he had to stay alert. Nobody was going to kill him right here in these people's minivan; eventually someone would have to cut him free of this seat, and he could pretend to be asleep when they did, and then jump for freedom in the instant that the tape was cut.

He was in control of himself again, coldly and deeply angry at the Fussels and already ashamed at having gone to pieces in front of them.

And so, he was surprised when he began weeping. His

"If you," Kootie gasped, his heart hammering, "let me go—I won't tell the police—that you hit me—and tied me up."

Mr. Fussel had to duck his head to stand in the back of the minivan, and now he rocked on his feet and slapped the ceiling to keep his balance. "Drive carefully!" he shouted at his wife. "If a cop pulls us over right now, we're fucked!"

Kootie could hear Mrs. Fussel crying. "Don't talk like that in front of the boy! I'm pulling over, and you're going to let him out!"

"Do as she says," Edison grated, "or I'll say you gave me the shiner, too. Kept me for days."

Mr. Fussel was pale. For a moment, he looked as though he might hit Kootie again; then he disappeared behind the rear seat and began clanking around among some metal objects. When he reappeared, he was peeling a strip off a silvery roll of duct tape.

A sudden intrusive vision: *two stark figures strapped into chairs with duct tape, eye sockets bloody and empty . . .*

Edison was blown aside in Kootie's mind as the boy screamed with all the force of his aching lungs, clenching his fists and his eyes and whipping his head back and forth, dimly aware of the minivan slewing as the noise battered the carpeted interior—but the strip of tape scraped in between Kootie's jaws and then more tape was being wound roughly around the back of his head, over his chin, around his bucking head again and over his upper lip.

Kootie was breathing whistlingly, messily, through his

Mr. Fussel turned around in his seat and faced Kootie. He was frowning. "What's the matter, Kootie? Do you want us to drive you back to that corner and let you out?"

"Yes," Kootie's voice said firmly, and then Edison kept Kootie's jaw clamped shut so that his *No!* came out as just a prolonged "Nnnnn!"

"That's a dangerous neighborhood," Mr. Fussel said.

"Then let me out—dammit!—right—here! Kootie, let me talk! It's kidnapping if you people keep me in this vehicle!"

Mrs. Fussel spoke up. "Let's let him out and forget the whole thing."

"Eleanor, he's sick, listen to him! It would be the same as murder if we left him out on these streets. It's our duty to call the police." The man had got up out of the passenger seat and turned swayingly to face Kootie. "And even if we have to call in the police, we'll still get the twenty thousand dollars."

Kootie spun toward the sliding door in the side of the van, but before he could grab the handle the man had lunged at him and whacked him hard in the chest with his open palm, and Kootie jackknifed sideways onto the back seat; he was gasping, trying to suck air into his lungs and get his legs onto the floor so that he could spring toward Mrs. Fussel and perhaps wrench at the steering wheel, but Mr. Fussel gave him a stunning slap across the face and then strapped the seat belt across him, and pulled the strap tight through the buckle, with Kootie's arms under the woven fabric. The boy could thrash back and forth, but his arms were pinioned. He was squinting in the new brightness, for the man had knocked his sunglasses off.

In the moment of opening up the jaws of his mind for the kill, for the forcible extraction of another self from its living body, his plain physical vision always became a superfluous blur, and he relied on the sensed identity coordinates of the other self, like a pilot making an instrument landing by following a homing beam in bad weather.

Just when he would be zeroing in on the thing that was "Houdini," it became something else, and the real Houdini would be gone.

Once, in Paris in 1901, Oaks had psychically traced Houdini to a sidewalk café—but when Oaks walked up to the place with a gun in his pocket, seven bald men at the tables in front simultaneously took off their hats and bowed their heads, revealing the seven letters H-O-U-D-I-N-I painted one apiece on their shining scalps, and that grotesque assembly was the only "Houdini" that was present.

Always in his stage act Houdini was untraceably switching places with his wife (whom he had taken care to marry in three different ceremonies); another favorite trick was escaping out of a big milk can that was filled with water and padlocked shut—so that each escape was confusingly like a reexperienced birth. (*Slippery!*) In Boston in the fall of 1911, Oaks had been closing in on Houdini—the magician was weakened with a fever and haunted by dreams of his dead older brother—when suddenly the magician's psychic ground-signal was extinguished; Oaks had panicked, and expended far too much energy trying to find the ghost, and then, recuperating in defeat afterward, learned that the magician had had himself *chained inside the belly of a dead sea monster* during the eclipsed period. (The creature had washed up dead on a Cape Cod beach, and was described as "a cross between a whale and an octopus.")

In the 1920s, Oaks had got closer. Houdini had begun a new career as an exposer of phony spiritualist mediums who weren't entirely phony, and ghosts themselves had begun to threaten him. The famous Boston medium Margery gave a séance near Christmas of '24, and the ghost of her dead brother Walter announced that Houdini had less than a year to live. Houdini lived out the year, but on Halloween of '25, he was stricken with a "severe cold," and after a brief, restless sleep stayed up all night. Oaks had managed to get into Houdini's hotel room, but the sick magician had climbed out the window and disappeared until showing up protected at the Syracuse train station the next day.

On the following Halloween, in 1926, Oaks had managed to end the chase. Houdini's wife, Bess, got ptomaine poisoning from rat excrement that Oaks had managed to put into her dinner, and the magician had to travel without her masking presence. On October 11, in Albany, a ghost had been coached to walk translucently out onto the stage where a manacled Houdini was being hoisted into the air by his bound ankles and lowered into his Water Cell, a glass-sided tank from which he was supposed to escape; the ghost got itself caught in the pulleys, and Houdini was joltingly dropped a foot before the rope retightened, and a bone in his left ankle was broken. Houdini didn't try to complete that trick, but bravely went on with the rest of his act. Then, on October 22 at the Princess Theatre in Montreal, a blurry-minded religious student was induced to visit the magician in his dressing room and try Houdini's claim to be able to withstand the hardest punches; the student struck without giving Houdini any warning so that he could brace himself, and the four solid blows ruptured the magician's appendix.

Houdini of course didn't stop performing. He finished the run in Montreal the next day, and on the twenty-fourth, he opened at the Garrick Theater in Detroit. But Oaks had known that the man was dying now. That night Houdini was admitted to Grace Hospital, diagnosed with streptococcal peritonitis.

And so Oaks had got what might have been the first of his janitorial jobs at a hospital. It took Houdini a week longer to die, and in that time, Oaks managed to snag a few fresh ghosts—but when Houdini finally did die, at 1:26 P.M., he died masked. Oaks was ready to catch him, and strained numbingly hard after Houdini's ghost when the magician died, but the old magician had been as slick as ever, and his ghost had darted away from Oaks's grasp in a flicker of false memories and counterfeit dates and assumed identities.

Oaks had seized and devoured a splash of fresh ghosts—but they had nothing to do with Houdini. Later he learned that a baby girl had been born in the same instant as Houdini's death, and he realized that what he had caught was the natal explosion of stress-thrown ghost-shells emitted by the newborn infant.

It had been tasty, but it had not been Houdini.

Spiritually depleted by the decades of that useless pursuit, Oaks had gone hungrily after the other psychically conspicuous figure of the time—Thomas Alva Edison. And he had had no luck there either.

Sherman Oaks boosted himself down off the cinder-block wall and shambled across the parking lot.

At some weary point last night, he had got on a bus. He had dozed off, and when he'd snapped awake, he had been sitting in a moving streetcar, one of the old long-gone Red Car Line, and he had passively ridden it south to the Long Beach Pike on the shore of Long Beach Harbor. He had got out of the streetcar and dazedly walked up and down the arc-lit midway, among the tattoo parlors and the baseball-pitch booths, startled repeatedly by the ratcheting clank of the Ferris-wheel chain and the *snap-clang* of .22 rounds being fired at steel ducks in the shooting gallery. The only lighted construct against the blackness of ocean had been the Cyclone Racer roller coaster—the *Queen Mary* had still been somewhere on the other side of the world, steaming across the sunlit face of the Atlantic.

On the street in front of him this morning, he was seeing Marlboro billboards with slogans in Spanish, and Nissans and the boxy new black-and-white RTD diesel buses; the Mexican teenagers at the corner were wearing untucked black T-shirts and baggy pants with the crotches at their knees, and from the open window of a passing Chevy Blazer boomed some Pearl Jam song. He was living in 1992 again—the bus trip last night had been a brief tour through long-lost snapshots, requickened memories.

Yesterday, in the minivan in the back of the truck, he had animated one of the memories that had been tumbling back into him since Monday night—a moving-picture snapshot of the old Angel's Flight cable car that used to climb the hill from Third Street to Bunker Hill in downtown Los Angeles, until it was torn down for redevelopment schemes in the sixties. He had projected the hallucination to help awaken the clathrated ghost inside the boy, *excite* the ghost like an atom in a laser tube, so that Oaks would be sure of sucking the big old ghost out, along with the boy's trivial ghost, when he would finally succeed in killing the boy. And then Edison's ghost had countered by animating a relevant and defensive snapshot-memory of its own.

As much as it had been a shock to Oaks to realize that it was a memory they happened to have in common, it must also have been a shock to the ghost of Thomas Edison.

Oaks had gone after the world-famous inventor in late 1926—but the memory that the Edison ghost had projected had shown Oaks trying to get that ghost at a far earlier time, when Edison had been an anonymous but obviously strong-spirited boy selling snacks and papers on a train somewhere near Detroit.

Oaks thought about that now. In that surprisingly *shared* memory, the boy Edison had been . . . twelve? Fifteen? God, that would have to have been in the early 1860s, during the Civil War! Oaks had been an *adult* . . . a hundred and thirty years ago!

How old *am* I? wondered Oaks bewilderedly. How long have I been *at* this?

And, I was no more successful with damnable Edison in 1929 than I was on that train during the Civil War.

Or in the truck yesterday.

As soon as he had recovered from the loss of Houdini's ghost, Oaks had made his way to Edison's home in East Orange, New Jersey; and then down the coast to the "Seminole Lodge" on the Caloosahatchee River in Fort Myers, Florida, where Edison and his wife spent the winters.

Edison had been eighty years old then. He had retired from the Edison Phonograph Company only weeks earlier, leaving it in the hands of his son Charles, and was planning to devote his remaining years to the development of a hybrid of domestic goldenrod weeds that would yield latex for rubber, to break the monopoly of the British Malayan rubber forests.

The old man might as well have been *made* of rubber, for all the dent Oaks had been able to put in him during the next couple of years.

Edison had invented motion pictures, and voice-recording, and telephones, largely for their value as psychic masks, and with a transformer and an induction coil and a lightning rod with some child's toy hung on it he could have ghosts flashing past as rapidly as the steel ducks in the Pike shooting gallery, confounding any efforts to draw a bead on the real spirit of Edison behind all the decoys.

But Oaks had managed to sneak carbon tetrachloride into the old man's coffee in the summer of 1929, and as the kidneys began to fail and the doctors speculated about diabetes, the psychic defenses had weakened too; like the van der Waals force that lets an atom's nucleus have a faint magnetic effect when its surrounding neutralizing electrons are grossly low in energy, the old man's exhaustion was letting his real *self* gleam through the cloud of distracting spectral bit-players and simulations.

Oaks had begun to move in—but Edison's friend Henry Ford had moved more quickly. As an exhibit in his Ford Museum, in Dearborn, Michigan, he had built a *precise duplicate of Edison's old Menlo Park laboratory.* It couldn't even be dismissed as a replica, for he had used actual boards and old dynamos and even *dirt* from the original. And Edison *visited* the place, and was emotionally *moved* by it, thus grievously fragmenting his psychic locus.

Ford had arranged a gala "Golden Jubilee of Light" to be celebrated on the 21st of October at the Dearborn museum. Oaks had *met* Edison—along with Ford and President Hoover!—at a railway station near Detroit, and in Edison's honor the whole party had transferred to a restored Civil War vintage wood-burning locomotive.

In the instant when Oaks was poised to kill Edison and inhale the man's ghost—and then escape somehow—a period-costumed trainboy had walked down the aisle of the railway car carrying a basket of traveler's items for sale. Edison, sensing Oaks's momentarily imminent attack, snatched the basket from the boy—and then the eighty-two-year-old inventor tottered a few steps down the aisle, weakly calling, "Candy, apples, sandwiches, newspapers!" And so the image in Oaks's psychic sights was fragmented in the instant of his striking; there were suddenly two Edisons in the car, or else perhaps two boys and no Edison at all. Oaks managed to keep from uselessly, blindly firing the gun in his pocket, but he was unable to restrain his long-prepared psychic inhalation.

Edison had been ready for him, too. He must have set up this replay of the remembered train scenario as a trap. The old man smashed a doctored apple against a wooden seat back and shoved the split fruit into Oaks's face, and Oaks helplessly inhaled the confined, spoiled ghost that had been put into it.

Oaks had been . . . *jammed up.*

Not yet sure what had happened to him, knowing only that he had failed to get Edison, Oaks had stumbled off the antique train at Dearborn and disappeared into the crowd.

And he had discovered that he couldn't eat ghosts anymore—and that he *needed* to. The Bony Express had begun to assail his identity inside his head, and he could feel himself fragmenting as their power increased and his own declined.

Desperately reasoning that what Edison had done, Edison could undo, he had tried to get an audience with the great man—after all, he hadn't done anything obviously overt on the train, and he had actually worked for a while at Edison's Kinetoscope studio in the Bronx in the early nineteen-teens, to make pocket money and calculate countermasking techniques, while keeping up his pursuit of Houdini—but Ford and Charles Edison had kept him away, and kept Edison secluded and effectively masked.

And so Oaks had returned to Los Angeles in despair,

to commit suicide while he "still had a *sui* to *cide,*" as he had grimly told himself.

The method he chose was sentimental. He went to his stash box, a rented locker in a South Alameda warehouse in those days, and selected a choice smoke he'd been saving—and then he drew it into a hypodermic needle and injected the five CCs of potent air into the big vein inside his left elbow.

He expected the air bubble to cause an embolism and stop his heart.

Instead, the ghost he had injected, perceiving itself to be in a host that was about to fragment into death, spontaneously combusted in idiot terror.

The detonation had blown most of the flesh off the bones of Oaks's arm, and the doctors at Central Receiving Hospital on Sixth Street had amputated the limb at the shoulder.

Oaks had been put in the charity ward with drunks and bar-fight casualties, and when he woke up after the surgery, it wasn't long before one of his wardmates expired of an infected knife wound.

And Oaks caught the ghost, ate it, assumed it, got a life. The explosion had cost him his arm, but it had also unblocked his psychic windpipe.

He could do *that* again, any time; bottle one of the palindrome-confounded ghosts, bum a needle somewhere, and then shoot the lively ghost into his . . . leg, this time? *Right* arm? And then be missing *two* limbs. And what was to prevent the ghost from being propelled the short distance to his *heart* before it blew up?

Oaks was twitching with the urge to try once more to inhale a ghost. Maybe it would work now—now that the sun was up, now that he'd remembered all these things, now that his goddamn teeth ached so fiercely from being clenched that he couldn't see why they didn't crumble to rotten sand between his jawbones, which seemed intent on crashing *through* one another—maybe that's why he was clamping them shut, because otherwise they'd stretch *apart* just as forcefully, swing all the way around and bite his head off—

No. He had proved that it didn't work anymore, he couldn't ingest ghosts the way he was right now. He would shoot one into a vein if he had to, before the Bony Express could crash in through the walls of his identity and make a shattered crack-webbed *crazed* imbecile of him . . .

But first he would see if Edison couldn't undo what Edison could do. At least Edison was a ghost now, without the resources he'd had as a living person; and he didn't have Henry Ford protecting him anymore.

Just some kid. Some *bleeding* kid.

Oaks sighed, flinching at the multitude of outraged and impatient voices that shook his breath. His trembling left hand wobbled to the compass-pommel of his knife, and brushed the bulk of the revolver under his untucked shirt. Three more shots in it. One for himself, if everything worked out as badly as it could and even a ghost injected right into a vein didn't unjam him.

But I found the kid once, he thought dully. I can find him again. And I *can* make Edison tell me how to get unjammed.

And then I can eat him at last.

Oaks reached his hand into the pocket of his baggy camouflage pants and dug out his money. He had a five and three ones and about three dollars in change. Enough for bus fare south, and a can of bean soup.

Better make it two cans, he thought. Tomorrow's Halloween. This might be a demanding twenty-four hours, and already you feel like shit.

CHAPTER 35

✦

"There's nothing like eating hay when you're faint," he remarked to her, as he munched away.

"I should think throwing cold water over you would be better," Alice suggested, "—or some sal-volatile."

"I didn't say there was nothing better," the King replied. "I said there was nothing like it."

—Lewis Carroll,
Through the Looking-Glass

"RUBBERS," said Neal Obstadt, using a pencil to push a tightly latex-sleeved vial across his desk. The roof of his penthouse office was folded back again, but the breeze out of the blue sky was chilly, and a couple of infrared space heaters had been rolled in and now glowed like giant open-walled toasters in the corners. "Why do they pack 'em in rubbers?"

The vial was empty. All ten of the ghosts Sherman Oaks had paid as his November tithe had been compressed and sealed inside glass cartridges, along with some nitrous oxide for flavor, but Obstadt had kept one of the vials to roll around on his desk.

"The guys in the lab say they don't," said Canov impatiently. "They say it must be some kind of special gift wrap. Listen, I've got two urgent things. You said to monitor deLarava's calls. She—"

Obstadt looked up sharply. "She's said something? What?"

"No, nothing that seems to be important. She's talked to that Webb guy in Venice, but he still hasn't sensed the ghost she's apparently got cornered there, the one that drove all those sea creatures onto the beach Wednesday morning. Mainly she's busy setting up for her shoot on the *Queen Mary* tomorrow. But we—"

"Gift wrap," Obstadt interrupted. "*Gift* wrap. Is it sarcasm? Disrespect? I've snorted nine of 'em already, and they've been primo, every one. A diorama of Los Angeles citizens. No complaints about the merchandise, and I'm a connoisseur. Still, *rubbers*. What do you think? Does he mean, *Go fuck yourself*? Go fuck yourself *safely*?"

"*She has a telephone line we weren't aware of.* Her listed office lines, and the phones in her stateroom on the *Queen Mary*—" Canov paused to peer nervously down at Obstadt, but Obstadt was staring at him with no expression. "She got another," Canov blurted. "JKL-KOOT, that's the number—"

"On those billboards. The famous Parganas kid." Obstadt tried to think. "I'm like a cat," he said absently. "I've got nine lives." *Nine* of them he had snorted up,

since yesterday afternoon! No wonder he couldn't think—
he was awash in other people's memories, and the Los
Angeles he pictured outside didn't have freeways yet, and
Truman or Eisenhower or somebody was president. "The
Parganas kid! Are the cops still buying that Edison driver's
hijack story?"

"It looks like it. He's been let go, after questioning,
anyway."

"Why does Loretta want that kid? Why did Paco Rivera
want him, why *really?*" He waved his hand. "I know, his
name was Sherman Oaks. A joke. We assumed it was Oaks
that murdered the kid's parents, and that he wanted to kill
the kid because he could identify him; but . . . They both
got away, right? Yesterday? Oaks and the Parganas kid?"

"Not together."

"And *Loretta* wants the kid, too?"

After a pause, Canov shrugged. "Yes."

Obstadt stuck his pencil into the opened vial and lifted
it up. "The big smoke that hit town Monday night . . ." he
said thoughtfully, whirling the vial around the pencil shaft.
"Oaks would have been . . . *terribly* . . . aware of that. How
old is the kid?"

"Eleven."

"Not puberty yet, probably." He was nodding. "The *kid*
has got to have the *big ghost.* Either he's carrying it, or
he's inhaled it and it's grafted onto him, not assimilated.
That's why Loretta wants him, and why Sherman Oaks
wanted him. Oaks can't have *got* the ghost yet, or not as
of yesterday afternoon, anyway, or the kid would be dead,
not running around."

Obstadt looked up from the spinning, condom-sheathed vial, and smiled at Canov. "Your guys *caught* the kid yesterday! Took him away from that yuppie couple, the dead Fussels! And you *gave* the kid to Sherman Oaks!" Obstadt was speaking in a wondering tone, still smiling, his eyes wide. "And if you had done what I told you, monitored fucking *all* of Loretta's phone lines, *I'd* have the kid, *I'd* have the big ghost, which is probably goddamn *Einstein* or somebody, do you realize that?" Obstadt was still smiling, but it was all teeth, and he was panting and his face was red.

Almost a whisper: "Yes, sir."

"Good. Good." Obstadt knew that Canov must be aching to say, *But you got a thousand and ten smokes! How big can this one be in comparison?* You weren't there, Obstadt thought, Canov my boy—you weren't there Monday night, you weren't *aware,* anyway, when that wave swept across L.A. and every streetlight dimmed in obeisance, every car radio whirled off into lunatic frequencies, and every congealed-ghost street bum fell down hollering.

"There's another thing," said Canov in a strangled tone. "You told me to check out any kids deLarava might have. No, she doesn't seem to have any—but she's looking for this Peter Sullivan, and she's got a description of the van he's driving, and the license number. He used to work for her, along with a twin sister of his named Elizabeth who everybody called Sukie, who killed herself in Delaware Monday night."

"She did? Now, why—"

"Listen! The Sullivan twins were orphans, their father was a movie producer named Arthur Patrick Sullivan, okay? He drowned *in Venice* in 1959. Now Sullivan the Elder was the godfather of this Nicky Bradshaw character—"

"Who Loretta's also looking for, right. Spooky, in that old TV show."

"And . . . and Sullivan the Elder had just got married to a starlet named Kelley Keith. He drowned, while she was on the beach watching, and then she took a lot of his money and disappeared."

"In '59," said Obstadt thoughtfully. "He drowned at Venice, and now Loretta's . . . after the son, and the godson, and a big-time ghost that apparently came out of the sea . . . in Venice."

"And she was obviously after the daughter too, but she killed herself. Clearly you follow my thinking."

"Okay!" Obstadt opened his desk drawer and took out the glass cartridge that contained the last of Sherman Oaks's tithe ghosts. The lab boys had painted a blue band around it to distinguish it from the others—the vial its smoke had come in had been tucked into a different kind of condom: Trojan, while the others were all Ramses. How do the lab boys know? he wondered. Nobody should be an expert at recognizing different kinds of *rubbers*.

Trojan—it reminded Obstadt of something, but Canov was speaking again.

"Loretta deLarava is almost certainly Kelley Keith," he was saying, "and she seems to be unwilling to have that fact known."

"Maybe she's got crimes still outstanding," mused Obstadt aloud, "hell, maybe she killed the old movie producer! Any number of possibilities. Whatever it is, we can use it to crowbar her, and she would be a useful employee. Meanwhile! *Tomorrow* is Halloween. Get all your men out—find the Parganas kid, and this Peter Sullivan, and Oaks, and bring 'em all to me. Alive, if that's easily convenient, but their fresh ghosts in glass jars would be fine. Better, in a lot of ways."

"But the Sullivan guy is masked, deLarava said so; he ditched one of her top sniffers outside of Miceli's yesterday. And the big ghost and the kid can mask each other, and Sherman Oaks is nothing *but* a walking mask—he's got no name or birth date, and the ghosts *inside* him probably have more personality definition than *he* does. We'd never catch their ghosts in vials, they'd be everywhere, like a flashlight beam through a kaleidoscope."

"I don't care," said Obstadt, opening another drawer and lifting out the thermoslike inhaler. "I want Oaks out of the picture, by which I mean dead. He's not just a dealer, he's fallen into the product and become a junkie, a heavy smoker, a rival. And I want deLarava working for me, severely subservient to me." He laid the glass cartridge into the slot at the top of the inhaler. "Do you know why water in a bucket hollows out and climbs the walls and gets shallower when you spin the bucket real fast?"

Canov blinked. "Uh, centrifugal force."

"No. Because there's other *stuff around,* for it to be spinning in relation *to;* the room, the city, the world. If the bucket of water was the only thing in the universe, if it *was* the universe, the water would be still, and you couldn't tell if it was spinning or not. Spinning compared to *what?* The question wouldn't have any meaning."

"Okay," said Canov in a cautious tone.

"So—" So I'm tired of being hollowed out, thought Obstadt, and of climbing the walls, and of getting shallow. I'm tired of not being the only person in the universe. "So I need to *contain* them, don't I? As long as they're existing at all. DeLarava I can contain by just *owning* her."

"She's doing her shoot aboard the *Queen Mary* tomorrow," Canov reminded him, "the Halloween thing, about ghosts on the ship. Anything about that?"

"Ummm . . . wait, on that. I don't think there's anything much on the *Queen Mary* right now. Let's see how you do at finding these people before sundown tonight, hm?"

"Okay." Canov visibly shifted his weight from one foot to the other, and he scratched his beard. "I'm sorry about not finding the other phone line sooner—we—"

"Get out of my sight," said Obstadt gently, with a smile.

After Canov had tottered out the door, Obstadt leaned back in his chair and looked up into the cold blue vault of the sky, wishing that the tiny crucifix of a jet would creep across it, just to break up the monotony of it.

Then he sighed and twisted the valve on the inhaler. He heard the hiss as the pressure from the punctured cartridge filled the inside of the cylinder, and then he lifted the tube to his lips.

The hit was cold with nitrous oxide, but nausea-sweat sprang out on his forehead at the hard, static *absence* of the rotted thing that rode the rushing incoming stench and wedged itself hopelessly sideways in the breech of his mind. The back of Obstadt's head hit the carpet as his chair went over backward, and then his knees banged against a bookcase and clattered sideways to the floor, and he was convulsing all alone on the carpet under the high blue sky.

CHAPTER 36

✺

*"I love my love with an H," Alice couldn't
help beginning, "because he is Happy. I hate
him with an H, because he is Hideous . . ."*
                              —Lewis Carroll,
                              Through the Looking-Glass

AT EYE-HEIGHT on one of the glass shelves was a
white bas relief of Jesus done in reverse, with the face
indented into a plaster block, the nose the deepest part—
as if, Elizalde thought, Jesus had passed out face first into
a bowl of meringue. Someone had at some time reached
into the hollow of the face to paint the eyes with
painstaking lack of skill, and as Elizalde shuffled across
the linoleum floor the head gave the illusion of being
convex rather than concave, and seemed to swivel to keep
the moronic eyes fixed on her.

What household out there, she asked herself nervously,
is decorated to *near* perfection, lacking only this fine *objet
d'art* to make it complete?

*Frank Rocha's house had been full of things like that—
prints of Our Lady of Guadalupe, tortured Jesuses painted
luridly on black velvet.* Elizalde nervously touched the
bulge of her wallet in her back pocket.

The old woman behind the counter smiled at her and
said, *"Buenas días, mi hija. Cómo puedo ayudarte?"*

"Quiero hacer reparaciones a un amigo muerto," said
Elizalde. How easy it was to express the idea *"I want to
make amends to a dead friend"* in Spanish!

The woman nodded understandingly and bent to slide
open the back of a display case. Elizalde set down her
grocery bag and clasped her hands together to still their
trembling. Already she had stopped at a tiny corner
grocery store and bought eggs and Sugar Babies and a pint
of Myers rum and a cheap plastic compass with stickum
on the back so that it could be glued to a windshield; and
in another *botánica,* she had bought a selection of herbs
in cellophane packets, and oils in little square bottles, that
she had been assured *habría ojos abrir del polvo,* would
open eyes out of the dust—all of it had been set out on
the counter in response to her request for something that
would call up the dead.

Out of the display arrangement of stones and garish
books and cheap metal medallions, the old woman now
lifted a plastic bag that contained a sprig of dried leaves:
YERBA BUENA, read the hand-lettered sticker on the bag,
and Elizalde didn't even have to sniff it, just had to look
at the dusty, alligator-bumpy leaves, to be surrounded by
the remembered smell of mint; and, for the first time, she
realized that the Spanish name meant *good herb*—over
the generations her family had smoothed and elided the

words to something that she would have spelled *yerra vuena,* which she had always taken to mean something like "fortunate error," with the noun given an unusual feminine suffix.

"*Incapácita las alarmas del humo en su apartamento,*" the woman told her—quietly, though they were alone in the shop. "*Hace un te cargado, con muchas hojas; anade algún licor, tequila o ron, y déjalo cocinar hasta que está seco, y deja las hojas cocinar hasta que están secas, y humando y quemadas. Habla al humo.*"

Elizalde nodded as she memorized the instructions— *disable smoke alarms in the apartment, make a strong mint tea with booze in it, then cook it dry and let the leaves smoke, and talk to the smoke.*

Jesus, she thought; and then in spite of herself, she glanced at the disquieting bas-relief-in-reverse, which still seemed to be turned toward her, staring.

I still like "fortunate error," she thought helplessly as she took the bag from the woman and handed her a couple of dollar bills. She tucked the dried mint into the bag with her other purchases, thanked the woman, and shuffled out of the store. Bells hung on the doorframe rang a minor chord out into the sunlight as she stepped down to the Beverly Boulevard sidewalk.

Two young boys whirled past her on bicycles, giggling, one of them riding with one hand on the handlebars and the other clutching the metal box of a car stereo. Looking in the direction they'd come from, she saw a blue scatter of car window glass on the sidewalk, and a white-haired old woman wrapped in a curtain scooping up the bits of glass and eating them.

Up ahead of her on the other side of Beverly was the two-story, fifties-vintage building where she had rented her psychiatric office. She could see a vertical edge of it from here, and a corner of glowing green neon—it was still standing, apparently still occupied.

Well, she thought with a shudder of nausea, the fire trucks did get there damn quick.

Elizalde had rented a suite there for only a couple of months *(before that final night, two years ago tomorrow)*—a tiny reception room, her office, a bathroom, and the big conference room with windows looking out over Beverly *(the glass of which had burst out in the intense heat of the flames)*.

At her Wednesday-night séances, she would have the six or eight of her patients sit around the conference table, and after lighting a dozen or so candles on the shelves she would turn out the lights and have everyone hold hands. They took turns "sharing with the dead"—reliving old disagreements, talking with the dead sometimes, crying and praying sometimes—and Elizalde had tried to insist that if someone felt the need to say *Fuck you, fuck you* to the group and then storm out of the room, that it at least be done quietly.

Frank Rocha had always tried to get the seat next to Elizalde, and the palm of his hand was often damp and trembling. At the penultimate séance, a week before Halloween, he had passed her a folded note.

She had tucked it into her pocket, and only read it later, at home.

It had been painstakingly handwritten, and some misguided idea of formality had led him to draw quotation marks around nearly every noun (. . . *my "love" for you . . . the lack of "understanding" from my "wife " . . . my concern for your "needs" and "wants" . . . my "efforts" to make a "life" for you and me . . . the "honor" of "marrying" you . . .*), which gave the thing an unintended tone of sarcasm. Elizalde had telephoned him at his job the next day and, as gently as she had been able, had told him that what he had proposed was impossible.

But she had cried over the note, alone in her living room late that Wednesday night, and she had kept it in her wallet through all the subsequent horrors and flight and migration.

Elizalde hadn't wanted to leave the Long Beach apartment this morning—or at worst go any farther outside than to where Sullivan had parked the van, to fetch his meager food and some instant coffee and then hurry back inside—until the dawning of Sunday morning, when Halloween would safely be passed. But when Sullivan had begun to speculate on things that they ought to go buy before sundown today, his own readiness to be talked out of leaving Solville was so palpable that she had pretended to be unaware of it, and she'd made herself agree brightly to his proposed shopping trip. New socks and underwear, she noted, would be a necessity.

The apartment's toilet had indeed proved to be hooked up to the hot-water pipe—the bathroom window was steamy. They took turns showering and getting back into yesterday's unfresh clothes, and by the time they had moved the plaster hands away from the door and opened it to the fresh Friday-morning breeze, Sullivan was tight-lipped and grumpy and Elizalde was brittle with imitation cheer.

Sullivan had furtively switched license plates with a pickup truck in the Solville parking lot, and then the two of them had driven off north into the skyline-spiked brown haze of Los Angeles, Sullivan to buy some "electronics" and Elizalde to cruise the *botánicas* and *hierverias* for any likely looking séance aids.

"I think that, in addition to being wisps of *stuff*, ghosts are an electromagnetic phenomenon," Sullivan had said nervously as he steered the van along the middle lane of the Harbor Freeway, "something like radio waves. When *they focus* somewhere, like they do when something energizes them and wakes them up, gets them into their excited state, they're located—a particle rather than a wave, for our purposes, or maybe a standing wave with perceptible nodes, sort of low-profile ball lightning—and they're detectably magnetic. Sometimes strongly so." Sullivan had been sweating. "I've seen them around the step-up transformers at power plants out in the desert, just a bunch of indistinct guys standing around blinking on the concrete, and if there's enough of them their magnetic field can interfere with the power readouts. What I'm going to . . . *try* to do is scrounge together some gear that'll isolate an individual ghost's signal, step it up, and hook it to a speaker. Meanwhile, you can pick up whatever sort of voodoo stuff it is that . . ."

He had paused then, at least having the grace to be embarrassed . . . *that you used when you killed your patients two years ago,* she had thought, mentally finishing his sentence for him.

She had given him a hooded gaze under one raised eyebrow. "You just be sure you get some spare big-amp fuses for your *electronics, gabacho* . . . she'd said quietly.

He had pursed his lips and nodded, clearly intimidated by her supposed connections to some vast, secret, potent *brujeria folklórica.*

Now, standing on the sidewalk in her stale clothes and stringy long hair, among the baby carriages and beer signs, watching the progress of all the old beat Torinos and Fairlanes with defeated suspensions and screeching power-steering belts, she wondered if she could accomplish anything at all.

Sullivan had told her about "bar-time," and had explained that experiencing it was one of the consequences of being a spiritual antenna, with a psychic guilt-link to some dead person or persons; when hungry ghosts or ghost hunters focused their attention on her, she couldn't help but put some of her spiritual weight on her "one foot in the grave," so that she lived just a fraction of a second outside of time, *ahead* of time. He said it happened to all ghost-bound people.

And Sullivan had told her how dormant ghosts could be excited into fitful agitation by people such as themselves, and had told her how to spot the elusive creatures, once that had happened.

She had been careful not to make any of the moves that would rouse the things—she had not whistled any old Beatles tunes (Sullivan had told her that "The Long and Winding Road" was particularly evocative), nor, in this neighborhood, Santana's "Oye Como Va"; she'd been careful not to pick up stray coins on the pavement, especially very shiny ones; and she had not stared into the eyes of the faces, faded to washes of pink and blue, in the photos taped up in the windows of the little hairstyling salons, for Sullivan had told her that frightened new ghosts would cling to those paper eyes and then wait to meet and hold on to an unguarded gaze.

She *had* bought the compass, though. Sullivan had told her that when a compass needle pointed in some direction besides north, it was very likely pointing at one of the awakened ghosts. She had kept it in her pocket and glanced at it frequently—and at one point during her shopping stroll she had walked wide around a dusty old Volkswagen sitting on flat tires in a parking lot, averting her eyes as she skirted it, and a few minutes later she had crossed Beverly to avoid the open front door of a corner bar because the needle had swung away from north to point at these things.

Sullivan had told her to wait for him by the video games in the Raphael's liquor store at the corner of Lucas Avenue, and now she started angling through the crowd in that direction. It would be better for her to be waiting for him inside than for him to have to idle in the parking lot in the conspicuous van. Her bag of purchases was heavy enough now, and her hip and shoulder still ached from her fall on the Amado Street sidewalk two days ago; and she was walking awkwardly, for she had tucked the thing that Sullivan swore was *Houdini's dried thumb* into the high top of her left shoe, to balance the can of mace in her right one.

Un buen santo te encomiendas, she thought, quoting an old saying of her grandmother's. A fine patron saint you've got.

At a red light, she leaned her elbow on the little steel

cowl over the signal-change button on a curbside traffic-light pole—and then gasped with dizziness and heard the thump of the seat of her jeans and the grocery bag hitting the sidewalk in the instant before her vision jumped with the jar of the impact.

People were staring at her, and she thought she heard *borracha!*—drunk!—as she scrambled back up to her feet. The light box on the pole across the street had finally begun flashing walk and she hoisted her bag in both arms and marched between the lines of the crosswalk toward the opposite curb, sweat of embarrassment chilly on her forehead. Not until she heard a wet *plop* on the pavement by her foot, and looked down just in time to see an egg from her torn bag hit the asphalt, did she realize that she was on bar-time again.

She stepped up the curb so carefully that any bar-time effect was imperceptible, and then she crossed the sidewalk and leaned against the brick wall of a *mariscos* restaurant, panting in the steamy squid-and-salsa-scented air that was humming out of a window fan.

It could be just Sullivan nearby, she told herself nervously; he said we can have that effect when we're together, our antenna fields overlapped and making "interference fringes"—it happened with him and his twin sister all the time, he said. Or it could be Frank Rocha, resonating in the sidewalk in forlorn response to the scuff of my sneakers (though the dried thumb in my shoe should be keeping any spiritoids from *recognizing* me). Maybe I just got *confused,* and *thought* I heard the egg break on the street before it really did; I haven't had a decent night's sleep, a decent meal, in—

But, of course, she was standing right across the street now from 15415 Beverly. She looked up, slowly and sullenly; the two-story building had been repainted, but she couldn't recall now anyway whether the fire had streaked the outside walls with soot. The windows of what had been her conference room had glass in them again, and between the glass and the curtains hung a green neon sign reading: PSYCHIC PALM READER

Good luck to you, she thought bitterly to the present tenant. You'll never host as good a show as I did.

On that final Wednesday evening, that Halloween night, Frank Rocha had arrived very drunk. A week had passed since the night when she had read his clumsy letter, and, mostly out of guilt and uncertainty, she had let him stay at the meeting in spite of his condition. At one point early in the evening, he had taken his hand out of hers and had fumbled at something inside his leather jacket; after a muffled *snap!*, he had shuddered and coughed briefly, then returned his hand to hers, and the séance had proceeded. The smoke from the candles and incense had covered any smell of cordite, and Frank Rocha had continued to mumble and weep—no one present had realized that he was now dead, that he had neatly shot himself squarely through the heart with a tiny .22 revolver.

Later, in the darkness, he had again pulled his hand free, but this time it had been to squeeze her thigh under the table; not wanting to hurt his feelings, she had thought for a while before reaching down and firmly pushing his hand away. Luckily, she had had her face averted from him.

With a blast of scorching air that hit her like a mailbag dropped from a train, Frank Rocha's body had exploded into white fire. Elizalde and the person who had been sitting on the other side of him were ignited into flame themselves and tumbled away in a screaming tangle of bodies and folding chairs, and everyone was dazzled to blindness by the man-sized, magnesium-bright torch that had been Frank Rocha.

And then the séance had started to be for real.

Elizalde looked away from the white building across the street and made herself take deep, slow breaths. Hoping to reassure herself, she dug the plastic compass out of her jeans pocket and looked at it—

But it was pointing southeast, straight ahead down Beverly toward the Civic Center.

The compass needle didn't wobble in synch with any of the cars or pedestrians she could see. Unlike the readings she had got earlier at the abandoned Volkswagen and the barroom door, this one seemed to be some distance away.

There's a . . . a *ghost* down that way, she thought carefully, trying to assimilate the idea. A big one.

A furniture truck made a ponderous low-gear left turn onto the boulevard from Belmont Avenue, and little Toyotas and big old *La Bamba* boat cars rattled along the painted asphalt, up toward Hollywood or down toward City Hall, and crows and pigeons flapped around the traffic lights or pecked at litter on the sidewalks in the chilly sunlight . . . but there was a big *ghost* awake and walking around somewhere down Beverly in the direction of the Harbor Freeway.

✳ ✳ ✳

The ghosts had arrived at the séance sometime during the confused moments when curtains were being torn down from the windows and bundled around the people who had been set afire; Frank Rocha himself was a roaring white pyre that no one could get close to.

Half of Elizalde's hair had been burned off, and after she'd been extinguished herself she had scorched her hands and face in a useless attempt to throw a curtain over Frank Rocha, but what she today remembered most vividly was the agony of listening to the shattering, withering screams.

The hallway doors had opened, and a lot of people had begun to come in who didn't even seem to notice the fire; and they hadn't *walked* in, but seemed to glide, or float, or flicker like bad animation. The light had been wrong on most of them—the shadows on their faces had not been aligned with the flaring corpse on the floor, and when their faces had happened to turn toward it, the incongruously steady shadows had abruptly looked like holes.

Others appeared from the ceiling—several of these were oversized infants, impossibly floating in midair, with the purple umbilical cords still swinging from their bellies, and their huge faces were red and their mouths hideously wide as they howled like tornadoes.

Bloody, mewling embryonic chicks pecked and clawed at Elizalde's scorched scalp, and fell into her face when she tried to cuff them off.

Instead of running for the ghost-crowded doors, everyone had seemed to be scrambling to the corners, down on their hands and knees to be below the churning burnt-pork-reeking smoke. The clothing burst away from three of her patients, two women and a man, to release long fleshy snakes, which lifted like pythons as they grew, and then dented and swelled to form grimacing human faces on the bulbous ends.

The faces on the flesh-snake bulbs, and the shadow-pied faces of the intruding ghosts, and the red faces of the giant infants, and the blood-and-smoke-and-tear-streaked faces of Elizalde's patients, all were shouting and screaming and babbling and praying and crying and laughing, while Frank Rocha blazed away like a blast furnace in the middle of the floor. By the time his unbearably bright body had shifted and rolled over and then fallen through the floor, the big windows had all popped and disintegrated into whirling crystalline jigsaw pieces and spun away into the darkness, and people had begun to climb out, hang from the sill, and drop to the flower bed below. Elizalde had dragged one unconscious woman to the window, and had then somehow hoisted the inert body over her shoulder and climbed out; the jump nearly broke her neck and her knees and her jaw, but when the fire trucks had come squealing across the parking lot, Elizalde had been doing CPR on the unconscious patient.

Elizalde blinked now, and realized that she had been standing for some length of time on the curb, shivering and sweating in the cold diesel breeze.

That was all two years ago, she told herself. What are you going to do right now?

She decided to backtrack up Belmont and then walk on down to Lucas along some other street; Houdini's thumb was still there tickling her, down behind her sweaty ankle bone, but something had paid attention to her a few moments ago, and she didn't want to blunder into some supernatural event. She turned around and walked into the mariachi jukebox noise of the *mariscos* place and bought a couple of fish tacos wrapped in wax paper just so as to be able to wheedle from the counterman a plastic bag big enough to slide her ruptured grocery bag into.

The next block up was Goulet Street, gray old bungalow houses that had mostly been fenced in and converted to body shops and tire outlets after some long-ago zoning change. As she hurried along the sidewalk past the sagging fences, a young man stepped up from beside a parked car and asked her what he could get her, and half a block later another man nodded at her and made whip-snapping gestures, but she knew that they were both just crack cocaine dealers, and she shrugged and shook her head at each of them and kept walking.

On the morning after the séance, she had been remanded from the hospital into the custody of the police, charged with manslaughter; she spent that night in jail, and on the following day, Friday, she had put up the fifty-thousand-dollar bail—and then had calmly driven her trusty little Honda right out across the Mojave Desert, out of California. She hadn't had a clue as to what had happened at her therapy session—she had known only two things about it: that Frank Rocha and two of the other patients had died, and—of course—that she herself had had a psychotic episode, suffered a severe schizophrenic perceptual disorder. She had been sure that she had briefly gone crazy—and she had not doubted that diagnosis until this last Monday night.

Walking along the Goulet Street sidewalk now, she wondered if she might have been better off when she had thought she was crazy.

At Lucas she turned right, and then turned right again into a narrow street that curved past the rear doors of a liquor store and a laundry, back to Beverly. Raphael's liquor was across the Beverly intersection, and she was hurrying, hoping Sullivan wasn't parked there yet.

But the compass was still in her hand, and she glanced at it. The needle was pointing behind her, which was north.

Good old reliable north, she thought. She sighed, and felt the tension unkink from her shoulders—whatever had been going on was apparently over—but she glanced at it again to reassure herself, and saw the needle swing and then hold steady.

Grit crunched under her toes as she spun around to look back. A hunched, dwarfed figure was lurching toward her from around the corner of the liquor store.

Duende! she thought as she twisted to lean back the other way; it's one of those malevolent half-damned angels the women on the beach told me about last night!

Then she had crouched and made a short hop to get her footing and was striding away toward Beverly, in her retinas burning the glimpsed image of a gaunt face behind glittering sunglasses under a bobbing straw cowboy hat.

But a battered, primer-paint-red pickup truck had turned up from Beverly, its engine gunning as the body rocked on bad shocks, and she knew that the half-dozen mustached men in wife-beater undershirts crouching in the back were part of whatever was going on here.

Elizalde sprinted to the back wall of the laundry, leaning on it and hiking up her left foot to dig out the can of mace; but the men in the truck were ignoring her.

She looked back—the *duende* had turned and was hurrying away north, but it was limping and clutching its side, and making no speed. The truck sped past Elizalde and then past the *duende,* and made a sharp right, bouncing up over the curb. The men in the back vaulted out and grabbed the dwarfish figure, whose only resistance was weak blows with pale little fists.

The hat spun away as the men lifted the small person by the shoulders and ankles, and then the oversized sunglasses fell off and she realized that the men's prey was just a little boy.

Even as she realized it, she was running back there, clutching the bag in her left arm, her right hand thumbing the cap of the mace spray around to the ready position.

"Déjalo marchar!" she was shouting. *"Qué estás haciendo? Voy a llamar a policía!"*

One of the men who wasn't holding the boy spun toward her with a big brown hand raised back across his shoulder to hit her, and she aimed the little spray can at his face and pushed the button.

The burst of mist hit him in the face, and he just sat down hard on the asphalt; she turned the can toward the men holding the boy and pushed the button again, sweeping it across their faces and the backs of their heads alike, and then she stepped over the spasming, coughing bodies and shot a squirt into the open passenger-side window of the truck.

A quacking voice from the bed of the truck called, *"No me chingues, Juan Dominguez!"*—but she didn't see anyone back there, only some kind of cloth bag with a black Raiders cap on it. The *bag* seemed to have spoken, in merry malevolence.

The boy had been dropped, and had rolled away but not stood up; Elizalde's own eyes were stinging and her nose burned, but she bent down to spray whatever might be left in the can directly into the faces of the two men who had only fallen onto their hands and knees. They exhaled like head-shot pigs and collapsed.

Elizalde dropped the emptied can and hooked her right hand under the boy's armpit and hoisted him up to his feet. She was still clutching her bag of supplies in the crook of her left arm.

"Gotta run, kiddo," she said. "Fast as you can, okay? *Corre conmigo, bien?* Just across the street. I'll stay with you, but you've got to motivate with your feet. *Vayamos!*"

He nodded, and she noticed for the first time the faded bruise around his left eye. Not stopping to retrieve the hat and the sunglasses, she frog-marched him back around the liquor store to the Lucas Avenue sidewalk and started down it toward the stoplight.

Across the wide, busy street she could see the dusty brown box that was Sullivan's van in the liquor store parking lot.

She looked behind her—there was no sign of the pickup truck.

The boy seemed to be able to walk, and she let go of him to dig the compass out of her pocket. The needle was pointed straight east. *The ghost's still ahead of us,* she thought nervously; then she held it out in front of them, and the needle swung back toward north.

She moved it around, to be sure—and it was consistently pointing *at the boy who was lurching along beside her.*

She knew that she would change her pace, one way or the other, when she gave that new fact a moment's thought—so she instantly gripped the compass between her teeth and began to walk faster, dragging the boy along, lest she might otherwise stop, or ditch him and just flat-out run.

This *boy* is the ghost, she told herself; Sullivan said they can accumulate mass from organic litter, and eventually look like solid street people.

But Elizalde couldn't believe it. For a moment, she pulled her attention away from the sidewalk pedestrians they were passing and craned her neck to look down into his pinched, pale face—and she couldn't believe that a restless ghost could have made those clear brown eyes, now pellucidly deep with fear, out of gutter puddles and sidewalk spit and tamale husks. And his eye socket was bruised! Surely the bogus flesh of those scarecrows couldn't incorporate working capillaries and circulating blood! He must have a ghost . . . *on* him, somehow, like an infestation of lice.

A *big* ghost, she reminded herself uneasily, remembering how steadily the compass needle had pointed at it from blocks away.

She still couldn't see the red pickup truck, behind or ahead. Apparently, the mace had worked.

They had nearly reached the corner. She spat the compass into her shopping bag. "What's your name?" she asked, wondering if she would even get a response.

"The kid's in shock," said the boy huskily, his voice jerking with their fast steps. "Better you don't know *his* name. Call me . . . Al."

"I'm Angelica," she said. Better you don't know my last name, she thought. "A friend of mine is in that brown van across the street. See it?" She still had her hand under his arm, so she just jerked her chin in the direction of the van. "Our plan is to get out of here, back to a safe place where nobody can find us. I think you should come with us."

"You've got that compass," said the boy grimly. "I've been *in* a 'van,' and I can scream these lungs pretty loud."

"We're not going to kidnap you," said Elizalde.

They shuffled to a rocking halt at the Lucas corner, panting and waiting for the light to turn green. Elizalde was still looking around for pursuit. "I don't even know if my friend would want another person along," she said. She shook her head sharply, wondering if it could even be noon yet. "But I think you should come with us. The compass—anybody in the whole city who knows about this stuff can track you."

The boy nodded. At least he was standing beside her, and hadn't pulled away from her hand. "Yeah," he said. "That is true, sister. And if I put my light back under the bushel basket, if I—*step out of the center-ring spotlight,* here, this kid will collapse like a sack of coal. So, you've got a place that's safe? Even for *us?* How are you planning on degaussing me? This damned electric belt's not worth *one* mint."

Hebephrenic schizophrenia? wondered Elizalde; *or one of the dissociative reactions of hysterical neurosis?* MPD would probably be the trendy analysis these days—multiple personality disorder.

She floundered for a response. What had he said? Degaussing? Elizalde had heard that term used in connection with battleships, and she thought it had something to do with radar. "I don't know about that. But my friend does—he's an electrical engineer."

This seemed to make the boy angry. "Oh, an *electrical engineer*. All mathematics, I daresay, equations on paper to match the paper diploma on his wall! Never any dirt under his fingernails! Maybe he thinks he's the only one around here with a *college degree!*"

Elizalde blinked down at the boy in bewilderment. "I—I'm sure he doesn't—I have a college degree, as a matter of fact—" Good Lord, she thought, why am I bragging? Because of my rumpled old clothes and dirty hair? Bragging to a traumatized street kid? "But none of that's important here—"

"B.S.," said the boy now, with clear and inexplicable pride. "Let's go meet your electrical engineer."

"Shit, yes," said Elizalde. The light turned green, and they started walking.

CHAPTER 37

※

"But that's not your fault," the Rose added kindly. "You're beginning to fade, you know—and then one can't help one's petals getting a little untidy."

Alice didn't like this idea at all . . .

—Lewis Carroll,
Through the Looking-Glass

SULLIVAN HAD SEEN ELIZALDE crossing the street, and when he saw that the reason she was moving slowly was because she was helping a limping *kid* along, he swore and got out of the van.

He had noticed the onset of bar-time as he'd been driving, five or ten minutes ago, when he reflexively tapped the brake in the instant before the nose of a car appeared out of an alley ahead of him; he had then tested it by blindly sliding a random cassette into the tape player, cranking the volume all the way up, and then turning on the player—he had not only cringed involuntarily, but had

496

even recognized the opening of the Stones' "Sympathy for the Devil," just before the first percussive yell had come booming out of the speakers. He had switched the set off then, wondering anxiously what was causing the psychic focus on him, and if it was on Elizalde too.

And now here she was with some kid.

He met them by the traffic-light pole at the corner, and he took the shopping bag from her. "Say goodbye to your little friend," he said. "We've gotta go *now*. Bar-time, you feel it?"

"Yes, I do," she said, smiling. "Other people out here probably do too. Act natural, like you *don't* feel it."

She was right. He smiled stiffly back at her and hefted the bag. "So, did you get your shopping done? All ready to go?"

Two teenage Mexican boys swaggered up to them, one of them muttering, *"Vamos a probar la mosca en leche, porqué no?"* Then one of them asked her, in English, "Lady, can I have a dollar for a pack of cigarettes?"

"Porqué no?" echoed Elizalde with a mocking grin. She reached into her pocket with the hand that wasn't supporting the sick-looking boy and handed over a dollar.

"I need cigarettes too!" piped up the other teenager.

"You can share his," said Elizalde, turning to Sullivan. "We're ready to go," she told him.

We're *not* taking this sick kid along with us! he thought. "No," he said, still holding his smile but speaking firmly. "Little Billy's got to go home."

"Auntie Alden won't take him today," she said, "and it's getting very late."

Sullivan blew out a breath and let his shoulders sag. He looked at the boy. "I suppose you *do* want to come along."

The boy had a cocky grin on his face. "Sure, plug. On your own, you might get careless and open a switch without turning off the current first."

Sullivan couldn't help frowning. He had spent the morning at an old barn of a shop on Eighth Street called Garmon's Pan-Electronics, and he wondered if this boy knew that, somehow. Was the boy's remark the twang of a snapped trapwire?

"I told him you're an electrical engineer," said Elizalde in a harried voice. "Let's *go!*"

After a tense, anguished pause: "Okay!" Sullivan said, and turned and began marching his companions back across the liquor store parking lot toward the van. "The collapsing magnetic field," he told the boy, in answer to the boy's disquieting remark, "will induce a huge voltage that'll arc across the switch, right?" Why, he wondered, am I bothering to prove anything to a kid?

"Don't say it just to please me," the boy told him.

When they had climbed into the van and pulled the doors closed, Sullivan and Elizalde sat up front, and the boy sat in the back on the still-unmade bed.

"Why did you give that guy a buck?" asked Sullivan irritably as he started the engine and yanked the gearshift into drive.

"He might have been Elijah," Elizalde said wearily. "Elijah wanders around the Earth in disguise, you know, asking for help, and if you don't help him, you get in trouble at the Last Judgment."

"Yeah?" Sullivan made a fast left turn onto Lucas going

south, planning to catch the Harbor Freeway from Bixel off Wilshire. "Well, the *other* guy was probably Elijah, the guy you *didn't* give a buck to. Who's our new friend, by the way?"

"Call me Al," spoke up the boy from the back of the van. "No, my name's Kootie—" The voice sounded scared now. "Where are we going? It's all right, Kootie, you remember how I didn't trust the Fussels? These people are square. I'm glad you're back with us, son. I was worried about you."

Sullivan shot Elizalde a furious glance.

"He's magnetic," she said. She seemed near tears. "Compasses point to him. And I used up my mace spray on a crowd of bad guys who were trying to force him into a truck."

"It's okay," Sullivan said. "That's good, I'm glad you did. I wish I'd been there to help." Good God, he thought. "Did you get some likely . . . groceries?"

"I think so." She sighed deeply. "Did you hear what those two *vatos* said? They described you and me as *la mosca en leche*. That means fly-in-milk—like 'salt-and-pepper,' you know, a mixed-race couple. They thought I was a Mexican."

Sullivan glanced at her. "You *are* a Mexican."

"I know. But it's nice that they could tell. How did you do, did you get some good electronic stuff?"

Sullivan was looking into the driver's mirror on the outside of the door. A new Lincoln had sped up to make the light at Beverly, and it was now swerving into the right lane as if to pass him. He was glad of the distraction, for he didn't want to talk about the ragtag equipment he'd bought.

"Not bad," he said absently, "considering I didn't know what I wanted." When the Lincoln was alongside, Sullivan pressed the brake firmly, and the big car shot ahead. "They had some old carborundum-element bulbs there cheap, so I bought a few, and I got an old Ford coil for fifty bucks, and a Langmuir gauge." He made a show of peering ahead with concern.

But the Lincoln ahead had actually *slowed,* and now another one just like it was speeding up from behind. "Other stuff," he added—nearly in a whisper, for something really did seem to be going on here. His palms were suddenly damp on the wheel.

There was a cross street to the right ahead, and he waited until the last instant to touch the brake and whip the wheel around to cut directly across the right-hand lane; the tires were screeching, and a bar-time jolt of vertigo made him open the sharp turn a little wider before the van could roll over, and then he had stamped the gas pedal and they were roaring down the old residential street.

A glance in the mirror showed him the second Lincoln coming up fast behind him. He could hear the roar of the car's engine.

"Bad guys," he said breathlessly. "Fasten your belts— kid, get down somewhere. I'm gonna try to outrun 'em. They want us alive."

The other Lincoln had somehow looped back, and was now rushing up behind the nearer one, which was swerving to pass Sullivan on the left. Sullivan jerked the wheel that way to cut the car off, and he kept his foot hard on the gas pedal.

A loud, rapid popping began, and the van shuddered and rang and shook as splinters whined around the seats. Sullivan snatched his foot off the gas and stomped the brake; Elizalde tumbled against the dashboard as the front end dropped and the tires screamed, and then as the van slewed and ground to a halt, and rocked back, he slammed it into reverse and gave it full throttle again.

The closer Lincoln had driven up a curb and run over a trash can. Sullivan had to hunch around to watch the other one through the narrow frames of the back windows, for the door mirror had been blown out; the van's rear end was whipping wildly back and forth as Sullivan fought the wheel, and he heard five or six more shots, but then the second Lincoln too had driven up onto a lawn to get out of Sullivan's lunatic way, and the van surged back-end foremost right out into the middle of Lucas Avenue.

A hard, smashing impact punched the van, and as Sullivan's chin clunked the top of the seat back, he heard two more crashes a little farther away. The van was stalled and he clanked it into neutral and cranked at the starter. Feathers were flying around the stove and the bed in the back, where he had last seen the kid. At last the engine caught.

Sullivan threw the shift into drive again and turned around to face out the starred windshield, and he hit the gas and the van sped away down Lucas with only a diminishing clatter of glass and metal in its wake.

Sullivan drove quickly but with desperate concentration, yanking the wheel back and forth to pass cars, and pushing his way through red lights while looking frantically back and forth and leaning on the horn. When he was sure that he had at least momentarily lost any pursuit, he took a right turn, and then an immediate left into a service alley behind a row of street-facing stores. There was an empty parking space between two trucks, but his sweaty hands were trembling so badly that he had to back and fill for a full minute before he had got the vehicle into the space and pushed the gearshift lever into park.

"Kid," Sullivan croaked, too shaky even to turn around, "are you all right?" His mouth was dry and tasted like old pennies.

In the sudden quiet, over the low rumble of the idling engine, he could now hear the boy sobbing, but the boy's voice strangled the sobs long enough to choke out, "No worse than I was before."

"They want us alive," said Elizalde from where she was crumpled under the dashboard. She climbed back up into the seat and shook glass out of her disordered black hair. "I'm glad you've got these guys figured out, you asshole."

"Are you hit?" Sullivan asked her, his voice pitched too high. "They were shooting at us. Am I hit?" He spread his hands and looked down at himself, then shuffled his feet around to see them. He didn't see any blood or feel any particular pain or numbness anywhere.

"No," said Elizalde after looking herself over. "What do we do now?"

"You—you left your jumpsuit in Solville. Get a jacket of mine from the closet in the back, and a T-shirt or something for the kid. Disguises. I got a baseball cap back there you can tuck your hair up into. You two take a bus back; you'll look like a mother and son. I'll drive the van, and—I don't know, take backstreets or something. I think I'll be out of trouble once I get on the freeway, but you'd be safer traveling in something besides this van."

"Why don't we all take the bus?" asked Elizalde. "Abandon the van?"

"He'd have to abandon the stuff he bought," said the boy, who was still sniffling, "and a couple of these things aren't useless rubbish."

"Thanks, sonny," said Sullivan, not happy that the kid had been examining his purchases. Then, to Elizalde, he said, "Oh—here." He unsnapped the fanny-pack belt and pulled it free of his waist. "Have you ever shot a .45?"

"No. I don't believe in guns."

"Oh, they do exist, trust me." He pulled the loop and the zippers sprang open, exposing the grip of the pistol under two straps. "See? Here's one now."

"I saw it last night, remember? I *meant* I don't *like* them."

"Oh, *like* them," said Sullivan as he popped the snap on the straps and drew the pistol out of the holster sewed inside the fanny pack. Pointing the pistol at the ceiling, he managed to push the magazine-release button beside the trigger guard, but missed catching the magazine as it slid out of the grip. It clunked on the floorboards and he let it lie there. "*I* don't *like* 'em. I don't *like* dental surgery, either, or motorcycle helmets, or prostate examinations."

He pulled the slide back, and the stubby bullet that had been in the chamber flicked out and bounced off Elizalde's forehead.

"Ow," she said.

"Sorry."

"That's a Colt," said the boy, who had shuffled up behind Sullivan's seat. "Army-issue since 1911."

"Right," said Sullivan, peripherally beginning to wonder who the hell this boy was.

The slide was locked back, exposing the shiny barrel, and he tripped the slide release and it snapped forward, hooding the barrel again. He held the gun out toward her, grip first and barrel up, and after a long moment she took it.

"It's unloaded now," he said, "but of course you always assume it is loaded. Go ahead and shoot it through the floor—hold it with both hands. Jesus, not that way! Your thumbs have got to be around the *side;* that slide on the top comes back, hard, and if you've got your thumb over the back of it that way . . . well, you'll have another severed thumb to stick in your shoe."

She rearranged her hands, then pointed the pistol at the floor. Her finger visibly tightened on the trigger for several seconds—and then there was an abrupt, tiny *click* as the hammer snapped down.

Elizalde exhaled sharply.

"Nothing to it, hey?" said Sullivan. "Now, it's got a fair recoil, so get the barrel back down in line with your target before you take your second shot. The gun recocks itself, so all you've got to do is pull the trigger again. And again, if you need to. You'll have seven rounds in the magazine and one in the chamber, eight in all. If you *hit* a guy with one of 'em, you'll knock him down for sure."

She took hold of the slide with her left hand and tried to pull it back as Sullivan had done; she got it halfway back

person, which undoubtedly would have been Houdini's wife, Bess! *What a mask!* (May thieving Sukie Sullivan's ghost be snorted up by a shit-eating rat!) Was Pete in Venice looking for his father's ghost? Did he *find* Apie's ghost? What—

"*Ratatouille,*" said Webb, "is an eggplant-based vegetable medley. I tried to write MISTER ELEGANT once on a T-shirt, and it was days before I realized that I'd got it wrong, and I'd been walking around labeled MISTER EGGPLANT."

"Shut *up*, Joey." The Parganas kid, she thought, and Pete, and the "Mex gal," will be running scared now, keeping low; but maybe I can still get a line on Nicky Bradshaw. I'll have to check my answering machine, see if there have been any Find Spooky calls.

And and and—Obstadt's coming to the shoot on the *Queen Mary* tomorrow. He wants to know about some "problem that can arise with this ghost-eating business." (How vulgar of him to speak plainly about it!) I'll have to watch for a weakness in him, and be ready to assert myself. There'll be high voltage, and steep companionways—and the whole damned ocean, right over any rail.

"You don't seem to be *getting ahold* of anybody, do you?" Webb said, smiling and shaking his head.

"Joey, *shut* the fuck *up* and get *out* of my stinking *face*, will you?" She levered her bulk off the bed and swung herself toward the door of the motel room. "Keep looking for *Arthur Patrick* Sullivan. He's got to be here, or be coming ashore in the next twelve hours—you haven't left this area, and you'd have sensed him if he was *awake* anywhere within several blocks of here, wouldn't you?"

"Like American Bandstand." Webb hopped down from atop the TV set, agile as an old monkey. "He can't have got past the walls of my awareness," he said, nodding mechanically. "Unless someone opened the gate to a Trojan horse. A Trojan sea horse, that would be, locally."

"A Trojan . . . sea horse." Her face was suddenly cold, and a moment later the marrow in her ribs tingled.

"Oh my God, *that fish*, that goddamn *fish!*" she whispered. "Could Apie have been hiding inside that fish?" *I am in control of nothing at all*, she thought dazedly.

Webb gave her a look that momentarily seemed lucid. "If so, he's gone."

"If so," she said, pressing her temples again, "he's in L.A. somewhere." She was panting, clutching at straws. "He'll probably try to find Pete."

"Oh well then," said Webb with a shrug and a grin. "Find one and you've found them both, right? It's that simple!"

"That simple," echoed deLarava, still panting. Tears were spilling down her shaking cheeks again, and she blundered out the door.

CHAPTER 38

> *"What else had you to learn?"*
> *"Well, there was Mystery," the Mock Turtle replied, counting off the subjects on his flappers,—"Mystery, ancient and modern, with Seaography . . ."*
> —Lewis Carroll,
> *Alice's Adventures in Wonderland*

SULLIVAN had parked the van in the shade under one of the shaggy carob trees at the back of the Solville parking lot, and then he had got out and looked the old vehicle over.

The back end was a wreck. The right rear corner of the body, from the smashed taillights down, was crumpled sharply inward and streaked and flecked with blue paint. Apparently, it had been a blue car that had hit them when he had reversed out onto Lucas. The doors were still folded-looking and flecked with white from having hit Buddy Schenk's Honda in the Miceli's lot yesterday; and

511

the bumper, diagonal now, looked like a huge spoon that had been mauled in a garbage disposal.

In addition to all this, he could see four little-finger-sized holes in and around the back doors, ringed with bright metal where the paint had been blown off.

Forcing open the left-side back door, he had found that the little propane refrigerator had stopped two nine-millimeter slugs, and he had disconnected the appliance and laid the beer and Cokes and sandwich supplies out on the grass to carry in to the apartment; the sink cabinet had a hole punched through it and the sink itself was dented; and a solid ricochet off of the chassis of the field frequency modulator he'd just bought had ripped open one of his pillows, the deformed slug ending up shallowly embedded in the low headboard. One of the back-door windows was holed, and the slug had apparently passed through the interior of the van and exited through the windshield; and one perfectly round, deep dent in the back fender might have been put there by a bullet. And, of course, the driver's-side mirror was now a half-dozen fragments dangling from some kind of rubber gasket.

These were the extent of the damage, and he shivered with queasy gratitude when he thought of the boy having been crouched on the van floor in the middle of the fusillade, and of Elizalde's head nearly having been in the way of the one that had punched through the windshield. They had been lucky.

Sullivan had made several trips to the apartment to stack his electronic gear in a corner with Elizalde's bag of witch fetishes beside it, and put the drinks and the sandwich things into the refrigerator. Finally, he had locked the van up and covered the whole vehicle with an unfolded old rust-stained parachute, trying to drape it as neatly as he could in anticipation of Mr. Shadroe's probable disapproval.

Now he was sitting on a yellow fire hydrant out by the curb across Twenty-First Place, holding one of Houdini's plaster hands and watching the corner of Ocean Boulevard. There was a bus stop at Cherry, just around the corner. Clouds like chunks of broken concrete were shifting across the sky, and the tone of his thoughts changed with the alternating light and shade.

In shadow: they've been caught, Houdini's thumb can't deflect the attention the boy was drawing; they're being tortured, disloyal Angelica is leading bad guys here, I should be farther away from the building so I can hide when I see the terrible Lincolns turn onto Twenty-First Place.

In sunlight: buses take forever, what with transfers and all, and Angelica is a godsend; how nice to have such challenging and intelligent company if you've got to be in a mess like this, even if this séance attempt *doesn't* work; and even the kid, Shake Booty or whatever his name is, is probably going to turn out to be interesting.

It's been an hour just since I came to sit out here, he thought finally—and then he heard a deliberate scuffing on the sidewalk behind him.

His first thought as he hopped off the hydrant and turned around was that he didn't have his gun—but it was Elizalde and the boy who were walking toward him from the cul-de-sac at the seaward end of Twenty-First. The boy was carrying a big white bag with KFC in red on the side of it.

"You stopped for food?" Sullivan demanded, glancing around even as he stepped forward; he had meant it to sound angry, but he found that he was laughing, and he hugged Elizalde. She returned the hug at first, but then pulled away.

"Sorry," he said, stepping back himself.

"It's not you," she said. "Just use your left arm."

He clasped his left arm around her shoulders and pulled her close to himself, her head under his chin.

When they turned to walk across the street to the old apartment building, she nodded toward the white plaster hand that Sullivan was holding in his right hand. "I just don't like strangers' hands on me," she said.

"I don't like people with the wrong number of hands," said the boy.

Sullivan looked dubiously at the boy, and then at the Kentucky Fried Chicken bag the boy was carrying, and he tried to think of some pun about *finger-lickin' good;* he couldn't, and made do with saying, "Let's get in out of the rain," though of course it wasn't raining.

When they had got inside the apartment and dead-bolted the door and propped the Houdini hands against it, the boy set the bag on the painted wooden floor and said, "Has either of you two got any medical experience?"

"I'm a doctor," said Elizalde cautiously. "A real one, an M.D."

"Excellent." The boy shrugged carefully out of his torn denim jacket and began stiffly pulling his filthy polo shirt off over his head.

Sullivan raised his eyebrows and glanced at Elizalde.

Under the shirt, against his skin, the boy was wearing some kind of belt made of wire cables, with a glowing light at the front.

"What are your names?" came his voice from inside the shirt.

Sullivan was grinning and frowning at the same time. "Peter Sullivan, Your Honor," he said, sitting down in the corner beside his boxes. He had opened all the windows when he had carried the things in here earlier, but the heat was still turned on full, and the air above about shoulder height was wiltingly hot.

"Angelica Elizalde."

"This kid is—I'm called Koot Hoomie Parganas." The boy had got the shirt off, and Sullivan could see a blood-stained bandage taped over his ribs on the left side, just above the grotesque belt. "A man cut us with a knife yesterday afternoon. We treated it with high-proof rum, and it doesn't seem to be infected, but the bleeding won't quite stop."

Elizalde knelt in front of him and pulled back the edge of the bandage—the boy's mouth tightened, but he stood still.

"Well," said Elizalde in a voice that sounded irritated, even embarrassed, "you ought to have had some stitches. Too late now, you'll have a dueling scar. But it looks clean enough. We should use something besides liquor to prevent infection, though."

"Well, fix it right," Koot Hoomie said. "This is a good little fellow, my boy is, and he's been put through a lot."

" 'Fix it right,' " echoed Elizalde, still on her knees beside the boy. She sighed. "Fix it right." After a pause, she shot a hostile glance at Sullivan, and then said, "Peter, would you fetch me a—damn it, an unbroken egg from my grocery bag?"

Wordlessly, Sullivan leaned over from where he was sitting and hooked the bag closer to himself, dug around among the herb packets and oil bottles until he found the opened carton of eggs, and lifted one out. He got to his hands and knees to hand it across to her, then sat back down.

"Thank you. Lie down on the floor, please, Kootie."

Kootie sat down on the wooden floor and then gingerly stretched out on his back. "Should I take off the belt?"

"What's it for?" asked Sullivan quietly.

"Degaussing," said Elizalde.

"No," said Sullivan. "Leave it on."

Elizalde leaned over the boy and rolled the egg gently over his stomach, around the wound and over the bandage, and in a soft voice she recited, "*Sana, sana, cola de rana, tira un pedito para ahora y mañana.*" She spoke the words with fastidious precision, like a society hostess picking up fouled ashtrays.

Sullivan shifted uneasily and pushed away the bullet-dented field frequency modulator so that he could lean back against the wall. "You're sure this isn't a job for an emergency room?"

Elizalde gave him an opaque stare. "*La cura es peor que la enfermedad*—the cure would be worse than the injury, he wouldn't be safe half an hour in any kind of public hospital. Kootie is staying with us. *Donde comen dos, comen tres.*"

Sullivan was able to work out that that one meant

something like "Three can live as cheaply as two." He thought it was a bad idea, but he shrugged and struggled to his feet, up into the hot air layer, and walked into the open kitchen.

"There you go, Kootie," he heard Elizalde say. "You can get up now. We'll bury the egg outside, after the sun goes down."

Elizalde and the boy were both standing again, and Kootie was experimentally stretching his right arm and wincing.

"Voodoo," said the boy gruffly. "As useless as the hodgepodge of old radio parts Petey bought."

Sullivan turned away to open the refrigerator. "Kootie," he said, pulling a Coors Light out of the depleted twelve-pack carton, "I notice that you refer to yourself in the first person singular, the third person, and the first person plural. Is there a—" he popped the tab and took a deep sip of the beer, raising his eyebrows at the boy over the top of the can "—*reason* for that?"

"That's beer, isn't it?" said Kootie, pressing his side and wincing. "Which costs a dollar a can? Aren't you going to offer any to the lady and me?"

"Angelica," said Sullivan, "would you like a beer?"

"Just a Coke, please," she said.

"A Coke for you too, sonny," Sullivan told Kootie, turning back toward the refrigerator. "You're too young for beer."

"I'll start to answer your question," said Kootie sternly, "by telling you that one of us is eighty-four years old."

Sullivan had put down his beer and taken out two cans of Coke. "Well it's not me, and it's not you, and I doubt if it's Angelica. Anyway, you can't divvy it up among people socialistically that way. You gotta accumulate the age yourself."

Kootie slapped his bare chest and grinned at him. "I *meant* one of *us*. First person plural."

A knock sounded at the door then, and all three of them jumped. Sullivan had dropped the cans and spun toward the door, but he looked back toward Elizalde when he heard the fast *snap-clank* of the .45 being chambered. An ejected bullet clicked off the wall, for she hadn't needed to cock it, but it was ready to fire and her thumbs were out of the way of the slide.

He sidled to the window, ready to drop to the floor to give her a clear field of fire, and pushed down one slat of the Venetian blinds.

And he sighed, sagging with relief. "It's just the landlord." He was whispering, for the window beyond the blinds was open. He wondered if Shadroe had heard the gun being chambered.

Elizalde engaged the safety before shoving the gun back into the fanny-pack holster and zipping it shut.

Sullivan unbolted the door and pulled it open. Gray-haired old Shadroe pushed his way inside even as Sullivan was saying, "Sorry, I'm having some friends over right now—"

"I'm a friend," Shadroe said grimly. He was wearing no shirt, and his vast suntanned belly overhung his stovepipe-legged shorts. His squinty eyes took in Elizalde and Kootie, and then fixed on Sullivan. "Your name's *Peter Sullivan*," he said, slowly, as if he meant to help Sullivan learn the syllables by heart. "It was on the . . . rental agreement."

"Yes."

"It's a common enough name—" Shadroe paused to inhale. "Wouldn't you have thought so yourself?"

"Yes . . . ?" said Sullivan, mystified.

"Well, not today. I'm your godbrother."

Sullivan wondered how far away the nearest liquor store might be. "I suppose so, Mr. Shadroe, but you and I are going to have to discuss God and brotherhood later, okay? Right now I'm—"

Shadroe pointed one grimy finger at the also-shirtless Kootie. "It's him, isn't it? My pigs were—starting to *smoke*. I had to pull the batteries out of 'em—and I sent my honey pie to my boat—to take the batteries out of the pigs aboard there. Burn the boat down, otherwise." He turned an angrily earnest gaze on Sullivan. "I want you all," he said, "to come to my office, and see. What your boy has done to my television set."

Sullivan was shaking his head, exhaustion and impatience propelling him toward something like panic. Shadroe reeked of cinnamon again, and his upper lip was dusted with brown powder, as if he'd been snorting Nestle's Qwik, and Sullivan wondered if the crazy old man would even hear anything he might say.

"The boy hasn't been out of this room," Sullivan said loudly and with exaggerated patience. "Whatever's wrong with your TV—"

"Is it 'godbrother'?" Shadroe interrupted. "What I mean is, your *father*." Sullivan coughed in disgust and tried to think of the words to convince Shadroe that Sullivan was not his son, but the old man raised his hand for silence. "Was my *godfather*," he went on, completing his sentence. "My real name is Nicholas Bradshaw. Loretta deLarava is after my. Ass."

Sullivan realized that he had been almost writhing with insulted impatience, and that he was now absolutely still. "Oh," he said into the silence of the room. "Really?" He studied the old man's battered, pouchy face, and with a chill realized that this *could* very well be Nicholas Bradshaw. "Jesus. Uh . . . how've you been?"

"Not so good," said Bradshaw heavily. "I died in 1975."

The statement rocked Sullivan, who had not even been completely convinced that the man *was* dead, and in any case, had only been supposing that he'd been dead for a year or two at the most.

"*Amanita phalloides* mushrooms," Bradshaw said, "in a salad I ate. You have bad abdominal seizures twelve . . . hours after you eat it. Phalloidin, one of the several poisons. In the mushrooms. And then you feel fine for a week or two. DeLarava called me during the week. Couldn't help gloating. It was too late by then—for me to do anything. *Alpha-amanitine* already at work. So, I got all my money in cash, and hid it. And then I got very drunk, on my boat. Very drunk. Tore up six telephones, ate the magnets—to keep my ghost in. And I climbed into the refrigerator." His stressful breathing was filling the hot living room with the smell of cinnamon and old garbage. "A week later, I climbed out—dead, but still up and walking."

Elizalde walked to the kitchen counter, put down the egg, and picked up Sullivan's beer. After she had tipped it to her lips and drained it, she dropped the can to clang on the floor, and held out her right hand. "I'm Angelica Anthem Elizalde," she said. "The *police* are after *my* ass."

Shadroe shook her hand, grinning squintingly at Sullivan. "I'm gonna steal your *señorit*er, Peter," he said, his solemnity apparently forgotten. "What are you people doing here? Hiding here? I won't have that. You'll lead deLarava and the police to me and my honey pie." He was still smiling, still shaking Elizalde's hand. "Your van is an eyesore, even under the parachute. I can't understand people who have no pride at all."

Sullivan blinked at the man's random-fire style, but gathered that he was on the verge of being evicted. He tried to remember Nicky Bradshaw, who had been a sort of remote older cousin when Pete and Elizabeth had been growing up. Their father had always seemed to like Nicky, and of course had got him the Spooky part in "Ghost of a Chance."

"Listen to me, Nicky. We're going to try to build an apparatus, set up a séance, to talk to dead people, to ghosts," he said quickly. "To get *specific* ones, *clearly,* not the whole jabbering crowd. I want to talk to my father, to warn him that deLarava is devoting all her resources to finding him and eating him, tomorrow, on Halloween."

And then an idea burst into Sullivan's head, and suddenly he thought the séance scheme might work after all. "*You* should be the one to talk to him, Nicky, to warn him—he always liked you!" Sullivan's heart was still pounding. I might need to buy another part or two, he thought excitedly. This changes everything.

"You should talk to him yourself, Peter," said Elizalde, who was standing beside him.

"No no," Sullivan said eagerly, "the main thing here isn't what I'd prefer, it's what will work! This is a huge stroke of luck! He'll listen to Nicky more seriously than he'd listen to me, Nicky's twelve years older than I am. Aren't you, Nicky? He always took you seriously."

Bradshaw just stared at him, looking in fact a hundred years old these days. "I'd like to talk to him," he said. "But you should be the one—to warn him. You're his son."

"And he's your father," Elizalde said.

Sullivan didn't look at her. "That's not the *point* here," he snapped impatiently, "what *matters*—"

"And," Elizalde went on, almost gently, "Nicky presumably isn't linked to your father by a consuming guilt, the way you clearly are."

"You're the antenna," agreed Kootie. "The variable capacitor that's fused at the right frequency adjustment."

Sullivan clenched his fists, and he could feel his face getting red. "But the machinery *won't work* if it's—"

For a moment no one spoke, and the only sound was a faint fizzing from one of the cans of Coke that he'd dropped when Bradshaw had knocked on the door. Sullivan's forehead was misted with sweat. *You're not Speedy Alka-Seltzer,* he thought. *You won't dissolve.*

"You weren't going to do it," said Elizalde, smiling. "You were going to go through the motions, set it all up so plausibly that nobody, certainly not *yourself,* could accuse you of not having done your best. But there was going to be some factor that you were going to forget, something no one could blame you for not having thought of."

Sullivan's chest was hollow with dismayed wonderment. "A condensing lens," he said softly.

"A condensing lens?" said Kootie. "Like in a movie projector, between the carbon arc and the aperture?"

Sullivan ignored him.

Without a condensing lens set up between the Langmuir gauge and the brush discharge in the carborundum bulb, the signal couldn't possibly be picked up by the quartz filament inside the gauge. But wouldn't he have *thought* of that, as soon as he saw the weakness and dispersion of the flickering blue brush sparks in the bulb? Even if Elizalde hadn't said what she had just said?

In this moment of unprepared insight, while his bones shivered with an icy chill in spite of the hot air and the sweat on his face, he was bleakly sure he would *not* have thought of it, or would at least have contrived to set the lens up incorrectly.

He wouldn't be able to do it wrong now, now that he was aware of the temptation.

But maybe it *still* won't work! The thought was almost a prayer.

Kootie limped forward and held his right hand up to Bradshaw. "Pleased to meet you, Mr. Bradshaw," he said. "I'm two people at the moment—one of 'em is known as Kootie—"

"That's an I-ON-A-CO belt you got on," said Bradshaw, shaking the boy's hand. "They don't work. You got it from Wilshire?"

"We *were* on Wilshire," said the boy in a surprised tone, and it occurred to Sullivan that this was the first time the voice had really sounded like a little boy's. "Right by MacArthur Park!"

"I meant H. Gaylord Wilshire himself," said Bradshaw. "That was his original tract. From Park View to Benton, and Sixth down to Seventh. My godfather bought one of those fool belts. From him, in the twenties. What's old man Wilshire like, these days?"

"Insubstantial," said the boy, and his voice was controlled and hard again. "But I didn't get to introduce my other self." He looked around at the other three people in the room. "I'm Thomas Alva Edison," he said, "and I promise you, *I* can get your ghost telephone working, even if Petey here can't."

Sullivan was relieved that everyone was staring at the boy now, and he went back to the refrigerator and took the second-last beer and popped it open. I shouldn't have said *condensing lens,* he thought bitterly. I should have blinked at her in surprise, and then acted insulted. *Edison.* I'm *sure.* No doubt the kid *is* a ghost, or has one on him, but I'll bet every ghost that knows anything about electricity claims to have been Thomas Edison.

"Cart all your crap to my office," said Bradshaw wearily. "You can set up your gizmo there. It's the most masked room in this whole masked block. Electric every which way, water running uphill and roundabout—even hologram pictures in a saltwater aquarium under black light. And bring your bag of fried chicken, Mr. Edison— Johanna loves that stuff. Did you get Original Recipe—or the new crunchy stuff?"

"Original Recipe," said Elizalde over her shoulder as she stepped past Sullivan and opened the refrigerator.

"Good," said Bradshaw. "That's what she likes. I hope you brought enough."

An hour later Sullivan was sitting cross-legged on the dusty rug in Bradshaw's dim office, staring idly at the featureless white glow of the old man's TV screen and gnawing a cold chicken wing.

Bradshaw's "honey pie," a heavy young woman in tight leotards and a baggy wool sweater, had burst in shortly after they'd carried all the supplies to the office, and after the introductions (*Johanna, this is Thomas Edison—Mr. Edison, my honey pie, Johanna*) she had told Bradshaw that "the pigs on the boat were just burping, not smoking yet."

After that, Johanna and Elizalde had gone out again in Bradshaw's car to buy supplies—bandages, hydrogen peroxide, a secondhand portable movie projector, a pint of tequila for Elizalde, more beer and more Kentucky Fried Chicken, and a box of sidewalk chalk, which Kootie had insisted on.

When they had got back, Elizalde had cleaned the cut in Kootie's side and secured it with the bandages and put on a more expert-looking dressing, and then they had torn open the KFC bags.

The chicken was now gone, and Sullivan had had several of the beers.

He tossed the chicken bone onto his newspaper place mat and took a sip of his latest beer. "Angelica," he said, "could you pass me that muffin?"

Elizalde looked at him coldly. "Why do you call it a *muffin?*"

He stared back at her. "Well, it's . . . a little round thing made out of dough."

"So's your head, but I don't call *it* a *muffin*. This is a *roll.*" She picked it up and leaned across the newspapers to hold it out. "Don't get drunk for this," she added.

"Keep the roll," he said. "I had my heart set on a muffin."

"I wish *I* could get drunk," said Bradshaw grumpily. He had crunched up a succession of red cinnamon balls as the others had passed around the chicken and mashed potatoes and gravy, and now he poured himself another glass of whatever it was that he was drinking—some red fluid that also reeked of cinnamon. "My pigs and TV are useless while Mr. Edison's here."

Sullivan had decided not to ask about the smoking pigs, but he waved his beer at the white-glowing television. "What're you watching?"

"Channel Two," said Bradshaw. "CBS, my old alma mater."

"I'll bet I could mess with it and get you a better picture." Sullivan felt tightly tensed, as if any move he made would break something in the cluttered office.

"It's not on for the picture," wheezed Bradshaw. "Ghosts are an electrical brouhaha in the fifty-five-megahertz range—and Channel Two is the—closest channel to that. The brightness control on that set is—turned all the way to black, right now—believe it or not."

"That's awfully shortwave," commented the boy who claimed to be Edison.

"You're a shortwave critter," Bradshaw said. "And a damn big one. Even if you were a dozen miles away—you'd still show up on the screen here as a—white band. But standing here, you're hogging the whole show. We could have the ghost of—goddamn Godzilla standing right outside, and I wouldn't have a clue."

"Don't you people have a telephone to build?" asked Elizalde.

Sullivan looked irritably across the newspapers at her—but then with a flush of sympathy he realized that she was as tense as he was. He remembered how she had bravely pretended to be eager to go witchcraft-shopping this morning, when he had been ready to sit holed up in the apartment all weekend; and for a moment, before he sighed and got to his feet, he felt a flicker of pitying love for her, and of disgust with himself.

"Yeah," he said. "Household current should be enough—I bought a train-set transformer, and there's the Ford coil."

Elizalde had got up too, and was lifting candles and herb packets and tiny bottles of oil out of her shopping bag.

"What did you have in mind?" asked Kootie, who was sitting crouched like a bird up on the back of the old couch. "Let's be speedy, it's less than twelve hours to midnight, and I want to be clathrated damn deep, out of range of any magnets, when church bells are ringing the first strokes of Halloween."

"You're not Speedy Alka-Seltzer, you won't dissolve! I'll race you into the water!" It had been a man's voice that had said it, calling happily. Sullivan remembered the two Coke cans he had dropped on the floor back in the apartment, and he didn't want to remember whose voice it had been that had said, *"I'll race you into the water!"*

"A bulb with a carborundum button instead of a filament," he said loudly, "charged, with the eventual brush of electric discharge . . . focused through a goddamn *condensing lens . . .* onto the quartz filament, which we'll blacken with soot, inside a Langmuir gauge. It'll work like the vanes in a radiometer, wiggle in response to the light coming through the lens. We can break a thermometer to get a drop of mercury to put in the gauge, and then we can evacuate it to a good enough rarefication with a hose connected to the sink faucet . . ."

But the twins had been feeling nauseated ever since eating the potato salad at lunch, and were queasy even at the smell of the Coppertone lotion, and they had decided to stay out of the surf and just lie on the towels, on the solid bumpy mattress of the sand.

Kootie had been listening as Sullivan had been describing his proposed device, and he now interrupted: "You don't want a magnet in the receiver. This is such a sensitive thing you're talking about that an actual *magnet* in the same room would draw the voices of all the ghosts in Los Angeles. We'll have enough trouble with fields caused by the changing electrical charges. Use chalk, I had the ladies buy some." He paused, and then said, "We still have some of the Miraculous Insecticide Chalk, Mr. Edison. That won't do, Kootie, this has to be round, like a cylinder. Good thought, though."

"Chalk?" asked Sullivan, trying to concentrate.

Their father had shrugged, and his remark about Speedy Alka-Seltzer had hung in the air as he turned away from them, toward the foam-streaked waves, and young Pete had been able to see the frail white hair on the backs of his father's shoulders fluffing in the ocean breeze.

"The friction of a piece of wet chalk varies with changes in its electric charge," Kootie said. "Without a charge it's toothy and has lots of friction, but it's instantly slick when there's a current . . ."

The three cans of Hires Root Beer were laid out like artillery shells, awaiting their father's return from his swim. There was one for him, and one each for Pete and Elizabeth. Their stepmom had explained that she didn't drink soda pop, so there were only three cans.

". . . a spring connected to the center of the diaphragm," Kootie was saying, drawing with his hands in the stale dim air, "with the other end pressed against the side of the rotating chalk cylinder. The fluctuations in the current from your Ford coil will change the mechanical resistance of the chalk, so the needle will wiggle, you see, as the chalk rapidly changes from slick to scratchy, and the wiggle will be conveyed to the diaphragm."

"It sounds goofy," quavered Sullivan, forcing himself to pay attention to what Kootie was saying, and not to the intrusive, unstoppable, intolerably resurrected memory.

"It works," said Kootie flatly. "A young man named George Bernard Shaw happened to be working for me in London in '79, and maybe you've read his description of my electromotograph receiver in his book *The Irrational Knot*."

Sullivan shivered, for he was suddenly sure that the ghost this boy carried was, in fact, Thomas Edison. Sullivan's voice was humble as he said. "I'll take your word for it."

But he didn't add, "sir." Aside from police officers, there was only one man he had ever called "sir."

Their stepmother didn't even bother to act very surprised when Pete and Elizabeth screamed at her that their father was in trouble out in the water. The old man had swum out through the waves in his usual briskly athletic Australian crawl, but he was floundering and waving now, way out beyond the surf line, and their stepmother had only got to her feet and shaded her eyes to watch.

". . . and the carborundum bulb should be sensitive enough to pick the ghost up," Kootie was saying, "and reflect his presence in the brush discharge. He should easily be able to vary it, so it's a *signal* that's going through the lens into the Langmuir viscosity gauge . . ."

Sullivan blinked stinging sweat out of his eyes.

Their stepmother hadn't eaten any of the potato salad, and she seemed to be fine; but she wouldn't even take one step across the dry sand toward the water, and so the twins had gone running down to the surf all by themselves, even though cramps were wringing their stomachs . . .

Kootie had asked Sullivan a question, and he struggled to remember what it had been. "Oh," he said finally, "right. We'll have primed the quartz filament with a ground vibration, set it ringing by waving a magnet past the little swiveling iron armature in the gauge, and then I guess we get rid of the magnet, outside the building. The quartz starts from a peak tone, and then the vibration will damp down as the quartz loses its initial . . . its initial *ping*. We'll gradually lose volume, but even with the damping radiometer effects of the signal it's getting from the focused light, and from friction with the trace of mercury gas in the gauge, the sustaining vibration should last a good while."

Both twins had paused when they were chest deep and

wobbling on tiptoe in the cold, surging water. But Elizabeth let the buoyancy take her, and began dog-paddling out toward their distant suffering father; while Pete, frightened of the deep water that was frightening their father, and of the clenching pain in his abdomen, had turned and floundered back toward shore.

"You're the antenna," said Kootie, who was now looking down at him curiously from his perch on the couch back, "but you'll need a homing beacon too, a lure."

And after a while, Elizabeth had dragged herself back, exhausted and sick and alone.

"I'm that as well," said Sullivan bleakly. "I'm still his son."

They had not, of course, opened the three Hires cans, though the twins were destined to glimpse the cans again twenty-seven years later. . . again in Venice.

And Sullivan's face went cold—the memory of Kelley Keith's face blandly observing the drowning of her husband had overlaid memories of deLarava's face, and at long, long last he realized that they were the same woman.

"Nicky!" he said, so unsteadily that Elizalde shot him a look of spontaneous concern. "Loretta deLarava is Kelley Keith!"

"Shoot," said Bradshaw. "I've known that since 1962."

"When we were ten? You could have told us!"

"You'd have wanted to go back to her?"

Sullivan remembered the pretty young face looking speculatively out at the old man drowning beyond the waves. "Jesus, no."

"She killed your father," said Bradshaw. "Just like she

killed me. And now she wants to erase both guilts. Both reproaches, both awarenesses. If we're gone, see, it can be not true. For her."

"She, no, he *drowned*, she didn't *kill* him—"

"She fed you and your sister and your father. Poisoned potato salad. All in the golden afternoon."

Kootie bounced impatiently down off the couch, and as he began pacing the floor he picked up Sullivan's pack of Marlboros. Now he shook one out and, with it hanging on his lower lip, slapped his pants pockets. "Somebody got a match?"

"It's the kid's lungs!" protested Elizalde.

"One cigarette?" said Kootie's voice. "I hardly think— It's all right, Mrs. Elizalde, I've smoked Marlboros before. Really? Well, she's right, you shouldn't. Don't let me catch you with one of these in your hand again!" He took the cigarette out of his mouth and put it back in the pack. "You started it, you were working my hands. Don't argue with your elders, the lady was right. I was out of line . . . dammit." He turned a squinting gaze on Sullivan. "I think your plan will work. It's better than mine was, in some ways. I like the carborundum bulb to focus just the one signal—it just *might* eliminate the party-line crowd. Let's get busy."

Bradshaw volunteered to clear off the top of his desk, and soon Kootie and Sullivan were laying out globes and boxes and wires across the scarred mahogany surface. Bradshaw even dragged a couple of old rotary-dial telephones out of a cupboard for them to cannibalize. Twice Sullivan went out to the van, once for tools and once to disconnect and tote back the battery so as to have some solid twelve-volt direct current, and at one point, while he was doing some fast, penciled calculations on the desktop, Elizalde stepped up behind him and briefly squeezed his shoulder. She'd been intermittently busy with something in the little added-on kitchen, and the stale cinnamon air in the office was getting sharp with the steamy fumes of mint and hot tequila.

As his fingers and brain followed the inevitable chessboard logic of potentials and resistances and magnetic fields, Sullivan's mind was a ringing ground zero after the detonation of his hitherto-entombed memories, with frightened thoughts darting among the raw, broken ruins of his psyche.

I was there when he drowned! The Christmas shoot in '86 was not *the first time I was ever at Venice Beach—no wonder I kept seeing deja-vu sunlit overlays of the Venice scene projected onto those gray winter streets and sidewalks. I had* been there *when he drowned on that summer day in '59, and Loretta deLarava is Kelley Keith, our stepmother, and she killed him, she poisoned him and watched my father die! I was there—I watched my father die! At least Sukie tried to swim out and save him—I gave up, ran away, back to the towels.*

O car-bolic faithless, he sang in his head, echoing Sukie's old misremembered Christmas carol.

He was suddenly sure that Sukie had all along remembered some of that day, possibly a lot of it. Her drinking (*"What you can't remember can't hurt you"*), her celibacy, and her final feverish attempt to force Pete into bed and have sex with him after he had confronted her with the lies she had told to Judy Nording—even her

eventual suicide—must, it seemed to him now as he
screwed the Ford coil onto the surface of the desk, have
been results of her remembering that day.

By midafternoon, the assembly had been wired and
screwed down and propped up across the desktop, and
the carborundum bulb was plugged in. Edison pointed
out that when the evacuated bulb warmed up, the line of
its brushy interior discharge would be sensitive to the
motion of any person in the room, so they ran wires around
the doorway and into Bradshaw's little fluorescent-lit
kitchen, and set up the chalk-cylinder speaker assembly on
the counter by the sink, with a rewired old telephone on a
TV table in the middle of the floor. Sullivan had
ceremoniously slid a kitchen chair up in front of it.

Elizalde had made a steaming, eye-watering tea of mint
leaves and tequila in a saucepan on the old white-
enameled stove and had turned off the flame when all the
liquid had boiled away and the leaves had cooked nearly
dry. She and Johanna were standing by the stove,
hemmed in by the wires trailing across the worn linoleum
floor.

Elizalde's eyes were big and empty when she looked
up at Sullivan, and he thought he must look the same way.
"When you're ready," she said, "Johanna and I will go light
the candles in the other room, and splash the *vente aquí*
oil around. Then we should disconnect any smoke alarms,
and I'll turn on this stove burner again, high, under this
pot of *yerra vuena*. You want to be talking into the smoke
from it."

Sullivan had been making sure to take each emptied
beer can to the trash before furtively opening the next, so

that Elizalde wouldn't be able to count them. *O rum key, O ru-um key to O-bliv-ion,* he sang shrilly in his head.

He took the latest beer into the office, which was very dark now that Bradshaw had unplugged the television set and carried it out to one of the garages, and he pried the can open quietly as he checked the discharge in the carborundum bulb. The bulb had indeed warmed up, and the ghostly blue wisp of electrons was curling against the inside of the glass, silently shifting its position as he moved across the carpet.

"I guess we're ready," he said, sidling back into the bright lit kitchen past Bradshaw, who was standing in the doorway.

CHAPTER 39

"She must be sent as a message by
the telegraph—"

—Lewis Carroll,
Through the Looking-Glass

"I DON'T REMEMBER the old man's number,"
Bradshaw said. "We could call the reference desk at a
library, from a regular phone, I guess."

"I know the number," said Sullivan. Running and
running, he thought, running with Sukie since 1959, and
then running extra fast and alone since 1986. All over the
country. To wind up here, now, in this shabby kitchen,
staring at a gutted old black bakelite telephone. "It's April
Fool's Day, 1898."

He looked at Elizalde. "My father's birthday. That and
his full name will be his telephone number." He looked
down at the rotary dial on the telephone. The old man
would be summoned by dialing April the first, 1898, A-R-
T-H-U-R—P-A-T-R-I-C-K—S-U-L-L-I-V-A-N.

Slowly, looking at the rotary dial, he read off, "411898, 2784877287425-78554826."

"A lot of numbers," said Kootie, and Sullivan thought it might actually be the boy talking.

"It's very long distance," he said.

"I remember I always thought God's phone number was Et cum spiri 2-2-oh," said Elizalde nervously. "From the Latin mass, you know? *Et cum spiritu tuo.*"

"You can call Him after I'm done talking to my dad."

"Can magical calls out of here be traced?" asked Bradshaw suddenly.

Kootie cleared his throat. "Sure," he said. The boy was sitting up on the kitchen counter beside the chalk cylinder, which had been mounted on the stripped frame of an electric pencil sharpener; he was pale, and his narrow chest was rising and falling visibly. Sweat was running in shiny lines down over his stomach, and the bandage over his ribs on the left side was spotted with fresh blood. "You've got— what, three? four?—antennas sitting around in this kitchen, and they do broadcast as well as receive."

"Don't worry, Nicky," said Sullivan, "we'll use a scrambler. Angelica, could I have Houdini's thumb?" When she had dug the thing out of her shoe and passed it to him, he laid it on the table beside the telephone. "We can dial with this."

"It would be good if we could make a test call first," Kootie said thoughtfully. "Anybody got any dead people they got to get a message to?"

Visibly tensing before she moved, Elizalde stepped forward away from the stove, placing her sneakers carefully among the looped wires, and sat down in the chair. "There's a guy I took money from," she said steadily, "and I didn't do the work he paid for."

Kootie hopped down from the counter. "You know his number?"

"Yes."

"But you'll need a lure," he said, "remember? A 'homing beacon.' "

She leaned sideways to pull her wallet out of her hip pocket, and then she dug a tattered, folded note out of it. "This is in his handwriting," she said. "His *emotional* handwriting." She looked over at Johanna by the stove. "Could you light the candles and . . . smear the oil over the door lintel, or whatever's required?"

"Better than you, maybe," said Johanna with a merry smile.

Elizalde looked at Sullivan. "Drop the dime."

He was grateful to her for going first. "Okay. Kootie, turn up that fire."

Sullivan stepped past Bradshaw into the dark office, and while Johanna struck matches to the candles on the shelves and shook out the oil and muttered rhymes under her breath, he dug out of his pocket the magnet they had pulled from the old telephone. He crouched beside the upright Langmuir gauge and waved the magnet past the tiny iron armature, and heard the faint contained *ting* as it rocked against the dangling quartz filament. Then he opened the outside door, sprinted out through the glaring sunlight to the covered van and set the magnet down on the asphalt beside it.

Seven seconds later he was back in the kitchen, panting in the hot fumes of cinnamon and mint.

Kootie had connected the modified pencil sharpener, and the speaker was resonating with a flat sound like a sustained exhalation; the mint in the saucepan was steaming and sputtering.

Elizalde took the receiver off the hook, then picked up Houdini's thumb and began dialing the telephone; somehow the speaker behind her made a fluttering sound in synchronization with the rattle of the dial. Belatedly, Sullivan realized that privacy would not be possible here, and he took a hasty sip of the beer to cool his heated face.

Elizalde was still dialing numbers into the telephone, but already a whispering voice was rasping out of the speaker.

"*Cosa mala maca muere,*" it said. "*Me entiendes, Mendez?*"

Sullivan felt moving air on his sweaty scalp at the back of his head, and he realized that his hair was actually standing on end.

"It's the damned crowd effect," said Kootie irritably, "that can't be your man yet." He frowned at Elizalde. "Do you recognize this voice?" Then Kootie's eyes were wide, and he spoke with a scared boy's intonation: *"It's that laughing bag!"*

Elizalde's hand sprang away from the dial, and Houdini's thumb landed in the sink. "Jesus, he's right," she said. "The cloth bag in the truck bed!"

Sullivan didn't know what they were talking about. "What did it just say?"

"It said, a—a bad thing never dies," said Elizalde rapidly, hugging herself, "and then it said, 'You understand?' " She threw Sullivan a frightened look. "Can't I quit this and just go away?"

He spread his hands. "Can't *I?*" he asked, really hoping that she would find some way to say *yes*.

But she was rubbing her eyes with the heels of her hands; and then she said, "Could you bring that thumb back here?"

As Sullivan stepped over to the sink, Bradshaw growled, "Is this somebody you two *(gasp)* tracked in on your shoes?" The mint leaves in the pot on the fire were smoking and popping now.

Kootie shrugged. "It's . . . yes, something, somebody, that was paying attention to me this morning, and it would have seen Mrs. Elizalde."

"Miss," said Elizalde.

"Let a dead guy clear the line for you," Shadroe said. He stumped into the kitchen—carelessly stepping all over the wires, his bare belly swinging ahead of him—and he took the receiver and blew sharply into the mouthpiece. "Hello?" he said. "Hello?" Then he dialed *Operator*, twice.

He set the receiver back down beside the telephone. "Try it now."

Sullivan had fetched the thumb, and handed it to her, and she began shakily dialing again. It took nearly a full minute for her to dial all the numbers of her man's birth date and full name, but Bradshaw's breath had apparently chased away any stray ghosts.

At last she was finished dialing, and she hesitantly picked up the receiver.

A musical buzz sounded from the speaker by the sink;

it stopped, and then began again, stopped, and began again.

"My God," said Sullivan softly. "It's *ringing!*"

"Cultural conditioning," muttered Kootie. "It's what everybody expects, even the man she's calling."

"Who is that?" came a startled voice from the speaker, and Sullivan was peripherally impressed with the fidelity of Edison's chalk speaker.

"Frank?" said Elizalde into the mouthpiece. "It's me, it's Angelica."

"Angelica!" The initial surprise in the voice gave way to petulance: *"Angelica, where are you? Who is this old man?"*

Sullivan saw Elizalde glance bewilderedly from Bradshaw to Kootie. "Who do you mean, Frank?"

"He comes in your clinic every day! He does the séances all wrong, reading palms of people's hands, and . . . taking liberties *with the pretty women!"*

"Oh, that would be—that's not my clinic anymore, Frank, I don't—"

"I saw you today, from here, from the window. You fell on the curb when I saw you coming. I live here, and I waved, but you didn't come in."

"I'm sorry, Frank, I—"

"You didn't come in—you don't respect me anymore— you never did respect me! I didn't speak to you in the sewer, and I shouldn't speak to you now. You didn't come visit me after I hurt myself in your clinic. You have other boyfriends now, in your fine house, and you've never once thought of me."

Elizalde's face was contorted, but her voice was strong. "Frank," she said, "I failed you. I'm sorry. Do you remember why you came to my clinic, why you were sent there?"

"Uh . . . well, because I always had to keep checking over and over again if my shoes were tied and if I locked doors and turned off the headlights on my car, even in the daytime—and I went to bed and didn't come out for a month—and I tried to kill myself. And then after I got out of the hospital they said I should be your outpatient."

"I failed to help you, and I'm terribly sorry. I haven't had any boyfriends. I've been hiding, running. And every day I've been thinking about what I did to you, how I let you down, and wishing I could go back and make it right."

"You can make it right—right now! We can get married, like I said in my note—"

The mint had flared up in the pan. Sullivan took the pan off the fire and clanged the lid onto it for a moment to snuff the flames.

"No, Frank," said Elizalde. "You're dead now. I think you know that, don't you? Things like marriage are behind you now. You didn't *hurt* yourself in my clinic that night, you *killed* yourself. You remember when you went to bed and stayed there for a month—you weren't supposed to *relax* yet, then, it wasn't time for that yet. It's time now. You're dead. Go to sleep, and sleep so deeply that . . . there won't be room or light for any dreams."

For several long seconds, the kitchen was silent except for the background hissing of the speaker, and Sullivan saw Kootie glance speculatively at the spinning chalk cylinder.

Then the voice came back. *"I've thought I might be dead,"* it said quietly. *"Are you sure, Angelica?"*

"I am sure. I'm sorry."

"You've thought about me? Been sorry?"

"You've been behind all the thoughts I've had. I came back here to ask you to forgive me."

"Ah." Again there was silence for a few seconds. *"Goodbye, Angelica.* Vaya con Dios."

"Do you forgive me?"

The hissing went on for a full minute before Bradshaw shifted his weight on his feet and cleared his throat; and finally the speaker began making a dull rattle, which ceased when Elizalde reached out and pressed the hang-up button on the telephone cradle.

Sullivan tipped up his can of beer to avoid having to meet anyone's eye, and he could hear Bradshaw's knees creak as he shifted his weight again. The mint smoke was billowing thickly under the low ceiling.

Elizalde pushed back the chair and stood up. "I fucking don't—" she began in a choking voice—

And the musical buzz started up from the speaker by the sink; it stopped, and then started again.

She bent to snatch up the receiver again. "Hello?"

From the chalk-and-pencil-sharpener speaker behind her a cultured man's voice said, *"Could I speak to Don Tay, please?"*

"That's for me," said Kootie, stepping forward and sitting down in the chair. Elizalde mutely handed him the receiver. He cleared his throat. "This is Thomas Edison," he said.

The voice on the speaker exhaled sharply. *"For God's sake, this is an open line! Use elementary caution, will you? My son—"*

"—Is safe," said Kootie. His face was composed, but tears had begun to run down his cheeks. "We've got the line masked and deviled on this end."

"God, and you're speaking physically! *With his voice! What—in hell—did we do?"* Louder now, the voice called, *"Kootie! Can you hear me, boy?"*

Kootie's reddening face relaxed into a grimace and he burst into tears. "I'm here, Dad, but don't yell or—or the speaker might break, we've got it hooked up to a pencil sharpener. Mr. Edison is taking good care of me, don't worry. But Dad! Tell Mom I didn't mean to do it! I'm the one that should be dead! I tried to tell you before, but you were b-both d-d-drunk!" His head was down and his stiff poise was gone, and he was just sobbing.

Elizalde got on her knees beside him and put her arm around his bare narrow shoulders and rocked him gently.

"Boy, boy," said the voice on the speaker shakily, *"we're fragmented here, we blur and break, and some of the pieces you talk to may be minimal. Your mother has gone on ahead, and perhaps has . . . found the white light, who knows? She told me to make you understand that she loves you, and I love you, and you were . . ."*—the voice was still loud, but blurring—*"mot to vlame for what haphened. Ee-bay areful-kay. Isten-lay oo-tay Om-Tay . . ."*

Gradually the hissing background had been becoming textured with clinking and mumbling, and Sullivan thought he heard a voice in the middle distance say, *Te explico, Federico?*

"I love you!—Dad?" said Kootie loudly into the receiver; then he fumbled at the telephone until he had found and pushed the disconnect button. The speaker

Keith; and even if Obstadt told no one, *he* knew, *he* could—intolerably—see it.)

"The van," she said dully; then she blinked. "The *egged* van, Pete's van! You didn't call me? He was *here in Venice!* What was he doing?"

"Relax, ma'am! He wasn't here. He must have loaned the van to a friend. This was a curly-haired shorter guy in a fancy coat with breakaway sleeves."

"Breakaway sleeves . . . ? Oh, Jesus, that was *Houdini* you saw! It was Sullivan wearing *my* goddamn *Houdini* mask!"

"That was Pete Sullivan? This guy didn't look anything like your pictures of him." Webb frowned in thought. "Not at first, anyway. He did get taller."

"Damn it, it was him, trust me. What was he doing?"

"Oh. Oh, chatting up a bird. A-sparkin' and a-spoonin', I'm assumin'. Mex gal. She got taller too, after a while. She was trying to reason with a guy who was in love with her, a sulking man hiding in a drainage pipe. But when Neat Pete showed up with his joke dinner jacket and fine white hands, she decided to chat with him instead. They stood in a parking lot that was in a traffic whirlpool, so I couldn't intuit what they said. Dig this—there was a Venice Farmer's Market in that very parking lot this morning! I bought various vegetable items. I will cook a *ratatouille.*"

"Shut up, Joey, I'm trying to think." Who on earth, she wondered, could this "Mex gal" be? Not just someone he met by chance, if the two of them took the precaution of talking in an eye of traffic. And the mask seems to have covered her too, giving her the appearance of some other

"Me too, babe, but do they come when you call? Face it, Loretta, nobody gives the least particle of a rat's ass about your. . . . *magical prowess.*"

Over the line she heard a familiar metallic splashing. The man was urinating! He had *begun* urinating during the conversation! He went on in his new, labored voice: "You work for me, now, Miss Keith—sorry, Mrs. Sullivan—oh hell, I guess I know you well enough to just call you *Kelley,* don't I?"

DeLarava just sat perfectly still, her damp handkerchief in front of her eyes.

"I know you're busy tomorrow," Obstadt said, "so I'll drive down and say . . . 'Hi!' . . . at your ghost shoot on the *Queen Mary.* I need to quiz you about a problem that can arise in this ghost-eating business. And you'll tell me everything you know."

The line went dead. Slowly she lowered the phone back down onto the cradle. Then her hands flew to her temples and pressed inward, helping the rubber bands constrict her skull and keep the pieces of her mind from flying away like a flock of baby chicks when the shadow of the hawk was sweeping the ground.

"The egged van was at the canals yesterday," remarked Webb, who was sitting cross-legged on top of the TV set.

She dragged her attention away from the stark fact that her false identity had been blown. (If Obstadt talked, and Nicky Bradshaw stepped forward and talked, she could conceivably be arraigned for murder; and, even worse, everyone would see through the deLarava personality to the fragmented fraud that was Kelley

"Fine. Grab the clothes and scoot." To his own surprise, his head bobbed forward as if to kiss her; but he caught himself and leaned back.

She blinked. "Right." To the boy, she said, "Is your name Kootie or Al?"

The boy's mouth twitched, but finally he said, "Kootie."

"All right, Kootie, let's outfit ourselves and then get the hell out of here."

In the dim living room of Joey Webb's motel room off Grand Boulevard in Venice, Loretta deLarava sat on the bed and blotted her tears with a silk handkerchief. Obstadt's man Canov had put her on hold, and she had been sitting here now for *ten minutes* it seemed like, and the room reeked because Joey Webb, suspicious in an unfamiliar environment, had resumed his old precaution of hiding half-eaten Big Macs and Egg McMuffins behind the furniture.

"Hello, Loretta," said Obstadt at last. His voice was echoing and weak.

"Neal, I *know* about it, so don't even waste a moment with lies. Why are you trying to impede me? You had your people try to *kill* Sullivan and the Parganas boy an hour ago! You should thank God that they got away. Now I want you to help me find them—and they'd better not be dead!—or I'll call the police about the incident. I want, immediately, all the information you have—"

Obstadt inhaled loudly, and coughed. "Shut up, Loretta."

"You can't tell *me* to shut up! I can call spirits from the vasty deep—"

against the compression of the spring, and had to let go.

"Try it again," said Sullivan, "but instead of pulling the slide back with your left hand, just hold it steady, and push the gun forward with your right." He was nervous about having the pistol unloaded for so many seconds, but wanted her to have as much sketchy familiarity with it as might be possible.

This time she managed to cock it, and again dry-fired it at the floor.

"Good." Sullivan retrieved the fallen magazine and slid it up into the grip until it clicked, then jacked a round into the chamber and released the magazine again to tuck into the top of it the bullet that had bounced off Elizalde's forehead. He slid the magazine into the grip again and clicked the safety up.

"Cocked and locked," he said, handing it back to her carefully. "This fan-shaped ridged thing behind the trigger is the safety; pop it down, and then all you've got to do is pull the trigger. Keep it in the fanny pack, under the jacket, and don't let the kid play with it."

Sullivan's chest felt hollow, and he was sweating with misgivings about this. He could have set up the pistol with the chamber empty, but he wasn't confident that she'd be able to work the slide in a panicky second; and he could have left the hammer down, along with the safety engaged. but that would require that she remember two moves, and have the time for them, in that hypothetical panicky second.

"You still got money?" he asked her.

"Three or four of the twenties, and some ones and some change."

clicked and resonated hollowly, and faintly a woman's voice said, *"If you would like to make a call, please hang up and dial again."*

Elizalde helped Kootie out of the chair, and to Sullivan she seemed to be hurrying the weeping boy, clearing the way so that he could finally call *his* father. She's a psychiatrist, Sullivan thought. She probably figures this is all good therapy, all this awful idiot pathos.

As he sat down on the warmed chair seat he noticed that Edison was letting Kootie cry, not taking over the boy's body again. Sullivan frowned—he knew the fused quartz filament would hold its initial vibration for quite a while in the rarefied mercury-vapor atmosphere inside the gauge, but it had to be picking up noise, random interference, to judge by the way the crowd effect kept creeping in.

But there was nothing Edison would have been able to do about it. At least the speaker was giving out only an even hiss right now.

Sullivan held out his open palm like a surgeon in the middle of an operation. "Thumb?"

Over Kootie's shaking shoulder, Elizalde gave him a glance of exhausted pique. *"Thumb,"* she said, slapping Houdini's black thumb into his hand.

Sullivan began dialing. *Hide, hide,* he thought, *the cow's outside?* Or, *Dad, I'm sorry I wasn't out there, treading water beside you, even if it would just have been to drown with you.* Or simply, *Dad, where have you been? What on earth am I supposed to do now?*

He dialed the last numbers of SULLIVAN and laid the thumb down.

The speaker beside the sink buzzed as the woman's voice came back on the line. *"What number were you trying to reach?"*

Her tone was palpably sarcastic now—and with a sudden emptiness in his chest he realized that, for the second time in four days, he was talking on the telephone to his twin sister, Sukie.

Impulsively, he replied in a falsetto imitation of Judy Garland: "Oh, Auntie Em, I'm frightened!"

And Sukie came back quickly enough to override his last couple of syllables with, *"Auntie Em! Auntie Em!"* in the sneering tones of the Wicked Witch of the West.

Sullivan sneaked a glance to the side. Everyone in the smoky kitchen, including fat Johanna in the office doorway, was staring at him; even Kootie had stopped crying in order to gape.

"He put her in a Leyden jar," Sukie went on in a sing-song voice, *"and there he kept her near yet far."*

What? thought Sullivan bewilderedly. Put who in a Leyden jar? Auntie Em, in that crystal ball in the movie? A Leyden jar was an early kind of capacitor for storing a static electric charge. "What the hell, Sukie?" he said.

"This root beer will not pass away, Pete. Have you drained it yet?"

"—Yes." The blood was thudding in his ears, and he felt as though he were standing behind his own body, leaning over its defeat-slumped shoulder. "At least *you* swam *out.*"

"We will not regret the past nor wish to shut the door on it. You should have drank more.

"'We are but older children, dear,
Who fret to find our bedtime near.'"

"That's from *Alice*," said Sullivan.

"Through the Looking-Glass, *actually*," Sukie said.

"Why do—you all—quote those books so much?"

"They're not nonsense here, Pete. The little girl who
falls down the deep well that's lined with bookshelves and
pictures—call it 'your whole life flashing before your
eyes'—the collapse of all the events of your timeline, down
to an idiot unlocated point that occupies no space—the
Alice books are an automortography. And then you're in
a place where your . . . 'physical size' is a wildly irrational
variable, and distance and speed are problematical. And
you can't help but go among mad people."

The volume was perceptibly diminishing; the vibrations
of the quartz filament in the Langmuir gauge in the other
room were becoming increasingly randomized.

"I—" said Sullivan, "wanted to talk to Dad, actually . . ."

"He doesn't want to talk to you, actually. You're just
going to have to be a little soldier about this. Lewis Carroll
wasn't dead, but he knew a little girl who did die—he had
taken photographs of her, and he caught her ghost in a
Leyden jar, just like Ben Franklin used to do. She told
Lewis Carroll all those stories, and he wrote 'em down."
She paused then, and when she spoke again her voice was
gentler. *"You're probably looking Commander Hold-'Em*
in the eye right now, aren't you?"

Sullivan was. (He felt even further removed from his
seated body than he had a few minutes ago, and he

knew that, if Elizalde refused to give him back the .45, he could easily find something else—hell, he could walk in two minutes from here to the ocean, and just swim out.) His father had not forgotten nor forgiven. Over the reeks of burnt mint and Bradshaw's cinnamon-and-rot breath and his own beery sour sweat, Sullivan could smell Coppertone lotion and mayonnaise and the terrible sea.

"If you care," he whispered.

"I've got to take a moment to say . . . good. But! It's just that he doesn't want to talk to anyone over this open line, Pete. He wants you to go pick him up. He says Nicky Bradshaw will know where he is, he has apparently dreamed about Nicky. Dream a little dream of me . . . not." Her voice was definitely fading now.

"Beth," he said loudly, "I ran away from you too, can you—"

At the same time she was saying, *"I worked hard to ruin your whole life, Pete, can you—"*

With their old skill of each knowing what the other was about to say, they paused—Sullivan smiled, and he thought that Sukie was smiling somewhere too—and then they said, in perfect unison, "Forgive me?"

After a pause, *"How could I possibly not?"* they both said.

Sukie's voice faded away into the increasing hiss of the speaker; for a few seconds everyone in the kitchen heard a dog barking somewhere deep in the amplified abyss, and then the roaring hiss was all there was.

For some reason Kootie whispered, "Fred?" and began crying again.

Sullivan hung up the telephone. He lifted his head and looked at Bradshaw's impassive, squinting face. "I need to go pick up my father," he said hoarsely. "Apparently, you know where he would be."

"Turn off your telephone," whined Bradshaw aggressively. "Every psychic from San Fran to San Clam is probably picking all this up."

Sullivan stood up and pushed the sweaty hair back from his forehead. "True. Hell, it's probably been breaking in on TV sets and radios," he said, "like CB transmissions." He walked stiffly into the dark office and crouched to unplug the transformer from the wall socket. The air in here was sharp with the oily, metallic, but somehow also organic-smelling reek of ozone.

Bradshaw had followed him, and now swung open the outside door. Late-afternoon sunlight and the cold sea breeze swept into the room, and Elizalde and Kootie and Johanna shuffled blinking out of the smoky kitchen onto the office carpet.

Sullivan twisted the cable clamps off the van battery's terminals, and then began disconnecting the wires that linked the components of their makeshift device. "We're off the air," he remarked.

"If I'm supposed to know where he is," said Bradshaw, "then he must be at his grave in—the Hollywood Cemetery. I've been visiting the grave ever since he died—even after *I* died."

Nettled, Sullivan just nodded his head. "That's fine. Hollywood Cemetery, I know where that is, on Santa Monica, right over the fence from Paramount Studios. Straight up the Harbor Freeway to the 101. I should easily be back before dark." He would even have time to stop at Max Henry's on Melrose for a shot or two of Wild Turkey and a couple of chilly Coors, before going on, north a block, to—to the cemetery.

It occurred to Sullivan that he had not been within the walls of that cemetery since the day of his father's funeral, in 1959. "Uh," he asked awkwardly, "where's his . . . grave marker?"

"North end of the lake—by Jayne Mansfield's *cenotaph*—that means empty grave—she's buried somewhere else."

"Okay. Now I wonder if I could borrow your—"

"Explain to him," interrupted Bradshaw, "that I couldn't come along. Tell him I'm waiting here, and I—(*gasp*)—I've missed him." He raised his hand as if fending off an argument. "And you can't drive that van."

"No, I was just going to ask if—"

"No," Bradshaw insisted, "the van is out. It's a . . . a disgrace. Take my car, it's a Chevy Nova. Full tank of gas. It drives a little sideways—but that'll help keep anyone from being able to see—which way you're going."

"Great," said Sullivan, wishing he had a beer in his hand right now. "That's a good idea, thanks." He squinted through the open doorway at Elizalde, who had walked out across the asphalt and was taking deep breaths of the fresh air. "Angelica," he called, "can I have back the . . . machine in the fanny pack?"

She gave him an opaque look—she probably couldn't see him in the dim interior—and then she walked back and stepped up inside. "What is Commander Hold-'Em?" she asked quietly.

"My sister's slang for death, the Grim Reaper. Is it back in the apartment?"

"You've *named* the gun that?"

Psychiatrists! he thought. "No," he said patiently. "I was talking about the gun, and then you asked a question about my sister's term for death and I answered you, and then I was talking about the gun again. Which I still am. Could I have it?"

"You showed me how to use it," she said. Her brown eyes were still unreadable.

"I remember. After you said you didn't believe in them." Suddenly, he was sure that her patient, Frank, had killed himself with a gun.

"Kootie would be safer here," she said, "in this masked area, with Bradshaw or Shadroe or whoever your 'godbrother' is."

"I agree," said Sullivan, who thought he could see where this was going. "And so would the famous Dr. Elizalde, whose face I saw on the network news, night before last."

"I'm coming with you," she said. "Don't worry, I won't intrude on you and your father."

Bradshaw started to speak, but Sullivan cut him off with the chopping gesture. "Why?" Sullivan asked her.

"Because you should have a gun along with you when you go there," Elizalde told him, "and I won't let you go by yourself with a gun, because I think you're still 'looking Commander Hold-'Em in the eye.'" She was staring straight at him, and she raised her eyebrows now. "That is *to* say, I think you might kill yourself."

"No," interjected Bradshaw worriedly, "I won't take responsibility for the kid. I told you no kids."

"I won't be any trouble, mister," said Kootie, "just—"

"That's . . . hysterical," Sullivan said to Elizalde. "Give me the goddamn gun."

"No." Elizalde jumped out into the yard and sprinted across the asphalt; when she was ten yards away, she turned and shaded her face with her hand to look back at him. She lifted the hem of her untucked old sweatshirt, and he saw that she was wearing the fanny pack. "If you try to take it from me, I will shoot you in the leg."

His face hot, Sullivan stepped down out of the office. "With a .45? You may as well shoot me in the chest, Angelica!"

Her hand was under the flapping hem of her sweatshirt. "All right. At least you won't die a suicide and go to Hell."

He stopped, and grinned tiredly at her. *"Whaa?* Is this a psychiatric thing or a Catholic thing?"

"It's me not wanting you *dead*, asshole! Why won't you let me come along?"

Sullivan had lost his indignity somehow, and he shrugged. "Come along, then. I hope you don't mind if I stop for a drink on the way."

"Your sister drank, I gather?"

His exhausted grin widened. "You want to make something out of it?"

"I've got to make something out of *something.*"

Bradshaw stepped down to the pavement behind Sullivan. "Take the kid!" he wheezed. "With you!" He seemed to be at a loss for words then. "On Long Beach sands," he said finally. "I can connect nothing with nothing."

Sullivan turned around. "What's the matter with you, Nicky? Kootie can stay in our apartment. He won't be any trouble. He'll probably just take a nap."

"Sure, mister," said Kootie. "I didn't get a lot of sleep last night anyway; I could use a nap. I won't be any trouble, mister."

Bradshaw just shook his head. After a moment he shook himself and dug into the pocket of his ludicrous old shorts, and then tossed a ring of keys to Sullivan. "Gray Chevy Nova right behind you," he said. "The blinkers don't work right—the emergency flashers come on if you try to signal. Use hand signals, okay?"

Sullivan frowned. "Okay. I guess we'll *for sure* be back before dark."

Bradshaw nodded bleakly. "Leave a dollar in the ashtray for gas."

CHAPTER 40

❦

"It's only the Red King snoring," said Tweedledee.
"Come and look at him!" the brothers cried, and
they each took one of Alice's hands, and led her up
to where the King was sleeping.
"Isn't he a lovely sight?" said Tweedledum.
Alice couldn't say honestly that he was.

—Lewis Carroll,
Through the Looking-Glass

THE CEMETERY in the late afternoon was full of ghosts, and at first Sullivan and Elizalde tried to avoid them. Even before they parked Bradshaw's goofy car, while they were still hardly past the office, they saw semi-transparent figures clustered around the big white sculpture of a winged man sexually assaulting a woman. The smoky figures might have been attempting to stop the winged man, or help him subdue the woman, or just conceal the atrocity from the street.

Sullivan swore softly and looked for a place to park.

The broad lawns he remembered out front along Santa Monica Boulevard were gone, those spaces now stacked full of shops—a Mexican market and a Chinese restaurant shouldering right up to the east side of the ivied stone buildings of the cemetery entrance, muffler and bodywork shops to the west—but there was still a sense of isolation here inside, in this silent, far-stretching landscape of old sycamores and palms and canted gravestones. Looking through Bradshaw's windshield at the ghosts that could hold their shapes in this still air, Sullivan wished the noise and smoke and spastic motion of the boulevard could intrude their vital agitations here.

Elizalde had Houdini's plaster right hand in her lap, and Sullivan was gripping the left one between his knees; the dried thumb was in his shirt pocket.

Past the ghosts was a crossroads, and he turned left onto the narrow paved lane and parked. "The lake's ahead of us," he said, hefting Houdini's plaster hand. "Let's *walk* up to it—the noise of the engine might spook him—" He winced at the unintended pun. "—and anyway, this car keeps looking like it's in the process of running off onto the grass."

Actually, he simply didn't want to get there. His father's ghost was to *meet* him? Would it be a translucent figure like the ones climbing on the statue?

I was only seven years old! he thought, with no conviction. *It was thirty-three years ago! How can I—still—be to blame?*

Still, he was profoundly sorry that he had let Elizalde talk him out of the preliminary drinks, and remotely glad that she was holding the gun.

"Okay." Elizalde seemed subdued as she climbed out of the car, and the double slam of the doors rang hollowly in the quiet groves. "Do normal people see that crowd by the entrance?"

"No," said Sullivan. "They're just visible to specimens like you and me."

Looking north, Sullivan could see the distant white letters of the HOLLYWOOD sign standing on the dark hills, and the words *holy wood* flickered through his mind. To the south across the stone-studded hillocky lawn, past the farthest palms, was the back wall of Paramount Studios, with the red Paramount logo visible on the water tower beyond the air conditioning ducts.

"It's . . . somewhere ahead of us," said Sullivan, starting forward. He glanced to his left, remembering that Carl Switzer was buried right there by the road somewhere. Switzer had been "Alfalfa" in the old Our Gang comedies, and had been shot to death in January of '59. Alfalfa's grave had been only five months old when Arthur Patrick Sullivan was buried, and the twins, big fans of the Our Gang shows, had found the still-bright marker while silently wandering around the grounds before their father's graveside service. Neither of them had said anything as they had stared down at Switzer's glassy-smooth stone marker. It had been obvious that anybody at all could die, at any time.

"This is very pretty," said Elizalde, scuffing along next to him and holding Houdini's plaster right hand like a flashlight.

"It's morbid," snapped Sullivan. "Burying a bunch of *dead bodies,* and putting a fancy marker over each one so the survivors will know where to go and cry. What if the markers got rearranged? You'd be weeping over some stranger. *Not* some stranger, even, some cast-off dead *body* of a stranger, like a pile of fingernail clippings or old shoes, or the dust from inside an electric razor. What's the difference between coming out *here* to think about dead Uncle Irving, and thinking about him in your own living room? Okay, here you can sit on the grass and be only six feet above his inert old body. Would it be better if you could dig a hole, and sit only *one* foot above it?" He was shaking. "Everybody should be cremated, and the ashes should be tossed in the sea with no fanfare at all."

"It's a sign of respect," said Elizalde angrily. "And it's a real, tangible link. Think of the Shroud of Turin! Where would we be if they had cremated Jesus?"

"I don't know—we'd have the Ashtray of Turin."

She swung Houdini's plaster hand and hit Sullivan hard in the shoulder. One of the fingers flew off and bounced in the coarse green grass.

Sullivan had let out a sharp *Hah!* at the impact, and he sidestepped onto the grass to keep his balance. "Goddammit," he whispered, rubbing his shoulder as he stepped back down to the asphalt, keeping away from her, "give me back the fucking .45, will you? If you go trying to make some theatrical gesture with *that*, you'll kill someone." He noticed the gap in the hand, and looked around until he spotted the finger. "Oh, good work," he said, stepping across and bending to pick it up. "It didn't half-cost my dead sister and I any trouble to get hold of these things, go ahead and bust 'em up, by all means."

"I'm sorry," she said. "We can glue it. I'm tired, I didn't

mean it to be more than a tap. But you weren't saying what you believed, just what you *wished* you believed— that dead people go away and stay away, canceled. Are these ghosts or not?"

He thought her question was rhetorical until she repeated it in an urgent whisper. Then he stopped fiddling with the plaster finger and looked ahead.

"Uh," he said, "my guess is ghosts."

Three fat men in tuxedos were walking toward them, a hundred feet ahead, where the road was unpaved; the man in the middle had his arms around his companions' shoulders, and they were all walking in step, but no dust at all was being kicked up, and their steps made no sounds in the still air. Their mouths gaped in wide, silent smiles.

"Let's slant south, toward Paramount," said Sullivan.

He and Elizalde set off diagonally across the grass to their right with a purposeful air.

The sun was low over the mausoleum along the distant Gower Street border of the cemetery—the shadows of the palm trees stretched for dozens of yards across the gold-glowing grass.

Griffith's magic hour, Sullivan thought with a shiver.

Flat markers stippled the low luminous hills in meandering ranks, like stepping-stones, and some graves were bordered with ankle-high sections of scalloped pink concrete, and the interior space of these was consistently filled with broken white stones; a few, the graves of little children, had plastic dinosaurs and toy cars and miniature soldiers set up on the stones to make pitiful dioramas.

Mausoleums like ornate WPA powerhouse relay stations stood along the dirt road ahead of them, and the brassy sunlight shone on the wingless eagle atop the Harrison Gray Otis monument; Sullivan was sure that the eagle had had wings in 1959. The cypresses around them rustled in the gentle breeze and threw down dry twigs.

Sullivan and Elizalde had by now wandered into a marshy area, back by the corrugated-aluminum walls and broken windows of the Paramount buildings, that seemed to be all babies' graves, the markers sunken and blurred with silt.

Houdini's maimed hand was shaking in Elizalde's fists. "We've passed those ghosts," she whispered. "Let's get to the lake."

At that moment, a wailing laugh erupted from somewhere far off among the trees and gravestones behind them. Elizalde's free hand was cold and tight in Sullivan's.

They hurried back to the dirt road, and over it, onto a descending slope of shadowed grass. Ahead of them was a long lake, with stone stairs at the north end and, at the south end, tall white pillars and a marble pedestal rising out of the dark water. A white sarcophagus lay on the pedestal.

"Douglas Fairbanks, Senior," panted Sullivan as he and Elizalde hurried along the marge of the narrow lake.

Human shapes made from dried leaves were dancing silently in the shadows of the stairs, and curled sections of dry palm fronds swam and bobbed their fibrous necks out on the dark face of the water.

"Just up the hill and across the next road," Sullivan said, "is the other lake, the one my father—"

He couldn't finish the sentence, and just pulled her along.

✳   ✳   ✳

Nicholas Bradshaw had been standing for several minutes, watching Kootie breathe in his sleep as he lay curled on the wooden floor, before he crouched and shook the boy's shoulder.

The boy's eyes opened, but Bradshaw was sure that the alert, cautious intelligence in the gaze was Thomas Edison's.

"A car went by twice," said Bradshaw, "slow. I don't think it was bad guys—but it did make me think you'd be—safer back in the office."

Kootie got lithely to his feet and glanced at the blinds, which glowed orange around the slats. "They're not back yet."

"No," said Bradshaw. The empty living room echoed hollowly, and he didn't like to talk in here.

"The boy's asleep," said Kootie. "I suppose I can be out in the air for a few minutes—your place does seem to be a deceptive one for trackers to focus on."

"I've tried to make it so," said Bradshaw, opening the door. "And it helps that I'm a dead man."

"I reckon," said Kootie, following him outside.

Parrots fluttered past overhead, shouting raucously, and the mockingbirds on the telephone lines had learned the two-note chirrup that car alarms emitted when they were activated by the key-ring remotes, and which always sounded to Bradshaw like the first two notes of the "Colonel Bogie March."

Bradshaw was remembering the early days of working on "Ghost of a Chance," in '55 and '56. CBS had filmed the show's episodes on a couple of boxy sets on a sound-stage at General Service Studios, and in spite of the depth-and-texture look that Ozzie Nelson had pioneered for "The Adventures of Ozzie and Harriet," the director at General Service had held to the old flat look of early television—bright lighting with minimal shadow and background.

During the show's tightly scheduled first two years, Nicky Bradshaw had seemed to spend most of his waking hours on those sets, and it had been a deepening and expanding of his whole world when CBS had given the job of filming the show to Stage 5 Productions in 1957. The Stage 5 director had used a series of sets that had been built for Hitchcock's *The Trouble with Harry*, and often filmed scenes at local parks, and occasionally at the beach.

His world had gone flat again when the show was finally canceled in 1960, a year after his godfather's death. (He hurried Kootie toward the office—he must do this thing before his godfather's ghost arrived.) And then it had flattened to the equivalent of sketchy animation in a flip-book after his own death in 1975.

Most of all—more than sex, more than food—he missed dreams. He had not allowed himself to sleep at all in the last seventeen years, for if he were to have a frightening dream while he wasn't consciously monitoring the workings of his dead body, he wouldn't be able to wake himself up—and the inescapable trauma would surely be strong enough to cause him to throw ghost-shells in his fright . . . and, since he had continued occupying his body past the end of his lifeline, the ghosts would have no charged line to arc back to.

They would collide, collapse into jarring interference, implode in fearful spiraling feedback.

He knew of several cases in which a person had

suffered a profound trauma *only a few moments* after unacknowledged death, and had burst into flames. Bradshaw had accumulated *seventeen years*.

But he could still remember laying his weary body down and closing his eyes and letting sleep take him, remember awakening in darkness and seeing by a luminous clock face that there were hours yet to sleep, remember drifting to wakefulness on sunny mornings with the images of dreams still dissolving before his eyes as he stretched and threw back the covers.

After seventeen years, he wasn't sure he remembered what dreams were, any more than he really remembered what the sensations of taste had been like. Dreams had been . . . visions, it seemed to him now, like vivid daydreams over which one had little or no control; scary sometimes, it was true—but also, as he recalled, sometimes achingly erotic, sometimes luminous with a wrenching beauty that seemed to hint of some actual heaven somewhere. And in dreams he had been able to talk and laugh again with people he'd loved who had died.

His hand was on Kootie's bony shoulder, propelling the boy toward the main building.

When they had both stepped up into the dark office, Bradshaw ducked into the kitchen to fetch Elizalde's pint bottle of tequila, which was still more than half-full.

"You're how old?" he asked gruffly.

"Eighty-four," said Kootie.

"Old enough to have a drink." Bradshaw actually took an involuntary breath. "If you'd like one."

"A shot won't hurt the boy," assented Kootie. "It seems I've acquired a taste for the stuff, since my expiration."

You ghosts always do, thought Bradshaw as he poured a liberal slosh of the yellow liquor into a Flintstones glass.

"You're not going to have any?" asked Kootie alertly.

"Oh," said Bradshaw, "sure. I've just got to find a cup for myself." On a bookshelf he found one of the coffee cups from which he'd been drinking his Eat-'Em-&-Weep Balls tea, and he poured an ounce of tequila in on top of the red stickiness.

Kootie raised his glass, but waited until Bradshaw had tipped up his coffee cup and taken a mouthful of the tequila.

What do I do now, thought Bradshaw—swallow it?

He glanced up at Kootie, who hadn't even taken a sip yet. Bradshaw sighed and swallowed, feeling the volatile coldness in his throat and trying to remember what tequila tasted like. Pepper and turpentine, as far as he could recall.

That will do, he thought. I suppose that stuff will just sit in my stomach until it . . . evaporates? Soaks into my dead tissues like a marinade? For the next day or two, he thought seriously, I'll have to be careful about burping around any open flame.

Flame, he thought, and he remembered those cases of "spontaneous combustion" that had occurred when a newly dead person experienced an emotional trauma. In a number of the cases, the person had been drinking alcohol.

He put down the cup. "I'm too old for tequila," he said. He inhaled, feeling again the chill of the fast-evaporating alcohol in his mouth. "I'll be regretting even just that one sip."

Edison took another swallow from his glass. "Well, I'm eighty-four years old, but I'm working with an eleven-year-old stomach. The boy will probably sleep through until morning, so another drink or two will do no harm. I've got something to celebrate anyway."

Too weary to speak, Bradshaw raised his eyebrows.

"I received a Bachelor of Science degree on Sunday."

Bradshaw couldn't imagine what Edison was talking about, but he nodded ponderously as he reached for the bottle to refill Kootie's glass. "That's good." He sucked air into his lungs. "A college degree can make all the difference in the world."

There was a broader lake in a shallow green meadow on the north side of the cemetery lane, and its water was still enough that Sullivan could clearly see the vertical reflections of the tall palms on the far shore. There were two more palm trees reflected in the water than there were standing on the shore.

Marble benches stood here and there on the grass slope, and there seemed to be figures sitting on every one. Some stared at Sullivan and Elizalde, while others silently went through the motions of talking or laughing, and a couple were bent over notebooks, perhaps writing poetry. Sullivan supposed that one or two of them might be living people who saw this place as solitary.

Past the urns and markers and statues he hurried, holding Elizalde's free hand as they made their way down the slope. Around the north curve of the shore, only a few hundred feet ahead, he could see another rectangle of broken white stones, and he was sure that his father's grave was very near there.

He and Elizalde were striding along the shoreline now

to stay away from the ghosts on the slope, though the animate palm fronds swam in closer to them, creaking woodenly in eerily good imitation of the grumble of ducks.

Rope-wide grooves were curled and looped across the muddy bottom of the shallow lake, as if big worms had been foraging earlier in the day.

Sullivan blinked around at the marble-studded slopes, and he sniffed the chilly jasmined air—then realized that it was a *sound* that he had become aware of, a low vibration as if a lot of people hiding behind the nearer stones and trees were humming the same bass note.

Clustered red water lilies hid the lake floor at this north end of the lake, and his father's grave was just on the far side of a bushy gray-green juniper that overhung the water.

"Got to go back up the slope for just a few steps," he said tightly, "to get around this shrubbery."

"I'd rather wade across," whispered Elizalde.

He thought about the worm tracks, and for a moment he wondered if there even *was* a bottom right here, under the blanket of water lilies. "It's just a few steps," he said, tugging her uphill around the juniper. Two ghosts were pirouetting on the Cecil B. DeMille crypts, but no one was paying any evident attention to Sullivan and Elizalde.

Back down beside the water on the far side, he saw that a knee-high white statue of the Virgin Mary had been propped up on the rectangle of white stones, with red flowers in the little stone hands and a black cloth hood tied around the head.

Jayne Mansfield's etched pink cenotaph lay at the feet of the stone Virgin; the surface of the marker had apparently once had a reproduction of Mansfield's face bonded to it, but the image had been crudely chipped off. In the shadows under the juniper Sullivan could see a couple of empty cans of King Cobra malt liquor and a dozen white candles in a clear plastic bag.

Off a few steps to the east of Mansfield's marker lay a low black-marble square that, from the way its placement jibed with his thirty-three-year-old memories, must be the one that would have his father's name on it.

Kootie's head seemed to be bobbing in time to a slow pulse, and Bradshaw stood up and fetched a jar from the kitchen. It was a Smucker's orange marmalade jar, scraped nearly empty.

"How're you doing," he said as he plodded back into the office with it. "Mr. Edison."

Kootie was frowning intently, and the expression made him even look like an old man, in the dim sunlight that filtered in through the lantana branches clustered outside the windows. "I'm afraid," he said with evident care, "that I've stuck poor Kootie with . . . what I trust will be . . . the first hangover of his life."

Bradshaw knew that if his flesh had still been alive, his hand would have trembled as he held out the marmalade jar. "Best thing for the boy would be," he said. There was no heartbeat in his chest, but it should have been knocking. "For you to get sick now, while the booze is still. Undigested. Cough yourself out into this jar. The boy will feel better for it."

"There never has been a vacuum produced in this country that approached anywhere near the vacuum which is necessary for me," said Edison, articulating each

"He's in my ear," Sullivan told her. And he remembered the scene in the railway carriage in *Through the Looking-Glass,* and he added with weary certainty, "He's a gnat."

Elizalde obviously hadn't understood what he had said, but let herself be hurried along down the east shore of the lake.

Trying to run smoothly so as not to jar his head and possibly dislodge his father, Sullivan nevertheless kept glancing across the lake, toward the setting sun. The figures on the far-side slope were beginning to fragment; an old woman would take a tottering step and then abruptly be a child running, and a figure on a bench would close a book and stand up and suddenly be two figures. One pedestrian became a motorcycle and rider, and silently sped away over the grass, bounding over gravestones as if they were hurdles.

Up by the Cathedral Mausoleum, Sullivan and Elizalde crossed the grass through a cluster of stones with Armenian names, each of which had an unlit candle in front of it and a dish for burning incense, and then they ad sprinted across the road and were hurrying past the st side of the mausoleum, toward the stairs above the grave of Douglas Fairbanks.

cuttle fast and low through the little valley past these " Sullivan whispered, "and then when we're among es—"

lden, shocking racket from the west slope of the Fairbanks lake made them both instantly crouch their teeth—it was a loud metallic squealing t by idiot laughter.

syllable meticulously with Kootie's mouth. "A hundred-thousandth of an atmosphere was enough to let the filament burn. I need to find my vacuum."

"This jar is evacuated," said Bradshaw. "Hop in. You've had too much to drink. Carry the hangover into the jar. To free the boy."

"Physicists and sphinxes in majestical mists. Nothing wrong with my . . . sibilant syllables." Kootie's eyes were half-closed.

"Dammit," said Bradshaw. "Mr. Edison. *Exhale yourself. Get in the jar.*"

But Kootie's chin wobbled downward, lifted once with a questioning whine, then dropped to his chest. A hoarse snore blew out through the boy's lips, but Bradshaw knew it was just breath, not Edison's ghost.

"Mr. Edison," said Bradshaw, his voice droning flatly as he tried to speak louder. "Wake up. It's just a hop, skip, and a sigh. To bed."

Kootie was unconscious, though, and didn't stir even when Bradshaw reached out to nudge his head with the empty jar.

Bradshaw's face was immobile, but a red tear ran down his gray cheek as he set the jar carefully on the cleared-off desk.

Horribly, there still was something he could do.

ARTHUR PATRICK SULLIVAN
"And flights of angels sing thee to thy rest"
1898-1959

Sullivan waved a circling gnat away from his face and

stared down at his father's gravestone. He was tightly holding Elizalde's hand.

His father's stone had a picture attached, too; a playing-card-sized greened-brass plaque with an engraving of the old man's face etched on it. Sullivan recognized the smiling likeness; it was from a Fox Studios publicity still taken in the forties.

The breeze paused, and when it came back it was chillier. The palm-frond swans scudded away toward the ring of inert fountain jets that stuck up above the surface of the water; Sullivan had at first glance thought the nozzles were a cluster of baby ducklings, and perhaps they still appeared so to the creaking frond-birds.

Sullivan released Elizalde's hand, crouched, and touched the inset plaque—and it was loose, simply resting in the shallow rectangular recess in the stone. He pried it out with a fingernail and stood up again, tucking it into his shirt pocket and retaking hold of Elizalde's hand.

Sullivan's mouth was dry and tasted of pennies. When he began to speak, he found that his voice had a rusty flippancy: "So where are you, Dad?" he asked, aware that Elizalde was listening. "We want to be on the road before the evening traffic gets heavy."

The breeze twitched at his hair, and then a small voice in his ear said, *"Call me Fishmeal."*

Sullivan didn't move. The voice might be that of any random ghost. He seemed to remember that the line was from the beginning of *Moby Dick*.

"On the freeways," the voice went on, *"there you feel free."*

Sullivan's heart was suddenly beating hard enough to

shake his shoulders. *That* phrase was familiar—it was something his father had always said to the twins, though the old man had only lived to see the earliest of the Southern California superhighways—the 110 to South Pasadena, and the one that he had always stubbornly gone on calling the Ramona Freeway, though it had been renamed the San Bernardino Freeway four years before he died.

Sullivan's mouth opened, but all the things there were to say overwhelmed him, and he just exhaled a descending "Ssshhhhh."

"You're a good boy," said the tiny buzzing voice, *"and I know you won't slap me, even though I* am *an insect."*

Sullivan's hand was cold and shaking in Elizalde's, and he guessed that she was looking at him in concern, but he held his head still.

"What kind of insect?" he whispered.

"Good, then you don't—" began the voice—

But it was interrupted by the wailing hyena laugh from the shadowy trees.

Elizalde's free hand gripped his, hard. "I[ ] laughing bag," she whimpered. "The thing K[ ] saw today—the thing that spoke on the pho[ ]

"Swing south," buzzed the voice, *"po[ ] the Paramount wall, there's a tunneli[ ] field of the movies overlaps a bit a[ ] just cut north to the entrance."*

"Back the way we came," sai[ ] away from the juniper bush [ ] can go around this other side [ ]

"What about your father?"

syllable meticulously with Kootie's mouth. "A hundred-thousandth of an atmosphere was enough to let the filament burn. I need to find my vacuum."

"This jar is evacuated," said Bradshaw. "Hop in. You've had too much to drink. Carry the hangover into the jar. To free the boy."

"Physicists and sphinxes in majestical mists. Nothing wrong with my . . . sibilant syllables." Kootie's eyes were half-closed.

"Dammit," said Bradshaw. "Mr. Edison. *Exhale yourself. Get in the jar.*"

But Kootie's chin wobbled downward, lifted once with a questioning whine, then dropped to his chest. A hoarse snore blew out through the boy's lips, but Bradshaw knew it was just breath, not Edison's ghost.

"Mr. Edison," said Bradshaw, his voice droning flatly as he tried to speak louder. "Wake up. It's just a hop, skip, and a sigh. To bed."

Kootie was unconscious, though, and didn't stir even when Bradshaw reached out to nudge his head with the empty jar.

Bradshaw's face was immobile, but a red tear ran down his gray cheek as he set the jar carefully on the cleared-off desk.

Horribly, there still was something he could do.

ARTHUR PATRICK SULLIVAN
"And flights of angels sing thee to thy rest"
1898-1959

Sullivan waved a circling gnat away from his face and

stared down at his father's gravestone. He was tightly holding Elizalde's hand.

His father's stone had a picture attached, too; a playing-card-sized greened-brass plaque with an engraving of the old man's face etched on it. Sullivan recognized the smiling likeness; it was from a Fox Studios publicity still taken in the forties.

The breeze paused, and when it came back it was chillier. The palm-frond swans scudded away toward the ring of inert fountain jets that stuck up above the surface of the water; Sullivan had at first glance thought the nozzles were a cluster of baby ducklings, and perhaps they still appeared so to the creaking frond-birds.

Sullivan released Elizalde's hand, crouched, and touched the inset plaque—and it was loose, simply resting in the shallow rectangular recess in the stone. He pried it out with a fingernail and stood up again, tucking it into his shirt pocket and retaking hold of Elizalde's hand.

Sullivan's mouth was dry and tasted of pennies. When he began to speak, he found that his voice had a rusty flippancy: "So where are you, Dad?" he asked, aware that Elizalde was listening. "We want to be on the road before the evening traffic gets heavy."

The breeze twitched at his hair, and then a small voice in his ear said, *"Call me Fishmeal."*

Sullivan didn't move. The voice might be that of any random ghost. He seemed to remember that the line was from the beginning of *Moby Dick.*

"On the freeways," the voice went on, *"there you feel free."*

Sullivan's heart was suddenly beating hard enough to

shake his shoulders. *That* phrase was familiar—it was
something his father had always said to the twins, though
the old man had only lived to see the earliest of the
Southern California superhighways—the 110 to South
Pasadena, and the one that he had always stubbornly gone
on calling the Ramona Freeway, though it had been
renamed the San Bernardino Freeway four years before he
died.

Sullivan's mouth opened, but all the things there were
to say overwhelmed him, and he just exhaled a descending
"Ssshhhhh."

"You're a good boy," said the tiny buzzing voice, *"and
I know you won't slap me, even though I* am *an insect."*

Sullivan's hand was cold and shaking in Elizalde's, and
he guessed that she was looking at him in concern, but he
held his head still.

"What kind of insect?" he whispered.

"Good, then you don't—" began the voice—

But it was interrupted by the wailing hyena laughter
from the shadowy trees.

Elizalde's free hand gripped his, hard. "It's that
laughing bag," she whimpered. "The thing Kootie and I
saw today—the thing that spoke on the phone."

"Swing south," buzzed the voice, *"past Fairbanks to
the Paramount wall, there's a tunneling effect there, the
field of the movies overlaps a bit and blurs things; then
just cut north to the entrance."*

"Back the way we came," said Sullivan, pulling Elizalde
away from the juniper bush and the stone Virgin. "But we
can go around this other side of the lake."

"What about your father?"

"He's in my ear," Sullivan told her. And he remembered the scene in the railway carriage in *Through the Looking-Glass,* and he added with weary certainty, "He's a gnat."

Elizalde obviously hadn't understood what he had said, but let herself be hurried along down the east shore of the lake.

Trying to run smoothly so as not to jar his head and possibly dislodge his father, Sullivan nevertheless kept glancing across the lake, toward the setting sun. The figures on the far-side slope were beginning to fragment; an old woman would take a tottering step and then abruptly be a child running, and a figure on a bench would close a book and stand up and suddenly be two figures. One pedestrian became a motorcycle and rider, and silently sped away over the grass, bounding over gravestones as if they were hurdles.

Up by the Cathedral Mausoleum, Sullivan and Elizalde crossed the grass through a cluster of stones with Armenian names, each of which had an unlit candle in front of it and a dish for burning incense, and then they had sprinted across the road and were hurrying past the west side of the mausoleum, toward the stairs above the lake grave of Douglas Fairbanks.

"Scuttle fast and low through the little valley past these stairs," Sullivan whispered, "and then when we're among the trees—"

A sudden, shocking racket from the west slope of the Douglas Fairbanks lake made them both instantly crouch and bare their teeth—it was a loud metallic squealing drowned out by idiot laughter.

A thing was flapping toward them from the trees beyond the road to the west, about ten feet above the grass and muscling its way rapidly through the twilight air; it flexed through a slanting beam of golden sunlight, and Sullivan saw that it had long metal wings but its body was a swinging burlap bag with a baseball cap bobbing on top.

Elizalde's razory scream seemed to shake leaves out of the overhanging willow branches, and she let go of Houdini's plaster right hand—and it disappeared.

Sullivan's hand was abruptly empty too; but when he glanced down he saw that he was wearing a black formal jacket with white shirt cuffs just visible at his wrists.

And then he felt the sleeves of the jacket snap loose above the elbows when the jacket and pants twisted him to his left, toward the stone stairs that led down to the lake.

"Whoa, Nellie!" buzzed Sullivan's father in his ear.

Elizalde too had turned toward the stairs. She was shorter suddenly, and plump, and her hair was up in a wide bun above the high collar of her lacy white blouse; but the eyes in the unfamiliar round face were Elizalde's brown eyes, and white showed all the way around the irises.

"It's the mask," said Sullivan jerkily as he found himself scuffing down the stone steps toward the water. "Relax and go with it—I think we're about to start wading."

His unfamiliar shoes stepped right off the bottom step into the warm water, and sank to the ankles in silt; then his long shirtsleeves pulled his arms forward and he was diving.

He braced himself to land flat and not strike his knees or elbows on the bottom—but there was no bottom, and he was swimming breathlessly in choppy *cold* water. Cold *salt* water.

He gasped in sudden shock, stiff with vertigo even though he was supported by the water. He didn't know where he was, or even if he was still conscious and not hallucinating.

The splashing of his clumsy strokes was echoed back to him by a close wall which was not the wall of the Cathedral Mausoleum but, only yards away, the vertical black steel hull of a ship too vast to be comprehended from way down here.

Someone on a deck far above cried, "Get out of town tonight!"

Sullivan could hear Elizalde splashing along next to him, but in the quickly lowering darkness he couldn't see her. Some current kept bumping him against the steel hull of the ship and bumping Elizalde against him, even when they both swam sharply out away from it—and then he heard a metallic boom as Elizalde collided with a wall on *her* side; apparently the two of them were now swimming through some narrow channel.

And the walls were sharply concave now, curling up around him. The light was gone, and Sullivan's knees had somehow got jammed up under his chin by the rounded metal that was now underneath him too.

He was shivering violently at the speed and force of whatever was happening—but then it stopped, and he was encapsulated underwater, in darkness.

He could feel the struggling bony pressure of Elizalde crowding hard at his back, and he knew that she was being tightly constricted by the wall on her side. They were completely submerged in solid water now, with no smallest pocket of air.

A metal floor was shoved up against Sullivan's shoes, and the echoes of his scraping soles told him that there was a lid very close over his head. He and Elizalde had got trapped inside some kind of closed cylinder full of water. Sullivan's ear canals chugged and bubbled as they were icily filled, and his heart hammered at the mental image of his father lost again under seawater.

Sullivan reached out to push against the wall in front of his face, and he felt tightly ratcheted handcuffs cut into the skin of his wrists. Elizalde was thrashing furiously against his back.

With her shaking him, he couldn't even get his legs under himself to batter his head against the lid, and he was about to lose the breath that was clenched inside his lungs by blowing it all out in a helpless scream—when he became aware that his hands were busy.

His right hand had dug in the kinky hair over his ear and pulled free something that felt like a hairpin; and his fingers now worked carefully as they straightened the bit of wire. He knew that they were working more slowly and carefully because one finger was now missing.

He managed to nudge Elizalde in the back of her ribs with his left elbow, hoping the gesture conveyed, *Hold still!*

Then the fingers had deftly poked the wire into the receiver slot of the left cuff, between the close cowl and the knurled outer side of the swing arm, and, without letting go of the wire, his fingers had gripped the sides of the cuff and compressed it painfully tighter—and a moment later the swing arm had sprung back out, and his left wrist was freed. His left hand took the wire then, and, with all of its fingers to work with, freed his right wrist even more quickly.

He pushed Elizalde back and braced his feet. Now his hands thrust up past his head, scraping his elbows against the claustrophobically close metal walls, and pressed strongly upward against the metal lid—and *twisted*. The forceful torque released a catch, and then he was turning the whole lid and the upper edge of the cylinder, bracing his feet against the floor. He straightened his legs, and he was lifting the lid off them, pushing it up with his hands, which were out in rushing cold air to the wrists—and only then did Sullivan realize that he and Elizalde had been upright rather than lying horizontally.

And then *up* abruptly became *down,* and both of them were falling headfirst out of the narrow can while air bubbles clunked and rattled past them; Sullivan's shoulders jammed in the narrower neck for a moment, but the water and a lot of loose metal disks coursing past him pushed him free—

And he fell through sunlit air and splashed heavily into shallow water, twisting his neck and shoulder against a muddy bottom and catching Elizalde's knee hard in the small of his back.

When he struggled up to a sitting position the water was rocking around his chest and his eyes were blinking in the golden light of late afternoon. He was leaning back against vertical stone, wheezing and panting, and through the sopping tangles of his hair he could see two branching tree trunks standing up from the shadowed brown water a couple of yards away from where he sat, and, a couple of yards beyond them, a low cement coping and a hedge; a few of the top leaves shone golden green in the last rays of sunlight.

His hands were spasmodically clawing in the silty mud under him, trying to find a tree root to grip in case the world was going to turn upside down again.

Elizalde sat up in the water beside him and held on to his shoulder while she coughed out muddy water and whoopingly sucked air into her lungs. Her mud-matted hair was long again, and the lean, tired face was her own. When he could see that she would be able to breathe, Sullivan cautiously leaned his head back and looked up. He was sitting against a square marble pillar that supported a marble crosspiece far overhead. He and Elizalde were apparently in the south corner of the lake, in the tail-end lagoon behind the marble walls of the Douglas Fairbanks monument.

The world was holding still, and he began to relax, muscle by muscle.

There was a twisting itch in his ear then, and he nearly thrust his finger into it; but the buzzing voice said, *"You've got to get to the Paramount wall—but first grope around in the water and get Houdini's hands."*

"Okay, Dad."

Sullivan pushed away from the pillar and slowly waded on his knees out across the pool, his face bent so closely over the water that his harsh breaths blew rings onto the surface, and he swept his hands through the velvety silt. Elizalde was just breathing hoarsely and watching him.

Faintly, he could hear a rapid creak of metal and

quacking laughter, but the sounds were distant and not drawing closer.

The silt was thick with pennies and nickels and dimes, but he tossed them aside—Elizalde inhaled sharply when she saw the first handful of them—and at last he found the plaster hand with the missing finger and silently handed it to her, and then a few moments later he found the other.

"Up this far slope to the service road," he whispered to Elizalde, "and then turn right and hug the wall all the way back west. The car is—"

"You were *in* there, *with* me," interrupted Elizalde tensely, "right? The can was full of *salt water* this time, wasn't it?"

Sullivan sucked the elastic cuff of his leather jacket; and he thought that it still tasted of salt. "I don't know if it really *happened* or not," he said, "but I was in there with you."

In Sullivan's ear the voice resonated again: "*At the end there, that was Houdini's famous escape from the padlocked milk can. Big news in the teens and twenties.*"

Sullivan helped Elizalde stand up in the yielding mud, and then he waded to the coping, stepped up onto it, and threw one leg over the hedge. "My dad says that was Houdini's famous escape from the milk can," he said quietly.

"This time it was ours," Elizalde said, reaching up from the water for Sullivan to give her a boost. "Happy birthday."

Nicholas Bradshaw had shambled slowly out across the

shadow-streaked parking lot to Pete Sullivan's shrouded van, and by the back bumper he crouched to pick up the little magnet they'd taken out of the telephone. Before turning his steps toward one of the garages, he put the magnet in his mouth.

I wonder, he thought stolidly, if you're held entirely accountable for sins you commit after you're dead. Kids before the age of reason aren't considered capable of knowing right from wrong, so if a five-year-old kills a playmate, he's not blamed. Or not much. He's just a little kid, after all. So what about adults past the age of . . . expiration? We're just *dead* guys, after all.

He thought of the "beasties," the solid ghosts who wandered up from the beach in the evenings and hung around outside his office door, waiting for Bradshaw to set out paper plates with smooth pebbles on them. The poor old creatures could be vindictive—they sometimes pulled license plates off parked cars, and once or twice had got into incomprehensible squabbles among themselves and left broken-off fingers and noses to be swept up in the morning along with the usual litter of rocks and beer cans—but it would be folly to assign *blame* to them. "Wicked" was too concrete an adjective to be supported by the frail nouns that they were.

He tugged open the creaking garage door, and dug out a folded tarpaulin and a big paint tray from behind the dusty frame of a '55 Chevy. He carried them outside and pulled the door back down.

When he had lugged everything across the lot and up into the office, Kootie was still snoring heavily in the Naugahyde chair by the desk.

Bradshaw dropped his burdens and stumped into the kitchen and shook a steak knife free of the litter in one of the cabinet drawers.

He would work without thinking—he would spread the tarpaulin out across the rug and lay the paint tray in the middle of it; then he would lift Kootie out of the chair . . .

But he himself was *not* one of those mindless solid ghosts. He couldn't honestly take refuge in that shabby category. He was dead (through no fault of his own), but his soul had not ever vacated his body.

His face was cool, and when he brushed his hand across his forever-unstubbled jowls, it came away wet. Tears or sweat, it was Eat-'Em-&-Weep juice either way.

Bradshaw would, he was determined that he would, simply lean over the boy's face and, with the telephone magnet between his teeth, inhale the boy's dying breath.

Bradshaw would thus get Edison. And Edison could monitor Bradshaw's body during the long nights aboard the boat, so that Bradshaw himself could sleep, and dream—just as Kootie had been able to sleep while the old ghost walked and spoke and looked out for him.

I've never eaten a ghost, Bradshaw thought; well, why *would* I, none of the average run of ghosts could responsibly *watch the store* while I slept. But Thomas Edison could.

Thomas Edison is probably the *only* ghost that I'd do this to get, he thought, and certainly the only very powerful one *I'll* ever get a shot at; the only one that could let me safely dream. I wouldn't . . . *sell my soul,* ever, except for this. It's God's fault, really, for putting this within my reach.

He remembered the boy saying, *I won't be any trouble, mister.*

Bradshaw stood over the snoring boy, staring at the pulse under his ear; and then he looked down at his right hand, which was gripping the steak knife.

For the first time since his death in 1975, his hand was trembling.

Hunching along through the shadows under Paramount Studios' corrugated aluminum back wall that was streaked with rust stains and gap-toothed with broken windows, Sullivan thought of the broad sunny lanes and parking lots and white monolithic soundstages on the other side. When he had last been on the Paramount lot, in about 1980, there had even been a dirt-paved street of Old West buildings under a vast open-air mural of a blue sky.

"We made a hundred and four pictures there in 1915," said his father's tiny voice in his ear, *"back when it was Lasky, DeMille, and Goldfish in charge, and we'd moved everything here from the barn at Vine and Selma. Sixteen frames a second, the old Lumiere standard. Now because of sound reproduction, it's twenty-four frames a second, ninety feet a minute, and nobody needs to know how to read in order to see a movie, and the purity of the silent silver faces is gone. For us, the graveyard extends all the way south to Melrose."*

Sullivan glanced back through the trees toward the Douglas Fairbanks lake. "Keep your voice down, Dad."

"Keep *your* voice down," whispered Elizalde, who of course couldn't hear what his father was saying.

Gravestones stood in thickly clustered ranks outside the Beth Olam Mausoleum, and Sullivan felt as though he and Elizalde and his father were hiding behind a crowd. The shadowy human-shaped figures that stood among the stones seemed to be facing away almost vigilantly, as though guarding Arthur Patrick Sullivan's retreat, and the multitudinous bass humming was louder.

"You got a lot of friends here, Dad?" Pete Sullivan whispered.

"Oh, sure," said the voice in his ear. *"Go up to the doors there, and rap* shave-and-a-haircut."

"Just a sec," Sullivan told Elizalde, and then he sprinted up the steps to the locked door of the mausoleum and rapped on the glass: *knock, knock, knock-knock, knock.*

From inside came the answering *knock, knock.*

Elizalde was smiling and shaking her head as he rejoined her and they began walking north along the broad straight lane; receding perspective made the curbs seem to converge in the distance, and on the blue hills above the implicit intersection point stood once again the familiar white letters of the Hollywood sign. Why, Sullivan thought, can't I get away from it?

"It's a gravestone, too," said Sullivan's father.

For a minute they trudged along in silence through the gathering twilight. A couple of cars were parked ahead, and real people were opening the doors and climbing in; Sullivan no longer felt that he and Elizalde were conspicuous intruders.

As they walked up to Bradshaw's car Sullivan thought he heard laughter in the remote distance, but there was no triumph anymore in the cawing; and, from some radio or tape player a bit closer, he heard the opening notes of Al Jolson's "California Here I Come."

I been away from you a long time . . . Sullivan thought.

They climbed in and closed the doors gently. Sullivan started the engine, and as they drove out onto Santa Monica Boulevard and turned right, making oncoming cars swerve because of the way the Nova's skewed front end seemed to be about to cross the divider line, Sullivan said, impulsively, "Dad, I don't know if you knew it or not, but I didn't swim out, to help you."

Elizalde was looking out the window at the Chinese restaurant they were passing.

"I knew it," buzzed the gnat in his ear. *"And we both know it wouldn't have done any good if you had swum out, and we both know that isn't an excuse you'll look at."*

Sullivan hiked up a pack of Marlboros from the side pocket of his jacket and bit one cigarette out of it. "Did Sukie—Elizabeth—tell you that Kelley Keith is gunning for you?"

"I knew she'd be waiting for me. So I came ashore hidden inside a sea monster. Grounded and damped to a flat magnetic line."

Sullivan pushed in the cigarette-lighter knob. "What . . . brings you to town?" he asked, unable to keep the defensive flippancy out of his tone. He didn't look at Elizalde.

"Why, I got a free ticket to the coast," droned the gnat's voice, possibly trying to imitate Sullivan's tone, *"and I thought I'd look you kids up."* The voice was silent, then said, *"A big one was switched on here, and all of us were sympathetically excited by it. I came out of the ocean, after*

God knows how long; to find that the broken stragglers of Elizabeth had joined me, and that you had never—" The voice lapsed again.

"Had never what, Dad?" Sullivan asked softly, looking almost across Elizalde to see where he was going through the windshield. "Stopped running? Away from the surf, that would be, Angelica." His smile was stiff. "I didn't want to look back, that's for sure. 'I said to Dawn: Be sudden—to Dusk: Be soon,' remember that, Dad? Francis Thompson poem. I've always tried to . . . what, to have nothing permanent, leave nothing behind that would, like, *hang around.* I always hated things to be . . . etched in stone."

"Uh," said Elizalde hesitantly, "I think the car's on fire."

Smoke was trickling, then billowing, from the slots on the top of the dashboard. "Shit," said Sullivan—he snatched the cigarette lighter out of its slot, and blinked for a moment at the flaming, gummy wad on the end of it; then he gripped the wheel with his free fingers while he cranked down the driver's-side window with his left hand, and he pitched the burning thing out onto the street. "That *was* the cigarette lighter, wasn't it?" he asked angrily.

Elizalde bent over to look at the still-smoking ring in the dashboard. "Yes," she said. "No—it's a cigar lighter. Wait a minute—altogether it says, L.A. CIGAR—TOO TRAGICAL. What the hell does that mean?"

Sullivan waved caramel-reeking smoke away from his face, and he was remembering the tin ashtray that had briefly burst into flame at Los Tres Jesuses on Wednesday morning. "Let's remember to ask Nicky."

"Freeway coming up," said Elizalde.

❉ ❉ ❉

And so, thought Nicholas Bradshaw as he tucked the still clean knife back in the kitchen drawer, *I* don't get the renewal, *I* don't get a rebirth. I have heard the candy-colored clowns they call the sandmen singing each to each—I do not think that they will sing to me.

Cinnamon tears were still running down his slack cheeks, and his hands were still trembling, but, when he had plodded back into the office, he crouched and picked up Kootie's limp, breathing body and straightened up again with no sense of effort. He even stood on his bad right ankle long enough to hook the outside door open with the left, and felt no twinge of pain.

Shutting down, he thought.

The boy whined in his sleep as the chilly evening air ruffled his sweat-damp hair. Every step Bradshaw took across the shadowed asphalt seemed to be the snap of a television being turned off, the slam of a door in an emptied building, the thump of a yellowed copy of *Spooked* being tossed out of a vacated apartment onto a ruptured vinyl beanbag chair in an alley. I am unmaking myself, he thought. I am looking at a menu and pointing past the flowing script on the vellum page, past the margin and the deckle edge, right off the cover of the menu, at, finally, the crushed cigarette butts in the ashtray.

"I believe I feel like Death Warmed Over this evening," he said out loud.

Aside from a remote sadness that was almost nostalgia, he had no feelings about his decision not to kill Kootie and inhale the Edison ghost: not guilt at having considered doing it, nor satisfaction at having decided not to. He had held the knife beside the boy's ear for several minutes, knowing that he could hide the body in one of the several freezers in the garages, and that Pete Sullivan and the Angelica woman would believe him when he told them that the boy must have run away; knowing too that he would be able thereafter to sleep again, and dream.

Had it been the thought of the sort of dreams he might have had, that had made him finally pull back the knife? He didn't think so. Even if the dreams had proved to be uniformly horrible—of the day he learned of his stepfather's death, for example, or the summer-of-'75 week he had spent drunk and freshly dead inside the refrigerator on the Alaskan trawler in the Downtown Long Beach Marina, or whatever detail-memories the murdering of Kootie would have given him—he still thought he could have *lived* with them.

In the end, he just hadn't been able to justify extending the mile-markers of his personal highway by reducing this living boy to one of them.

At the apartment door now, he set the boy upright against the wall, and held him in place with one hand while he opened the door with the other. Then he got his arms under the boy's arms and knees again and carried him inside.

Bradshaw knelt to lay Kootie on the floor where he had been napping earlier. The boy began snoring, and Bradshaw got to his feet and left the apartment, being sure that the door was locked behind him.

Back in his office he sat down on the couch without bothering to turn on any lights. The desk was bare—the components of the telephone had been disassembled and laid in a cardboard box, and Bradshaw had not brought the television set back in. His charred pigs, relieved of their malignant batteries, lay in a heap in the corner. Distantly he wondered if he would ever again marshal his warning systems.

He reached around behind the arm of the couch and pulled free the broom, then clutched the straw end and boomed the top of the stick twice against the ceiling.

Tomorrow, he thought, I'd like to drive to the Hollywood Cemetery myself, and lie down on one of those green slopes and just sleep. But I've been dead for seventeen years—God knows how bad it might be. The explosion might knock half the mausoleums off their foundations.

He heard Johanna's door slam upstairs, and then in the quiet night he could hear the faint ringing of the metal stairs. There was silence when she had got down to the asphalt, and then came a knock at the door.

"Come in," he said. "It's not locked."

Johanna pushed the door open and stepped inside. "Not by accident?" she said in a concerned voice. "Always you lock it. And won't you get your pigs and TV back up?"

"I don't think, so," he said. "Sweetie-pie." He inhaled, and then made words of the sigh: "Bring me a can of snuff, would you please? *(Gasp)* And then sit here by me."

The couch shifted when she sat down. "And no lights," she said.

"No." He took the snuff can from her extended hand and twisted the lid. "Tomorrow is Halloween," he said. "All these things we've had up through this night—will be broken up and lost. Like a rung bell finally stopping ringing—but. When dawn comes. Find it a sweet day, Johanna. Find it a blessed day. Live in the living world. While it lasts for you. I hope it may see you happy, and not hungry. Not hurt, not crying. Every one of me will be watching over you. To help, with all of whatever I'm worth then."

He tapped a little pile of snuff out onto his knuckle and sniffed it up his nose. Almost he thought he could smell it.

Johanna had tucked her head under his jaw, and her shoulders were shaking. "It's all right if I cry now," she whispered.

He tossed the little can out onto the dark rug and draped his arm around her. "For a while," he said.

After a time, he heard the crunch of the Nova's tires on the broken pavement outside, and he kissed her and stood up. He knew it must have got cold outside by now, and he went to the closet to put on a shirt.

CHAPTER 41

❖

"—then you don't like all insects?" the Gnat
went on, as quietly as if nothing had happened.
"I like them when they can talk," Alice said.
"None of them ever talk, where I come from."
"What sort of insects do you rejoice in, where
you come from?" the Gnat inquired.
"I don't rejoice in insects at all," Alice explained,
"because I'm rather afraid of them . . ."

—Lewis Carroll,
Through the Looking-Glass

IN SPITE of their muddy clothes, Sullivan and Elizalde
had stopped to buy a couple of pizzas and a package of
paper plates and an armload of Coke and Coors six packs,
and when they had turned on the chandelier light in the
apartment living room, Sullivan carried the supplies to the
open kitchen. He was glad of the heat being on so high in
the apartment. "Wake up Kootie," he called, "he'll want
some of this."

Elizalde crouched over the boy and shook him, then

587

looked up blankly. "He's passed out drunk, Pete. Tequila, by the smell."

Sullivan had unzipped his sodden leather jacket, and now paused before trying to pull his hands through the clinging sleeves. "How did he—? Could he be a drunk already, at his age?"

"I suppose. Did you bring the bottle back here?"

"No, didn't think of it." He worked his arms free and tossed the jacket into a corner, where it landed heavily.

They had left the front door open, and now Nicky Bradshaw spoke from the doorstep. "I gave it to him," he said. "He was Edison. We were talking, and he said he could have a couple."

Elizalde stood up, obviously furious. "That's . . . *criminal!*" she said. "Edison should have had more sense. He's *in loco parentis* here—I wonder if he let his own kids drink hard liquor." She squinted at Bradshaw. "You should have known better, too."

"I wasn't watching him pour," Bradshaw said. "Can I come in?"

"*Nicky!*" buzzed the gnat in Sullivan's ear, and then it was gone.

"Yeah, come in," Sullivan said. "Where's Johanna?"

"She's fixing her makeup." Bradshaw stepped ponderously in, creaking the floorboards. "Did you find—" His hand jerked up toward his head, then stopped, and suddenly his weathered face tensed and his eyes widened. "Uncle Art!" he said softly.

Sullivan looked down at Elizalde, who was still crouched over Kootie. "My father flew over to him," he explained. "How is Kootie?"

"I think he's waking up. You've got instant coffee in your van? Could you go get it?"

"Sure." She had carried in Houdini's hands and laid them by the door, and he hefted one up as he stepped outside, but though the night breeze chilled him in his damp clothes he didn't feel peril in it, here. He walked shivering across the lot to the van and lifted the parachute to get at the side doors with his key; in the total darkness inside, he groped like a blind man, finding the coffee jar and a spoon and a couple of cups by touch, with Houdini's hand tucked under his arm.

Before he climbed down out of the van, he stood beside the bed and sniffed the stale air. He could smell cigarette smoke, and the faintly vanilla aroma of pulp paperback books, and the machine-oil smells of the .45 and the electrical equipment he had bought today. It occurred to him that it was unlikely that the van would ever be driven again, and he wondered how long this frail olfactory diary would last. On the way out, he carefully pulled the doors closed before lifting the parachute curtain to step away from the van.

Kootie was awake and grumbling when Sullivan got back inside, and Bradshaw was sitting against the wall in the corner, muttering and laughing softly through pink tears. Sullivan pursed his lips and narrowed his eyes, but didn't go over to where Bradshaw and his father were talking, instead striding on to the kitchen. Elizalde stood up from beside Kootie to help Sullivan unpack the supplies.

They took turns washing their hands in the sink, then opened the pizza boxes. "Edison says he doesn't want any," Elizalde said as she lifted a hot slice of pepperoni-and-onion pizza onto a paper plate, "but I think he will when he sees it."

Sullivan had measured a spoonful of powdered coffee into one of the cups, and now he turned to frown at the water he had left running in the sink. "I wonder if this is even connected to a hot pipe," he said, putting a finger into the cold stream from the tap.

"You could always make it from the back of the toilet," she said. "That's plenty hot. And it's what Edison deserves."

"Kootie *is* still in there?" Sullivan asked quietly.

"Yes. It was him that first woke up. Edison's planning to 'go into the sea' tomorrow, and I think it's doing Kootie good to have him run things in the meantime, so Kootie can get a lot of sleep."

"You're the doctor." The water was still running cold, so Sullivan put down the coffee cup, jacked a Coors out of one of the six-pack cartons, and popped the tab on top. "Do you figure you've laid Frank Rocha?" He stepped back before her sudden hot glare. "What I mean is, you know, is the ghost laid. Is he R.I.P. now? Can we just . . . buy some kind of old car and leave California?"

"You and me and Kootie?"

"Kootie? Is he part of the family?"

"Are we a family?" Her brown eyes were wide and serious.

Sullivan looked away, down at the pizza. He lifted another triangle of it onto a paper plate. "I meant partnership. Is he part of the partnership?"

"Is your father?"

"Jesus, is this what you psychiatrists *do?* Take the night off, will you?" He looked across the room just as Johanna stepped up to the front door. "Here, Johanna, you want a piece of pizza?"

"And a beer, please," she said, walking in. Her blue eye shadow looked freshly applied, but her eyes were red, and she was wearing a yellow terry-cloth bathrobe.

Sullivan pushed the paper plate across the counter to her and opened her a beer. He didn't want to talk to Elizalde; he was uncomfortable to realize that he *had* meant the double entendre about laying Frank Rocha, though he had acted surprised and innocent when she had glared at him. Was he jealous of her? He knew he was jealous of Bradshaw's easy conversation over in the corner with his father, though he didn't want to take Bradshaw's place.

Then abruptly his ear tickled, and his father's tiny voice said, *"Nicky's got to go to some other building here. Let's you and me walk along. Your girl can talk to Nicky's girl."*

My *girl,* thought Sullivan. "That's not how it is," he said. He was sweating in spite of his clinging, wet clothes—for his father would want to talk seriously now— and he picked up the can of Coors.

"Your sister went on to drink a lot, didn't she?"

Sullivan paused, with the beer halfway to his mouth. "Yes," he said.

"I could tell. Do you know why I came back, out of the sea? There goes Nicky, follow him."

Bradshaw was at the open doorway. "Nick," said Sullivan, putting down the beer and stepping past Elizalde out of the kitchen area. "Wait up, I'll—we'll—walk you there."

"Thank you, Pete," said Bradshaw. "I'd like that."

Bradshaw began clumping heavily across the dark lot toward the office, and Sullivan walked alongside, his hands in his pockets. "Nick," he said. "What does 'L.A. CIGAR—TOO TRAGICAL' mean?"

"Damn it," said Bradshaw in his flat voice. "Did you burn up the car?" He stepped up to his office door and pushed it open.

"No, but I threw your cigarette lighter out onto Santa Monica Boulevard." Sullivan followed him inside to the kitchen, where Bradshaw opened a cupboard to pry a finely painted china plate out of a dusty stack.

"It's a . . . mercy thing," said Bradshaw, not looking at him. "That some people do. It's a hippodrome, where it reads the same forwards as backwards. I don't know who started it, or even who else does it. But you write it around . . . *(gasp)* . . . ashtrays, and lighters, and chimneys. I've seen little shops on Rosecrans, where you. Can buy frying pans with it written. Around the edge." He had opened a drawer and lifted out a handful of shiny pebbles. "The hippodrome words attract new ghosts. They hang around—trying to figure it out how the end can be the same as the beginning. And then when the fire comes. They get burned up." He spread the pebbles on the china plate, and then carried it back out through the dark office and right outside to the parking lot.

"Beasties!" he called in a harsh whisper. "Din-din, beasties!" He put the plate down on the pavement. "It's a mercy thing," he said again. "They're better off burned up and gone. If they hang around, they're likely to get caught by people like Loretta deLarava. That's Kelley Keith, Uncle Art, what she calls herself now. Caught, and digested, to fatten the parasite's bloated, pirated personality. And if they *don't* get caught by somebody . . ."

He stepped back, almost into the doorway of the office, and Sullivan joined him in the shadows.

From around behind an upright old car hood on the other side of the yard, a lumpy figure came tottering uncertainly into the glow of the parking-lot light. It was wearing a tan trench coat over its head, with apparently a broad-brimmed hat under that to hold the drapery of the coat out to the sides like a beekeeper's veil. Its groping hands looked like multi-lobed sweet potatoes.

And from the overgrown chain-link fence on the other side of the lot came a rattling and scuffling, and Sullivan saw more shapes rocking forward out of the darkness.

Bradshaw turned and walked into the dark office, and when Sullivan had followed him inside, he closed the door. "They're shy," Bradshaw said. "So's your dad. I'll be back at the party."

"Nicky, wait," said Sullivan quickly. When the fat old man turned his impassive face toward him, he went on almost at random, "Have you got copies of the Alice books? *Alice in Wonderland, Through the Looking-Glass?*"

Bradshaw walked around to his desk and opened one of the drawers. After rummaging around, he looked up and called, "Catch," and tossed a paperback toward Sullivan.

Sullivan did catch it, and he tilted it toward the light

from the kitchen; it was both of the Alice books published together. "Thanks," he said, tucking it into his hip pocket.

Bradshaw left the building through the kitchen so as not to disturb the timid ghosts at their pebble buffet, and Sullivan sank cautiously into the Naugahyde chair in the middle of the office floor.

"You still got that brass plate from my gravestone?" said the tiny voice of his father.

Sullivan slapped the front of his damp shirt, and felt the heavy angularity still there. "Huh! Yes."

"Don't lose it, I'm tethered to it. It's my night-light. If I stray far from it, I'll get lost."

Sullivan took it out of his pocket, then began unbuttoning his shirt.

"Do you know why I came back, out of the sea?" his father's voice said.

"Because Thomas Edison lit up the sky here Monday night." Sullivan slipped the brass plate down inside the soaked front-side wallet of his scapular and buttoned his shirt up again.

"That's how I was able to find my way back. That's not why."

Sullivan was shivering, and the cinnamon-and-rot smell of the office seemed to be infused with the smells of suntan lotion and mayonnaise. "Okay," he whispered to the insect in his ear. "Why?"

"Because I . . . abandoned you and Elizabeth. I was a white-haired old fool showing off like a high-school Lothario, trying to impress this thirty-three-year-old girl I had married! With three-score and ten, I would have

had nine more years with the two of you, seen you reach sixteen. But I had to be Leander, swimming . . . a Hellespont that turned out to be . . . well, I only just this week got back to shore."

Sullivan's eyes were closed, but tears were running down his cheeks. "Dad, you're allowed to go swimming—"

"And I hoped that . . . that it would have been okay, that Kelley would have taken care of you two, and that you'd have grown up to be happy people. I hoped I would come ashore and find you both with . . . normal lives, you know? Children and houses and pets. Then I could have relaxed and felt that I had not done you any real harm by dying a little sooner than I should have."

"I'm sorry we weren't able to show you that."

Sullivan was thinking of Sukie, drunk and grinning wickedly behind dark sunglasses in a late-night bar, perhaps singing one of her garbled songs; he thought of the way the two of them had watched out for each other through the lonely foster-home years, each always able to finish the other's interrupted sentence; and he thought of the two of them running away from the sight of their father's intolerable wallet on the Venice pavement in '86, running away separately to live as solitary shamed fugitives. And he imagined Sukie at forty years of age (he hadn't even seen her since they'd both been thirty-four!) hanging up a telephone after having called Pete to warn him about deLarava's pursuit—and then putting a gun to her head.

"Kelley Keith was to have been our stepmother," Sullivan said aimlessly. "And she did . . . *adopt* us, in a way, after we got out of college." He wondered if he meant to hurt his father by saying it; then he knew that he did, and he wondered why.

The gnat was just buzzing wordlessly. Finally, it said, *"What can I do, what can I do? I've come back, and Elizabeth's killed herself; she's in the house of spirits with all the other restless dead, idiots jabbering over their pretend drinks and cigarettes. You're a rootless bum. I gave you kids a mother that was—that was nothing more than a child herself, a greedy, mean, selfish child, and then I left you with her. And it's wrecked you both. Why did I come back? What the hell can I do?"*

Sullivan stood up. "We've got to get back to the party." He sighed. "What you can do . . . ? Sukie and I let you down, even if you don't see it that way, even if it plain *is not* that way. Tell us . . . that you don't hold it against us; that there are no hard feelings. I bet Sukie will hear you too. Tell us that you . . . l-love us anyway."

"I love you, Pete, and not 'anyway.' Don't hold it against me, please, that I left you, that I abandoned you to that woman."

"We never did, Dad. And we always loved you. We still do."

The thing in his ear was buzzing indistinctly again, but after a moment it said, *"One last favor for your old man?"*

Sullivan had crossed to the door, and paused with his hand on the knob. "Yes. Anything."

"See that I get back in the ocean tomorrow, on Halloween. Say goodbye to me willingly and at peace, and I'll do the same. That's the way we'll do it this time. And then—Lord, boy, you're forty years old! Stop running, stand your little ground."

"I will, Dad," Sullivan said. "Thanks."

He opened the door. The humped ghosts were crouched around the plate, clumsily picking up pebbles, and they shifted but didn't flee as Sullivan stepped around them and strode back toward the apartment.

"You asked why you came back," he said, "remember? I think you came back so that we could finally get this done."

When they got back to the apartment, the pepperoni pizza was gone and everyone had started on the sausage-and-bell-pepper one. Sullivan took a piece of it with good enough grace, and he retrieved his beer.

Bradshaw and Johanna were standing by the window. Elizalde was sitting with Kootie and they were talking amiably; either it was Kootie animating the boy's body now, or she had got finished yelling at Edison for getting the boy drunk.

"Join you two?" said Sullivan shyly, standing behind her with his beer and his paper plate. His father had flown away when they had reentered the hot apartment; Sullivan had seen the flicker of the gnat looping away toward Bradshaw, but he was no longer jealous.

"The electrical engineer!" said Kootie. Apparently, he was still Edison.

Elizalde looked up at Sullivan with a rueful smile. "Sit down, Pete," she said. "I'm sorry I got into my psych mode there."

"I asked for it," he said, folding his legs and sitting next to her. "And your questions were good. I've got answers to 'em, too."

"I'd like to hear them later."

"You will, trust me."

Sullivan guessed that Edison was still a bit drunk; the old man in the boy's body resumed telling some interrupted story about restoring communications across a fogged, ice-jammed river by driving a locomotive down to the docks and using the steam whistle to toot Morse code across the ice to the far shore, where somebody finally figured out what he was up to and drew up a locomotive of their own so that messages could be sent back and forth across the gap. "Truly wireless," Edison said, slurring his words. "Even electricless. We're like the people on the opposite banks, aren't we? The gulf is torn across all our precious math, and it calls for a very wireless sort of communication to get our emotional accounts settled." He blinked belligerently at Sullivan. "Isn't that right, electrical engineer? Or did I drop a decimal place somewhere?"

"No, it sounds valid to me," Sullivan said. "We're . . . lucky, I guess, that you were there with a whistle that could be heard . . . across the gap."

After an hour or so, Kootie's body curled up asleep again, and Sullivan boxed up the remaining pizza and declared the party over. They all agreed to meet again early in the morning for a walk down to the beach, and then Bradshaw and Johanna plodded away toward the main building, hand in hand, and Elizalde told Sullivan to lock the door, and went into the bathroom to take a shower. When Sullivan leaned the Houdini hands against the closed door, he noticed that the broken finger had been glued back on. Elizalde must have borrowed glue from Johanna.

Sullivan took the Alice book out of his hip pocket and leaned against the kitchen counter to start reading it. When Elizalde came out of the steamy bathroom, wearing her relatively clean jumpsuit, she switched off the living-room chandelier and lay down on the floor near Kootie.

"Will this kitchen light keep you awake?" Sullivan asked quietly.

"An arc-welder wouldn't keep me awake. Aren't you . . . coming to bed?"

He raised the book. "*Alice in Wonderland,*" he said. "I'll be along after a while, when I'm done with my homework."

She stretched on the floor and yawned. "What were your answers to my pushy questions?"

He was tired, and the paperback book was jigging in his trembling fingers. He laid it face-down on the counter. "Here's one. We are a family, rather than a partnership, if you would like us to be."

She didn't say anything, and her face was indistinct in the dark living room. Sullivan got the impression that his answer had surprised her, and pleased her, and frightened her, all at once.

"Let me sleep on that," she said finally.

He picked up the book again. "I'm not going anywhere."

He stared at the page in front of him, but he wasn't able to concentrate until she had shifted around to some apparently comfortable position, and her breathing had become regular and slow with sleep.

EPILOGUE
Burn Rubber, Sweet Chariot

※

If they go faster than my machine, I will be able to go downhill as fast as they dare to and for hill climbing the electric motor is just the thing, so I will beat them there. On rough roads they will not dare to go faster than I will; and when it comes to sandy places, I am going to put in a gear of four to one which I can throw in under such circumstances, and which will give me one hundred twenty horsepower of torque, and I will go right through that sand and leave them way behind.

—Thomas Alva Edison,
Electrical Review,
August 8, 1903

CHAPTER 42

⊚

*"I mean," she said, "that one can't
help growing older."*

*"One can't, perhaps," said Humpty
Dumpty; "but two can . . ."*

—Lewis Carroll,
Through the Looking-Glass

THE MORNING AIR was raucous with the cries of the
parrots that were swooping like livid green Frisbees from
the telephone wires to the branches of the shaggy old carob
trees along the Twenty-First Place curb, but when one of
the apartment doors finally opened, the gray-haired fat man
who came shuffling out ignored the clamoring exotic birds
as though he were blind and deaf. He was clutching a sheaf
of white business-size envelopes, and he tucked them into
a rack under the bank of mailboxes out front.

The old man's punctual in paying his bills, thought J.
Francis Strube. The first of November isn't until tomorrow,
but tomorrow will be a Sunday, with no mail pickup.

Strube's dark blue BMW was idling almost silently a

hundred feet away from the apartment building, and certainly wasn't blowing any telltale smoke out of the exhaust, but still he slid down a little in the leather seat, just peeking over the dashboard at the old man.

And he wasn't sure. This fellow fumbling with the mail was about the right age, but Nicky Bradshaw had been athletically slim—and *healthy*. This man . . . he didn't look well at all; he moved slowly and painfully, squinting up and down the street now with impotent ferocity. Strube slid down even lower in his seat.

The old man by the apartment building was plodding back along the walkway toward the door he had come out of; but he paused halfway there, and just stood, staring down toward his feet.

Strube's lower back was cramping, and he sat up a little straighter in the seat.

And the old man curled one arm over his head and stretched the other out with his fingers spread, and turned on his heel in a three-hundred-sixty-degree circle; then he paused again, let his arms fall to his sides, and opened the door and went back inside.

Strube had steamed the inside of his windshield by whispering a deep, triumphant, "Hah!"

That had been the Spooky Spin, and even someone like himself, who had only seen reruns of the old "Ghost of a Chance" show, had to remember the way the Spooky character had always executed that move just before the primitive stopped-camera trick photography had made him seem to disappear into thin air.

Strube was whistling the "Ghost of a Chance" theme music—*dooo-root-de-doodly-doot-de-doo!*—as he punched into the telephone the Find Spooky number. Probably no one would be answering the line until nine or so, but he couldn't wait.

It rang twice, and then, to his surprise, someone did answer. "Have you seen Spooky?" a woman asked with practiced cheer.

"Yes," said Strube. "I've found him."

"Well, congratulations. If we verify that it really is Nicky Bradshaw, you'll be getting two complimentary tickets to the filming of the reunion show. Where is he?"

"It's him. My name is J. Francis Strube, I'm a Los Angeles-based attorney, and I worked for him as a legal secretary when he had an office in Seal Beach in the mid-seventies. Also, I just this minute *saw* him do the Spooky Spin, if you're familiar with the old show."

After a pause, the woman said, "Really? I'm going to transfer you to Loretta deLarava." The line clicked, and then Strube was listening to a bland instrumental version of "Mr. Tambourine Man."

I should think so, Strube thought, sitting back in the seat and smiling as he kept his gaze locked on Bradshaw's door. I imagine Loretta deLarava will have room for a quick-witted attorney on her staff.

"This is Loretta deLarava," said a harsher woman's voice now, speaking over background static. "I understand you're the clever person who has found our missing Spooky! Where is he?"

"Ms. deLarava, my name is J. Francis Strube, and I'm an attorney—"

"An attorney?" There was silence on the scratchy line. Then, "Are you *representing* him?" deLarava asked.

"Yes," said Strube instantly. Spontaneity wins, he thought nervously. Trust your instincts.

"Where is he?"

"Well, we want certain assurances—"

"Look, Mr. Strube, I'm on the E Deck loading dock of the *Queen Mary* right now." Good God, Strube thought; she's hardly two miles away across the harbor! "I'm doing a Halloween-related shoot about famous ghosts on board the ship today, and I had been hoping to find Bradshaw in time to at least get him in a couple of shots there, film him doing his trademark Spooky Spin on the Promenade Deck, you know?" She was sniffling. "You're not going to take a piss, are you?"

Strube assumed this was some showbiz slang, meaning *be an obstruction* or something. *Rain on my parade.* "No, of course not, I just—"

"So what? Do you want us to interview you, too? It'd be a cinch. Prominent local attorney, right? 'The man who tracked down Spooky.' And then we could discuss your client's possible role in the reunion show later. How does that sound?"

Strube didn't like her tone, or her apparent assumption that he was motivated by a desire for publicity; and he wished he could say something coldly dismissive to her.

But, of course, he couldn't. "That sounds good," he said. Then, despising himself, he went on, "Do you promise?"

"You have my word, Mr. Strube. Now where is he?"

"Well—in Long Beach, in the Twenty-First Place cul-de-sac by the beach." Strube read her the address from the stenciled numerals on the curb. "I'll be there, too," he said, "and I'm confident—"

"Good," she interrupted. "I knew somebody was confident. I should have guessed it'd turn out to be a lawyer." And the line went dead. I guess she'll be here soon, Strube thought timidly.

The shouting of the parrots made Sullivan open his eyes. He knew that he had been very nearly awake for some time; he remembered having dreamed of Venice Beach sometime during the night, but he couldn't remember now if it had been Venice of 1959, 1986, or 1992, and it didn't seem important.

A faint *thwick* from the kitchen made him lift his head—Kootie was sitting cross-legged on the kitchen counter, looking at Sullivan over the top of the Alice paperback, a page of which he'd just turned. Kootie touched a finger to his lips.

Sullivan turned his head sideways, and his neck creaked, and Elizalde opened her eyes and smiled sleepily.

"I guess we're all awake, Kootie," Sullivan said, speaking quietly just because it was the first remark of the day. He rolled over, got stiffly to his feet, and stretched. "How are you feeling?"

"Fine, Mr. Sullivan—Pete, I mean. Could I have cold pizza and Coke for breakfast?"

Maybe Edison is sleeping off the hangover, Sullivan thought. "Sure. I think I'll pass, though. We'll probably be leaving here in an hour or two, after a . . . a walk down to the beach. You sure you wouldn't like to wait, and get something hot?"

"I like cold pizza. We hardly ever have pizza at home."

"Tear it up then." Sullivan yawned and walked into the kitchen to turn on the hot-water tap. He couldn't remember now whether the water had ever got hot last night; well, there *was* always the hot water in the toilet tank.

"Uh," said Kootie. "Could you help me down? My cut hurts if I stretch. I was halfway up here before I knew I couldn't climb up."

"Sure," Sullivan said.

"Kootie," said Elizalde, who had got up and now hurried over to the counter, "didn't I tell you not to put any strain on it?"

"No, miss," the boy said.

"Oh. Well, once we get you down from there—"

Suddenly a fourth voice spoke, from the bedroom doorway. "Leave him where he is."

Sullivan spun, and then froze. A man was standing there, pointing at them a handgun made from a chopped-down double-barreled 12-gauge shotgun. Focusing past the gun, Sullivan saw that the man had only one arm; then that he was wearing baggy camouflage pants and a stained wind-breaker, and that his round, pale face was dewed with sweat. His gaze crawled over Sullivan's face, to Elizalde's, and to Kootie's, like a restless housefly.

"*Harry Houdini* made a call from Long Beach last night," the man said in a high, calm voice, "and as it happens I'm a big Houdini fan. But when I came down here I kept getting deflections, I couldn't get any consistent directional for him. So, I remembered this dead spot by the beach, like the wood where Alice lost her name. And then you all had a party last night. A man went to an Armenian restaurant, because his friends told him to order the herring; when it was served, it was alive, and the herring opened its eye and looked at him. He left, but his friends told him to go back the next night, so he did, and he ordered the herring again. But on the plate, it opened its eye again, and he ran away. The next night he went to a Jewish restaurant instead, and ordered herring, and when the waiter brought him his plate the herring opened its eye and looked at him and said, 'You don't go to the Armenian place anymore?' "

Sullivan felt a drop of sweat roll down his ribs under his shirt, and he kept staring at the sawn muzzles of the gun, each barrel looking big enough for a rat to crawl down it. Elizalde had stepped in front of Kootie, but now none of them were moving.

"What do you want?" asked Sullivan in an even voice.

"I want to speak to Thomas Edison."

"This is the guy that stabbed me," whispered Kootie; then he shivered, and in a louder voice he said, "You have my attention. What did you want to talk about?"

"Unplug me," the man said. "The rotten ghost is jammed in my mind, and I can't . . . eat. When you did this to me in '29, I cleared it inadvertently, by injecting a quick ghost into a vein in my arm; that worked, but it blew my arm off. I can't afford to do that again, even if I could be sure the ghost would only blow off another limb, and not detonate inside my heart. You did this, you must know how to undo it." His wheezing breath was a hoarse roar, punctuated with little whistles that sounded like individual cries in an angry crowd.

"And then you'll stab me again, right?" said Edison

with Kootie's voice. "Or just blow out my middle with that scattergun and catch the boy and me both, when we breathe our last breath. It's a Mexican standoff." Kootie looked up at Elizalde. "No offense, Angelica."

Elizalde rolled her eyes in angry frustration. "For God's sake, Edison!"

"I won't," said the one-armed man. Distant voices shouted in his lungs. "I'll leave you alone, and subsist on ordinary ghosts. How can I assure you of this?"

Sullivan saw Elizalde's eyes glance across the room, and he looked in that direction. The .45 was lying against the wall where she had slept. He knew she was thinking that a dive in that direction would make the one-armed man swing the shotgun away from Kootie and himself.

But she couldn't possibly get the gun up and fire it before the shotgun would go off; and the shotgun wouldn't have to be aimed with any precision for the shot pellets to tear her up. He spread his fingers slowly, to avoid startling the gunman, and closed his hand firmly on Elizalde's forearm.

A whining buzz tickled Sullivan's ear, and he restrained his free hand from slapping at it.

"What the hell is this?" said the tiny voice of Sullivan's father's ghost. *"I can't get to the beach by myself—I'm tethered to my grave portrait, and it's way too heavy for me to carry."*

Sullivan looked anxiously back at the one-armed man—but the man was apparently unaware of the ghost in Sullivan's ear.

The barrels of the shotgun wobbled. "Well?" The man's tiny eyes were fixed on Kootie's face.

"I could write the procedure down," said Kootie's voice thoughtfully, "after you let us go, and leave it in some pre-agreed place. You'd have to trust me to do it, though."

"Which," said the one-armed man, "I don't." He kept his little eyes fixed on Kootie, but he rocked his head back and *sniffed* deeply. "There's another ghost in here. If you tell me how to get unjammed, I'll just eat *it*. That'll keep me alive until I can go get more."

"No good," said Kootie's voice. "That's Pete's dad, and Pete's sentimental about it. Besides, the procedure involves a bit of work on your part." The boy's face kinked in a crafty grin. "It's not just crossing your eyes and spitting."

The one-armed man stared impassively at the boy sitting on the counter. Finally, he sighed. "Let me tell you a parable," he said. "A man had a new hearing aid, and he was telling a friend how good it was. 'It cost me twenty thousand dollars,' the man with the hearing aid said, 'and it runs on a lithium battery that's good for a hundred years, and it's surgically implanted right into the skull bone and the nerve trunk at the base of my brain.' And his friend said, 'Wow, what kind is it?' and the man with the hearing aid looked at his watch and said, 'Quarter to twelve.'"

Sullivan wished the story had been longer. Surely Nicky would . . . would somehow come along soon, and perceive this, and put a stop to it. The shotgun was steady, and the man was standing just obviously too far away for Sullivan to have any hope of leaping forward and knocking the short barrels aside before the gun would be fired.

"I'll give you twenty thousand dollars," the one-armed

man said. "I'll take that automatic that's against the wall there, I can hold that on you without being conspicuous. We'll go out and get the money, and you can tell me then, once I've handed it over to you. We'll be out in public, I won't be eager to shoot you out in a street. Once I'm un-jammed, I can kill *anybody* and eat 'em, I won't need you."

Kootie's head swung back and forth. "No. You'd still want Thomas Edison."

The man's pale face puckered in a derisive smile. "For that much money you'd have told me. You don't even *know* how to do it, do you?" He shifted his stance and raised the gun slightly.

"Yes, he does!" said Elizalde shrilly.

Kootie turned on her, scowling. "Damn it, Angelica, I *do* know how this fellow can do it. You don't need to think you're . . . helping some *old fool* run a *bluff.*"

"No, no," said the one-armed man. "You might have known once—but you're senile now. Hell, you're what, a hundred and fifty years old?" He snickered. "I can *see* that you're wearing a big set of those geriatric diapers right now."

Kootie's hands flew to the buttons on his shirt. "I can—damn you—*prove* you're wrong." He was smiling tensely, but his face was red. "This is an electric belt, urine would short it out!" His shaky fingers were making no progress at undoing the buttons. "You're talking to someone who understands electricity, believe me! I recently received—"

"He's just taunting you, Edison!" said Elizalde urgently. "Don't let him get you excited. It's not worth—"

"You just *hired* people who understood electricity," the

man with the shotgun interrupted, shaking his head with evident good humor. "You were always just doing dumb stuff like . . . what was it, trying to make tires out of milkweed sap? *That's* proved to have been a real breakthrough, hasn't it?"

"It happens I recently received a B.S.—"

"Oh really? Where's your diploma?" The man laughed. "B.S. is right. Bullshit. Why don't you go ahead and add a Ph.D.? 'Piled higher and deeper.'"

Kootie was squirming furiously. "It's not a, a '*dip*shit *dip*loma,' you ignorant—"

"So how do I *do* it, then, if you're so smart?"

"Edison, don't—" said Elizalde quickly—

But Kootie's mouth was already open, and with it, Edison said, "I already told you—cross your eyes and spit."

And now the one-armed man was doing just that. His eyes crossed until the irises had half-disappeared in the direction of his nose, as if the pupils might *touch* each other behind his nose, and his mouth opened wide.

The barrels of the stumpy shotgun lifted and swung back and forth, and Sullivan pressed himself back against the kitchen counter. He glanced at Kootie, who just shrugged, wide-eyed.

It was as if the one-armed man had a speaker surgically implanted in his larynx—men's angry voices, crying children, laughing women, a chaotic chorus was shouting out of his lungs.

He might have been trying to spit. His lower jaw rotated around under his nose, and his tongue jerked— and finally one of the voices, a woman's, shrill and jabbering as if speeded up by some magical Doppler effect, rose and became louder and clearer.

And the one-armed man *spit*—and then gagged violently, convulsing like a snapped whip—

—As a glistening red snake shot out of his mouth. It was smoking even before it slapped heavily onto the floor, and the instant reek of ammonia and sulfur was so intense that Sullivan, who had involuntarily recoiled from its abrupt appearance, now involuntarily flinched from its fumes. And a chilly, laughing breeze punched past him and instantaneously buckled the blinds and shattered out the window.

Everyone was moving—Kootie had leaped from the counter and was colliding with Elizalde out on the floor in the direction of the broken window and the .45, the red snake-thing was slapping and hopping in front of the one-armed man, who was hunched forward with a rope of drool swinging from his mouth, and Sullivan made himself push off from the kitchen counter and vault over the spasming snake-thing to kick the hand that held the chopped shotgun.

Both shells went off, with a crash like a far-fallen truck slamming through the ceiling. Sullivan had jumped with no thought of anything beyond kicking the gun, and the air compression of the shotgun blasts seemed to loft him farther—his knee cracked the one-armed man's head and then Sullivan's shoulder and jaw hit the bedroom doorframe hard, and he bounced off and wound up half-kneeling on the floor.

The room was full of stinging haze, and through squinting, watering eyes he could see Elizalde and Kootie.

They were up, moving, opening the front door, in the ringing silence of stunned eardrums. Unable to breathe at all, Sullivan crawled around the wet red snake, which was already splitting and falling apart, and scuttled painfully on his hands and knees toward the daylight and the promise of breathable air. His hands bumped against Houdini's plaster hands, and he paused to grab them—but they disappeared when he touched them.

He hopped and scrabbled out through the door into the fresh air, rolling over the doorstep onto his back on the chilly asphalt. The breeze was cold on the astringent sweat that spiked his hair and made his shirt cling to him.

Nicky Bradshaw, wearing a sail-like Hawaiian shirt, was standing on the sidewalk, looking down at him with no expression on his weathered old face. Behind Bradshaw were two tensely smiling men in track suits—and each of them held a semiautomatic pistol.

Some kind of the new nine millimeters, Sullivan thought bleakly; Beretta or Sig or Browning. Ever since Mel Gibson in *Lethal Weapon*, everybody's crazy about nine millimeters. He looked down past his belt buckle, and saw Elizalde slowly crouching to place his old .45 on the pavement, watched closely by another of the smiling, trendily armed young men.

Sullivan's nostrils twitched to a new smell—the burning-candy reek of clove-flavored cigarettes. And when a woman's voice spoke, barely audible over the ringing in his ears, Sullivan didn't even need to look to know whose it was. She had, after all, been his boss for eleven years.

"I'm glad they've come without waiting to be asked,"

said Loretta deLarava. "I should never have known who were the right people to invite! Cuff 'em all," she added, "and get 'em into the truck, fast. Nicky and Pete I recognize, and this must be the famous Koot Hoomie Parganas, found at last—but I want all of them. Get anybody who's inside. Find Pete's van, and search it and this apartment for my mask. You know what to look for."

Sullivan at last rocked his head around to look up at her. Pouches of pale flesh sagged under her bloodshot eyes, and her fat cheeks hung around her sparking cigarette in wrinkly wattles.

"Hi, stepmother," he gasped, hardly able to hear his own voice. He hadn't wanted to speak to her, or even look at her, but it was important to let the ghost of his father know who this was. He wasn't sure how well the ghost could see, and in any case Loretta deLarava didn't look anything like the Kelley Keith of 1959.

DeLarava frowned past him, sucking hard on the cigarette, and didn't reply.

On one of the second-floor balconies, a white-bearded man in jeans and a T-shirt was looking down at this crowd in alarm. "Sol!" he yelled. "What's going on? Was that a gunshot? What's that terrible stink?"

"You're the manager here, Nicky?" said deLarava quietly. "I don't want your people to get hurt."

Bradshaw squinted up at his alarmed tenant. "Health-code enforcement," he grated. "Stay inside. These new renters have some kind of. Bowel disorder."

"Jesus, I'll say!" The man disappeared from the balcony, and Sullivan heard a door slam.

More by vibration in the pavement under his back

than by hearing, Sullivan became aware of someone else striding up now, from the direction of the street. "Ms. deLarava?" a man said brightly. "My name is J. Francis—" The voice trailed off, and Sullivan knew without looking that he had noticed the guns. "I'm an attorney. I think somebody here is going to need one."

"Cuff that asshole too," said deLarava.

CHAPTER 43

❂

*"Consider what a great girl you are.
Consider what a long way you've come
today. Consider what o'clock it is. Consider
anything, only don't cry!"*

—Lewis Carroll,
Through the Looking-Glass

A COUPLE OF DELARAVA'S MEN hustled the
handcuffed attorney to a new Jeep Cherokee at the curb
out front; three others opened the back of a parked truck
and tossed about a thousand dollars' worth of red-and-
black cable coils and clattering black metal light doors out
onto the street to make room for the rest of her captives:
Kootie, Sullivan, Elizalde, the one-armed man, and
Bradshaw. Sullivan noted that Johanna had eluded
capture, and he wondered if Nicky had in some sense
anticipated this, and sent her safely away; if so, Sullivan
wished Nicky had conveyed his misgivings to the rest of
them.

A Plexiglas skylight cast a yellow glow over the interior of the truck. The captives were arranged along the truck's right wall, with their cuffed wrists behind them; each pair of ankles was taped together and then taped at two-foot intervals onto a long piece of plywood one-by-six, which was then screwed into the metal floor with quick, shrill bursts of a Makita power screwdriver. The one-armed man wasn't cuffed—deLarava's men had simply taped his right arm to his body, with his hand down by his hipbone.

And deLarava stayed in the back with the captives when the truck door was pulled shut, leaning against the opposite wall while her driver backed and filled out of the cul-de-sac and then made a tilting right turn onto what had to be Ocean Boulevard.

"Nicky," she said immediately, "remember that you've got an innocent woman and child in here with you. If you feel any kind of . . . psychic crisis coming on, I trust you'll be considerate enough to let me know, so that my men can transfer you to a place where you won't harm anyone."

"Nothing ever excites me when I'm awake," said Bradshaw, who was slumped below some light stands up by the cab. "And I'm not feeling sleepy."

"Good." She reached into the bosom of her flower-patterned dress and pulled out a little semiautomatic pistol, .22 or .25 caliber. "If anyone wants to scream," she said, sweeping her gaze back and forth over the heads of her captives, "this will put a fairly quick stop to it, understood?"

"Lady," said the one-armed man weakly, "I can help you. But I need to eat a ghost, bad. I just threw a couple of pounds of dead ectoplasm, *and* a *good* ghost, and I'm

about to expire." He was sitting next to Sullivan, against
the door, and each one of his wheezing breaths was like a
Wagnerian chorus.

DeLarava's mouth was pinched in a fastidious pout,
but without looking down at him she asked, "Who *are* you,
anyway?"

The man was shaking, his right knee bumping Sullivan's
thigh. "Lately, I've been calling myself Sherman Oaks."

"How can Sherman Oaks help me?"

"I can . . . well, I can tell you that the boy there is
carrying the ghost of Thomas Alva Edison."

DeLarava gave a hiccupping laugh. "That I already
knew," she said, greedily allowing herself to actually stare
at Kootie.

Sullivan looked angrily past Elizalde at Kootie. "Why
in hell did you tell him how to unclog himself, anyway?"

Kootie flinched, and said defensively, "Mr. Edison
didn't tell him *exactly* how. He—" Kootie choked and
spat. "I can speak for myself, Kootie. He did *more* than
what I *told* him, Pete. He kicked the rotted one out by
throwing out a good one."

"After you told him the right . . . posture to assume,"
said Sullivan.

"Pete," said Elizalde, "let it go, it's done."

Meaning, Sullivan thought, don't torment a senile old
man who made a mistake out of wounded vanity.

"What do you all mean by 'unclogged'?" asked
deLarava, still staring at Kootie.

Sullivan looked up at her, and realized that Kootie and
the one-armed man were looking at her too. This might
conceivably be a bargaining chip, he thought.

"When you suck in a ghost that has rotted in an opaque container," said Sherman Oaks, "your ghost-digestion gets clogged. Impacted, blocked. You can't eat any more of them, and the ghosts already inside you get rebellious. I was that way. Now I know how to get clear of it, how you can Heimlich yourself. *Ptooie*, you know?"

"Could we refer to them as 'essences'?" said deLarava stiffly. "And use the verb 'enjoy'?"

"Where are we going?" asked Elizalde in a flat voice.

DeLarava squinted at her as if noticing her for the first time. "Pete's Mex gal! One of my boys tells me you're the crazy psychiatrist who's been on the news. We're all going to the *Queen Mary*."

Sullivan's leather jacket had been left back at the apartment, probably still balled up on the floor from having served as a pillow; and now through his thin shirt he felt fingers fumbling weakly at his left shoulder.

He looked at the man next to him, surprised that Oaks could have freed his single arm from the tape—and he saw that Oaks's hand *wasn't* free, was in fact still strapped down against his right hip; but Oaks was hunched around toward Sullivan, as if miming the act of reaching toward him with the arm that wasn't there.

Breath hissed in through Sullivan's teeth as he jerked away from Oaks in unthinking fright.

"What—" snapped deLarava, convulsively switching her little pistol from one hand to the other, clearly startled by his sudden move. "What is it?"

Sullivan realized that she hadn't once looked directly at him, and that she apparently didn't even want to speak his name. She plans to kill me at some point today, he thought; and because of that she's too fastidious to *acknowledge* me.

He turned back to look at Sherman Oaks, and the tiny eyes returned his gaze with no expression; but the man now sniffed deeply.

You smell my father's ghost, Sullivan thought. You know he's in here with us.

At least the phantom fingers had moved away from him. "My shoulders are cramping up something terrible," Sullivan said, deliberately, still staring at Oaks. *Have we got a deal?* he thought into the little eyes. *I won't tell her you've got a "hand" free if you won't tell her about the ghost.*

"Any discomfort is regretted," said deLarava vaguely.

Sullivan looked back at the old woman. She was blinking rapidly, and her eyes, again fixed on the wall over the captives' heads, were bright with tears.

"They could only find the thumb," said deLarava hoarsely, looking right up at the skylight now. "Where are the hands?"

"Lost in the Venice canals," said Sullivan at once. "I tried to fish them out, but they dissolved in the salt water like . . . like Alka-Seltzer." Jammed behind him, his left hand was digging in his hip pocket; all that was in there was his wallet—containing nothing but ID cards and a couple of twenty-dollar bills—and his pocket comb.

"*Why* are we going to the *Queen Mary?*" asked Elizalde.

"To enjoy—" began deLarava; but her hair abruptly sprang up into a disordered topknot, drawing startled gasps from Kootie and Elizalde. And deLarava began to sob quietly.

Sullivan was aware of an itch in his right ear, but his father's ghost didn't say anything.

The Jeep Cherokee was leading the procession, and when it turned left off Ocean onto Queen's Way, the two trucks followed.

J. Francis Strube didn't dare hunch around in his seat, for the man in back was presumably still holding a gun pointed at him, but he could peer out of the corners of his eyes. They had driven past the new Long Beach Convention Center on the left, and past Lincoln Park on the right, and now they were cruising downhill toward a vista of bright blue lagoons and sailboats and lawns and palm trees. Out across the mile-long expanse of the harbor he could see the black hull and the white upper decks of the *Queen Mary* shining in the early-morning sunlight.

The car radio was tuned to some oldies rock station, and the driver was whistling along to the sad melody of Phil Ochs's "Pleasures of the Harbor."

For the past five minutes, Strube had been remembering how cautious Nicholas Bradshaw used to be, when Strube had worked for him in 1975—refusing to say where he lived, never giving out his home phone number, always taking different routes to and from the law office. Maybe, Strube thought unhappily, I should have taken his paranoia more seriously. Maybe I was a little careless today, in the way I blundered into this thing. "Are we actually going to the *Queen Mary?*" he asked in a humbled voice.

The driver glanced at him in cheerful surprise. "You've never been on it? It's great."

"I've been there," Strube said, defensively in spite of everything. "I've had dinner at Sir Winston's many times. I meant, are we really going there now."

"DeLarava's scheduled a shoot there today," the driver said. "I understood you were to be interviewed, along with that Nicky Bradshaw fellow. He was the actor who played Spooky, the teenage ghost in that old show. You must have seen reruns. He's to do some kind of dance, was my understanding."

Strube was squinting against his bewilderment as if it were a bright light. "But why am I *handcuffed?* Why all the guns?"

The man chuckled, shaking his head at the lane markers unreeling ahead of him. "Oh, she can be a regular Von Stroheim, can't she? What's the word? Martinet? I mean, you wanna talk about *domineering?* Get outta here!"

"But—what are you saying? What happened back there at that apartment building? You people threw all those wires and metal shutters out of the truck onto the street! And what was that awful smell?"

"Ah, there you have me."

Strube was dizzy. "What if I try to get out, at the next red light? Would this man behind me *shoot* me?"

"Through the back of the seat," said the driver. "Don't do it. This isn't a bluff, no, if that's what you're asking. The new automatics are ramped and throated so they have no problem feeding hollow-points, and it might not even make an exit wound, but it would surely make a hash of your vital organs. You don't want that. In fact—" He slapped the wheel lightly and nodded. "In fact, if Sir

Winston's is open for lunch, we might be able to get her to spring for a good meal!"

"Never happen," said the man in the back seat gloomily.

After they had been driving for about ten minutes, stopping and starting up again and making some slow turns, Sullivan felt the truck stop and then reverse slowly down a ramp; and the skylight went dark, and he could hear the truck's engine echoing inside a big metallic room. Then the engine was switched off.

Car doors chunked in the middle distance, and he could feel the shake of the truck's driver's-side door closing; footsteps scuffed across concrete to the truck's back door, and the door was unlatched and swung open. The chilly air that swept into the truck's interior smelled of oiled machinery and the sea.

"E Deck," called a young man who was pulling a wheeled stepladder across the floor of the wide white-painted garagelike chamber. "We chased off the ship's staff for the moment, and we've got guys around to whistle if they come back. They say they've turned off the power in the circuit boxes on the Promenade and R Decks, and the gaffers are off to patch in and get the Genie lifts and the key lights set up for the first call at ten."

Test it with a meter anyway, thought Sullivan as his constricted left hand fingered his pocket comb. You don't want to be hooking your dimmer-board to the lugs if somebody forgot, and there's still a live two hundred twenty volts waiting for you in the utility panel.

Behind the fright that was dewing his forehead and

shallowing his breathing, he was vaguely irritated at his suspicion that these efficient-looking young men might be better at the job than he and Sukie had been.

DeLarava was still sniffling as she clumped heavily down from rung to rung of the stepladder. "Get a couple of runners to take . . . the kid, and the old guy up by the front, and Pete Sullivan, he's the guy in the white shirt . . . to that room they're letting us use as an office. Gag the woman and the one-armed guy and leave them where they are for now."

Sullivan looked at the one-armed man seated awkwardly beside him. Sherman Oaks seemed to be only semiconscious, and his breathing was a rattling, chattering whine, like a car engine with a lot of bad belts and bearings. But the fabric of the man's baggy brown-and-green trousers was bunching and stretching over the left thigh, as if kneaded by an invisible hand.

Does he have fingernails on that hand? wondered Sullivan. If so, are they strong enough to peel off the tape that's holding down his flesh-and-blood arm? If he frees himself, and he's left in here with Angelica, he'll surely kill her to eat her ghost.

Should I tell deLarava about Oak's unbound— unbindable!—hand? If so, he might in return tell her that my father's ghost is on my person, and she'd fetch in some kind of mask and eat the old man with no delay.

Elizalde was sitting at Sullivan's right, her taped ankles screwed down next to his, and he rocked his head around to look at her. Her narrow face was tense, her lips white, but she crinkled her eyes at him in a faint, scared smile.

"I'd bring Dr. Elizalde too," Sullivan said. He was

peripherally aware of an increasing ache in his left forearm; his fingers seemed to be nervously trying to pry the thick end-tooth off his comb, which was a useless exercise since the comb was aluminum.

"Why would I want to bring Dr. Elizalde?" deLarava mused aloud.

"She's a medical doctor as well as a psychiatrist," Sullivan said, at random.

Sherman Oaks was singing in a whisper with each scratching exhalation now, without moving his lips at all, and his voice seemed to be a chorus of children: ". . . *Delaware punch, tell me the initials of your honey-bunch, capital A, B, C-D-E . . .*"

"In that case bring them all!" cried deLarava; though Sullivan thought it was Oaks's eerie singing rather than his own suggestion that had changed the old woman's mind. "Put cats in the coffee," she sang wildly herself, "and mice in the tea, and welcome Queen Kelley with thirty-times-three!"

Sullivan recognized the bit of verse—it was from the end of *Through the Looking-Glass*, when Alice was about to be crowned a queen.

DeLarava kept her little pistol pointed at her captives, as a runner hopped up into the truck and knifed the tape off everyone's ankles.

"You want that lawyer that's in the Cherokee?" the man asked.

"Leave him where he is," deLarava said. "Lawyers are for after."

The fingers of Sullivan's left hand suddenly strained very hard at the end of the aluminum pocket comb, and with a muffled snap it broke, cutting his thumb knuckle. He palmed the broken-off end when the runner hopped down from the truck and began hauling Oaks's legs out over the bumper.

After Oaks had been propped upright against the side of the truck it was Sullivan's turn, and when he had been lifted down he stepped back across the floor to make room for Elizalde and Kootie—and Bradshaw, the shifting of whose bulk across the truck floor required the summoning of a second runner.

Down on the deck at last, Bradshaw hopped ponderously to shake the legs of his shorts straight. "I bet those guys were gay," he muttered.

"Don't try to shuffle away, Pete!" said deLarava sharply; and Sullivan was tensely sure that this direct address meant that she intended to kill him very soon indeed.

"Not me, boss," he said mildly.

When at last Bradshaw was standing next to Kootie and Elizalde on the concrete deck, deLarava pirouetted back, then mincingly led the way down a white hallway while the runners prodded the captives along after her. "O Looking-Glass creatures," called deLarava shrilly over her shoulder, "draw near. 'Tis an honor to see me, a favor to hear."

Sullivan managed to catch Elizalde's glance as they fell into step, and he gave her an optimistic wink.

It wasn't completely an empty gesture—it had just occurred to him that the hands sticking out of his shirt cuffs might well be Houdini's. The mask wasn't complete— he wasn't wearing the jacket with the detachable sleeves—but that was probably because he didn't have the whole outfit, he wasn't carrying the magician's dried thumb; nevertheless, the plaster hands had disappeared when he had touched them, back there in the fumy apartment, and now *somebody's* left hand was clutching a bit of broken metal.

Lurching along up at the head of the procession, Sherman Oaks was tall enough to have to duck under a couple of valves connecting the pipes that ran along under the low ceiling, but the room deLarava led them into was as roomy as a TV studio. Fluorescent lights threw a white glow over two low couches against the walls, and a metal desk out in the middle of the floor, and rolls of cable on stacked wooden apple-boxes in a corner; deLarava waved toward one of the couches and then crossed ponderously to the desk and lowered her bulk into the chair behind it.

To the pair of her employees who had herded her captives into the room, deLarava said, "Loop a cable through their cuffs—under the arm of the one-armed fellow—and sit them down on the couch and tie the cable where they can't reach it."

As soon as Sullivan had been tethered and pushed down onto the couch, again sitting between Elizalde and Oaks, he felt his thumb begin to pry at one of the narrow comb-teeth that had broken away with the thick end-tooth. To explain any muscular shifting of his shoulders, he leaned forward and looked to his right—Elizalde and Kootie were whispering together, and Bradshaw, at the far end of the long couch, was just frowning and squinting around at the walls as if disapproving of the paint job.

DeLarava waved the runners out of the room with her

little gun. From the floor behind the desk she lifted a big leather purse, and with her free hand she shook it out onto the desktop. Three cans of Hires Root Beer rolled out, two of them solidly full and one clattering empty; and then a brown wallet thumped down beside the cans, followed by a ring of keys.

"You recognize these, Pete?" deLarava asked, staring down at the items on the desk.

CHAPTER 44

. . . and she had a vague sort of idea that they must be collected at once and put back into the jury-box, or they would die.

—Lewis Carroll,
Alice's Adventures in Wonderland

SULLIVAN didn't answer. He took a deep breath—and thought he caught a whiff of bourbon on the air-conditioned breeze.

"And I've got an electromagnet," deLarava went on, "and some very specific music, and a schizophrenic who's a better mask than you and your sister ever were. I don't want a *glut* today, just your father—and, as long as they're here, Thomas Alva Edison and Koot Hoomie Parganas." She lifted her pouchy face and stared right into Sullivan's eyes. "And, wherever he is, Apie will come when I call him," she said. "Did you know that he and your mother had their honeymoon aboard the *Queen Mary,* in 1949?"

"No," said Sullivan. Their father had never liked to talk

to the twins about their mother, who had died in 1953, when they were a year old.

His left hand had broken off one of the narrow comb-teeth, and his fingers were prodding the tiny sliver of metal into the gap between the hinged single-blade swing-arm and the pawl housing of the cuff on his right wrist.

Sullivan was trying to remember what he'd read last night about Alice's coronation party; he wished he could lean across Elizalde and ask Kootie, who'd been reading the book this morning. Sullivan's fingers were still pushing the comb-tooth against the cuff, and, recalling the trick his hands had done yesterday inside the magically projected milk can in the cemetery lake, he tried to help—and immediately the tooth sprang out of his grip, and was lost forever down between the couch cushions.

A young man who was apparently the second assistant director leaned in at the doorway. "That producer guy, Neal Obstadt, is here," he said. "He says you're—Jesus!—expecting him!" the young man finished as a burly man in a business suit pushed right past him into the room. The newcomer's iron-gray hair was clipped short, and the cut of his jacket didn't conceal broad shoulders that Sullivan guessed were probably tattooed.

Sullivan's heart beat faster at the thought that this intrusion might mean rescue—but the surge of hope died when the tanned cheeks spread back at the sight of deLarava's five captives, baring white teeth in a delighted smile.

"Why, Kelley!" he said. "I don't see how that boy there could be anyone but the famous Koot Hoomie Parganas! What a thoughtful," he added, frowning abruptly, "tithe."

He glared across the room at her now. "You've been eating ghosts for years, right? You know how it works?"

"That will be all, Curtis," deLarava said hastily to the young man in the doorway, who seemed relieved to be able to hurry away.

Neal Obstadt waved at the captives. "They're secured?"

"Cuffed to a cable," said deLarava.

"And I assume," he went on, "that all five of your guests here will be dead before sundown?"

DeLarava rolled her eyes. "If you insist on subverting the civilized circumlocutions of—"

"You gonna kill 'em or not? I don't have all day, and neither do you, trust me."

"Fuck you, Neal. Yes."

"I can talk freely then. Some smoke dealer named Sherman Oaks sold me a dead ghost. Well, they're *all* dead, aren't they? But this one had gone rotten, and now it's stuck in my head; it's *in the way,* and I can't eat any more ghosts. All that happens when I try is that I get the nitrous oxide—but I don't get a life. The *life* in the dose just gets exhaled away. Does me no good. Have you run into this problem?"

"I've heard of it, yes," deLarava began.

"I know how to undo it," said Sherman Oaks— surprising Sullivan, who had thought the ragged one-armed man was nearly unconscious.

"So do I," said Sullivan and Kootie in quick unison.

"My name is Sherman Oaksssss . . ." said the one-armed man. He went on exhaling past the end of his sentence, and the breath didn't stop, but kept whistling out of him as if his mouth were an opening in a windy

canyon; and on that wind came the chanting voices of half
a dozen little girls:

> *"There was a man of double deed*
> *Sowed his garden full of seed.*
> *When the seed began to grow,*
> *'Twas like a garden full of snow."*

Obstadt had reached into his jacket and smoothly
drawn a stainless-steel .45 semiautomatic, cocked and
locked. Sullivan blinked helplessly at Elizalde and
nodded. *Same kind of gun,* he thought. *God help us.*

"*When the snow began to melt,*" the girls' voices
chanted on out of Sherman Oaks's slack mouth,

> *" 'Twas like a ship without a belt;*
> *When the ship began to sail,*
> *'Twas like a bird without a tail."*

Behind Sullivan's back, the strong fingers of his left
hand quickly broke another narrow tooth off the comb-
end, and again began working the end of it into the
handcuff housing, in under the pawl wheel. This time he
didn't try to help his hands.

> *"When the bird began to fly,*
> *'Twas like an eagle in the sky;*
> *When the sky began to roar,*
> *'Twas like a lion at the door."*

"The fuck is he doing?" shouted Obstadt. He pointed

the pistol at Oaks and yelled, "Shut up!" Sullivan could see that the safety lever was down now.

The voices continued, with the businesslike diligence of a child's jump-rope ritual; and Oaks's mouth was slack, and his throat wasn't visibly working, as the soprano syllables stitched his outrushing breath:

"When the door began to crack,
'Twas like a stick across my back;
When my back began to smart,
'Twas like a pen-knife in my heart;
When my heart began to bleed,
'Twas death and death and death indeed."

Oaks's eyes were crossed sharply together behind his nose. He was frowning and shaking his head, and Sullivan was sure this performance wasn't voluntary; Sullivan guessed that it was some kind of after-effect of the unclogging the man had done back in the apartment.

DeLarava had stood up, and now Sullivan looked away from Oaks at her. Her face was as pale as bacon fat, and her mouth was trembling.

"My little girls!" she screamed suddenly. "That's them! He's the one who ate my little birthday girls!"

Then she was end-running around the desk, her blubbery arms swinging horizontally and her belly jumping under the flowered dress, and she flung herself onto her knees in front of Oaks and planted her lips over his still-exhaling mouth.

And the wind out of Oaks must have increased, for deLarava's head was flung aside, and she teetered and windmilled her arms for a moment before sitting down heavily on the deck—and a smell of flowers and green grass tickled Sullivan's nose, and the room was full of flickering shadows and quick tapping and anxious little cries.

All at once Sullivan could see several skinny little girls in white dresses—or it might have been one, very quick, skinny little girl—flashing around the room, like a carousel of hologram photographs spinning under a strobe light; then the apparition was gone, and he heard sobbing and laughter and light fluttering footsteps receding away down the hallway beyond the door, away from the direction of the trucks, farther into the maze of the ship.

Sullivan felt the tiny metal blade trip the pawl inside the cuff mechanism, and then the fingers of his left hand squeezed the cuff tight, and released it—and his left hand was free.

"You can have the Parganas," wheezed deLarava as she rolled over onto her hands and knees and began dragging one big knee, and then the other, under herself, "kid. And Oaks." She raised her obese body to her feet in one steady straightening, though the effort sent bright blood bursting out of her flaring nostrils and down the front of her dress. "Leave me the others."

Then she took a deep breath and went charging out the door after the girl-ghosts. "Wait," she was bellowing hoarsely as she clumped and caromed down the hall, "wait, I'm one of you too! Delaware punch! Tell me the—goddammit—"

Obstadt was still pointing the .45 at Sherman Oaks's round face, but his finger was out of the trigger guard and he was looking after deLarava.

"Like that," said Oaks in a frail voice.

Obstadt looked down at him over the sights. "What?"

"What I just did. That's how you do it. I just now spit out those ghosts. To get cleared of the rotten one, hike one of your quick ones up to the top of your mind. Cross your eyes, hard, so you can *see* the quick one standing there on the diving board of your mind, and then exhale and *spit.* The live one goes, and knocks the rotten one out with it."

Sullivan was still sure that Oaks's latest seizure had been involuntary, and that the little girl-ghosts had simply forced their way out of him, past the now-compromised containment of his will; Sullivan guessed that the one-armed man was simply incontinent now, and would leak ghosts whenever he so much as sneezed. Nevertheless, Sullivan was a little surprised that Oaks would give the crucial information away with no security.

Sullivan had got his toes well back in under the couch, and he was watching Obstadt intently.

Obstadt stepped back, leaned against the desk, and crossed his eyes.

Sullivan heard a creaking from down the couch to his right, and when he glanced that way he saw Bradshaw squinting and gathering himself as if for a rush, as if he'd forgotten that he was tethered. Sullivan caught the old man's eye and frowned hard, shaking his head slightly.

Obstadt exhaled, leaning forward with the .45 pointing at the deck, and coughed; and he shook spasmodically, and his shoulders went up and his chin dropped onto his chest, then his shoulders fell and his head snapped forward and a black cylinder with ribs or folded legs ridging its sides came inflating out from between his gaping jaws, balanced for a moment on his teeth, and then fell and slapped onto the floor, where it flexed muscularly. The irregularities on its sides separated and proved to be legs that waved uselessly in the fouled air.

Sullivan had flinched at the sight and the smell of the thing's sudden appearance, but before Obstadt could straighten up Sullivan had sprung from the couch and whipped his right hand down in a fast arc past Obstadt's jaw, so that the freed cuff cracked solidly against the back of the man's head. Sullivan's bar-time jolt of surprise, halfway through the move, had only made him hit harder.

The .45 went off with an eardrum-hammering bang and blew the black thing to wet fragments, and the ricochet rang around the metal room and punched a hole in the couch where Sullivan had been sitting; Obstadt was on his hands and knees, and from somewhere a fist malleted the back of his bloodied head, sending Obstadt's face snapping down to the deck like a smacked croquet ball. Wind and a man's shouting voice were blowing out of his mouth now.

Sullivan looked up—Oaks had freed himself from the gaffer's tape, and it had been he that had punched Obstadt.

Sullivan's right arm was paused across his body from the follow-through of his blow, and now he lashed it back up hard at Sherman Oaks's face, which was looming over his own; the cuff just tore Oaks's cheek, for Sullivan's fingers had snatched at the chain, but Sullivan followed the blow with a solid kick of his left knee into Oaks's groin, and the one-armed man convulsed double and fell over sideways into the stinking mess that had been the buglike expelled ghost. The other ghost Obstadt had exhaled, the one with a man's voice, whirled gasping around the room and cycloned away in the hall.

Sullivan took one hitching half-breath, and the instant sting in his lungs made him decide not to breathe. He fished his comb out of his pocket and broke off another tooth, and when he had freed his right wrist he crouched to ratchet one cuff tightly around Oaks's wrist and the other around Obstadt's left ankle.

Then he tried to pick up the .45—but his fingers had suddenly gone limp, and all he could do was to push the weapon around clumsily; even by pressing the heels of both hands together, he couldn't get a grip on the gun. *Fuck it,* he thought in despair, straightening up.

Still not breathing, though his eyes were watering from the harsh fumes of the sizzling, evaporating ghost, he reeled back to the couch, and his hands were suddenly strong and dextrous again as he leaned behind Elizalde and then Kootie and then Bradshaw and sprang free the left wrist of each of them.

He expelled the last exhausted air in his lungs in croaking to Elizalde, *"Get the gun!"*

Her nostrils were whitely pinched and her eyes were teary slits, but she nodded and quick-stepped to crouch by where Obstadt and Oaks, linked, were writhing in the wet, smoking mess. Elizalde snatched up the .45 without difficulty and tucked it into the waistband of her jeans, pulling the untucked sweatshirt hem over it.

"Out," she barked, leading the way out the door and into the hallway.

Sullivan couldn't tell how much of the screaming racket in his ears was external and how much was just the internal overload-protest of his eardrums, but at least the appalling smell seemed to be keeping deLarava's employees back at the garage end of the hall.

Then he did hear something, from back in the direction of the garage—a familiar wailing laugh.

Elizalde was hurrying down the hall away from the garage, in the direction deLarava had gone, and Sullivan and Kootie and Bradshaw went stumbling hastily after her.

The Jeep had been parked well in, right up against the inboard bulkhead of the garage area, and the trucks had parked behind it. At the boom-and-echoes of the gunshot, Strube's guards had climbed out and rushed toward the hall; but they had been stopped by the fumes, and had joined the general rush out into the fresh air on the sunlit loading dock. Some men in undershirts had come inside from the dock carrying a burlap sack with a baseball cap on it and something thrashing inside it, and they hurried into the vacated hall.

Strube didn't mind the smell. He hiked his left arm behind himself until he could reach the door handle with his right hand, and when he had timidly opened the door and stepped down to the deck, he wandered down the hall himself—slowly, so that any of deLarava's men who might see him would be likelier to yell at him than shoot.

But apparently no one saw him. He walked past an open doorway and glanced in at two men rolling in a black puddle. The odd smell was strongest here, and one of the struggling men had only one arm, but Strube wasn't curious. If he kept walking, he was sure to find an elevator or stairway that would lead him up to the tourist decks, where he could surely get someone to call the police for him; maybe he would be able to get a security guard to unlock the handcuffs.

And then what? He could refuse to press charges, and take a cab back to Twenty-First Place, where he had left his car. Then he would drive back to his office, to think. His venture into show-business law was proving to be more difficult than he had anticipated.

CHAPTER 45

"If that there King was to wake," added
Tweedledum, *"you'd go out—bang!—just like
a candle!"*

—Lewis Carroll,
Through the Looking-Glass

BY THE FLUORESCENT TUBES overhead, Sullivan
could see that the hallway broadened out ahead of
Elizalde—the port walls slanted outward with the hull and
were riveted steel with vertical steel crossbeams welded
on, and the edges of the empty doorways on the inboard
side were knobby from having been cut with torches—
and in the far bulkhead, beyond a row of wheeled
aluminum carts, he saw a tiny recessed booth with
accordion bars pulled across it.

"Whoa, Angelica!" he called. "That's an elevator."

Elizalde nodded and skidded sideways and sprinted to
the elevator. By the time she had pulled back the bars
from the little stall, Sullivan was right behind her, and he

took her arm as the two of them stepped into the telephone-booth-like box.

The walls were paneled in rich burl elm that was dinged and scratched at the tray-level of the wheeled carts. He folded up a hinged wooden seat and flattened himself against the elevator wall to make room for Kootie; and over the boy's head he saw Bradshaw shuffling slowly across the deck.

"Come *on*, Nicky," Sullivan called, thinking of the winged bag that had flown after them in the cemetery yesterday. "Hurry!"

"I don't," said Bradshaw, scuffling to a stop. "Feel so good. Motion sickness. I'd throw up in there. I'll meet you. Later."

The ringing in Sullivan's ears had decreased to a shrill whining . . . and he was suddenly aware of an airy absence. He slapped his chest, feeling the angular hardness of the brass grave-portrait plaque, still in his scapular. "My father!" he said. "Is he with you, Nicky?"

Bradshaw paused, then shook his head. "But I'll watch for him," he said. "Go on now."

Sullivan bared his teeth and clenched Houdini's fists. His father might be anywhere down here. *DeLarava* might be anywhere down here. "Nicky, get in the elevator!"

Bradshaw smiled. "You know I won't, if I say I won't."

"—Okay." There's nothing I can do, Sullivan thought. "Okay. *Vaya con Dios,* amigo."

"*Y tu tambien, hermano,*" said Bradshaw.

Sullivan pulled the folded gate out again across the gap until it clanged shut, and said, "We've got to go down a deck."

"*Down?*" panted Elizalde. Her breaths were frightened sobs. "No, Pete—up! Sunlight, normal people!"

"I should have thought of this before," said Sullivan. "Kootie, do you remember how Alice's coronation ceremony got wrecked?"

The boy's brown eyes blinked up at him. "The food at the banquet came to life," he said, "and it didn't want to be eaten."

"Right, the leg of mutton was talking and laughing and sitting in the White Queen's chair, and the pudding yelled at Alice when she cut it, and—and the White Queen dissolved in the soup tureen, remember? The *bottles* even came to life, and took plates for wings and forks for legs. And Queen Alice was knocked right out of the Looking-Glass world." He punched the button that had a downward-pointing arrow on it. "We've got to find the after steering compartment."

The little booth shook, and then with a hydraulic whine the deck outside started to move upward; before his vision was cut off by this ascending fourth wall, Sullivan heard the sirenlike laugh again, closer, and he saw Bradshaw shift heavily around to face the way they had come.

The bare bulb in the shelved, inlaid elevator ceiling made the faces of Kootie and Elizalde look jaundiced and oily, and Sullivan knew he must look the same to them.

Elizalde was shaking. "Goddamn you, Pete, what's in this after steering compartment?"

"The degaussing machinery," said Sullivan, trying to speak with conviction. "They'd have had to install it when the *Queen Mary* was a troopship during the war, to keep her hull from attracting magnetic mines, and there's no way they'd have gone to the trouble of tearing it out, afterward. And the after steering room is the electrical spine of any ship—there'd have been a diesel engine there to run a sort of power-steering pump, so they could steer the ship from down there if the bridge was blown away. It's the backup bridge, in effect, and I don't suppose they're using the real one for anything at all now, with tourists dropping snow cones all over everything. There'll be live power down below still." It's certainly possible, he thought.

"So what?" Elizalde was leaning against the back of the car, her sunken eyes watching the riveted steel of the elevator shaft rising beyond the frail bars of the gate, and she spoke quietly in the confined space. "What the hell good is this old anti-mine stuff going to do us? Jesus, Pete, tell me you know what you're doing here!"

"How did this apparatus keep the ship from attracting magnetic mines?" asked Kootie.

Sullivan looked down at the boy. "The mines had a specific magnetic polarity," he said. "Once that was known, it was easy enough to forcibly reverse the ship's own natural magnetic field by passing a current through a set of cables around the hull."

"But it's turned off now?"

"Sure, it'll be disconnected, but it'll still be there."

"And you think there'll still be power there too. So, you're planning to reconnect it and crank up a big magnetic field; and," it was Kootie's little-boy cadences that went on, "you're gonna wake up every dinner aboard."

"It'll draw 'em out," Sullivan agreed. From the walls,

he thought, from the closets in the old staterooms, from the deck planks weathered by three decades of sunny summer cruises and North Atlantic storms. "And none of 'em will want to be eaten. It'll be a mass exorcism." Once drawn out, he thought, they'll dissolve away in this alien Long Beach air. He remembered Bradshaw's explanation of the L.A. CIGAR traps, and he hoped the dim old ghosts might somehow understand that this was . . . rescue? Liberation? Finishing the job of dying, say.

A breeze on his ankles made Sullivan look down past Kootie, and he saw that an edge of the elevator shaft had appeared down by their feet; the gap below it rode up until he could see another deck, dimly lit by electric lights somewhere. The elevator floor clanged against the painted steel deck, and he pulled the accordion gate aside. The bulkheads of the silent old corridors were ribbed and riveted, painted gray below belt-height and yellowed white above.

"This has got to be as close to water level as you can get," he said, instinctively speaking quietly down here so close to the sanctum sanctorum of the vast old liner. "It'll be right behind us, directly over the rudder."

"Get these cuffs off us," said Kootie.

"Oh, yeah." Sullivan took out his comb, broke off another narrow tooth, and quickly opened the handcuff that was still on Kootie's right wrist; then he did the same for Elizalde.

"Where did you learn that?" Elizalde asked as the cuffs clanked to the floor and she massaged her freed wrist.

Sullivan held up his hands, palms out, and wiggled the fingers at her. "If you hadn't glued that plaster finger back on, I'd be missing one right now." He started down the corridor toward the stern. "Come on."

Ancient bunks, with brown blankets still tumbled on them, were bolted on metal trays to the steel bulkheads down here, and as he led Elizalde and Kootie past them Sullivan shuddered at the thought of coming back this way if he got the field up and at maximum intensity.

"That's serious electrical conduit," said Kootie, pointing at the ceiling.

Sullivan looked up, and saw that the boy was right. "Follow it," he said.

A few steps farther down the hall the conduit pipes curved into the amidships bulkhead over a dogged-shut oval door, and Sullivan punched back the eight dog clips around the door's perimeter; the door rattled in the bulkhead frame, and Sullivan realized that the rubber seal had rotted away. He prayed that he wasn't the first person to open this door since the ship was docked here in Long Beach in 1967.

But there were lights burning inside the twenty-foot-square room beyond the door when he pulled it open; and they were new fluorescent tubes, bolted up alongside the very old lights, which were hung on C-shaped metal straps so that the recoil of the big wartime guns on the top deck wouldn't break the filaments.

A diesel engine the size of a car motor sat on a skid supported by two I-beams laid down near the left bulkhead, with two banked rows of square batteries on shelves behind it; and Sullivan saw a new battery charger bolted to the bulkhead over them.

"They're live!" he said, his shoulders slumping with

relief. "See? This must be the ship's backup power supply now, in case the AC from ashore goes funny. UPS for their computers, uninterrupted power supply so they don't lose their data."

"Groovy," said Elizalde. "Hook it up and let's get out of here."

"Right." Sullivan looked around and identified the reduction-gear box and the steering pump and the after steering wheel to his left, and so the three-foot-by-four-foot box on the right-hand bulkhead had to be the degaussing panel. He walked past it and began unlooping heavy coils of emergency power cable from the rack riveted to the bulkhead.

Sullivan was remembering another exorcism he had helped perform, at the Moab Nuclear Power Station in Utah in 1989.

The Public Utilities Commission had claimed that it would be cheaper to produce power elsewhere than to spend the millions needed to bring the reactor up to current safety standards—but the real reason had been that the site had become clogged with ghosts attracted to the high voltage. The things had clustered around the big outdoor transformers, and some had got solid enough to fiddle with the valves and switches and steal the employees' cars.

The power line from the degaussing panel had been cut, just beyond the breaker, disconnecting the panel from the rest of the ship; but a post stuck out above the hacksawed conduit, and Sullivan pulled the dusty canvas cover off the emergency power three-phase plug on the end of the post.

"They call these things biscuits," he told Elizalde defiantly.

"Call it a muffin if you like," she said. "Today I'm not arguing."

He picked up one end of the cable and separated the inch-thick wires protruding from the end of it. The red one he shoved into the positive hole in the biscuit, and the black one he shoved into the negative hole. They fit tightly enough to support the weight of the cable. He would be getting direct current from the batteries, so he let the white wire hang unconnected.

The Moab station had in its time produced more than fifty-billion-kilowatt hours, enough power to light half a million homes for a quarter of a century. But he had stood in the control room and watched the dials as the power had fallen from fifty to twenty to three percent of capacity, and then a voice on the intercom had said, "Turbine trip," and Sullivan's gaze had snapped to the green lights on the control panel in the instant before they flashed on, their sudden glow indicating that the circuit breakers were open and no electricity was being produced.

And as the superintendent reached for the switch that would drive the cadmium rods into the reactor core, killing the uranium fission, Sullivan alone among the technicians in the control room had heard the chorus of wails as the resident ghosts had faded into nothing.

He was setting up the same devastation now. The current he would shortly be sending through the degaussing coils in the length of the hull would wake up all the dormant, undisturbed ghosts aboard the ship; focused, they would venture timidly out of their housekeeping-tended graves, only to evaporate into nothingness when the drain on the batteries outstripped the ability of the recharger to counter it, and the magnetic field collapsed.

Perhaps sensing his unhappiness, Kootie and Elizalde wordlessly stepped aside as he dragged the other end of the cable across the painted steel deck to the stepped ranks of batteries against the left bulkhead.

Steel bars connected the terminals of each battery in a row to the next, and he wedged the inch-thick end of the red wire under the bar on the first battery in the top row, then did the same with the black wire to the first battery on the bottom row. He had now hooked up the degaussing panel, at the expense of the diesel engine's starter motor.

As he straightened up, he softly whistled, in slow time, the first notes of reveille.

He walked back across the deck to the panel and, with a sigh, pushed the master switch up into the on position. There was a muffled internal click.

The needle of the first DC voltmeter on the face of the panel jumped to 30, but that one was only indicating full power from the batteries. Then he took hold of the rubber-cased rheostat wheel and started turning it clockwise; the second voltmeter's needle began to climb across the dial toward 30, as the needle on the ammeter next to it moved more slowly up toward 150. For the first time in more than forty years, current was coursing through the wartime degaussing cables that ribbed the hull all the way from back here by the rudder to the bow a thousand feet north of him.

The deck had begun to vibrate under his feet, and a droning roar was getting louder; when he had cranked the wheel all the way over as far as it would go clockwise, the noise was so loud that Elizalde had to shout to be heard.

"What are you doing?" she yelled. "You've turned something on!"

"My God," said Kootie, loudly but reverently, "that's the noise of the screws. You've waked up the ghost of the ship herself!"

CHAPTER 46

❖

*"What matters it how far we go?" his
scaly friend replied.
"There is another shore, you know, upon
the other side."*

—Lewis Carroll,
Alice's Adventures in Wonderland

"OH," Elizalde moaned, "let's get *out* of here!" Sullivan
backed away from the panel, and even Houdini's hands
were trembling. "Yes," he said. Sullivan led the way out
of the after steering compartment and back down the
corridor toward the elevator. The hallway reeked of
sweaty bodies now, and he could hear a scratchy recording
of Kitty Kallen singing "It's Been a Long, Long Time"
echoing from somewhere ahead of them.

Bony figures were shifting among the blankets on the
bulkhead-hung bunks as Sullivan and Elizalde and Kootie
hurried past; hands still translucent groped at Elizalde,
and voices blurred by unformed mouths mumbled
amorously at her.

The elevator motor was buzzing and rattling when they rounded the corner, but the car was coming down to this deck—and through the bars Sullivan saw the burlap sack with the black Raiders baseball cap on it slumped on the elevator floor, shifting furiously and yowling as if it were filled with cats.

Before he could grab Kootie and Elizalde and run, the cat noises stopped and the front flap of the bag fell away, and as the car clanked down to the deck a naked young woman, slim and dark-haired, stood up in it and blinked through the bars at Sullivan and beyond him. Her body wasn't solidified yet—ribs showed faintly through the white softness of her breasts, and her loins were a wash of shadow.

Her eyes were bewildered brown depths, and already solid enough for Sullivan to see tears on the lashes. *"Es esto infierno?"* she asked.

Elizalde pulled back the gate. *"Esto es ninguna parte,"* she said. *"Y esto pasara pronto."*

Is this hell? the ghost-woman had asked; and Elizalde had told her that this was nowhere and would soon pass. Sullivan stared at the woman nervously, remembering the thing that had flown over the grass at the cemetery yesterday, laughing and clanking metal wings—and she stared back at him without any recognition, her imprinted malice having fallen away with the burlap sack under her bare feet.

The woman stumbled out of the elevator car, looked blankly around, and then walked uncertainly back toward where the bunks were hanging, and Sullivan paused as if to stop her or warn her; but Elizalde grabbed his arm and pulled him into the car.

"Tumble a bunch of old books together," she said. "Books so old and fragile that nobody can read them anymore. The pages will break off and get mixed up. Does it matter?"

Sullivan was sweating as he stepped into the car, crowding the wall to make room for Elizalde and Kootie. These limitless dim lower decks, with all their forgotten alcoves and doors and passageways, were suddenly potent, and darkly inviting, and he pushed the up button hard. "Let's go all the way to the top," he said hoarsely.

"Amen," said Elizalde.

J. Francis Strube had found a carpeted hallway and he had started running downhill along it, past silent doors recessed in the wood-paneled walls. The hallway curved up ahead of him to disappear behind the gentle bulge of the glossy ivory ceiling, as if he were sprinting around the perimeter ring of a very elegant space station, and he had assured himself that somewhere between here and the eventual bow he must run across someone who could help him.

But a grinding roar had started up under the carpet and the whole ship had *moved* slightly, as if flexing itself, and he had lost his footing and fallen headlong; his hands had still been cuffed behind him, and though he had managed to take the first hard impact on his shoulder, his chin and cheekbone had bounced solidly off the carpeted floor.

Now he was up again, and walking, but he had to step carefully. Perhaps it was some Coriolis effect that made walking so difficult; he had to plant his feet flat, with the toes pointed outward, to keep from rolling against the close walls.

Over the droning vibration from below the deck he could presently hear children laughing, and when he came to a gleaming wooden staircase he saw a little girl with blond braids come flying down the banister; she rebounded from the floor and the wall like a big beach ball, and her long white dress spread out in an air-filled bell to let her sink gently to the carpeted, landing.

Another girl came zooming down right behind her to do the same trick, and a third simply spun swan-diving down through the vertical space of the stairwell, graceful as a leaf.

"Up, up!" cried girl voices from the landing above, and when Strube stepped forward to tilt his head back and peer in that direction, he saw three more blond little girls stamping their feet with impatience.

All six of the girls seemed to be identical—sextuplets?—and to be about seven years old. How could they be doing these impossible acrobatics? They were a little higher up than he was—was the gravity weaker up in that ring? When he counted them all again, he got seven; then five; then eight.

"Girls," he said dizzily; but the three or four on his level were holding hands and dancing in a ring, chanting, "*When* the *sky began* to *roar,* 'twas *like* a *lion* at the *door!*" and the three or four above went on calling, "Up, up!"

"Girls!" he said, more loudly.

The several who had been dancing dropped their hands now and stared at him wide-eyed. "He can see us!" said one to another.

Strube was dizzy. His neck was wet, and he couldn't shake the notion that it was wet with blood rather than sweat, but with his hands cuffed behind him he couldn't reach up to find out.

"Of course, I can see you," he said. "Listen to me. I need to find a grown-up. Where's your mother?"

"We don't think we have a mother," said one of the girls in front of him. "Where is *your* mother, please?"

This was getting him nowhere. "What are your names?"

One of the girls at the landing above called down, "We're each named Kelley. We all became friends because of that, and because we couldn't sleep, even though it was pitch dark."

"In most gardens," spoke up a girl in front of Strube, "they make the beds too soft, so the flowers are always asleep."

"We came from a hard, noisy garden," put in one who was sliding slowly down the banister. "We've got to go up," she told her companions. "If there isn't the sun, there'll be the moon."

"Who is taking *care* of you?" Strube insisted. "Who did you come here with?"

"We were thrown out of a dark place," said one of the girls above. The four or five below were climbing the stairs now with graceful spinning hops. "Again," put in another.

At least they seem to be well cared for, Strube thought. Then he looked more closely at a couple of them and noticed their pallor and their sunken cheeks, and he saw that their dresses were made of some coarsely woven white stuff that looked like matted cobwebs.

"Where do you *live?*" asked Strube, speaking more shrilly than he had meant to. His heart was pounding and his breath was fast and shallow; he realized that he was frightened, though not of these girls, directly.

"We live in Hell," one of the Kelleys told him in a matter-of-fact tone. "But we're climbing out," one of her companions added.

Strube wasn't able to think clearly, and he knew it was because of the bang his head had taken against the floor back up the hallway. His stomach felt inverted; he would have to find a men's room soon and throw up. But he felt that he couldn't leave these defenseless, demented children down here in these roaring, flexing catacombs.

"I'll lead you out of here," he said, stepping up the stairs after them. He had to hunch his left shoulder up and stretch his right arm to hold on to the banister, for the ship was rolling ponderously. "We've all got to get out of here."

The girls looked down at him doubtfully from the landing. One of them said, "Would you know the sun, or the moon, if you saw either of them?"

Jesus, thought Strube. "Yes. Definitely."

"What if it's just another painted canvas?" one of the girls asked.

"I'll tear it down," Strube said desperately. "The real one'll be up there, trust me."

"Come on, then," a Kelley told him, and the girls whirled and leaped around him as he climbed on up the stairs. The gravity did seem to be weaker as one ascended higher, and he had to restrain himself from dancing with them.

✖ ✖ ✖

A lift attendant had abruptly appeared in the elevator, cramping things terribly. He was an elderly man in a white shirt and black tie, and in a fretful English accent he demanded to know what class of accommodations Sullivan and Kootie and Elizalde had booked.

Sullivan glanced bewilderedly at Elizalde, and then said heartily, "Oh, first class!"

"All the way!" added Kootie.

The old man stared at their dirty jeans and disordered hair, and he said, "I think not." He pushed the button for R Deck, and a moment later the elevator car rocked to a stop. "The Tourist-Class Dining Saloon is down the hall ahead of you," he said sternly as he leaned between Sullivan and Kootie to slide open the gate, "just past the stairs. See that you go no higher up."

Sullivan hesitated, and considered just throwing the old man out of the car and resuming their upward course; but he and Kootie and Elizalde were deep in the ghost world now, and they might well find the solid ghosts of security guards from the 1930s waiting for them on the higher decks.

"I think we'd better play along," he said quietly to Elizalde. "We're in good cover so far, and I doubt that Edison's field shows up at all in this chaos." He stepped out of the car onto a carpeted hallway.

After an agonized, tooth-baring whine, Elizalde followed him out, tugging Kootie along by the hand.

Behind them the gate slid closed, and the car began to sink away down the shaft.

The ship was alive with voices now, and Sullivan and

his companions seemed to have left the rumble of the screws below them.

Many of the room doors were open, and laughter and excited shouting shook the tobacco-scented air, but when they peeked into the lighted staterooms they passed, they could see only empty couches, and mirrored vanity tables, and paneled walls with motionless curtains over the portholes.

At the open, polished burl walnut stairway they could hear children's voices ascending from below; but the dining-room doors were ahead of them, and a steamy beef smell and a clatter of cutlery on china was accompanying the voices from beyond the closed doors, and Sullivan led the way around the stairs and pushed the doors open.

The noises were loud now, but the tables and chairs set across the ship's-width hardwood floor were empty; though a chair here and there did occasionally shift, as if invisible diners were turning their attentions from one companion to another.

Sullivan took Elizalde's cold hand, while she took Kootie's, and he led them between the noisy tables toward the service doors in the far bulkhead; and though there were no diners visible, Sullivan tried to thread his way exactly between the tables, and not violate the body spaces of any ghosts.

They exited the dining room through the starboard service door, and now, among the kitchens, they saw people.

Nearly solid men in white chef's hats were pushing carts in and out of open kitchen doorways, apparently oblivious of the unauthorized intruders; the dishes on the carts were covered with steel domes, and, since the kitchen staff didn't seem able to see Sullivan and he hadn't eaten at all today, he reached out and touched one of the covers on a cart that had been momentarily left against the hallway bulkhead. The cover handle was warmly solid, and he lifted the dome away.

From a bed of baby carrots and asparagus, a woman's face was smiling up at him. Her eyes were looking directly into his, and when her lips opened to puff out a bourbon-scented whisper of, "*Hi, Pete,*" he recognized her as Sukie.

Elizalde tugged at his arm, but he pulled her back, feeling the relayed shake as Kootie was stopped too.

"Hi, Sukie," he said; his voice was level, but he was distantly surprised that his legs were still holding him up. He glanced sideways at Elizalde's face, but she was looking down at the plate, and then at him, in frowning puzzlement.

"I guess she can't see me," said Sukie's face. "You've spilled it all out onto the floor, haven't you? How long can this magnetic charge last? Who's your chick, anyway? She's the one who was on the phone last night, isn't she?"

"Yes." Sullivan squeezed Elizalde's hand. "The charge—I don't know. An hour?"

"When I consider how my light was spent! And then I'll be gone, and you'll probably be sorry, but not near sorry enough. You're in love with her, aren't you? How do I look in a halo of vegetables? I'll see if I can't wish you something besides misery with her; no promises, but I'll see what I can muster up. Haul your ass—and hers, too, I guess—and you got a kid already?—up to the Moon Deck. We also serve who only stand and gaff."

Elizalde barked a quick scream and her hand tightened on Sullivan's, and then the face was gone, and all that was on the plate was steaming vegetables.

"You saw her, didn't you?" said Sullivan as he hurried on down the kitchen corridor, pulling Elizalde and Kootie along.

"Just for a second," said Elizalde, having to nearly shout to be heard over the feverish clatter of pots and pans, "I saw a woman's *face* on that plate! No, Kootie, we're not going back!" To Sullivan, she added, "You were . . . *speaking* to her . . . ?"

"It was my sister." Sullivan saw a door in the white bulkhead at the end of the corridor, and he tugged Elizalde along more quickly. "She says I'm in love with you. And she says she'll try to wish us something besides misery."

"Well," said Elizalde with a bewildered and frightened grin, "this *is* your *family,* after all—I hope she tries hard."

"Yeah, me too, in spite of everything." They had reached the door. "Catch up, Kootie, I think we've got another dining room to pass through." He pushed open the door.

This dining room too was as wide as the ship, but the ornate rowed mahogany ceiling was fully three deck-heights overhead; ornate planters and huge, freestanding Art Deco lamps punctuated the middle height—and there were visible diners here.

All the men at the tables were wearing black ties and all the women were in off-the-shoulder evening dresses. The conversation was quieter in this vast hall, and the air was sharp with the effervescence of champagne. On the high wall facing them across the length of the dining room, a vast mural dominated the whole cathedral chamber; even from way over here Sullivan could see that it was a stylized map of the North Atlantic, with a clock in the top of it indicated by radiating gold bars surrounding the gold hands, which stood at five minutes to twelve.

"I'm not dressed for this," said Elizalde in a small voice.

Sullivan looked back at her, and grinned at how humble she looked, framed in the glossy elm burl doorway, in her jeans and grimy Graceland sweatshirt. Kootie, peering big-eyed from behind her, looked no better in his blood-stained polo shirt, and Sullivan found that he himself was sorry he hadn't found time to shave yesterday or today.

"Probably they can't see us," he told her. "Come on, it's not that far."

But as they strode out across the broad parquet floor, a white-haired gentleman at one of the nearer tables caught Sullivan's glance, and raised an eyebrow; and then the man was pushing back his chair and slowly standing up.

Sullivan looked away as he hurried past the table and pulled Elizalde along, glad to hear Kootie's footsteps scuffing right behind her.

Men were standing up at other tables, though, all looking gravely at Sullivan and his two companions as they trotted through the amber-lit vista of white tablecloths and crystal wineglasses, and now the women were getting to their feet too, and anxiously eyeing the shabby intruders.

"Halfway there," gritted Sullivan between his teeth. He was staring doggedly at the mural above and ahead of them. Two nearly parallel tracks curved across the golden clouds that represented the Atlantic, but only one track had anything on it—one miniature crystal ship, all by itself out in the middle of the metallic sea.

How could there be a room this big in a *ship!* he thought as he strode between the tables, tugging Elizalde's hand. Polished wooden pillars, the vaulted ceiling so far away up there, and it must be a hundred tables spread out on every side across the floor to the distant dark walls recessed at the lowest level . . .

Someone among the standing ghosts began clapping; and more of them took it up, and from somewhere the full-orchestra strains of "I'll Be Seeing You" began to play. All the elegantly dressed ghosts were standing and applauding now, and every face that Sullivan could see was smiling, though many were blinking back tears and many others openly let the tears run down their cheeks as they clapped their hands.

When he was close to the far doors, a crystal goblet of champagne was pressed into Sullivan's hand, and when he glanced back, his face chilly with sweat, he saw that Elizalde and Kootie each held a glass as well. The applause was growing louder, nearly drowning all the old familiar music.

Elizalde hurried up alongside Sullivan and turned her head to whisper in his ear: "Do you think it's poison?"

"No." Sullivan slowed to a walk, and he lifted the glass and sipped the icy, golden wine. He wished he were a connoisseur of champagnes, for this certainly seemed to be first-rate. He blinked, and realized that he had tears in his own eyes. "I think they're grateful at being released."

At the door, on an impulse, he turned back to the resplendent dining room and raised his glass. The applause ceased as every ghost raised a glass of its own; and then the rich tawny light faded as the lamps on the Art Deco pillars lost power, and the music ceased (with, he thought, a dying fall), and finally even the background rustle of breathing and the shifting of shoes on the parquet floor diminished away to silence.

The dining hall was dark and empty now. The tables were gone, and a lot of convention hotel chairs were nested in stacks against the bulkheads.

Sullivan's lifted hand was empty, and he curled it slowly into a fist. "The field is beginning to fail already," he said to Elizalde. "We'd better get upstairs fast." He pushed open the door at his back.

Across a broad foyer was a semicircular bronze portal like the entry to a 1930's department store. Its two doors were open wide, and on the broad mother-of-pearl ceiling within, Sullivan could see the rippling reflection of brightly lit water, and hear splashing and laughter; these doors apparently led to a balcony over the actual pool, which must have been one deck level below. Sullivan thought the swimmers must be real people, and not ghosts.

Elizalde looked in the same direction and whispered, "Good Lord, stacked like a slave ship!"

An imposingly broad mahogany stairway opened onto the foyer to their left, and Sullivan waved Elizalde and Kootie up—the stairs were wide enough for all three of them to trot up abreast, though Kootie was stumbling.

"Did you see some bathing beauty in there?" Sullivan

asked Elizalde as he hurried up the stairs, pulling Kootie along by the upper arm. " 'Stacked' I get, but 'like a slave ship'—is that good or bad?"

"I meant those bunks," she panted, "you pig. Stacked to the ceiling in there, with soldiers all crammed in, trying to sleep. I didn't notice any—damn *bathing beauty.*'"

"Oh . . . ? What I saw was a balcony over a swimming pool," he told her. Apparently, the field *hadn't* yet collapsed, but was out of phase. "What did you see, Kootie?"

"I'm looking nowhere but straight ahead," said the boy, and Sullivan wondered which of the personalities in Kootie's head had spoken.

Maybe one or more of the degaussing coils *have* been disconnected, Sullivan thought uneasily, at the substations along the length of the ship. I've got a big wheel spinning—is it missing some spokes? Is it going to fly apart? "All we can do is get out of here," he said. "Come on."

They jogged wearily up two flights of the stairs, and then paused just below the last landing. Peering around the newel pillar, Sullivan assessed the remaining steps that ascended to the broad Promenade Deck lobby area known as Piccadilly Circus.

From down here he could see the inset electric lights glowing in the ceiling up there, and he could hear a couple of voices speaking quietly. Far up over his head on the other side, on the paneled back wall of the stairwell, hung a big gold medallion and a framed portrait of Queen Mary.

"Up the stairs," he whispered to Elizalde and the boy,

"and then fast out the door to the left. That'll lead us straight off the ship onto the causeway bridge, across that and down the stairs to the parking lot. Ready? Go!"

They stepped crouchingly across the landing, then sprang up the last stairs and sprinted wildly across the open floor, hopping over loops of cable to the wide open doorway out onto the outdoor deck—and then all three of them just stopped, leaning on the rail.

The rail had no gap in it, and the causeway to the parking lot stairs was gone. The stairs, the parking lot, all of *Long Beach* was gone, and they were looking out over an empty moonlit ocean that stretched away, to the horizon under a black, star-needled sky.

CHAPTER 47

❖

"I wish I hadn't cried so much!" said Alice,
as she swam about, trying to find her way out.
"I shall be punished for it now, I suppose, by
being drowned in my own tears! . . ."

—Lewis Carroll,
Alice's Adventures in Wonderland

FOR A LONG MOMENT, the three of them just clung
to the rail, and Sullivan, at least, was not even breathing.
He was resisting the idea that he and Elizalde and Kootie
had died at some point during the last few seconds, and
that this lonely emptiness was the world ghosts lived in;
and he wanted to go back inside, and cling to whoever it
was whose voices they had heard.

He heard clumsy splashing far away below, and when
he looked down he thought he could see the tiny heads and
arms of two swimmers struggling through the moonlit
water alongside the *Queen Mary*'s hull. The sight of them
didn't lessen the solitude, for he guessed who they must be.

Hopelessly, just in case the cycle might be breakable,

he filled his lungs with the cold sea breeze and yelled down to the swimmers, *"Get out of town tonight!"*

He looked at Elizalde, who was half-kneeling next to him, stunned-looking and hanging her elbows over the rail. "Maybe," he said, "I'll listen to me this time."

She managed to shrug. "Neither of us did yesterday."

The spell broke when sharp, heavy footsteps that he knew were high heels on the interior deck approached from behind Sullivan, and he didn't need to smell a clove cigarette.

He grabbed Elizalde's shoulder and Kootie's collar and shoved them forward. "Wake up!" he shouted. "Run!"

They both blinked at him, then obediently began sprinting down the deck toward the lights of the bow, without looking back; he floundered along after them, his back chilly and twitching in anticipation of a shot from deLarava's little automatic.

But the big silhouette of deLarava stepped out of a wide doorway *ahead* of Elizalde and Kootie, and deLarava negligently raised the pistol toward them.

They skidded to a halt on the worn deck planks, and Sullivan grabbed their shoulders again to stop himself. He looked behind desperately—

And saw deLarava standing back there too.

"I'm not seeing a railing at all," called both the images of deLarava, in a single voice that was high-pitched with what might have been elation or fright. "To me, you're all standing straight out from the Promenade Deck doorway. From your point of view, you can walk here by coming forward or coming back. Either way, get over here right now or I'll start shooting you up."

Elizalde's hand brushed the untucked sweatshirt at her waist. The night sea breeze blew her long black hair back from her face, and the moonlight glancing in under the deck roof glazed the lean line of her jaw.

"No," whispered Sullivan urgently. "She'd empty her gun before you half drew clear. Save it." He looked at the forward image of deLarava and then back at the aft one. "Tell you what, you two walk forward, and I'll walk back."

"And I'll be in Scotland afore ye," whispered Kootie. Sullivan knew the remark was a bit of bravado from Edison.

As Elizalde and Kootie stepped away toward the bow, Sullivan turned and walked back the way they had run; and as he got to the open Piccadilly Circus doorway he saw that Elizalde and Kootie were stepping in right next to him, both blinking in exhausted surprise to see him suddenly beside them again. The soft ceiling lights and the glow of another freestanding Art Deco lamp kindled a warm glow in the windows of the little interior shops at the forward end of the lobby.

DeLarava had stepped back across the broad inner deck, and she was still holding the gun on them; though Sullivan could see now that the muzzle was shaking.

"Do you know anything about all this, Pete?" deLarava asked in an animated voice. "There's some huge magnetic *thing* going on, and it's broken the ship up, psychically. Right here all the ghosts have waked up, with their own stepped-up charges, and they've curved their bogus space all the way around us, and this lobby area of this deck is in a . . . a closed loop—if you walk away from it, you find yourself walking right b-b-back into it." She sniffed and touched her scalp. "Goddammit."

The only other person visible in the broad lobby was a white-haired little old fellow in a khaki jacket, though the area had at some time been set up for a shoot—a Sony Betacam SP sat on a tripod by the opposite doorway, and the unlit tic-tac-toe board of a Molepar lamp array was clamped on a sandbagged light stand in the corner next to a couple of disassembled Lowell light kits; and power and audio cables were looped across the deck, some connected to a dark TV monitor on a wheeled cart. Nothing seemed to be hot now, but Sullivan could faintly catch the old burnt-gel reek on the clove-scented air.

It seemed to him that the ceiling lights had dimmed from yellow down toward orange, in the moments since he had stepped in from the outside deck.

With her free hand, deLarava snicked a Dunhill lighter and puffed another clove cigarette alight. "Is Apie here, Joey?" she asked.

Sullivan nervously touched the brass plaque under his shirt.

The old man in the khaki jacket was grimacing and rocking on his heels. "Yes," he said. "And he can no more get out of here than we two can. We toucans." He sang, "*Precious and few are the moments we toucans sha-a-are . . .*" Then he frowned and shook his head. "Even over the side—that's not the real ocean down there now. Jump off the port rail and you land on the starboard deck."

"I think he tried it," whispered Kootie bravely, "and landed on his head."

Sullivan nodded and tried to smile, but he was glancing around at the pillars and the stairwell and the dark inward-facing shop windows. *Keep your head down, Dad,* he thought.

The ceiling lamps were definitely fading and the lobby was going dark—but reflections of colored lights were now fanning above the wide throat of the open stairwell on the aft side of the lobby, gleaming on the tall paneled back wall and the big gold medallion and the framed portrait, and from some lower deck came the shivering cacophony of a big party going on.

DeLarava stumped across the glossy cork deck to the top of the stairwell—a velvet rope was hung doubled at the top of one of the stair railings, and she unhooked one brass end, walked across to the other railing with it, and hooked the rope there, across the gap.

"Nobody go near the well," she said, her voice sounding more pleading than threatening. "Joey—*where is Apie?*"

The Piccadilly Circus lobby was almost totally dark now, the lamps overhead glowing only a dull red, and Sullivan could see reflections of moonlight on the polished deck.

Then, with the echoing clank of a knife switch being thrown, the white-hot glare of an unglassed carbon-arc lamp punched across the lobby from the forward corridor between the shops, throwing deLarava's bulbous shadow like a torn hole onto the paneling of the stairwell's back wall.

The lamp was roaring because of working off alternating current, but from the darkness behind and beyond the cone of radiance, a strong, confident voice said, "I'm here, Kelley."

DeLarava had flung her hand over her face, and now reeled away out of the glare, toward the doorway that led out onto the starboard deck, on the opposite side of the lobby from Sullivan.

He spun away from the glaring light toward Elizalde and Kootie—and stopped.

Angelica Elizalde was still standing where she'd been, her hair backlit now against the reflected glare from the stairwell wall, but a portly old man stood between her and Sullivan, where Kootie had been a moment before, and Kootie was nowhere to be seen. Sullivan blinked at the old man, wondering where he had appeared from, and who he was.

Sullivan opened his mouth to speak—then flinched into a crouch a moment before a hard *bang* shook the air, and he felt the hair twitch over his scalp.

He let his crouch become a tumble to the deck, and he reached for Elizalde's ankles but she was already dropping to her hands and knees. The old man who'd been standing between them had stepped forward into the glare, the tails of his black coat trailing out behind him as if he were walking through water.

Sullivan's father's voice boomed from the forward darkness behind the light. "Step forward, Kelley!"

"Fuck you, Apie!" came deLarava's shrill reply. "I just killed your other precious stinking kid!"

Sullivan grabbed Elizalde's upper arm and pulled her into the deeper penumbra behind the cone of light. "Where's Kootie?" Sullivan hissed into her ear as they crawled toward the wall.

"That's him," Elizalde whispered back, waving out at

the old man in the center of the deck. Sullivan looked up, and noticed two things: the old man's jowly, strong-jawed face, which in this stark light even looked like a figure in a black-and-white newsreel, was instantly recognizable from the photos he'd seen of Thomas Alva Edison; and the shadow the old man cast on the far aft wall above the stairs was the silhouette of a young boy.

This was the Edison ghost out and solid, and Sullivan knew deLarava would not want to damage it. "Give me the gun," he whispered to Elizalde.

The two of them had scrambled forward to the wall below one of the little interior windows on the port side, and Elizalde sat down on the deck and pulled the .45 from the waist of her jeans and shoved it toward him.

His hands wouldn't close around it. "Shit," he whispered, panting and nearly sobbing, "Houdini must have been a fucking pacifist! I guess he didn't want his mask to be able to *kill* anybody! Here." He pushed it back to her with the heels of his limp hands. "You've got to do it. Shoot deLarava."

He looked up and squinted, trying to see the old woman on the far side of the pupil-constricting glare. Then a movement above the stairwell, out across the deck to his right, caught his attention.

A rapid clicking had started up, and the light narrowed to a beam as if now being focused through the lens of a projector.

In a wide, glowing rectangle of black and white and gray on the stairwell wall, Sullivan saw an image of the corner of a house, and a fat man frustratedly shaking the end of an uncooperative garden hose; Kootie's shadow-silhouette had been replaced with a projected image of a boy, who was standing on the lush gray lawn with one foot firmly on the slack length of the hose behind the fat man. The man scratched his head and looked directly into the nozzle—at which point the boy stepped off the hose, and a burst of water shot into the man's face.

"Plagiarism!" called the ghost of Edison, which, though solidly visible in the light, was itself now throwing no shadow at all. "That's my 'Bad Boy and the Garden Hose,' from 1903!"

"Lumiere made it first, in 1895," called Sullivan's father's ghost from the blackness behind the carbon-arc radiance to Sullivan's left. "Besides, I've improved it."

In the projected movie scene, the water was still jetting out of the hose, but the figure holding the nozzle was now a fat woman, and the gushing flow was particulate with thousands of tiny, flailing human shapes, whose impacts were eroding the fat woman's head down to a bare skull.

Across the deck, deLarava screamed in horrified rage—then another gunshot banged, and the light was extinguished.

"Is that supposed to be sympathetic magic?" deLarava was screaming. "I'm the one that's going to walk out of here whole, Apie! And everything will be what *I* say it is!"

"*Shoot* her, goddammit!" said Sullivan urgently, though Elizalde surely couldn't see any more than he could in the sudden total darkness.

"I *can't*," said Elizalde in a voice tight with anger, *"kill* her."

Sullivan jumped then, for someone had tugged on his shirt from the forward side, away from Elizalde; but even as he whipped his head around that way he smelled bourbon, and so he wasn't wildly surprised when Sukie's voice said, "Get over here, Pete."

"Follow me," he whispered to Elizalde. He grabbed the slack of her sweatshirt sleeve and pulled her along after the dimly sensed shape of Sukie, stepping high to avoid tripping over cables, to the narrow forward area behind where the light had been.

Sukie proved to be solid enough to push Sullivan down to his knees on the deck, and into his ear she whispered, "Not hot."

He groped in the darkness in front of his face, and his fingers touched a familiar shape—a wooden box on the end of a stout cable, open on one face with a leather flap across the opening. It was a plug box of the old sort known as "spider boxes" because of the way spiders tended to like the roomy, dark interiors of them. Like the carbon-arc lamp, this was an antique, and had surely not been among deLarava's modern equipment. The spider-box devices had been outlawed at some time during the mid-eighties, when he and Sukie had still been deLarava's gaffers, because of the constant risk of someone's putting their hand or foot into one and being electrocuted.

But Sukie had said *Not hot,* so he pulled back the leather flap with one hand, then rapped the box with the other hand and held it out palm up.

Sukie slapped one of the old paddle plugs into his hand, and he tipped it vertical and shoved it firmly into the grooves inside the box. Then he let the flap fall over it and pulled his hands back.

"Set," he said.

"Hot," said Sukie, "now."

And again, a knife-switch clanked across a gap, right next to him now, and another carbon-arc lamp flared on with a buzzing roar, the sudden light battering at Sullivan's retinas.

By reflected light he could see his father standing over him; Arthur Patrick Sullivan looked no more than fifty, and his hair was gray rather than white. He glanced down at Pete Sullivan, who was crouched over the spider box, and winked.

"I think we need a gel here," said Pete's father; and the old man reached around in front of the lamp and laid his palm over the two arcing carbon rods in the trim clamps.

Sullivan winced and inhaled between his teeth, but the hand wasn't blasted aside; instead it shone translucently, the red arteries and the blue veins glowing through the skin, and his father was looking down the length of the room and smiling grimly.

On the stairwell wall another scene was forming—this time in color. (Flakes falling from the ceiling sparked and glowed like tiny meteors as they spun down through the beam of light.)

Glowing tan above, blue below—the bright rectangle on the wall coalesced into focus, and Sullivan recognized Venice Beach as seen from the point of view of a helicopter *(though no helicopter had been in the sky on that afternoon).*

In the colored light it was just Kootie standing and blinking in the middle of the deck; the boy shaded his eyes and glanced wildly back and forth.

"This way, Kootie!" called Elizalde, and the boy ran to her through the rain of flakes and crouched beside her, breathing fast.

In the projected image on the stairwell wall at the other end of the lobby, Sullivan could see the four tiny figures on the beach; three were staying by the patchwork rectangles of the towels spread on the sand, while the fourth, the white-haired figure, strode down to the foamy line of the surf.

One of the flakes from the ceiling landed on the back of Sullivan's hand, and he picked it up and broke it between his fingers; it was a curl of black paint (and he remembered his father describing how Samuel Goldwyn's glass studio had been painted black in 1917, when mercury-vapor lamps superseded sunlight as the preferred illumination for filming, and how in later years the black paint had constantly peeled off and fallen down onto the sets like black snow).

Loretta deLarava was clumping out into the light now from the far side of the lobby, her face and broad body glowing in shifting patches of blue and tan as she took on the projection.

"Nobody but me is getting out of here alive, Apie," she said, pointing her pistol straight at the glowing hand over the light. "Prove it all night, if you like, to this roomful of ghosts."

The white-haired little image in the projection had waded out into the surf, and now dived into a wave.

Just then from down the stairs behind deLarava came a young man's voice, singing, *"Did your face catch fire once? Did they use a tire iron to put it out?"* It was a tune from some Springsteen song—and Sullivan thought he should recognize the voice, from long ago.

A movement across the lobby caught Sullivan's eye—five or six little girls in white dresses were dancing silently in the open doorway on the starboard side, against the black sky of the night.

Now something was coming up the stairs; it thumped and wailed and rattled as it came. DeLarava glanced behind her down the stairwell and then hastily stepped back, her gun waving wildly around.

Even way over on the forward side of the lobby, Sullivan flinched away from the spider box when a lumpy shape with seven or eight flailing limbs hiked itself up the last stairs onto the level of the deck and knocked the velvet rope free of its hooks.

Then Sullivan relaxed a little, for he saw that it was just two men, apparently attached together; they were both trying to stand, but the wrist of one was handcuffed to the ankle of the other. He thought they must be Sherman Oaks and Neal Obstadt, but the man cuffed by a wrist had two arms with which to wrestle his companion, had one fist free to pummel against the other man's groin and abdomen, two elbows with which to block kicks to the face.

Behind them, as if shepherding them, a young man stepped up the stairs to the deck, into the projected glare; he was broad-shouldered and trim in a white turtleneck sweater, with blond hair clipped short in a crew cut.

"Kelley Keith," said this newcomer in a resonant baritone, and from childhood memories and the soundtrack of the old TV show Sullivan belatedly recognized the youthful voice of Nicky Bradshaw. "Listen to the hookah-smoking caterpillar—this mushroom's for you. And it won't pass away."

The carbon-arc lamp over Sullivan's head was roaring, and the paint flakes were falling more thickly, and, down the length of the lobby, projected right onto the blood-spattered fabric of deLarava's broad dress now, the little figure in the surf was waving its tiny arms.

Crouching up forward by the spider box, Sullivan was clasping Elizalde's hand in his right hand, and Sukie's in his left.

"It's not the real moon!" cried several of the little girls visible through the open doorway out on the starboard deck. "It's painted! We're still in Hell!"

"No, look!" shouted a man at the rail behind them. "It's crumbling! The real sun is out there!" By the now-rumpled business suit and necktie and the blood-streaked white shirt, Sullivan recognized him as the lawyer whom deLarava's men had driven away in the Jeep Cherokee; the man's hands were still cuffed but he had got them in front of him, and he was holding a long broom that he was waving over his head as high as he could reach. Black paint chips fell down onto him like confetti.

"My baby ghosts!" screamed deLarava; she started ponderously out of the projected light toward the half-dozen little girls, but the man with the broom had swept a hole in the night sky out there, and a beam of sunlight (cleaner and brighter, Sullivan thought, than a 3200 Kelvin lamp through a blue gel) lanced down to the deck. The girls flocked to it, then broke up and dissolved in white mist and breathless giggling, and were gone, in the moment before deLarava ran through the spot where they had been and collided with the still-shadowed rail.

The carbon-arc lamp, working off AC and no doubt a choke coil or a transformer, was flickering and glowing a deepening yellow. Sullivan's father's ghost lifted his hand away from the carbon rods, and the beam of light now just threw a featureless white glow down the lobby onto the far wall. Sullivan felt Sukie reach off to the side, and with an arcing snap the light went out, the carbon rods abruptly dimming to red points.

In the sudden silence, the fat old woman backed across the exterior deck from the starboard rail, and in the open doorway she turned around to face the dark Piccadilly Circus lobby.

Her dress still glowed with the image that had been projected onto it, and the tiny white-haired swimmer, carried on her dress right out of the rectangle that had shone on the stairwell wall, was floundering below the shelf of her breasts.

She stomped slowly back in through the doorway and started across the lobby floor. "I will at least have Edison," she said.

CHAPTER 48

❈

Come, hearken then, ere voice of dread,
With bitter tidings laden,
Shall summon to unwelcome bed
A melancholy maiden!
We are but older children, dear,
Who fret to find our bedtime near.
                              —Lewis Carroll,
                              Through the Looking-Glass

FROM AFT BY THE STAIRS, the ankle-cuffed man stepped forward (dragging his flailing companion) into the dim glow projected by deLarava's dress, and Sullivan saw that he *was* the gray-haired Obstadt. "No, Loretta," Obstadt said hoarsely, kicking at the man attached to his foot, "you said I could have him. You work for *me* now. Get back—"

And, crouched on the floor, the two-armed man who must nevertheless have been Sherman Oaks was jabbering urgently in what sounded to Sullivan like Latin.

DeLarava shoved her little gun at Obstadt's belly and

681

fired it. The *bang* was like a full-arm swing of a hammer onto the cap of a fire hydrant, and Obstadt stopped and bowed slightly, his mouth working. The man on the floor took the opportunity to lash his free fist twice, hard, into Obstadt's groin, and Obstadt bowed more deeply.

Beams of sunlight lanced into the lobby from behind Sullivan, reflecting off the floor to underlight deLarava's jowls, and he realized that the night sky was breaking apart on the port side too.

"Koot Hoomie Parganas," said deLarava, moving forward again. Her dress still glowed in surging fields of tan and blue, and the tiny swimmer was waving its arms under her breasts.

Sullivan glanced past Elizalde at Kootie, who was sitting cross-legged in a nest of cables, his hair now backlit by reflected daylight. The boy seemed to have been forsaken by Edison—his wide eyes gaped in horror at the approaching fat woman, and his lips were trembling.

Elizalde stood up from her crouch beside Sullivan. "No," she said loudly, stepping in front of the boy, "*Llorona Atacado.* You won't replace your lost children with this boy." And she jabbed her hand in the air toward deLarava's face, with the first and little fingers extended. "*Ixchel se quite!* Commander Hold-'Em take you," she said, and she spit.

The saliva hit the deck between them, but deLarava reeled back, coughing and clutching the glowing fabric over her stomach as if the tiny drowning figure were sinking into her diaphragm. She blinked up at Elizalde from under her bushy eyebrows, and the barrel of the little automatic came wobbling up.

Sullivan was on his feet now, and he could see that Elizalde was not even going to think of raising the .45.

DeLarava's gun was pointed from less than two yards away at the center of Elizalde's Graceland sweatshirt—and as Sullivan leaned forward to grab Elizalde and yank her out of the way, his scalp contracted with the bar-time advance-shock of deLarava's gun going off.

And so, instead of trying to pull Elizalde back, he made his forward motion a leap into the space between the two women (in the moment when both of his feet were off the deck he whiffed suntan oil and mayonnaise and the cold, deep sea—and, faintly, bourbon), and then the real gunshot punched his eardrums and hammered his upper arm.

The impact of the shot (and bar-time anticipation of the second) spun him around in mid-air to face the glowing figure of deLarava, and her second shot caught him squarely in the chest.

His feet hit the deck, but he was falling backward, and as he fell he heard the fast *snap-clank* of the .45 at last being chambered; and as his hip thudded down hard and he curled and slid and the needlessly ejected .45 round spun through the air, he saw Elizalde's clasped hands raise the weapon toward deLarava, her thumbs safely out of the way of the weapon's slide; the .45 flared and jumped, and the gunshot in the enclosed lobby was like a bomb going off.

Sullivan's knees were drawn up and his right arm was folded over his chest, but his head was rocked back to watch deLarava's fat body fly backward, sit boomingly on the deck, and then tumble away toward the starboard doorway in a spray of blood—

—Sullivan slid to a tense halt, staring—

But deLarava was at the same time still standing in front of Elizalde, and still holding the little automatic, though her arm was transparent; she was looking from Elizalde to the automatic in puzzlement, and the weight of the gun was pulling her insubstantial arm down toward the deck.

Then the top of her head abruptly collapsed from the eyebrows up, as the rubber bands imploded the frail ectoplasmic skull.

Sullivan's chest felt split and molten, but he rolled his head around to scan the sunlight-spotted deck for a glimpse of his own freshly dead body. Surely deLarava's chest-shot had killed him, and he was now a raw ghost about to blessedly dissolve into the fresh daytime air that was streaming in through the cracking night sky; after all, he wasn't able to breathe—his lungs were impacted, stilled, and the only agitation in him was the thudding heartbeat that was jolting his vision twice every second . . .

My heart's beating! he thought, with a shiver of dreadful hope. Suddenly, he realized that he wanted to live, wanted to get away from here with Elizalde and Kootie and live . . .

DeLarava's grotesquely pinheaded ghost was staring at its arm, which had been stretched all the way down to the deck by the weight of the little automatic. The translucent figure stumbled away forward toward where the carbon-arc light had been, and her arm lengthened behind her as the automatic slid only by short jerks after her across the polished cork deck.

Obstadt had reeled out through the open lobby doorway to the starboard rail. Beyond him, the induced black sky was breaking up, and Sullivan could see whole patches of luminous distant blue showing through it.

Obstadt's tethered companion was up and hunching along beside him like a wounded dog—now the companion only had one arm, and Sullivan realized that it had certainly been Sherman Oaks all along, with his missing arm only temporarily provided by the ship's degaussing field, which had been so magically stepped-up in this one segment of the ship. Oaks was wheezing like a hundred warped harmonicas, and his windbreaker and baggy camouflage pants were rippling and jumping and visibly spotting with fresh blood, as though a horde of starved rats were muscling around underneath.

The battered-looking lawyer who had been standing with the little girls was still holding the broom and staring stupidly up at the fragmenting sky—and Obstadt's right hand lashed out and caught the man by the necktie. Obstadt strongly pulled him along the rail toward himself and opened his mouth wide over the lawyer's throat.

But Nicky Bradshaw lumbered over to them and pulled Obstadt away. Bradshaw's crew-cut had lengthened messily in the last few seconds and was shot with gray now, and his turtleneck sweater was beginning to stretch over his belly, but he grabbed Obstadt's coat lapels with both hands and boosted him up until the wounded man was nearly sitting on the rail; and then he braced his feet and pushed Obstadt over backward.

With a tortured roar and a useless flailing of arms and legs, Obstadt tumbled away out of sight below the deck, and Sherman Oaks was abruptly dragged upright and slammed belly-first against the rail, his single arm stretched straight downward as it took Obstadt's pendulous weight.

"Nicky," Oaks wheezed, "I worked with you at Stage 5 Productions in '59! I can get you a ghost that'll make you young again! *Thus from infernal Dis do we ascend, to view the subjects of our monarchy!*"

In the brightness of the sunlight that was shining over there, Sullivan saw tears glisten on Bradshaw's cheek—

But Bradshaw took hold of Oaks's belt and lifted him over the rail—Oaks kicked, but had no free hand with which to grab anything, and howled, though all his voices seemed to have lost the capacity to form words—and Bradshaw effortfully tossed the tethered pair away into the brightening abyss.

Away on the other side of the Piccadilly Circus deck, Sullivan cringed at the receding scream of a thousand voices.

Sullivan couldn't roll over, but he saw Kootie look back toward the port deck to see if Obstadt and Oaks would land there—but there was no sound of impact from that direction. The supernaturally amplified magnetic field was obviously breaking down, and the two men had certainly fallen all the long way down into the walled lagoon that lay like a moat around the ship.

Sullivan heard Elizalde gasp, and looked across the lobby again—to see that Bradshaw had now climbed right up onto the starboard rail outside and was standing erect, balanced on it, with his arms waving out to the sides.

Bradshaw's recently youthful and trim body was visibly deteriorating back into the gross figure of Solomon Shadroe, and with every passing second it became a more incongruous sight to see the fat old man tottering up there.

Bradshaw squinted belligerently down at the disheveled attorney, who had lurched back across the narrow section of outdoor deck and was leaning in the Piccadilly Circus doorway, panting. The attorney had evidently wet his pants.

"You okay, Frank?" asked Bradshaw gruffly.

The lawyer blinked around uncertainly, then goggled up at the fat old man standing on the rail; and he seemed to wilt with recognition. "Yes, Mr. Bradshaw. I—I brought all this—"

"Good." Bradshaw blinked past him into the shadows of the Piccadilly Circus lobby. He was probably unable to see in even as far as where deLarava's gorily holed body lay tumbled on the polished cork floor, but he called, "Pete, Beth—Angelica, Kootie—" The freshening breeze ruffled his gray hair, and he wobbled on his perch. "—Edison. I don't want to spoil the party, so I'll go. This here just won't last much longer."

He might have been referring to the psychically skewed magnetic field, but Sullivan thought he meant his control over his long-dead body and his long-held ghost; and nervously Sullivan thought of the descriptions of the way Frank Rocha's body had finally gone.

Then Bradshaw's face creased in a faint, self-conscious,

reminiscent smile—and he curled one hand over his head and stuck his other arm straight out, and he spun slowly on the rail on the toe of one foot; and, almost gracefully, he overbalanced and fell away out into empty space and disappeared.

Sullivan found himself listening for a splash— irrationally, for the water was a good hundred feet below, and Sullivan was sprawled on the other side of the Piccadilly Circus lobby, closer to the port rail than the starboard one from which Bradshaw had just fallen—but what he heard three seconds later was a muffled *boom* that vibrated the deck and flung a high plume of glittering spray into the morning sunlight up past the starboard rail.

The lawyer seemed to be sobbing now, and he ran away aft, his footsteps knocking away to silence on the exterior deck planks, and the footsteps didn't start up again from some other direction.

Sullivan discovered that he was able to sit up; then that he could get his legs under himself and get to his feet. Elizalde hurried around to his right side and braced him up, and at last he dared to look down at his chest.

A button hung in fragments on his shirtfront and a tiny hole had been raggedly punched through the cloth, but there was no blood; and then with a surge of relief he remembered the brass plaque from his father's gravestone, tucked into his scapular, over his heart.

"Your arm's bleeding," said Elizalde. "But somehow that seems to be the only place you're hit." Her face was pale and she was frowning deeply. Sullivan could see the lump of the .45 under the front of her sweatshirt.

He looked down at his left arm, and his depth perception seemed to flatten right down to two dimensions when he saw that his shirtsleeve was rapidly blotting with bright red blood. "Hold me up from that side," he said dizzily, "and maybe no one will notice. You're a doctor, Angelica—can you dig out a bullet?"

"If it's not embedded in the bone, I can."

"Good—Jesus—soon." He took a deep breath and let it out, feeling as disoriented as if he'd had a stiff drink and an unfiltered Pall Mall on an empty stomach. "Uh . . . where to?"

"The bridge is there again," said Kootie anxiously, "the one that leads to the stairs and the parking lot. Let's get off this ship while we can."

Sullivan looked up, across the wide lobby. DeLarava's body was still sprawled out there in the middle of the deck, but the lights and camera gear at the forward end of the room were all her modern equipment again. The little old man in the khaki jacket was crouched over one of the Lowell light kits, busily packing away the scrims and light-doors, and humming. He didn't look up when Kootie ran back there, snatched up a half-used roll of silvery gaffer's tape, and hurried back to Sullivan and Elizalde.

"Kootie's right," said Elizalde, scuffling back around to Sullivan's left side and hugging his bloody arm to her breast. "Let's get back to Solville before people are able to wander in here and find this mess."

"*Joey,*" said a frail voice behind Sullivan, "*stop them.*"

Sullivan looked back at the film equipment and saw that deLarava's fat ghost was leaning on the tripod, her translucent chin resting on the black Sony Betacam. Her head ended right above the eyebrows, constricted to a short, stumpy cone by the rubber bands; and her translucent ectoplasmic right arm was still stretched out for yards across the deck, the limp fingers of the ghost hand twitching impotently on the grip of the automatic pistol.

The old man by the light kit looked up. "Oh, I've seen these before," he said cheerfully, speaking toward the ghost. "I should pop it into a marmalade jar, so somebody can sniff it. Crazy. No more point to it than catching somebody's shadow by slapping a book shut on it. *If* you ask *me.*"

"*Joey,*" said the ghost in a peremptory but birdlike tone, "*you work for me. You gentlemen—why, you all work for me. Joey, I seem to have dislocated my wrist— take the gun from my hand and kill those three.*"

"I hear a voice!" exclaimed Joey, smiling broadly. "A blot of mustard or a bit of undigested beef, speaking to me! A sort of food that's bound to disagree—not for me." He stood up and bowed toward Kootie, who was nervously holding the roll of gaffer's tape. "Thanks a lot, boy," Joey said, "just the same."

DeLarava's ghost was fading, but it straightened up and drifted across the floor straight toward Sullivan, and its eyes, as insubstantial as raw egg-whites, locked onto his. "*Come with me, Pete,*" the ghost said imperiously.

Sullivan opened his mouth—almost certainly to decline the offer, though he was dizzy and nauseated at the hard sunlight, and giving a lot of his weight to Elizalde's right arm—but the breath that came out between his teeth was sharp with bourbon fumes, and it whispered, *"What number were you trying to reach?"*

DeLarava's ghost withered before the fumy breath, and the gossamer lines of the fat face turned to Kootie. *"Little boy, would you help an old woman across a very wide street?"*

"Physicists and sphinxes in majestical mists," came the old man's voice out of Kootie's mouth. *"I will go right through that sand and leave you way behind."*

The smoky shred that was deLarava's ghost now swung toward Elizalde, and the voice was like wasps rustling in a papery nest: "You *have no mask.*"

The bloody fabric of the sweatshirt over Elizalde's breasts flattened, as if an unseen hand had pressed there, and then a spotty handprint in Sullivan's blood appeared on the sweatshirt shoulder, and smeared. Elizalde cocked her head as if listening to a faint voice in her ear, and then said, almost wonderingly, "Yes, of course."

Sullivan felt the bourbon-breath blow out of his mouth again. *"This one is my family, too,"* the voice said softly.

Then Elizalde's shoulder twitched as if shoved.

—And out of Sullivan's mouth Sukie's ghost-voice added, *"A.O.P., kids."*

As quick as an image in a twitched mirror, deLarava's ghost folded itself around past Kootie and stood between the three of them and the roofed causeway off the ship. *"No one passes,"* it whispered.

Kootie looked back at Sullivan fearfully; and in spite of his own sick-making pain, Sullivan noticed that the boy's curly black hair needed washing and combing, and he noticed the dark circles under the haunted brown eyes;

and he vowed to himself, and to the ghosts of his father
and sister, that he would make things better.

"There's no one there, Kootie," he said. "Watch." He
stepped forward, away from Elizalde's arm, and faintly felt
the protesting outrage as deLarava's fretful substance
parted before him like cobwebs and blew away on the
strengthening sea breeze.

Kootie and Elizalde hurried after him. Kootie looked up
at Elizalde with a strangely lost look, and he waved the roll
of gaffer's tape he had snatched off the deck. He held it
gingerly, as if he didn't want to get any more of the glue on
his fingers than he could help. "When we get to the stairs,"
he said, "I figured you could tape Pete's arm with this."

Elizalde looked startled. "Of course. That's a good idea
. . . Edison?"

"No," said Kootie, trotting along now between the two
grown-ups. "Me."

Halfway across the elevated walkway, Sullivan paused
and began unbuttoning his shirt. "One last stop," he said
hoarsely.

He fished out the front-side wallet of his scapular and
pried free of the torn plastic sleeve the brass portrait-
plaque that he had taken off his father's gravestone
yesterday evening. DeLarava's bullet, a .22 or .25, had
deeply dented the center of the metal plate, and the
engraved portrait of his smiling father was almost totally
smashed away.

Sullivan rubbed his own chest gingerly, wondering if
the blocked gunshot had nevertheless cracked his
breastbone; and he held the brass plate between the
thumb and forefinger of his right hand.

"Goodbye, Dad," he said softly. "I'll see you again, after a while—in some better place, God willing."

The piece of brass was warm in his hand. He hefted it and looked down at the shadowed water between the dock and the ship.

"I'll take that," said a whisper from behind Kootie.

Sullivan whipped his head around in exhausted alarm, but it was the ghost of Edison who had spoken, a smoky silhouette hardly visible out here in the breezy sunlight; the hand the old ghost was extending was so insubstantial that Sullivan doubted it could hold the brass plate, but when he held the plate out and let go of it, Edison supported it.

"I'll take him, and go, at last," Edison said faintly. *"I hope it may be very beautiful over there."* Sullivan thought the ghost smiled. *"On the way,"* it whispered, *"your father and I can talk about the . . ."* and then Sullivan couldn't tell whether the last word was *silence* or *silents*.

Kootie wanted to say goodbye to Edison, but was shy to see the ghost standing out away from himself, tall and broad in spite of being nearly transparent.

But the ghost bent over him, and Kootie felt a faint pressure on his shoulder for a moment.

In his head he faintly heard, *"Thank you, son. You've made me proud. Find bright days, and good work, and laughter."*

Then the Edison ghost stepped right through the railing and, still holding Peter Sullivan's piece of brass, began to shrink in the air, as if he were rapidly receding into the distance; the image stayed in the center of Kootie's vision no matter which direction he looked in—

down at his feet, toward the buildings and cranes on the shore, or up at the mounting white decks and towering red funnels of the ship—so he turned to the walkway rail and gripped it and stared at the glittering blue water of the harbor until the image had quite shrunk away to nothing there.

And at last he stepped back, and took Peter Sullivan's hand in his left hand and Angelica Elizalde's in his right, and the three of them walked together to the stairs that would lead them down to the parking lot and away, to whatever eventual rest, and shelter, and food, and life these two people would be able to give him.